REAL COWBOYS GET THEIR GIRLS

Wyoming Rebels

STEPHANIE ROWE

Authenticity Playground, LLC

COPYRIGHT

Stephanie ROWE

A Real Cowboy Never Says No

WYOMING REBELS

COPYRIGHT

the author or the artist. There are excerpts from other books by the author in the back of the book.

To Lily, who reminded me what love is.

CHAPTER ONE

MIRA CABOT'S first thought when she saw him was that cowboy hats didn't belong at this funeral.

Her second thought was that it was fantastic he was wearing one.

There was nothing like watching a genuine cowboy saunter boldly into a conservative southern church full of overpriced black suits and expensive leather shoes to remind her that life was not over just because someone she loved was dead.

She grinned, her first smile in what felt like years, knowing that AJ would have been thrilled to see the cowboy ignoring the rigid society rules at his funeral. He'd give the white cowboy hat two thumbs up, and he'd probably even toss in a bonus if the man didn't take it off when he met AJ's domineering father.

She knew AJ had always figured he'd wind up being fêted in a small service by the river, where they'd spent hours as kids. His funeral of choice would have been kids, dogs, bare feet, and a local band playing his favorite country music as a reminder to everyone to get off their butts and live life.

Instead, his father had taken over the largest church in town, and he'd booked the finest ballroom in five counties for everyone to retire to after the burial, because he was more concerned about status and money than he was about his dead son's desires.

The line inched forward, dragging her inexorably forward into the church where AJ's dad was presiding, but the cowboy didn't move from the doorway. Mira watched him standing in the doorway, surveying the church with methodical precision, as if he were taking stock of every person present. He was wearing jeans, but they looked sharp and crisp. His face was clean-shaven, but there were already hints of whiskered shadows caressing his jaw. His dark hair was barely visible beneath his hat, but it was clearly cut short. His blue eyes were shrewd and assessing as he scanned the occupants, apparently searching for someone. There was a life and energy exuding from him, as if he got up every morning and somehow managed to cram forty-eight hours of life into every single day.

He made her feel weary and bone-tired in comparison, but at the same time, it was energizing. She hadn't been around someone that alive in a long time, and it was a good reminder to get off her butt and get outside in the sunshine, just like AJ was probably shouting at her to do right at that very moment, stalking her from heaven.

The usher, one of AJ's cousins, took her arm. "First row, Mira? AJ always considered you his sister."

"You really think I'd be welcome in the family seats?" She almost snorted as she glanced at the front of the church. AJ's dad, Alan Joseph Wentworth, Sr., was flanked by his attorney and his only remaining son, Thurston Wentworth, the hard-drinking underachiever who would now inherit the business, much to the dismay of the clan's patriarch. Thurston looked presentable in a navy suit, and his hair was greased back to hide the unruly curls. Alan, however, was sheer, unassailable properness. His silver hair was precisely coiffed, and his crisp black suit fit him with the precision of a custom-made specialty.

Alan looked up, catching her gaze, and his face hardened.

She shot him a winning smile, the same "you don't bother me" grin she'd been giving him for years, which was a bald-faced lie because the man scared the hell out of her. He was a man who got what he wanted, and he was willing to hurt anyone to get it, including his own son or the family who had given him refuge.

Yeah, there was no chance she was going to sit with Alan today. "You know, that's a great idea to sit in the front, Todd, but I might have to leave early. I wouldn't want to disturb the service." And she didn't want her last tribute to AJ to be tainted by Alan. Instead, she gestured to the last pew. "I'll just slide in the back here."

Not waiting for assent, she ducked into the last row of benches, breaking protocol since the seats in front of her weren't full yet. Not that she cared, and neither would AJ. She wasn't here for his family. She was here for him.

She scooted into the far corner, letting the shadows of the balcony conceal her. She knew almost everyone who walked in, but very few of them would bother to notice her. Unlike Mira, the rest of the attendees were from the south end of town, the section of mansions and gated driveways that wished her end of town didn't actually exist. A few of her friends from high school were there, but they'd moved beyond their shared teenage angst. Not a single one bothered to look over into her dark corner. There was a smattering of sharply dressed twenty-something men and women she didn't know, and she figured those had to be AJ's friends and co-workers from Boston, people from the part of his life she'd never known.

As she sank onto the thick, well-worn cushion, she glanced back again toward the entrance, but the cowboy was no longer in the doorway. Without his energizing presence galvanizing her, the enormity of what she was facing settled heavily onto her shoulders once again. Grim reality wrapped around her like a shadowy cloak trying to suck the last remnants of energy from her soul. She sighed and closed her eyes, trying to summon the inner strength that had gotten her through so much.

She needed a plan. She needed to take action. But what action? What was she going to do?

Sudden tears threatened, and she instinctively lifted her chin in defiance, willing them away.

She knew exactly what she had to do, and she'd known it for the last four hours. She was going to have to quit her job, pathetic as it was, and move away from the only place she'd ever lived, and the only place she'd ever wanted to live, to somewhere that AJ's dad would never, ever find her.

~

CHASE STOCKTON KNEW he'd found the woman he'd come to meet.

There was no mistaking the depth of loathing in the gaze of AJ's dad when he'd glared at the woman in the pale blue sundress. There was only one woman Alan could despise that much, and it was Mira Cabot.

Chase grinned. After more than a decade, he was about to meet Mira Cabot in person. *Hot damn.*

Anticipation humming through him, Chase watched with appreciation as she ducked into the last row of pews, her pale shoulders erect and strong as she moved down the row. She was a little too thin, yeah, but there was a strength to her body that he liked. Her dark blond hair was curly, bouncing over her shoulders in stark contrast to the tight updos of the other women in the church. He'd noticed her flip-flops and hot pink toenails, a little bit of color in the chapel full of black and gloom.

Chase had hopped a plane to attend the funeral, but it hadn't been just to honor AJ. He could have done that from his ranch in Wyoming. Nope, he'd come here to meet Mira, because he'd had a feeling this was going to be his only chance.

He ignored the line of churchgoers waiting to be seated. Instead, he strode around the back of the last pew to the far side, where his quarry was tucked away in the shadows. As he approached, someone turned up the lights in the church, and the shadows slid away, casting her face in a warm glow, giving him his first view of the woman he'd been thinking about for more than a decade.

Chase was shocked by the raw need that flooded him. Her eyes were the same chocolate brown as in her photo. Her nose had that slight bump from when she and AJ had failed to successfully erect a tire swing in her front yard, resulting in her crashing to the ground and breaking her nose. Her lips were pale pink, swept with the faintest hint of gloss, and her eyelashes were as long and thick as he'd imagined. Her shoulders were bare and delicate in her sundress, and her ankles were crossed demurely, as if she were playing the role that was expected of her. Yet, around that same ankle was a chain of glittering gold with several blue stones. He knew that anklet. He'd helped AJ pick it out for her twenty-first birthday.

She was everything he'd imagined, and so much more. She was no longer an inanimate, two-dimensional image who lived only in his mind. She had become a real, live woman.

Mira was eyeing the crowd with the faintest scowl puckering her lips and lining her forehead, just as he would have expected. She didn't like this crowd any more than AJ had.

Chase grinned, relaxing. She was exactly what he'd imagined. "You don't approve?" he said as he approached her.

She let out a yelp of surprise and jumped, bolting sideways like a skittish foal. "What?"

Chase froze, startled by the sound of her voice. It was softer than he'd expected, reminding him of the rolling sound of sunshine across his back on a warm day. Damn, he liked her voice. Why hadn't AJ ever mentioned it? That wasn't the kind of thing a guy could overlook.

She was sitting sideways, her hand gripping the back of the pew, looking at him like he was about to pull out his rifle and aim it at her head.

He instinctively held up his hand, trying to soothe her. "Sorry. I didn't mean to startle you." He swept the hat off his head and bowed slightly. "Chase Stockton. You must be Mira Cabot."

"Chase Stockton?" Her frown deepened slightly, and then recognition dawned on her face. "AJ's best friend from college! Of course." She stood up immediately, a smile lighting up her features. "I can't believe I finally get to meet you."

He had only a split second to register how pretty her smile was before she threw her arms around him and hugged him.

For the second time in less than a minute, Chase was startled into immobility. Her body was so warm and soft against him that he forgot to breathe. He had not been expecting her to hug him, and he hadn't had time to steel himself. He flexed his hands by his sides, not sure how to react. It had been so long since anyone had hugged him, and it was an utterly foreign experience. It was weird as hell, but at the same time, there was something about it that felt incredible, as if the whole world had stopped spinning and settled into this moment.

When Mira didn't let go, he tentatively slipped his arms around her, still unsure of proper protocol when being embraced by a woman he'd never met before. As his arms encircled her, however, a deep sense of rightness settled over him. He could feel her ribs protruding from her back, and he instinctively tightened his grip on her, pulling her into the shield of his embrace. In photographs, she'd always been athletic and solid, but now she was thin, thinner than he liked, thinner than he felt she should be.

She tucked her face in his neck and took a deep breath, and he became aware of the most tempting scent of flowers. It reminded him of a trail ride in the spring, when the wildflowers were beating back the last remnants of a stubborn winter.

The turbulence that constantly roiled through his body seemed to quiet as he focused on her. He became aware of the desperate nature of her embrace, reminding him that she was attending the funeral of her best friend, and she was no doubt being assaulted by the accompanying grief and loss.

He bent his head, his cheek brushing against her hair. "You okay?" he asked softly.

She took another deep breath, and then pulled back. Her blue eyes were full of turbulent emotion. "It's just that seeing you makes me feel like AJ's here again." She brushed an imaginary speck of dust off his shoulder. "You were his best friend, you know. You changed his life forever."

He wasn't used to anyone touching him with that kind of intimacy, especially not a woman. Women never got familiar with him. *Ever*. He simply didn't allow it. But with her, it felt okay. Good even. He shrugged, feeling completely out of his depth with her. "He changed mine," he said. "He did a hell of a lot more for me than I ever did for him." AJ had been a lifeline in an ugly existence that had been spiraling straight into hell. He knew exactly where he'd have been without AJ: dead, or in prison. It was a debt he could never repay.

She nodded, still not stepping away from his embrace. She lightly clasped his forearms, still holding onto him. "He was like that, wasn't he?"

"Yeah, he was." Unable to make himself release her, Chase studied her face, memorizing the curve of her nose, the flush of her cheeks, and the slope of her jaw. "You were his rock, you know. The only person in this world he truly trusted."

And that was it, the reason why he'd wanted to meet her. He was bitter, tired, and cynical, and he'd needed to see if the Mira Cabot his friend had always talked about actually existed. He needed to know whether there was someone in this world, anyone besides his brothers, who a man could actually believe in. Hearing that AJ had died had derailed Chase more than he'd expected, and he'd needed something to hold onto, something that connected him back to AJ and the hope that something good still existed in this world.

Her cheeks flushed, and she smiled. "Thanks for telling me that. We didn't keep in touch much over the last few years, but he's always been in my heart."

He stared at her, uncertain how to respond. Who talked about things in their heart? And with strangers? But he knew the answer to that. Mira did, and that was why he'd wanted to meet her.

She finally pulled back, and he reluctantly released her, his hands sliding over her hips. She moved further into the pew and eased onto the bench. "Sit with me," she said, patting the seat beside her.

"Yeah, okay." Instead of taking the aisle seat, he moved past her and sat on the other side of her, inserting himself between Mira and AJ's dad. The old man was across the church, but he hadn't stopped shooting lethal stares in her direction. AJ wasn't there to protect her, so it was now Chase's job.

He draped his arms across the back of the pew, aware that his position put one arm behind Mira's shoulders. Not touching, but present. A statement.

He looked across the church at AJ's dad, and this time, when the man looked over, he noticed Chase sitting beside her. The two men stared at each other for a brief moment, and then Alan looked away.

Satisfied, Chase shifted his position so he could stretch his legs out, trying to work out the cramps from the long flight. He was glad he'd come. It felt right to be there, and he'd sent the message to AJ's dad that Mira was under his protection.

He glanced sideways at her as she fiddled with her small purse. Her hair was tumbling around her face, obscuring his view of her eyes. Frustrated that he couldn't see her face, he started to move his hand to adjust her hair, and then froze. What the hell was he doing, thinking he could just reach out and touch her like that?

Swearing, he jerked his gaze away from her, a bead of sweat trickling down his brow as he realized the enormity of what was happening. *He was attracted to her.* For the last decade, Mira had simply been AJ's best friend, an angel of sorts who Chase had idealized from a distance, never thinking of Mira as anything more personal than simply a bright light in a shitty world.

But now?

He wanted her.

He wanted to brush her hair back from her face. He wanted to run his fingers over her collarbone. He wanted to feel her body crushed against his again. He wanted to sink his mouth onto hers, and taste her—

Hell. That spelled trouble, in a major way.

Suddenly, he couldn't wait to get on the plane and get out of there, and back to his carefully constructed world.

He hadn't come here for a woman. He'd come here for salvation, not to be sucked into the hell that had almost destroyed him once before. Mira Cabot might be the only woman on the planet worth trusting, but that wasn't reason enough for him to risk all that he'd managed to rebuild.

Nothing was worth that risk. *Nothing.*

∾

USUALLY, Mira didn't mind being alone. She treasured her solitude, and had no problem standing on her own. Coming to the service by herself had been preferable to faking her way with acquaintances who didn't really care that AJ was dead.

But with Chase sitting next to her, his broad shoulders taking up half the pew, and his long legs stretched out to the side, she had to admit, it felt good to be beside him.

It was almost as if the sheer magnitude of his presence could keep the noise at bay, letting her settle into the shield he gave her, so that she could actually slow her mind long enough to think. His presence made it safe to take the time to *feel*.

She stole a glance at him as he watched the gathering congregation. He started to take his cowboy hat off, then he saw AJ's dad glaring at him. He immediately dropped his hand, leaving the hat in place as he shot a silent, unrelenting stare at AJ's dad. Her heart softened with the realization that Chase had gone against his instincts and left the hat on in a silent statement of solidarity with AJ, and his enduring battle to survive his controlling, abusive father. The hat would infuriate Alan, and it would make AJ's presence real at his funeral.

It was perfect, and she wanted to cheer at Chase's willingness to stand up for AJ in this church full of Alan's minions. His white shirt was unbuttoned at the collar, showing a gold chain against his tanned skin. He was rough and untamed, the antithesis of everyone in the church. It was weird to feel so comfortable with a complete stranger, but they weren't really strangers. AJ had connected them, and she knew that Chase was the only other person in the world that AJ had truly cared about. AJ's faith in Chase meant she could trust that he was a good guy.

He bent his head slightly toward her, but didn't look at her. "Is that Thurston? AJ's brother?"

She looked toward the front to where Alan and Thurston were talking with the minister. "Yes. They pulled him out of rehab to attend the service."

Chase laughed softly. "Alan must be angry as hell that AJ died before the old man could force him into the family business. Thurston will ruin the company if he ever takes over."

"I know." She shared his amusement. "AJ would appreciate that."

Chase glanced over at her, still smiling. Her heart skipped a beat at how handsome he was. She hadn't noticed a man for a very long time. The last thing she'd have expected was to be attracted to Chase Stockton, but she definitely was. It was a little unnerving, but her reaction also gave her hope that the part of her that was a woman was still alive inside her, and someday, she might even come back to life.

Chase leaned back against the pew, shifting his legs. The movement made his arm brush against her shoulder, and she stiffened, not sure whether she should pull away. A part of her didn't want to retreat, but the feel of his shoulder against hers was so distracting she couldn't focus on anything else. She pretended to cough, and used the movement as a way to reposition herself without making it look like she'd done it on purpose.

"Well, that's one thing that AJ can die knowing he did right," he said, apparently not noticing her strategic shift.

She raised her eyebrows. "What's that?"

"He never had kids that his father could get his claws into. Remember what AJ used to say? He'd never bring a child into this world so that Alan could destroy it. Alan's stuck without a decent heir, and his business is going to die because of it. Can you imagine if AJ had left behind a kid?" He whistled softly. "His widow would have had no chance of keeping the kid safe from Alan."

Mira felt the blood drain from her face, and she instinctively clutched her belly.

Chase's eyes sharpened, and his gaze shot to her hand, and then back to her face.

She froze, her heart pounding, as she frantically tried to think of a casual response.

Nothing came to her. Her mind was utterly blank.

"AJ lived in Boston," Chase said slowly, as if measuring every word. "Not here."

She nodded, her mouth bone dry as she forced herself to take her hand off her stomach. "Right."

"He never came home to visit," Chase continued with a casualness she didn't believe. "He despised everything in this place, except for you."

She managed a smile. "Yeah, I know."

Silence, but he didn't take his penetrating gaze off her. "Did you ever go there?" he finally asked. "Visit him in Boston? Recently, perhaps?"

"No," she said quickly. "My mom's been an invalid for the last eight years, as I'm sure you know. I was her caretaker until she died a few weeks ago. I couldn't ever leave town. She needed constant care." Her voice broke unexpectedly at the thought of her mother, and she turned away, clenching her hands in her lap. "The service is starting," she said, her voice snappier than she intended.

She focused intently on the minister, her lips pressed tightly together as she fought not to cry.

"Two funerals in a month? I didn't know your mom had died." Chase's voice was soft now, as were his eyes. "I'm so sorry, Mira. I know how much she meant to you."

She glared at him. "Don't be nice, unless you like it when a woman bursts into tears and sobs uncontrollably all over your crisp white shirt," she hissed.

His eyes widened in the moderate terror she'd expected, and he closed his mouth, cutting off his next question.

She folded her arms across her chest, her eyes blurring as she tried to listen to a bunch of strangers talk dispassionately about her best friend, and as she tried not to notice that Chase was intently watching *her*, and not paying any attention to the service at all.

CHAPTER TWO

CHASE HAD ABSOLUTELY INTENDED to leave town once the church service was over.

There had been no chance he was going to go to the highbrow after-funeral gala and socialize with the bastards who had driven AJ out of town. *No chance.* He had no time for people who were superficial, drank too much, and cared about nothing but themselves and their own agendas.

And yet, there he was, leaning moodily against one of the white pillars, watching Mira circulate through the lavishly decorated ballroom. Her chin was held high, and her curls were bouncing. She was animated and charming in her conversations with people, but he wasn't buying it.

Whenever she had a moment to breathe, her shoulders slumped, and her face became lined with exhaustion and grief. She'd kept careful track of Alan, and had made sure not to run into him.

Chase had been watching the old man as well, and he knew that Alan was not going to let Mira leave without cornering her. He'd been watching her with dangerous hostility all night, a predator stalking his prey, waiting for the chance to isolate her.

Mira excused herself from her latest conversation, and started working her way toward the restroom. As Chase watched, she put her hand on her stomach.

That was the twenty-seventh time she'd done it in the last ninety minutes.

Shit.

He suddenly realized that Alan was striding across the floor toward her, his face determined. Chase jumped forward, almost sprinting through the crowd to get to Mira before Alan did.

They arrived at the same moment, but Alan didn't notice Chase's approach. He grabbed Mira's upper arm and jerked her to him. "I know my son came to town for your mother's funeral, and I know he stayed at your place. Two days later, he changed his will to give all his money to charity." He jerked her closer, ignoring her yelp of pain. "If I find out that you convinced him to change his will, I promise you will suffer—"

"Hey." Chase stepped between them, using his body to force the older man back. "Let go of her."

Alan stared at him, and his fingers tightened around Mira's arm. "Who the hell are you?"

Chase's hand balled into a fist instinctively. "Let her go," he repeated, his voice lethally soft. All the lessons he'd learned about violence from his piece-of-shit dad came rushing back, and his knuckles tingled, anticipating the impact before he even moved to strike.

The old man glared at him. For a long moment, they simply stared at each other, and then Alan's eyes widened, apparently seeing in Chase's eyes exactly the kind of no-good, bastard genes that ran through him.

With a low swear, Alan released Mira, shoving her back hard enough to make her stumble.

Chase caught her before she could fall, pulling her against him as she rubbed her upper arm. He could feel her trembling against him, and it made more anger roll through him. "Mira Cabot is under my protection," he said, an unspoken threat lacing his words. "Remember that."

Alan gave him a thin smile. "I own this town, cowboy. You

remember that." He shot another vicious glare at Mira, and then spun on his heel. A woman draped in diamonds accosted him, and he graced her with a smile charming enough to win over the most bitter of old women.

"Bastard," Chase muttered.

"Thanks," Mira said, leaning into him for a brief moment.

He nodded, not taking his gaze off Alan, daring the old man to come back. "No problem. Glad I was here."

"Me, too." She paused, drawing his attention to her. There were circles beneath her eyes, and she looked exhausted.

He frowned. "Are you okay?"

"Fine. I just need to get out of here." She managed a smile that didn't reach her eyes. "Thanks again. It was good to meet you. Have a good flight back to Wyoming." Dismissing him, Mira ducked past him, no longer heading for the bathroom, but for the exit. She was walking fast, not even noticing the people who tried to engage her in conversation.

Chase hesitated. He could let her go. He could allow her to walk out the door, and she wouldn't be his problem. He didn't trust women. Ever. He couldn't afford to take on her problems. He had rules that he hadn't strayed from for fifteen years. He'd made a promise, and he couldn't risk being derailed from it. Following Mira out that door was the wrong choice on every damn level... except for the fact that she was in trouble, she was AJ's best friend, and he owed AJ his life.

Shit. He had only one choice, didn't he?

Swearing, he jammed his hand into his pocket for his car keys, and followed her out the door.

TWENTY MINUTES LATER, Mira slammed her car door shut, the sound reverberating in the dark night. She kicked off her high heels, and then broke into a run, her bare feet sinking into the damp grass. She didn't slow down until she got to the edge of the river.

The water was rushing, churning violently after the recent rainstorm. The familiar sound wrapped around her like a blanket, easing the tightness gripping her so ruthlessly. She slowed to a jog and then finally stopped beneath the huge willow tree on the edge of the river.

Her initials were carved into the trunk just below AJ's, and she traced her fingers over them, remembering how many times they'd hid by the river when his father was looking for them. The old pieces of wood they'd used for a ladder were still there, crookedly nailed to the tree trunk. AJ had been three years older than she, so she'd climbed that tree by herself many times after he left for college. It had always made her feel closer to him, despite the fact he was gone. Maybe it would work today as well.

She grabbed one of them, testing it. The wood was cracked and rotting a bit, but it seemed strong enough. Besides, what was the worst that could happen? That she'd fall a few feet to the muddy ground? Not exactly a mind-numbing tragedy.

Almost hoping for the distraction of a fall, she quickly pulled herself up the ladder they'd built for themselves so long ago.

A few seconds later, she was perched in the crook of the tree, her knees pulled to her chest. She took a deep breath, letting the damp air fill her lungs. She hadn't come here in so long, but suddenly, tonight, she'd had to return. She looked up into the starry sky, barely visible through the thick branches. How many nights had she sat in that tree, making wishes about a future that had never unfolded to match her dreams? "AJ," she whispered. "I don't know what to do. This was really bad timing for you to die, you know that, don't you?"

Of course he didn't answer. It was just a lonely, empty silence.

Headlights swept across the riverbank, and she glanced over her shoulder as a black pickup truck swung in beside her battered sedan. Stiffening, she sat up, watching as the driver's door opened. The broad-shouldered silhouette that emerged from the car was immediately recognizable, and it wasn't simply because of the cowboy hat. There was a lithe grace and rugged strength that emanated from Chase, as if he were a man who could barely contain his true self long enough to survive in polite society for an evening.

She nestled deeper into the crook of the tree as he scanned the area, then grimaced as he stepped into the grass and headed right for her. She watched with growing dread as he walked straight to the tree, and peered up at her. "Got space up there?"

His deep voice rumbled through her just as it had at the church. There was something so warm in his voice. It seemed to wrap around her like a blanket, at the same time it rolled through her belly like a searing kiss designed to make her insides burn. "Not really," she said. Between the shadows and the brim of his hat, she couldn't really see his face. "I'm not feeling sociable right now."

"Yeah, me either. I hate crowds of superficial bastards. They always make me cranky."

To her surprise, she found herself laughing, despite her cranky mood. "Okay, fine, you can come up, but I can't promise I'll be good company."

"No problem. I'm rarely good company myself." He swung up the ladder with the practiced ease of a man who was used to a physical life. He settled in beside her in the crevice that had always had plenty of room for her and AJ. Now, however, it felt cramped and tiny. Chase's shoulder was against hers, and there wasn't enough space for her to move away.

Then he leaned back against the tree trunk, adjusting so they weren't touching. Although she was grateful for the space, at the same time, a part of her wanted to inch just close enough to him to feel the heat of his body against hers, penetrating the cold that seemed to be buried so deeply inside her.

Chase clasped his hands behind his head and propped his feet up on another branch. He tipped his hat over his eyes, as if he were stretching out in a hammock for a nap instead of invading her personal space in a tree fifteen feet in the air.

He said nothing, and after a few moments, she began to relax. The night sounds returned to her. She listened to the roar of the river, the chirp of birds, and the rustling of the leaves in the tree. With Chase beside her, the moment felt complete. This place had been meant for two people, and she was used to a comforting male presence beside her.

Chase wasn't AJ, but in a way he was, and that made him safe enough for her to relax around. She rested her chin on her knees and thought about the last few weeks, trying to figure out what she was going to do. Somehow, with Chase beside her, her life didn't feel so overwhelming. She still didn't have any answers, but at least she felt composed enough to think clearly.

"He'll figure it out, you know," Chase said after a while.

She jumped, startled by the sound of his voice, and his hand shot out to steady her, settling around her elbow with effortless ease. "Sorry. I was in my own world," she said, her heart hammering at the sensation of his fingers grasping her arm.

"I noticed."

"You did?" She realized that although his hat was tipped forward, it didn't obscure his eyes. He was watching her intently.

Awareness tingled over her skin. "Who will figure what out?" She didn't actually care what he was talking about. She just wanted a distraction from how she was reacting to him.

"Alan."

She frowned. "AJ's dad? He'll figure out what?"

Chase's eyes bore into her, and with sudden dread, she knew what he was going to say before he said it. *Oh, no.* She definitely didn't want to get into that discussion with him. "I'm getting tired," she said quickly, faking a yawn. "I think I'll be heading home." She pushed lightly at his legs, urging him to move out of the way.

He didn't. Instead he sat up, moving with a slow, relaxed ease that was in direct contrast to the sudden pounding of her heart. He leaned forward, his gaze boring into her relentlessly. "Alan's going to figure out that you and AJ slept together when he was here for your mom's funeral. He's going to realize you're pregnant with AJ's kid, who happens to be Alan's grandchild, and his best chance for an heir to his throne."

Mira felt like her entire world had congealed into horror. "I'm not —" She stopped herself before she'd even completed the lie. What was the point? Chase would never believe her. Instead, she sagged back against the tree, too exhausted to fight the battle she'd already lost. "How did you figure it out?"

He shrugged. "I'm a master of observation." His words were light,

23

but his eyes were still boring into hers. "Alan's a bastard. He'll have legal custody of that kid before it's even born."

Mira bit her lip. "I know he'll try." She managed a smile. "It's okay. I've already figured it out. I'll leave town. He won't bother to track me." But even as she said it, she remembered Alan's accusation at the hotel ballroom. If he thought she'd influenced AJ's will, he *would* pursue her relentlessly, no matter where she went.

No, no, no. She couldn't worry about that. She and AJ had never discussed his will, and she had to believe Alan would realize that and let her disappear.

Chase said nothing for a long moment, and she began to relax. Then, he said. "What are you going to do for money? Last I heard, you had to quit even your part-time admin job to take care of your mom. You've been moonlighting as in the office of the middle school, but with school budget cuts, there hasn't been much work. Do you even have savings?"

"I'll find something." She lifted her chin, annoyed that AJ seemed to have shared so much about her situation. "There's no reason for me to stay in town, now that my mom and dad are both gone." Well, there was no reason except for her one, dear friend, Taylor Shaw. New tears threatened. Taylor had been her rock over the last few years. How could she leave her behind? How on earth would she ever start over by herself? She managed a perky grin. "It'll be an adventure."

Again, Chase was silent, and she wondered if he believed her. Even she didn't believe it, but she had to.

"And if Alan finds you in six months with a swollen belly? Or in a year with an infant on your hip? What happens then?"

Mira swallowed. There was no good answer to that. They both knew what Alan was like.

Chase finally tipped his hat back, so she could see his face more clearly. His jaw was angular, and the moon was casting his face into shadows. He looked dangerous and lethal, the kind of man who would walk beside her with a machete if that was what it took to keep her safe.

"I owe AJ my life," he said quietly. "You're the only person in this world who really mattered to him, and now, he has a kid on the way. You're both in danger, and he's not around to protect you. So it's my job."

"Danger?" She managed to laugh. "I think you're being a little melodramatic."

He unfastened the cuff of his shirt and jerked the sleeve up. His muscular forearm was covered with dozens of small round scars, just like the ones that had covered AJ's back. Her heart clenched, and she put her hand over the marks. His muscle flexed beneath her touch, but neither of them pulled away. "Cigarette burns?" she asked softly.

He nodded. "I know what AJ's dad is like, because mine wasn't that different."

Sadness bore down on her, and she wanted to hug this man she'd just met. She knew the kind of pain a man like Alan could inflict on his son, and it made her sad to think Chase had endured the same things as AJ. "I didn't know. He never told me that about you."

Chase shrugged, dismissing her sympathy as he pulled his sleeve back down. "There's no chance in hell I'm leaving you unprotected," he said. This time, there was no hesitation. He just looked right at her. "Tonight, I'll spend the night at your place, and leave my truck in your driveway for the whole town to see."

She gaped at him. "If you do that, everyone will think that I picked you up, and we had sex the night of my best friend's funeral."

He nodded. "I'm a couple weeks late, but the timing should work okay for the baby."

Tears filled her eyes as she realized what he was offering. "You want the world to think you're the biological father of AJ's baby?" Then she could stay in town. She didn't have to leave.

He looked at her, and her words died in her throat at the expression on his face. There was something else he hadn't said. "What?"

"It's not enough," he said. "You know that won't be sufficient against Alan. It's a start, but it needs more. He'll know damn well that there's an equal chance it could be AJ's baby, and he won't stop until he's certain. A DNA test is going to tell him what he wants to know."

Mira bit her lip, the fleeting hope abandoning her. "You're right."

25

"There's only one way." He brushed his fingers through her hair, ever so slightly. His face was dark and intense, his eyes turbulent with emotions she couldn't begin to decipher. "After we set the stage tonight, you're going to have to move to Wyoming and marry me."

CHAPTER THREE

CHASE ALMOST LAUGHED at the expression of absolute horror on Mira's face. It wasn't that different from what he'd felt the moment he'd proposed to her. Shock, surprise, and yeah, maybe a little horror. He hadn't intended to offer to marry her. He hadn't intended to ever offer to marry *anyone*, but now that he'd done it, it felt right. He knew in his gut that it was his duty to be there for both of them.

She, however, didn't appear to agree with him. "Oh, no. *No.*" She shook her head, scrambling backward so fast she almost fell out of the tree.

Chase caught her arm just as she started to slide backwards. "Why not? I'm a great guy. You know I am."

Her mouth dropped open. "Marry you? Seriously? No." She twisted her arm free, and scrambled over his legs. Her breasts brushed over his arm, and desire clenched through him. For a brief moment, her body was pretzeled up with his, and then she was over him and flying down the makeshift ladder.

For a brief moment, he considered not following her. He really didn't want to get married any more than she did. He never had. But he thought of the cigarette burns on AJ's back, and he knew there was no way he was going to leave AJ's kid to face that future.

Swearing, he swung down from the tree, not even bothering with the ladder. He sprinted after Mira, who was running toward her car. He caught up to her just before she got her door open.

He leaned against the door and folded his arms across his chest, blocking her access to the car. Her face was pale in the moonlight, and something tugged inside him at the vulnerability of her expression. "I didn't mean to scare you," he said softly, using the same tone he reserved for frightened horses.

Mira backed up, then set her hands on her hips, visibly summoning her strength. One strap of her dress had slid off her shoulder and down her arm, a visceral reminder of both her femininity and her vulnerability. "I am not going to marry you," she said.

"Why not? It seems like a logical choice." He wanted to slide his fingers beneath that strap and coax it back in place. He could imagine how soft her skin was...shit. He dragged his gaze off her shoulder and pinned it to her face.

"It's not just you," she explained. "I'm not going to marry anyone."

He frowned at her blanket statement, which sounded way too much like something he'd say. "Why not?"

"Don't you know?" She cocked her head, apparently confused. "You seem to know everything about me."

"I have no idea what you're talking about." He shrugged, and held out his hands in a gesture intended to make him appear harmless, despite the fact he was still firmly blocking her car door. "Tell me."

She sighed, and pulled the strap back up over her shoulder. "When I went to college, I fell in love freshman year. I got engaged. We were going to get married the summer after my sophomore year."

Sudden jealousy surged through Chase. She'd been engaged? Why the hell hadn't he known about that? "What happened?"

"What happened?" Her voice became slightly high-pitched, revealing emotion he could tell she was struggling to contain. "I got a call that my parents had been in a car accident. My dad was dead, and my mom was paralyzed."

Chase swore under his breath. He remembered that call. AJ had been absolutely devastated. Mira's parents had been the only source of love and family AJ had ever had, especially Mira's dad. As sheriff, he'd been the one man in town with the power to stand up to Alan and protect AJ from him, and he'd done it repeatedly. The tragedy had derailed AJ. Maybe that was why AJ had never mentioned Mira's romantic entanglements at the time. During that period, AJ hadn't cared about anything other than the loss of Mira's dad.

"I decided to drop out of school to take care of my mom," Mira continued, her voice becoming calmer now, as if she'd somehow managed to separate herself from the memories. "My fiancé refused to even come to the funeral, because it was too close to exams and he needed to study. After two months, he called and announced he didn't want to marry someone who was stuck caring for an invalid. He said I had to come back to school and live a real life, or he was calling off the engagement." Tears filled her eyes. "I loved him, and my family had been taken away from me. I had no one to lean on except him. How could I let him go? I told him I would come back to school, but I needed more time to get things settled with my mom. For two weeks, I tried frantically to find a way to secure care for her, but I was really struggling to find someone I trusted. I wasn't fast enough, and he broke up with me. He married my roommate three months later."

Shit. Chase shook his head in empathy. He knew what it felt like to be hit when he was down. It sucked. "Bastard."

A strangled laugh choked out, a breath of humor breaking through the pain in her blue eyes. "I won't do that again."

"Get engaged?"

She shook her head. "No, count on a man like that and commit to him. I was actually willing to give up taking care of my mom for him. What if I'd done it? What if I'd left my mom to wither and die in some nursing home so I could marry some jerk?"

He touched her arm. "You didn't do that. It's okay, Mira."

"But I *would have* if he hadn't dumped me." She sighed, searching his face for understanding. "I'm so scared of how close I came to marrying someone who would have taken me away from what was important to me. I won't ever give someone that kind of power again. My parents loved each other unconditionally. It was so beautiful, and I thought I had that with Brian, but I was wrong. I was stupid and desperate, and willing to marry a jerk just to have the fairy tale." She ran her fingers through her hair, her hands shaking. "I realized that it's better to never be married than to settle for less than what my parents had." She met his gaze, and he saw the depth of torment in her eyes. He realized then how deeply she'd been traumatized. "I know you're AJ's best friend, but how on earth can I trust you with my life and my child's? Because it's not just AJ's baby. It's mine, too."

Chase was stunned by her story. AJ had told him how she'd stepped up to take care of her mom, but Chase had never comprehended how much she'd had to endure. He had always thought of her as the rock, the steady balance in life, and yet she'd suffered greatly. He felt her pain, the betrayal she'd endured, and her genuine fear of being married to someone who would betray her. "I get it," he said. And he did. She'd been burned badly, and she was smart enough not to want to risk it again.

She blinked. "What do you mean?"

He sighed at the question, realizing that she'd read more into his statement than he'd meant to share. But she'd been honest with him, and she deserved the same thing in return. "My mother died when I was born," he explained. "I never knew her. But my dad married three more times, and all three of my stepmothers were brutal, on many different levels, not to mention some assorted girlfriends that he mixed in." He didn't want to go into the details, because he'd long ago stopped wasting energy on them, but he needed Mira to understand. "I watched them tear my father apart, and destroy what was left of my family. I watched my brothers suffer as each one was born, and I fought so hard to protect them all from the women my dad had chosen. As bad as my dad was, the women he married made him worse. I don't trust women. I don't trust marriage. And I'd never give a woman any power over me."

He couldn't keep the coldness out of his voice, and she cocked her head, listening intently. "Then why would you ever offer to marry me?" She didn't sound scared. She actually sounded relieved, as if his antipathy toward marriage eased some of her fear.

"Because you're Mira Cabot." He walked over to her and took her hands. Her fingers were cold, but her hands weren't trembling anymore. "I've known you vicariously through AJ for over a decade, and I know what kind of person you are. You're the one person in the world he trusted, and that means you're the one person in the world that I know I can trust as well."

Her eyes glistened with sudden moisture. "I'm not an angel, Chase."

"No. I know that. I know you get cranky as hell when you're hungry or tired. I know you stole a gun from your dad's squad car when you were fourteen because you were going to shoot Alan with it. I also know you cheated on your seventh grade geography test."

Her eyes widened. "You know all that, but you didn't know I was engaged?"

He paused at her question. Why hadn't AJ told him that? Had it just been because AJ had been distracted, or had it been something else? And what else didn't he know about her? Suddenly, he wanted to know. He wanted to sit her down and grill her with a thousand questions, discovering everything about this woman who had existed only in his imagination for the last ten years.

Mira pulled her hands out of his. "Listen, Chase, it's very heroic of you to sweep in and rescue me, but we both know it won't work—"

"I'll have my lawyer draw up a contract. Child support, alimony, and everything you'll need. We'll live together at my ranch for a year. Once the baby is born, and we've solidified my fatherhood, we'll get 'divorced.' This won't be a real marriage, Mira. Just a business partnership designed to protect you and the baby."

She cocked her head, studying him. For the first time, she looked thoughtful. "A business partnership?"

"To protect you and the baby," he repeated. Alan was lethal, and his tentacles were strong and powerful. Chase knew he'd have to address every possible eventuality to ensure Alan could never take the child. "I owe AJ a life debt. You can trust that, if nothing else. AJ was a distrustful loner, and you know he wouldn't have trusted me unless I deserved it."

She studied him for a long moment, then she reached into her purse. She pulled out a cell phone encased in a cracked, black case. Silently, she scrolled through it, and then held it out to him. He looked down and saw his name, cell phone, and current address listed in her contacts. He frowned. "How did you get this information?"

"AJ always believed he would die young. He knew his time on this earth would be short, and he worked hard to make his imprint in the time he had." Her voice trembled slightly, and she cleared her throat. "After my dad died, AJ was concerned that there was no one to protect me. He told me that if I ever ran into trouble and he wasn't around to help, then I should go to you. He made sure I always had your updated contact information. Every time you moved, I knew how to find you at any hour of the day."

Son of a bitch. Chase closed his fingers around the phone. "He didn't tell me he gave you my info."

"He said you didn't need to know. He said you'd just say yes." She managed a smile. "What he didn't say was that you would come riding up gallantly on your white horse and throw yourself at my feet in a desperate attempt to save me when I didn't even ask for help."

"My horse isn't white. He's a bay, and he'd be highly insulted to know you called him white." Chase knew why AJ hadn't told him that he was first in line as Mira's savior.

If he had, Chase would have found a way to talk him out of it. He wasn't a protector, and he didn't have time to do anything but focus on repairing the damage his father had done to him and his brothers. And yet, Chase had decided to rescue her anyway, all on his own. "You would never have come to me for help, would you?"

She shook her head. "Never." She shrugged. "I'm kind of an independent girl. I like to save the world on my own."

"Yeah, I suspect you do." He cocked his head thoughtfully. "AJ knew you'd never ask, didn't he?"

She nodded slowly. "Yes, he probably did." She looked at him. "So why did he give me your information?"

Chase rubbed his jaw. "He knew that I'd offer. By telling you that I was the guy to ask for help, he was setting the stage for you to trust me, so that when I offered to help, you'd let me. He had it planned all along, didn't he? Manipulative bastard." He couldn't keep the affection out of his voice. AJ had known them both too well.

She laughed then, her fingers brushing against his as she retrieved her phone from him. "You're much more stubborn than I'd have expected you to be, getting all insistent on marrying me."

He grinned. "You're a hell of a lot more difficult to convince than I'd have anticipated. AJ led me to believe you had the ability to think logically. I had no idea you would get all emotional on me. I'm not really into the emotional thing, just so you know."

"Well, you'll have to learn to deal with it," she said, poking the phone into his chest. "I'm highly emotional. I find it cathartic. Suppressing emotions will never get you anywhere."

Her words made something leap through him. "I'll have to learn to deal with it? Is that your way of saying, 'Yes, Chase, I am willing to sully my pristine reputation by getting knocked up by you and then running off to Wyoming to be your shotgun bride?'"

She laughed out loud then, a sound that made him chuckle. Damn, she had an engaging laugh. "A shotgun bride sounds so romantic," she remarked with a deadpan expression. "I've always dreamed of it."

He stiffened at her words, knowing full well how women fantasized about their weddings. He didn't want her to have expectations that he would inevitably fail to meet. "I'm busy on the ranch," he warned her. "I can't be the husband type, so don't expect it. One year of cohabitation while you get big and fat with my kid."

"Well, I have no interest in turning my loyalties over to a husband, so we're even." She cocked her head, and he saw her eyes soften. "*Your* kid? You said that like it was already true, like you mean it."

He nodded, possessiveness surging through him. "There's no halfway in my book. Yeah, I'm claiming that baby that's in your belly. Obviously, I have sperm of steel to knock you up long distance, but hey, I've always been an overachiever." He reached out and put his hand on her stomach, feeling the softness of her flesh beneath his touch. "That's my kid in there, Mira. From this moment onward, there is no other truth."

"I believe you," she said softly as she put her hand over his, not to pull him off her belly, but to hold his hand there. It was an intimate moment, one he'd never thought he'd experience, but it felt right. "You truly will stand beside AJ's child as your own, no matter what."

"Of course."

She bit her lip. "One year?"

Hope surged through him, and fear, but also something else. A feeling of anticipation that he hadn't experienced in a long time. A year of Mira living in his house sounded good. Really, really good. "One year. Then you're free, but even after we divorce, I'll always, *always*, be Dad. I won't fail either of you."

She stood on her tiptoes and pressed a kiss to his cheek. Her lips were warm and soft, and the kiss far too fleeting. "Well then, cowboy, you better get your shotgun, because you just got yourself a bride."

CHAPTER FOUR

MIRA WAS SITTING on her living room couch, grimly studying the stack of moving boxes in the corner, ready to be put into storage. Prior to Chase's proposal, she'd already had almost the entire house packed up to be sold. The house was going on the market in three days, regardless of whether she left town or not.

She had no choice but to let go of the house she'd grown up in. She needed the money from the sale of the house to pay off her mother's remaining medical expenses. It was the right thing to do. But sitting there, surrounded by the things that reflected her past, including the last remnants of her parents' belongings, it suddenly felt clinical and cold to be packing up and moving out, to be leaving so she could marry a man she didn't even know.

It had been bad enough selling the house when she was at least going to stay in town and do something heroic like try to get a job filing permits at the town office. But to be leaving behind every last memory of her family to marry a stranger and possibly raise a child in the barren, friendless world of the untamed west? It felt a little barbaric.

She looked around the living room. The walls were empty now, but the outlines of the picture frames had left marks on the formerly white paint that had since turned yellow and stained. Thirty-two years of sunlight had left their mark.

She knew every photograph that had once hung on the walls. Her parents' wedding picture. Her baby picture. Her dad's first day on the job as sheriff. A photo of her and AJ at their high school graduation, bedecked in their black gowns and huge smiles.

Every memory of a lifetime was now packed away. She was taking only one photograph, the one taken of her and her parents the day they'd dropped her off at college. It was the last time she'd seen them both alive and healthy. Her mother's clothes were already bagged up to be donated to charity. Her life, her world, stripped away—

The front door slammed open, making Mira jump as her best friend, Taylor Shaw, strode in. "You slept with him? After all these years, you finally met Chase Stockton, and then slept with him? Why didn't you tell me?"

Mira grinned at Taylor's energetic, unapologetic entrance. The mere appearance of her friend made her feel better. "You were on a transcontinental flight at the time," she said. "I figured it could wait."

"Sex can never wait, especially for you, my celibate friend." Taylor was wearing jeans, her favorite pink sweatshirt, and a pair of old flip-flops, indicating that she'd just arrived home from her trip to Indonesia. Taylor always went for her comfy clothes after spending an eternity on a plane. Her curly mop of blond hair was somewhat bouncing irreverently around her face, but the three-inch gold hoops dangling from her ears added that hint of femininity she never seemed to lack. "I had to hear about it from Octavia, who accosted me before I even pulled into my driveway. Apparently, the whole town saw his truck in front of your house all night after the funeral. You're a complete slut, and I mean that in the most affectionate, supportive way." She flopped down on the couch, then glanced around at the boxes. "Did you find a place yet? Clock's ticking."

Mira grinned at the change in subject. Taylor never worried about societal proprieties. She just dealt with life straight on, and she loved that about her friend. "I sort of found a place," she said, hesitating before explaining further. She still hadn't decided whether to tell Taylor the truth about the pregnancy. Chase had been adamant that no one could know AJ was the biological father, because Alan was just that good. But Taylor was her best friend, the one who had stood by her all the years while she'd been taking care of her mom. "I'm moving to Wyoming to live with Chase," she said carefully, testing the waters. "To marry him, actually." The words tasted thick and muddy on her tongue, and for a moment, she felt like she was going to throw up. What had seemed like a solid, logical solution two nights ago now sounded...less than sane, pretty much.

Taylor's blue eyes widened. "*What?*" Then she sighed. "Oh, man, I know you're devastated by AJ's death, but marrying his best friend isn't going to bring him back, not for either of you. One night of sex doesn't create that kind of bond. Just because AJ loved Chase doesn't mean that you would automatically love him. You've hated every boyfriend I've ever had, right? Love doesn't translate across third parties."

"Yeah, true, but that's because you have singularly bad taste in men."

Taylor wrinkled her nose. "This is about you, not me, and the fact you're having a thinly disguised emotional collapse. To be expected, of course, but marrying a hot cowboy is a bit of a permanent solution, you know? Although, as bad decisions go, I guess it could be worse, like throwing yourself off a cliff, for example. "

Mira picked up a tape gun and dragged it across one of the few remaining boxes, locking away more of her past. "It's kind of a trial thing. For a year." She sliced the tape off, then grabbed a marker to jot a note about the contents on the side of it.

"A year? What?" Taylor stood up, her hands on her hips. "This is completely unacceptable. I'm going to kidnap you. We're going to have a crazy girls' weekend and you'll realize that you can handle your life just fine, even though it kind of feels overwhelming right now." She held out her hand, and wiggled her fingers for Mira to take them. "Come on. Let's leave now. We'll be back in two days, enough time to finish clearing out the boxes before it goes on the market."

"I'm pregnant." The words burst out of her mouth before she'd even decided to say them.

Well, so much for not telling Taylor the truth. But just saying it felt like a thousand burdens had fallen off her shoulders.

"What?" Taylor's mouth dropped open, and her hand fell limply to her side. "How could you possibly know already? It's been twenty-four hours since he left."

God, here it came. Was she really going to tell her? Mira dragged another box over to her to tape it, avoiding Taylor's gaze. "Yeah, well, when my mom died last month, AJ came to town to see me. He stayed over."

Taylor sank back onto the couch beside her. "You slept with *AJ*? But you guys are completely platonic. Like siblings, though not actually siblings, for which I think we're both eternally grateful given the fact that he *knocked you up*. Dear God. How is this possible? There's no connection between you guys."

"Was," Mira corrected. "And I know there was no romance between us. It was a one-night thing. We were both in bad shape, because you know how much he loved my mom. She was more his mom than his own mother was. We cried, we held each other, and then it just happened."

"Oh, God." Taylor leaned forward, searching her face. "Was it good? Was it worth a ten-year dry spell?"

"Eight years, and it was perfect, in the way that it was, but no, nothing really sexy about it." She still couldn't believe she'd been naked with him, but being held in his arms when the grief had been so overwhelming was a gift she'd never forget. Neither of them would have made it through that night alone.

"Wow." Taylor rubbed her forehead. "It's AJ's baby, for sure? Did he know before he died?"

"No. I just found out Wednesday morning."

"Oh, *God*. On the morning of his *funeral?*" Taylor shook her head. "You know, AJ would probably have loved that timing. He'd want you to be looking toward the future instead of wallowing in the past. Can't you see him in heaven, cheering you on as you peed on a stick right before his funeral?"

Mira managed a smile. "This is true. He would have enjoyed that."

"Knowing AJ, he probably did it on purpose. He decided to leave behind a legacy, and figured you were the one woman with enough cojones to kick his dad's ass if he came after the kid. So, yay, girl power, I guess? Maybe you could get like an award or something?"

This time, the laughter bubbled out. "You're insane, Taylor."

"I know. It's my gift. But I'm guessing that since you discovered your MTB status after his skydiving accident, you weren't able to scrape any money from him? All to charity?"

"Yep. And what's MTB status?"

"Mother-to-be, of course. Hello, get with the times." Taylor eyed her belly. "Is it kicking yet?"

"Talking actually. Asked me for cash yesterday. I told it to get a job. I feel like I need to set some standards early on, you know? My dad would never approve of being soft with the kid."

"Amen, sistah. Sheriff Cabot will be watching you." Taylor leaned back and propped her feet up on a cardboard box. "So, what's the old bastard's status?"

"Alan? He knows AJ spent the night after the funeral. He thinks I used my body to convince AJ to change his will. I suspect he's going to try to use me to invalidate the will."

Taylor nodded. "Rock on. So he's after you for money, but in the process of trying to expose you for the deceitful fraud we all know you are, he'll get the delightful surprise of figuring out that when you croon to your uterus, you're actually talking to his grandchild. How fun is that? It's like a cat and mouse game, but he's this shape-shifting, immortally deadly panther, and you're like, a stuffed mouse, staked out in the yard, waiting to be munched."

Mira blinked. "I think my odds are a little better than that."

"Sweetie, no one's odds are better than that when it comes to Alan. Your dad was the only one who could stop Alan. The only reason Alan respected your dad was because he knew that your dad would shoot him if necessary, all in the name of duty, of course, but still. Once your dad died, there was no one to stop Alan. AJ had to forget to open his parachute in order to escape him. You think you can dodge that bullet?"

Mira frowned. "AJ didn't forget to open his parachute. It was faulty." But even as she said it, she remembered all too clearly the Christmas Eve she'd found him on the South Bridge, ready to jump into the freezing water when he was thirteen. If she'd been five minutes later, she would have lost him that night, instead of a few days ago. Deflated, she sank down. "You think AJ killed himself?" She hadn't thought of that, but it was possible.

Taylor shrugged. "I don't know, Mira, but it wouldn't surprise me. You know perfectly well that Alan was trying to buy AJ's company so he could steal it from him and force AJ home. He almost did it too. His reach is incredible. AJ believed in life after death, so, yeah, I think it's very possible he figured the next life was better than this one." She cocked her head. "And now you have to take on Alan yourself. You'll lose, you know. You'll lose the battle, and you'll lose the kid."

Well, there was nothing like stark honesty from a best friend to make a girl more convinced that marrying a total stranger might actually be the least insane choice at the moment. "That's why Chase and I set it up to make it look like I slept with him. He's claiming to be the dad."

"Seriously? You didn't sleep with Chase?" Taylor looked at her thoughtfully. "That's sort of heroic of him."

"Isn't it? After I stopped freaking out at the sound of the words, 'marry me,' I came to the same conclusion."

"It may be control-freak, hero-complex, overcompensating-male 'heroic,' but it also could be simple super-nice-guy 'heroic.'" Taylor settled more deeply into the couch. "Girl, I think you need to tell me everything."

Mira did. Forty minutes and a pint of ice cream later, the entire sordid story had been replayed. Just retelling the facts had reinforced the enormity of the situation she was facing, and the magnitude of the decision she'd made with Chase. "So, I'm heading off to Wyoming to enter into a one-year business contract involving illusionary sex and marriage vows that are total lies. I think it's the perfect foundation for a relationship, don't you?"

"Absolutely. We need more marriages based on lies, abstinence, and the exchange of money." Taylor folded her arms across her chest. "But I have to admit, I'm going to have to veto it. You can't marry him."

Mira's heart fell. "What are you saying? I needed your support. I thought you were on board with it. I'm a little freaked out about moving to Wyoming to marry a guy I barely know. I need a kick in the pants, not someone telling me I can't do it. AJ trusted him, so—"

"I know, I know." Taylor waved her hand dismissively. "I'm sure Chase is a great guy, and he'll fulfill his part of the bargain. I trust AJ's judgment. And you do need help dealing with Alan, or you're never going to see your child again. I'm on board with all that."

Mira frowned. "Then why did you say I can't go?"

"Because, my dear friend, of how you look when you talk about him."

Something clenched in Mira's belly, and heat suffused her cheeks. "How I look?"

"Yes. You got a little starry-eyed, girl."

"What? I so did not. I don't even have that gene anymore when it comes to guys."

"You do, and you did." Taylor pried herself off the couch and knelt in front of Mira, putting her hands on Mira's knees, searching Mira's face with the earnestness of a best friend. "You believe in him, Mira. You don't know him, but a little part of you is a little bit in love with him."

"*What?*" She gaped at her friend. "You're insane—"

Taylor rolled her eyes. "Yes, we already covered that, and I concur. However, I'm also right. Insane people can be correct a large percentage of the time. And you, my dear friend, are looking at Chase like he's going to swoop in and whisk you off to the land of magic and fairy tales, just like you did with Brian."

Mira snorted, laughing at her friend's description, refusing to give credence to it. "Seriously with that, Taylor? I'm not like that anymore. I don't get dreamy about guys, and I am very clear on the fact that I do *not* want to be rescued by any man, ever again. I'm using Chase to rescue myself. There's a difference. He's like a hammer. Or a roll of duct tape. Things you can use in an emergency to save your life."

Taylor's eyebrows shot up. "Chase is duct tape? Really?"

"Yeah. Not the boring gray kind. He's like that crazy kind with the cool colors. He's pretty duct tape that smells good." She shrugged, recalling his scent when he'd climbed into the tree with her. "Duct tape with a nice voice, too. And shoulders. Great shoulders. He's like designer duct tape—you appreciate how fantastic it looks, but in the end, you use it to tape the fender on your car just the way you'd use any other duct tape. I'm marrying duct tape for the sake of my unborn child. It's pretty basic. No love involved."

Taylor snorted. "You're pregnant, broke, and alone. Your mom just died. Your best friend and the father of your baby just died. You've spent all your money taking care of your mom, and selling the house will barely even cover medical expenses. You are incredibly resourceful and practical, and yes, Chase is definitely duct tape of the highest quality, but you're *seeing* him with your hopeful little heart instead of your practical Girl Scout hands." She sighed. "Besides, what woman wouldn't want to be rescued by a handsome cowboy? Because I heard he was devastatingly handsome, and his rental car wasn't exactly cheap."

Mira bit her lower lip. "I did notice that he's handsome," she admitted. "And nice. I definitely noticed both of those things." Crud. Was Taylor right? Was she really being stupid again, like she'd been with Brian? She was too smart to get emotionally invested in another man, especially when something this important was at stake.

Taylor tucked Mira's hair behind her ear. "You don't need to tie yourself down forever to a man just to get out of this current situation. Marriage is forever, babe. Even if you get divorced, he'll be on record as that baby's father, which gives him rights. Trust me, you don't want that with the wrong guy."

"Parental rights?" Wow. She'd forgotten about that. Weight settled on Mira's shoulders, dragging her down. "I can't fight Alan on my own. You know that." Her hand settled protectively over her belly.

"We'll think of something." Taylor squeezed her hand. "You have several months before you'll start to show. Rushing off to marry Chase is the wrong choice. You're panicking, and you're seeing him through rose-colored glasses because you're desperate."

Mira closed her eyes, trying to quell the rising sense of panic. "I'm not wrong about him. I can trust him."

"Just like you could trust Brian?"

"Dammit, Taylor!" Mira pulled away and stood up. She walked across the room and braced her hands on the window frame, staring out at the tiny, weed-filled yard that her parents had once tended so lovingly. Was Taylor right? Was she being stupid again? Was she overreacting to her situation? She'd always managed to pull herself through every situation. Why would this one be different?

But it was different, because it wasn't only her own life that she had in her hands. It was her baby's. AJ's baby. A child with a horrible, horrible enemy who was stronger than she was.

"I'll help," Taylor said. "You're not alone."

Mira laughed softly, and turned to face her. "Taylor, you travel almost all the time for your job. I love you, but your life is on the road, in every country but this one. You couldn't even get your boss to let you off to come home for the funeral. I'm the one living here, who has to face my life."

Taylor didn't give up. "I have money. I'll give you some."

"Even if you gave me every last cent you had, it wouldn't be enough to fight Alan, and we both know it."

Taylor bit her lip, and gave a slight nod. "He is a pretty rich bastard," she acknowledged with a grimace.

Mira looked around the room. This time, instead of lost memories, she saw only the faded paint on the walls and the tattered carpet. The air was tinged with the scent of hospitals and sick people, and the odor of mold that could never quite be cleansed. "I don't want to be here anymore, Taylor. I almost got out and started a life when my parents got in the accident, and now I am not only free to go, but I have motivation to leave." She met her friend's gaze. "I want to get out. I want to do this. Chase is giving me the chance to start a new life, and I want to do it."

Taylor studied her, then sighed. "Okay, then. Go to Wyoming, but put off the wedding. Get your freedom, get your feet under you again, but don't trap yourself or that baby. Escaping Alan is worth nothing if you get yourself in a trap that will haunt you forever." Involuntarily, Taylor rubbed her ring finger on her left hand. It was empty now, but it hadn't always been.

A chill crept over Mira, remembering what Taylor had endured at the hands of a man that the entire town had loved. "You have a point," she conceded.

"Of course I do. We've both made terrible, terrible mistakes when it comes to men. They were both men we had every reason to believe in, and we were wrong. You don't even know Chase, other than what AJ has said about him." She gave Mira a steely look. "Protect yourself, Mira. Don't fantasize that he's some fairy tale hero. Chase is a man, and by definition, that means he's flawed. Never forget that." She sighed wistfully. "Your dad's not around with his gun anymore to rescue us."

She laughed softly. "I know. He was handy for that, wasn't he?"

Taylor smiled. "He was. Your dad was awesome. That's what your baby deserves, a man with a gun who isn't afraid to use it. Hang on until you find that guy, okay? Don't marry Chase tomorrow."

"Chase is a cowboy," Mira felt compelled to point out. "I'm sure he has guns. He didn't seem the type to resist using them."

Taylor raised her brows. "Fine, he has guns. Will you at least do me the favor of stalling the wedding until you make sure you like what he aims them at? Two months."

Two months felt like an interminable time to acquire the protective shield of marriage to Chase. "Two weeks."

"One month. You won't even be showing by then. It will be more believable if you wait long enough to find out that you got pregnant from your night with him. If you get married *after* you 'find out' you're pregnant with his child, then it makes sense you guys would get married in a hurry. Otherwise, it doesn't ring true."

Mira considered this. "That idea has some validity, from a strategic perspective."

"At last!" Taylor clapped her hands in mock celebration. "The girl finally sees the light!"

"I can't lie to Chase, though. I'm not going to go out there under false pretenses." She walked over to the table and pulled out her phone. "I'm going to tell him that I'm not going to marry him right away."

Taylor stayed her hand. "Maybe you should wait until you're out there. You don't want him to change his mind—"

"I'm not going to lie to him," Mira insisted. "If he decides not to help, then I'll think of something else." She started to dial his number, when a movement outside caught her eye. She glanced up in time to see a long, black limousine pause in front of the house. Her heart started to pound as she watched Alan roll down the back window and peer at the house.

She caught her breath, her heart pounding as his gaze met hers. He gave her a small salute, and then rolled up the window and the car drove off.

Sweat broke out down her back and slithered down her spine. "He's not going to give up," she said, softly. "He hates me for taking AJ away from him, and now it's his chance for payback. He wants to invalidate AJ's will and get his money, and he's going to use me to do it." She looked back at Taylor, who was standing up now, concern etched on her face. "He'll dig deep enough that he'll find out I bought the pregnancy test in town, won't he? He'll know I bought it before Chase ever came to town." Suddenly, she felt sick, sick all the way to the depth of her soul.

"Dammit, girl." Taylor walked over to the window and put her arm around Mira's shoulder. "You better get on that plane to Wyoming, and because I love you dearly, I'm going to hope like hell that Chase is the man you think he is, because if he's not, you might be out of your league."

Mira looked at Taylor. "You think I should marry him? Right away?"

"Right away sounds like an awfully risky step, but so is leaving yourself exposed to Alan." Taylor bit her lip. "I don't know, Mira. I just don't know."

"Yeah, me either." She put her arm around Taylor's waist and leaned her head on her shoulder, watching Alan's car disappear down the decrepit road.

"He's hot, right? Chase?"

Mira smiled. "Very."

"Good kisser?"

"Apparently. He managed to seduce me the night I met him, right?"

"Powerful?"

"He exudes power. He stood up to Alan at the reception, and Alan backed down."

"Really?" Taylor grinned. "I'd have loved to see that."

Mira smiled. "It was a good moment." She had been so shocked when Alan had grabbed her that she hadn't had time to prepare herself. When Chase had stepped in, it had been an amazing respite from the crush of emotions flooding her.

"Well, then, maybe this time, you're supposed to leap without a net." Taylor glanced at her. "You've been to hell and back, and you're going to be a mom. At some point you need to trust your gut."

"My gut says he's a good man." She didn't even hesitate.

"Then, my friend, just maybe it's time for you to get married." Taylor grimaced. "Or just buy a big gun. One or the other. I'm not sure which is the best choice."

Mira sighed. "Me either."

Taylor raised her brows. "So what are you going to do?"

Mira looked down at the phone still clutched in her hands, the one that AJ had programmed Chase's phone number into. "I'm going to call him," she said.

"And say what?"

She started to dial. "I don't know." But she did. She knew in her gut exactly what she needed to say to him. The shadow from Alan's drive-by still lurked, reminding her exactly how bad a wrong choice could be. Could she really bind herself to a stranger just to hide from Alan?

She couldn't. It wasn't worth the risk.

She knew what she had to do...but as she dialed the phone, she felt her stomach sinking, telling her that the choice she was about to make was wrong. Dead wrong. But she knew she had to do it anyway.

CHAPTER FIVE

WHAT THE HELL had he done?

Wearily, Chase drove up the long driveway to his ranch, his mind still spinning. When he'd left Mira's house that morning, he'd been feeling like a gallant hero doing the right thing. But the further he'd gotten from that small southern town, the more the doubt had set in.

What the hell was he doing? Marrying a woman and offering himself up as a father? He had no business doing either one. He didn't want to get tangled up with a woman, and he had no damned idea how to be a dad.

Swearing, he slammed his truck door shut and strode across the dirt toward his front door, his boots crunching into the rock. He vaulted up the front steps, then paused when he saw a familiar motorcycle parked in the shadows by the door.

Irritation flooded him at the sight of the motorcycle that belonged to one of his brothers.

He wasn't in the right frame of mind to deal with Zane tonight...shit. Had he really just thought that? He'd been working on his brothers since he'd bought the place, trying to get them to move to the ranch. Zane's appearance was a rarity, something Chase had been trying to cultivate for years. He should be fired up that Zane was at his place waiting for him, but he just felt *annoyed?* It was because of his preoccupation with Mira. Was he really going to let the distraction of a woman interfere with his relationship with his brothers? His reaction to Zane's motorcycle made it obvious that he couldn't go through with the deal with Mira.

He couldn't marry her or claim fatherhood of the kid. He'd give her money, set her up in a different town, but he was not going to bring her into his life. He couldn't afford it.

In an even worse mood now, he flung open the front door and strode into the foyer. He didn't bother to call out. He just walked straight into the family room. Sure enough, Zane was stretched out on the couch like he owned it, except for the fact that his boots were still on, as was his thick leather jacket, always ready to leave on a moment's notice. His jeans and his plaid shirt were the only cowboy left in him, but he'd been one of the best bull riders in the region at one time. He'd traded the bulls for a bike, and claimed to never think about his old life at all.

Chase didn't believe him. He'd seen Zane watching the horses in the corral when he'd thought Chase wasn't around. What he didn't know was why Zane had walked away from that life, and refused to ever look back.

"I poured you a drink." Zane nodded toward the tonic water sitting on the coffee table. "I brought you the hard stuff. Raspberry flavored, I think."

Chase sat down on the black leather couch and studied his brother, ignoring the water. He didn't drink alcohol, thanks to the lessons he'd learned from his father. "Where have you been? It's been six months. I thought you'd cracked up your bike for the last time. You good?"

"Always." Zane swung his feet to the floor, his motorcycle boots thudding on the polished wood. His dark brown hair was cut short for once, but the diamond earring glittered in his left ear. Where the hell was the guy who used to wear a cowboy hat and well-worn boots? "You look like shit," Zane commented. "What happened?"

Chase sighed, the weight of his recent decision returning with no mercy at the question. "A good friend died. He knocked up his best friend before he bit it. She's got no money, and his dad is like ours, only with serious leverage and power."

Zane whistled softly as he took a swig of the cold beer he'd helped himself to. Chase always kept his favorite brand in the fridge, for the occasions when he stopped by. "Brings back memories, doesn't it?"

"Yeah, it does." Chase watched his brother swig the beer, and suddenly, he wanted one as well. He wanted to feel that bitter taste coat his tongue and burn down his throat. Shit. He hadn't wanted a drink in years. Scowling, he tossed his hat on the table, and then bent his head, running his hands through his hair as he tried to pull himself together. "I told her I'd marry her and claim the kid. I gave her a plane ticket for tomorrow to move out here."

Zane didn't answer, and after a long moment, Chase looked up. His brother was spinning the bottle between his fingers, leaving prints on the condensation. He was studying the bottle intently, as if he hadn't even heard what Chase had said.

But Chase knew he had. That was Zane's way. Silence until he had something to say.

Zane finally looked up. "You heard from anyone else lately?"

Chase knew Zane was asking about their seven half-brothers, the legacy of their bastard father. "No." Chase had bought the ranch five years ago with the goal of bringing his family back together. He had enough acreage for every Stockton man to have his own ranch, but so far, no one had come. Granted, Steen was in prison, so he had a valid reason, but no one else had come back to the town they'd grown up in. Chase wasn't giving up, though. The bond between the brothers was intense and unshakeable, and he knew that every single one of them would drop everything for each other, if one of them needed help. The connection was there, and someday he was going to bring them back together. "You going to move into the ranch?" he asked Zane, knowing the answer, but unwilling to let his brother off the hook.

"No. I like the road." Zane raised his eyebrows. "At some point, you have to stop trying to fix what's broken, bro. Broken's okay."

"Yeah, I know broken is okay, but fixed can be better."

"You so sure about that?" Zane leaned forward, his beefy forearms resting on his muscular quads. There was a tattoo on his arm of his favorite bull, the one that had dumped every single cowboy, except for Zane, who'd ridden him three times. "You want to bring a woman into this house? You want to marry one?" He raised his hand. "Blood oath, bro, remember? Never let a woman come between us? Or did you forget that?"

Chase rubbed the mark on his palm that all the brothers carried. "I remember."

Zane studied him for a long moment. "So, you think she's different, then? You think she doesn't make you violate the oath?"

The oath had been a promise to never allow a woman to bring negative energy between the brothers or to take a position of power in any of their lives, which basically banned marriage or a significant relationship. All the Stockton men knew how badly women could screw things up, but none of them were willing to go celibate. Hence, the creatively worded oath that basically translated to "brothers first, women last, every single time."

"I'm not sure. I barely know her." But he felt like he did know her. She *was* different. This was the woman he'd known for a decade, and yet, at the same time, he'd known her only for a few hours. Shit. He stood up, restless. "I'm going to go for a ride."

Zane didn't move. "Sit down. It's almost midnight, and your pony is napping."

Slowly, Chase sat down, surprised by Zane's command. His brother never wanted to talk about anything. "What's up?"

"How bad's the dad?" Zane asked.

"Bad."

Zane was quiet for another moment. "How about her?"

"I trust her."

Zane looked sharply at him. "No shit?"

He shrugged.

"They won't come if there's a woman here," Zane said. "None of them will come."

He was referring to their brothers, the ones Chase had been working so hard to bring home. Chase ground his jaw, not answering, but he knew Zane had a valid point. His ranch offered a respite from women, a place for the brothers to bond. Although none of them had moved back, they all stopped in from time to time, just as Zane had done tonight. They were linked by a brutal childhood that had required them to fight for each other and protect each other. Nothing came between their commitment to each other, especially a woman. "I —" His phone rang suddenly, and he looked down. His pulse quickened when he saw it was Mira. "It's her." He answered it immediately. "You okay?"

"I can't marry you." She spoke without preamble, direct and to the point.

Something plunged through his gut like a knife, and he tightened his grip on the phone. "What?"

"I don't know you. I can't bind myself to you for life, or give you parental rights to my child. Forever is a long time." There was a panicky edge to her voice, and she was talking so fast that he knew she was on the verge of falling apart. "I'm running from one nightmare. How do I know I'm not running into another one? I can't risk it, Chase. I mean, I know you through AJ, but what does that mean? We don't know each other. This is my life, my baby, my everything. I just... I just can't."

Based on his conversation with his brother, her backing out should have relieved him, but it hadn't. It felt completely wrong, edging him toward panic. He felt like he was sinking into quicksand and it was closing over his head. "Mira, just get on the plane. Come out here. We'll give it four weeks. If you feel like you can't trust me by that point, then we'll call it off."

There was a moment of silence, then she took a deep breath. "Really? We don't have to get married right away? You're okay with that?"

"Of course I am." There it was. Such an easy solution. Bring her out there, but not tie himself down. It gave him time to see if he could find a way to repay his debt to AJ without sacrificing what mattered to him. If not, the marriage was off. "We won't even tell anyone you're pregnant. We'll just do a test run and see if it can work."

She laughed softly, her voice filled with relief. "Okay, then. I wanted to come, but I sort of panicked. I didn't want to come under false pretenses and not marry you once I got there. I feel better now. We'll just see how it goes, then."

He smiled at the sound of her laugh. The fact that she'd been panicking as well made his own tension abate, replaced by a need to step up and protect her. "It'll be okay. We'll get it right."

"Okay." She was smiling now. He could hear it in her voice. "I'll see you tomorrow, then, okay?"

"I'll meet you at the airport...unless you want me to fly down there and get you?"

She laughed again. "I'm very capable of navigating an airport by myself, but that's a very nice offer. I appreciate it, but I'm fine. See you tomorrow night. And...Chase?"

"Yeah?"

"Thanks. For all of it."

He smiled. "My pleasure." He was still grinning when he hung up the phone, then his smile faded when he saw his brother studying him. "What?"

"The mighty has fallen."

~

MIRA SAW him the moment she walked through the gates into the luggage area.

Chase was leaning against the far wall, his hands jammed into his pockets as he carefully scanned the faces pouring through the gate. He was wearing a brown cowboy hat this time, and his faded jeans sat low on his lean hips. His plaid shirt was open at the collar, revealing tanned skin and the same gold chain she'd noticed before. He looked like a real life, untamed cowboy, and a ripple of anticipation pulsed through her. This man was here for *her*.

He finally saw her, and his gaze stopped, pinned to her. Heat flushed her body, and she lifted her chin, trying to quell the thudding of her heart. He levered himself off the wall and strode toward her, the languid, easy gait of a man who could saunter across a thousand miles of barren country and never break a sweat. He never took his gaze off hers as he neared, but his expression was unreadable.

He came to a stop in front of her, still studying her face.

She pulled back her shoulders, craning her neck to look up at him. "You're taller than I remembered."

"Am I?" He slid his hand behind her neck, his touch warm and seductive. "My dear Mira," he whispered. "I know everyone in this town, and this is a small airport. If we decide to go through with it, it needs to be set up from the start, or there will be holes for Alan to find."

Her heart started to pound even harder. "What are you saying?"

"We slept together two nights ago, and now you're moving out here to live with me." His fingers tightened on the nape of her neck, drawing her closer. "I have to greet you the right way. You on board?"

Oh, God. *He was going to kiss her.* Why hadn't she thought of that before? But he was right. "Okay," she managed, her voice no more than a nervous squeak. "Lay it on me, cowboy."

He grinned. "Be careful what you ask for, sweetheart. A cowboy has a lot of talents, and kissing just happens to be one of them." Then he lowered his head and kissed her.

Her heart leapt the moment his lips touched hers. The kiss was tender and tantalizing, his lips so warm and soft against hers that she melted into him. His fingers tightened on the back of her neck, and she felt his other arm wrap around her waist, tugging her against him.

The well-muscled hardness of his body was in sharp contrast to hers, and he seemed to tower over her, wrapping her up in an embrace that was so delicious she never wanted to leave it.

He angled his head and deepened the kiss, sending spirals of electricity running through her. Instinctively, she slid her arms around his neck, leaning into him. His tongue slipped through her parted lips, and for a split second, she almost melted right there. Dear God. Was this what a real kiss was supposed to be like? It had been so long she'd completely forgotten what it felt like to be thoroughly kissed by a man. She wanted more, more kisses, more of him, more touching, more—

"Who in the hell's this?" A deep, raspy male voice blasted in her left ear, and she jumped back, completely embarrassed to be caught nearly climbing into Chase's skin in the middle of an airport next to a baggage claim.

Chase, however, pulled her right back against him, tucking her under his arm before he swung around to face whoever had interrupted them.

A weathered cowboy in well-worn jeans and scuffed boots was standing beside them. His salt-and-pepper hair was just visible beneath his black cowboy hat, and his denim shirt looked like it had been through a thousand washings. There was a sparkle in his blue eyes, and his grin was engaging as he surveyed them.

Chase tightened his arm around her shoulders. "Evening, Gary. This is my cousin, Mira Cabot. Mira, this is Gary Keller."

Cousin? She blanched. Was Chase *that* kind of guy, the kind who lived in a world where people made out with their cousins on a regular basis?

Gary burst out laughing, and he slammed his hand onto Chase's shoulder. "Always think you're funny, don't you, Stockton? Cousin, my ass." He swept off his hat and bowed low to Mira. "Welcome to Wyoming, my lady. If Chase gives you a hard time, you feel free to ring me up. He's never too old to get his hide tanned."

She grinned with relief, realizing it had all been a joke. "Thank you. I appreciate it."

Gary set his hat back on his head, gazing at her more intently now. "Haven't seen Chase around women much," he said thoughtfully. "You must be somethin' special."

She felt her cheeks turn red. "I, um—"

"She is." Chase pressed a kiss to the top of her head. "It took me ten years to get her to come out here, but she finally made it. The right bribe makes all the difference."

Gary guffawed again, and she smiled, relaxing against Chase. It had been a long time since she'd had much to laugh about, and it felt good to be around a man who wasn't going to get weighed down by what they were embarking upon.

"Ten years, eh?" Gary eyed her. "Why'd you keep him waiting ten years?"

She grinned. "My mom always told me that the right guy will wait. So, I had to test him. I figured ten years was about long enough."

"Shoot, I married my lady two weeks after I met her. I'd never have waited ten years for her." He flexed his arms. "She knew she had to grab me while the grabbing was good, or I'd have been gone forever."

Chase laughed. "It took you nine years to get her to say yes, you old liar. Don't mess with Mira, or I'll have to hunt you down."

Gary feigned fear, clasping his heart. "Oh, I'm scared now. Watch out, Mira, the man's a force to be reckoned with." The older man winked. "Sunday dinner? The little lady would love to meet the woman who finally got Chase's attention."

Dinner? Mira started to panic. How could she go to dinner and keep up a façade with such a nice man. "Oh, I don't—"

"You bet," Chase said. "I'll bring the pie."

"Excellent." Gary winked at Mira again. "I invite Chase only because he makes the best apple pie in the county. It's the only reason anyone invites him anywhere." He tipped his hat, his affection for Chase evident. He was so warm and engaging that Mira knew he was the real deal, a genuinely nice cowboy who lived by the code of loyalty. "Welcome again, Mira. If you're good for Chase, then you have my vote. See you guys on Sunday."

Sunday? As she watched him walk away, the enormity of what she'd just stepped into suddenly seemed to loom up. This wasn't a simple façade between the two of them. This was an intention to deceive an entire world, one by one, laying the seeds for a deception that had to be strong enough to last the lifetime of her child.

Good God, what had she done?

CHAPTER SIX

CHASE LEANED MOODILY on his kitchen counter, watching Mira inspect his kitchen. He'd spent a lot of time refinishing the cabinets and installing the granite countertops. He was proud of how the kitchen had come out, but right now, he didn't even care what she thought of it. All he could do was focus on her. Her hair was loose, tumbling around her shoulders. She was wearing old jeans that fit her with enough sensual perfection to make his gut clench every time she turned around. He'd noticed her bright pink toenail polish, and her bare ankles made it clear she was still wearing the anklet she'd had on when he'd first met her.

At the funeral, she'd been gorgeous, all fancied up in her dress, but now that she was casual and walking through his house, it was different. It was real now. She was real, and accessible.

He hadn't meant to kiss her when she'd arrived, but when he'd seen her standing there looking both terrified and brave as hell, kissing her had made sense. He'd wanted to claim her, right there, in front of everyone. Kissing her had set her up as being under his protection, and he'd wanted to do that.

Ah, hell, who was he trying to kid? It hadn't been a conscious, strategic decision. It had been a raw, visceral need to imprint himself on her before anyone else could do the same.

The kiss had been incredible. Amazing. Best moment of his life...and then Gary had interfered. After Gary had left, Mira had withdrawn. She'd been careful not to even brush against him as they walked, and her smile had been taut and distant.

The warm, open woman he'd met at the funeral was gone, and he didn't like it.

He wanted the Mira he knew back, but as he watched her walk through *his* house, he had no idea what to do to make it happen. "I'm not used to having a woman in my house," he said finally, hoping that she might take pity on him and help him figure out what to say.

She glanced over at him, and for the first time since the kiss, he saw a small smile curve her mouth. "I'm not used to being in a man's house, so we're even." She turned to face him, her eyes finally meeting his. "I'm not comfortable going to Gary's, Chase. I feel like we're spiraling too fast into a situation that's out of my control."

Ah...so that was it. He considered her concerns for a moment, but it took him less than a split second to dismiss them. He didn't know what it was, but something was burning in him that he hadn't expected. Going to Gary's would cement their connection in the public eye, and he wanted that to happen. Yeah, it wasn't real, and it was, as he'd said, a business partnership only, but he wasn't going to leave her high and dry. His need to protect her and the baby was growing stronger every minute he was with her. "You don't turn down an invite from Gary," he said simply.

She blinked. "Why not?"

He shrugged. "He's a good guy." He didn't want to explain any more than that. To explain what Gary meant to him was to go places he didn't go with people, especially not a woman he barely knew.

Awkward silence settled between them, and he shifted. He had no idea what the hell to do with her. He hadn't been lying when he'd said that he didn't know what to do with a woman in his house. He was so out of his league. "How are you feeling?"

"Fine." She sighed, and he suddenly noticed how tired she looked. There were shadows under her eyes, and her shoulders were slumped.

"You're tired." He walked over to the front hall where he'd dropped her luggage. "Sorry for being an insensitive ass. I'll take you to your room." He swung her bags off the floor and headed down the hall toward the bedrooms. His suite was at the far end, taking up one entire end of the house. "This way."

There were two guest bedrooms. One in the basement, and one right next to his room. The basement would give her privacy and space. It even had a kitchenette so she could make her own meals, and its own bathroom. He'd never even have to see her if he put her down there. They could both live their lives and do their own thing. It would be like not even having her in the house.

He glanced over at her as she walked beside him. His gaze fell on her mouth, and he remembered what it had been like to kiss her. She seemed to sense his perusal, and she caught his eye. Neither of them spoke, but a sensual awareness slithered down his spine and wrapped itself around his gut.

This wasn't simply a woman. It was Mira Cabot, the woman who'd been a part of his consciousness for over a decade.

She wasn't going in the basement.

She was going in the room next to his.

MIRA AWOKE AT MIDNIGHT, her heart hammering.

The moonlight was streaming across her bed, casting an eerie glow across the rustic furnishings. A light breeze was making ripples flutter across the surface of the navy bedspread. For a moment, she forgot where she was, and then the events of the last two days came flooding back over her. How could she forget? She was in cowboy country now, shacking up with the father of her child...potentially. Possibly about to embark on the façade of her life...

Not something that happened to a girl every day.

Sighing, she rolled over onto her side, staring out the window. What had awakened her? The utter silence of the night? The lack of fluorescent lights outdoors? Or the sense of sheer isolation descending upon her like a great weight suffocating her? Was she running away like a wimp? Or taking the brave plunge of a woman who would fight for those she loved? Or was she simply just a confused sod wandering cluelessly through life?

Yeah, any of those could have been enough to drag her out of a well-needed sleep. She'd never been a good sleeper through stress—

An eerie haunting howl drifted through the night. She bolted upright in bed, her heart hammering as the creepy sound sent chills racing down her spine. What in heaven's name was that?

Another howl filled the night, and she listened intently, trying to discern what it was. Wolves? Or was it the tortured ghost of an old west outlaw who had met his demise on the gallows and then committed his eternity to haunting the progeny of all those who had betrayed them?

Wolves would probably be better.

There was another echoing howl, and then another, until the night was filled with the mournful wail of the wild animals.

Definitely wolves. Beautiful, but also chilling.

She climbed out of bed, and padded over to the window in her bare feet. She peered outside, searching the night for four-legged shadows. It had been dark when she'd arrived, and she'd been too tired to look around, but now that the moon was full, it was casting the ranch into silvery, glistening shadows.

There was a massive barn several hundred yards away, and numerous corrals, some with grass and others with soft-looking dirt for riding. Beyond the barns stretched dark hills with rocky outcroppings, the perfect place for wolves...or rattlesnakes...or mountain lions.

A loud thud sounded from the barn, jerking her attention back there.

The door slid open. She gripped the windowsill in sudden nervousness, but quickly realized it wasn't a jet-black panther intent on making her his midnight snack. It was a huge dark horse, trotting easily out the massive barn doors. Chase was silhouetted on his back, a figure so imposing that she shivered in awareness. He spun the horse deftly around to close the barn door behind him, his cowboy hat and broad shoulders creating a breathtaking silhouette. He moved in perfect unison with the animal, as if they were one.

After shutting the door, he swung the horse toward the hills, and she caught her breath, leaning forward to get a better look. The pair went still, poised in suspended animation as they prepared for flight. The moment was pure, unbridled freedom, a man and his horse, unlike anything she'd experienced in her life.

She was used to a life of service, never being away from home for more than an hour, in case her mother needed her. And yet, this was Chase's life, climbing onto his horse for a midnight ride, just because he wanted to.

Yearning coursed through her, an almost painful craving for a life beyond what she'd lived. She wanted to be more than she was, to live more than she'd done, to be brave enough to step out over an abyss just to see what would happen when she went airborne. Suddenly, the night didn't feel like the oppressing constraint of isolation. It felt like a fresh start, a chance to live again.

Chase turned his head suddenly, looking directly at her window. She stiffened. Could he see her? She knew she should probably duck inside and pretend she hadn't been playing the part of a voyeur, but she didn't move.

A part of her wanted to be caught by him, to be swept into this surreal moment of magic and moonlight, of cowboy and horse.

He swung his horse toward her, and urged the animal into a lope. Anticipation pulsed through her as he neared. He reined the animal into a sliding halt just outside her window. Since it was a ranch house, she was almost exactly level with him. He was so close, she could almost touch him if she reached out.

"Can't sleep?" he asked, his voice somehow deeper and sexier in the shadows of the moon.

"The wolves woke me up." She was in awe of his mount. The horse stood quietly, intently focused on his rider, awaiting the next command. He had a white blaze on his face, and a sock on his left hind leg. Other than that, he appeared to be a deep, rich, beautiful brown. "What's your horse's name?"

"Red Devil, but he lets his friends call him Red." Chase's face was shadowed beneath his hat, hiding him from her. "Did the wolves scare you?"

She shook her head. "It was beautiful."

"Want to go see them?"

She caught her breath, jerking her gaze from his horse to him. "Now?"

"Yep."

Her instinct was to refuse, and retreat responsibly into her bed, so she would be rested and capable of handling life in the morning, as she'd been doing for the last eight years. But instead, she smiled, unable to keep the anticipation off her face. "I'd love to." Somehow, in the darkness of the night, immersed in the vastness of his ranch, real life didn't seem to matter. The only thing that mattered was embracing this moment.

He grinned, his teeth glistening white against his shadowed face as he held out his hand. "Hop on, then." He edged his horse closer, clearly intending to have her ride with him.

Excitement rippled through her. Ride double with him into the moonlight to look at wolves? This was so not her life, was it? "Okay." She started to reach for him, and then suddenly remembered that she was wearing only a light camisole, no bra, and a pair of thin, cotton sleep pants. Embarrassment flooded her cheeks "I'm not dressed. I should put on jeans—"

"You look perfect to me. It's unseasonably warm for this time of year. You don't need anything else." There was a sensual undertone to his voice that made her belly tighten, but before she could dive back into her room in search of a sweatshirt, he held out his hand. "Come on. The wolves don't stay put for long, and they don't care what you're wearing. I'll catch you."

I'll catch you.

Rightness rippled through her, and she knew, in that moment, she wanted to be caught by him. "Okay, but if you drop me, I'll shoot you." She climbed up on the windowsill and swung her legs over the side, gripping the windowsill as she perched precariously, her bare feet dangling above assorted bushes that, for all she knew, could be thick with thorns. "Are you sure about this?"

"Never doubt a cowboy. It offends us and forces us to overcompen-sate, which is never a good thing." He leaned over, grabbed her around the waist, swept her off the windowsill, and settled her in front of him in the saddle. "This okay?"

"Um...yeah. Sure." Her back was flush against his chest, and her bottom was wedged up against his crotch. The thin material of her pants gave her little protection from the heat of his body cascading through her, and the sensation of so much physical contact was almost overwhelming. His arm was wrapped securely around her waist, anchoring her against him. Any hope she had of being proper and leaning forward so she wasn't using him as a lounge chair was completely eliminated by how securely he had her tucked against him. She had a feeling his horse could fling them to Georgia and Chase still wouldn't lose his grip on her. "It's been a long time since I've ridden a horse."

"Well, lucky for you, I've got that angle covered." He swung his horse around toward the hills. "If you get scared or need a break, let me know, okay?"

She nodded, looking ahead toward the rocky hills. Was she really going to do this? Ride into the night with a man she didn't know? He could abduct her, and no one would ever find her body in the vastness of this land.

Then he nudged his horse into a lope, and the time to retreat was gone.

By THE TIME they reached the southern ridge, Chase knew he had a problem on his hands.

Or, more accurately, in his lap.

It had taken exactly twenty-five yards of riding double with Mira for his cock to get hard, and it hadn't chilled out in the hour they'd been riding. He hadn't had a never-ending hard-on since he was a hormonal teenager, but the feeling of Mira's body snuggled against his had stirred up a need in him that wasn't going to stand down.

Even though she said she hadn't ridden in years, she moved naturally with the movement of the horse, relaxing into Chase and letting her body follow his. It was seductive as hell, and tempting beyond words.

The fact that her shirt was so thin it felt as if his hand was on her bare stomach didn't help. Nor did the fact that her hair was whipping against his cheek, and he couldn't stop breathing in the smell of lilacs that seemed to be clinging faintly to her.

In her white pajamas and bare feet, she was so feminine he didn't even know how to respond. As they got further and further from the ranch, and the terrain got rougher, he realized she was completely dependent on him to keep her safe. She didn't even have shoes on. What the hell had he been thinking, taking her out on the range at night, while she was wearing something so thin and sexy that even the buzzards would have a hard time not noticing?

Protectiveness surged over him, and he locked his arm more tightly around her waist. She'd trusted him enough to let him bring her out here. He wasn't going to let her down.

"What's that one called?" She pointed to a three-pointed outcropping to the north. "It's so beautiful."

The awe in her voice was genuine, and intense satisfaction settled more deeply through him. She'd been peppering him with questions about the ranch the entire ride, noticing things about his land he hadn't noted in years. Mira appreciated his ranch the way he did, and that got him right in his gut.

"It's called Triple Threat. It's a really steep drop off on the other side. If you went over, it'd be a bad day for you." Again, his arm tightened reflexively around her, in a gesture that was fast becoming habit.

He reined in his horse and paused. "Listen. We're almost there."

They sat quietly together as Red went still, the three of them in total sync. The night was pregnant with silence, and then he heard the howl directly off to his right.

Mira tensed and turned sharply, scanning the night. "It sounds like it's right next to us," she whispered.

"It almost is." He kept his mouth right by her ear, a whisper meant for her alone. "Stay quiet." He urged Red ahead, and the horse deftly navigated the rocky terrain, his bare hooves almost silent on the boulders.

They rounded the corner, and he felt Mira suck in her breath as he reined in Red. Less than twenty yards away, on the butte aptly called Wolf Hill, were six wolves. Two of them had their noses turned toward the sky, and their low, echoing howl filled the night.

Red stood absolutely still, trained to perfection, and Mira was immobile against Chase. The only sign that she'd seen the wolves was the reflexive tightening of her hand around his forearm.

He grinned, leaning forward to rest his cheek against hers. "See the one with the white chest?" he whispered against her ear, keeping his voice so low he could barely hear the words himself.

She nodded.

"I call her Sheera. She's the alpha female of the pack. Jam, the alpha male, isn't up there right now. Gorgeous, aren't they?"

"Incredible." She squeezed his hand. "Thank you for bringing me here, Chase. It's unbelievable." The genuine awe in her voice made him grin.

Even his brothers had never seen Sheera or Jam. The wolves had never paid a visit when his brothers had been in town, and it felt good to share them with someone. With her, specifically.

"What are the names of the others?"

He rested his chin on her shoulder, pointing out each one. She nodded, relaxing against his chest as he explained the personalities of each wolf. He couldn't believe how interested she was, and how appreciative. He loved the solitude of his midnight rides, and never in his life would he have wanted to share them with anyone, but having Mira with him had cast the night into another light, one that was unexpected, but not so bad.

This woman as his wife?

Maybe she'd fit in okay. Maybe it wouldn't be so bad. Maybe his brothers would learn to accept her. But even as Chase thought it, he knew that his brothers would never get on board. Their scars ran too deep, and survival had taught them lessons they would never unlearn.

His phone rang, blasting out into the silence. The wolves scattered, Mira jumped, and even Red flicked an ear.

Swearing, he dug the phone out of his pocket, instinctively responding to the ring that he'd assigned only to his brothers. He looked down and saw it was Travis, one of his brothers. "Hey." He took the call, as he always did when it was one of his brothers.

Travis didn't waste time on pleasantries. "Is she there?"

He frowned. "Who?"

"Mira. The wife. Is she there already?"

Chase realized that Zane must have already talked to Travis. "Yeah. What's up? Something wrong?"

Travis swore. "You realize you have money, bro, don't you? Lots of it. Enough that women will want it. You're a target, just like dad was."

Mira leaned back against him, resting her head on his chest. Instinctively, Chase tightened his grip on her, breathing in that lilac scent. He turned Red toward home, the idyllic moment shattered. "She's not like that."

"I'm coming out there," Travis said. "I'll be there tomorrow night. Don't get married tomorrow."

Chase frowned. "You're coming here?" Travis hadn't been to the ranch in two years.

"Yeah. I'll see ya." The phone clicked, and Travis was gone, leaving Chase staring at his phone. What the hell had just happened?

CHAPTER SEVEN

THE WEIGHT SETTLED MORE DEEPLY in Mira's chest the further they got from the wolves. The magic of the night had vanished, replaced with the reality of life. "Who was on the phone?" she asked.

"My brother." Chase had been quiet since the call, but his hold on her was still secure.

"I didn't mean to eavesdrop, but I could hear the whole conversation. Should I buy a gun before tomorrow night?"

She felt him chuckle at her words, and a tiny bit of the tension eased from his body. "You know how to shoot a gun?"

"My dad was a sheriff. I can shoot anything."

He whistled softly. "You can borrow one of my guns if Travis gets out of line. He'd appreciate a woman with a gun." He was silent for a moment, and she closed her eyes, lulled by the smooth gait of the horse and the warmth of Chase's body.

She didn't want to think about choices, the future, or a hostile brother coming to the ranch to drive her away. She just wanted to be in this moment, enjoying the sensation of being held in Chase's arms, and breathing in air so fresh it seemed to make her lungs twenty pounds lighter each time she inhaled.

"I have eight brothers," he said finally.

"Eight? I don't have any. Well, I had an older brother, but he died when he was six months old." Nine kids growing up in the same house. She couldn't imagine what that would be like. "Are you close?"

"Yeah. Hell forges unbreakable bonds."

His words brought back the memory of the cigarette burns on his forearms. Instinctively, she rubbed her hand over the marks that were hidden by his shirt, as if she could erase them simply with her touch. Eight boys trapped in a life of abuse? "Where's your dad now?"

"Dead."

"Good." Even as she said it, she felt a wave of sadness that anyone could be in a situation where their dad's death made life better. When her dad had died, it had been devastating. As terrible as the grief had been, it had also meant that she'd had an amazing father who had meant everything to her, and she'd never trade that for less grief. If her dad were around, he could show Chase what a dad could be like, just as he'd done for AJ.

"Yeah."

Again, they fell into silence, but there was an edge to it now, a darkness of the past hovering over them. A chill began to creep through her bones, and she wasn't sure if it was because of the turn in the conversation, or the temperature of the night.

"I killed him," Chase said finally.

The chill turned into a knife. "What?" She twisted in his arms, turning so she could see him. His face was hard and chiseled, still shadowed by the brim of his hat in the moonlight.

"When I was twenty-two, my youngest brother called me. My dad had beat the hell out of him, and locked him in the garage. Travis's ribs were broken, and he couldn't breathe. He called me to tell me what happened and ask me to send the cops. My dad's wife at the time wouldn't let the cops in, and he sat there in that garage until I got there the next night from New York. He was almost dead." Chase's voice was so hard that she was almost afraid of him. "I had to break the door down to get to him, and my dad came after me. He was drunk off his ass, and he had a gun. He shot me. I got the gun, he wound up dead, and the shit was over."

His voice was so even, as if he were telling a story about picking up a can of beans at the store, but she didn't believe it. She'd heard similar stories from AJ too much, and she knew the depths of suffering that made a man become so impenetrable. "I'm sorry," she said softly.

His gaze flicked to hers, and for a moment, she saw anguish in those blue eyes, but he shuttered it almost immediately. "My dad married three times, and had countless other women. He used his fists and belts, sometimes cigarettes. They used cigarettes, too, but also irons, and other shit that caused damage no one could see, the kind that eats away inside until there's nothing left."

Tears filled her eyes. "Oh, Chase—"

"I didn't have it as bad because I was older by the time things got really ugly. I wasn't home much, and I was big enough to defend myself. But some of my brothers were pretty young, products of assorted women. Sometimes, the women took them when they left. Other times, they left them behind, but they were all my brothers, no matter what." He shook his head once, silencing her when she started to respond. "With each woman, my dad became worse. They took his money, they fucked him over, and they twisted him deeper into the pit he was falling into. The day I left for college, my brothers and I took a blood oath that we would never let a woman destroy us, and we would always protect each other from any enemy, but especially women." He held out his hand, and she saw a small scar on his palm.

She traced the mark silently, his palm roughened from all his ranch work. "He's coming here to protect you from me, isn't he? Your brother? The one who called you?"

"Yeah."

She looked up at him. "Will he hurt me?" It wasn't a question based on fear. It was a question designed to help her understand exactly what she was about to face. She'd been the daughter of a sheriff for too long not to know the questions to ask.

Anger flashed in Chase's eyes, and he flipped his hand over, trapping hers against his thigh. "No one will hurt you, Mira. I swear it on my life. Do you understand? *No one will ever hurt you.*"

The vehemence in his voice sent chills down her spine, and she knew that the abused child had become the protector of the innocent at any cost. His brothers were his posse, but somehow, because of AJ and the baby, she had come into his circle of protection.

But at the same time, the bond between the Stockton men was obvious, and she had inadvertently stepped right between them. She had a feeling it wasn't a good place to be. "Chase," she said slowly. "I think maybe getting married isn't the right thing to do. I won't come between you and your brothers. They mean too much to you. Maybe I should just go into town or something." She managed a shrug. "Now that I'm in Wyoming, I'm probably safe."

Probably? That might be a little strong. Possibly safe? Still too much. Not likely. Hardly at all. But being in Wyoming bought her time to figure out a more permanent solution.

For a long moment, Chase stared at her, his face inscrutable. She could almost hear the thoughts roaring through his head as he tried to reconcile his loyalty to both his brothers and to AJ, trying to find a way to balance it.

She sighed. "If it takes that long to decide, then we know the answer. I'll leave in the morning." She managed a smile. "At least I didn't unpack." She turned back toward the front of the horse, leaning forward slightly so she didn't lean against Chase. Suddenly, she felt hugely embarrassed that she'd hopped on a plane to come live with him. She felt even more embarrassed by how she'd responded to his kiss, and how she'd snuggled into him on the ride.

She realized that Taylor had been right. She'd let it get personal with him already. If she hadn't, she wouldn't feel so empty inside just because she was going to leave in the morning, and start a new life, her real life, without him.

~

MIRA SMELLED GOOD.

Really, *really* good.

Way better than any of his brothers ever had.

Chase gritted his teeth as they rode in silence back to his ranch. Mira was stiff, holding herself away from him, even though he still had his arm around her waist. Her hair was drifting against his face, tickling his skin. He missed the feel of her body against his. Somehow, even though she was a woman and she was in his space, she'd given him a sense of peace tonight that he didn't usually have.

He wanted her around.

But his brothers had suffered enough. How could he take away their safe haven?

He swore under his breath, urging his horse into a faster lope. The easy rhythm rocked Mira back against him, and he took advantage, leaning into her. She slid back into him, her bottom nestled against his crotch, just as it had been on the ride out. Rightness settled through him, an absolute sense of everything being in equilibrium. It was the feeling he'd been striving for ever since he'd bought the ranch, but it had eluded him at every turn.

Mira had given it to him.

Suddenly, it was no longer about AJ or the baby. It was about Mira, and what he wanted. He wanted her for himself. No, he *needed* her. His entire body craved every inch of physical contact he could steal from her.

He had no idea how he could make this fly, but he knew with absolute certainty, that he had to find a way.

He reined Red in as they neared the ranch. "Want to come to the barn, or be dropped off at your window?"

She leaned forward again, trying to put space between them, but he didn't let her. "Window, please."

"I've never dropped a woman off at her bedroom window before," he mused as he navigated Red across the rustic landscaping. "As a cowboy, that's probably a big failure on my part. Seems like something I should have done before."

He was rewarded with a small laugh. "Yes, well, now you can say you've done it."

He paused Red a few feet away from the window, too far for her to jump. "Okay."

She was still for a moment, then twisted around to look at him. Her hair was tousled and sexy, tangled over her shoulders from the ride. "I know I look really athletic, but I'm not actually capable of leaping from a horse's back, over a row of bushes, into an open window, without causing severe damage to myself."

The moonlight was dancing across her features, showcasing her long, thick lashes, the cute upturn of her lips, and the weary shadows beneath her eyes, indicating a woman who had pushed herself to the edge. Slowly, he slid his hand around her neck, just as he'd done at the airport.

She stiffened, but didn't pull away as he stroked his fingers over the nape of her neck, almost unable to believe how soft the strands were. "Like silk," he said softly. "The most delicate spun silk."

"What are you doing?" She didn't sound mad. Confused. And something else he couldn't quite decipher. Intrigued? Interested? Burning with need for him? God, he hoped so.

"Cowboys survive on instinct," he said, sliding his fingers deeper into her hair. Soft, and thick, and so sexy. "It's all I know. I'm not a thinker. I just listen to my gut, and I do."

She swallowed, and her hand went to his chest, her fingers digging in ever so slightly. "Stop," she said. "I need to stay focused. You aren't a knight in shining armor, and you're not going to rescue me."

"I'm no knight," he agreed, spreading his fingers over the back of her head, lightly, ever so lightly, drawing her closer to him. "And you're much too strong to need to be rescued. But even your dad would say it's always good to have a backup plan." And with that, he bent his head and kissed her.

Her lips were so soft, a sensation utterly foreign to him. In the airport, the kiss had been hot and fiery, but it had been in the midst of the frenetic bustle of crowds and travelers. Now, in the silence of the night, there was nothing but the two of them. There was no assault on his senses to distract him from the utter perfection of her mouth beneath his.

He kissed her again, silently urging her to kiss him back. The need for a response from her was hammering through him. He didn't just need physical contact. He needed to know that she wasn't immune to him, despite her independent ways. He *needed* that connection.

He nibbled at her lower lip, and pressed a kiss to each corner of her mouth. She started to tremble, but still didn't kiss him back, though her fingers were digging more fiercely into his chest, and she wasn't pulling away.

"Don't leave tomorrow," he whispered against her mouth.

"You're trying to seduce me into staying?" she whispered. "That's a little unethical."

He kissed her jawbone, then her earlobe. She tasted fresh and untainted, like the mountains after a spring rain. He trailed kisses down the side of her neck. "Seduction and staying are completely unrelated," he said between kisses. Her shoulder was bare, and he brushed his kiss over her collarbone. The strap of her camisole was thin, so delicate, it would snap with the slightest tug. It was pure femininity, and his gut literally clenched at the sight of it. "You're such a woman," he said as he thumbed the strap off her shoulder, watching it drift down her bare arm. "Incredible."

"Incredible that I'm a woman?" Her eyes were closed, and she was utterly still, not fighting him, but still not responding, as if she was doing everything she could to hold herself aloof.

"No. Just incredible." He pressed a kiss to the curve of her shoulder where the strap had been. Her skin was so soft, and he grinned when he felt the goose bumps pop up. "Are those from me?'"

"No. I'm cold." Her voice was throaty and breathless, making him smile wider.

"I'm not doing my job if you're cold." He reached around her, and slid his hand around her thigh as he pressed a kiss to the side of her neck. He grasped her leg and lifted it across Red's neck, turning her sideways in his lap.

From this angle, he could see her nipples through the thin fabric, tight and visible. Raw desire hit him, a need so deep he felt like the axis of his world was shifting. "Come here," he said, unable to keep the gruffness out of his voice. "Face me."

He grasped her other calf, and she moved her leg between them across to Red's other side, so she was facing him. Her legs were over his thighs, a seduction of heat and warmth that was sheer perfection. They were close to each other now, too close in the saddle, and there was nowhere for her legs to go except where they were, draped over his thighs. Her eyes were wide, and he could see both fear and anticipation in them.

He had no words to reassure her. He was in a place he was pretty sure he'd never been in before, and he had no tools to manage it. All he knew was that he wanted her. He needed her. He burned for her. He dropped the reins, and set his palms on either side of her face. "This isn't about the baby," he said. "Or AJ. This is just us, here, right now."

She swallowed. "Okay," she whispered.

Okay. Raw desire coursed through him, and he bent his head, unable to stop himself, unwilling to deny himself this moment. He took her lips in his, and was nearly stunned by the sensation of her mouth against his once again. "So incredibly soft," he whispered against her mouth. He felt huge and awkward in comparison to her delicate frame. "I'm afraid I'll break you just by breathing on you."

She smiled then, a flash of warmth in those gorgeous eyes. "Such a sweet man," she said softly.

It was the tenderness in her voice that broke him. He couldn't remember anyone ever using that tone with him in his life. With a low groan, he swept his arm behind her back, pulling her against him, and kissed her like his very survival depended on it.

And this time, she kissed him back.

~

CHASE'S KISS WAS AMAZING. Mira couldn't believe how incredible it felt to be in his arms. His kiss poured fire and heat into her, igniting a need deep inside her, a need she didn't even know was a part of her... until he'd awoken it.

There was no way for her to resist what he offered her: strength, passion, and a sense of connection that had eluded her for so long. She slid her arms around his neck, and sighed when he locked his arms around her lower back, crushing her against him. His chest was rock hard against her breasts, and her nipples were burning at the feel of his rough shirt against her. His hands were hot against her back, searing her skin through her thin fabric of her top.

Her pulse was hammering so fast she couldn't even feel the separate beats. She was nervous, sort of terrified, by her reaction to him, but the fear wasn't enough to supersede how his kiss made her feel. Sexy, desirable, protected. *Feminine.*

He lightly nipped her lower lip, and then his tongue slid over hers, a sensual caress that made her belly tighten. Tentatively, she responded, and he let out a low groan, deepening the kiss. Within moments, the kiss seemed to turn to fire. His mouth seemed to burn her everywhere he kissed: her mouth, her neck, her collarbone. Her entire body was humming with desire, a need for him that trumped almost a decade of fear and hesitation.

He grabbed her hips and pulled her further onto his lap. She could feel his erection pressing through the thin material of her pants, and the zipper on his jeans was digging into her sensitive flesh. His hands flanked her hips, trapping her against him. His grip was strong and unyielding, but she didn't feel like she was trapped, just protected.

He kissed her throat, and she leaned her head back, giving him full access. She closed her eyes, all her senses riveted on his mouth as he kissed down her throat, and then lower, moving down between her breasts.

She started to tremble again, and he palmed his hand between her shoulder blades, holding her up as he pressed a kiss to the swell of her breasts. *Oh, God. Really?* Every inch of her skin was tingling in anticipation, as he swirled his tongue across her skin, lower, and lower, until it brushed over her nipple.

Her entire body clenched in response as he pulled the taut bud into his mouth, lightly biting the sensitive tip.

"Feels good?" He swept his tongue across her nipple, a damp seduction of incredible softness.

"Of course not. Why would you say that— Oh!" She let out an involuntary yelp as he bit her nipple again.

"Don't lie to me, woman. A cowboy has ways of extracting the truth." He pulled her up again, and caught her mouth in a searing kiss that obliterated the last of her defenses. She kissed him back, desperate now, pouring herself into the kiss. The kiss grew harder, deeper, so urgent that it was almost violent, but not quite, never quite crossing that line to someplace that scared her.

He swept his hand under the loose waistband of her pants, sliding his hand over her bare bottom, never letting up his relentless assault on her mouth as he gripped her hips again, this time, skin against skin in a dazzling seduction of sensation and strength.

Red stomped his foot once, the sound jerking her back to the present. She was on a horse! "Chase, we have to stop—" He cut off her protest with another kiss, sliding his hands under her bottom and lifting her so tightly against him that his clothes seemed to merge with her own skin.

Sensation flooded her senses, and all she could do was cling to him as he continued his sensual, delicious assault on every level. She was vaguely aware of a rocking motion, and realized that Red was walking, but Chase gave her no time to think about it. He wrapped his arms around her, and then swung her off his lap in an effortless move that made her feel like she weighed about five pounds. He swept her through her window, depositing her inside the room. For a brief moment, she felt the cool night air sweeping over her now, filling with regret and loneliness. Why had he ended the kiss so quickly? Even as she thought it, however, she took a deep breath, steeling herself against the turbulence of emotions as she turned away from the window.

It was better this way. She needed space from him to think, to figure out, what she needed to do—

Suddenly, she heard the thud behind her, a thud that sounded suspiciously like Chase coming through her window after her. Her heart leapt in anticipation, and she spun around, but she didn't have time to fully turn before his arms wrapped around her, sending heat rushing through her. Before she could decide whether to protest, he scooped her in his arms and carried her toward the bed.

CHAPTER EIGHT

OH, God, was she going to do this? They were just going to leave his horse in the middle of the ranch? "Red—"

"He's well-trained. He's fine. I took off his tack before I followed you in. He'll head to the barn and settle down for the night." He set her on the bed, and pulled back, his blue eyes gleaming at her. "But I appreciate the fact you were concerned about him."

It was such a small thing for her to have done, but she could see from the intensity of his gaze that he meant it. By thinking about his horse's well-being, she'd somehow passed some test she doubted he even knew he had. Her heart tightened for him. This wasn't simply a man whose kisses ignited a passion in her. It was a man who'd suffered greatly as a child, and dedicated his life toward keeping his family together, a man who was touched by the fact she'd cared about his horse...a man who was afraid he'd break her if he breathed on her.

She smiled, her heart softening as she ran her fingers over his cheek. "You're a good man," she said softly. "Your brothers are lucky to have you."

He went still, and for a moment, she thought she'd said the wrong thing by bringing up his brothers. Of course it had been a mistake. His brothers were his reality, the meaning of his life, the rock that had held him together for so long...and she was not a welcome part of it. "Listen, I don't want to interfere—"

He cut her off with a kiss, a kiss that was almost desperate with need. The fierceness of the kiss broke through her walls, and she wanted to cry with the intensity of her response. She understood the loneliness that drove him, because she'd lived it with AJ, and because she'd experienced it in the years since her parents' car accident.

Chase was so alive, so passionate, a survivor who had transcended his past and become an indomitable force. Still kissing her, he eased her backward, until he was on her, his weight pressing into the bed. It felt so good to be beneath him, to feel his warmth and strength enveloping her. Her entire body practically vibrated with a need for him, a need that was nothing like what had driven her into AJ's arms.

AJ had been about finding comfort with a friend in the midst of devastating grief. This moment with Chase was about her own need as a woman. It was about Chase as a man. It was lust and desire, and something more, an attraction and a source of strength greater than she was. She tugged at his shirt, pulling it out of his jeans, needing to feel the man beneath the rugged exterior.

He eased off her and dragged his shirt over his head, showing a lean body cut with the muscles of a man accustomed to a physical life. Scars crisscrossed his flesh, and her heart tightened at the reminder of all he'd suffered. She instinctively sat up and pressed a kiss to the one over his heart, a jagged line that looked like a knife had torn his flesh apart. "I'm so sorry," she whispered.

His fingers tangled in her hair, and he went still as she kissed another mark on his ribs. "It's okay," he said softly. "It was a long time ago."

"Never long enough," she said, as she kissed a scar on the front of his shoulder. "It's always too raw," she said. "I know it is."

Chase felt his entire body shudder as Mira kissed each of his scars. He didn't even think about them anymore, but having her isolate them one by one brought them all roaring back to life. But it felt different now. Instead of flashbacks of the pain and fear he felt as a kid, his muscles relaxed, releasing the tension that he'd been holding for so long. His muscles trembled as they let go, as if they didn't even remember how to be normal.

Then, she rose to her knees, as if to go around him and see his back. He stopped her, pulling her against him. "My turn," he said.

She smiled as he bent his head, the intoxicating smile of a woman who had stopped his world on its axis. He kissed her, this time a slow seduction. He tasted her lips with careful purposefulness, taking the time to slide his tongue across every inch of her mouth, memorizing the feel and taste of her.

He started to lower her to the bed again, and she pushed at his chest. "Boots?"

"Boots?" He nibbled his way down her neck. "What about them?" He had no idea what she was talking about. All he could focus on was *her*.

"I think they're super sexy and everything, but I don't want to be the woman who isn't even worth taking boots off for."

"What?" He pulled back, then grinned when he saw the twinkle in her eyes. "You know you're completely worthy of ditching the boots." He swung off the bed, and yanked off his cowboy boots. He didn't waste time, sliding his jeans off as well, leaving behind only his boxer briefs.

She was propped up on her elbows, watching him, her face shadowed by the moonlight as if she were an ethereal goddess who had come to earth just to ease his pain.

"You are one fine woman," he said as he eased onto the bed, crawling across the navy comforter until he was above her, suspending himself, not quite touching, but almost, a temptation so great his muscles were actually shaking with the effort he was exerting to restrain himself.

Mira placed her palms on his chest, a sensual, incredibly delicate touch that made his abs tighten. "Kiss me, Chase."

"A cowboy never says no to his woman," he said, lowering himself on top of her. This time, it was pure heat between them, the thin fabric of her top and pants no more than a tease. Her skin was hot, a sinful temptation. Her breasts were straining against her camisole, her nipples hard and ready.

"I'm not your woman," she whispered.

Yes, you are. He didn't say it aloud. He just kissed her, a kiss that staked his claim on the woman he'd coveted since the first time he'd seen her picture on AJ's desk during orientation week their freshman year.

She sighed in capitulation, and wrapped her hands around his neck, pulling him closer. Her kiss was as fervent as his, stoking the embers already burning within him. This time, when he slid his palm beneath the hem of her silky top, he moved his hand upward, sliding her top aside. Her breasts spilled free, and he pulled the shirt over her head, tossing it to the floor.

He cupped her breasts softly, stunned by the sight of them. Petite and soft, they filled his palms as if they were meant for him. "Perfection," he whispered, as he bent his head to place a reverent kiss on each nipple.

Mira stiffened beneath him, a soft gasp slipping from her lips as he kissed her breasts. Satisfaction poured through him as he drew her nipple into his mouth and bit lightly.

"Oh, wow." She gripped his shoulders, twisting beneath him. "I can't believe how good that feels."

He grinned. It felt right to have her responding to him so completely. She was entirely accessible to him, allowing herself to feel every sensation he stirred up. He wanted her to feel amazing, to drift to the heavens in ecstasy. He wanted to give her everything he had to offer.

New furor surging through him, he kissed his way down her belly to the waistband of her pants. Her skin was so soft and smooth, her muscles trembling as he moved lower. He thumbed the waistband of her pajama bottoms, and ever so slowly began to slide them downward as he kissed her.

The soft tuft of hair tickled his chin, and then he pressed a kiss to the swollen nub between her legs. Mira's body jerked, and she let out a soft cry, and tried to pull away, even while her fingers dug into his hair, holding him right where he was.

He grinned, and wrapped his arms around her thighs, holding her still as he kissed her, sweeping his tongue across her folds. She tasted like the sweetest honey, one that was created just for him. It was intoxicating perfection, stirring up a sense of possession inside him. He wanted to claim her as his own, forever and ever, locking her down against him. His muscles were taut with need, as he continued to kiss her, intense satisfaction roaring through him as she responded to him, giving herself over to him completely. Her trust in him settled in his gut, and it felt so right. This was his woman, the one he'd been waiting for his entire life. *Mine.*

Her body started to tremble, and she gripped his shoulders. He took advantage, upping his assault, driving her relentlessly, tightening his grip on her hips as she bucked against him. Anticipation roared through him and he bit lightly, just enough, just right, exactly how he knew it should be. "Chase!" She gasped his name, and then her body shuddered under the sudden, ruthless, orgasm.

Red-hot desire roared through him as she came apart in his arms, and raw need pulsed at him. He needed more. He needed to be inside her, to make her his in the only way he knew how.

He ditched his underwear, and then moved up her body, kissing as he went. She opened her eyes, and smiled. Her cheeks were flushed, and her eyes were half-lidded as she held out her arms to him. "Make love to me, Chase."

"God, yes." He slid his knee between her thighs, parting them.

She immediately wrapped her legs over his hips, and his heart seemed to stutter at her complete trust of him.

His cock pressed against her damp entrance, but he didn't enter her. Instead, he took her face in his hands and kissed her, the gentlest kiss he knew how to deliver. It wasn't a kiss of untamed lust. It was a kiss that was for her, and her alone. He didn't have words to describe it. He didn't know how to articulate the promise he was making, because he wasn't even sure what it was.

He poured it all into the kiss, and she responded with equal passion, until the world seemed to vanish, and all that remained was the woman in his arms. Need coiled within him, escalating with each moment until his muscles ached and screamed for release.

He shifted his hips and slid right into her, their bodies coming together in the perfect synthesis of desire, lust, and partnership. She gasped, her legs tightening around him as he sank deeper inside her.

The feeling of being so connected with her was almost surreal. It was so incredible, as if this were the moment his entire life had been building toward. She was the one he'd been waiting for, the one who could somehow strip him of all the hell that haunted him. She was the one who could make him whole again.

He thrust again, pulling out, then driving even deeper, again and again, until he couldn't think of anything but her. She seemed to fill his entire existence, a great flash of sunlight burning up all the crap searing into him. He needed more. He needed everything. He needed this moment. He needed *her*.

She gasped his name, and her body went rigid as the second orgasm flooded her. The moment she found her release, he released his iron-clad control over his own lust. His orgasm hit him so hard that her name tore from his throat. He bucked against her, holding her tight in his arms as he rode the wave that seemed endless and merciless, dragging him into her spell until there was nothing left but the two of them, and the fire that had marked him forever.

MIRA AWOKE to a heavy weight wrapped around her, suffocating her. Her eyes snapped open, and she saw rustic wooden walls, and a masculine room she didn't recognize. Where was she? Panic rushed through her, and she tried to sit up, but the weight tightened around her.

"It's okay," Chase muttered, sleepily. "Just me."

Chase? She turned her head to see him beside her. He was on his side, facing her, his leg draped across her hips, and his arm tucked around her torso. His eyes were closed, and thick whiskers lined his jaw.

Relief rushed through her and she sank back onto the sheets. She became aware of the fact they were both naked. The heat from his body was burning through her, and the hair on his legs was prickling her thigh. She could even feel his erection pressing against her hip.

Desire and awareness licked through her as she recalled the previous night. What had she done, sleeping with him like that?

Embarrassment flooded her cheeks, and she rested her arm across her eyes, half-wishing she could sink into the mattress and disappear. She didn't even know him. Her grand plan had been to come out to Wyoming and start her own life, not fall into his arms less than five hours after arriving.

What would he think of her? He already knew she'd slept with AJ less than a month ago, and now she'd jumped him like a dog in heat? Granted, AJ had been her first in years, but still, how would he know that? Her chest tightened, and she fisted her hand in frustration. What kind of standard had she set? How could she possibly protect herself from him now? Would he want her to jump into bed with him every night? Because it would be really difficult to maintain a "business partnership" marriage if she was getting naked with him every night. Not that it would be bad, because sex with him was amazing, but she couldn't do this.

Chase moved his hand, spreading his palm over her left breast.

She tensed, hating the way her nipple tightened at the contact. She wouldn't have sex with him again right now. She couldn't. She needed her space—

"Your heart is racing," he mumbled, his voice still heavy with sleep. "What's wrong?"

Her heart was racing? That was why he'd spread his hand over her breast? To check on her, not seduce her? Tears suddenly filled her eyes, and exhaustion overwhelmed her. "Don't be nice."

He grunted, and shifted. Before she could react, he pulled her onto his chest, so she was looking right at him. His eyes were at half-mast, and he looked so sinfully sexy that she wanted nothing more than to scoot up his body and kiss him until he made love to her again.

He reached up, gently moving her hair off her face. He sifted through her curls, his fingers deftly untangling the knots. As sleep wore off, his eyes were becoming more alert, roaming her face carefully. "Why are you panicking?"

She cleared her throat. "I'm not panicking."

He smiled, a half-smile that showcased the dimple in his left cheek.

"Sweetheart, I make a living by knowing how to read the physical cues of my horses. I'm really good at it." His fingers were comforting as they worked through her hair, and she couldn't help but begin to relax. "I wake up after the best sex of my life, to find that your entire body has gone rigid, your heart is racing like a filly in flight, and you don't even want to look at me. So, yeah, panicking. It's my job to make that go away. It's what I do."

She immediately dragged her eyes off his chin and met his gaze. "The best sex of your life?"

"Hell, yeah." His gaze was thoughtful, still roaming over her face and her hair, as if he were trying to imprint her on his memory. "This complicates things," he said.

"I know." She bit her lip, trying desperately not to lose herself in the magic he was weaving in her hair. "I'm not ready for this."

His fingers stilled. "You loved AJ," he said quietly. "Shit. Sorry. I rushed you into this."

"Well, of course I loved him..." She saw his face become shuttered, and realized what he was thinking. "Not like that. He was my best friend, but I didn't love him romantically." She suddenly saw a chance to try to explain. "We'd never even kissed before a month ago. We were both so devastated by my mother's death. It was like we were trying to hold onto her through each other. It's weird to say, but it wasn't sex. It was more like...survival, trying not to drown in the grief. I don't know if that makes sense." She felt her cheeks redden. "I don't sleep around. AJ was the first guy I'd been with since Brian, and then you. I mean, that's it. I—"

She stopped when he brushed a kiss over her knuckles, her belly clenching.

"Mira."

She swallowed. "What?"

He pressed another kiss to her knuckles. "I know who you are. You don't need to try to explain it. I've seen you through the eyes of a man who respected and trusted you more than anyone else on the planet. There's no chance that I'd be judging you."

For a moment, she started to relax, and then his words sank in, the truth behind his beautiful speech. "You know me through AJ," she said.

"Of course. I've known you for more than ten years." He brushed a tendril of hair back from her face. "You're the one who saved him. You brought him back home to your family and you welcomed him. You never cared about his deformed foot, and you taught him to look past it." He frowned, searching her face. "I've been waiting for you for ten years, Mira. I didn't know it, until I saw you in that church two days ago."

"Ten years?" She frowned.

He nodded. "Since the first week of college, when AJ first mentioned you. I was bitter, and I hated women. You seemed to be an exception, though, a woman worth trusting. AJ didn't believe in anyone except you, and I soon realized you were someone I had to meet." He grinned. "It took ten years, but at least we finally met."

Betrayal seemed to wrap around her heart, and she bit her lip, reality finally sinking in. She now, finally, understood why he'd brought her back to Wyoming. It wasn't simply because of AJ, which she had been able to accept. It was also because he saw her as some magical fantasy woman who would save his world. He wanted her to rescue him, the way she'd rescued AJ.

The hurt bit deep, as deeply as it had when Brian had betrayed her. Her college love had wanted her to be a fun-loving co-ed, and he'd tossed her aside when he'd realized she wasn't always the carefree socialite she'd been in college. Now, Chase was the opposite. He saw her only as a salvation who could soothe the scars he still carried from his terrible childhood. He wanted her to save him, like he thought she'd done for AJ, like she'd tried to do for her mother.

She had nothing left to give him, nothing left to give anyone else. She wanted him, someone, *anyone,* to see her as she really was. She wanted someone to see that the woman who put on a brave front was terrified. She wanted someone to realize that the woman who took care of other people wanted someone to hold her up. She needed someone to realize that even though she cried, sometimes she just wanted to forget life and be a little irresponsible and fun.

"I'm not a goddess," she said, rolling off him. "I'm just me. I get angry. I cry. I yell. I break promises. I'm not perfect, Chase. Not at all. I'll make terrible mistakes as a mother, and I'm sure I'll make my kid cry. I can't save anyone. I can't save you. I'm not this fantasy woman that you have created in your mind. I'm real, and I'm a mess."

She sat up, grabbed the nearest item of clothing, which was his plaid, button-down shirt. She yanked it on and held it closed over her breasts.

Chase frowned as he watched Mira withdraw from him. What had just happened? He leaned over the bed and grabbed her wrist as she tried to climb out of the bed. "Mira," he said gently, trying not to spook her any more than she already was. "Come back here."

She looked down at his fingers wrapped around her arm. "Please let me go."

"What happened? What's going on?" A rising sense of urgency pulsed through him. She was slipping through his fingers. After all these years, he'd finally found her, and he was already losing her. "Mira. Talk to me."

She looked over at him. "For ten years, you've had this vision in your head about who I am. You don't see me."

He frowned. "Of course I see you—"

"No." She touched his lips, silencing him. "You don't. You had a terrible childhood, which I understand, and my heart breaks for you. You see me through the eyes of AJ, not for who I am." She sighed, realizing the truth of the words before she even spoke them. "I see you the same way. I never would have slept with you last night or even come out here if it wasn't for everything AJ had said about you."

He nodded. "Yeah, of course. He connects us more deeply than we would have been able to do on our own this quickly. But that's okay. It means we know who we really are, and we don't have to do that stupid dance while we figure each other out."

"That's my point! Don't you get it?" She pulled her wrist free of his grasp, and he reluctantly let her go. "I'm not the woman you've created in your head. I can't save you. I didn't save AJ. He saved himself, and I was just his friend." She touched his face. "And you can't save me, either. I have to go figure out who I am, Chase. I can't live in the shadow of who I once was, which is who you want me to be."

Swearing, he rolled out of bed, catching her arm as she walked toward the door. "I don't want you to be anyone but yourself," he said. "What are you talking about? It's you that I made love to last night, not some figment of my imagination."

She turned to face him, and he went cold at the resolution he saw in her eyes. "No, you didn't. And I didn't make love to you. I made love to a sense of safety and trust created by AJ. And I'll be honest, all I want to do is fall into your arms right now and let you make love to me a thousand more times, until the rest of the world disappears and all that's left is you."

Something twisted in his gut at her words. He would have expected it to be fear, maybe even terror at the thought of getting irrevocably entwined with a woman, but fear wasn't what he felt. It just felt...right. The most intense feeling of satisfaction. "That's a problem?"

"Yes. I need it to be real, Chase. I need you to be with *me*, not a fantasy, and it needs to be the same for you." With a sigh, she laid her hand on his cheek. Her fingers were so soft that it was almost surreal. "I think I fell a little bit in love with you the moment you said your name at the church, and that's how I know it's not real. It's too soon for how strongly I feel about you, which means I've fallen in love with a fantasy who isn't real, and it's the same for you." She dropped her hand and stepped back. "I'll leave today, Chase. I have to. I can't live under false pretenses anymore."

Before he could respond, she grabbed some clothes from her luggage, and ducked out into the hall. He heard the bathroom door shut, and the shower began to run.

With a deep sigh, he sank down on the bed, and ran his fingers through his hair. Was she right? Was he making shit up because of ten years of idealization? He wasn't a fool. He knew that she was flawed. She had to be. So what would he do the first time she did something that triggered a memory, one of those hot spots that made him shut women out? Would he still believe she was different from all the other women? Or would he react instinctively to protect himself and his brothers from a perceived threat, and boot her to the curb without giving her a chance, like he'd done with every other woman he'd ever been with? She deserved more than that, so much more.

But could he give her more? Could he give her the trust she deserved and was worthy of, when the shit got difficult, which he knew it would?

He turned his head to look at the picture on the nightstand. It was a photograph of him and two of his brothers from when they were kids. They were on the Johnson ranch, standing around Killer, the dead-mean old bull that ran the place. All three of them were grinning their heads off, each of them with a hand on the bull that they'd once been too scared of to go near. He picked up the photograph and looked at it, running his finger over the faces of his brothers.

Without the Johnson ranch, he would be dead now, and so would his brothers. Old Skip Johnson had chosen to put him to work on the ranch instead of turning him over to the cops when he'd found him drunk and trying to steal his booze. That ranch had been Chase's salvation, and that was the ranch he now had his home on. He'd bought it from Skip five years ago, giving his former mentor one year to live his fantasies out as a retiree in Florida before he'd died.

Was Chase really willing to risk the dream of rebuilding his family just for a chance at a fantasy with a woman, a fantasy that was so lofty that he knew it wasn't based on reality? Mira was right. There was no way she was the flawless woman he'd created in his mind, and there was no way she, or any woman, was worth risking his relationship with his brothers for. Silently, he set the picture back down.

The answer had to be no.

It wasn't only his life. It was his brothers' as well. He couldn't do this thing with her. He would have to let her leave. It had all been a mistake.

Regret pouring through him, he stood up and strode across the room to retrieve his jeans, which were in a pile on top of her suitcase.

He grabbed his pants off it, but the belt buckle caught on the suitcase, jerking it off the table. It landed with a thump, dumping the contents across the pine flooring.

Swearing, he scooped everything up, trying to shove it all back inside before she returned to the room. He tried not to notice the black lace bra or silk underwear. He ignored the bottle of nail polish that was in the exact shade of his favorite wild flower in the spring.

And he refused to contemplate how that crazy-soft light cream sweater would hug her curves.

But when he picked up a pair of light blue baby socks, he couldn't toss them aside. He just stared at them, shocked by how tiny they were. How in the hell could a kid be small enough to fit in them? Then he noticed another pair. Pink. Slowly, he reached down and pulled those free of the pile.

He held both pairs in the palm of his hand, two tiny pairs of socks. They were so small, it was as if they were for dolls. He instinctively cupped his hand around them, already prepared to protect the tiny being who would wear socks that small. She'd bought one of each, ready for whatever gender she was carrying. Even though she was facing hell, she was set to take on the challenge.

Those socks would be on the feet of the kid she carried, the one who had no dad, and was saddled with a true bastard of a grandfather. Chase looked at the burn marks on his forearm. He looked back at the socks, then back at his arm. He was going to sentence a kid to that? AJ's child? The baby of the first woman he'd trusted enough to allow into his house and his bed? Yeah, technically, it was the guest bedroom, but it was the same thing. His world. His sanctuary.

He wasn't a fool. He was a bitter, cynical bastard who didn't trust anyone. If there was *any* reason for him not to trust Mira, he would have seen it. But instead, he'd brought her into his world.

Yeah, maybe he saw her through his fantasies, but he knew he was right about her being worth trusting. She was willing to walk away from his help and face AJ's dad herself, rather than lose her freedom to a man.

He gently laid the socks on top of her clothes, and he knew what he had to do.

He'd won over a lot of battered horses, and gained their trust. It was time to do the same with Mira. He could make this work.

CHAPTER NINE

MIRA LEANED against the wall in the shower, letting the hot water wash Chase's scent off her skin. She felt surprisingly, achingly alone. She knew she had to leave the house, but last night in Chase's arms had been amazing. It was the first time she'd felt alive in a long while.

She hadn't been lying when she'd said a part of her wanted to lose herself in the moment with him, but Taylor's words kept ringing in her ears. She was falling too hard and too fast for him, and there was so much at stake. Her own life, and her baby's.

The truth was, she was a complete mess right now, from her mom's death, and then AJ's, and then the baby thing. Of course she was latching onto Chase. What woman wouldn't? But that could only lead to bad things. She couldn't even find her own feet right now. How could she trust her judgment?

She wanted to be saved, and the last time that had happened, she'd wound up pregnant. The time before that? She'd wound up engaged to a man who'd wanted her to abandon her paralyzed mother to go party with him at college. So, what would it be with Chase? What more did she have to lose?

Her baby. He'd already said he'd go on record as the baby's father.

That would give him all the power in the world when it came to her life.

There was a light knock at the bathroom door, making her jump. "Who is it?" Dumb question. There was only one person in the house besides her.

"It's me." Chase's deep voice rumbled through her, making goose bumps pop up on her skin.

Why did the blasted man have to affect her like that? "What do you want?" The glass door to the shower was fogged up, but not enough for privacy.

"We need to talk."

She almost laughed at his timing. "I'm in the shower."

"I know. Can I come in?" The door opened as he asked it, and she instinctively covered her breasts as she saw him step into the room. He was blurred from the steam on the shower door, but she could tell he was wearing only his jeans. His chest was bare, and she could see the shadows of his muscles and the breadth of his shoulders, even through the distortion of the fogged glass.

"Can't you wait until I get out?"

He leaned against the sink and folded his arms over his chest, facing the shower. "No."

"I'm naked."

"I know. I'm not blind." He held up something pink and blue. "You bought these?"

She couldn't tell what they were. "Chase, seriously, I'm not comfortable with you in here. Can you wait outside?"

"I spent half the night kissing every inch of your body. I made love to you three times, and I know what every part of you tastes like. I know every curve on your body. I know you have a scar on your left breast, and a freckle on the inside of your right thigh. I know you have a birthmark on your left butt cheek in the shape of a butterfly, and I know the sound you make when you have an orgasm, and how it changes depending on whether it's an orgasm from oral sex or making love. The feel of your naked body entwined with mine while we slept will be imprinted upon my mind forever, as will the color of your skin in the moonlight. Having me wait outside won't change any of that, no matter how much you wish it could, so yeah, I want to talk, and I want to talk now."

By the time he finished his little speech, her cheeks were hot, her skin was tingling, and her lower belly was clenched in memory of all the sensations he'd evoked in her last night. "Yes, we were naked last night, but this is different. You've never seen me in the shower—"

The shower door slid open before she could finish her sentence, and she found herself face-to-face with him. His blue gaze was intense, drilling into hers so deeply she felt like ducking behind a tree. He wasn't even looking at her body. Just her face. "Now I've seen you in the shower," he said. "We need to talk, Mira."

She wrinkled her nose at him. "You have no sense of personal space."

He didn't even acknowledge her point. "You can't leave."

She blinked, startled by his change in topic. "Leave where?"

"My house. You said you were moving out." He frowned. "You're not?"

"Oh, that, right." She cleared her throat, and gave up arguing with him about the shower. He was right. There wasn't any part of her left that he hadn't claimed last night, and he was clearly a man on a mission. "Go away." She grabbed the door and slid it shut.

He opened the door back up and held up what she now recognized as the baby socks she'd spontaneously picked up at the gift shop at the airport on her way to Wyoming.

Embarrassment flooded her cheeks. "It was just a whim."

"It's a baby." His gaze finally left her face and went to her belly. "You're carrying a baby, Mira."

Her hand instinctively went to her stomach, which was still in its ordinary, "a little too much chocolate" rounded state. "I know."

"Sex last night was great," he said. "I'm not going to deny that I'd move you into my bedroom in a split second if you'd do it."

Something inside her twisted, and she couldn't tell if it was stark, raving terror, or the deepest, most beautiful desire. "Chase—"

He held up his hand. "I know the arguments. I was just saying it like it is." He folded his arms over his chest and leaned back against the sink, giving her the illusion of a little bit of personal space. "Here's the truth. I'm not going to lie and try to claim that I'm not attracted to you. I never let myself get a hard-on for a woman. I make sure it doesn't happen. But it's going on with you, and that's the way it is. But —" He again held his hand to silence her when she opened her mouth to protest. "I get that there are issues here. I've been obsessed with you for a decade. I'm not going to lie about that either, but I get your point that we've both been living in a fantasy land about each other."

Something tightened in her chest. A decade? He'd really thought about her for a decade? She didn't know what AJ had said about her, but she knew it wasn't glamorous. He'd seen her with dirt under her toenails and sweat stains under her arms hundreds of times. "Okay, so—"

He flipped the baby socks in his hand. "But what's reality is this kid, and the fact that he's got a grandfather who will abuse him if he gets his hands on him. You can't stop Alan alone. I can't stop him alone. But together, we have a chance."

She sighed. "So, we're back to where we started."

"No, we're not." He caught the socks, snatching them out of the air. "I spent the night making love to you. We're not back to where we started. We'll never be back there, and I don't want to be."

Suddenly, the water seemed too hard against her skin. Too hot. Her skin felt sensitive and on fire. "I do."

"No, you don't." He levered himself off the sink and walked over to her, stopping on the threshold to the shower. This time, his eyes burned over her body, searing her with the raw desire in his gaze. "It's complicated, but it's good."

She lifted her chin, letting the water run over her body, refusing to cower before him. "It's not good." At his raised eyebrows, she sighed. "Okay, it *was* good. Great. But—"

"They're two different things," he said. "Us, and the baby. For the baby, you need to stay here. For us..." He shrugged, his gaze boring into her. "We need to figure that out, but I'll never let what happens between us affect my commitment to making sure that kid wakes up every morning of his or her life feeling safe."

Her throat tightened at the passion in his voice. He meant every word. "Does that mean safe from you?"

He blinked, his brow furrowing. "What?"

She couldn't help blurting out the fear that had been gnawing at her since her conversation with Taylor. "What if you wind up being the bad guy, too? What if you're the baby's father on paper, and you wind up being the bad guy? Who protects us from you?"

He stared at her, and a cold, cold mask settled over his face. "You think that just because my father was an abusive drunk that I'll be that kind of father? You think I'd actually do something to hurt another living being? A *child?*"

At his words, a deep feeling of foreboding settled over her. "I didn't mean it like that—"

"No?" His voice was cool. "What did you mean, exactly?"

"I just meant that I've judged people incorrectly before. I believe in you, but how do I know I'm right? To give you parental rights to my child when I don't even know you is terrifying on any level. It has nothing to do with what kind of father you had, and everything to do with the fact that I don't know you."

He stared at her, and said nothing, and she began to realize that she'd just touched upon a nerve that was buried deep inside him.

"Chase." She shut off the water and stepped out of the shower, not even caring that she was naked anymore. "I grew up with AJ. His father is a terrible man, but AJ inherited none of his anger, his violent tendencies, or his lack of humanity. I know from personal experience that a person's parents don't define who they are. I *know* that, so please don't ever think I'm judging you based on that."

Again, he said nothing, but she felt the wall that was building between them.

Fear rippled through her, and she realized that he was slipping out of her grasp. Too late, she realized that she'd already begun to count on his support and his loyalty. Without him as backup, she was in a really precarious position. "Chase." She set her hands on his chest, and his muscles flexed beneath her palms. "Don't judge me based on your own past. I'm really scared right now, and struggling to make choices with my head, and not with my heart. My heart wants to trust you, but I don't know you that well. Please understand that."

He closed his eyes for a moment and inhaled deeply. His skin was damp from the steam of the shower, making her fingers want to slide off his chest.

"Chase?"

He opened his eyes, and his gaze bore into her. "I'll have my lawyer draw up a contract that protects you from me. I'll pay for you to have another lawyer look it over. In the meantime, we need to get you a doctor in town. I'll ask around, and find out who's the best. We'll hold off on getting married until you're far enough along. That would be what, the third month? That's when things are usually pretty confirmed? In the meantime, you need to stay here and make the world believe that we're in love, having sex all the time, and I knocked you up. Sound good? Safe enough?"

Gone was his warmth and affection. She could practically see his shields going up between them. It was what she wanted, right? His protection but not risking her heart? But it felt terrible. She hated it. "I'm not the women who betrayed you so many times, Chase," she said softly. "I'm just me."

Something flickered in his eyes, and for a moment, she thought she saw the old Chase, the one who made her feel like the most cherished woman in the world. Then it was gone. "I know." He reached out and brushed his finger across her cheek. She went utterly still, her heart pounding in anticipation.

When he'd first walked into the bathroom, she wanted nothing more than for him to leave. Now, all she could think about was how much she wanted him to kiss her.

His gaze dropped to her lips, and she went still. Tension rose between them, thick and steamy, and her pulse quickened. *Kiss me, Chase. Don't give up on me.*

She couldn't ask him to do it. She couldn't reach out. She was too scared. He needed to make the first move and bridge the gap between them, to hold them together while they battled through the scars they both carried.

His gaze met hers, and she saw decades of abuse in his eyes. Hurt, pain, suffering, and a fierce, indomitable will to survive and protect. "Chase?"

He sighed. "What the hell am I going to do with you?" His fingers slipped under her chin, and he bent his head to kiss her.

His lips were like velvety magic against hers, his kiss a seduction that swept through her like a sensual caress. She instinctively melted against him, needing the physical connection with him. She clasped her hands behind his neck as his arms locked around her, pulling her against him. Her breasts were flush against his bare chest, and her nipples hardened instantly at the sensation of his body against hers. They were both damp from the shower, and the wetness made her breasts slide over his chest as he backed her against the sink, deepening the kiss.

He lifted her onto the counter, cupping her buttocks as she wrapped her legs around his hips. Last night, making love to him had felt like a fantasy drifting through her life for one moment. This time, it felt different. This time, in the light of day, it was real. She felt almost desperate, as if she were trying to hang onto the first good thing that life had given her in such a long time.

His kiss was equally desperate, almost rough, as if he were driven by a need beyond what he could control. He cupped her breasts, pinching her nipple. Desire leapt through her, and she fumbled for the fly of his jeans. She didn't want foreplay. She didn't want to think that much. She just wanted him inside her, as if that would bind him to her.

He helped her with his zipper, and then freed himself. His jeans were still around his thighs as he pulled her onto his cock and thrust inside her. She gasped at the invasion, her whole body clenching at the feel of him inside her, filling her so completely. He drove deep and hard, holding her tightly to keep her from sliding on the granite counter. His kisses were relentless, intermixing with his thrusts to spiral her out of control, until she could barely even think. She was overwhelmed by the enormity of his being, and the strength of his body.

He moved one hand between her thighs, sweeping over her folds. "Come with me, Mira. Let it go."

The orgasm leapt through her so fast she screamed.

"That's my girl." He kept his hand between them, driving deeper and faster, taking her further and further over the edge, not letting up his assault, until her whole body was on fire with the orgasm that sucked her into its endless cycle of ecstasy.

She screamed again, digging her fingers into his shoulder, and then he came as well. He bucked against her, locking her tight against him as he drove so deep inside her that she felt like he would be a part of her forever. He buried his face in her hair, whispering her name over and over again as he came, his orgasm lasting as long as the ones that had taken her.

It felt like an eternity of heaven before the final aftershocks faded. His arms were still around her, his hands palming her butt. He rested his forehead against hers, and she closed her eyes, stunned by the impact of their lovemaking.

She ran her hands over his chest. The bumps from his scars mingled with the sweat rivulets trailing over his skin, and her fingers tangled in the dark hair accenting his chest. She didn't even know what to say. Making love hadn't changed what they were facing, but at the same time, she felt better, as if the wall that had grown between them had been torn down by their lovemaking.

Chase pressed a kiss to her forehead, and slipped one hand through her hair, lifting the curls off the back of her neck. He lightly massaged the nape of her neck, releasing tension from her muscles that she hadn't even realized she was carrying.

"Chase?"

"Yeah."

"I'm really not judging you based on your dad." She pulled back to look at him. "I'm just scared."

He said nothing for a moment, seemingly distracted by untangling her hair with his fingers. "Your point was valid."

She frowned. "What?"

He finally stopped playing with her hair and stepped back, his cock sliding out of her body in an agonizing sensation of loss. "When I was sixteen, I was already drinking heavily. I'd slept with six girls by then, and I couldn't remember half of them because I'd been drunk. My friends and I snuck onto this ranch to steal alcohol and joyride his tractor. I was the one who volunteered to go through the kitchen window, and I wound up with the rancher's shotgun wedged in my chest."

Her heart ached for the expression on his face. There was so much torment and guilt. "What happened?"

"He gave me the choice of going to jail, or working for him twenty hours a week for two years, until I graduated from high school." Chase pulled his jeans back up over his hips. He didn't fasten them, but they rested low on his waist. "Old Skip had strict rules, and I followed them, because I'd seen my dad go to jail and I knew what it was like. I didn't want to be my dad, so I shaped up. I never would have done it without being forced to. I'll never forget the day Old Skip handed me my first pair of cowboy boots, telling me to earn them." He looked at Mira. "I had never thought I was capable of earning anything, but I'd wanted to be worthy of those damned boots, so I started working my ass off for him." He ran his hand through his hair, remembering. "Gary was Old Skip's buddy, and he used to keep us in line when Old Skip wasn't around. He's a good man." He gestured to the walls. "I bought the place five years ago. This is the ranch that saved me, but without AJ, I never would have taken it this far. I never would have believed I could buy it and make it mine."

She smiled, accepting a towel when he handed it to her. "So, you should feel proud. You broke free from your past."

"No." He leaned forward and planted his hands on either side of her hips, staring intently at her. "Don't you get it? I *was* my dad for a while, and then I cleaned myself up. But my dad was okay too, until my mother died. He loved her, and she died when I was born. That's what put him over the edge and started the spiral that he never came out of." His fingers dug into the sink. "I'm one bad choice away from being my dad, Mira. One sliver of a breath." He ran his finger over her jaw. "A woman broke him, and I never understood how that could happen, until now."

Her heart tightened, and for a moment, she couldn't seem to breathe. "Chase, it's been a long time since you were that boy. You're not your dad—"

"No?" He traced a circle above her breast. "Then why, when I thought you saw me as a monster a few minutes ago, did something inside me simply snap?" He cupped her breast, a tender, possessive touch that made her belly tighten. "I don't think I'm capable of handling how I'm beginning to feel about you, because you're right. You're human, and I'm not sure I can handle anything except the fantasy."

His words were like cold water being dumped over her naked body. So, he didn't want her, the woman she was? That felt fantastic to hear after having sex with him four times in the last twelve hours. "I see."

"Do you?" His voice was urgent, almost desperate. "Do you understand the depths of how far I could fall? Do you know how bad I could be? Because I do. I have the scars to prove it, and so do all my brothers." He picked up the blue baby socks from the floor where they'd fallen, and he set them in her hand. "I never thought about it until now, until I realized the impact I could have on those that I've sworn to protect if I screw up." He closed her fingers over the socks. "One mistake, Mira. That's all it would take for me to fall into the pit that consumed my dad."

She crushed the socks in her hand. "You really think you'd make that mistake? After all you've endured?"

He looked at her. "When I was a freshman in college, I met a girl. I fell in love. She cheated on me with one of my teammates. When I found out, I was devastated. I went straight to a party and started drinking. It was the first time I'd touched alcohol since I was sixteen, and I didn't even pause. AJ found me and dragged me out of there before I finished my first drink. Without him, I'd have been down that path again. So, yeah. I think I have that potential." He looked down at the socks. "And now there's going to be a child," he said softly.

The cotton was rough and damp in her hand, no longer soft and pristine. They were wrinkled and wet. "Yes, there is," she said quietly.

A door slammed somewhere in the house, making them both look toward the door. "Chase!" A man's voice echoed. "You around?"

Chase swore under his breath. "That's Travis."

She stiffened. "Your brother? The one who has come to drive me away and save you from me?"

"Yeah." He raised his voice. "I'm in the bathroom," he called out.

"I'll be out in a second." He turned back toward Mira. "Promise me you won't leave the house, that you won't move out."

She hesitated, confused. "But you just said—"

"We'll keep it professional. I'll keep my distance." His gaze swept over her nakedness one more time. "I don't know how the hell I'm going to keep my hands off you, Mira, but I won't risk you or the child. I'll find a way to be the man my father never was."

Her chest tightened at his promise, and suddenly she wanted to cry for the past that haunted him so ruthlessly. He was such a good man. Was it really possible he could betray himself and her and cross that line?

The door suddenly opened, and she yelped, jerking the towel over her breasts as Chase leapt in front of her, using his body to shield her as a man walked into the bathroom. He was even taller than Chase, and his hair was rough and unkempt. His visage was harder than Chase's, but he had the same blue eyes and straight nose. He was wearing crisp blue jeans and cowboy boots, with a white hat that was tipped low over his face. His gaze swept right past Chase and bore into her.

She stiffened and raised her chin. "You must be Travis. I'm Mira Cabot."

Travis's eyes narrowed, and he looked from her to Chase, swiftly noting her nakedness and Chase's low slung, unfastened jeans and shirtless torso. "Zane said this was a business arrangement," he said. His voice was rough, lazy with a cowboy drawl that didn't conceal his burning intelligence. "This looks like a hell of a lot more than a business partnership."

"Get out of here, Travis." Chase's voice was mild, but it carried a steely edge that made her shiver in appreciation that he was on her side. "I'll be out in a minute."

Travis looked at her again, and she saw a promise in his eyes, a promise to do whatever it took to protect his brother. "I'll be in the kitchen." He stepped backward, his boots thudding on the floor as he pulled the door shut behind him, just hard enough to make a point.

As his footsteps echoed down the hall, Chase ran his hand through his hair. "Tell me you'll stay, Mira."

She sighed. "I don't want to get in the middle—"

He wrapped his hands around her upper arms, pulling her against him. "Tell me you'll stay." His voice was edged with desperation, and she saw something in his eyes that drained the last of her resistance.

"I'll stay for now," she said, finally. "I won't leave without telling you."

He held her for a moment longer, then finally acknowledged her comment with a brief nod. "Okay. We'll talk more later, but I have to go see Travis." There was an edge of excitement to his voice that made her smile.

"How long has it been since you've seen him?" she asked as Chase reached for the doorknob.

He looked back at her. "Five years," he said. "He's only here because of you, so thank you for bringing him back." He gave her a brief smile, then ducked out of the bathroom, pulling the door shut behind him with a soft click.

Mira leaned back against the sink with a sigh. Two Stockton brothers in one house? Because one hadn't been more than she could deal with, right?

She looked up at the ceiling. "AJ, you brought him into my life, so what am I supposed to do now?"

Of course, he didn't answer, but she could almost hear him chuckling. He'd always claimed life was meant to be lived, but what exactly did that mean?

She wasn't entirely sure, but at least one thing was certain: there could be no more sex with Chase. That much she was sure of. But then what?

The low murmur of male voices drifting down the hall told her that she was about to find out.

CHAPTER TEN

TRAVIS WAS LEANING against the counter, his arms folded across his chest, waiting, when Chase walked into the kitchen. He wasn't eating, or doing anything. Just waiting.

Something tightened in Chase's chest at the sight of his younger brother. "Good to see you." He walked over to him, and dragged him into a rough hug.

Travis stiffened, then hugged him back, gripping tightly.

After a moment, Travis pounded him on the back and the brothers released each other. "You're getting old, bro," Travis said. He touched his temple. "Got some gray going on there?"

"Not as much as you. You look like you've got some miles on you." Chase released his brother and stepped back, scanning him. The last time he'd seen Travis, his kid brother been nineteen years old, with a backpack and a guitar, heading off to Nashville. Travis was carrying another thirty pounds of muscle on his once lanky frame, but his face had some lines on it now. In fact, there were shadows beneath his brother's eyes, and his face was thin, almost too thin. He didn't simply look older. He looked worn. "What's the scar on your jaw from?"

Travis touched the mark. "Bar room brawl."

Chase tensed, and then Travis laughed. "Shit, bro, you need to chill.

You really think I'd be in a bar room brawl? I'm not that guy. You know I'm not a drinker."

"Yeah, but it's been a while. People change." Chase turned away and started the coffee machine. "Want something to eat?"

"I won't change that way," Travis said. "That's a line I don't cross. And are you offering one of your famous omelets? I'll never turn that down. You got any jalapeños in that fridge of yours?"

"Always." Chase opened the fridge and pulled out the ingredients. He started mixing the eggs, and then decided to add some more for Mira. After cooking for himself for so long, it looked like the biggest batch of eggs he'd made in years. It wasn't a fraction of what he used to whip up for his brothers, but it was a start. It was good. "How's the yodeling going?"

Travis shrugged. "I'm on tour through the end of October." He sat down on one of the bar stools that lined the granite bar. "Fifty-two cities, ninety-six shows in the last four months."

Chase didn't miss the bitterness in his brother's tone, and he cocked an eyebrow at him. "Not going well?" Travis had busted his butt in Nashville for years before signing a deal. It was all he'd ever wanted, and he'd gotten it, and a whole lot more.

"It's fine. I sell out everywhere. Got a couple nominations this year." Travis shrugged. "Living the dream, bro, right?" He looked around. "Place looks good," he commented, changing the subject. "Better than I remembered."

Chase didn't push the topic, but he wondered what was going on. "I've been fixing it up." Even though Travis was a few years younger than Chase, he'd still followed the path of the Stockton boys and started working on the ranch as soon as he was old enough. Old Skip had taken every one of the boys on as help, and they'd all had more than a few hot meals in that kitchen. Some weeks, Skip's chili had been the only decent thing they'd eaten. "Skip hadn't done much to it over the years. He was sick for a while before he passed away." The coffee ready, he poured a cup for Travis and slid it across the counter to him. "Can you stay for a while?"

Travis shook his head. "Have to be in Millingham, Alabama tomorrow night. I blew off tonight. Said I had food poisoning." He inhaled the coffee, and closed his eyes. "You still make the best damn coffee on the entire planet, bro. There's no place in this country that's better than your kitchen in the morning."

"Yeah, thanks." Chase pulled out a mug for Mira, then started chopping onions. "She's okay, you know."

Travis didn't bother to pretend he didn't know what Chase was talking about. Neither of them bothered with small talk anymore. Life didn't slow down enough to waste time dancing around when things had to be covered. "You can't bring her here," Travis said, without preamble.

"I can."

"Shit, man." Travis put down his mug, and gestured around the kitchen. "Look at this place. You've sunk every dime you have into it. You've got a viable business going on with the horses. You've got every-thing to lose. If you marry her and claim that kid, she's got a knife aimed at your back for the rest of your life."

Chase ground his jaw. "She's not like that—"

"How the hell do you know? This place is *our* history. What if she takes it? It's all we've got."

"The ranch matters to you?" Chase looked up, surprised by his brother's comment. "You've never come by even once since I bought it."

"I know, but it's always *here*." Travis leaned forward, his expensive watch glistening on his wrist. "I talk to Zane. I talk to some of the others. We all know this place is here. If the shit blows up, we got this. If we lose the ranch, the thin, fragile tie that binds us together will break, and we'll all scatter for good."

Chase stared at his brother. "When did you become so poetic?"

Travis shrugged. "I write songs. It's what I do. It's not that hard." He thumped his chest. "You have to feel it to write it. You know my song, *Fence Sittin'*?"

"Your first number one? Yeah, I know it." Chase would never forget the first time he heard Travis's song on the radio. He'd been driving to the train station to head into the city, and they'd said his little brother's name and played that song. He'd pulled over and sat in his car, listening to every single word of it. That moment had been one of the best experiences of his life. Travis had gotten out, and he'd made it.

"That song is about this place. It's what it means to me." Travis stood up and walked over to the window. He braced his hands on the sill and looked out over the front porch. "I still remember sitting on that porch with Old Skip the day he brought out his old guitar and put it into my hands. He said I had talent and I was a stupid bastard for sitting on my ass and chasing girls." He looked back at Chase. "If you marry Mira, she has rights to this place, no matter what you put in the contract. With the right lawyer, she could get it."

Chase put down his knife. "I'm not going to lose the ranch, Travis."

"How do you know?" Travis turned back toward him. "Those women took everything from Dad. Every last thing he had. They can do that."

"Shit, Travis, this isn't like that." Anger rushed through him, and he grabbed the knife and started slicing tomatoes. "Mira's not like that. Hell, she doesn't even want to marry me. I'm the one trying to force her."

"Really?" Travis's eyes narrowed. "Then what the hell are you doing? If she doesn't want to marry you, then take that gift and get out while you can." Travis's voice was hard.

"Really? You think I should just walk away?" Chase slammed down the knife. "That baby she's carrying is the child of my best friend, who I owe my life and this ranch to. You think I should walk away and let that kid live the same life we did? You think that's what I should do?"

"You can save the kid in other ways than marrying her! Hell, Chase, you don't even like women. What the hell has she got on you?"

"Nothing!"

"Then why don't you use your damned head and think of a solution that doesn't put any of this place at risk?"

"Because I don't want to!" The words burst out before he could stop it, and then hung in the air, suspended between them.

Travis whistled softly, understanding dawning on his face. "You've fallen for her. Completely and totally. It's not about the baby. It's about *her*."

"Shut the hell up." Chase jammed the knife through the bell pepper, chopping it up into jagged pieces.

"You don't even *know* her." Travis walked over and leaned on the counter next to Chase. "Talk to me, bro. What's going on?"

Chase kept chopping. "Just doing my civic duty." Even as he said the words, his conversation with Mira came tumbling back. He set down the knife yet again, looking at his brother. "Do you think we'll all end up like him? You ever hit a woman? Or a kid?"

Travis was silent for a long moment, then shook his head. "No. I never have." He met Chase's gaze. "But I get pissed. A lot. I have a punching bag in my tour bus. I use that."

"You think a kid would be okay with you as a dad?"

Again, a long silence, then Travis shrugged. "I hadn't thought about it, but I don't know. What do we know about being good for anyone, let alone a kid?"

"Nothing." Chase picked up the knife again, and started slicing the jalapeño. "Not a damn thing."

Travis sighed, and leaned against the counter, his arms folded loosely over his chest. "This thing with Mira is wrong on a thousand different levels, bro. You know that. It's wrong for the ranch, for us, for you, for her, and for that kid."

Chase said nothing as he dumped the vegetables into the bowl of beaten eggs. Travis's words made sense, but he couldn't own them. The thought of walking away from Mira felt wrong all the way to his gut. Was it just because he'd had her in his head as a fantasy for so long? Or was it a real response to the woman he'd made love to all night? He added his signature spices, stirring the mixture until it was well-blended.

"Some of us aren't meant to get married and be a dad," Travis said. "Some of us are meant to live a different life."

Chase poured his concoction into the frying pan. "Yeah, maybe." He'd always thought that of himself, but Mira had made him think differently. Now he was thinking about things he had no business contemplating, but he couldn't stop himself.

"That's us," Travis said. "The nine Stockton fuck-ups. We're meant to be solo, and to come back here and recharge and make sure our roots are secure. You're the anchor, and so is this place. It's just how life is." He reached across the counter and snagged his mug. "We're meant to drink good coffee and try not to fuck up the world we live in, and you know it."

Chase grabbed a spatula, watching the omelet begin to sizzle and bubble around the sides. Travis was simply repeating the truth they'd all come to accept as they'd gotten older and realized how close to the edge they all treaded. Only Steen had realized it too late, winding up in prison due to a battle over a woman. The poor bastard was still there, but the clock was ticking down on his release. What did a man become after four years in prison? "I know."

"Let Mira go, Chase. Give her a wad of cash if you want, but let her go. She deserves more than what you can give her, and we all deserve more than what a woman will bring into our lives—" He stopped suddenly, cutting himself off, staring past Chase toward the hallway.

Chase looked over his shoulder, and his gut sank when he saw Mira standing in the doorway. She was wearing jeans and a tank top. Her hair was still wet, and her feet were bare. Without makeup or any adornments, she looked so young and vulnerable that his heart tightened.

She was staring at Travis, and he knew that she'd heard at least the end of the conversation. He quickly replayed it in his mind, trying to recall what they'd said.

Slowly, she pulled her gaze off his brother and looked right at him. He saw the question in her eyes, asking him what he wanted her to do.

He didn't need to ask what she felt. She was prepared to walk out and leave him to the life he'd worked so hard to accomplish. Travis's comments had made him realize that his efforts to create a homestead for his brothers was working. It would be a slow process to get them all back there and reconnected, but it was already working. He had what he wanted. He had *everything* he wanted.

Would he really risk it for a woman he barely knew? A woman who wasn't even ready to trust him, or even trust her own feelings for him? A woman who was so tightly entwined through his soul that he didn't even know which parts were his fantasy and which were real? For a child who could embroil him in a legal battle that could decimate his finances if he fought it all the way through? Alan was a formidable opponent, far more than his own father had ever been, but just as rotten to the core.

Mira raised her eyebrows, and he knew she was waiting for his answer. She wanted it now. She needed it, because she had a life she had to figure out, and the clock was ticking. All he had to do was nod, and she would walk away without a single look back.

Travis looked over at him, and he saw his brother's dark expression, already retreating from the presence of a woman in their sanctuary. "Tell her, Chase."

Mira pressed her lips together and raised her chin. "Tell me what?"

He looked back and forth between them, and he knew that the only two things in the world that made him feel alive were standing there, and he had to choose between them.

⁓

"I'VE MADE A DECISION," Mira cut Chase off just as he opened his mouth to answer.

Travis raised his eyebrows. "Did you?"

"No." Chase interrupted. "Mira—"

"There's no need to get married." She blurted out the words before Chase could speak. She'd heard enough of the conversation between the brothers, and she'd seen the look of torment on Chase's face when she'd walked in. She didn't know what he would choose, but either one was unacceptable. If he'd stood up for her against Travis, he would lose his brother. If he'd told her to leave... God, the mere thought of it made something inside her want to cry with loss. There was no way she could handle him cutting her out, but there was no way that she'd be responsible for coming between the brothers. Which meant she had to take herself out of the equation before Chase could be forced to make a choice.

Chase shot an angry look at Travis, whose relief was obvious. "Don't listen to my brother," Chase said. "He's—"

"He cares about you," she interrupted. She stepped into the kitchen, knowing what she had to say. She'd realized the moment

Travis had cut himself off and looked at her. Everything had become clear when she'd seen the bond between the brothers. She'd been touched by the depth of their fear of how broken they both were, and she now understood how important the ranch was to all of them. It had been beautiful seeing their connection, but at the same time, she'd felt like an intruder into their space.

She deserved more than to live life as an outsider, and so did her child.

"The issue with the baby is not whether I'm married to Chase. It's whether we can convince Alan that Chase is the biological father. If I stay here for a few months, it sets up our relationship sufficiently." She didn't look at Chase as she talked. She couldn't. It was harder than she thought to pull away from him, even after this short time. "I don't need to marry him." She looked at Travis. "And I don't need his money."

Chase swore under his breath. "You do need money."

"Just a roof over my head and food until I can get a job. Selling my parents' house should cover most of the medical bills." Her throat suddenly tightened, and she felt a wave of sadness at her mother's death, but she lifted her chin. "It's clear that I can't put AJ's name on the birth certificate, and I feel that leaving it blank is too dangerous." She met Chase's gaze. "The only thing I think I really need from you is your name on the birth certificate. With any luck, nothing more will ever happen, but it gives us the ammunition if we need it."

She knew the risk of giving him parental rights over the child, but she couldn't think of any other way. Chase's name had to be on there, or the child would always be vulnerable to Alan.

Chase's eyes narrowed. "It might not be enough, if Alan comes after him."

"Marriage doesn't change whether you're the baby's biological father or not. If we make our relationship clear and visible, and your name is on the birth certificate, then it's just as good as if we were married. The only issue will be that the baby will be born 'early,' so we need to lay low until then. Alan has to forget about me." She shrugged. "If he forces a DNA test, then it doesn't matter whether you're married to me or not."

"It might help." Chase was gripping the spatula so hard that his knuckles were white.

"The omelet's burning," Travis said. "Needs to be flipped."

Chase glared at him, then turned back to the stove. He flipped the omelet deftly, making it apparent that he didn't lack kitchen skills, which was a little surprising. It made him seem softer, and more human, which she really didn't need.

Travis walked past her, poured a cup of coffee, and then held it out to her. "You want cream or sugar?"

She was so surprised by his offer that for a moment, all she could do was stare blankly at him. "What?"

"You drink coffee? Chase makes the best."

She glanced at Chase, then accepted the mug. "Black is fine."

Travis inclined his head, then returned to his place at the counter. "The omelet is worth hanging around for, too."

Chase frowned at his brother, as if he were as confused as she was by Travis's sudden congeniality. "I made enough for you," he said, glancing back at Mira.

Okay, she was completely confused. She'd been in the middle of a great speech, and now the guys were talking about food? "Great. I love omelets." Were omelets and coffee actually part of a secret code she knew nothing about? Had she just agreed to a midnight bloodletting ceremony in the hayloft? She looked at Travis. "Are you trying to poison me, or do you suddenly not think I'm a curse cast upon this place and your brother?"

Travis grinned, and tapped the brim of his hat in a salute. "It was a good speech, Ms. Cabot. I believed it. You don't want my brother, his money, or his ranch, so yeah, I'm good."

She blinked. "Just like that? You believe me?"

"Yeah." He picked up his coffee. "People don't impress me much, but I know good stock when I see it." He raised the mug in a toast. "To bastard fathers who bring people together."

Mira glanced at Chase. He didn't look nearly as pleased as Travis did. "I think you should stay until the baby is born," he said tersely. "No point in risking it."

Relief rushed through her at his words, and she felt herself relax.

She'd meant every word of her speech, but the truth was that a part of her wanted nothing more than to stay on his ranch in his protective circle. Staying until the baby was born, without getting married, gave her time to get her feet under her and set up her life. "I can live with that." Instinctively, she looked over at Travis and raised her brows.

He scowled, a moody look that made him look vaguely familiar. "Nine months? That's kind of a while."

"Is it?" Chase flicked off the burner with a little too much force. He jerked up his sleeve and shoved his arm in front of Travis's face, showing him the cigarette burns. "The baby's father had these all over his fucking back, his cheekbone had been broken in two places, and his left foot didn't even fucking work anymore, all because his daddy was as bad as ours. The baby's father, my best friend, is dead, but the bastard who messed him up isn't. Mira's spent the last eight years caring for her paralyzed mother. Every last cent she had went into taking care of her, and now she's got a child to protect. And you want to put a fucking time limit on the protection we give the two of them? Did all your limousines make you forget exactly how shitty life is as a kid without anyone to protect you?"

Travis stared at Chase's arm for a long moment, and when he looked up, his expression had changed. He looked cold and hard, as if he were ready to strike out at the first person who looked at him the wrong way. She wondered where *his* scars were. "I'm in," he said, his voice hard. "It doesn't get to happen again."

His voice was so unrelenting, that she knew he wouldn't change his mind. Suddenly tears filled her eyes, and she didn't even know what to say.

Travis looked at her, and his eyes narrowed. "You have a phone?"

She lifted her chin, refusing to let him see that she was almost ready to cry just because the two of them were willing to stand by her. "Yes, why?"

"Get it."

She pulled it out of her back pocket. "I have it. Why?"

"Put my number in it. If you can't reach Chase, you call me. Just put it under Travis Stockton, not Turner, just in case anyone sees your phone." He rattled off his phone number, but she was so surprised she forgot to type it in.

He frowned at her. "What?"

"You're Travis *Turner?* The famous country music star?" She'd heard of Travis Turner many times, and some of his songs were on her play list. "No wonder you looked familiar." She actually felt a little bit fan-girl for a moment.

Chase plunked a plate with part of an omelet down in front of her. "He's Travis Stockton," he said firmly. "Travis Turner is a stage name because we're a bunch of anti-social hermits who don't want the public in our business." He gave Travis another plate, and then filled the last one for himself.

Travis nodded at her phone. "Put the number in your phone, Ms. Cabot. I want it in there before I leave."

She quickly typed his number in her phone. Travis *Turner's* mobile number was in her phone? How insane was that? "I won't share it."

"I know." He took a sip of his coffee. "That's why I gave it to you." He picked up his coffee and omelet. "Front porch," he announced. "It's a damn fine day." He headed out the door. She grabbed her plate to follow him, but Chase stopped her with a hand to her arm.

Her belly clenched at his touch, and all thoughts of Travis-the-superstar fled until all that remained was Chase. She swallowed and forced herself to look up at him. With Travis in the room, she'd been able to avoid intimacy with Chase, but now that it was just them, the night of lovemaking with him flooded her mind and senses. Heat radiated from her skin, and she felt her cheeks flush with embarrassment and more than a little desire. "What is it?"

He slid his hand through her hair, and cupped the back of her neck. "I haven't given you a proper good morning, yet," he said.

She swallowed. "Good morning—"

He bent his head and kissed her. It wasn't a platonic, "hey, we're roommates now," kind of kiss. It was a kiss intended to shred every last one of her defenses, and to plunge straight to her core and ignite the same firestorm of passion that he'd unleashed last night. She had no defenses against him, and she sank into him as he kissed her. His mouth just tasted so good, and the strength of his body as he pulled her into his arms was irresistible.

She sighed in capitulation, and kissed him back.

The kiss turned carnal within seconds, and she felt his hands on her hips, drawing her against him as he backed her against the counter. God, not in the kitchen! She pushed at his chest, and was surprised when he stopped.

He broke the kiss and pulled back just enough so he could look at her. Without his cowboy hat, he looked younger. His dark brown hair was disheveled from a night of lovemaking, and his jaw was dark with whiskers. "Nine months," he said. "I have nine months."

"Nine months to do what?" Make love to her until she died of ecstasy? Because right now, she felt like that might be an okay way to meet her demise.

"To figure this out." He kissed her once more, breaking the kiss before she had time to respond. "Travis is waiting. Let's eat." He gave her a wink that made her belly flip over, then he grabbed both their plates, forks, and napkins, and headed out the door. "Grab our coffee, will you?"

He didn't wait for an answer. He just walked, leaving her with a body that was still tingling from his assault.

What? She was so not okay with those terms. "Chase!"

He paused at the door, turning back to look at her. "Yeah?"

"Don't kiss me again."

His eyes narrowed thoughtfully, as he turned back toward her. She stiffened as he walked back over to her, still holding the plates. "Why not?"

She raised her chin. "Because I can't do that. I can't be sleeping with you and trying to establish my life. You're just too...overpowering."

"Mira—"

She held up her hand to silence him. "What were you going to say when I walked in? If I hadn't announced I wasn't going to marry you, what would you have said? Were you going to risk the ranch and your brothers to marry me?" Whoops. She hadn't meant to ask that. She didn't want to hear him say it. "Never mind." She grabbed the coffee mugs and brushed past him, heading out to the porch, ignoring his shocked look at her bold question.

She waited for him to call her back and answer her question.

He didn't.

He could have stopped her if he'd wanted to answer.

He hadn't, which means she knew what he would have said.

He had been planning to choose his brothers, which was exactly why she simply could not kiss him again.

Taylor was right.

She did like him, far too much.

CHAPTER ELEVEN

A WEEK LATER, Chase was tired, sweaty, and his hip hurt like hell from being tossed from his newest horse too many times. He raked the back of his hand across his brow, reining in his mount as dust kicked up at the end of his driveway. He shaded his eyes, watching the approaching vehicle. The moment he saw his red pickup, the tension that had been caked on him all day eased from his tired muscles.

Mira was back.

She hadn't left him.

He knew that she'd committed to staying at the ranch until the baby was born, but every day that she left in search of a job, he found himself on edge until she reappeared. Tonight, she was late, and his tension had been mounting with each passing hour of her absence.

Needing to connect with her, he reached down to unhook the corral gate, then slipped Red through the opening. He urged the horse into a lope, arriving at his front door just as Mira stopped the truck. She'd left the house while he'd been feeding the horses breakfast, and it was almost seven o'clock now. It was the fourth day in a row that she'd been gone all day, and he was getting cranky about it.

Ever since the morning when she'd announced she wasn't going to marry him and had laid down the law of no more kissing, she'd been as elusive as a hare, sidestepping him every time he tried to talk to her about anything significant. She was cordial, but there was a distance that he didn't like.

Yeah, he understood why she'd pulled back. He knew he'd failed the test when she'd asked him whether he would have married her over Travis's concerns. He should have said yes, but he didn't lie, no matter what. He had no idea what his answer would have been if she hadn't taken control, but he knew that he liked coming in from the barn at night and seeing her curled up by the fire reading. In the short time she'd been living with him, he'd gotten used to making dinner for two people. He even enjoyed testing recipes he thought she might like. It hadn't been so bad having a woman in his house, but the truth was, it wasn't enough to simply have her there. He wanted her to be *his*.

He wanted her accessible to him like she'd been when he'd first met her at that church, when she'd jumped up and hugged him, and let every emotion she felt show on her face. He needed her to look at him as if he mattered, and he craved the freedom to touch her whenever he wanted, even if it was simply to tuck a strand of hair behind her ear when her hands were full. Cohabitation wasn't enough, not by a long shot.

Today had been the longest day yet. She'd been gone for twelve hours, and he'd been getting worried. He'd dialed her cell phone three times to check on her, but had never pressed "Send." He didn't know if she would be okay with him checking up on her, and he was skittish as hell about driving her further away. All he knew was that he wanted her home, where he could keep an eye on her and make sure she was okay.

And now she was back.

He reached down from his saddle and opened her door, swinging it open with an agile move from his mount. "Hi." He couldn't keep the smile off his face, he was so relieved to see her.

She beamed up at him, and for a split second, he was stunned by how beautiful she was. He'd never seen her smile like that before, and it was as if the sun itself had poured itself into her. "I got a job!" she announced.

He blinked. "You did?" Tension locked around his gut. Yeah, he wanted her to get her life going, but a job gave her independence from him. "What kind of job?"

"Managing O'Doul's hardware store. Apparently Howard, who was running it, fell into a canyon after drinking too much."

He frowned. "Howard's a lush."

"Yes, well, now he's in a body cast, and they needed someone." She jumped out of the truck, still grinning. "I know absolutely nothing about screws or types of wood, but apparently, I'm charming enough that Mick figured I might steal business from Stevens Hardware Supply, which apparently is his biggest competitor." She looked so happy that he wanted to break out the champagne and raise a toast to her...at the same time he wanted to handcuff her to him so she couldn't leave. "He said if I like the job, I can keep it even after Howard recovers. Apparently, this was Howard's last chance. How about that?" Her smile widened. "Less than a week of job hunting, and I'm employed. How awesome am I?" She held her arms over her head and did a little hip-swaying dance that was ridiculous, adorable, and sexy as hell at the same time.

"Mick's a good guy, but not easily impressed. You did good." Chase had to give her credit. O'Doul's was one of the better gigs in town. With three locations in the state, Mick could even afford to pay health insurance to his full-time employees. "Nice job."

"Thank you." She gave him a sweeping bow that made him want to reach over and haul her into his arms for the kind of kiss he'd been fantasizing about constantly ever since she'd put the brakes on their relationship.

He didn't reach for her, though, afraid of pushing her away. Apparently oblivious to how hard his cock was and how much effort it was taking not to drag her into his arms, she reached into the back of the truck and hauled out some brown paper bags. "Do you know Eva Carter, who works at the café across the street from O'Doul's? Well, she has an apartment over her garage, and the tenant is moving out at the first of the year. She's so nice. She reminded me of my friend, Taylor, from back home. I'll bet I could rent the space from her. She said she's not going to re-rent the apartment because her current tenant is a complete scumbag and she's tired of dealing with renters, but I bet she'd rent to me, don't you think?"

A cold, bitter feeling settled in his gut. "That place only has a space heater. You can't live there with a baby. Winter is brutally cold in Wyoming."

"Oh...a space heater?" She frowned. "She didn't mention that." She wrinkled her nose. "Well, still, it shows me that there are some options out there, you know? Everyone is so nice in this town." She grinned. "You have no idea what it's like to walk down the street and have people smile at me. After all those years taking care of my mom, no one here is looking at me with this great veil of sadness, and no one sees me as the daughter of the local sheriff. It feels good to be able to start a new life without any baggage following me."

He smiled, the tension in his gut easing at the genuine joy on her face. "There are good people in this town," he acknowledged. Some bastards too, but he wasn't going to bring that up. Mira made him want to stop thinking about the crap, and that felt good. He swung down off his horse to take the paper bags from her. "I'll get these. What's in them?"

"So, I also stopped at the grocery store. Apparently, I'm deficient in iron, so I need more red meat. Burgers tonight." She handed him the bags, and turned to gather more.

He frowned. "Deficient in iron? What are you talking about?"

She grabbed her purse, slung it over her shoulder, and picked up one more grocery bag. "Well, I went to see Doctor Murdoch today. I hadn't been to a doctor yet, and I wanted to set up a baseline. She's so fantastic. Anyway, I'm a little anemic, so I need to fix that. Other than that, I'm in great health. The baby is totally fine. I don't have to go back for a month, but I just wanted to establish a relationship with her, in case anything went wrong, you know?"

Something twisted in his gut, and all his amusement vanished. "You went to the doctor today? To check on your pregnancy?"

Her smile faded at his tone. "Was I not supposed to do that?"

"No, you should. It's just..." Shit. Why was he so pissed that she hadn't asked him go along with her? "If it's my baby, then I need to go to your appointments with you." Yeah, that was it. For appearance's sake, he needed to accompany her. "I didn't even know you were going."

She bit her lip, and she lifted her chin in a hint of defiance that sent waves of apprehension tumbling through him. "It's not your baby."

Her words were like a sharp hit to his gut. Yeah, he knew it was true, but he felt like she was slipping out of his fingers, and so was the child. "If my name is on that birth certificate," he said evenly, carefully selecting his words, "it's my baby to the world. Anyone who knows me is well aware that I'd be there with you at every appointment. It's how I am. In addition, I've committed to that baby's well-being, and I want to be there, because I want to make sure everything is okay."

The smile completely vanished from her face, and he saw fear flicker in her eyes. "If you can't even let me go to an appointment by myself, how would you let me move out with the baby, then? Would you do that? If that's not your style, then how are you going to do that?"

Shit. He felt like things were spiraling. "Irreconcilable differences," he said. "If we can't make it work, then that's the way it is. But right now, you're living with me, and we're a happy couple. So, yeah, I need to go."

She fell silent, and tension seemed to build between them. After a moment, she looked at him. "After my parents' car accident, I felt like my entire world collapsed. I had nothing to lean on, and it was absolutely terrifying. I've had to learn to be strong, and I feel like I'm pretty good at it. But every night when I go to bed, and I lie there thinking about how I'm single and pregnant, I'm terrified. I don't know how I'm ever going to do this on my own, Chase. If you start coming to appointments with me and acting like a devoted dad and partner, I'm going to get used to having you to lean on. Then when I'm on my own again, I don't know if I'll be able to do it. I can't rely on you, and then suddenly not have you there. It's too hard."

Chase swore under his breath and set the bags down. He took her bag and set it beside his, then took her hands. They were trembling and cold, and suddenly he felt like such an ass for being pissed that she was out there in his town, building her life. "You need to understand something, Mira. I will do *anything* for those who I've committed to. For my whole life, it's been only my brothers and AJ. And now it's you and that baby. You're in my circle of protection, and no matter what you do, you'll never be outside of it. You don't have to do this on your own, and it doesn't make a difference whether you're living here or not. I'm here for you and the baby, all the way through."

Tears brimmed in her eyes. "It's not the same thing, Chase."

"What's not the same thing?" He didn't understand how he was failing her.

She carefully extracted her hands from his. "Having you to back me up is wonderful, but it's different than having a partner who is there just for you, someone who is that special confidant who always puts you before anyone else. Going to the doctor's appointments is so personal. Sharing it with you would make it feel...well...it would feel like we're a couple, not simply that you're a great guy who has my back. I'm not made of steel, Chase. I would love to have someone by my side, so if you play that role, it's going to be too hard for me to remember that it's all a lie."

He ground his jaw. He didn't quite grasp the difference of what she was saying. He had no experience, either as an observer or a participant, in the kind of relationship she was describing. He just knew that he wanted to be a part of this with her. "I'd like to go." Was that better? Asking instead of demanding?

Something flickered in her eyes, a vulnerability that made his protective instincts flare up. "Chase, you aren't hearing me."

"I'm trying. I don't have background in this stuff." His horse nudged at his shoulder impatiently, reminding Chase that he still needed to feed him. "I want to go with you," he repeated. Instinctively, his gaze flicked to her belly. "I want to know that the baby's okay, too, you know. The kid doesn't have a dad. He's going to need someone."

The corner of her mouth curved up. "He might be a she."

"Girls need dads too." He frowned, suddenly thinking back to the days when he was in high school. "They need dads with big guns actually. I don't want anyone to mess with her." His gaze settled on her face, and he noted the shadows under her eyes and the weariness of her shoulders. "Or you."

His words fell into the silent chasm between them. After a moment, she managed a smile. "I'll go make dinner while you feed Red." She picked up two of the grocery bags, then turned and hurried into the house, without even looking back, leaving all his promises and offers dangling in the cool evening air, untouched and unacknowledged.

Grimly, he stared after her as the screen door swung shut behind her. What the hell was he doing wrong? The further she drifted from him, the more he wanted to pull her back. He was beginning to think that his agreement to her proposal that they didn't have to get married hadn't been the best decision. If they were married, he'd at least feel that he had some way to hold onto her.

Red nudged him, and he rubbed the horse's nose. "I think you're lucky you've been gelded," he muttered, as he swung back into the saddle. He turned the horse back to the barn, half-wishing that gelding really would solve his problem...

Or not.

He wasn't ready to give up yet, and when he got Mira back, he was going to need all his parts functioning just fine.

Because he would get her.

He *had* to get her.

MIRA BRACED her hands on the dashboard of Chase's truck, peering at the old farmhouse as his truck bounced up the dirt driveway. "I really think this is a bad idea. I don't think I can lie to Gary." She'd managed to put off the dinner invitation that Gary Keller had issued at the airport when she'd arrived, but when he'd found her at the hardware store earlier in the week, he'd cornered her and she'd had no escape.

And now they were here, about to disillusion one of the nicest men she'd ever met.

"You don't need to lie." Chase put his truck into park, his muscles flexing beneath his denim shirt. He was showered and freshly shaved, and he smelled amazing. He looked younger with his clean shave, and a part of her wanted desperately to run her hand over his jaw. What would it feel like to have him kiss her when his face was so soft?

He raised his brows at her, then lightly grasped her wrist. She was too surprised to pull away, and then, when he pressed her hand against his face, she didn't want to pull away. She slid her fingers along his jaw. "So smooth," she whispered.

"You don't have to hold back," he said, his gaze riveted to her face, and his voice deliciously husky. "You can touch me anytime you want."

Sudden desire rushed through her, and she quickly pulled her hand away. She'd been at the ranch for three weeks, and it had been increasingly difficult to keep her distance from Chase. He was charming at dinner, gruff and cranky before his coffee, and ridiculously sexy in his dusty jeans and cowboy hat whenever he came in from the barn. He didn't appear to have anyone else on the ranch helping him, and he worked literally from sunrise to sunset training horses, caring for them, and keeping the physical structure in good repair.

He reminded her of her dad, in a way, with his unflagging, steady energy to do his job. He never seemed to get flustered when a horse was difficult, and she'd never seen him lose his temper with an animal or anyone else. He was dependable and solid, and she was already starting to rely on him.

His constant, unabashed efforts to seduce her didn't help. She was attracted to him, and it was getting harder to remember to keep her distance. She had to keep reminding herself that he'd refused to choose her over his brothers, so she knew that she would never come first to him. Not that she wanted him to walk away from his family, but she couldn't marry him, or anyone, unless she knew that she would come first if she needed it.

He smiled slightly, the corners of his mouth curving up in a most insanely tempting fashion. "Did I mention that you look sexy as hell in those jeans?"

Heat flooded her cheeks. "I don't think so." She knew he hadn't. She clung to every compliment he gave her, even though she pretended not to hear most of them.

He leaned closer, his fingers gliding over the nape of her neck. "You look sexy as hell in those jeans, sweetheart." His breath was warm against her mouth, and her heart started to race.

"Don't call me sweetheart," she whispered.

He cocked an eyebrow. "Why not?"

"Because I like it." The admission slipped out, and she bit her lip, but it was too late to take back. Chase's face softened, and a hungry gleam appeared in his eyes. Oh, God. He was going to kiss her, wasn't he? He was going to kiss her, and she was going to let him and—

"Chase!" The front door of the gray farmhouse swung open with a bang, and Mira leapt back from Chase, both relieved and horribly frustrated by the interruption. She didn't want to have time to think about kissing him. She wanted it to just happen without her making the decision that she wanted it, because she couldn't make that decision.

Chase didn't look annoyed, however. He was studying her with a thoughtful look on his face, as if he realized that she would have let him kiss her, and he was contemplating exactly what he was going to do with that bit of information.

"You two ever going to get out of that truck?" A red-haired woman in blue jeans and cowboy boots was striding energetically toward the truck. The wrinkles on her face suggested she was in her seventies, but her flaming red hair was fit for a teenage rodeo queen. "It's about time you brought Mira around."

Mira quickly turned away from Chase, wishing that the moment had never happened. She wasn't sure which moment it was that she regretted. Was it the fact she'd almost kissed him, or the fact that she'd been interrupted before it had happened? She didn't know. God, she was so confused.

Taking refuge in their visitor, she opened the door and climbed out of his truck before Chase could make it around the truck to escort her, as he liked to do. "Hi," she said, forcing cheerfulness into her voice. "You must be Martha Keller."

"I am!" Martha swept Mira into a bear hug that surprised her, but felt amazing. "It's so good to see you, my darling." She tucked her arm through Mira's and winked at Chase. "Did you bring my pie, young man?"

Chase grinned, a devilish grin that was so sexy that Mira actually felt a little weak in the knees. "Would I ever let my favorite lady down?" He reached into the backseat and pulled out three pies that he'd baked last night, even though he'd been so tired that he'd nearly fallen asleep in the bowl of apples. Mira had helped him, and it had been fun cooking together. A lot of fun. "Two apple and one blueberry."

"Three pies? For that you get a second helping." Martha beamed at Chase as he leaped ahead of her so that he could hold the front door open, flirting with the older lady as she ducked under his arm.

Mira was startled by Chase's warm affection with Martha. He was so doting and sweet it was a little heart melting. It was a side she hadn't seen of Chase, or maybe a side she hadn't let him show. Either way, it was not what she needed to see. Endearing was not a quality she wanted to add to his list of attributes.

Gary was waiting for them with a roaring fire, some delicious wine, and a cheese plate containing more delicious cheese than she'd ever had in her lifetime. His hug was as warm as his wife's, and Mira felt her tension rising. How could she lie to these people?

Ten minutes into pre-dinner conversation around the fire, it became too much for Mira to cope with. Gary and Martha were so warm and caring that they reminded her of her parents. It was so cozy and homey, a domestic scene that she hadn't been a part of in so long. The camaraderie between Gary, Martha, and Chase was so evident, making her increasingly aware that her sense of belonging over the past few weeks had been such a superficial farce.

This was the kind of home she'd grown up in. This was the kind of warmth she craved. But this wasn't her world. It was a lie, a fabrication set up to protect a baby. What would Martha and Gary think of her when they found out the truth, that she'd been knocked up in a grief-induced one-night stand, and Chase was playing the hero for a child who wasn't even his? All this would be snatched away from her, and she'd be alone before she'd even had a chance to become a part of this world. Nausea churned in her belly. "Excuse me. May I use your bathroom?"

At Martha's direction, Mira stumbled to her feet and made it to the room in question. She was just shutting the door when Martha appeared over her shoulder.

Mira jumped, startled by the presence. "I'll be right out—"

"Oh, nonsense." Martha took her by the elbow and propelled her right past the bathroom and into the kitchen, plunking her down on a stool at the counter. "You don't need to go to the bathroom, and we both know it. Sit, girl, and talk to me."

Mira stared at her. "Talk? About what?"

"About what? Really?" Martha picked up two potholders and opened the oven. She retrieved a roast, keeping her voice deceptively casual as she addressed Mira. "Oh, how about the fact that you're pregnant, but barely even talking to Chase? Is that a good place to start the conversation?"

CHAPTER TWELVE

MIRA FELT her cheeks flame up. "What?"

Martha set the roast down on the stove and gave Mira a look. "How big do you think this town is? You're living with Chase. You were all in love when you greeted each other in the airport. You're seeing a doctor because you're pregnant. Despite all that storybook romancing, you and Chase aren't even sitting on the same couch in my living room. What's going on?"

Oh, God. This was what she'd been worried about. How could she lie to this lovely woman? "I just... I don't..." What to say? She hadn't been expecting Martha to know *everything*.

Martha jammed two meat forks into the roast and hoisted it onto a cutting board. "Those Stockton boys have issues," she announced, her voice warm with affection. "I'll be the first to tell you that they all deserved to be in jail at some point in their lives, but they're cleaning up well." She handed Mira a paring knife and three fresh tomatoes. "Slice."

Mira immediately began to cut, grateful for the distraction. "Yes, well, they aren't real high on the idea of a woman in their space."

"Of course not. They learned not to trust them." Martha wagged a baster at Mira. "Looks like you got the job of teaching them that not all women are she-devils from hell."

"That's not my job—"

"What?" Martha slammed the baster on the counter, making Mira jump. "Chase has never so much as let a woman breathe on his truck, let alone move into his house. He might not be able to show it, but he's head over heels for you. He's the oldest in that family, and he's the one who kept the boys together when all that hell was going on. He's got the word 'responsible' carved all the way to the marrow of his bones, but that's not all life is." Martha leaned forward, her eyes twinkling. "He needs to learn that life is also about long, moonlight kisses, late night conversations under the covers, and the kind of intimacy you can get with only that one special someone."

Mira bit her lip against the sudden longing in her chest. "I know that's important, but—"

"Then show him."

"No!" Mira set down her knife. "I already like him. A lot. But he's going to break my heart, and I can't go through that again."

Martha raised her brows. "You're so sure he's going to break your heart? And why is that?"

"Because his brothers have to come first."

"It's a different kind of first," Martha said, shrugging off her concern. "There's space for lots of people to come first."

Mira thought back to her college fiancé, and his demands, and she knew Martha wasn't entirely right. Sometimes, choices had to be made. "Chase and I had the same best friend, but we didn't meet until recently. He still sees me as the woman that my friend described. I don't even know if he sees me for who I am in real life."

Martha cocked her head. "Fantasy versus reality? You're not sure you measure up?"

"I know I don't. Who would?"

"Don't sell him short, Mira. Chase is no fool, and he's too gun-shy to shack up with a woman unless he knows in his gut that he's right about her."

A tiny, tiny flicker of hope fluttered inside Mira's chest. Was it really possible that at some point, Chase had begun to see the real her?

But that wasn't the entire issue. "He feels very responsible for the baby," she said quietly.

"I'll bet he does."

She looked at Martha. "If I let myself fall in love with him, how would I ever know if he married me for the baby, or for me?"

"Ah..." Martha leaned back against the counter, folding her arms over her chest. "And therein lies the problem, doesn't it? You got pregnant too early, before you two were able to solidify what you had together."

Mira shrugged. "It hasn't been very long." It hadn't, but at the same time, she still felt like he'd been a part of her heart forever.

"Huh." Martha picked up a white serving bowl and began to scoop potatoes out of the dish the roast had been in. "Then, I think it's time for you and Chase to start dating."

"Dating?" She shook her head, trying to ignore the flicker of anticipation at the idea. "I'll be honest, Martha, I don't feel like there is a place for me in his life, not with all his brothers. I'm trying to save some money, and then I'll move out after the baby is born. Right now, we're just cohabitating for convenience." There, she'd said it, as close to the truth as she could afford to get.

Martha raised a silvery eyebrow. "Is that how you want it, my dear? Do you see Chase as nothing more than a sperm factory?"

Mira burst out laughing. "A sperm factory? No, I don't think he's a sperm factory."

"Do you think he's a handsome, caring, honest, dependable man who made your entire world turn upside down when he made love to you all night long?"

For what felt like the thousandth time in five minutes, Mira felt her cheeks heat up, and this time, there was no way to deny the ache in her chest for him.

Martha clapped her hands in delight. "That's a yes, if I've ever seen one." She leaned forward, resting her elbows on the counter. "Girl, you need to stop being a pathetic martyr. Yes, so, you've got a baby to complicate things. So what? Trying to protect yourself from hurt will just leave you a bitter, old lady who lives with cats who urinate all over her basement and a child who pretends he isn't related to you. Is that really the life you aspire to?"

Mira blinked. "No, not really."

"Then go date Chase. Seriously. It's not that complicated." Martha set a gravy boat in Mira's hand. "But first, serve up the gravy. I'll give you a can of whipped cream to take home for a private dessert." She winked, ducking out of the way as Mira burst out laughing.

Whipped cream and Chase?

Martha was insane.

But as Martha opened the fridge to retrieve the salad, Mira couldn't help but notice a can of whipped cream sitting on the top shelf.

No.

She couldn't do that.

She wouldn't.

Urinating cats were better than having her heart shattered, she was sure of it.

∾

Dinner had been awkward.

Chase wasn't going to lie.

The entire night, Mira had sat on the edge of her seat, looking like a mouse about to bolt.

Gary had pulled him aside and lit into him that he wasn't treating Mira right, and he had a headache from the lecture that Martha had given him to start dating Mira.

Dating her.

Dating her.

Chase looked over at Mira. She was leaning back against the seat, her eyes closed, the bag of leftovers clutched to her chest. It wasn't even nine o'clock yet, and she was already beat.

He frowned as he turned into his driveway. "You feeling okay?"

She nodded, not even opening her eyes. "Martha thinks we should go on a date. She thinks there's magic between us that we're destroying by being stubborn and afraid of being hurt."

128

He rubbed his jaw as he pulled the truck into his driveway. "She said the same to me."

Mira opened her eyes and looked at him. "What do you want, Chase?"

Her expression was soft and vulnerable, as if she were too tired to keep up the façade she'd been perpetuating all evening. Her dark eyelashes framed her vibrant blue eyes, making her appear vulnerable. She looked utterly feminine, and his instinct to protect thundered through every part of his body. He eased the truck to a stop in front of the house, and turned to face her, resting his arm along the back of the bench seat, behind her. "What I want is for you to be in my bed every night, and at my breakfast table every morning." There. He'd said it. He couldn't believe he'd admitted it aloud, but he had. The words felt weighty and significant, damned terrifying if he was honest, but he didn't want to take them back. He wanted them out there. He wanted her to know.

She raised an eyebrow. "That's it?"

He frowned at her weary, unimpressed response. Didn't she under-stand the magnitude of what he'd just said? He'd admitted he wanted her to be part of his personal life, immersed in his personal space, the space he guarded from everyone. "That's a lot."

"It's not enough." With a shuddering sigh, she opened the car door. "There's too much at stake to risk it, Chase. What if we try, but we decide we hate each other? This baby will need both of us, so maybe it's best to just keep things even so that we can support each other as needed?"

"What? No way." He jumped out of the truck, jogging around to catch the door before she could get out. He held out his hand to help her down. "I want more."

She didn't take his hand, helping herself down instead. "What exactly is it that you want? More what? More sex? More intimacy? A great big family of love with your brothers?"

He swore under his breath. "I'm not the kind of guy your dad was, Mira. I don't bring that to the table. I have no clue how to have a family, and my brothers have to come first. I owe them, but I also want you. You matter. A lot."

She nodded, giving him a forlorn smile that tore at his heart. "I get it, but coming in second isn't what I want. I want it all."

He sighed, deflation settling deep in his chest. That was it. The truth. He'd laid it all out there, and it didn't matter. It wasn't enough. "Then I'm not your guy." But for the first time in his life, he wished he could be.

~

MIRA BOLTED UPRIGHT IN BED, certain that something was terribly wrong. The house was silent, almost eerily so, but the lights in the barn were blazing. She rolled over to check her phone, and saw it was two in the morning. What was Chase doing? Riding?

She hurried to the window and looked out. The barn doors were wide open, but there was no activity. Fear rippled through her, and she had a sudden feeling that something was very wrong.

Without hesitating, she yanked on her jeans and boots, grabbed a sweatshirt, and then raced down the hall. She flung the front door open and hurried across the dried-out grass to the barn, rushing through the open door.

Horses were up, with their heads out the doors. The barn was immaculate, without even a stray piece of hay in the corner. Pride of ownership gleamed from every surface, and her heart tightened at the sight. It was obvious how much Chase cared about the ranch. She'd never been in the barn, because she'd spent her days at work, trying to keep herself emotionally divested from the ranch that she was going to have to leave.

But now that she had seen it, she knew that she'd made a mistake in not coming in before. This place was Chase. This amazing stable defined who he was. The only way she would ever have answers about him was to see what made him thrive.

She realized suddenly that he wasn't around. "Chase?"

"Mira?" His voice was tense and strained, echoing from the last stall.

She hurried down the aisle, noticing now that the last door was open. She reached it, and then gasped when she looked inside. Chase was gripping the halter of a beautiful black stallion, who was trying to lie down. The animal's flanks were coated in sweat, and his nostrils were flared as he fought for breath. "What's wrong?"

"Spy has colic," Chase said tersely. His face was lined with tension, and he looked fearsome as he gripped the horse's halter. "Stomach ache," he clarified. "He wants to roll, but that could twist his intestines and kill him. I need to keep him on his feet."

Urgency surged through her, and suddenly, all the distance she'd tried to erect between them dissolved. "What can I do?"

Sweat was pouring down his temples, and he shook his head. "I've got it—" Just then, the horse groaned and his knees buckled. Chase swore and shouted at the horse, dragging on his halter to try to keep him up.

Instinctively, Mira ducked past Chase into the stall and shouted at the horse, shoving against his hip and trying to startle him. Their joined efforts worked, and the horse lurched back to his feet again.

Chase dragged the horse's head to the side, pulling him to the left to try to get him off balance enough to take a step. "Stay beside him," he commanded. "Keep working it. I'm going to try to get him to walk out of here." He tugged on the lead shank, and Mira got behind the horse, clucking as she dragged off her sweatshirt, and waved it behind Spy.

The animal lurched forward, his front hooves making it past the stall door. Chase shouted with victory, and together they got the animal moving forward. They made it down the aisle, but the horse was still fighting, still trying to go down with each step. Each time his knees began to buckle, she shouted and flapped her sweatshirt, while Chase urged him on in front.

"Outside," Chase said. "Let's get him to the ring."

Together, working as a unit, they got Spy to the corral, but it was a battle for every step. The air was cool, but the horse was still drenched in sweat.

"I gave him some medicine," Chase said. "If we can keep him moving until it kicks in, he should be okay. Come on, Spy!" He tugged on the horse as he tried to go down again. "Shit, come on, boy. You can do this!"

They got him going, and then one minute later, the horse dropped to his knees before they could stop him. He rolled onto his back with a groan, kicking his feet in the air as if he were itching his back, instead of risking his own life. Mira's heart dropped, and she and Chase leapt at Spy, shouting and pushing at him.

"Get up," she screamed. "Come on!"

For an agonizing moment, Spy continued to roll, and then he lurched to his feet with a groan, staggering as he tried to regain his balance. "Good boy!" Chase urged him forward, and Mira stayed by the horse's side, each of them working together to try to keep him moving.

As the horse stumbled forward, Chase looked over at Mira. His face was gray with worry. "Good job back there, Mira."

She nodded. "No problem."

They fell into a grim, tense partnership, working together to keep the horse moving. Twice, he managed to get down and start to roll, but both times they got him going again. After what felt like an eternity, Mira finally noticed that Spy was moving less laboriously now, and he wasn't trying to stop anymore. She looked over at Chase, who was rubbing the horse's ears and talking softly to the animal as they walked, his voice soothing and calming. He was so nurturing, that her own heart tightened. She'd never seen him be so soft, and it was amazing to see the big, strong cowboy being tender. "Chase?"

He glanced over at her, and she saw his face was lined with dirt and grime, with streaks down his temples from the sweat. "He's getting better," he said. "Can you see that?"

She nodded, relief rushing through her. "I didn't know if I was imagining it or not."

"Nope. He's made it through the worst." Relief was heavy in his voice, as was exhaustion. "I think he's going to make it."

She smiled, joy rushing through her. "We did it, eh, boy?" She rubbed her hand over Spy's coat, which was caked with sweat and dirt. His skin was cold, and she realized the sweat was beginning to dry. "Should I get a blanket or something for him?"

Chase hesitated, and then nodded. "I think it's safe for you to go into the barn. Thanks. There's a sweat sheet on a rack outside his door.

It's a cotton blanket with holes in it. It keeps him warm, while letting the air circulate to dry him."

"Got it." Mira patted Spy once again, and then hurried into the barn. As she reached the barn door, she glanced back over her shoulder at the ring. The sun was just beginning to rise, casting the arena in a faint orange hue. She watched Chase run his hand down Spy's neck, and the horse lightly nudged Chase's hip. Her throat tightened with pride. She and Chase had done that. Together, they'd helped that horse live. What an incredible night.

Smiling for the first time in what felt like forever, she turned and hurried into the barn, humming to herself.

CHAPTER THIRTEEN

CHASE LEANED over the stall door, resting his arms on the wood as he watched Spy doze peacefully in the back corner. The animal's head was down, and he was exhausted, but his body was relaxed.

The worst was over.

He was going to make it.

"I brought you coffee." Mira leaned over the door beside him, holding a steaming mug. "Thought you might need some caffeine."

"Thanks." He glanced over at her. She was covered in sweat and dirt from the long night, and there were shadows beneath her eyes, but there was a radiance on her face that nearly glowed. "You were great. I don't think I could have done it without you."

She smiled, and mimicked his position, resting her arms over the top edge of the door as she watched Spy rest. "Could he really have died?"

"Yeah. It was bad." Chase let out a breath, finally able to acknowledge the depth of what had been at stake last night. "He's my breeding stallion," he explained. "I paid a lot of money for him when he was a colt, but it was far less than he's worth. The guy who owned him was short on cash, and I was in the right place at the right time. He's my future. I could never afford to replace him if he'd died last night. The

134

entire future of this ranch is riding on him." Instinctively, in a move that was so natural he didn't even think about it, he draped his arm over Mira's shoulders, drawing her against him as they watched Spy. "Thanks for your help, city girl."

She relaxed against him, and he could tell she was as weary as he was. "I'm glad I was here."

"Me too." As he stood with her tucked up against him, Chase had a sudden feeling of contentment. Mira had been a star all night, fighting as hard as him to save Spy. She'd never complained, and had never shown a sign of fatigue, even when she'd worked tirelessly beside him to help with the morning feeding. Not a single one of his brothers had ever been here to help him, but Mira had been by his side all night, without hesitation, and her satisfaction in saving Spy was evident.

He realized suddenly that she fit on the ranch. She fit in his life. She was an asset, not a liability. Mira, the Deep South lady he'd coveted for so long, wasn't who he'd thought at all. Yeah, she had the huge heart he'd always expected, but she was also gritty, strong, and tough enough to fight off death.

Was she also tough enough to survive him and his brothers? Was he tough enough to survive her? Shit. He didn't even know how everything was supposed to fit together anymore. He'd had a plan for his life, and now things were skewing in different directions, ones he wasn't prepared for.

His phone rang. He pulled it out of his pocket and saw it was Zane. He moved his thumb over the "Send" icon to answer, then realized Zane was probably calling to give him grief about Mira.

He didn't want to hear it.

He didn't want his brothers in this moment.

He turned off his phone and slid it back into his pocket, Gary's words echoing in his mind about how he needed to treat Mira better. He thought of Martha's orders to start dating her. Maybe he would try. Maybe he was supposed to try. "You hot?"

She glanced over at him. "Hot, sweaty, and dirty, yes."

"Want to go for a swim? I know a place. Just for an hour, then we'll be back to check on Spy. It'll work better than caffeine to pick you up."

She eyed him for a moment, those sexy blue eyes studying him. He tensed, his entire body on edge, waiting for her to accept his offer. *Say yes, Mira. Say yes.*

After a moment, she nodded. "Okay."

"Okay." He couldn't suppress his grin, or the rush of energy that flooded his body. "Two horses or one?"

She raised her eyebrows. "Two."

Two? Bummer. Looked like he still had some work to do.

But she'd said yes.

It was a start.

"I AM SO NOT JUMPING off this rock." Mira stared uneasily over the edge of the boulder that loomed above the natural pool nestled in the cliffs near Chase's house. The boulder was at least fifteen feet above the water, and despite Chase's suggestion, there was no chance she was jumping off there.

Maybe in her youth, but now? She'd probably need a wheelchair if she did it.

Chase walked up beside her. He'd already shed his jeans and shirt, leaving on only a pair of black boxer briefs that didn't hide the fact that he was walking around with an erection. He didn't seem to care that she could tell, so she tried to ignore it.

Not so easy, when she could remember lots of details about that particular part of his anatomy.

His body rippled with muscle, and his neck and arms showed the layers of grime where his collar and shirt sleeves had ended, exposing his skin to the dirt of the previous night. He looked sexy beyond words, a rugged cowboy who was a part of the earth that he rode on every day.

Suddenly, she didn't feel like a woman who wanted to park her butt on the top of the rock and sit. She wanted to be the woman who jumped out there with him.

Chase raised his eyebrows. "You stay out all night battling colic, but you're afraid of a little jump? The water's deep. It's safe."

She grimaced, still wearing her jeans, boots, and tank top. Why hadn't she thought of a bathing suit when Chase had suggested swimming? He'd had the horses saddled up and ready in minutes, and she'd been too busy second-guessing her acceptance of his invitation to actually consider the logistics of swimming.

Dirt caked her body, and the water was so clear she could see all the way to the rocks on the bottom. A waterfall was cascading on the far side of the pool, and the high red rock surrounded it, an oasis of perfection in the middle of a harsh landscape. In truth, it looked unbelievably appealing, but to rip off her clothes and charge off the rock was so not her. At least, it wasn't the grown-up her. As a youth, she used to swing out in a tire swing she and AJ had tied to their tree and careen into the river, but that was a long time ago.

Chase stepped in front of her, and held out his hands, his eyes twinkling. "Come on."

She bit her lip. "Leaping off massive cliffs into tiny pools isn't really my thing." She peered past him. "Is there a way down on the side? I can meet you down there." Then, at least, she could swim.

"It's worth it." He wiggled his fingers, clearly trying to tempt her. "Do you trust me?"

His question jerked her attention back to him. She'd used those very words with Taylor such a short time ago when she'd justified packing her life up and moving out to Wyoming. She'd barely even met him at that point, and yet she'd boldly announced how much she trusted him.

How ridiculous to trust someone who was a virtual stranger with her life and her baby's. But now, staring into his blue eyes, she realized the answer was still yes. She did trust him. This time, it was real trust, not trust built simply upon a legend created by their shared mutual best friend. She'd seen Chase care for his horse, bond with his brothers, and stand by her. It was Chase she trusted, the real life man. Slowly, she nodded. "I do."

A smile flashed across his face. "Then come with me."

"Oh, jeez. Really?"

He grinned wider. "Come on, babe. You'll love it."

She made a noise of exasperation, even as her heart was starting to hammer in anticipation. "Okay, fine. But if I break both my legs and wind up in a body cast, you have to be my manservant for the rest of my life." She poked at his chest, and he caught her finger.

"I'll even massage your numb, lifeless feet," he said. "And I'm great at massages. It would be worth it."

"I doubt it." She took a deep breath. Her heart was pounding, but a part of her really did want to jump. "Give me a sec." Trying not to think about what she was doing, she stepped back from him and unfastened her jeans. Her cheeks burned as she peeled her pants off, glad she'd grabbed her pink low-cut bikinis instead of her white, cotton oh-so-comfy ones. And heaven help her if she'd put on a thong. A little bit of modesty was a good thing, right? Yes, she was well aware that he'd seen her completely naked, but that time, she'd been stripped bare by his roving hands while he was seducing her in the dark of night with tempestuous kisses and whispered temptations. Peeling off her clothes in the broad sunlight, while standing on a barren rock with Chase watching her, was completely different.

She tossed the jeans aside and turned back to face him. Her heart immediately started pounding when she saw the heated expression on his face. His gaze seemed to bore into her, and she caught her breath. "Don't." Even as she said it, another part of her was screaming for him to *do, do, do*. Her body remembered exactly what it was like to have his hands on her, and her heart missed that intimacy between them.

Chase didn't leap across the rock and sweep her up in his arms. In fact, he said nothing. He simply held out his hands to her again in an invitation that suddenly seemed much more personal than it had a few minutes ago.

She decided to leave her tank top on. In her middle-of-the-night rush to the barn, she hadn't put on a bra. Yes, Chase had been best friends with her breasts, but in the bright light of morning, standing on a rock ledge with the man who was turning her life upside down, she needed a shirt. "You swear I won't land on a rock or something?" Her hand went protectively to her belly, and the tiny swell that was beginning to show.

Chase walked over to her and put his hand over hers. His palm dwarfed hers, sending heat pulsing through her. "I swear I won't let anything happen to either of you."

She nodded, her heart pounding at how close he was. She could see scars on his chest, and she wondered what those had been from, what horrors he'd endured when he'd received them. "Okay."

He smiled and took her hands, walking backward as he drew her toward the edge of the rock. "I used to come here all the time when I was a teenager. After Old Skip worked me all day, I'd get an hour off, and this was my spot. My brothers came here too, when they took their turns working at the ranch. We called it Stockton Rock. It was usually cold as hell, but we swam anyway. We got lucky today with this weather. It's a rare gift for it to be this warm here."

The warmth in his eyes as he spoke about his brothers made her smile. "How did you manage to stay so close to your brothers when you grew up in a rough situation? Where did you learn about that kind of loyalty?"

He shrugged. "I was the oldest. They needed me to protect them. It worked out okay." He dropped her right hand and turned to face the pool, still clasping her left hand as they stood together. "We'll jump side by side. On three. One."

She tightened her grip on his hand, peering down at the still water. "Um...okay."

"Two."

Did she really want to do this? She didn't. She really didn't think she did. "Chase—"

"Three." He jumped.

With a small yelp, she leapt with him, carried far out over the water by the force of his leap. For a split second, she lost her balance, and then he steadied her with their clasped hands. She had a moment of experiencing the sheer beauty of freedom as they sailed through the air, and then they plummeted into the water. The cold water sucked the breath from her, shocking her system as she went under.

She seemed to sink forever, a slow, peaceful descent into water so clear she could see Chase grinning at her through the bubbles rising around them.

She finally stopped descending, giving her the chance to kick to the surface. She broke through, and gasped in the fresh air as Chase surfaced beside her. He flipped his wet hair out of his eyes, his grin so boyish and charming that she found herself laughing at him. She felt energized and brave, filled with life she hadn't felt in so long.

He grinned. "Fun, wasn't it?"

She nodded, treading water. "It was awesome. Can we do it again?"

He threw back his head and laughed, a gorgeous, irresistible laugh that made her belly curl with delight. "Of course. Follow me, my princess." He stroked his way across the pool toward the base of the rock and grabbed an outcropping.

When she reached him, he grabbed her hand and hauled her against him. "One kiss per jump. It's the toll." He kissed her once, a hard, fast kiss that was over just as her toes were starting to curl. "Now, up you go." He pointed out the footholds, and then she grabbed the rock.

To her surprise, there was a natural path of foot and hand holds up the side of the rock, and she found herself at the top before she'd even realized she was climbing. Chase was right behind her, water streaming over his bare chest, making it glisten in the sunlight.

He was unbelievably sexy, and the way his gaze raked across her made her feel just as desirable. Her shirt was plastered to her body, and she could feel that her nipples were hard from the cold water.

"Aren't you hot in that shirt?" he asked. "You look hot."

She grinned at the double word play. "I'm keeping it on." She turned away from him, aware of his heated gaze on her almost naked bottom. "You coming?"

"Wouldn't miss it." He caught her hand, and they stood side by side again. "On three?"

"No. Now!" She let go of his hand, ran two steps, and leapt into the air, sailing far out into the pool. The wind was rushing by her, flinging her hair aside as she waved her arms for balance. Again, a moment of perfect suspension, and then she plummeted into the water. The cold closed in around her again, but this time it felt like it was cleansing all the silt from her body and her soul. She felt like she was a child again, leaping out in the river with AJ, using the rope swing they'd hung themselves. She'd felt so free and happy back then, and she felt the same way again: young, carefree, and connected with the man she was with.

There was a loud splash as Chase plunged in beside her, and he caught her ankle as he went past, jerking her down toward him.

She had only a split second to protest, and then she was in his arms, being assaulted by his kisses as he kicked them both to the surface. They broke the surface of the water, and she pushed off him, laughing as she caught her breath. "Let's do it again!" She stroked toward the rock, laughing as Chase caught up to her and then effortlessly passed her, reaching the rock while she was still several yards out.

He pulled himself halfway out of the water, and it streamed in sensual rivulets over his body. His biceps flexing from gripping the rock, he swung out over the water, extending his hand toward her. "Time to pay the toll, my pretty."

She laughed at his wicked voice. "This is a really expensive theme park."

"You're in Wyoming. We're the land of pricey resorts." He caught her hand and pulled her in for another kiss.

It lasted longer this time, and got a little bit steamier. By the time the toll was satisfied, there was no way to blame her perky nipples on the cold water. "Should we do flips this time?" She scurried up the rock, laughing as he sped up past her, apparently finding a second path in the rocks.

"You can flip?" he asked.

"Yep. I did gymnastics as a kid, and some cheerleading." She reached the top of the rock and shook her hair out as she walked over to the edge.

"Cheerleading? You seem much too serious for cheerleading," Chase said as he walked up beside her. "I could see you being editor of the school newspaper."

She grinned. "I was that as well, but yes, cheerleader. I liked the flips." She cocked her head. "Didn't you play football?"

"I did. College and high school." He studied her. "I think football players are supposed to date the cheerleaders. Want to share an ice cream sundae with me on Sunday afternoon?"

She burst out laughing. "I want my own ice cream." She patted her belly. "I have to eat for two, you know."

"Damn. And here I thought I'd just come up with a brilliant way of getting close to you. I'm going to have to work on my skills." He managed to look cranky, which just made her laugh even more.

"Ready?" She turned toward the water, taking a breath to calm herself and focus. It had been a long time since she'd been upside down. She flexed her muscles, activating memories long stored.

Chase was still beside her. "Together?"

She glanced at him, and something tightened in her chest. "Side-by-side flips? You don't think we'll kill ourselves?"

"Nope. I don't."

She nodded, a sense of rightness settling over her. "I don't either. Side-by-side then."

"You call it."

"Okay." She flexed her hands. "On three. One."

He moved a few inches away from her, giving them both space. "Two."

They both bent their knees slightly, stabilizing their balance. "Three!"

She took three steps, swung her arms, and launched herself off the rock, tucking her chin. To her delight, her body rotated just as she'd intended, and she had executed a complete somersault before her feet even hit the water. Chase flipped in perfect synch with her, grinning at her as they went upright. She let out a whoop of laughter, throwing her arms above her head in victory as her feet broke the surface of the water and she plunged beneath the surface.

Perfection, in every way.

CHAPTER FOURTEEN

THE MOMENT WAS HEAVEN.

Chase stretched out on the blanket he'd brought with him, the rough surface warm against his back. Mira lay against him, using his stomach as a pillow as she pointed out shapes in the clouds.

He grinned contently as he played with her drying hair. He was valiantly trying to discern the animals she could see in the sky, but all he could see were floating balls of white fluff, constantly changing shapes.

It wasn't that he had no imagination. It was that all he could think about was the woman who'd spent the last hour leaping off the rock, doing more acrobatics than he could ever hope to do without breaking his neck, though he'd certainly tried. He'd crashed more times than not, completely schooled by her talent.

But it had been hilarious.

He couldn't remember the last time he'd laughed so hard. Mira's laughter had been infectious, each of them igniting more humor in the other, until finally, exhaustion had done them in. Well, not him, but he'd been carefully tracking her energy level, aware that her body was supporting two.

The moment he saw her energy dip and her shoulders start to slump, he'd suggested a break, and she'd agreed right away.

And now...what had been high-octane fun had morphed into quiet, peaceful intimacy that was equally perfect. She fit, he realized. She fit the ranch, she fit the horses, and she made him happier than he'd ever been.

He reached down and placed his free hand on her belly. There was a slight swell now, but it was still, devoid of any telltale movement. "When can you feel it start to kick?"

She went still, and he felt her stiffen slightly. "Around four to five months, I think. A while."

"I bet that's wild." He rubbed his thumb over her belly, almost unable to believe that a live human being was forming inside her body. He didn't want her to feel threatened by his touch. He wanted to be the one to ease her stress, not magnify it. "Pretty amazing, isn't it?" He kept up the slow, deliberate caress on her belly.

She relaxed slightly. "It is."

They were both silent for a moment, but it was no longer a tense silence.

"Chase?"

"Yeah."

She put her hand over his. "I think you'll be a great father."

His hand stilled on her belly. "You do?"

"I do." This time, it was Mira who began a slow caress, tracing her fingers over the back of his hand. "Even if we don't get married, I'm going to put you in my will as the baby's guardian. I can't think of anyone else I'd rather have look out for it if something happens to me. Is that okay?"

A ball seemed to lodge itself in Chase's throat. "Yeah, sure. Of course it's okay."

"Good." A faint smile played at the corners of her mouth, a smile so sweet that he found himself wanting to lose himself in it.

He grinned, untangling the ends of her hair. A lock fell free and floated over his chest, across a long scar from the horsewhip his father had found at the town dump one day. His smile faded, and that old, familiar fear clamped across his chest. As idyllic as this moment was, it didn't hide the truth of her life, and of the demon chasing her and the baby. He knew suddenly that it didn't matter what his brothers thought. Mira and her baby deserved to be protected, and he was all they had. He was their protector, end of story. He knew it, without any doubt whatsoever, whatever the repercussions were with his brothers. "Mira?"

"Hmmm..." Her eyes fluttered closed, and he felt her head become heavier against his stomach as she began to doze off.

"I think we should get married."

Her eyes snapped open, and she turned her head to look at him. "Why?"

He shrugged. "It feels right."

She smiled slightly, and his heart seemed to stutter in his chest at her relaxed smile. "It's felt right all along, hasn't it? You think it's all because of AJ?"

He took time to consider her question, then finally he gave her the truth. "I don't know how much of it is the last ten years, and how much of it has been the last few weeks. I don't think I can divide it." He lightly squeezed her belly. "I just know that I want to protect both of you." His gaze flicked to his scarred forearm. "We can't leave anything to chance."

She stared up at the sky, watching the clouds. "What has changed with your brothers?" she asked. "I can tell you meant it just now, when you said we should get married."

"Nothing has changed with them, but I've changed. I know it's right, and if I know it's right, they'll come around. You saw Travis. He understood."

"He understood for a few months of free room and board. Not for the full nine months, let alone marriage."

"It was a start. We've all been knocked around by our father. They'll get it." He knew they would, because they had to. "There's no way on this earth that I can do anything but commit every last resource I have to you and the baby."

He saw a tear trickle out of the corner of her eye, but she didn't look at him. "Do you love me, Chase?"

"I've always loved you." The words were automatic and natural, a truth that he'd lived with for over a decade.

She turned her head to look at him again. "Not like that. Do you love me so desperately that you feel like you'll never be whole again unless I'm by your side?"

Fear clamped down on him, even though a part of him burned to say yes, to acknowledge that she'd described exactly what he felt like, putting into words that which he couldn't articulate himself. But he didn't. Because he knew he couldn't. Instead, he shook his head. "I can't do that. I can't even let anyone that close, even if I want to." But if he were capable of letting someone matter that much to him, it would be her.

"I see." She closed her eyes, putting distance between them, distance that made him want to shout in denial.

Swearing, he caught her hand, drawing her attention back to him. "Don't you understand, Mira? I know I can't give you promises of soul-searing love, but I'm giving you every last thing I have to give. Whatever love I'm capable of, it's yours. My money. My home. My family. My brothers will become yours. I'm offering you my circle of protection. It's everything to me. It's all I have to give, and it's yours."

He knew it wasn't enough, not for Mira the woman, but maybe, just maybe, it would be enough for her as a mother who needed to protect her child.

Mira bit her lip. "Chase—"

"Can you afford to say no? What if Alan comes for you? What if he finds you living in town, and your only safety is my name on the kid's birth certificate? A name on a line isn't going to be enough, Mira. Are you willing to risk it for the baby?" He knew he was being unfair, pushing her at her most vulnerable, but he didn't know what else to do. All he knew was that he *had* to make her a part of his world. He knew that he alone wasn't enough, but his protection might be. It *had* to be. "You know we get along. We have great sex. We fit okay, and the baby will be safe."

Gone was the hesitation that had plagued him at first. He knew, without a doubt, that Mira was the missing piece of his life, the very thing he'd been waiting for all these years. She made him laugh. She made his house feel like a home. She enriched the life he wanted to live.

His brothers would get on board, one by one. She could be the anchor that held them all together in a way he could never do, because he couldn't articulate or express the warmth that she could. "Marry me, Mira."

She didn't answer, and he felt his soul freeze, hovering in terrified anticipation of what she might say. Had he pushed her too far to the edge? She had a job now, and was on her way to supporting herself. Soon, she wouldn't need him, except to deal with Alan.

She sat up, facing him, her blue eyes searching his face. "Chase—"

The sudden roar of a motorcycle broke through the moment. They both turned to see a bike hurtling across the plains toward them. It took Chase only a split second to realize it was Zane.

Alarm ripped through him, and he lunged to his feet. What in the hell was his brother doing out there on his bike?

Mira grabbed her jeans and yanked them on. "Who is it?"

"My brother." Chase jerked his own pants on, watching the dust spiral from Zane's tires as he sped toward them. "He never comes out here. Something's wrong." Instinctively, he shaded his eyes to look toward his ranch, half-expecting billows of smoke to be filling the air, but the sky was blue.

The relief that his ranch wasn't on fire was fleeting, replaced by the gnawing realization that it had to be something else equally wrong. He jerked on his shirt and shoved his feet in his boots as Mira got dressed.

The horses were dancing in agitation as Zane roared up. Chase suddenly recalled that he'd silenced a call from Zane just before they'd headed out to ride.

He grabbed Mira, pulling her back as the back tire came to a stop inches from her bare toes. "What's wrong?"

Zane jerked his helmet off and dragged his forearm across his sweaty forehead, his face lined with absolute fury as he shot Mira a look so deadly that Chase stepped in front of her. "What's going on?" Chase asked.

His brother jerked his gaze off Mira. "Steen's been stabbed. Some altercation in the prison yard. They think he's going to die. We can't get in to see him, because you're the only one on his visitor list. I've been trying to reach you all fucking morning, and you've been out here with *her* while your own brother is dying? What the fuck, man? We have to go!"

Chase felt the bottom drop out of his gut. "Son of a bitch." Without hesitation, he swung his leg over the back of the bike as Zane gunned the engine. "Can you take the horses back?"

Mira's face was ashen. "Of course," she said. "I'll take care of everything. Go!"

Chase just had time to shout his thanks over the roar of the engine, and then the bike was hurtling across the high desert, bouncing over ruts as they raced back toward the ranch in a race for the life of one of the few people in the world who mattered to him, who had been dying alone while he'd been swimming with a girl.

STEEN LOOKED like he was already dead.

Stunned by the state of his younger brother, Chase sank down next to the hospital bed. Despite his attempts to visit, Steen had refused to see him for over two years. His head was shaved, several new scars marked his skull, and his skin was ashen. Tubes were coming out of his arms, and his bare torso was wrapped in bandages. Around his wrist was a handcuff, locking him down to the bed like he was a fucking criminal who would rip off his tubes and start shooting up the hospital.

Of anyone who he thought would wind up in prison, it wasn't Steen. Son of a bitch. "Steen." Chase leaned forward in his chair, whispering urgently. "You with me?"

"He goes in and out of consciousness." A nurse walked up, carrying a clipboard. Behind her, Chase could see the police officer on duty to guard his brother. "You must be Chase Stockton."

"Yeah, what's going on?"

She smiled. "Excellent. I'm so glad you're here. Steen was asking for you when he first came in for surgery, before he lost consciousness. We tried to call at the time, so he could at least hear your voice, but we were unable to get through. We had to go ahead with the surgery.

There was a lot of damage, and he's already showing signs of infection. We're doing what we can, but he has to want to live in order to fight through it. He has a long recovery ahead even with the right attitude."

Guilt shot through Chase. How long had Steen been lying here, dying, while he'd been screwing around with Mira? Shit. "When did this happen?"

She looked at her chart. "He was stabbed just before six o'clock. He was in surgery by six thirty. We tried to call several times yesterday evening but we weren't able to go through."

Chase ground his jaw. It had probably happened right after they'd left to go to dinner with Gary and Martha. He'd never checked the messages on his landline, which was the number that the prison had. *Shit.* "Can we get his other brothers in?" He thought of Zane and Travis, sitting out in the waiting room of the hospital, desperate for news, unable to come in because Steen had refused to name them on his list of approved visitors. They were still trying to reach the others, calling them in. Every Stockton they'd reached was on his way. The brothers were finally coming together, but it was for the wrong reason.

"If it appears that he's close to death, yes, they can come in. Right now, we're waiting. You're the only one who's approved." The nurse checked the machines. "We were hoping you could get here earlier. The first few hours are critical. It's all about a will to live, and Steen, quite frankly, doesn't have it. He awoke briefly, just long enough for us to remove the breathing tubes, but we haven't been able to rouse him since." Her voice was clinical and non-judgmental, simply educating him as to the current situation so he'd be prepared. "Talk to him. Hold his hand. Play songs that matter to him. It sometimes works." She sighed. "Prison sucks the will out of many of the inmates. He may simply want to go, so be prepared."

Fear clenched Chase's gut and he took his brother's hand. "Steen, man. You can't check out. You have less than five months left in that shithole, and then you're coming home. You and me, bro, at the ranch, like old times, with the horses. Got a new young one that I'm saving for you. He's had a tough life and won't trust anyone. He needs you." All the Stocktons were horse people, but Steen had a special touch that the rest of them didn't have.

149

Steen didn't respond, not even a blink of his eyelids.

"His name's Superman. I figured he needed a badass name, because he's got a long way to go. I can't even get near him. Someone beat the hell out of him, and he's still losing weight. He *needs* you, Steen."

There was still no response, and Chase bowed his head, fighting off the grief. He'd tried so fucking hard to hold his family together, and now, he was losing Steen, for good, for real, forever. "Come on, man. I got this big ranch, and I need help on it." He swore under his breath. Steen, of any of his brothers, had suffered more at the hands of their stepmothers and their father. He'd wound up in prison because a woman he'd loved had betrayed him. There was no one who had less faith in women than Steen, and now he was dying because of it.

Grimly, Chase realized that there was no way in hell Steen would come back to the ranch if Mira were there, no matter what the reason for her presence.

If he even lived.

~

EXHAUSTED BEYOND WORDS, Mira sank down on the couch in Chase's living room, her muscles actually shaking with exhaustion. She'd fed all the horses, walked Spy and made sure he was still recovering, cleaned the stalls, and watered the horses.

It had taken all day, and it was almost six now. There had been no word from Chase all day, and she hadn't dared call him, not after the look of absolute horror on his face when he'd realized that Zane had been trying to reach him while he'd been with her. The accusation in Zane's lethal stare had clearly stated what he thought about Chase being with her when their brother was dying.

No room for her. *No room at all.*

Mira rested her head against the back of the couch, staring at a photograph of a young Chase and two other teenage boys. They were wearing cowboy hats, and holding the reins of three scrappy looking ponies. Hoodlums in cowboy boots, she was sure. Was one of them Steen?

God, she would never forget the depth of anguish in Chase's eyes when Zane had told him that Steen was dying. His fear had plunged right into her heart. She knew that terror. She'd felt it the day she'd gotten the phone call that her parents had been in a car accident. The hospital had said the same words about her own father, that they didn't think he'd live through the night.

He hadn't.

She knew the shock of losing a loved one in an instant. She knew it too many times over.

Again and again, she'd replayed their car accident in her mind, wondering if it would have been different if she hadn't gone to college, if she'd stayed home, if she'd called her parents that night and made them three minutes later. No matter how many times she revisited the situation, she was never able to make the accident go away. It had taken time, but she'd eventually accepted that she couldn't blame herself for it.

But she'd seen the look on Chase's face, the stricken horror at the realization that his brother had been dying, but he hadn't answered his phone because he'd been with *her*.

If Steen died, a part of Chase would always blame her. And if he didn't die, Chase would realize that it had been a close call. There was no room for her and them in his life. After tonight, Chase would be sure to always put them first. *Always.*

Tears filled her eyes as she looked around the room. She had become accustomed to the ranch, and it had started to feel like home. Some of her books were on the shelves, and her magazines were on the coffee table. Her sweatshirt was draped over the armchair, and a picture of her parents was on the mantle next to Chase's pictures. The fridge now held her favorite kind of yogurt, organic milk, and flaxseed meal for her oatmeal, and there was now fabric softener in the laundry room.

At some point, this ranch had become home, and Chase was a part of it. She hadn't even been aware of it, until now, until she was facing a future without it. She'd assumed she had time to find her way. She'd rested comfortably on the knowledge that Chase would fight for her and the baby, that she didn't need to commit to him because he would wait for her.

But now that opportunity was gone. She'd hesitated, and the window had closed. After spending the night helping Chase save Spy's life, and then playing at the swimming hole, she'd realized that she wanted to be with him, that she wanted to find a way to make it work. Yes, she knew he was damaged and bruised when it came to relationships, but there was such beauty in his soul and in their connection, that she'd realized she had to be brave enough to try.

And now...what would happen after today? Had she lost her chance?

Her phone rang suddenly, jerking her out of her reverie. Was it Chase? Hope leapt through her. She jumped up and raced across the room, sweeping it off the kitchen counter. Her heart fell when she saw Taylor's name on her caller ID, not Chase. With a sigh, she declined the call and walked back over to the couch.

Her old life seemed so far away now. She didn't want to go back there.

Her phone started ringing again, and again, hope leapt through her as she looked down. Taylor again. Fear trickled through her at the repeat call. With foreboding weighing in her heart, she answered the call. "What's up?"

"Did you get my message? Tell me you left."

"Left? What message? I didn't see one from you." Tires rolled on the gravel outside, and she leapt up. "I have to go. I think Chase is back."

"No! Don't answer it! Alan found you! He found the record of the pregnancy test! He's on his way to the ranch!"

"What?" Mira's heart dropped and she raced to the window. A long, black limousine was pulling up in front of the ranch. "Oh, God, he's here."

"Get out the back door," Taylor said. "You have to go."

Mira watched as the rear door of the car opened and Alan got out, along with two other men in suits. Lawyers? "Oh, God," she whispered. "Where would I go? He'd find me."

"Don't answer any questions!" Taylor said. "You'll need a lawyer. Don't let him bully you!"

The doorbell rang, making Mira jump. She backed away from the door, clutching the phone. Dear God, why hadn't she married Chase already? Why had they waited? "I have to go. I have to call Chase."

Someone pounded on the door, and she ducked into the kitchen, leaning against the fridge as she tried to catch her breath, pressing her hand to her stomach. She wasn't prepared to face him. Dammit. She shouldn't have underestimated him. Her hands shaking, she dialed Chase's number.

It went straight into voicemail, and she realized he probably had to turn it off in the hospital. She immediately hung up. Could she really bother Chase when his brother was dying?

"Mira Cabot! Open the door!"

She closed her eyes, trying frantically to decide what to do. Call Chase again? Add to his stress? But then she thought of his reaction when he'd realized he hadn't been there for Steen. It was in his blood to take care of those in his circle, and she knew that the baby was in that circle. Regardless of whether there was a place for *her* in his life, she knew that he would do anything to protect the baby. She had to give him the chance. Ignoring the furious pounding on the door, she dialed his number again. "Chase," she said into his voicemail, her voice shaking. "Alan's here. He found out I bought the pregnancy test before you came to town. I don't know what to do. Call me, as soon as you can. And, I hope Steen's okay. I've been thinking about you all day."

She hung up, trying to calm her mind enough to think clearly. She could call the hospital, but she had no idea what facility his brother was in.

Footsteps sounded on the back porch, and she blanched when she saw shadows fall across the kitchen window. Before she could move, a face appeared in the glass, and she found herself staring straight into the bitter, angry eyes of her baby's grandfather. His gleam of satisfaction twisted right in her gut, and she instinctively covered her belly with her hands.

His gaze followed her movement, and then he smiled. "Open the door, Mira." He held up a manila envelope. "I have a document for you to read and sign."

She knew what that document was.

It had to be a waiver turning guardianship of her baby over to Alan, and she knew that he would have a way of forcing her to sign it right then and there. He had something on her, something she wouldn't be able to defeat, because he wouldn't have come until he had everything in line. What would it be? Her parents were dead. Taylor? Chase? What did he have on them? What card was he going to play? What knife was he going to plunge in her belly and twist until she caved?

Frantically, she dialed the only other phone number she knew in town.

Gary Keller picked up on the first ring. "Coming for dinner tonight, my dear?"

Before she could say another word, the back door crashed open, and the man who had beat his son so badly that he'd never walked right again strode into her kitchen.

It was too late.

CHAPTER FIFTEEN

"CHASE?"

He looked up in surprise as Zane and Travis walked into Steen's hospital room. For a split second, relief rushed through him, and then the reality crashed down on him. "Why are you here? They said you couldn't come in unless he was dying—"

Fuck.

He looked down at Steen, at the machines pumping life through him, and he felt his world begin to crush in on him. "They came and got you?"

Zane looked ashen, and Travis had dark shadows beneath his eyes, even more so than when he'd been at the ranch a few weeks ago. "They said he's giving up." Zane punched his fist against the wall, leaving a dent.

"What the hell, Steen? Why aren't you trying?" Zane dropped his muscled frame into a folding chair, and braced his forearms on his thighs, staring at their brother. Steen's muscle had wasted away, and his chest wasn't even moving perceptibly. "Steen," he said urgently. "We need you, man. Don't give up. It's just a knife wound. You've healed worse than that."

Still no response from their brother.

Zane and Chase exchanged grim looks. "I've said everything I can think of," Chase said. "I don't know what else to say."

Zane ran his hand through his hair. "It's Rachel, isn't it? He gave up the day all that went down."

Chase ground his jaw at the name of the woman who had landed Steen in prison. "Yeah. He changed that day. You could see it in his eyes. They went dead."

"Well, fuck it." Zane hunched forward. "She's just a woman, Steen. Forget her. You want to give her the satisfaction of dying? Your best payback will be to go live and reclaim your life."

Still nothing from Steen.

Travis leaned against the wall, keeping back. "He looks like he's been sick. That can't all be from the last twenty-four hours, can it? He's thin as hell."

"I don't know. I haven't seen him in two years." Chase looked around at his brothers. How long had it been since the four of them were in the same room together? Years, and years. It had to come to this to get them together? It was what he'd been striving for, but hell, not this way. "What about the others?"

"Quintin will be here tonight. Logan's coming in tomorrow. Maddox and Ryder should be here any minute. I can't find Caleb. His number has been disconnected. You got a more recent number?"

"I don't know." Chase dug his phone out of his pocket and tossed it at his brother. "You can check the one in my phone and see if it's different." He looked at Zane, who had been in a coma in high school after a motorcycle. "You think he can hear us? Does he know we're here?"

Zane shrugged. "I don't remember anything from when I was out. If I heard you guys, I don't remember. All I remembered was you standing over me when I was on the side of the highway, shouting at me not to die or you would come to hell and kick my ass." Accusation flashed in his eyes. "You had that chance with Steen, to tell him not to give up, but you didn't answer your phone when they called. If you'd talked to him then, he'd have known we cared. But no one was there, and now he's given up."

Chase gritted his jaw, guilt wrenching away at him. "I know."

"What the hell, man? What were you doing with her at that pool?" Zane shook his head in disgust. "I went through the house looking for you. Her shit's everywhere. It's like she's claimed the place."

Images of Mira's fuzzy pink blanket draped over the back of the couch popped into Chase's mind, and a sense of rightness settled over him. He liked her belongings in his house. It made the house feel less empty. Suddenly, a yearning to talk to her rushed over him. He was in over his head, and he wanted to hear her voice. She'd lost her father, and she'd somehow kept her mom from giving up after the accident. Maybe she would have an idea. He suddenly wanted to talk to her, to get her advice, to hear her voice—

"Hey, Chase?" Travis interrupted. "Mira called and left a message. You want to listen to it?"

"Yeah." Instinctively, Chase reached for his phone, but he paused when he saw Zane's hostile glare.

"Really?" Zane challenged. "You're going to take her call while Steen could be taking his last breath? Dad put his women before us. Don't do it. Don't fucking be him, Chase." There was a hard edge to his voice, but beneath it was something stronger, the weight of a child-hood they had all suffered.

Chase swore under his breath. Maybe Zane was right. Maybe Steen just needed it to be about him right now. But hell, he didn't know, and he couldn't afford to make a mistake. He needed to reach Steen, and he didn't know how. He looked over at Travis, who was holding out the phone. "She's been through something like this. Maybe she can help."

Travis's eyebrows went up. "Call her then."

"Help? Really? You think a woman can help Steen? A woman destroyed him." Zane's voice was bitter. "What the hell happened to you, bro? Since when do you call upon women as your savior? We're all we need. Us." He gestured to the three of them. "A woman is the reason Steen's given up in the first place, and now you want to bring one into this room?"

Chase ground his jaw, and shook his head at Travis, knowing that an argument with Zane wasn't what Steen needed to recover. "I'll get it later. Just check Caleb's number."

Travis's eyebrow went up. "You didn't take the hospital's call, and that was a mistake. You sure you want to skip this one?"

Chase frowned, studying his brother, fighting to think clearly. Right now, all he wanted to do was get on that phone and talk to Mira, but Zane's words made sense too. "You think I should?"

"I think that you made a promise to her kid, and that means you always take the call. You take mine, you take Zane's, you take Steen's, but you also take hers. I made a promise to her as well, and if you don't take the call, then I will." He held out the phone. "You or me."

Zane sat up, looking back and forth between them. "What are you talking about Travis? You're in with her too?"

"It's not about her. It's about that kid who is going to end up like us if we don't step in, so yeah, I'm in with her too." Travis took the phone back, and touched the screen. "I'll listen to her message." He began to put the phone to his ear, and Chase lunged to his feet.

"I'll do that." He grabbed the phone from his brother and put it to his ear, walking a few feet away to listen to her message. The moment she said his name, he knew something was terribly wrong, and his heart clenched in fear.

By the time she finished her message, he was already racing toward the door. He'd just reached it when Zane barked out his name. "Where the hell are you going?"

Chase stopped abruptly and looked back at the room. He looked at Zane, with his angry scowl. He looked at Travis, who appeared exhausted and drained. And he looked at Steen, who was dying in front of him.

If he left, Steen might die, and if so, he'd die without Chase by his side. He'd never know if staying could have given Steen the motivation to fight for his life. He'd hold his brother's death in his hands for the rest of his life.

If he stayed, Mira and the baby would be Alan's forever. He knew the old man would waste no time. The trap would be sprung within moments.

And yet, he had to choose.

~

ZANE STOOD up and walked over to Chase. "Don't you dare leave."

His muscles straining with the need to run to Mira, Chase met his gaze. "The baby's grandfather is at my house. He found her. He's going to claim the baby."

Zane stopped, his eyes flashing with sudden anger. "He's there? At the ranch?"

"Yeah." Images of what was going down flooded Chase's mind, and panic surged over him, so intense he could barely think.

Travis swore. "You gotta go."

"What about Steen?" Zane said, not moving out of the way.

All three brothers looked at him. He was so still, he looked as if he were already dead. His face was sunken, his skin pale, his arms limp. He looked beaten, not just from the stabbing, but from the last four years in prison. Sudden anger flooded Chase, and he looked at his brothers.

"I've been mortgaged up the ass on that ranch for five years," he snapped. "I've been holding over a thousand acres for you guys to come home to, and no one ever does. Steen won't even fucking let me visit him." He strode over to the bed and grabbed his brother's shoulders. "You fucking gave up before you even got stabbed, didn't you? Did you jump in front of that knife just to get it over with more quickly? Well, fuck that!" He released Steen and whirled around to face Zane and Travis, who were gaping at him as if he'd lost his mind. "Mira is the only one who has moved into that house and let me help her."

Zane's face darkened. "We don't need help, Chase. We're not kids anymore."

"No, you're not. I get it." He looked around the room at his three brothers, his family, the only people who had ever mattered to him. "But you know what? It's not just that. I've sacrificed everything to hold onto that damned ranch for you guys, for me, and for us. None of you have dropped a dime or broken a sweat over there. Mira was up all night with me saving my best stud, even though she's pregnant." As he spoke, he realized it was true. For the first time in his life, he had an equal relationship. "She's there for me as much as I'm there for her, and I'll be damned if I'm going to let her down."

He spun toward the bed and leaned over his brother. "Listen to me,

Steen. I love the hell out of you, but you've been wasting away for too damn long. If you want to die, that's your choice. I can't stop you, and neither can the others. If you want to live, we're here for you, but you have to make the choice yourself, because I need to go save a life. Yours is up to you." His throat tightened as he set his hand on his brother's shoulder. "I love you, bro, no matter what you choose, but right now, it's up to you."

He squeezed Steen's shoulder, and then turned away. Zane was blocking the door, but Travis was nodding. "You gotta go," he said. "I'll keep you posted."

Chase nodded and strode toward the door. "Move, Zane."

"It's your *brother*."

"As you said, he's a grown man, and he has to make his choice. I can't hold his hand anymore. I can't hold any of yours." He grabbed his cowboy hat off a hook by the door and jammed it on his head. "I can't change the past, but right now, I can change the future for one kid, and that's what I'm going to do."

Travis pulled the door open and stepped aside. "Keep in touch."

"Will do." He slammed his hand on Travis's shoulder, and then, after a moment, the brothers embraced. It was quick, but real, a bond that would never die.

He raced out the door, and he didn't look back.

He wanted to. Hell, he wanted to look back at the brother he might never see alive again, but he didn't.

He knew what he had to do.

MIRA PRESSED her phone to her chest as Alan walked into the kitchen, his smoothly polished black shoes clicking on the floor that belonged to cowboy boots, not dress shoes. Her heart thudding almost uncontrollably, she went still, watching him approach. "What do you want?" she asked, somehow managing to keep her voice steady.

He was wearing a custom suit, and his gray hair was perfectly coiffed. His skin had a slight grayish tint to it, and it was sagging more than it had the last time she'd seen him. He looked old, but deadly. "I want my grandchild."

Oh, God. Her stomach dropped to her feet. "What are you talking about?" She met his gaze, not looking away.

"You're pregnant with AJ's child." Anger flashed across his face, but he quickly masked it. "Do you really think you could hide it from me by coming out here?" His voice was cold with loathing.

She schooled her features into a blank look, still trying to calm her mind. Panic wouldn't serve her. "Pregnant with AJ's child?" she repeated. "What in the world are you talking about?"

This time, he couldn't hide the flash of anger, and he stalked across the room toward her, his fingers curving as if he intended to grab her.

She quickly stepped around the granite island in the middle of the kitchen. "Don't touch me," she snapped. "This is my house, and you're trespassing. Leave now."

"It's not your house. It's Chase Stockton's, and he still owes a considerable amount on his mortgage."

His mortgage? Could he take Chase's ranch? No. That was impossible. He was bluffing. "I live here. You don't. Leave." She looked at her phone, saw that she was still on the call with Gary, and spoke again, more loudly. "I am going to call 9-1-1 if you don't leave here in one minute—"

Alan moved suddenly, lunging across the island and grabbing her arm. He ripped the phone out of her hand and threw it across the room. It shattered against the stone fireplace, and he grabbed her arm, his fingers digging into her skin like talons. "Shut the hell up, Mira. I'll give you one chance to make the right choice." He shoved the envelope at her, pressing it against her breasts. "For one million dollars in cash, you will assign me guardianship of my grandchild. The moment it's born, you walk away, and never come back."

Her mouth dropped open. He actually believed she would abandon her own child for money? Obviously, he did, which showed exactly where he placed the value of his own child in that hierarchy. "First of all," she snapped. "I would never trade money for my child. Second, it's not AJ's baby. It's Chase's, and we're getting married." Her voice didn't waver, and her gaze was unyielding.

For a moment, Alan's eyes narrowed. She could tell she'd taken him by surprise, and she waited, resisting the urge to babble in defense of her lie. She'd learned from her dad that liars usually talked too much, wrapping themselves up in fabrications that unraveled when more information was revealed. People who told the truth let the facts speak for themselves.

So, she said nothing else.

"A DNA test will clear up that situation, won't it?"

Crap. How dare he be intelligent enough to know about basic science?

He jerked his chin toward the back door, and she was startled to see that his two suited escorts were now in the doorway, waiting for his command. "Find out how old an unborn baby has to be before we can do a DNA test. I'm sure we don't have to wait until it's born."

Bastard! Of course he'd want a DNA test. "You can't run one without my permission, and I'm not giving it to you."

"You're unfit to be a mother," he said, his fingers still digging in. "I have reams of evidence of you buying illegal drugs, coming home drunk, and using your dying mother's pain killers to fund your own habit." He released her to pull a document out of his envelope. "I have over twenty affidavits from people who will attest to your substance abuse problem, as well as evidence that you were defrauding the insurance companies to steal money from your mother's medical funds to pay for it."

He slapped the document in her hands, and she looked down, her heart sinking when she saw the names of assorted prominent people from town listed, and their quotes. How much money had he paid them? Were there so many people willing to sell themselves for money? Apparently, there were. "They lied."

"They swore under oath." Alan leaned forward. "You have two choices, Mira. Take a million dollars cash and disappear. Or you can fight me, and I'll destroy your reputation until the courts ban you from ever coming near the child again. That kid will grow up knowing that his mother was an addict who thought her next high was more important than her own kid. I can do it. You know I can."

Her mind started to spin, and she felt dizzy. She wanted to protest that Chase would never let it happen, and that Alan couldn't violate the sanctity of the marriage vows, but the words died in her throat. If she roped Chase in deeper, he'd destroy Chase as well. He'd take the ranch, destroy his reputation, and steal everything that mattered to him. Especially because it *was* AJ's child and that might give Alan power she didn't want him to have.

"If you sign the papers giving me guardianship, I'll tell the kid that his mom was a good woman who died in a plane crash. He'll never know otherwise."

Never know her own child? Or have it grow up thinking that she was an addict? "Chase is the father," she managed. "Not AJ. You have to leave."

Alan grabbed the front of her shirt and jerked her over to him. "You will sign the papers, Mira. If the DNA test shows Chase is the father, then I'll walk away and tear up the contract, because I don't want his filthy spawn. You can keep the money. If it's AJ's kid, then the deal is a go."

"No!" She tried to twist out of his grasp, but his grip tightened. "I'm not signing anything!"

Alan snapped his fingers, and one of the other men walked up. He was holding a tablet computer. Silently, he turned it so that Mira could see what was on the screen. It was a detailed email outlining countless instances of substance abuse, including an incriminating paragraph about how she was pregnant with the heir to one of the most dominating empires of the south, and how the baby's future was at risk because of her substance abuse problems. The recipient of the email was the editor-in-chief of a major national newspaper, and the producer of a national investigative television show. "I have twenty-two more emails ready to send right now to other media outlets. The campaign will begin this instant. Once word gets out about how messed up you are, you'll have *no chance* to ever see the kid again, and you'll be locked down in my house until the baby is born."

Oh, *God.* "You're going to look like a fool once the DNA test says it's Chase's child." Her breath was tight in her chest, and she was having trouble getting oxygen. "And it's all lies, so I can sue you for libel and slander. No one will publish that. They'll all be liable."

Alan smiled. "They're only lies if you can prove they're lies. I have proof that it's all true, and I can afford to fight a very lengthy legal battle in the process. Can you?"

She felt sick. "You're the bastard," she snapped. "If you drag me into a court battle, I swear I'll expose you for the father you truly are. I've seen AJ's scars, and I know his foot was messed up because of what you did to him." His face darkened with rage, and she leaned in toward him, anger surging through her. "I guarantee I'm not the only one who knows you beat him, and I'm guessing that your other son has told an awful lot of therapists that the reason he's such a mess is because his daddy beat the hell out of him. Is that worth it, Alan? You really want to go there? Because *that* is the truth, and we both know it, and I *will* make sure it gets out."

White-hot anger flashed over his face, and sudden fear ripped through her. She'd pushed the monster too far.

She had no time to back up before his fist came up and hit the side of her face.

No one helped her when she fell.

His two escorts simply walked out of the room, shut the door behind them, and left her alone with a bastard.

CHAPTER SIXTEEN

SHE WASN'T ANSWERING *her phone.*

Sweat trickled down Chase's spine as his truck hurtled down the highway toward his ranch. Mira's phone was going directly into voicemail, and he was still twenty minutes away. What if she stood up to Alan? What if she pissed him off?

Shit!

His phone suddenly rang, and he lunged for it, nearly losing control of the truck in his frenzy to get it. One glance told him it wasn't Mira, but he answered it anyway. "Maddox! Where are you?"

His brother, who he hadn't spoken to in several months, answered. "Heading toward the hospital. We're about forty-five minutes away. I have Ryder with me. How's Steen? Tell me he's gonna be okay." The edge to Maddox's voice bit deep, and Chase knew that the bond that tied the Stocktons together was soul deep.

He was going to have to ask his brother to break that bond. "How far are you from the ranch?"

"A couple minutes. Why? You need something?"

"There's a woman there. She needs help. I'm fifteen minutes away. You have to go help her."

There was a short silence. "What?"

165

"A woman. Mira Cabot. Get over there now!" His fingers were tight on the steering wheel, and Chase wanted to leap through the phone and grab his brother by the throat.

"You want us to go help a woman instead of coming to see Steen? What the hell? I thought he was dying."

"He is."

"Well, shit, Chase, why are you—"

"There's a bastard there who's going to beat her up! Get the hell over there! She's under my protection and she's pregnant with the guy's grandkid. He's like Dad, and he wants to hurt that baby!" And Mira. Son of a bitch. Alan wanted to hurt Mira as well.

There was more silence, and then he heard Maddox talking to Ryder. Chase gritted his teeth, pressing the accelerator even harder, but even he couldn't make the truck fly. "Travis and Zane are with Steen. I told them I was coming to help her. Come on, man. Do this for me." He couldn't keep the urgency out of his voice. "I can't get there in time."

Maddox came back on the phone. "The bastard's dead. We're on it."

Relief rushed through Chase. "Thanks."

"Tell Steen that if he dies before we get there, we're going to hunt him down in the Afterlife and make him pay," Maddox added. "Got it?"

"Got it." He hung up and immediately called Travis. When his brother answered, he gave him the message for Steen.

Something had to reach his brother. Maybe that was it.

～

PAIN RANG through Mira's head as she dragged herself backwards, trying to get away from Alan. "Every time you hit me, it digs your hole deeper, proving what you did to your sons," she snapped. "Get out while you can, Alan."

His face was grayish and pinched as he advanced upon her. "No, bitch. I've had enough of you interfering in my relationship with AJ. He rejected me because your family told him to. Your piece of shit father tried to steal my son, and you helped. Your entire family took him from me." He kicked aside a chair that went spinning across the kitchen floor. It slammed into the wooden cabinets with a sickening thud that made Mira jump. "It's over now. I'm taking what's mine."

Mira scrambled to her feet, staggering as a wave of dizziness hit her. Pain raked through her abdomen, and sudden fear knifed through her. What if he made her lose the baby? "Stop it!" she shouted, keeping the island between them. She pressed her hand to her belly. "Don't you dare touch me again," she snapped. "You want to hurt the baby?"

He lunged across the table and grabbed her hair. "Any grandchild of mine is tough enough to handle a few bumps."

She yelped and grabbed his hand, trying to stop him from pulling her hair, but he dragged her around the island anyway, jerking her to him. "Sign the papers," he snapped. "You have no idea what I'm capable of."

"Yes, I do." She slammed her elbow into his gut.

He grunted and released her hair. She immediately broke for the back door, her feet slipping on the polished wood. She grabbed the doorknob, but Alan caught her arm just as her fingers closed around it. He jerked her back, just as she heard shouting from outside. "Help!" she shouted. "Help me!"

There was more yelling, and she recognized Gary's voice, among others. She realized he'd come to help her, but Alan's men were blocking his path. "Gary!"

Alan threw her onto the couch, and she landed so hard she couldn't breathe. She just lay there, fighting for breath as Alan walked up and crouched beside her. Outside, the shouts continued, but no one came in to help her. She couldn't even yell for help. All she could do was try to regain her breath.

Alan's face was pale, deathly pale, his features contorted into a diabolical rage. He set the papers on the couch by her face, and shoved a pen into her hand. "I have dozens of witnesses who will swear you signed this of your own free will," he said, his voice pinched with anger. "I can keep this up all night, and if my grandchild doesn't survive it, then it's on you, not me."

She closed her eyes as a wave of nausea washed over her. She realized he was telling the truth. He would rather win than have his grand-child survive. He hated her and her family for the fact AJ rejected him, and it was finally his chance for payback. If she kept fighting, she would lose the baby. If she gave up, the baby might survive, and she might be able to fight back in courts.

She opened her eyes to look at Alan, and her heart fell. He had power and connections beyond comprehension, and she had nothing. Was there really a chance she could defeat him in a legal battle? She knew with sinking certainty that he'd never let it get that far. He'd never let her expose who he was. After the baby was born, there would be another night. Another visit. This time, with no witnesses. A night she wouldn't survive. "Did you kill my father?" The question popped out unexpectedly, as if she'd known it as a truth all along. "Did you cause that car accident?"

Alan stared at her for a long moment. He didn't answer, but she saw the truth in his eyes.

He'd killed her parents out of spite, out of hate, out of a psychotic insanity about his son, and now he was ready to do the same to her.

CHASE GUNNED the engine as he raced up his driveway, and his gut dropped when he saw Maddox and Ryder in a brawl outside his front door. Gary was slumped on the ground, not moving. Both his brothers were in a hard-fought hand-to-hand battle against two guys in suits who knew how to fight. It was clear his brothers were trying to get into the house, and the men were blocking them. Neither suit was Alan, but a long, black limousine was sitting ominously in front of the house.

Chase knew Mira had to be inside the house with Alan. Fear ripped through him, and he gunned the engine and jerked his steering wheel to the right. The truck plunged over the edge of the driveway and bounced across the rutted ground toward the back of the house. It bounced over rocks, careening dangerously to the side, but Chase didn't even slow down.

The truck skidded around the corner of the house, and Chase

plowed down a birdbath before slamming on the brakes. The truck crashed into his gas grill, knocking it over as Chase leapt out and vaulted onto the back porch. He exploded through the back door into the living room.

Mira was on the couch, and Alan's face was twisted in rage as he drew back his fist to hit her.

"No!" Chase leapt across the room and tackled the older man, throwing him back against the wall before he could land the blow. They crashed into the built-in shelves, and books rained down upon them.

He threw aside a hardcover book as it cracked against his temple and leapt to his feet. "Mira!" His heart seemed to freeze in his throat as he took in her bruised face and her bleeding lip. He vaulted over the coffee table and landed beside her, going down on one knee.

She managed a smile, but her eyes were pinched with pain. "Thanks for coming."

"I was late. Shit. I was late." Guilt poured through him, as he pressed his hand to her forehead. Her skin was cold, but sweat was trickling down her temples. He saw her hand pressed to her belly, and terror congealed in his gut. He set his hand over hers. "Tell me, hell, he didn't hit you in the stomach, did he?"

She shook her head. "No, not yet. I think the baby will be okay."

Chase felt his chest constrict, as he wrapped his arms around her, helping her sit up. Just as she sat up, she looked past him, and her eyes widened.

Chase spun around immediately, rising to his feet as Alan grabbed the fireplace mantle and dragged himself to his feet. His skin was ashen, and his cheeks were sunken. He looked like a man who'd been to hell and had never found his way back. Disgust poured through Chase for the man who was the replica of his own father, a bastard to the end. "Assault and battery is going to get you prison time, you piece of shit."

Alan grabbed his left shoulder, as if he'd hurt it in the fall. "I'll buy your mortgage, Stockton. You'll lose the ranch. You want to risk that?"

Chase froze. "What?"

"Your mortgage. Lenders sell them all the time." Alan tried to stand up more erectly, and his face pinched with pain. "I can own you by the end of the day."

His ranch? *His ranch?* Could Alan really find a way to take it?

Mira's fingers slipped into the waistband of his jeans, and she pulled herself to her feet. "Stay out of it, Chase. It's my battle. Don't risk the ranch."

Movement outside caught his eye, and Chase glanced out the front window. He could see Maddox fighting. Blood was trickling down the side of his face. His brothers were out there taking hits for him, because he'd asked them to. Could he really sacrifice his ranch, their ranch?

Then he looked down at Mira. Her jaw was clenched with pain, but there was a fire in her eyes, and he knew she wasn't going to give up. She was a fighter who had lost her family and her home, but she wasn't going to step down.

He realized suddenly that this was what family was about. Family wasn't a ranch. It was his brothers stepping in to help him, defending a stranger because he'd asked. It was Mira, willing to take whatever Alan dished out to protect her baby. It was the fact that every one of his brothers had rushed back to town when Steen needed them, without hesitation. Family was defined by the people who stood together against all odds, and it didn't matter whether they were standing on a ranch, or in a gutter somewhere. It was all the same.

It wasn't about a ranch, and it hadn't ever been. The front door suddenly flew open. Maddox and Ryder rushed inside, both of them battered, bruised, and bleeding. The brothers stopped when they saw Chase, but when they noticed Mira's black eye, their eyes narrowed in open hostility.

Chase nodded at them, and then slung his arm around Mira's shoulder, pulling her against him. "You can try to take the ranch," he said evenly to Alan. "I don't give a shit. But you need to know that you will *never* get through me to Mira or our baby."

Out of the corner of his eye, he saw Maddox and Ryder's faces go blank in shock at his announcement. He tensed, ready for them to resist, the way Zane and Travis had. But to his surprise, they walked right up, flanking him and Mira. Their cowboy hats were dirty, their faces were bruised, and knuckles were bleeding. They looked as mean as their father ever had, and Chase knew they could fight just as dirty.

"You have to go through me, too," Maddox said, wiping the back of his arm across a stream of blood trickling down his forehead.

"I'm in," Ryder agreed. "Don't touch what's ours."

Alan looked back and forth between them, then he glanced toward the door, where his men were limping in with torn suit jackets and more damage than either Maddox or Ryder had sustained. "This isn't over," he snapped.

"Yes, it is!" Mira pulled out of Chase's grasp and walked over to him. "Let it go, Alan. You almost destroyed AJ, and you're doing the same to your only living son. Get help. You won't ever get my baby—"

His lip curled in distaste. "I will. You wait." He lurched over to the coffee table, walking crookedly, as if he were drunk. He swept the computer off it. "I'll still send the email, Mira."

Mira stiffened, and Chase didn't need details to understand the threat. He strode over to Alan, and stopped beside Mira, angling himself between the bastard and Mira. "You don't get it, old man. You can blackmail her or any of us all you want, and we won't give in." He took Mira's hand, squeezing tightly. "We stand by each other, and every piece of crap you throw at us will have to go through all of us. You'll never do it."

"I have money," Alan snapped.

"Yeah, but I have more." Travis walked in the front door, wearing his pristine white cowboy hat and his pressed jeans. He looked every bit the country music superstar he was, and Chase grinned.

Mira gripped his hand. "Travis," she hissed. "Don't. He can ruin you."

Travis shrugged. "My pop tried to ruin me. He failed. Bullies suck." He walked up beside Mira, facing Alan. "We know what you're like," he said simply. "We don't like people like you."

Alan's upper lip sneered in distaste, and he looked at all of them, as if assessing whether he could take on all the Stocktons at once.

He couldn't, and Chase saw the moment the bully realized he was outnumbered.

Without another word, Alan spat on Chase's boots, and then turned and walked toward the door.

Mira's fingers tightened in Chase's, and he glanced down at her. Her face was pale as she watched Alan go, and he knew she was thinking that it wasn't over. He pulled her close and pressed a kiss to the top of her head. "You're not alone."

Tears shimmered in her eyes, and she nodded once, still not talking as she watched Alan lurch toward the door. He careened into one of his men, who caught him. As they helped him toward the door, Chase began to realize that something was wrong. Really wrong.

Alan collapsed before he made it through the front door.

"He's gone. Cardiac arrest." The paramedics passed the verdict on to Alan's men, who took the news of their boss's demise with stoic silence as they turned away and pulled out their cell phones.

Mira's heart, however, felt like it had been eviscerated. *Alan was dead.* She watched numbly as the paramedics pulled the sheet over Alan's face. Dead. Alan was *dead.* She was stunned, unable to tear her eyes off the shadowed figure beneath the stark white sheet. She could still see the ashen color of his skin as he'd fallen. She could still feel the hate from his bloodshot eyes burning into her as he fell, using the very last moment of his life to punish her with his loathing.

Her father had died in front of her. Her mother had died in front of her. And now Alan. Three deaths. Three times, she'd watched the life, the spirit, bleed from the body of someone, leaving behind nothing but an empty shell. Experiencing death again was like reliving her parents' death, a gaping wound flooded with tears, loss, and anguish. But at the same time, it was different, so different, because losing her parents had been like losing a part of herself. Watching Alan die was... "I feel happy," she whispered, horrified that she could feel joy upon someone else's death. "I just watched a man die, and I feel...happy."

"It's okay." Chase put his arm around her, pulling her tight against his side. "He was a sick bastard who hurt you and those you loved for a long time. You're finally free of him. Don't feel guilty."

She dragged her gaze off the stretcher and looked up at Chase. His face was grim as he watched them load the stretcher onto the ambulance. "Chase?" she whispered.

He looked down at her, and smiled, a smile that was loaded with the weight of death, but one that held the same relief she felt. "I'm not going to lie, Mira. I'm glad he's dead, and he got what he deserved. He owned his life, and he owned the way he died. He brutalized my best friend, stalked you, and he would have hurt a lot more people. The sun's going to shine brighter tomorrow because he's not in this world. I'm not going to waste a second mourning him." He touched her chin, his fingers so soft and gentle that they seemed to pull her back from the edge of her grief. "And you shouldn't either, okay?"

She nodded. "I know, but it's still—" She took a trembling breath, unable to articulate the miasma of emotions swirling through her.

"You're safe, sweetheart. Do you realize that?" Chase palmed her belly, his fingers spread across her stomach like a shield. "Do you understand? This little baby is safe, for the rest of his life. The enemy is gone. *Gone.*"

Tears suddenly filled her eyes, and her hands started to shake. She was safe. Forever. Alan could never come after her, and he could never hurt her child. The danger was *over.*

"Hey, it's okay." Chase pulled her into his arms, and she buried her face in his chest, clinging desperately to his strength. She wrapped her arms around his waist and held tight to the only stable thing she had in her life while the tears poured forth. They were tears of loss for AJ and her parents. They were also the cathartic release of a fear that had gripped her since she was a child and acquired him as an enemy after befriending AJ, a fear that had been tightening around her neck with each passing minute...and now it was over. *Over.*

Chase pressed a kiss to the top of her head, holding her tightly, until the strength and warmth from his body eased her trembling. She squeezed her eyes shut, breathing in his woodsy, masculine scent as the tears began to fade, replaced by a new, fragile sense of hope, of new life.

"Well, I think that's it for now," the sheriff said as the doors to the ambulance clanged shut.

Mira pulled back from Chase and looked around at the scene she'd been too upset to notice. The Stockton brothers were standing in grim silence, and Gary was sitting on the front porch, holding a frozen steak to his head. He'd been knocked out by one of Alan's men, but he'd recovered and refused to go to the hospital.

These men were the victors, the ones who had triumphed, the ones who deserved to win. Her heart softened for these men who had come to her rescue, strangers who hadn't hesitated to take on an enemy more powerful than they.

The sheriff tilted his hat back on his head and walked over to Chase. He'd already grilled them all on the situation, including failing to convince anyone to go to the hospital or press charges for assault, so there was no drama left. Mira and Chase hadn't mentioned the email threat, and neither had Alan's men. It didn't matter anymore, now that Alan was gone. It was all just...over. The officer was in his thirties, and his short brown hair reminded Mira of photos of her dad when he'd first made sheriff, back when she was a little girl. He'd been so proud in that photograph, a man ready to save the world. Then his life had been stripped from him too early because he'd dared to stand up against Alan. He would be proud of her, she realized. He would have been so proud of her refusing to give in to Alan, of aligning herself with Chase, of finding the strength to battle Alan for her baby. She smiled, almost feeling her dad smiling down upon her.

Sheriff Wilson extended his hand toward Chase. "Let me know how Steen is."

"You bet. Thanks." Chase kept one arm around Mira, tucking her tightly against his side as he shook the sheriff's hand.

The sheriff tipped his hat to Mira. "Welcome to town, Mira. I'm sorry it took this for us to meet." He gave her a little wink that was so much like her dad that tears suddenly burned in her throat.

"Thanks," she managed, trying desperately to hold her emotions together.

He eyed Chase's brothers. "I hope you ruffians stay in town for a while this time. It's been too long." To her surprise, he grabbed Travis's hand and yanked him into a bear hug. He did the same with Maddox and Ryder. There was no mistaking the bond between the men, making her wonder what past the men shared with the sheriff.

He saluted the brothers, then got into his truck and drove off, his tires spitting up dirt as he held his hand out the window in silent farewell.

Silence descended upon the small group. Mira looked around at them, the heroes who had been willing to fight for her. How had she been so lucky as to acquire such a formidable army to fight for her? "I don't know how to thank you all," she said, clearing her throat. "The way you came to help me—"

"It's no big deal," Ryder interrupted with a shrug, shifting uncomfortably. "It's how we work." He jerked his head at Travis. "Call Zane. See how Steen is." His attempt to change the subject was obvious, a man who wanted no thanks for being a hero.

"I'm on it." Travis stepped away from the group as he pulled out his phone.

As he did so, Mira saw Maddox and Ryder studying her. They were both tall and rugged, with heavy whiskers and jeans that were dusty and worn. They looked like men who had been out on the range when they'd gotten the call, throwbacks to the old west, to the days when men and their horses defined loyalty and teamwork.

"She's pregnant with your kid?" Maddox asked Chase. His dirty blond hair was brushing against the collar of his shirt, and his leather jacket was creased and old. "You called it 'our' kid when you were talking to the old man."

Chase didn't answer. He didn't give the party line they'd been planning for so long, about how the baby was his. Instead, he looked at Mira. She knew what he was thinking. With Alan dead, there was no longer a threat to her baby. There was absolutely no need for Chase to declare himself the father.

She didn't need a protector now.

It was over.

She was free...and suddenly felt like crying. She didn't need Chase anymore...but she did. How could she let him go? He was a part of her on so many levels. But how could she ask him to burden himself with her? Now there was no need. He deserved his freedom.

So, she lifted her chin and smiled at the Stockton brothers. "I really appreciate all your help. You guys go see to Steen. I'll clean up here and watch the horses until you get back." She glanced at Chase. "I should pack my stuff—"

"Let's go for a walk," Chase interrupted.

Mira shook her head, wanting them to leave. Everything had just shifted for her and she needed time to process it. Alan was gone, and her baby was safe. *Safe.* She had to look ahead to a life as a mom, starting her own family, without being forced to play house with a man who didn't love her, who was committed to her only out of a sense of obligation. "No, it's okay. I'm fine. You need to go back to Steen—"

Chase was already shaking his head. "No. We need to talk." He took her hand and started walking toward the barn. "I'll be back in a few," he informed his brothers. "Mira and I need a moment."

Travis grinned, watching them. "What about your brother?" he called out, his phone still in his hand. "You going to walk out on Steen for a girl?"

Chase paused, and looked back at his brothers. "I'll never walk out on any of you. Ever."

Satisfied, Travis nodded, as did Maddox and Ryder. It was all Mira needed to hear. She knew what Chase was going to say. She felt like her heart was fragmenting into a thousand pieces, and she knew she would never let him say the words.

She had to say them first.

CHAPTER SEVENTEEN

TENSION FLOODED Chase when Mira pulled her hand free even before they reached the barn. She turned to face him just inside the doors, her hands settling on her hips. "Listen, Chase," she said, her voice as steady as he'd ever heard it. "There's no need for you to do any more for us. Now that Alan's gone, we're all set. Thurston won't want any competition for the family business." She put her hand on her baby bump. "We're all set now," she repeated.

He ground his jaw, fighting against his reaction to drag her into his arms and kiss her until she took her dismissal back. "I think you should stay for a while, at least until you're sure you're okay."

She smiled, but there was sadness in her eyes. "Thank you and your brothers for saving me today. I really mean that. But I know there's no room for me in the Stockton world. I need to be in a place where I belong, and where everyone is fully invested in me." She shrugged. "That's what I grew up with, and that's what I need."

"How can you say that? Everyone showed up here for you. There is room—"

She put her finger across his lips, silencing him. "Chase," she whispered. "You don't need to protect me anymore. It's about your family, and it always has been. I need to find my way now. You guys were here for me tonight when I really needed it, but I'm okay now. You don't need to do any more for me."

Words flooded his mind, demanding that he claim her, that he refuse to let her walk away, but he couldn't articulate them. They just died in his throat, fading away into the same ugly place where the memories of his childhood lay haunting him. "Where are you going? Back home?"

There was a visible hesitation, and he felt his heart leap.

"I don't know," she said. "I might stay in town for a while. I've made some good friends, and there's nothing really left for me back home." She wrinkled her nose. "Just memories that hurt, you know?"

He thought of the night he'd made love to her so many times. He thought of the midnight ride to see the wolves. He remembered swimming with her that morning, an idyllic moment that felt like an eternity ago. He could picture her crazy hair when she stumbled into the kitchen for breakfast every morning. Every image was burned indelibly into his mind, and he knew they'd be there forever, a constant reminder of the moments that had given him the first peace he'd ever had. "Yeah, I know about memories that hurt."

She patted his arm. "Okay, so I'll just start to pack my stuff. I know it's everywhere in the house. I'll stay until you're back from the prison, so you can focus on him, okay?"

He wanted to say more. There were a thousand words rushing through him, words he didn't know how to say. "Do you want to go?" The question slipped out before he could stop it, and he grimaced. It was clear she was ready to leave, and he wasn't going to beg. When women wanted to leave, it never worked to talk them out of it. He knew that from the hell of his childhood.

She went still, watching him warily. "Go where? To see Steen?"

He leapt at the idea, grasping at it greedily. "Yeah. They say he's given up and isn't trying to live. I know you somehow helped your mom keep going even after the accident, so I thought maybe you could reach him." He didn't even bother to consider what his brothers would think if he showed up with her. He just knew he wanted her there. He wanted her with him. He needed her to be a part of whatever he was going to have to face in Steen's hospital room. "He's dying, Mira, and we can't save him."

Some of the stiffness faded from her shoulders, and she touched his hand. "I doubt I can reach him—"

"Will you try?" He flipped his hand over and cradled her fingers in his. "Please?"

She nodded. "Of course. What about the horses?"

"Gary will be in charge." Hope leapt through him. It felt so right to be bringing Mira back with him. "Let's go."

She looked past him, her gaze settling on his brothers, who were huddled in deep conversation. He felt her hesitation, and he swore under his breath. "I need you, Mira." The words came out rough, barely muttered under his breath, but when she looked at him, he knew she'd heard him.

Without another word, she squeezed his hand and started leading him back toward his truck.

MIRA HAD NEVER BEEN AROUND SO much testosterone or so many pairs of Wranglers in her life, especially in such a small, confined, somewhat hostile space. There were six Stockton men hovering around Steen's bed. Chase and Travis, along with her gallant rescuers, Maddox and Ryder, who were both sporting bruises and moving stiffly from the fight they'd endured on her behalf.

Her throat clogged when she looked at their injuries. They were complete strangers who had jumped in to help her, simply because their brother had asked them to. Such loyalty and commitment to each other was so amazing, and it reminded her of what she'd had with her own parents. She missed that feeling of connection, and a sad envy wrapped around her for the tightness of their bond.

They'd been joined by Quintin, whose tall, lean body reminded her of a wild stallion surviving on guts and courage out on the range.

Lounging against the wall, and giving her the most hostile glare, was a man Chase had called Zane. Unlike the others who were wearing cowboy boots and hats, Zane was in motorcycle boots, and a black leather jacket. He looked fierce and angry, and most of it was directed toward her.

Each of the brothers was well-muscled, carrying the air of a man who had been to hell and back, and would never forget it. Travis at least had a decent smile, but even he wasn't smiling. They all looked worried, almost scared, barely talking as they took over the area around the bed.

As she stood in the doorway, watching them, her heart tightened for what they had endured, and how they'd forged unbreakable bonds with each other for survival. Chase was arguing in low tones with Zane, and she could hear her name being batted around while he tried to convince his brothers to let her talk to Steen.

Her gaze slid to Steen, and her heart seemed to freeze in her chest. With the tubes and the bandages, and his sunken face, it was like seeing her father again in that bed, dying. Tears suddenly filled her eyes, and she put her hand over her mouth, fighting against the surge of emotion. She started to turn away, but then warm arms wrapped around her.

She looked up as Chase pulled her against him, ducking his head so that his face was beside hers. "I'm so sorry, sweetheart," he said quietly. "I didn't think about the impact it would have on you. I shouldn't have asked you to come. I'll take you home."

His voice was so tender, his concern so genuine, that it broke through the vise closing around her heart. She closed her eyes and rested her head against his chest, feeling the rise and fall of each breath and the steady thud of his heart. He held her tightly, pressing soft kisses to the top of her head, not asking anything of her, just offering his support.

Ever since the accident, she'd had to be so strong, and now, suddenly, Chase was there to hold her. The warmth of his body enveloping hers seemed to infuse her body with strength, taking the edge off the grief. She gripped his shirt, focusing on the feel of him, on the strength of his body.

As he held her, she began to understand the depths of what had happened. His brother, his beloved brother, was truly on the edge of death, and yet he'd left the hospital to come to her aid. Travis had come. Ryder and Maddox had come. These men, who claimed to have no room in their lives and hearts for anyone except their brothers, were liars.

They had room. They just didn't know it. They were born protectors, each and every one. They thought they had space only for each other in their sphere of protection, but they were wrong, and they'd already proved it.

And Chase...her dear, sweet, Chase. He'd been her protector since the very first moment, and AJ had known that.

Tears brimming in her eyes, she pulled back from Chase enough to look at him. His blue eyes were weary, and his face was lined with a lifetime of worry. She smoothed her fingers over his dark whiskers, each coarse strand like a promise of his strength. He'd been broken by women, and she knew he might never be able to cross that line and give her what she'd wanted: the superficial trappings and declarations of love.

But he gave her more. He gave her actions that spoke far more than words would ever speak. He was the man she'd been waiting for all this time. Did he love her? Or had his frantic, heroic rescue been because of the baby who reflected his own past?

She didn't know, but she needed to find out. If there was a chance, she would be brave enough to take it.

Chase frowned. "You want to leave?"

She shook her head. "I want to stay and talk to him."

The intensity of relief and gratitude that flooded his face made her heart turn over. This man cared, more than anyone would ever know, except, perhaps herself.

"But before I do," she said quietly, soft enough that the words were for him, but not so quietly that the rest of the room couldn't hear. She wasn't going to hide it, and she wasn't going to protect the others. "I have to tell you something."

She felt the attention of the room shift onto her, and Chase stiffened. She saw his jaw tighten, and his eyes cooled, putting distance between them. God, she knew it was a risk, but she was going to say it anyway. "I know that we got together because of the baby," she said. "I know that changes now that Alan's dead, but I just want you to know that I've fallen madly, deeply, truly in love with you. I don't need Alan and his threats to make me want to marry you. I think you'd be the most amazing father this child could ever have, and its uncles would be more than a mother could ever ask for. I would still marry you, if you wanted, and I would marry you for real."

Chase's face went impassive as he blocked his emotions from her.

Was he afraid of what she offered? Or did he want nothing of it? She stood on her tiptoes and clasped his face, forging onward with what she needed to say. "I know you might not love me like I love you, but I want you to know that you are worth all my heart. I love you, and my love will be with you no matter where our lives lead." There was utter silence in the room as she pressed a kiss to his mouth.

He didn't kiss her back, and her cheeks were flaming as she pulled back. His eyes were searching hers, brimming with emotions so turbulent she couldn't decipher them. She waited for a heartbeat, but he said nothing.

She turned away, feeling like her heart was shattering as she walked past the towering, silent masses of Stockton muscle and sat down on the edge of Steen's bed.

No one said a word as she leaned forward and placed her hands on Steen's cheeks. She leaned over and pressed a kiss to his forehead. "If you die now," she said softly, "you'll miss out on the chance to know what it's like to be truly loved by someone who will treat you well. And somewhere out there is a woman who needs you to hold her at night, to protect her, and to love her. If you die, then she'll never have the chance. She needs you, Steen. She needs you to get out of this bed, get out of this prison, and to rescue her, because there's no one else who can do it except for you. She's out there, right now, in this very moment, and she needs what only you can give her."

She took his inert hand and sandwiched it between her palms, pressing tightly. "Do you feel this?" she asked him. "This is what it feels like to be safe. She needs that from you, and she will be the one who will save you right back." She pressed a kiss to the tip of his finger, and couldn't stop the tears that started to fall. "Don't miss out, Steen. Life is so short, and opportunities are so fleeting. Don't miss her."

She bowed her head, trying to fight back the sobs. It was as if all the emotions that had been trapped inside her since her parents' death, AJ's death, the battle with Alan, and her feelings for Chase had suddenly surged to the surface, no longer willing to be crushed by sheer willpower.

Someone moved, and she looked up into Zane's face.

He'd sat down across from her, and she realized he'd heard every-thing she'd said.

"You tried to use a woman to save him? And love?" He sounded pissed, but also disbelieving.

"Yes." She kept holding Steen's hand.

"A woman is what destroyed him. That's what women do."

She met his gaze. "Don't be an ass, Zane. Not all women are evil, and you know it. So back off and let your brothers live a real life, even if you won't do it yourself." She knew it was probably a mistake to stand up against one of Chase's beloved brothers, but she didn't care. Someone had to, and it was going to be her, because they needed a protector, and she was going to claim the role.

MIRA HAD JUST CALLED his brother an ass?

Yeah, she had.

Chase grinned at the sudden irritation on Zane's face, and his brother looked over at him. "For real?"

"Yeah." He started walking across the room, ignoring his brothers, heading right toward her. Mira glanced over at him, and her eyes widened when she saw him coming.

Travis and Maddox moved out of his way, and he reached her in several short strides. He pulled her hand free of Steen's and knelt in front of her. The words that hadn't come before were tumbling through him, alive and vibrant, desperate to be spoken. "You're right," he said.

She frowned, her beautiful, tired face wary. "About what?"

"What you said to Steen."

Disappointment flickered across her face, and she lifted her chin. "It's what I believe."

183

"Well, it's true." He pressed a kiss to her palm. "I'm not going to lie, Mira. My brothers and I are fucked up when it comes to women."

She gave him a look. "Yes, I know that."

"But you've broken through that."

She blinked. "What?"

He chuckled, suddenly feeling the happiest he could ever remember being in his life. *She loved him.* "I've been waiting for you for ten years, Mira. Not just the fantasy woman, but the real life woman who leaves her coffee mug on the bathroom counter, and gets cranky when she gets hungry. I love the woman who can call my brother an ass when he's being one. I love the woman who's brave enough to ignore a room full of cynical Stocktons to give my brother the one message that none of us would have been able to give."

Some of the wariness left her face, and he saw hope in her beautiful eyes. Hope that he loved her back?

Hell, yeah, he did.

He shifted his weight so that he was on one knee, and he took her other hand, so he was holding both of them. He wanted this moment to be perfect, but he wasn't a poet, and he wasn't a romantic. All he could offer was himself. "I offered to marry you to protect the baby, but it was always about you. As Zane told me a thousand times, there were other ways to help you, but marrying you was the only one that felt right, because it was the only one that was right." He put his hand on her belly. "I love you, Mira, all on your own, and I've fallen more in love with you every day that we've been together. I want to be your husband, to be this baby's father, and to be a family."

Tears shimmered in her eyes. "But what about your brothers?"

He didn't even bother to look at them. He'd gotten his answer when Maddox and Ryder had headed toward the ranch at his request. It might be rocky, but his brothers would accept her because he loved her. "They're good."

She started to look toward Zane, but he caught her chin, directing her back toward him. "No, sweetheart. This is about us. You and me. It's no longer about anyone else." He took the plastic straw that he'd filched from the hospital tray and bent it into a disjointed circle. "I promise I'll get you a real one as soon as we leave here, but I want this done right." He held it up. "Will you marry me, Mira Cabot? I can't promise to be poetry and romance, but I promise you that I'll stand by you and love you every second of every day for the rest of my life. I love you with every last bit of my heart and soul, and I offer you my everything."

For a long moment, she said nothing, her eyes searching his desperately. He let her see the truth of his words, his promise of everything he was capable of giving. Would it be enough for her?

The silence in the room was overwhelming, everyone focused on her.

Finally, she held up her hand. "Yes," she whispered. "Of course, I'll marry you. It's always been you, Chase. Always. Since the first time AJ told me that his new roommate had told him that he should come to football tryouts with him, because his damaged foot would work the same in cleats as anyone else's. It just took ten years to find you."

Emotions flooded him, and he slipped the straw over her extended ring finger on her left hand. "AJ, the matchmaker."

She beamed at him. "He'd be happy right now."

Chase pulled her into his arms. "He'd be saying, 'it's about damned time,' and I tend to agree." Then he kissed her, the first kiss of the rest of his life.

When she melted into him, absolute rightness flooded him, and he knew that he'd finally found where he was supposed to be. He'd keep every scar on his body and soul, because without them, he'd never have ended up where he was, with Mira in his arms, loving him every bit as much as he loved her.

Love was a hell of a risk, except when it was with the right woman. Then it was the best, safest, purest emotion a man could ever have.

As for his brothers...well...he had a feeling that their time would come.

~

He needed to do something.

It was important.

He didn't know what it was, but it was pressing at him relentlessly.

It was difficult.

Impossible.

But he had to try.

Try.

Try.

There were voices in the distance, ones he recognized. And another. A woman. He had to talk to her. There was something he needed to say.

The urge grew stronger, pulsing through him, driving him. He became aware of a great weight pressing down on him, trying to hold him back. *No!* He screamed his outrage, fighting to get past it. He had to tell her. It had to be now. He felt like he was swimming through mud, fighting for breath that didn't want to come to him. He could do this. *He had to do it.*

Light suddenly burned his eyes. It was bright. Too bright. He tried to block it by closing his eyes, but he didn't want them closed. He needed to see. Shapes began moving, shifting in and out of focus. Shadows mixing with the light. Where was she? He tried to call her, but he didn't know her name.

Suddenly, a face came into focus in front of him. He recognized it. "Chase?" His voice was raw, and his throat hurt, as if he hadn't spoken in so long. Was it really Chase there with him?

His brother's face morphed into shock. "Steen?"

Yeah, yeah, it was really Chase. "Where is she?"

There was noise in the room, and suddenly there were faces crowding his vision. He recognized all of them. Ryder. Maddox. Travis. Zane. Quintin. They were crowding him, grinning those shit-eating grins that he remembered. "Where is she?" he asked again.

There was a shuffle, and then Chase pulled a woman forward. She was pretty. Dark blond hair. Blue eyes. She sat beside him. "I'm Mira."

Yes. Her voice rippled through him, and he took a deep breath at the familiar sound. Excruciating pain tore through his stomach from the attempt to inhale, and he couldn't hold back the grimace of agony. He shook his head at Chase's concerned look, trying to focus on the woman. "I heard you."

She nodded. "I know."

"What did you say?" He felt like she'd said something important, something slipping away at the edges of his memory, elusive but critical. Shit. His stomach hurt. And his side. He felt like he'd been sawed in half and left to rot on the side of the road. His vision began to fog, but he fought to stay conscious. He had to talk to her.

She smiled then, a smile so kind that he wanted to smile back through his cracked lips. "When you're ready to remember, you will."

"No." Desperation rushed through him, and he tried to reach for her hand, but he couldn't seem to move his arm. Pain tore through him again, and he pressed back in the bed, going utterly still as he waited for the pain to abate. *Jesus.* He clenched his teeth, fighting not to breathe and make it hurt more.

"I've got you, bro." Chase took his arm, moving it carefully until Steen's hand was in hers.

Steen forced his eyes open so he could see her. "I need to know. What did you tell me?"

She glanced at Chase, then leaned forward. "The day you walk into the kitchen of the ranch a free man, I will tell you."

"Free man?" he echoed. For a moment, he didn't know what she was talking about, and then his life came rushing back to him. Prison. The stabbing. He looked down and saw his body bandaged up and tubes coming out of him everywhere. Right. He'd forgotten. All the energy left him, and he sagged back into the bed. The pain from his wounds burned through him, and he wondered whether he'd ever be able to take a deep breath again. .

Chase leaned over Mira's shoulder, and Steen noticed that his arm was around Mira's shoulder and she was leaning into him. There was an intimacy between the two of them that made him think of Rachel, and pain echoed in his chest. "Steen," Chase said. "You have less than five months until you're out. This shit will be over, and you can start again."

"For what? I—" He cut off the familiar refrain when he saw the expression on Mira's face. "What?" She knew something. What did she know?

"Give it time," she said softly. "You'll figure out why you decided to live." She leaned forward and pressed a kiss to his cheek. He closed his eyes, stunned by how incredible it felt to be touched so softly, and so intimately. He went utterly still, afraid to break the spell, afraid to move, afraid of never feeling that kind of touch again. The pain that had been gripping him so fiercely eased slightly, allowing him just enough room to inhale slightly.

"Careful, buddy," Chase said. "She's mine."

Steen opened his eyes as Mira pulled back. She held up her left hand, which had a straw wrapped around her ring finger. "I'm marrying into your family, Steen. Zane is pissed, and most of your brothers are afraid of me. It seems as if you like me, so do me a favor and get healed, okay? I need you at the wedding so that Chase isn't the only one on my side. Got it?"

"Married?" He looked at Chase, who was grinning the biggest smile he'd ever seen in his life. Even as he studied his brother, he felt weariness stealing over him, and his eyes growing heavy. Shit, he was tired. He needed to sleep. He could feel his body screaming at him to let it heal, and he knew he had to shut it down. His eyelids began to drift shut, and his finger slackened in Mira's hand.

"Damn right," Chase said. "I need you there. You coming?"

Forcing his eyes open Steen looked at Mira again, and then he looked at each of his brothers, who he hadn't seen in years. He'd cut them out when he'd gone to prison, and yet there they were, all of them present, crowding his bed like they didn't give a shit about what'd he'd done. Only Caleb and Logan were missing. All the rest were there. Something rolled over inside him, something that had been dead for a long, long time. "Yeah, okay," he said, returning his gaze back to Chase and Mira. "I'll be there. At your wedding. But you're going to have to wait. Gotta get better. I'm not coming in a wheelchair." Pain stabbed through him again, and he gritted his teeth.

Chase's smile widened, and the others all seemed to take a universal deep breath. "You promise?"

He met his brother's gaze, knowing that in their world, a promise meant everything. "Yeah," he said. "I promise."

Did you enjoy Chase and Mira's story? If so, please consider leaving a short review on the eTailer and/or Goodreads. Reviews make a huge difference for authors!

∽

Do you want to know when Stephanie has a new book out, is running a sale, or giving away prizes? **Sign up for her private newsletter here!**

∽

Keep reading for the next Wyoming Rebels book!

Stephanie ROWE

A Real Cowboy Knows How to Kiss

WYOMING REBELS

COPYRIGHT

A Real Cowboy Knows How to Kiss (a Wyoming Rebels novel).
Copyright © 2016 by Stephanie Rowe.

ISBN 10: 1940968127
ISBN 13: 9781940968124

Cover design © 2016 by Kelli Ann Morgan, Inspire Creative Services.

the author or the artist. There are excerpts from other books by the author in the back of the book.

For Janet Juengling-Snell for all the amazing work and heart that you have spent on launching the Stocktons into the world. You ROCK!

CHAPTER ONE

STEEN STOCKTON TOOK a deep breath as he stepped outside the prison for the first time in four years. He'd forgotten what freedom tasted like, and he was sort of surprised that he even cared enough to notice the blue sky, the lack of walls, and the fact that he owned himself for the first time in too damn long. He'd thought his soul was dead, but the fact he was actually noticing the warmth of the afternoon sun on his face made him think that maybe he was wrong.

Maybe his soul wasn't dead. At least, not yet. He wasn't sure if that was a good thing, or not.

Being dead was easier.

And now that he was free? He had no idea what to do. He didn't even want to do anything. He simply wanted to walk away, and he didn't care where he ended up.

The long, winding road leading up to the prison was empty, and the parking lot was barren, except for a few staff cars and a shiny silver Mercedes that probably belonged to some hotshot lawyer slumming with the inmates.

Though he'd been officially sprung today, there had been mountains of forms to go through, so actual freedom had come late in the day. He was nothing but an inmate number to them, and he knew it. They didn't care how long it took to get him out the door, but since he'd been paroled, they couldn't keep him inside. Now, he was out.

His body felt like it had been to hell, and had gotten only halfway back. The walk down the steps felt interminable, but he managed to avoid the temptation of using the cement wall of the prison to support himself. Instead, he inched down the stairs, refusing to use the handrail, refusing to be weak.

When he'd been lying in that hospital bed a few months ago, he'd been ready to die. He'd made peace with the uselessness of his life, and he was done. But then somehow, some way, something had changed. He had only vague memories of what his brother's fiancée had said to him when he'd been unconscious, but her words had ripped open something in his gut and dragged him back to the land of the living.

And now, here he was. It had been only a few months since he'd almost died, a hellish period that had involved post-surgical complications and a second surgery. But now he was finally standing outside the prison he'd never thought he'd leave alive.

He was sure she'd said something about a woman. What woman? He needed to ask her. He needed to know, because otherwise, the fact he was still breathing made no sense.

Ignoring the pain from both the stab wound in his left side and the incision bisecting his stomach, he eased down the steps, almost laughing at how out of breath he was. Where was the former star athlete now, eh? The glory days were long past, not that those days had been all that glorious. He knew now they'd just been the setup for the fall.

He'd made it halfway down the flight of stairs, when a shadow moved across his path. Prison instincts flared up, and he stopped fast, his fists going up for protection as he jerked his head up to see who had cut him off.

It was a man in a suit, polished shoes, and a perfect white shirt. His dark hair was flecked with gray, and his smooth shave looked like it had been done in a grooming salon. His face had a few lines on it, but they were the kind of wrinkles a man got from too much stress, not from a lifetime in the sun. He studied Steen silently, evaluating him.

Steen let his fists drop, but his tension didn't lessen. He didn't trust men who paid more for their clothes than average people spent on their cars. He never had trusted people that like, and the last five years had made him even more cynical about human nature.

He was sure the man had never had to fight to save his own life. He almost envied the guy. What would it have been like to grow up having no idea how dirty life could be?

"Steen Stockton, I presume?" The man's voice was cultured and precise.

He knew who he was? Steen's tension rose another notch, but he hid it, giving only a non-committal shrug with one shoulder. "Maybe."

"They said you were getting paroled today."

Steen stiffened, as it occurred to him that the man could be associated with the people who had gotten him thrown into prison in the first place. He immediately raised his chin and relaxed his hands. There was no chance in hell he was going to be goaded into doing anything that could get his ass thrown back in prison. He was done with that. *Done.* "What's it to you?"

The man was unruffled by Steen's surly tone. "I've been waiting all day for you to come out. I wanted to thank you personally."

Steen paused at the unexpected answer. "*Thank* me? For what?"

The man cleared his throat. "I'm sorry. I've been remiss. My name is Thomas Smith." He held out his hand, and Steen reluctantly shook it. No one had shaken his hand in a long, long time.

"Okay," Steen said carefully, still unclear what the man wanted from him. He shifted restlessly, wanting to get away from the building that had trapped him for so long. He had no clue where he was going to go, but that didn't matter. He just wanted to hike down that long driveway and start over.

No, first he was going to find his brother's woman, and ask her what she'd said to him to pull him out of his coma. The words in his head wouldn't connect, and he didn't like it.

Thomas raised his brows. "My son is Joe Smith. He goes by Pointer."

Steen went still, looking sharply at the man. "Pointer?" He remembered Pointer all too well. The kid had walked into prison skinny and pale, the perfect bait for abuse on his first day. "He's your kid?"

At Thomas's nod, Steen relaxed. Pointer was a good kid, and Steen had known instantly that the younger man came from solid stock. Maybe Pointer wasn't exactly a kid. He was in his early twenties, but his cushy life had left him too young and inexperienced to face prison on his own. He'd been targeted from the first second he'd stepped in the door, and it was Steen who had met his gaze in that first second. It was Steen who'd seen the fear in the kid's eyes, as well as the rigid set to his jaw that hid his terror behind a mask of defiance.

He'd liked the kid instantly. Pointer reminded him of how he used to be, back when he believed that if you fought for what you believed in, you could make it happen. He hadn't wanted Pointer to lose that look within the first five seconds of being in prison.

Thomas gestured toward Steen's left side, which was heavily bandaged beneath his shirt. The knife blade had gone deep, causing injury that his body hadn't wanted to heal, resulting in a rough second surgery. "I want to thank you for saving his life," Thomas said.

"Oh..." That. Steen didn't want accolades. He didn't deserve any. He shrugged. "Right place at the right time. Nothing else."

Thomas laughed softly, the kind of amused laugh that called Steen on his bullshit. "Pointer said you'd say that, but he knows damned well that he wouldn't have survived his first day in prison if you hadn't seen that knife coming for him and stepped in front of the blade to take the hit instead of him. He was targeted because of my work, and I'll never forget that you're the reason I still have a son." He leaned forward, looking at Steen. "I've seen the tapes, Steen. I watched your eyes go to that knife, and I saw you decide to step in front of the blade and take the hit that was meant for my son, who you didn't even know. I know how badly you were hurt, and I know you almost died."

Steen shifted uncomfortably, not used to that kind of praise. "Yeah, well, it worked out okay." He realized there was no point in denying it. The kid had seen the move, and apparently, the damn cameras had immortalized it. Maybe it was good that Pointer knew he'd been saved. Maybe it would encourage him to pay it forward to someone else someday. "Pointer's a good kid," he said, trying to get the focus off him. He was too damn tired to be lauded as a hero. He'd just done what any decent human being would have done. Nothing special. Just basic shit.

"I know he is, and now, thanks to you, he has a chance to start over." Thomas slipped his hand inside his blazer and withdrew a fat envelope. He held it out to Steen. "Here's some cash to help you get started. It's tough to get going after you've been in prison. It's my thank you for saving my son's life. I'm deeply sorry that you almost died because of it. I will owe you a debt for the rest of my life."

Steen stared at the envelope for a moment, but he felt no temptation to take it. He shook his head. "Money ruins people," he said. "I don't want it."

Thomas must have heard the conviction in his voice, because he lowered the envelope without trying to push the money on him. "What can I offer you?"

"Nothing." The only thing Steen wanted was to turn back the clock to four years ago, and have him be smart enough to see what was coming before it happened. But there was no way to make that happen. Life had happened, and there was no way to go backwards.

Thomas raised his perfectly trimmed eyebrows. "I know a lot of people, Mr. Stockton. I can make phone calls. I can get you a job doing anything you want. I can help you start over. I have money, and I have contacts in every line of business."

Mr. Stockton? Steen almost laughed. Who called him Mr. Stockton? "Just call me Steen." But he had to admit he was mildly curious as to what Pointer's father did for a profession. Who had a business that resulted in so many connections and favors? Maybe he was trouble after all. "Why did your business get Pointer targeted?"

Thomas's face became shuttered. "I piss off a lot of people," he said simply. "I accept those consequences for myself, but seeing Pointer affected has caused me to think deeply about what I do. Please, allow me to do something in return for my son's life."

Steen shook his head. "I don't want anything." He started to walk past him, then turned around. "No, you can do something for me."

Thomas raised his eyebrows. "Anything."

"Be the father Pointer deserves."

Thomas frowned. "That's it?"

"That's everything. You seem like a good guy. He's lucky to have you. Be there for him. Put him first. That's it." Steen suddenly felt restless, and he wanted to leave. "Have a nice day." He nodded his farewell, and then walked past him, heading down the driveway toward the chain link fences that separated the world from those who weren't allowed to inhabit it.

Today, they would open for him. He still remembered the day he'd arrived in the van, watching those gates slide shut behind him, locking him away from the world.

Thomas didn't follow as Steen walked away, his legs growing heavier with each step. He hadn't realized how weak he still was, but there was no way he'd go back to the infirmary and ask them to call a transport to take him to a civilian hospital, like they'd originally planned. He'd rather die under the oak tree by the street than have anyone tell him what to do ever again.

He'd made it only about a hundred yards when the gates slid open, and a black pickup truck towing a two-horse trailer drove in the gate.

Steen stopped, a slow grin spreading on his face as he watched it roll up. He didn't need to see the *Stockton Ranch* lettering on the side to know it belonged to his brother, Chase, the only person who would be disrespectful enough to pick him up when he'd specifically told him not to.

The truck eased to a stop beside him, and Chase rolled down the passenger window. His beige cowboy hat was tipped back on his head, and those familiar blue eyes regarded him unflinchingly. Chase draped his wrist loosely over the steering wheel, turning just enough to face Steen. "Need a ride, little brother?"

"I don't know." Steen walked over to the window and leaned on the frame, his elbows resting on the door. "Where you going?"

"Stockton Ranch. We have room."

For a moment, Steen hesitated. How many times had Chase talked about getting him to the ranch? It wasn't his world, and he didn't feel like he was a Stockton like the others were. "You don't want an ex-con living at your place. It's bad for business."

Chase's smile disappeared, replaced by a dark scowl. "I'll say this one time, Steen, and then this topic is over. We both know damned well that you didn't do shit, and you didn't deserve prison. The fact that justice failed you doesn't change the fact you're a good man, an innocent man, and my brother. The ranch will always be a better place with you on it. Got it?"

Unexpectedly, Steen's throat tightened, and he had to look away. "You never give up, do you?" But there was no ire in his voice. Just weariness.

"No, I don't. You coming to the ranch or what?"

Steen took a deep breath, fighting off his gut instincts to climb into the truck and accept the life his brother offered. He wanted it, he burned for it, but it wasn't right. Despite Chase's words, he knew he was a black mark on the Stockton name, and he didn't warrant a piece of that land. He wanted to just walk away and forget who he was, but he couldn't make himself do it...not yet. There was something he needed to know, closure he needed to attain before he could walk away. "Is Mira there? At the ranch? I have some questions to ask her."

Chase grinned, his entire face lighting up at the mention of his woman. "Of course she is. She lives there now. We've been waiting for you to get out before we get married. She said you promised to come to the wedding, and she's holding you to it."

Steen considered that statement. Marriage carried nothing but bitterness for him. "You trust her?"

"Yeah, all the way."

He heard the conviction in Chase's voice, which surprised him. Chase had been more anti-marriage than any of them. "Then I hope you're right. You deserve a good one."

"I got one." There was a thud from the trailer, and the sound of hooves crashing into the metal. Chase swore, glancing back at the shuddering trailer. "White Knight doesn't like the trailer. You want to ride with him?"

Steen stiffened. It had been a long time since he'd done the horse thing. "Not really."

The horse crashed against the side of the trailer, making it shake. A panicked squeal split the air, and Steen instinctively called out to the animal and began heading toward the trailer. He'd never been able to walk away from a horse in need, and the old instincts came rushing back.

"Hey!" Chase called out.

Steen glanced back at him, still moving toward the horse. "What?"

"You'll need this." As he spoke, Chase tossed a battered old cowboy hat out the window. Steen recognized it immediately as the one he'd worn back in high school.

He caught it, surprised by the sensation of feeling that familiar shape in his hands again. "You still have this?"

Chase grinned. "I never gave up hope, bro."

Shit. It had been a long time. Steen studied the hat for a moment as images of his old life, his cowboy life, flashed through his mind. He remembered the horses, the competitions, the smell of worn leather and clean straw, all the things that had grounded him when nothing else had made sense. He felt like it had been in another lifetime, as if it had happened to someone else.

White Knight slammed against the side of the trailer again, jerking his attention back to the present. Steen jammed the hat down on his head and loped back to the trailer. He opened the door and swung inside without even thinking about what he was doing, moving as naturally as if he'd never walked away.

A dapple-gray horse was backed up against the rear of the trailer, his head up and his eyes wide with fright as the trailer began to lurch forward again. Steen instinctively began to talk, the words leaving his mouth without him even thinking of what to say. He just knew what the horse needed to hear, as he always had. The horse began to lower his head toward Steen, his ears flicking forward to listen, and suddenly, the day didn't feel so crappy.

For the first time in a long, long time, Steen felt like he was in the right place.

It wasn't much, and he knew it wouldn't last, but for right now, it was a start. He grinned at the animal. "Hey, boy. Sucks to be locked up in a cage, doesn't it?"

White Knight lowered his head even further, and he pushed against Steen's chest. Pain shot through his side, but he ignored it. Instead, he placed his hand on White Knight's nose, surprised by how soft it was. He'd forgotten what it felt like to touch a horse. He'd forgotten what soft was.

He'd forgotten a lot.

He just wished he'd forget the rest.

CHAPTER TWO

DESPITE HER VALIANT efforts to maintain a positive attitude, there was simply no way for Erin Chambers to see the bright side of the situation when the SUV she was driving lurched and slithered to an engine-coughing death on the edge of the Wyoming dirt road.

"Oh, come on. Please don't do this to me." She tried the ignition again, but there was no response from the vehicle that her best friend, Josie Mayers, had named "Faith" because the truck had gotten her out of so many sticky situations.

Well, Faith had bottomed out in a big way, and was so not living up to her name.

Erin grimaced as she flexed her hands around the steering wheel, trying not to freak out and collapse in a wail of self-pity at this latest sabotage to her attempts to make this day work out okay. She glanced at her watch, her heart sinking when she saw what time it was. It was almost six. It had been over an hour since she'd received the frantic call to stitch up a horse that'd had a trailer mishap.

As tempting as it was to surrender to Faith's refusal to move, she needed to get to the ranch, not sit by the side of the road awaiting the first Wyoming sunset she'd seen in over a decade.

Six weeks ago, it had sounded like a fantastic idea to use her upcoming sabbatical to run the Wyoming vet clinic so Josie could go to Chicago and help her mom recover from surgery. Erin had happily envisioned snuggly dogs, soft kittens, and long conversations with devoted pet owners, a situation that seemed so much more appealing than her stressful equine surgery practice in Virginia. She'd been excited to use her training to help animals that weren't under deep anesthesia all the time, and the thought of returning to the area she grew up in had sounded wonderful. She'd been struggling so much in her day-to-day life, and she was excited to reconnect with a life that used to make sense to her, hoping that maybe she'd be able to figure herself out in the process.

Today was her first day on the job. As she'd expected, she'd gotten conscious animals and the opportunity to drive around her old town, but other than that, it hadn't been anything like she'd hoped and expected, not by a long shot.

In the last twelve hours, she'd been knocked down and nearly impaled on the horn of a massive bull. She'd also been flattened into a mud puddle by a six-year-old girl practicing her barrel racing skills on whatever happened to be near her and her pony, which, at that time, had been Erin.

Her last stop had gone long when the sheep had escaped from the holding pen just before she'd arrived, necessitating almost an hour of watching sheepdogs do their stuff, which was incredibly cool, she had to admit, but not very helpful with her timing. She'd spent over two hours cumulatively being lost, since the spotty cell service in the region had rendered her reliance on her phone's GPS a poor decision. None of the landscape looked familiar to her, and she felt like a complete stranger in the land that had once been her home.

Except *this* life hadn't been her home. When she'd been a kid, she'd never been canvassing dirt roads, trying to locate assorted ranches. She'd been cloistered in the library, or at school, or at ballet class, or any of the proper training classes that her parents had thrust upon her. Everything about her return was wrong, nothing was as she'd imagined, and there was nothing she could do about it now.

Josie was gone, there was no one else to run the clinic, the engine was dead, and a horse named Ox's Ass needed stitches. A passing glance at her phone confirmed she had no reception, so there would be no white knight galloping to respond to a call for help. Grimly, she yanked open the glove box and pulled out the tattered spiral notebook that Josie had stashed inside as a makeshift owner's manual. She flipped the first page, quickly scanning Josie's notes. On the second page, she found a note stating: "When the engine dies while driving, there are three possible causes." Erin scanned the rest of the page, and her heart sank.

"Really? She wants me to connect wires in the engine? Seriously?" Josie's instructions seemed incredibly complicated, and Erin felt like tossing the notebook aside, crawling into the backseat, and sleeping until the three weeks were up.

But there was a horse with a torn shoulder, and she was the one who had to fix it. She sighed. Just because her parents were disgusted with her utter lack of mechanical ability didn't mean she couldn't manage to follow a few instructions, right? She pulled out her reading glasses and studied the notebook again. Sadly, and not surprisingly, the fact she could actually see the words clearly didn't make them any easier to understand.

No problem. She was an innovator. She could make this happen. She took a deep breath to fortify herself, and then popped the hood. Once she saw the engine, she was sure she'd be able to decipher Josie's notes. It was all good.

She pulled the door handle to get out...but the door didn't budge. "Oh, come on!" She twisted in her seat and then slammed her boot against the door. It opened with a reluctant creak of protest. See? She totally rocked it.

Trying not to think about the fact that feeling so triumphant over her ability to exit a truck maybe didn't bode well, she climbed out, her hiking boots kicking up dust balls in the roadside dirt. Ignoring the aches in her body, she strode around to the front of the vehicle, propped the hood up, and studied the engine.

Then she looked at Josie's drawings.

Then she looked at the engine again.

Then she looked at Josie's instructions.

Then she tried turning the notebook upside down.

"Seriously?" Was the drawing even of the same vehicle? Tears suddenly burned in her eyes, tears that had nothing to do with an engine, and everything to do with the fact that she'd been pressing on as hard as she could for the last twelve months since everything had fallen to pieces around her, and this stubborn engine was just one thing too much.

She gripped the grill of the truck and closed her eyes, willing herself to pull it together. She was not going to fail at this. Josie needed her, and Ox's Ass needed her.

Erin took a deep breath, and opened her eyes. "You can do this. It's not like Josie's a mechanic, right? If she can figure it out, then you can." She shook out her shoulders, then set the notebook on the engine. She stared at it. She willed it to make sense to her. But not one damned thing on Josie's drawing matched what she could see in the engine.

Dammit. She was not going to let Ox's Ass down, but what was she going to do?

Hike.

That was what she was going to do.

It was only a few miles, right?

She'd be there in two hours.

God, a two-hour hike carrying medical equipment? Really?

Yes, a two-hour hike carrying medical equipment. Really.

She was *not* going to let herself mourn for her sterile operating room and pristine working conditions. She'd left because that life was strangling her, and if it took hiking several miles in the dusk to find herself again, then that was what she was going to do.

Resolutely, she tossed the notebook on the engine and left it there, then marched around toward the back of the SUV. She'd just managed to get the stubborn tailgate open, when she heard the rumble of an engine.

She spun around, shielding her eyes against the sunset as a billow of dust filled the sky. A black truck pulling a horse trailer was heading right toward her. For a split second, she considered all the big city warnings about strangers and isolated roads, and then she decided that if she were kidnapped and held for ransom, it might help her to gain perspective on her own life. And, if she weren't kidnapped but got help instead, then that would be good, too. So, a win either way, no matter what quality of individual was in the truck.

Decision made, she stepped out into the road and began waving her arms to flag the driver down.

~

STEEN WAS in the middle of a deep conversation with White Knight about the crappiness of prison life and how much it sucked to have personal freedom ripped out of one's life, when he felt Chase slow down and stop the truck. Frowning, Steen glanced toward the window, knowing they hadn't gone far enough to reach the ranch, but there were no stop signs on these roads. When the truck stayed still, Steen raised the flaps on the side of the trailer and peered out, but all he could see were fields. Where were they?

He heard Chase's door slam shut as his brother shouted a greeting to someone. Apprehension flooded Steen, and he closed the flaps. The last thing he wanted to do was socialize. He had nothing to say to the world. He'd had nothing to say when he lived in it, and he had nothing to say now that he'd been removed from it for the last four years. How did a man make small talk when he had a prison record haunting him?

There was no chance he was getting out of the trailer.

He patted the horse's nose and resumed their conversation, keeping his whispers low so no one would know he was in the back. Knight was relaxed now, munching happily on the hay net that was dangling from the wall. His ears kept flicking toward Steen, listening to the conversation with more interest than anyone had shown in a long time.

Steen sat down on a hay bale, leaned back against the wall, and folded his arms over his chest as he stretched out his legs. His black motorcycle boots didn't fit with this environment, but it was what he'd been wearing the day he went to prison. He wondered idly if Chase had kept his old cowboy boots, in addition to his hat. Not that he'd wear them. His horse days were long past. Everything was long past.

He had no idea what he was supposed to do now. Everything he'd believed in was history.

He pulled his hat down over his forehead and closed his eyes. He'd spent four years waiting, and he had no problem with waiting some more while Chase socialized. He was in no rush to go anywhere.

As he sat there, however, the sound of a woman's voice drifted through the window. The moment he heard it, something inside Steen went utterly still. He held his breath, straining to hear her better, *needing* to hear her.

Knight snorted, and Steen instinctively put his hand on the horse's nose, willing him to be quiet. Everything inside him was screaming to hear more. Who was she? Something thundered through him, and he knew he'd heard her voice before.

He stood up and edged over to the side of the trailer, leaning his shoulder against the metal wall as he strained to hear the conversation. He couldn't decipher the words, but her voice rolled through him, melodic and beautiful. He felt the tension in his muscles ease, as if he'd found somewhere safe for the first time in years. Who was she?

Memories hammered at the edges of his mind, moments of his life from long ago. A face flashed in his mind, the image of a thin, homely girl with thick glasses, braces, fancy clothes, and a smile that could light up a room on the rare occasions when something made her grin.

Erin Chambers.

Steen grinned, remembering the girl who had been three years behind him in school, so young and innocent that she'd been more like a fragile china cup than an actual girl. She'd been a nerd and a brainiac, from a family with more money than the rest of the town had, collectively. They were the kind of family which had disdained kids like him who were from the wrong kind of family, and the wrong kind of life.

But not Erin.

Erin was different. Erin had never wanted anything from anyone. She wasn't the type of person he'd ever bothered to notice back in those days, and it had been sheer dumb luck that had brought her into his sphere of awareness. He'd never forget the day he'd first noticed her—

The door to the trailer swung open, and Steen jumped back as Chase stuck his head in the trailer. "You still know engines?"

"Engines? Yeah." He'd spent a lot of time in the mechanics' shop in prison, and he'd even fixed the guards' vehicles in exchange for a break from harassment. "Why?" He was still reeling from the thought of skinny Erin Chambers. How was she still in the area? He'd been so sure she'd be some high-ranking corporate exec on the East Coast by now.

"A car needs your help." Chase gestured him out. "I'll stay with Knight."

Steen instantly comprehended the situation. It was *Erin* who needed his help. Erin, who had once looked at him like he was a saint put on the earth to save the world. She was the only truly selfless human being he'd ever met in his life, the only one who'd ever looked at him as if she couldn't see all the worthlessness about him. Yeah, she'd been nothing but a kid, and he'd never exchanged more than a couple sentences with her, but in some ways, she had been one of the most pivotal parts of his high school existence. A part of him wanted to go out and see her, to find out what she'd become, but a deeper, stronger instinct kept him rooted.

There was no chance in hell he wanted Erin Chambers to see what he'd become. She'd known him as a star athlete, the first Stockton to break from the rut of cowboy-life. He'd been big time, on the way to a full ride at the college of his choice, fully prepared to make a career far away from the small, cursed life he'd been labeled with. Then had come his career-ending knee injury during his junior year of college, right in the middle of an ass-kicking season that had everyone short-listing him as a top draft pick destined for a Hall of Fame career. In one split second, every one of his dreams had come crashing to a stunned halt.

And that's when the real descent had begun, a series of events outside his control that had derailed him from everything that mattered and every dream he'd ever had.

Chase gestured again. "Come on. She's in a hurry."

"No."

Chase tipped back his hat. "No? Really?" It wasn't a question. It was a challenge, the kind that Steen never used to back down from.

This time, however, he didn't respond to the bait. "No," he repeated, even more firmly.

His brother's eyes narrowed. "I don't care if you've been in prison for four years. The only thing that separates us from our father is the fact that, despite everything, we value human beings. If you sit in there and refuse to help, then you're no better than he ever was."

Anger ripped through Steen. "I'm not him."

"You've got his genes. We all do. It's up to you to fight them. The first time he went to prison, it turned his soul black for good. You want to be him? You want to go there?"

Steen scowled at his brother. "You're a bastard."

"So are you." Chase stepped back, looking down the road. "Erin," he yelled out. "My brother's coming to help you. He's just got to get his pants on first."

He heard Erin yell something back, and Steen glared at his brother, who was now grinning broadly. "You're an ass."

Chase tipped his head. "Why, thank you. I appreciate the compliment."

Steen knew he had no choice now. He'd been busted. He gave Knight a final pat, then ducked out the door and stepped into the sunlight. Squinting against the brightness, he took a deep breath, and then turned toward the front of the truck, steeling himself for the sight of a skinny, intellectual rich kid who had moved far beyond his station in life.

What he saw was a woman in hiking boots and muddy jeans, with a thick ponytail cascading down her back as she leaned over the engine of a beat-up Chevy. The setting sun was igniting auburn streaks in her hair, making it look like fire was sizzling through the strands. Her hair was mesmerizing, the most insanely beautiful thing he could remember noticing in his life. The skinniness was long gone, replaced with the kind of womanly curves that he could spend hours memorizing. Her light blue tee shirt was muddy and torn at the hem, and she was muttering under her breath, talking to herself about something.

He grinned, remembering all those times he'd seen her talking to herself as she'd wandered through the school. Erin Chambers indeed.

At that moment, she looked up at him. The moment her brown

eyes fastened on him, he felt like his entire world had gone still. She wasn't the skinny geek he remembered. She was a woman who literally took his breath away.

~

IT WAS STEEN STOCKTON.

Erin couldn't believe the man standing before her. After all her years of fantasizing about him, wondering what had happened to him, searching the web for information about his football career after he'd blown out his knee in college, he was standing right in front of her.

An old, faded cowboy hat was pulled low over his forehead, almost shielding his dark eyes from her view. His face was clean-shaven, his jaw angular and defined. He was wearing a black tee shirt, black jeans, and boots that would fit more with a motorcycle helmet than a cowboy hat. His shoulders were still wide and his body angled down to a V toward his narrow hips, but he was lean, too lean, and his cheeks were sunken, as if he'd been in a bad place for a long time. He was all male, well over six feet tall, and his muscles were hard and cut beneath his shirt, despite his leanness.

He was no longer a boy, but the man she'd envisioned. He was raw heat, with a languid grace that she knew hid his lightning quick reflexes and innate physical grace. For the first time in years, she felt a pulse of physical attraction. Involuntarily, her gaze flicked to his mouth. His lips were pressed together, as if he were trying to contain the words that wanted to escape. Sexy and silent, just as he'd always been, only now, he was so much more.

In the face of the sheer strength of his presence, she suddenly felt like the ugly, geeky fourteen-year-old again, hopelessly outclassed by the only person she'd ever known who lived life on his terms and didn't care one bit what anyone else thought of him.

He frowned. "You okay?"

Erin suddenly realized she'd been gaping at him. Horrified, she snapped her mouth shut, trying to regain some semblance of self-respect. "Yes, fine. Thanks. It's so incredible to see—"

"You need some help with your engine?" he interrupted, cutting off her sentence before she could finish commenting on how good it was to see him.

It was her turn to frown now. Did he not recognize her? After all these years of fantasizing about him whenever she'd needed to escape from the reality of her life and marriage, he didn't even *remember* her?

Desolation flooded her, the kind of utter loss that happens only when a dream is shattered, a dream that had all its power because it was pure fantasy, and therefore could never be destroyed. And yet, in one instant, he'd shattered it, because *he* was reality now, standing in front of her. Steen had been the only one who'd ever looked *at* her, instead of *through* her, but it apparently hadn't meant anything to him, at least not enough for him to remember her.

She lifted her chin resolutely. It didn't matter. She knew her imagination had elevated him into the perfect man. Even though the real life man didn't even *remember* her, it didn't change the fact that he'd been her salvation and her escape throughout the years. She knew he was a good guy, and it wasn't his fault that she'd been such an insignificant blip in his life that he didn't remember her.

He tipped his cowboy hat back, giving her a clear view of his eyes for the first time. They were haunted. Deeply haunted. She was shocked by the change in them from the jaunty, arrogant boy she'd known in high school. There was no humor in his gaze. No life, even. Just emptiness. Her heart tightened, and instinctively, she reached out, touching his arm. "What happened to you, Steen?"

She'd never have believed anything could take him down, but something had, something that had broken the spirit of the man she'd believed in for so long, the one who had lived in her heart for over a decade.

CHAPTER THREE

STEEN FROZE, and his muscles went rigid under her touch, making her realize that she'd overstepped her boundaries in a major way. She quickly jerked her hand back. "Sorry, I didn't mean to—"

"You recognize me?" he asked.

She blinked. "What? Of course I do. How could I not?" Did that mean he recognized her? She wanted to ask, but she didn't dare. His gaze was too intense, and his silence was too unyielding.

After a few moments, she began to shift uncomfortably. She cleared her throat, and tried to change the subject to one that wasn't quite so incredibly awkward. "So, um, you know engines? Is that right?"

"Yeah." He still didn't take his gaze off her face, which she found both completely intimidating and wildly intoxicating. She used to catch him watching her when they were in school, but his face had always been inscrutable and distant. Now, however, there was so much intensity burning in his eyes that her heart started to race. No longer were his eyes empty and apathetic. They were simmering with heat, and all of it was directed at her.

So much for the fantasies not living up to reality. Even in her dreams, he'd never made her feel the way he was making her feel in this moment, like she was the only thing in his world that had ever mattered. Flustered, she pulled her gaze off him. "Well, um, here." She grabbed Josie's notebook from the engine. "I have this diagram of what I'm supposed to do if Faith dies, but I can't figure it out."

"Faith?" He still didn't take his eyes off her, not even to look at the notebook that she was waving at him.

"My car. Josie's car. Do you remember Josie? She was my only friend...I mean, she was my best friend in high school. Anyway, she's a vet out here, but she had to go to Chicago to help her mom through surgery, so I'm out here for a few weeks taking over her clinic while she's gone. So it's her car, and I don't know how to use it and—" She stopped when the corner of his mouth tipped up in a slight smile. "Sorry. I'm babbling."

"You used to be so quiet," he said. "I think you spoke more words just now than you uttered during your entire high school career."

"I used to be so quiet?" She stared at him as the meaning of his words sunk in. He remembered her from high school? The liar! *He remembered her!* Elation flooded her, and she couldn't stop the silly grin. "I'm still quiet," she said. "That was just a momentary babble because I'm nervous. So, don't get used to it. I'm not suddenly going to become a talker."

His right eyebrow quirked. "You're nervous? Why?" As he spoke, he plucked the forgotten notebook out of her hand and walked around her toward the engine.

"Because you make me nervous."

He glanced over at her as he leaned over the engine. "Me? Why?" There was an edge to his voice that was like steel.

"You always have." She leaned against the side of the truck and folded her arms over her chest, watching him as he looked back and forth between the notebook and the engine.

He tossed the notebook over his shoulder and braced his hands on the truck, his gaze methodically scanning every inch of the engine. "Why?" He repeated the question, not even bothering with polite preamble. He wasn't even looking at her, but she felt his intense awareness of her.

"Because you're you."

"That's not an answer." He bent over and fiddled with something in the shadowy recesses of the engine.

Her heart began to pound as silence built between them. She knew he was waiting for her answer, and a part of her wanted to give him the absolute truth. She'd never see him again after she left in three weeks, right? After so many years of suppressing every emotion and trying to be the woman who everyone in her life wanted her to be, now was her chance to speak up, to admit who she was, to let it all out. To take a chance. That's why she'd come out to Wyoming, right? Because she'd been dying inside, and she'd been desperate to find some kind of kick in the pants that would get her heart beating once again.

He twisted something and moved a wire, still waiting for her answer.

After a moment, he looked up. "She's all set," he said, his voice rumbling through her. His gaze was boring into her. "You're good to go." He waited a heartbeat, and she knew this was her last chance. In a split second, he was going to lower the hood, and she was going to drive away.

She swallowed and lifted her chin. "You made me nervous in high school because I had a huge crush on you," she said, speaking a little more quickly than she intended. When his eyebrows shot upward in surprise, she hurried onward, not wanting to hear him disdain her confession. "You always looked at me like you saw I was there. No one else did that. I mean, I was the new kid, only there for high school while my dad was starting up a new surgical unit at the hospital. I couldn't believe the captain of the football, basketball, and baseball teams noticed *me*. For a fourteen-year-old girl to be noticed by someone like you...well, it's huge. I always thought that you'd figure out I wasn't worth acknowledging, that someday you'd stop *seeing* me, that I was going to do something that would get me kicked off your radar." She couldn't read his expression at all, but he was watching her intently. "So, yeah, that's why."

He stood up, slammed the hood shut, and then leaned on it, still watching her. "And now? Why do I make you nervous *now*?" Again, that edge to his voice that made her want to both step away and also to reach out to him and take away whatever had caused it.

She swallowed and shrugged. "It's still the same."

Her words hung out there between them, silence mounting.

"You're not fourteen," he finally said. "It's not the same. It's completely different now." His gaze swept over her breasts in a swift, almost unconscious move that made her heart start to race. He'd noticed she was a woman. Dear heaven, *he'd noticed she was a woman.* When she was in high school, even though he'd noticed her, there'd never been anything romantic or sexual in the way he'd looked at her. But now? That last look from him had been searing hot.

"No," she agreed slowly, trying to keep her voice even. "I'm not fourteen. That's different, and that's why I'm nervous." When she was thirteen and he'd been a junior, he'd been untouchable, a crush that was safe because their worlds kept them too separated. When she'd been fourteen and he'd been a senior, they'd both been in high school, but the gap between them had been still be insurmountable. But now? The three years between their ages made no difference, and they both knew it. Not that she was going to say it. She'd said as much as she was brave enough to say. She was so far from bold, so not the kind of person who claimed what she wanted. She was actually really impressed she'd said that much.

Steen levered himself off the truck and walked around the grill, coming to a stop inches from her. She stiffened, trapped between the truck and his body. His gaze roamed her face, never, to her dismay, dipping below her chin, before it settled on her eyes again. "I'm not the kind of guy any girl...or woman...should have a crush on. I'm not one of the good ones."

Outrage rushed through her. In high school, he never would have said anything like that. He'd thought he owned the world back then. "What happened to you, Steen?" Again, she reached out instinctively.

When her hand landed on his upper arm, he didn't tense, and he didn't pull away.

He went still, but this time, she was pretty sure he leaned into her touch ever so slightly, as if his soul wanted it but his mind refused to accept it.

Time seemed to stand utterly still, and then he carefully lifted her hand off his arm. Her heart started to pound as he cradled her hand in both of his, his touch warm and soft, despite the strength of his hands.

"You always looked at me like I was a prince," he said, his voice rough. "And you're looking at me that same way right now."

She felt heat rise in her cheeks. "I don't—"

"No." He shook his head. "Don't apologize. It's incredible. I never want you to look at me any other way. It needs to stay that way. I need it to stay that way." He raised her hand to his mouth, and pressed a kiss to the back of her hand. "I'll freeze the expression on your face right now for the rest of my life, so that it's imprinted in my mind forever. Thank you for that. I wish you every last bit of good luck and good fortune with your life, wherever it takes you when you leave here."

For a moment, she forgot to breathe, stunned by the feel of his kiss. He smiled faintly, a smile of lost time and old memories, as he brushed his fingers over her cheek. Then, abruptly, he dropped his hand, turned, and walked back to the trailer and out of her life.

Again.

~

STEEN LEANED BACK against the chimney of the bunkhouse, clasping his hands behind his head as he watched the sun set over the hills. The roof was cool and hard, and it felt good, just uncomfortable enough to remind him he was alive.

So...Erin Chambers was a vet. He smiled, a deep sense of satisfaction pulsing through him. He'd always figured she'd succumb to her potential and run a billion dollar company somewhere. It had pissed him off to think of her selling out, and now he didn't have to have that on his list of things to hate about the world anymore. Erin had somehow stayed true to herself and had become a vet.

Damn.

Seeing her today had made things feel right in his world, even if it was just for a minute. His smile faded as he thought of the way she'd looked. Those jeans had fit her like pure sin, and the mud on her shirt had been sexy as hell. Her eyes had been vulnerable and honest when she'd watched him. Shit. He could still feel the heat from her gaze as she'd stared at him, the hunger in her eyes so obvious that it had taken all his willpower not to slide his finger along her jaw and take her mouth with his. She was all female, awakening every possessive and predatory male instinct he owned. He'd never reacted so strongly to a woman as he had today.

He'd wanted to pin her against that rusted truck with his body and sink his hips against hers. He'd burned to feel the softness of her body against his, to feel the curve of her hips beneath his palms. He'd wanted nothing more than to angle his head and kiss her. Not just a kiss. He'd wanted to breathe her soul into his, and wrap his entire being around hers, protecting her from how shitty the world really was.

He'd always felt protective of her, but today? Today had been about her as a woman, and him as a man. It had been pure desire, the kind of need that wound up with nakedness and endless nights of loving. He grinned, clasping his hands behind his head as he stretched his legs out on the shingled roof and thought about Erin. For four years in prison, he'd never had a moment like this. A moment of simply being still, without looking over his shoulder, thinking about something that made him smile.

Hell, there hadn't been anything to think about that would make him smile.

Not that he cared about the void that had been his life for so long.

It had been worth it to wait for this moment. He hadn't been lying when he said he'd remember the expression on her face for the rest of his life. He wasn't a prince, and he wasn't a good guy, but hell, to have Erin looking at him as if he was...it made him feel like maybe there was a chance there was something good left inside him.

He looked out across the ranch, his vantage point giving him a good view across the acreage. A few horses were grazing in a distant field, beside a massive rock he remembered sitting on as a kid, when he'd gotten pissed at Chase for dragging him out here to work on the ranch. He'd used the rock as a place to go when he was mad, but the truth was, he'd liked being on that rock. He liked being where no one could lay a hand on him or get in his face. Like now. On this roof, no one was in his space, and he hadn't had that for a long time. Four long years, to be exact.

"Steen?" A voice that felt distantly familiar caught his attention.

He looked down to see a woman standing in the dirt outside the bunk house, her belly sticking out so far it looked like she'd shoved a bowling ball under her shirt. She was wearing black leggings and sneakers, as if she were about to head off to a yoga class, not traipse around a ranch dodging dung. "Yeah?"

"I'm Mira Cabot, Chase's fiancée. He asked me to come out and tell you dinner's ready, if you want to come up to the main house and eat with us."

He sat up abruptly, studying her. So, this was Mira Cabot, the woman who had dragged him back from the edge of death? He didn't recognize her at all...except her voice. It seemed to settle around him like something soft and warm, and he knew he'd heard her talking to him that day in the hospital. He'd been consumed by the urgent need to find her and ask her what she'd said, but now that he could see her, he wasn't sure he wanted to. She looked like a normal person, not some soothsayer who had gifted him with some deep wisdom. He'd waited so long to ask her...and now...something in his gut knew that whatever she had to say wasn't going to live up to what was in his mind. So he shrugged casually, dismissing her invitation to dinner. "Thanks, but I'm all set. I don't need anything."

"Really?" She set her hands on her hips, glaring at him. "You're way too thin, your face is pale, and your cheeks are sunken. You look suspiciously like someone who almost died from a stab wound not too long ago, who bailed from the hospital before he was supposed to. Correct me if I'm wrong, but it seems to me that eating is a basic requirement to healing."

He stared at her, dread leaping through him at her comment. How much did she know? Yeah, he'd been in the prison hospital for a while, and then back in his cell, but recovery was slow in prison, especially since he'd been in bad shape before the injury, surgery, and then the complications had knocked him further on his ass. But before the panic could set in, he realized that she couldn't know his secrets. She was just being herself, irreverent and irritating...and perfectly her. He grinned, despite his crankiness. "You talk to Chase like that?"

"Only when he's pulling some manly crap that warrants it." She grinned back, her face creasing into a genuinely warm and welcoming smile. "Get down here, Steen. I didn't give you my best advice on your deathbed just to have you rot away out here on your roof."

Steen's smile vanished at her reference to their deathbed chat, which stirred up his curiosity again. He decided that maybe he did want to know. "Hang on a sec." He carefully inched down the roof, and then swung himself to the ground, successfully managing not to flinch or grimace at the stab of pain in his side. He landed beside her, surprised by how short she was. She'd seemed bigger when she was giving him attitude. "I have a question for you."

A question that had been gnawing at him for months. It was time to get it answered. He needed to know.

CHAPTER FOUR

SHE SMILED. "OF COURSE." She tucked her arm through his. "You can ask me as we walk to the ranch house."

Steen grimaced. "I'm really not feeling social—"

"No problem." She began to propel him toward the house. "You can be sullen and quiet the whole time, but as long as you eat, it's all good. Chase made some sort of beef stew he said was your favorite, so you better eat it."

Steen glanced toward the house that had once belonged to Old Skip Johnson, who'd owned the ranch when they were kids. Steen had been invited inside the main house only once, unlike Chase, who'd been buddies with the old man. Chase had really made him Old Skip's beef stew? He loved that shit. Guilt hammered through him. He knew Chase was reaching out, but he just couldn't meet his brother halfway. He didn't know how to bridge the gap he'd erected between him and his brother. "I'm not staying long," he said. "I won't be in your way."

"Not staying long?" Mira stopped and put her hands on her hips. "You have to stay. Who's going to watch the ranch while we're gone?"

"Watch the ranch?" Suspicion flared in Steen's mind. "What are you talking about?"

"I need to go back home to get the rest of my belongings and sort through my parents' stuff. I can't fly now." She patted her big belly. "So we're taking a road trip. Chase said you'd run the ranch while we're gone."

Steen narrowed his eyes and glanced at the house again. "I haven't been around horses since I was sixteen—"

Mira laughed, a laugh that was so genuine he almost felt confused. Who had a reason to be that happy? "I wasn't a horse person either, but I took care of things when Chase ran off to call you back from the dead." She poked his chest. "I think the least you can do is run the ranch for your brother. He was really worried about you, you know." Her brow furrowed. "He loves you, Steen. You know that, don't you?"

Hell, she was talking about love to him? He didn't want to have this kind of conversation. "Fine, I'll eat," he said gruffly, hoping that would get her to lighten up. He started stalking toward the front door, then gritted his teeth when Mira tucked her hands around his arm again, like they were best friends.

He didn't have best friends, and it made him feel trapped the way she was holding his arm. He didn't know how to respond to it, so he did nothing. He just walked, trying to focus on not accidentally bumping into her whenever the pain made him list to the side.

"What did you want to ask me?" she asked.

He glanced at her. She looked so happy, and so sweet. He was cynical as hell when it came to women, but there was something about Mira that he liked, and even trusted. He could see why she'd won Chase over.

She smiled encouragingly. "Chase is going to come out on the porch in a couple seconds, so ask me now if you want it to be private."

"Yeah, okay." He tipped his hat back and rubbed his forehead as he stopped. "So, yeah, when I was unconscious, Chase said he brought you to talk to me." He didn't want to say that he sort of remembered her being there. That felt too corny. He'd been dancing with death when she'd shown up, and everyone knew it. How could he possibly have heard what she said to him? But he had. He just couldn't remember what it was, but he knew it was important.

She nodded. "Yes. He thought I might be able to reach you. They were afraid you'd given up trying to live."

He didn't answer her unspoken question, knowing full well that she was right. That was exactly what he'd done. He'd used the injury as an excuse to pack it in, but his brothers had had other ideas.

She peered at him. "It's okay if you did give up for a bit, you know. Sometimes it's hard to keep going when you don't see hope."

"Yeah, well, sure." He cleared his throat, and then rubbed the back of his neck restlessly. He so wasn't used to these kinds of discussions, and he'd rather shove a pitchfork in his foot than talk personal with anyone, let alone a woman, but he couldn't walk away until he got his answer. "What did you say to me? Chase said you were the one who brought me back. What'd you say?"

She smiled, her eyes softening. "I told you that there was a woman out there who was waiting for you, someone who needed you, someone who only you could save. If you died, you'd leave her alone."

He was startled by her answer. She'd called him back by waxing on about a *woman?* "Really?"

She nodded. "Really."

That wasn't what he'd expected at all, on any level. Women had betrayed him so many times, so deeply, that the last thing he would ever do is stay alive for one. "Are you sure? Was there anything else?" This couldn't be what had been driving him to survive. It was impossible.

Mira's dark brows went up. "Of course I'm sure. I was there, and I was definitely paying attention to the words coming out of my mouth." She sighed. "I know that the men in your family have issues when it comes to women. I thought your brothers were going to shoot me when I told you to keep on living because a woman needed you. They all thought I was going to drive you over the edge." She beamed at him. "They were wrong."

He shook his head, feeling even crankier. "I'm not like my brothers." Although he'd come to live in the Stockton hellhole for good when he was twelve, he'd never felt that much of a bond with the other boys who'd lived in that shack and shared his last name. His mother had never been married to their dad. She'd been knocked up and gone on with life, dropping him off occasionally when she needed childcare. When he was twelve, she'd finally told him she couldn't deal with caring for him, so she was turning him over to his dad, an alcoholic bastard who took his rage out on his sons, who all bore the scars of his abuse. Steen had gotten lucky, because he hadn't moved in until later. The problem was that moving in so late in life, he'd never developed the same bond with the others. He didn't belong with them then, and he didn't belong with them now. He certainly didn't warrant a free handout of a hundred acres.

Mira was watching him, an expectant look on her face, as if she were waiting for him to tell her what woman he'd come back to life to rescue.

"Well, I appreciate your help," he said, somehow managing to be polite. There was something about Mira that made him want to be nicer than he actually was.

He was feeling strangely desolate after her answer. He'd been building so much into her answer, hoping that it would somehow shed light into the darkness that had no exit. Instead, she'd talked of women? "I'm done with women, though."

"Obviously not, since that's what woke you up." She tapped his chest, right over his heart. "You were meant to survive for a reason. Don't run away from it."

His head began to ache, and his side started throbbing. After years of never having any space to himself, all he wanted was to be alone. Away from people, away from conversation, away from those who thought they knew what was right for him. He was done with this, with all of it. "I'm going back to the bunk house. I'm beat. Long day."

"A long four years, more like," she said.

"Yeah, that too." He was restless and antsy, and he wanted nothing less than to go into that ranch house and sit around a table with Chase and his pregnant fiancée, like they were some happy little family. "Tell Chase I'm sorry I missed dinner." He was just turning to head back to the bunkhouse when the screen door opened and Chase walked out.

"You got him out here." Chase's cowboy boots clunked on the deck as he walked over to them. He'd cleaned up, and was wearing dark blue jeans and a collared shirt, like a respectable cowboy. He walked up to Mira and draped his arm over her shoulder to pull her against him. She beamed up at him, and he grinned at her, a moment of intimacy that made Steen look away.

He couldn't do this. He couldn't be around them. This was so not his world. "Listen," he said, risking a quick glance at his brother. "Can I borrow some car keys? I'm going to go into town."

Chase frowned. "I made dinner."

"Yeah, I know." Steen shook his head. "I need some space. I need to look around. Maybe get a job." Doing what? Pumping gas? Because that was what he'd been doing when the shit had gone down. Pumping gas. No, he wasn't doing that again. There was no way he was going back to that life. There had to be something more. Something else. But what? He felt like he was drowning.

Chase shook his head. "No way, man. This is your first night home. Dinner's on me. It's real food, bro. You've forgotten how good it tastes."

Steen thought of the thick stew that he used to love. He could still smell the rich aroma of it simmering, that mouthwatering smell of fresh baked bread for dipping... "Bread, too?"

"Yep. You in?"

Steen shrugged, his stomach rumbling despite his reluctance. How good would a home-cooked meal taste? Even if Chase totally messed it up, it would still be damn good. It had been forever.

"And you can't get a job," Chase added. "We need you on the ranch while Mira and I—"

"I know. Road trip." Steen glanced longingly down the long, dirt driveway. He wanted so badly to get on his old bike and drive, just drive until the world didn't exist. "Can't one of the other guys do it?" They had brothers. A lot of them. Too many. All of them who were closer with Chase than he was.

Chase shook his head. "They have other stuff." He set his hand on Steen's shoulder. "I need to do this for Mira, Steen," he said, his voice low. "She needs to go back, and I want to be there for her. Help me out. This place is yours as much as mine, if you ever want it. There's ten acres on the south side that's yours. It's got a great site for a house."

"Live here?" Resistance flooded Steen. "This isn't my world."

"It could be."

Steen met his brother's gaze, and shook his head once. He didn't want to make a scene in front of Mira, and he didn't want to be an ungrateful shit. "I appreciate it," he said finally. "I appreciate that you and Mira and the others pulled me back from the edge." Well, he wasn't so sure he appreciated that, to be honest. "I appreciate that you tried, and I'm sorry you got sucked into my crap."

"Yeah, you should be. You owe me." Chase grinned, looking entirely too happy. "The only way to pay me back is to eat my dinner, and then watch the ranch. If you still want to leave when I get back, I'll give you your old bike and you can go. Deal?"

Steen jerked his gaze to his brother. "You have my bike?"

"Yeah, I salvaged it for you." He held up a cell phone. "I also have one of these for you. It's not charity. It's necessary while you're managing the ranch, so don't argue."

Steen ignored the phone. "Where's my bike?" His fingers curled, as if he could feel the handlebars beneath his fingers.

But Chase shook his head and waggled the phone at him. "Dinner and ranch-sitting first."

Shit. He had no money to buy another one, and Chase knew it. His brother had him by the balls. He glanced down at Mira, who was watching him with a soft expression. He was surprised by the look in her eyes. She wasn't judging him, despite the fact he was being an ungrateful sod to the man she was going to marry.

Suddenly, he felt like a shit. Just because he'd failed at his life didn't mean Chase and Mira had to suffer. He took a breath, and managed a smile. He didn't want to be the guy everyone thought he was anymore. He had a chance to start over, and he wanted to take it. Dinner and ranch sitting for the brother who had saved his life seemed like a decent step in the right direction. With a scowl, he grabbed the phone out of his brother's hand and shoved it in his back pocket. "Yeah, okay. Dinner and I'll watch the ranch, but I'm not moving into your house."

Chase laughed and slammed his hand down on Steen's shoulder. "I'm almost a married man, buddy. I'm not going to complain about having you sleeping far enough away to give me a little privacy with my woman. The bunk house is all yours."

Mira's cheeks flamed red, and she poked Chase in the chest, much like she'd done with Steen. "You're such a pig, Chase. You're sleeping on the couch tonight just for that remark." She rolled her eyes at both men, and then marched inside. Steen thought he heard her giggle just before the door slammed.

Chase grinned as he pulled the door open and held it for Steen. "She never makes me sleep on the couch," he said with a wink. "But I like earning my way back into the bed."

"Shit, man." Steen grimaced. "I don't need to hear about stuff like that." Women? Dating? Romance? Stuff like that made his stomach turn, and all his alarms start ringing.

He'd learned his lesson, and he'd learned it well.

He might be willing to sit through dinner with his brother, and he could be coerced into watching over the ranch, but women? That was one road that had burned him badly enough that he was never going down it again. Ever. It didn't matter what Mira had said to him. It really didn't.

But as he followed his brother into the kitchen, Erin's face flashed through his mind. Had there been pain in her eyes when she'd looked at him? Was she the one who needed to be saved? Because if it was her...well...she was different.

Shit. He couldn't do that. Not even for Erin. *Not even for her.*

CHAPTER FIVE

FIVE DAYS LATER, Steen was pretty sure he'd made a colossal mistake in agreeing to watch over the ranch while his brother was gone. Chase and Mira had been gone less than two days, and Steen was convinced the job was going to kill him. He'd already gone the "almost dead" route, and now that he'd reclaimed his place in the land of the living, he wasn't sure he was ready to go down that road again. He wasn't ruling it out indefinitely, just not at the moment, and he really didn't want to die shoveling horse manure.

He set down the hay bale and leaned over, bracing his gloved hands on the hay as he tried to steady himself. His mind was spinning, and his back was drenched with sweat from the effort of fighting off the pain in his side. When had he become such a lame ass that he couldn't do basic physical labor? Yeah, true, he'd been feeling a lot stronger this morning than he had a few days ago, but he'd pushed it too hard and now he was paying for it. He hadn't even done that much. Shit. He was pathetic.

He bowed his head, struggling to catch his breath. A few minutes of rest, and he'd be fine. Just a minute—

"Hello? Is anyone here?"

Steen jerked upright the moment he heard Erin's voice echo

through the stables. He moved so fast that everything spun, and he had to grip the wall of the stable to keep from staggering. Swearing, he closed his eyes and wiped the sweat off his brow, hoping that Erin would just disappear and not walk down his aisle—

"Steen! What's wrong with you?"

He swore and turned to face Erin as she jogged down the aisle toward him. Her dark hair was in a loose ponytail, with the wavy ends pulled forward over her shoulder. Her jeans fit her just right, and her muddy tee shirt was much too snug over her breasts for his comfort. What did him in, however, was the look of concern on her face. She looked so damn worried about him that he felt the tension in his chest ease, and he was able to stand taller.

"Nothing. I'm fine." He made himself release the bars, and was pleased to discover he was perfectly capable of maintaining his balance unassisted. Score one for a quick recovery. "What's up? Why are you here?" The moment he asked the question, he winced. He sounded rude and obnoxious, which he generally was, but he didn't want to be that way with Erin. "I mean, yeah, good to see you again."

A small smile curved the corner of her mouth as she stopped in front of him. "Is it now? Delightful, in fact? Is that what you were trying to say?"

He watched the way the sunlight from the open barn door made the auburn highlights glisten in her hair. "Yeah, kinda. Delightful sort of works." Delightful wasn't a word he'd ever used in his life, but it seemed to fit the moment. He kind of liked it, actually. Delightful. *Delightful.* Erin the Delightful. Erin with hair that looked delightfully tempting, like it was begging for him to run his fingers through it. Yeah, delightful worked in a whole lot of ways when it came to Erin.

Her smile became wary, and she put her hands on her hips. "So, I'm here because Josie had the ranch on her schedule for a deworming treatment today. All the horses."

"All of them?" Steen dragged his attention from her hair and refocused on her face. He noticed that there were circles under her eyes, and she looked tired. He narrowed his eyes. "Late night?"

"What?" She frowned. "No, of course not. Do you have the horses ready?"

He glanced down the aisle at the empty stalls. "Not so much." There were at least thirty horses on the grounds right now, more if he counted the two small herds that were roaming the high plains. Almost all of them were turned out in the assorted fields on the ranch at the moment.

"Not so much?" She looked around, as if noticing the silence of the aisle for the first time. She sighed, giving him the kind of impatient look that made him want to grin. "Josie's notes said that Chase always brings them in so I'd be able to go right through them."

"Yeah, well, you didn't get Chase today. You got me." Steen tipped back his hat and wiped his forearm over his brow. "He's out of town for a few days, and he didn't mention it. I didn't see that on the schedule. We'll have to reschedule." A part of him wanted to ask her to stay until he could round them up, just so that he could be around her, but he wasn't that much of a fool. The longer she stayed, the more of him she'd see, and the less of himself he'd be able to hide from her. "See ya."

He turned away and gripped the hay bale, but when he lifted it, the pain was so great that he had to set it down again. Shit. He'd totally pushed it too hard today. He leaned on the bale, trying to catch his breath, grimacing when he heard Erin striding along toward him.

He didn't look up, hoping she'd get the point, but instead, she crouched down next to the hay bale and peered up at him, her brown eyes steady. "Guess what, Steen."

Damn, she smelled good. What was that smell? Lavender? It was so faint he almost couldn't catch it. Not perfume. Maybe just the soap she'd used in her shower. "What?"

"Did you know vets go to medical school? Did you know that we can tell when someone is in extreme physical distress? It's a handy talent sometimes, you know?"

He narrowed his eyes, and gave up the pretense. He eased down to his knees and braced his forearms on the hay, taking the strain off his body. "I'm recovering from an injury. I just need a sec. I tweaked something."

"An injury?" Her eyebrows went up, and he was annoyed to discover that he thought she was even sexier when she was looking stubborn and mutinous. The hero-worship thing she'd had going on in high school had had its own appeal, but her "don't mess with me" attitude was awesome. "And what would that injury be?" she asked dryly.

A stab wound in prison that nearly killed me, a surgery that saved my life but left a mile long scar down my body, and then a second surgery to clean up the shit from the first time around. The truth sounded so crappy he'd never say it aloud, not to her. So, he shrugged. "I got cut."

Her gaze flicked to his right side, where his most recent incision was, her intuition apparently not failing her at all. "I want to look at it."

His entire body went molten at the idea of her hands on his skin. "I don't think that's a good idea."

"Why not? Because my image of your manly prowess will be shattered when I see that you actually bleed like everyone else?" She made her way over to his left side and knelt beside him.

"No," he gritted out. "Because I'm afraid you won't be able to contain yourself when you see my incredible physique. You know, since you have such a crush on me and everything. I'm not in a dating mode right now, so I'd have to turn you down, and it could get awkward." Total lie. There was no chance he'd turn her down. It was the opposite problem entirely.

She laughed, breaking his tension. "I'll take my chances, hot stuff. I'll do my best to refrain from throwing myself at your feet and begging you to rip my clothes off and do lots of naughty things to me."

Naughty things? His imagination surged into overdrive as a dozen naughty ideas raced through his mind. Suddenly, his side didn't hurt anymore. All his blood had gone straight south, and was accumulating way too fast for a guy of his discipline.

She tugged lightly at his shirt. "You want me to disrobe you, or do you prefer to manage these things yourself?"

He looked over at her, trying to think about baseball and not the erection that he was starting to get. "Can't you go away?" Yeah, he was being completely rude, but he couldn't help it. He needed to get rid of her now, before she started seeing things about him that he didn't want her to know.

She grinned, entirely undaunted by his surliness, which, if he'd had to guess, he should have predicted. She'd never seemed intimidated by him, even when she was a gangly fourteen-year-old and he was being an arrogant jerk with his friends. That was one of the reasons he'd always been fascinated by her. He sensed that she saw right through his bullshit, which was intriguing as a general rule, but right now, it was decidedly inconvenient.

She patted his shoulder. "You're a worse patient than the Rottweiler I had this morning. Now shut up and be good, or I'll have to muzzle you."

"Vet humor," he muttered, barely hiding his grin. He was too cranky to laugh, but damned if she didn't make him want to do it anyway. With a melodramatic grimace, he dragged his shirt out of his jeans and pulled it up. He knew there were bandages on it, so she wouldn't be able to see that it was a knife wound.

She leaned forward, apparently inspecting his side. She said nothing, and he was just starting to relax, when he felt her hand on his side. He was so surprised by the touch that he jumped sideways.

"It's okay," she said softly. "I won't hurt you. I'm just looking."

Her voice was soft and gentle, just like she probably used on her animals, but it worked. He felt the tension ease from his body, and he went still, his entire being focused on the next touch. This time, when her palm flattened against his side, he was ready for it. He couldn't believe how warm her skin was, or how soft. He closed his eyes, drinking in her touch, absorbing every nuance of what it felt like. He couldn't remember the last time he'd felt anything so surreal, and so perfect. He bowed his head, his gloved hands digging into the prickly hay, tracking the movement of her fingers down his shoulder blade, along the bandage, and along his waist.

She spread her palm against his ribs, as if she were trying to hold his heart inside his body. It felt good...no, amazing...no, incredible.

"Steen?"

"Yeah." He wanted to tell her not to stop, but he had no words. The sensations had gone way beyond naughty things and disrobing. Her touch was searing deep into his soul, making parts of him respond that had nothing to do with his cock.

"The bandage is pretty soiled. You're bleeding through it. The skin around it isn't hot yet, so I don't think it's infected, but it's going to be if you don't get it cleaned." She moved her hand along the edge of the bandage again, a gentle touch that somehow seemed to strip the tension from his body. "You need to go to the doctor and have it checked."

"You do it." The words were out of his mouth before he'd even thought them, but the moment he said it, he knew it was what he wanted. "No doctor." He couldn't go back inside closed walls again, not yet. A hospital was like a prison, with locks on the doors and doctors who told you what should be done with your body. They'd ask him questions, and then it would go in his file that he was an ex-con with a stab wound. He didn't want to go there. He didn't want to be that guy, not anymore, not again. "You," he said again.

"Me?" She dropped her hand from his side. "I'm a vet."

He looked over at her. "Please."

She met his gaze, and he saw something in her eyes soften. Somehow, she'd understood the depth of his need without him having to explain it. "Okay, but don't complain if you wind up with fur and a tail by the time I'm finished."

Relief rushed over him. "Deal. Do you have time to do it now?"

"I have all afternoon, since we're not deworming." She stood up. "Wait right here. I'll get some supplies from Faith. Whatever you did to her worked. She's been rocking along perfectly."

"No problem." He stood up as she rose to her feet. She was less than a foot from him, and suddenly the air between them became heated and thick. Silence fell, and he felt that same urge overcome him, the need to touch her, taste her, and drink her into his soul.

Slowly, he pulled off one of his gloves and brushed his fingers over a loose tendril of hair that had escaped from her ponytail. He expected her to pull away, but she didn't. She sucked in her breath, but didn't retreat.

He rubbed the strands between his fingers. "So soft," he said. "I always wondered."

"You did?"

"Yeah." He met her gaze. "But now, it's a different kind of curiosity."

She swallowed. "Because I'm not fourteen."

"Because neither of us are teenagers." He opened his hand and slid all his fingers through her ponytail, watching the strands slide over his skin. He couldn't believe how soft it was, and he was mesmerized by the sensation of the strands against his skin. "I forgot that things this perfect existed."

"No. Don't say that," she protested, her body suddenly tensing. "I'm not perfect. I'm so tired of trying to be. Please, of anyone in the world to say that, don't let it be you."

The edge to her voice caught his attention, and his gaze moved from her hair to her eyes. This time, for the first time, he saw pain he hadn't seen before. Not physical pain. The kind of pain that etched itself deep in one's soul and never went away. He knew that kind of pain, because he lived with it every day. The realization that she carried that same kind of burden made his fingers curl more tightly in her hair. Suddenly, she wasn't the brilliant, rich girl who would always outclass him. She was a woman who carried the same burdens that he did. She was the same as he was, which made her reachable, touchable, and accessible.

His fingers tightened in her hair, and he tugged gently, needing more. "Is there a Mr. Erin back home waiting for you?"

Again, a flash of pain, but she shook her head. "Just me."

There were a thousand more questions he wanted to ask, and a thousand reasons to walk away, but he did neither of those things. Instead, he stripped off his other glove, and then did what he wanted to do most of all: he took her face in his hands and kissed her.

CHAPTER SIX

ERIN'S HEART hammered in her chest the moment she realized Steen was about to kiss her. Dear God, after all these years? It was really going to happen? She started to panic, but his fingers tightened in her hair, drawing her closer to him as he bent his head, trapping her.

His grip was so warm and gentle that all her fear fled, and she lifted her face to his. He closed the distance between them, and he kissed her, a true, perfect, real kiss that was so much more than anything she'd ever imagined. The moment his lips touched hers, all the years of fantasy dissipated, and all that was left was the reality of who he was, of this moment, and the feel of his lips on hers.

His mouth was decadently soft as he lightly kissed her, a touch so gentle that she was almost afraid she'd imagined it. It was beautiful and sensual, a caress so tender it belied the tough, arrogant attitude he worked so hard to convey. How could this rough cowboy possibly deliver a kiss so sensual and beautiful that it made her heart come alive? But he did.

Steen paused, his lips hovering over hers, as if giving them both the chance to back away.

She didn't retreat, and neither did he. Time hung in suspended animation as she waited, her entire soul yearning for more. Would he kiss her again? Or had this moment been all there would be? For a split second, she considered pulling away, not wanting to be the one who was rejected, but before she could do so, he kissed her again, his lips feathering over hers in the softest of kisses, like a butterfly that had just spread its wings for the first time.

He kissed one corner of her mouth.

And then the other.

It was the sweetest, purest, most innocent kiss of her life. It made her feel treasured and respected, as if she were an angel held in the palm of her guardian, protected against every negative moment in the world. It wasn't the kiss of a man who saw her only as breasts and a way to get off. It was the kiss of her knight, her salvation, a man who had declared himself her savior through one simple kiss.

Hope leapt through her as Steen kissed her again, hope that there was still beauty left in her, hope that there was still something magical in her world. Instinctively, she reached out and wrapped her fingers in the rough cotton of his shirt. She needed to touch him, to ground herself in his strength, to hold him close.

He pulled back slightly, not far, but enough that she could see into his eyes when she opened hers. His dark eyes searched hers, as if he was looking for the answers in her soul. Then he smiled as he lightly brushed her hair back from her forehead. "Erin Chambers," he said softly, his voice almost reverent.

It sounded so amazing to hear him say her name, and she smiled. "Yes?"

"You need to say no." His eyes darkened, and his expression became more intense. "You need to let go of my shirt, step back, and tell me that I'm not good enough for you. You need to do it right now, or I'm going to think I deserve this, and I'm going to kiss you again."

Her heart ached at his words, at the loss of arrogance he'd once carried with such pride. "I want you to kiss me again," she whispered. "I don't want to let you go."

He took a deep breath that mingled with a groan, then his hands came to her cheeks, his palms cradling her face as if she were a fragile crystal that could shatter at any moment. "Don't say that," he said. "I can't do this to you."

"Do what?" Kiss her? Make her feel like she mattered? Treat her like she was the most precious treasure he'd ever encountered?

"Drag you into my world." He traced his thumbs over her cheeks, a touch so soft and tender it made her entire soul burn for more. "It's such a bad place, where I live," he said, his voice low and rough. "I don't want you in it, and I don't want you to see it."

She knew he wasn't talking about his house, and her heart bled a little bit for whatever tragic lessons life had taught him since she'd last seen him. "I don't care." She tugged on his shirt to drag him closer, stood on her tiptoes, and then kissed him.

For a brief moment, one that felt like an eternity, he didn't respond at all. Embarrassment flooded her. Had she completely misread his reluctance? Had he actually *meant* it when he'd said he didn't want to kiss her again? Horrified, she started to pull back, but before she could retreat, he palmed the back of her head, cutting off her retreat, and then he kissed her the way she'd always dreamed of.

It wasn't chaste and sweet this time. There was nothing pure or innocent about it. This time, his kiss was searing passion and insatiable want, poured into an erotic temptation of tongues, lips, and need. His mouth tasted like sinful seduction, and his kiss was demanding and deep. He plunged past all her inhibitions and defenses, coaxing her into a tangle of tongues so intense she felt every nerve ending in her body ignite.

She released his shirt and slipped her arms around his neck. The moment her hands were no longer between them as a barrier, Steen wrapped his arms around her and hauled her against him. His torso was rock hard against her, a tower of strength and heat. Her breasts were tight against his chest, and her nipples became hard instantly, almost aching with need. He locked one arm around her waist, and his other hand slid beneath her shirt over her lower back. He traced her spine upwards, and then palmed her back between her shoulder blades, pressing her even more tightly against him.

The feel of his hand on her bare skin was incredible. Hot, rough, and demanding. His fingers kept catching on her bra, and she found herself desperate for him to find the clasp and unfasten it. She wanted his hands on her breasts, and his mouth on her nipples. She wanted every part of this incredible man to become hers. With him, maybe she could be the woman she'd never managed to be, the woman who was sexy enough to keep her man's interest—

Sudden memories flashed through her mind, dozens of incidents of embarrassment and failure, as a woman and as a lover. What would Steen do when he realized what she was really like? How fast would he run? Oh, God, no. She couldn't do that. She couldn't live through a rejection by Steen. She could handle being dismissed by anyone except him, because he was the light that had kept her going all these years.

Tears filled her eyes, and she pulled back, stepping out of his embrace. "I can't do this."

"What?" He stared at her, his eyes so dark and turbulent that she wanted to throw herself back in his arms and pretend she wasn't who she was. "What's wrong?"

"Nothing. I just—" She tucked her hair behind her ear, wishing she could be any place but in that barn with Steen. What had she been thinking by kissing him? Fantasies were better left as fantasies. She could never deliver on the intensity of what was sizzling between them. "I just remembered another appointment. That's all."

"Another appointment?" His eyes darkened, and he walked over to her, closing the distance she'd just managed to put between them. He caught her chin lightly between his thumb and forefinger, forcing her to look at him. "Don't lie to me, Erin. I can take it from anyone else, but not from you."

She saw the plea in his eyes, and the confusion, and her heart seemed to shatter. "I'm sorry," she whispered. "I'm just a mess. I just got out of a really terrible marriage, and I...I haven't been kissed in a really long time, let alone done anything more. It's just...I know you're..." She bit her lip, wanting to hit him for not looking away and giving her space. "God, Steen! You've been with so many women, and you're this great expert, and I just... I'm just extremely insecure when it comes to sex, and especially with you." She rolled her eyes and pulled away. "God, how could I even go there with you?" She started to walk away, then spun back to face him. "You've been my source of hope and strength for all these years. In my fantasies, I'm good enough for you. I don't want that shredded by reality. I couldn't take it if you rejected me, too." She gestured back and forth between them, trying to articulate what she was feeling for him. "This thing between us is amazing. I'm shocked that you've been thinking of me all this time, like how I've been thinking of you, but don't you get it? If we tried to make it real, then it disappears. We both lose what little hope it gave us."

He sighed, and ran his hand through his hair. "Erin, you've got it so wrong—"

"No, I don't." She held up her hand. "I don't want to talk about this anymore. Kissing you was amazing and incredible, but we're going to leave it like that, okay? I'm going to go get my supplies and fix your bandage, and then I'm going to leave, okay? Okay. Great. Fine." She flung up her hands and stalked out, not waiting for his response.

She didn't want him to call her back...but she did. She wanted more than anything for him to fight for her, to announce that he believed in her, to declare that he'd waited so long for this moment that nothing would hold him back from being with her, no matter how pathetic she was.

But he didn't say that.

He didn't say a word.

He simply let her walk away.

And her heart, which she hadn't thought could bleed anymore, crumbled into its last pieces.

STEEN BRACED his hands on the stall door, his mind reeling as he replayed Erin's comments. He didn't even know which one to react to first. He was furious that she'd been married to someone who made her feel like shit. What kind of bastard did that to a woman, let alone to *Erin*? She was an incredible woman, and he couldn't imagine how she'd been treated to make herself believe otherwise. What had she endured?

Then...oh, man, he couldn't believe her comments that she wasn't good enough for him. Was she insane? She'd always been so far out of his reach it had been laughable, but now he was an ex-con with a rap sheet? Yeah, he was even lower on the totem pole now. She should *never* feel less than the amazing woman she was. *Ever.*

But she did. Clearly, she did.

She was such a wreck that she'd come out to Wyoming to try to recover. She was halfway through her trip, and she was clearly no closer to getting her self-confidence back. Was he really going to let her walk away like that? Or was he going to do something about it?

He was going to do something about it.

"Okay, are you ready?" Her voice was brisk and business-like as she walked into the barn, carrying some sort of hard, plastic case. Her chin was up defensively, and she had pulled a baggy sweatshirt over her tight tee shirt.

He ground his jaw in irritation at the distance she was trying to put between them. He'd tried to stay away from her, but it was different now that he understood her situation. She needed him. He'd never been in a position to help anyone before, and he liked being that guy for her. He *wanted* to be that guy for her. Maybe Mira was right. Maybe Erin was the reason he was still alive...because he was supposed to help her.

Granted, he wasn't going to lie: he had liked kissing her. A lot. More than a lot. It had been the best kiss of his whole cursed life, and he wanted more because he simply couldn't get enough of her. But more than that, he wanted to be the guy to rebuild her.

Steen wasn't worth a lot, but he knew that one thing he could do would be to show Erin how incredible she was. He saw every amazing detail about who she was, and if she saw herself the way he saw her, she'd never again take shit from a guy who didn't honor her.

"Can you lift your shirt?" she said impatiently. "I'd like to get this done."

He studied her for a long moment, ideas swirling in his mind as he studied her. "How long are you in town?"

"Ten more days." She gestured at his shirt. "Can you lift it up, please?"

Ten days? He had less than two weeks until she was gone from his life. His gaze swept over her again, this time appraisingly. He noted again the circles under her eyes, the pain etched in her face. Could he take that away in such a short time? Make her realize how amazing she was, so she could go back to her life and claim it the way she deserved? For ten days, he could keep her from seeing who he really was and what he'd become. He could make it about her, and give her the gift that she'd always given him: hope of a better place in life, hope of being more than he thought he was.

"Steen?" She waved a hand in front of his face. "Are we doing this, or not?"

He grinned at her, unable to suppress the surge of anticipation. "Oh, yes," he said. "We are definitely doing it." And it was going to start right now.

He didn't bother to lift his shirt the way she'd instructed. Instead, he grabbed the bottom hem and dragged it over his head, so he was completely naked from the waist up.

Not surprisingly, Erin's eyes widened in a response so genuine and innocent that he wanted to laugh. This was going to be about her, for sure, but he was going to love every second of being with her. He was primed to reignite the fire that had once burned inside her. Yeah, he knew that helping her was going to require him to get in deeper than he wanted. When she left, she was going to take a piece of his soul with her, but at the same time, she'd leave behind something that would sustain him for the rest of his life.

He was in, and he was going to change her world, forever.

CHAPTER SEVEN

ERIN HADN'T BEEN ready for so much skin. She hadn't been remotely prepared for the sight of Steen's bare torso, rippling with muscle, and detailed with a stallion tattoo across his right pec. A long scar stretched across his abdomen, one that was somewhat recent, but definitely healed. It made him look even more dangerous, like a man who had survived hell and was still standing. He was pure male, and her stomach tightened instantly.

She wasn't used to responding to men. It had been so long since she'd been attracted to a man, but the awareness leaping through her was like fire igniting a part of her that had been hiding for a long time. When she'd walked in with her medical kit, she'd had lofty plans of focusing on his injury. She'd been so sure she'd be able to convince herself to remain detached, as if he were one of the horses she usually operated on.

She'd totally lied to herself. There was no chance she was going to be able to convince herself that the man in front her wasn't Steen Stockton. Not only was there no chance she was going to convince her subconscious that he was comparable to a horse, but she wasn't even going to be able to delude herself that he was simply a patient. He wasn't. Not to her.

He was Steen Stockton, in the living flesh. He was also half-naked, grinning at her as if he'd just figured out how to cause some serious trouble in her life.

Oy.

Men. More trouble than they were worth. But she couldn't help the thrill of anticipation at the way he was looking at her.

In a last ditch attempt to protect herself from him, she gave him a good, solid glare before turning her attention to the bandage. She'd just managed to get it off when he interrupted her focus.

"How long were you married?"

She sighed. This was why unconscious horses were better patients than conscious men. "I don't really want to talk about that, thanks." She studied his side. The bleeding was from what was clearly a surgical incision, but next to it was another scar, a jagged, rough-looking one that looked about the same age as the one on his stomach: somewhat recent. Her eyes narrowed thoughtfully as she assessed it. "Is that scar from a knife wound?"

"Yeah. How long were you married?"

"Six years," she said absently, her attention focused on his injury. "How did you get cut? This looks like it was very serious. Given the placement of it, if it had gone deep enough—" Her gaze jerked to his face in sudden understanding of why he appeared so lean. "Did you almost *die* from this? Is that why you look so thin? Is that what the scar on your stomach is from? Surgery to save you?"

He tensed ever so slightly. His reaction was barely noticeable, except for the fact she was studying him so intently. "Maybe. Check the new incision. That's the problem now. They had to fix stuff up. Just let me know if it's good. What was his name? Your ex-husband's? Are you actually divorced? Was he a vet as well?"

She bit her lip, unable to stop herself from tensing at the thought of the man she'd trusted enough to marry. "Yes, we're divorced. It's been over a year. His name's Louis, and he's a heart surgeon. He pioneered a new procedure that will save the lives of many people."

She couldn't quite keep the irritation out of her voice. He'd been such a star on every level, which made his betrayal even worse. She bit her lip against the sudden tightness in her throat. Damn it. Why did she still let him get to her? Why couldn't she just get over it? Well, she could, and she would. That was why she was in Wyoming on a working vacation, right? Because somewhere in the land of her messed-up childhood was the answer, or at least that was what she hoped. But first, more importantly, was Steen, a welcome distraction from the life she was trying to forget. "You almost died?" She set her hands on his, studying his face. "How on earth did you get cut badly enough to almost die?"

His gaze flickered toward hers, and she saw the evasiveness in his expression. "It's a long story. What did Louis do to you, Erin?"

"Nothing." She would not be a victim, and replaying her life just gave it power.

He cocked his eyebrow, and she knew he could tell she was lying. Guilt tumbled through her, and she sighed. Steen was right. She didn't want to lie to him. So, instead, she raised her eyebrows back at him. "Okay, so it wasn't nothing, but it's nothing I want to talk about." She would never forget that night, that moment, when everything had changed. Her hands started to tremble just thinking about it, so she shook out her hands, trying to keep her focus. "Why do you want to know so badly?"

"Because it helps me know how to get beneath those prickly spines you have up." He grinned. "I want to get under the spines, Erin."

She froze, her gaze snapping to his. "You do?"

At his slow nod, anticipation rolled through her. She suddenly felt a little warm. Yes, he was stubbornly ignoring her decision to keep a safe distance between them, but it was the most delicious sensation to have Steen pursuing her ruthlessly. It made her feel like there was something special about her, something that was worth going after.

Not that she was going to do anything with Steen, for a thousand reasons, most importantly because her soul was so fragile that she knew that even the slightest breeze would shatter it forever. She was holding on by the most delicate filament, and Steen had the power to sever that last hold she had on her ability to cope and be strong. "Don't."

He cocked an eyebrow. "Don't what?"

"You know what I'm talking about." When he continued to gaze at her intently, she flushed under his inspection. "Damn you." She cleared her throat, turned away, and began assembling her supplies to clean his still-healing incision, which was quite small and innocuous compared to his other scars. "I already told you that nothing is going to happen between us. No kissing or fondling of any nature. That means we don't need to have personal discussions about our past romantic lives, okay?"

"No, not okay. I'm not going to lie, I liked kissing you. A lot. I'm not ready to go away."

Despite her best efforts not to care, a little stab of excitement raced through her. She bit her lip, so frustrated she was responding to him. "I'm not ready for a relationship," she said quietly, almost not able to believe she was saying it. This was Steen, the man she hadn't stopped thinking about since he graduated high school and left town so long ago. How could she say no? Except she was. She had to. "Listen, Steen," she said as she began to clean the wound, "I'm too broken right now for anyone, including you."

He didn't flinch at her ministrations, but he turned his head to watch her. "I don't think so."

"But I know so." She said as she studied his assorted scars. She wanted to kiss away the pain she knew he must have endured. Her heart broke for what he'd suffered. Had there been anyone to sit by his side and tell him not to give up? She had a feeling he hadn't allowed anyone to come close, even if they'd wanted to. Was he like her? Keeping everyone at a distance? It was a terrible way to live, but she didn't know what else to do. "I came out here to heal and to find myself," she said as she laid the fresh bandage over his injury and rewrapped him. "I need space to be me." She finished and stepped back, needing desperately to retreat from the temptation he offered. "Looks great. You're all set. So, I'll see you around—"

He turned toward her and caught her wrist. "Who is the you that you're trying to find?" he asked, his dark eyes boring into hers with the same penetrating stare he'd always had. "Talk to me, Erin. I'm not a stranger."

A part of her wanted desperately to sit down and pour her heart out to him, to abandon the pretense of being the strong, amazing woman that she had always aspired to be. But at the same time, she couldn't afford to open the floodgates, or she was afraid she'd never be able to go back to her life and step back into the role she'd given everything to attain. Silently, she shook her head. "Steen, let it go. Please."

He frowned at her for a moment, still holding onto her wrist. Finally, he inclined his head ever so slightly. She wasn't sure if he was acknowledging her request, or if he was having a slight muscle spasm, because his stoic expression gave away nothing. "How about a trail ride?" he said. "I have to go check the herds at the far pastures."

She blinked. "Ride? Horses?" It had been so long since she'd ridden a horse. She operated on them almost every day, but her only focus was on them as patients who needed help, not them as animals that could be a part of regular life. "I'm not sure I remember how to ride. I've only done it a few times."

He grinned. "Me either. I haven't been on a horse since I was sixteen. You'll be my backup if I fall off and crack my head open on a rock." He raised his eyebrows. "You could take care of that, right?"

A little chuckle escaped at the image of Steen, who had once been one of the best calf ropers in the state, toppling off his horse and cracking his head open. "Yes, I could use prairie grass and saliva to tape you back together."

"Great. Let's do it. Yeah?"

She hesitated. The part of her that had spent her entire life working to prove herself and surpass the next hurdle recoiled from the idea of taking the afternoon off from work to simply enjoy herself. But another part of her, the broken part, cried for the chance to simply breathe, instead of frantically trying to accomplish one thing after another with no respite.

She felt like she was free-falling into an abyss, like a great black cloud was crushing her soul. She was desperate, and a little terrified that she couldn't seem to pull herself out of it. Maybe a horse ride was what she needed. Being out in nature, breathing in the fresh air, and feeling the wind on her face would give her clarity. She knew there had to be an answer as to how to reclaim herself, if she could just find it.

Steen grabbed his shirt and tugged it over his head. "I know you're free, because you had the rest of the day booked for this ranch. So, let's go. You need it. I can tell." He grinned, flashing her that old-school boyish grin that had made all the girls go weak. "Besides, this might be your only chance to see how hot my ass looks in chaps. It's worth it."

She burst out laughing then, a welcome relief from all the tension that had been building. "You have old-man saggy butt now," she retorted. "What woman wants to see that?"

"You do." He winked at her over his shoulder as he swaggered down the aisle, giving her a very good look at a rear end that looked every bit delicious as it had in high school. His jeans set low on his hips, owning his body with just the right amount of attitude.

She so should run for the hills, or at least try to get Faith to limp her way down the road and back to the clinic. But her feet wouldn't move. She didn't want to be the responsible, dignified Erin Chambers anymore. She wanted to be, for one day, the relaxed, devil-may-care woman who was daring enough to ride off into the sunset with a sexy cowboy who knew how to kiss.

Steen paused at the doorway to the tack room, looking back at her as he tipped his cowboy hat back, giving her a playful look that made her want to laugh. "You coming, Chambers?"

She grinned and made her decision. "Yes, I am. I definitely am."

Maybe it would be a mistake.

But maybe, just maybe, it would turn out to be the right choice.

She was tired of being afraid to try.

Fail or not, she was doing it. And as she closed her medical kit, she couldn't keep the grin off her face. Either way, it was going to be fun, and fun was something that she hadn't experienced in a long time... especially with a man who kissed like he was pure sin itself.

CHAPTER EIGHT

By the time Steen led his horse outside to mount up, he realized that he'd been a stupid, lust-crazed idiot to suggest a ride with Erin. Not because heading off into the hills with her was a bad idea. Nope, he was still on board with that. But getting onto a horse? Shit. It had been completely natural for him to suggest a ride at the time. The implications hadn't even occurred to him...but they were now...

He wasn't sure he could do it.

Erin was already mounted, sitting comfortably on a mare named Winter Storm that he'd recalled Chase mentioning was mellow enough even for him. He, however, was holding the reins of a skinny, wild-eyed horse named Rock, which he'd noticed his first day. Rock was a little thin, a lot hostile, and plenty scarred up, making Steen pretty sure that Chase had rescued it from somewhere. Steen had always been interested in the horses that had come from messed up places, and he'd been having some good chats with the animal. When he'd decided to take Erin out on a ride, his instinct had been to head right to Rock's stall to give the horse a chance for a little freedom.

But now, as he eyed the skittish animal, he realized he should have remembered he wasn't the same person he'd been when he'd ridden the rebels. Back then, he'd been a reckless teenager with a body that could absorb any hit. Today, he was a man who knew exactly how far he could fall.

Rock's hooves were dug into the dirt, and he was eyeballing Steen as if he was going to test him every inch of the ride.

"What's wrong?" Erin asked, too damned perceptively.

"Nothing." For a brief moment, Steen contemplated calling off the ride, but when he glanced over at Erin and saw the excitement gleaming in her eyes, he knew he'd do whatever it took to keep that light fueled. He'd made a promise to help her heal, and he wasn't going to fail within the first ten minutes.

But as he put his foot in the stirrup, his back began to ache, the age-old ache that never left. Swearing, he jerked his boot out and leaned on the saddle, his hands braced on the leather as Rock swung his head around to watch him warily.

"Steen? Is it your side?"

He gritted his jaw. "No."

"What's wrong?"

Frustration roiled over him, anger that he'd set himself up for Erin to see him like this. "I broke my back a few years ago," he snapped out, unable to keep the edge out of his voice. The memories were too vivid, dredging up the fear that had almost destroyed him. "I'm not sure it's a good call for me to ride. Rock's a little skittish." There. He'd said it. What a fucking pansy he was.

But in truth, he'd never forget what it had felt like to wake up after his motocross accident. He'd been battered as hell, but the worst moment of his life had been when he'd tried to move his legs, and nothing had happened. For two hellacious weeks, he'd been paralyzed from the waist down, and his doctors had told him he needed to prepare himself for the reality that he might never walk again.

Jesus. That day...those weeks...the fear had been insurmountable. His entire life had been built around physical activities. Every moment that anyone had ever looked at him as if he was worth something had come from sports: calf-roping, football, baseball, and then, finally motocross, when football had no longer been an option after his knee had blown out.

He'd been absolutely devastated the day he'd shattered his knee and learned that he'd never play football again. His career had ended less than two days before the NFL draft, in which he'd been highly touted to be one of the top picks and destined for a legit career as a pro ball player. He'd given every last breath in his body to football, knowing it was his best chance to break the cycle of the life he'd been born into, and to lose that ticket had been *crushing*. That devastation, however, had been nothing compared to the moment when he'd thought he would be paralyzed for the rest of his life. He'd felt like his world had just ended, and it had been a brutal road back to get his body working again.

Yeah, in the end, he'd proved the doctors wrong. They'd been impressed as hell, and said he wasn't at risk of becoming paralyzed again, any more than anyone else. What did they know? They'd been wrong about his ability to recover, right? What if they were wrong about his vulnerability, and he took a chance that wound up with him in a wheelchair forever? They weren't the ones who'd have to live with it if they were wrong. He couldn't take that chance again. Ever since that accident, he'd been living on edge, so careful not to ever take that chance again.

It hadn't even occurred to him ten minutes ago that horses would put him at risk...until he'd put his foot in the stirrup and thought about how many times he'd fallen off over his life. Would the wrong kind of fall do him in? *Jesus.* He closed his eyes, and fought off the rush of fear.

Erin didn't give him a break. "But you have such a way with horses. Just talk to it like you used to do. He'll be on your side."

He looked over at her, surprised by her comment. "Talk to them? How do you know I used to talk to them?"

Her cheeks turned red, and she shrugged. "One time, I was out at the ranch helping the vet. You were in the corral with a wild pony that people were calling Psycho. Everyone was watching, so I came over. He was totally freaked out and panicking, until you walked over to him and started to talk. You didn't do anything else. You just stood there and talked. His head came down, his body relaxed, and he turned his head to listen to you. After a few minutes, he walked over to you and pressed his head to your chest. It was absolutely incredible. I've never seen anything like that in my life, and I've worked with a lot of horses. Everyone said you had a gift that day, and I saw it too. You remember that day?"

He was shocked by her story. Now that she mentioned it, he did remember that horse. His real name had been something like Texas Hellion, but Psycho had been written on his halter when he'd shown up at the ranch, literally rescued from the proverbial glue factory by Old Skip, who felt it was his duty to rescue at least one hopeless, help-less horse per month. Psycho had gotten the golden ticket of a second chance that month, but by the time Steen had arrived, even Old Skip had given up on him. The trailer had been on its way to the ranch to take him away from his last hope...until Steen had connected with him. He'd saved that horse, and it had been the best damned feeling. He'd quit the horse scene a couple months after that, but he'd never forget Psycho.

Rock turned his head, studying Steen.

Steen studied him back, inspecting the animal's dark brown eyes. There was fear in there, but also curiosity, which was a good sign. As he and Rock inspected each other, he felt his own instincts taking over, rapidly assessing the animal, trying to ascertain what he would respond to.

"Talk to him," Erin suggested. "Do that thing you do."

"That thing I do?" He rolled his eyes at her vague, irreverent word choice to describe the depth of his connection with horses, but at the same time, her easygoing tone made him relax. He could talk to Rock. That was easy. It was what he did. He bent his head toward Rock's. The horse lowered his head, so that his cheek was pressed against Steen's. Steen grinned when he felt the horse's warm breath against his face. Shit, it had been a long time. "See, here's the thing, big guy," he said softly, too softly for Erin to hear. "I'm trying to impress a girl, but if I get paralyzed again, I'll be pissed as hell. I can't do that, buddy." Just the thought of it made a cold sweat break out across his brow.

Rock nudged his cheek, and blew on him again.

Sweat began to trickle down Steen's back, and he bent his head closer to the horse. "You with me?" he asked softly, using the same tone he'd used so many times before. "I need to know." He stared into the horse's eyes, and the animal didn't look away. There was a scar over his right eye, one that looked like it had taken a lot of stitches to heal. "You almost lose your eye, buddy?" Steen traced his fingers over the scar, and the horse's eyes closed slightly as he went still, letting Steen touch him.

Something inside Steen shifted, and he suddenly didn't want to be the guy who was grounded anymore. He didn't want to live in fear or regret, like he had for so long. He wanted to be in that saddle. He wanted to ride next to Erin and be the guy she needed for the next ten days. He wanted to be the man who saved her, and he wasn't going to do it living in terror of the shadows that had haunted him for so long.

He took a deep breath, shaking the tension out of his shoulders. "Okay, let's do this." He jammed his foot into the stirrup, grabbed the saddle, and then...paused.

Was he really going to do this?

He felt Erin watching him, and determination surged through him. Yeah, he was going to do this. What did he have to lose? If he got paralyzed, at least he'd know he'd fought to live instead of skulking in fear. He'd rather live for an hour with Erin by his side, than spend another thirty years existing in the half-life he'd inhabited for so long. So, yeah. He was doing this. With grim determination, he swung his leg over Rock's back, and settled into the saddle for the first time in years.

Rock tensed, and Steen instinctively leaned forward to stroke the animal's neck, talking under his breath. It took several minutes, but Rock's ribs finally expanded with a deep, shuddering sigh, and Steen knew that the trust had begun. He looked over at Erin, surprised to find himself wanting to grin. "Ready?"

She smiled back, her eyes so warm that something inside him slipped into place. He realized suddenly that she understood exactly how difficult it had been for him to get on that horse. She said nothing, giving him his privacy, but she *knew*. She always knew. She was the one person in the world who always saw through his shit to the real person beneath...and she was also the one who had always stood by him.

No wonder he'd been willing to risk paralysis for the chance to help her.

"You bet I'm ready," she said cheerfully. "Which way?"

Steen pointed toward the north cliffs as Rock shifted beneath him, dancing to the left with a few quick sidesteps. Steen instinctively moved with him, his body relaxed as he shifted his weight to keep himself perfectly balanced on the horse. So easy, so natural. He couldn't believe he'd been so afraid to try. "Lead the way, Doc."

Erin flashed him a grin, and swung Stormy's head toward the far pasture. She nudged the mare into a gentle lope, and Steen quickly caught up to her. It was surreal to feel the strength of the animal beneath him again, to be a part of such physical talent. He hadn't felt that kind of strength in a long time, not from himself or anything in his life. Riding the motocross bikes had been a rush, but that had involved a machine, not an athlete. With Rock, he could feel the flexing of muscles, the rush of adrenaline, and the sheer power that only a living being could create. God, he'd missed this. *He'd missed this.*

He took a deep breath, letting the clean air fill his lungs as Erin laughed with delight. "This is amazing," she called out to him. "I forgot what it was like to be riding instead of operating!"

"Want to go faster?" The thrill of the ride was building, that same rush that had galvanized him as a youth when he'd been calf roping, and then later when he'd tried the more socially and financially lucrative football field. He wanted to feel the wind on his face, and feel the power of the living creature beneath him.

"Yes!" She urged her horse onward, and the duo suddenly shot ahead. Stormy's neck stretched out as she lengthened her stride, and Steen grinned as Erin's laughter floated over the wind at him.

"Come on, boy," Steen said softly to his horse, gently urging him forward. After a moment of hesitation, Rock began to extend his legs, reaching farther and farther with each step, as if he, too, had forgotten what it felt like to be free. All hesitation dissipated as Steen and Rock raced across the fields. This was who he was. This was how life was supposed to be lived. It felt incredible, and he was suddenly so glad that he was out there. He never would have dared get on a horse if it hadn't been for Erin, and he was damned glad he had.

They caught up to Stormy and Erin in a few minutes, and the two horses naturally fell into the same rhythm, their hooves pounding in perfect sync as they thundered across the open field. Erin's hair was streaming behind her, and her smile lit up her face as they raced.

Steen had never seen her so relaxed, and he'd never seen that kind of joy on her face. He realized that even as a kid, shadows had lurked in her eyes, the same ones she was still carrying. But right now, as they raced across the dried grass, he knew he was seeing the true Erin, the one who craved the simple freedom of living. It was electric, and he knew he'd never forget the pure radiance and delight on her face, or the way it felt to know that he was the one who had put it there.

She looked over at him. "Thank you," she shouted over the pounding of the hooves. "You knew what I needed."

Her appreciation was so genuine and warm that something inside him softened, as if his soul was burning just for her. As he grinned back, he began to understand that he'd been lying to himself. His plan to rebuild her sense of self-worth wasn't just for her. It was also for him. There was something about Erin that made his heart want to beat again. He needed her. He needed to touch her, to hear her laughter, and he needed to save her.

Maybe Mira had been wrong. Maybe it wasn't that he was supposed to save Erin. Maybe she was supposed to save him, the damaged ex-con who had long given up any belief that there was anything left about himself or his life that was worth saving.

What if there was something worth living for? What if there really was?

For the first time in a very long time, he felt the tiniest sliver of hope.

CHAPTER NINE

ERIN STRETCHED out on her back on the warm, flat rock, watching the white clouds puff across the endless azure sky. Steen had taken a fleece blanket from his saddle roll and laid it over the rock, which had softened the surface, while still allowing the heat from the rock to penetrate. The moment was deliciously warm, soft, and perfect, especially since she was so aware of Steen beside her. She liked being with him, and she couldn't remember the last time she'd been so relaxed. "I think that's an ice cream cone." She pointed above their heads to a cloud that was changing shape even as she pointed it out.

Steen was stretched out beside her, taking up twice as much space as she was. His boot was resting against hers ever so lightly, and neither of them were pulling away. It was barely a touch, except that it was. Was he as aware of it as she was?

"It's a football," he said.

"Sports?" She laughed at his answer. "We're out in the most beautiful vista ever created, and you're thinking about sports?" She elbowed him playfully, just barely able to reach his side from her position on the rock. Of course he was thinking about sports. That was what had defined him through his whole life. He'd been a star football player, and had ruled the school from his athletic pedestal.

"Nope. I'm talking about sports to distract me from the fact I want to kiss you." He didn't move when he said it, and he didn't stop looking at the sky, but his words were heavy with intent. They seemed to slide beneath her clothes like a sensual caress of promise and temptation, and suddenly, she wasn't thinking about ice cream cones anymore.

Her heart began a steady thud of anticipation, but she didn't dare look at him. She didn't want to kiss him. Well, she did, more than she could practically fathom, but at the same time, there were a thousand reasons why she didn't want to, most importantly because she was terrified of how vulnerable she would be to him. He affected her more than anyone else ever had, and if she kissed him, the part of her soul that was still alive would be in his hands, at his mercy, to preserve or destroy. She was so close to the edge, so fragile, that she simply didn't have the resources to survive what Steen could do to her.

"Thinking about football isn't helping." His voice was low and rough, a seduction that was temptation beyond words. "All I can think about is what it would feel like to feel your lips against mine."

She swallowed hard. "Why is it that you want to kiss me so much?" It didn't make sense, quite frankly, and she didn't trust it. Oh, she trusted *him,* but not his need to kiss her. She wasn't the kind of woman that a man like Steen would lust after. She knew her long-standing crush on him made her more vulnerable to his attention than she might otherwise be. She didn't want her teenage fantasies to shove her into a new world of hurt, just when she was trying to regain her equilibrium from the one she'd been living in for so long.

He shrugged. "Not sure why I want to kiss you so much. Just do."

"Oh." His non-answer actually relieved her. He wasn't trying to sweet-talk her. He was simply being himself, and she was comfortable with that. She accepted his answer. He did want to kiss her, just because. She smiled up at the sky and clasped her hands behind her head. It felt so crazy to be lying in the sun with Steen, accomplishing nothing at all. "I haven't done this in a long time."

"Done what? Watched clouds? Or been coveted by a hot guy?"

She giggled. "Either of those, but I was actually just referring to the luxury of doing nothing at all."

Steen shifted, rolling onto his side toward her. He propped his head up on his elbow, so he could see her. His cowboy hat was tipped back, but his face was still shadowed from the sun's rays. "Tell me about your life, Chambers. When you were a kid, I thought you'd go out to New York City and start running some billion-dollar company. You were so damn smart." The tiny wrinkles around the corners of his eyes indicated a man who'd spent his life outdoors, squinting in the sun. She'd spent more time indoors in a year than he'd probably spent in his life.

She smiled, running her finger over the brim of his battered hat. It was soft to touch, and she wondered how many battles it had been through with Steen. "I went to med school and became a vet." Such a short answer that didn't begin to explain all that her life had been, but that was the answer she was used to giving. No one wanted the truth, and she, quite frankly, wasn't interested in anyone knowing about it.

He nodded. "Bet your parents were proud."

"My parents?" Her chest tightened, and suddenly, the beauty of the moment vanished. "The only thing they were ever proud of me for was marrying Louis." She couldn't keep the bitterness out of her voice, or that familiar sense of failure that she'd been free of so briefly while she'd been cloud watching.

"I'm sorry to hear that. They're fools, then." Steen's voice was soft, not judging, and she sighed, realizing it felt good to have said it aloud. Maybe she did need to talk about it. Steen wasn't like the other people in her life, the ones who saw her only as an asset or something to either brag about or condemn as inadequate. Steen seemed to simply accept her for who she was, and he didn't want anything from her at all.

Except, perhaps, a kiss, and she kind of liked that he wanted that from her.

At her sigh, Steen moved closer. He set his hand on her stomach and flattened his palm across her belly, on top of her shirt.

She jumped at the unexpected contact, but when he didn't make any further movement, she relaxed again, unable to stop the happy sigh that escaped from her. "It feels good to be touched," she said softly, loving the warmth of his hand through her shirt. "It's been a long time."

"What about your husband?"

"He wasn't a toucher." She closed her eyes, noticing how Steen's palm moved with each breath she took. "We had sex a few times in the first year of our marriage, but after that, there was nothing. He didn't like to touch in public, and that soon became the way he was in private, too." She wiggled a tiny bit to her left, scooting a bit closer to Steen. Words she had kept inside for so long seemed to tumble out of her now, spilling forth from the hidden chambers of her heart. "I remember one time I came home from work, and he was sitting on the couch watching the news. I'd had a horse die on the operating table, and I was really upset. It was the first time that it had ever happened, and I was devastated."

"I can imagine." Steen's hand was warm and reassuring on her belly, and he didn't pull away upon hearing of her failure.

"I sat down next to him, sobbing, but as soon as I did, he said he needed space, and asked me to sit on the other couch." She still remembered how cool and detached his voice had been, as if he were asking a stranger to move aside in a crowd so he could pass by. For a moment, she'd been too stunned to move, shocked that he would shove her away like that when her soul was breaking. He'd repeated it twice before she'd finally understood how completely he was cutting her off. "I went into the bedroom and cried in the shower instead."

"Bastard." Steen's voice was icy, but his touch was still gentle as he began tracing circles over her belly. "What happened when he came into the bedroom? Did he say something then?"

"No, he decided to go to work instead. He said he had some research to do. I didn't see him again for a couple days because our schedules didn't overlap. He never mentioned it again, and neither did I." She sighed, suddenly needing to tell the entire, sordid story, the one she hid from everyone, including herself. "I found out later that he was having sex with one of his residents at the hospital at the time. They'd been dating for four years. Everyone knew except for me."

Steen's hand stilled. "Bastard."

She smiled at his word choice. "I can't even tell you how stupid I felt the time I decided to surprise Louis at his hospital's holiday party, and discovered that the reason he'd told me to stay away wasn't because I hated events like that, but because he was taking his girlfriend as his date." She'd never forget the moment she'd seen Louis pull the young woman into his arms for a kiss beneath the mistletoe, his hands everywhere on her body that they shouldn't have been, while his buddies cheered him on. "You should have heard the silence in that party when I walked in while Louis was making out with his girlfriend under the mistletoe. Everyone just stood there, looking at me, waiting for him to notice. It took him a full minute."

Steen swore again, choice words that brought another smile to her face. He was voicing all the words that she'd never allowed herself to feel when she'd been fighting to be strong and to pretend she didn't care. "What did he do when he noticed you?"

"Nothing. He looked up, saw me, and didn't move. He knew that if he waited long enough, I'd walk out without causing a scene." She shrugged. "He was right. What could I do? I couldn't afford a scene, and he knew it."

"I'd have caused a scene. I'm socially unacceptable like that." There was no humor in his voice, just thinly veiled outrage. He touched her jaw, turning her head toward him. His eyes were blazing with such fury that her heart turned over. She realized he had meant it completely when he'd said he would have made a scene at the party. His fury on her behalf made her throat tighten. No one had ever wanted to defend her before. No one had ever been outraged on her behalf. She prided herself on being tough, but she wasn't going to lie. It was the best feeling ever to have Steen on her side.

"Erin, you do realize that he isn't worthy of you, don't you? He isn't even worth the time it took to tell that story." He searched her face, his fingers still clasping her chin, forcing her to meet his gaze.

She couldn't help but smile, a weary smile that acknowledged his words. "I know it intellectually, but it's not always easy to remember. It makes me so angry when I think of how hard I tried all those years to get his attention, or even a little affection. He wasn't interested in me. The only reason he married me was because I was the daughter of the famous Dr. Chambers, and he wanted to learn from my dad. The fact I was on my way to becoming a vet instead of a doctor was unforgivable, but Louis and my dad felt that the benefit of becoming family outweighed the appendage of me. I know that it's his problem, not mine, but it still hurts sometimes, no matter how hard I try not to let it."

Steen said nothing, but his hand began to move again across her stomach, gentle touching that seemed to take away that isolation that had plagued her for so long. "They're fools," he finally said. "Being a vet is amazing, and it's exactly what you should be doing."

She smiled at his support, hearing the truth in his voice. "When my dad found out that Louis had been having an affair for four years, you know what he said to me?"

His hand stilled as he looked at her. "What?"

"He said that it was my fault because how could Louis be expected to be fulfilled by a woman like me? He forgave Louis, and hated me for forcing Louis to do it." She managed a small laugh, trying to keep herself from caring. "I felt so stupid. I'd tried so hard to impress all of them my whole life, and I failed. Once my dad said that, and my mom agreed with him, I finally understood the truth. I realized I'd never be enough for them. I saw how stupid I'd been trying to win the approval of people who will never see it." She sighed and wrapped her hand around Steen's wrist, needing to ground herself in him. "After my divorce, I spent about a year burying myself in my work, but I was dying inside. That's why I came out here to help Josie. I needed to get away. I don't even know who I am anymore, Steen. I've spent my whole life trying to be good enough, and I'm not. So, if I stop trying, then who am I? I don't even know."

Steen sighed, and he bent over her, his blue eyes searching her face. "Listen to me, Erin. I know all about people who will use you for what they want. You can never win them over. You have to simply cut them out of your life and do what you want. You'll never win that battle."

"I'm learning that," she said. "But I need the reminder...a lot."

"No problem. I'll hammer it into you." His face became more serious. "Don't let them take away who you are. Never give anyone that power."

His voice was hard and bitter, and she thought back to all the rumors that had surrounded him as a child. She cocked her head, noticing the small scar above his left eyebrow. "Was your dad as horrible as everyone said? Is that who betrayed you?"

He shrugged noncommittally, as if the question didn't matter to him. "He was an abusive alcoholic who knocked up women as fast as he could. He allowed all his bastards to run around the house trying to find food while he drank, smoked, and took his hatred of life out on all of us, so yeah, not a good guy. He had no expectations for any of us, except to get out of his way, or to be target practice for his fists."

She felt her jaw drop open. "Really? He punched you?"

"When I was little, he did, but when I got bigger, no." He flexed his arm mockingly. "One of the advantages of being in prime physical condition is that an out of shape bum can't push you around, even when you're fifteen."

She felt like such a complainer. Her heart broke for what he'd endured, and for the casual way he blew it off. There was no way a child could endure that and not bear the scars on his heart. "I'm so sorry. Your situation was so much worse than mine. I had no idea what you were going through—"

"No. Don't belittle yourself." He leaned over her again, his face intense as he stared at her. "My life was easier, because by the time I came to live with him full-time, I knew he was a bastard and I didn't care what he thought. I stayed out of his way and lived my life. Your parents controlled you from the time you were a baby, and that's a hell of a lot harder to deal with. Conditional love is more destructive than no love, because they can use it to manipulate and destroy you. Just because they didn't shove cigarettes into your arm doesn't mean they weren't equally as shitty."

Her heart turned. "Your dad burned you with his cigarettes?"

"Once. I never let him do it again." There was a hardness to Steen's face that made her shiver. He may have been her childhood crush and the only boy in school that made her feel noticed, but there was a side to him that was so tough and hard, a world she had no experience with at all.

"I'm so sorry." She reached up and pressed her hand to his face. His whiskers prickled her palm, but she didn't mind. "You deserved so much more, Steen. I'm so glad that you were able to find your path and find a life with people who do see your value."

Something flickered in his eyes, something dark and dangerous.

He didn't answer, but instead, he took her hand and pressed his lips to her palm, tracing kisses across her skin. One kiss. Then another. Then another.

The moment he felt her hand against his lips, Steen knew he was lost. No one had ever looked at him the way Erin did, as if her heart was breaking for his pain. No one had ever assumed that he was the good guy that had found his path. He was so used to being the scum, and he knew that with his prison record, that would follow him throughout his life.

He had a feeling he should tell Erin about his stint in prison so she wouldn't hate him when she found out how wrong she'd been about him, but he couldn't bring himself to do it. He desperately needed her to look at him like he was a worthwhile human being. He'd thought he was long past caring what anyone thought about him, but he'd been wrong. He needed Erin to think he was okay, and he needed it with every fiber of his soul.

He couldn't break this moment, and this connection by poisoning it with who he really was. He wanted to be the guy who Erin saw when she looked at him, and he wanted to erase all the damage her parents and her ex had done to her.

She was watching him carefully, her gaze riveted to his as he kissed her palm. "That feels really good," she whispered.

"It's supposed to." He kissed the underside of her wrist, then pressed another kiss slightly further along her arm. "Touching is good."

She shook her head. "My family never hugged, and Louis never touched me. I'm not used to it. I didn't think I needed it." Her eyes were wide and vulnerable as she watched him. "But my whole body is crying out for you right now."

Her words were so honest and vulnerable that they seemed to plunge right past his shields, deep into the part of him that he'd shut down for so long. He went still, staring at her, searching her face for some kind of deception or manipulation, but there was nothing. Just stark honesty and need. He swore under his breath as he released her hand and leaned over her. He pressed a light kiss to her cheek.

Her eyes fluttered shut, and she put her hand over his, where it was still resting on her belly. "Why are you doing this?" she whispered, her voice breathy and shaky.

"Because I need to. I need to wipe away all the taint from your parents and Louis, and I need to feel what it's like to be with the one woman on this earth who has a good soul." He kissed the corner of her mouth, barely able to keep himself from rolling on top of her and taking her the way he wanted to. They were alone out in the wilderness, and their horses were tethered nearby. There was no one around for miles, and he knew that they had complete privacy under the brilliant blue sky that he'd barely seen for those four years in prison. "Tell me no," he said, kissing the other side of her mouth. "Tell me to stop. I won't stop on my own, but I know you deserve so much more than me."

Her eyes opened. "What do I deserve?"

He lightly bit her lower lip, then traced the tip of his tongue across it. "You deserve to feel like you are the sexiest, most treasured, and most brilliant woman on the face of the earth." He kissed along her jaw toward her ear. "You deserve to be kissed like the world will stop turning if the kiss ever ends." He grazed his teeth over her earlobe. "You deserve to be kissed by a man who makes you feel like there is no woman on earth who will ever, ever, matter to him, except for you."

Her fingers tightened around his hand. "Steen."

He pulled back far enough to look at her. "Yeah?"

"That's how you make me feel."

He went still, his heart suddenly thundering through him. He knew then that he was going to have to tell her right then, right there, who he really was and what he'd done. It didn't matter that he'd lose out on the way she looked at him. There was no way he was going to be one more black mark on her soul by betraying her. Swearing, he pulled back. "I'm not that guy, Erin. I swear, I'm not that guy. I can't be what you deserve—"

She put her finger over his lips, silencing him. "I know you have secrets, Steen. So do I. But right now, do they matter? Can't this moment just be what it is? I know who you are in your soul, and you see me for who I am. Isn't that enough?" Her eyes were shining with unshed tears. "Can't you just be who you are for now? Can't we forget about all the baggage and secrets, and put them aside for this moment? Can't you just kiss me? Please? I want this moment with you. It's the only way I'll ever know what it's supposed to be like to be kissed by someone who actually wants me just for me. I don't want anyone else. Just you."

Something shifted inside him, something that broke through his need to shield her from who he really was and made him want to be that guy, for her, right now. He knew that he saw in her things that no one else saw. He *knew* that. Yeah, he'd stand back and let her go home in ten days, but she knew she was leaving as well, so there were limits to what she could expect of this, and of him, especially when it came to a promise of forever. Could ten days change her life? His?

She smiled and slid her hands behind his neck, gently tugging him closer. "Face it, Steen, you need this as much as I do. There's always been something between us, and we both know it." She traced her fingers on the back of his neck, a gesture so tender and seductive that it almost broke him.

He had two choices right now. Get on his horse and get as far away as he could from her, or kiss her the way he wanted to.

There was no way he was going to reject her, not when what she wanted from him was exactly what he wanted to give her. He slid his free hand behind her head, tangling his fingers in her hair. "If you had any idea how much I want you, you'd never offer yourself up like this," he said softly, flicking the hem of her shirt aside so that his palm was spread on her bare skin.

Her stomach shuddered under his touch, and she sucked in her breath. "The fact that you want to touch me is the most incredible feeling," she said. "The fact you want me is...amazing."

"Oh, sweetheart, you have no idea." He finally succumbed to the need that had been coursing through him for so long, and he kissed her. It wasn't a chaste, innocent kiss. He was long past being able to do that. It was a kiss with no boundaries, a kiss that shattered any last remnant of resistance, a kiss that promised every inch of his soul.

CHAPTER TEN

THE MOMENT STEEN KISSED HER, Erin felt like everything she understood about the world had shattered. His kiss was so intense, so demanding, so incredibly intoxicating that she knew instantly that she was being kissed by a man who had never lived behind walls like those that had constrained her for so long.

He kissed her with an untamed, unashamed intensity that held nothing back. His lips were hot and demanding, coaxing her to let him in. The moment she parted her lips to kiss him back, he invaded her mouth with his tongue, a seductive, sensual assault that streaked through her body, tearing her from its protective, dead shell and catapulting her into a world of sensation and emotion that she'd never felt before.

She wrapped her arms around his neck, holding on desperately as she kissed him back, swept into passion so intense she could barely even think, let alone resist it. As he kissed her, he slid his hand across her torso, caressing every inch. His fingers brushed against the underside of her breast, and she almost gasped at the intensity of the sensation.

He gave her no time to react, and before she knew what he'd done, he'd unhooked the front clasp of her bra. Her breasts fell free, and exhilaration rushed through her at the sensation of being utterly free from constraint. He cupped her left breast and thumbed her nipple. The bud became hard instantly, and she squirmed, barely able to stand the intensity of her response to him.

"Sit up for a sec." His voice was low and thick as he grabbed her hands and pulled her upright.

She barely had time to find her balance before he'd grabbed her shirt and pulled it and her bra over her head. Embarrassment flooded her cheeks when his gaze went to her breasts, but before she could hide them, his face softened with such emotion that she was no longer afraid.

"They're beautiful," he whispered as he bent his head and pressed a kiss to each breast, his kiss so tender that she wanted to cry.

She ran her fingers through his hair. "How are you like this? How do you make me feel so beautiful and appealing? And wanted?"

He sat up, put his hands on her hips, and pulled her onto his lap. She wrapped her legs around his waist, faintly embarrassed to be sitting on his lap half-naked while they were outside in plain sight of anyone who happened by. At the same time, she felt wildly exhilarated to feel the breeze and the warm sun on her back, and the press of his erection against the juncture of her thighs through her jeans.

"Because I think you're amazing," he said. "I'm just letting you feel what I feel." Then, before she could talk more, he kissed her again, deeply, passionately, like a man who had been starved for her touch and couldn't go one more minute without her.

His hands were all over her upper body, tracing along her spine, cupping her breasts, and even sliding down over her hips to her butt. The sensation of skin on skin was incredible, and she wanted more. She wanted to touch him like he was touching her, to feel his skin beneath her palms, to taste him the way he was tasting her.

"Go ahead," he whispered against her ear. "Do it."

She realized suddenly that she'd been gripping the hem of his shirt, her fingers nearly shredding the material she was holding it so hard. "Is it okay?"

Steen laughed under his breath as he pulled back from her. "Sweetheart, it's more than okay." He peeled her hand from his shirt and pressed it to the front of his jeans. "Feel that?"

Her cheeks turned red. "Yes."

"That's your green light. You can do anything you want to me." He framed her face. "I'm not like Louis," he said, searching her face. "There's no chance on God's green earth that I would *ever* prefer to have your hands off my body instead of on it. Do you understand? I want this. I want your kiss. I want your touch. I want you to feel how amazing you are and how much I want you."

She stared at him in wonderment. "You mean that."

"Hell, yeah, I mean it." With a low groan, he released her face, grabbed the hem of his shirt, and ripped it over his head, just as he'd done in the barn. But this time, she wasn't looking at him as a patient. She was seeing him as a man, a man she'd been in love with since she was fourteen years old, a man who *wanted* her to touch him.

After growing up with parents who never hugged and living with a husband who'd banished her from physical proximity, let alone intimacy, it was so foreign to be with a man who didn't shut her out.

Tentatively, almost afraid he was going to stop her, she ran her fingers across his chest. His muscles were cut and defined, despite how lean he was, and she could only imagine the raw breadth of him when he hadn't been weeks from almost dying. She brushed her fingers through the hair on his chest, tracing its path toward the waistband of his jeans. His stomach tightened as she ran her fingers across his abs, and she felt the rock hard muscles beneath his skin. She glanced up at his face and saw he was watching her with smoldering eyes, as if he were doing everything in his power not to tear the rest of her clothes off and plunge right into her.

Exhilaration rippled through her, and a heady sense of empowerment. She worked her way back up his chest, then lightly pushed on him. "Lie down." His body was so rigid with need that she didn't expect him to acquiesce.

In fact, for a brief moment, all he did was quirk one eyebrow at her. "You're bossing me around?"

"I'm trying."

He grinned then, and stretched back on the rock, clasping his hands behind his head. "I'm all yours, sweetheart, but I have to warn you, at some point, you're going to push me beyond my limit."

She grinned in anticipation as she straddled his hips. His erection was straining against his jeans, and she instinctively shifted so it was pressing into her exactly where she wanted it. She couldn't quite contain her small gasp when she got her position right. "Then what happens?"

His eyes were hooded as he watched her. "Then I'm the boss."

Oh, wow, she kind of liked the sound of that. Grinning, she braced her hands on either side of his head and kissed him. She'd meant for it to be flirty and teasing, but the moment their lips came together, the kiss turned ravenous. She immediately forgot about being the seductress, and could think only about how much she wanted to be close to him.

He cupped her breasts, then broke the kiss and pulled her upward, so that he could take her nipple into his mouth. Desire rushed through her as he sucked and bit, and she tipped her head back, drinking in every feeling he was awakening in her. This was Steen, the man she'd idolized for so long. It was surreal to be touched so hungrily, by a man she craved so deeply. It was beyond anything she could have imagined, and she'd spent a lot of time imagining what it could have been like if she'd married someone else, anyone else, other than Louis. But never had she imagined it could be like this.

Still kissing her breasts, Steen's hands went to the fly of her jeans. She sucked in her belly when he unbuttoned them, and her heart started racing as he slowly unzipped them. Could she do this? Sleep with Steen? "I don't think—"

She cut herself off when he slid his hands over her hips, dragging her jeans and underwear down. His hands felt amazing on her hips, and the way he slid them over her thighs, like he wanted to own them, was exhilarating. She felt his possessiveness in every move he made, and she loved it.

Excitement rushed through her, and without thinking, she began to unbutton his jeans. He helped her, and within moments, the sensual kissing had been consumed by a frantic need for bare skin, without clothing in the way. She was vaguely aware of jeans going flying, and boots thudding off the rock to the ground below, but the sheer strength of Steen's presence obscured everything else from her mind.

This time, when he sat up and pulled her onto his lap, there were no thick pieces of denim between them. Just the unbelievable sensation of skin against skin, of his body against hers. His erection pressed against her belly as she wrapped her arms around his neck, kissing him so desperately, as if she could pour her entire soul into his. His response was equally intense, his hands spanning her lower back, then her hips, then her rear end, as if he needed to touch every part of her at once just to survive.

"I want to be inside you," he whispered.

Her heart leapt. Really? Was this really going to happen? "Me, too."

"I don't have any condoms."

She pulled back, her cheeks flooding. "I'm on the pill. Not because I'm having sex with anyone, because I'm not, but it's for cramps." God, did he think she did this all the time?

His expression softened, as if he'd read her mind. "Sweetheart, you could carry around entire cartons of condoms and sixteen different sexual aids, and I still wouldn't think you slept around." He grabbed her hips, pulling her closer. "I'm clean. When I was dying in the hospital, they tested me for every disease known to mankind. One of those invasions of privacy they do in pris—" He cut himself off, his face suddenly going hard.

She didn't know what he'd just thought of, but her heart wanted to cry for the sudden flash of torment in his face. She pressed a kiss to his mouth, refusing to give up until he responded. After a moment of hesitation, he grabbed her hair and turned the kiss carnal, as if he were running from whatever memory had just flared up. It was bruising, almost overwhelming, but instead of turning her off, his desperation seemed to ignite something inside her, something feral and wild, a side of her that she'd never before allowed to be free.

Their upper bodies were crushed against each other, her breasts smashed against his bare chest, her legs tight around his hips. She was trying to keep her thigh away from his injured side, but she could barely keep her focus as the kisses and touching intensified. Finally, desperately, she tried to break away to speak, but he barely gave her room to get the words out. "Me, too," she managed, before he kissed her again, so deeply and intimately it felt as if he were a part of her soul. "After Louis cheated..." Another kiss, deeper, more intense. His hands on her butt, gripping her. "I had to know. I got tested..."

"I don't give a shit if you have a thousand diseases," Steen said as he grabbed her hips and lifted her up. "Whatever happens after this moment doesn't matter. I'd give my life if it was the only way I could have this moment with you."

His eyes were intense and heated as he stared at her, and her heart tightened when she realized he meant every word. "Steen—"

"You're mine, Erin, and you always have been." And with that statement, he lowered her down onto his erection.

He slid inside perfectly, and she gasped when he filled her. He was so deep, deeper than she'd ever felt, and it was incredible. Tears filled her eyes as he moved her hips in a rhythm that brought him deeper and deeper, locking them together in a way that she knew would be imprinted upon her soul forever.

She wrapped her arms around his neck and kissed him, a searing kiss that consumed them both. She began to move on him, and his hips moved as well, tantalizing her with each thrust and tease. Desire pooled in her belly, building and building until she felt like her body was going to explode. She was gripping his shoulders, her entire body tense. "You can go ahead," she said, even as she was gasping for air. She didn't want him to wait for her, for the orgasm that would never come. What she was experiencing was beyond what she had ever expected, and she didn't want it ruined by both of them trying to get her to have an orgasm that would never happen. "I never have them."

"Never?" There was a low chuckle. "You've never been with me, sweetheart." He somehow managed to thrust even deeper, despite the fact that he was sitting up and she was on his lap.

She gasped, her finger digging into his shoulders. "Please don't put that kind of pressure on me," she said. "It will just ruin it. I want it to be perfect—"

He moved his hand between them and touched her clitoris. She yelped at the rush of sensation, and suddenly, she couldn't think, she couldn't breathe, she couldn't do anything but hold onto him as he rubbed the taut bud, his fingers sliding over the nub again and again, until her whole body was screaming for release.

"Now," he whispered, just before he lifted her up and thrust deep inside her again.

The orgasm exploded through her, a searing release that seemed to ignite every cell of her body. She gasped his name, but he swallowed her yelp in a blistering kiss as he came, his hips pounding into her as he poured his seed into her body, his arms wrapped so tightly around her she didn't even bother to hold herself up. She just gave herself completely over to the orgasm, to him, to the utter capitulation of her soul, until there was nothing left but one final shudder as she collapsed against him.

For a long while, they didn't move. They simply stayed entwined, with her leaning against him while he held her up. He laughed softly, nuzzling her neck as he locked his arms around her back, not letting her go. "Never?" he teased. "Did you say you *never* had them? Because I'm pretty sure that's what you said."

She sighed, smiling into his neck as she rested her hands limply on his hips. "Apparently, I lied."

"Apparently. I forgive you, this one time." He pressed his lips to her forehead, and she could feel the laughter rumbling in his chest. "But never do it again."

"Have an orgasm?" she teased. "Or lie?"

He slid his hand beneath her chin, lifting her head so she was looking at him. "Sweetheart, if I have anything to say about it, there are going to be a lot more orgasms in your future. Hundreds. Thousands. Maybe even millions."

There was no way to stop the thrill of anticipation. "A million? How am I going to take care of all the animals?"

He grinned. "We have time."

At his words, her smile faded. "Ten days," she said. "We only have ten days."

His smile faded as well, and for a long moment, there was only silence between them. Finally, he brushed the hair back from her face. "A million in ten days is going to take a lot of work." His voice was rough, now, almost hoarse. "We better get busy, don't you think?"

He tugged lightly on her hair. "I know it's just a bunk house, but I think you should stay with me tonight." His smile was completely gone now, and his expression was serious. "I mean it. Stay with me tonight."

The thought of crawling into bed with him, and waking up in his arms was intoxicating, but instead of excitement, Erin just felt a deep sense of loneliness settling down around her. She knew she had to leave in ten days. It was her choice to do so. It was her career, and her life. She didn't want Steen trying to stop her from living her life, but at the same time, she realized she was a little bit crushed that he hadn't issued even the slightest hint at having this thing they'd started go beyond the ten days, not even a whisper of remorse that it would have to end. Just a request to spend the night so that they could make the most of the ten days before it was over.

His eyes narrowed. "What did I say?"

"Nothing." She managed a smile as she raised herself off him and tried to stand up.

He caught her around the waist, rolled her onto her back on the rock, and pinned her down with his body. "No." His eyes were blazing again, as they had been every other time she'd tried to shut him out. "You don't share something as intimate as what we just shared and then lock me out. What just happened?"

She shook her head and pushed ineffectually at his arm. "Nothing. I just want to go."

Trying to budge him was like trying to move a mountain with a feather. He just settled more deeply on her, pinning her to the rock. Yes, he was lean from his injury, but even so, he was so much heavier and stronger than she was. She had no chance of extricating herself until he decided to let her go. "Steen, please, this isn't fair. I want to go."

He still didn't move. "You remember the girl I was dating in high school?"

She hesitated, trying to grasp the sudden change of topic. "Rachel? Yes, of course." She'd hated that red-haired cheerleader with every ounce of her soul. The girl had fondled Steen constantly, but she'd been mean and nasty to Erin every time they were alone. She had no idea what she'd done to make Rachel dislike her, but the cheerleader had been very good at punishing her for it.

"When I busted my knee in high school, she decided that I wasn't going anywhere, and she was done with me."

Erin frowned, remembering how they'd broken up in senior year. "Well, she wasn't very nice—"

"You know how I found out?" He met her gaze, and this time, she saw real emotion in them. Betrayal. Hurt. Pain. "I walked into her house to take her to dinner for our three-year anniversary, and she was messing around with the backup quarterback who had taken over for me when I got hurt. She laughed and said I was a fool not to realize what was going on, and that everyone knew." His voice was bitter.

Erin's heart tightened. "I'm sorry." She knew how awful that was. There was no pain that bit as deeply as having the person you loved and trusted most betray you.

He met her gaze again. "I didn't learn my lesson well enough that time," he said. "Five years ago, I ran into her at the local grocery store. She was in town for a wedding. I was in a bad place in my life, and I saw her as a sign from the angels. She talked a good game, and asked for forgiveness for what she'd done to me in high school. I believed she'd changed, and I thought she regretted it. I thought she had been sent to me to drag me back to the land of the living. We were in the middle of having sex when her husband walked into the hotel room. She had used me to make him jealous because she was pissed at him. She told him that I—" He stopped then, his face going hard.

She held her breath, fear prickling down her spine. Something terrible had happened that night, she was certain. Something that had eviscerated him. "What happened, Steen?"

He shook his head. "The day my mom left me at my dad's," he said, changing the subject again, "she told me that she'd be back in a week, like she had been every other time. I waited for her. Day after day after day. I believed she would come back for me, but she never did. I never heard from her again. She made me a promise to be there for me, just like Rachel had, and they both lied. So, I learned my lesson about believing in anyone, and I learned it well. I don't trust women, and I don't trust secrets." He searched her face. "But I trust you, Erin.

You're the only person on this God-forsaken planet that I trust, and I can't take it if you lie to me and shut me out."

There was an edge to his voice, something desperate, something far beyond the story he'd told about Rachel. What else had happened that night in the hotel room? "Steen—"

"Tell me what's wrong, Erin. I want to know what I did to make you pull away." He looked stricken, almost tormented. "Did I read the signs wrong? Did you not want to make love? Did I talk you into something you didn't want to do?"

"Oh, God, no. I wanted you to make love to me more than anything else I've ever wanted." She was horrified that she'd made him wonder that.

Relief rushed across his face, and she felt his body tremble as he bowed his head for a moment, gathering himself.

"I'm so sorry," she said. "I never meant to make you think that." She instinctively touched his head, running her fingers through his hair.

He looked up, searching her face, as if he were waiting for her to say the rest. "You can tell me anything, Erin. I've known you since we were kids." He pressed a kiss to her left breast, just above her heart. "Please tell me why you're pulling away. I don't know what I did. I need to know."

"I just..." God, how could she say the truth without sounding like a desperate fool?

"You just what?" He caught her hand and kissed her palm.

She watched him kiss her. His jaw was rough with stubble, unlike the first time she'd seen him when he'd been so clean-shaven, with his hair super short. It had been only a week and a half, but his hair was a little longer, and he looked rougher. The bones in his shoulders were protruding too much through skin that didn't have enough fat. His shoulder had an old surgical scar across it, and his side was bandaged. His cheeks were more hollow than they had once been. He was a man who had been through tough things, things that still haunted him. He was a man who had truly lived, and he made her want to live as well.

The person she'd been her whole life would never speak up about what was in her heart, for fear of upsetting or disappointing him. But he made her want to be brave, and not hide from who she was or what she felt. "When I said that we only had ten days..." She stopped, and bit her lip. Dammit. She didn't want to sound needy and pathetic. What if it drove him away?

His eyebrow quirked. "Yeah?"

She cleared her throat, forcing herself to continue. "You didn't seem to care that we only had ten days, other than trying to figure out how to fit in as much sex as possible." There, she said it. Well, she hadn't exactly spelled it out, but she'd said enough.

His face darkened, and he pulled back, his body tensing.

The moment he withdrew, she knew she'd made a mistake. The reason he hadn't mentioned anything after ten days was because *he didn't want it*. She shouldn't have said anything. Damn him for making her say it!

But it was too late. There was no taking it back.

CHAPTER ELEVEN

STEEN SAW the hurt in Erin's eyes, and he felt it in the sudden softness of her voice. Regret poured through him. Son of a bitch. This wasn't supposed to happen this way. He was supposed to rebuild her, not tear her down.

"Never mind." She pushed ineffectually at his shoulders, but he didn't move off her. "Forget I said it. It's fine. I'm leaving. I get it—"

"No, you don't." He knew he was being a bastard by using his weight to keep her from leaving, but he knew that if she got up, she'd shut him out and disappear from his life. There was no way he could let her run away from him, not before he'd had the chance to make this right.

She glared at him, her chin held stiffly. "I don't what?"

"You don't get it."

"Oh, really? What don't I get?" Her voice was cool and distant, and he knew it was his fault.

Swearing, he struggled to think of how to phrase it. The last thing he wanted was to let her walk out of his life after ten days. It had been only a few days since they'd reconnected, and he couldn't get her out of his mind for even a split second. After another ten days, letting her go would be like carving out his own heart with a pitchfork and leaving it in the hot sun to fry, but he knew he had to do it. She was better than his world, and she didn't deserve to be trapped in his life. He couldn't ask her to stay, but he couldn't go with her, for a whole host of reasons, including the fact that she deserved more than to be saddled with him. There was no future for them, but he, somehow, had to make her understand that it wasn't *her* that was the issue.

"Steen!" She smacked his shoulder lightly. "Let's just let it go. The sex was great. We finally did it. I need to get back to work—"

"Stop it!" He grabbed her wrist, anger roiling through him. "Don't talk like that. It wasn't sex. It was much more than that." Then he paused...sudden fear knifing through him. What if he was wrong? What if he was the only one who'd thought it was more? "Wasn't it? Or was that all it was to you? Sex?"

Her mouth opened, and then closed. Confusion flickered across her face. "I don't understand you. What do you want from me?"

"What do I want?" Swearing, he finally rolled off her. "I don't want anything *from* you. I just wanted to rebuild you after that piece of shit tore you down."

"What?" She sat up and grabbed her bra and shirt from the pile nearby. "That's why you had sex with me? As part of a restoration project or something?"

"Shit, no." He ran his hand through his hair. Hell, he was making a mockery of this. What the hell was he supposed to say to make this right? "I haven't been with a woman in years. It's not worth it to me. There's no other woman on this planet that I would have made love to today except for you. No one."

She paused with her shirt half on, staring at him. "What are you trying to say, Steen? I don't understand."

Swearing, he turned toward her. "The first time I noticed you was on the third day of my junior year. You were in eighth grade, still in middle school, and you crossed the street to the other side when you saw me walking with my friends."

Her eyes narrowed. "You and your friends were loud and obnoxious. You scared me. I always avoided you guys...until you started being different."

Guilt shot through him at the memories of the guy he had once been. "I watched you cross the street, and as soon as you got there, you stopped and knelt down. There was a baby bird that had fallen out of a nest. Do you remember?"

She blinked, her forehead wrinkled in confusion. "You were there that day?"

"Yeah, I was." He'd never forget it either. "You picked it up and made a nest for it on the handlebars of your bike. Then, you rode off down the street with it." He had been so fascinated by the gentle way she'd handled the bird. He'd never seen anyone touch a living creature with such care. "I followed you. I wanted to see where you were going."

Her eyebrows went up. "You *followed* me?"

"Yeah. You went to the nearest vet. They were closed, but you banged on the door until the vet came out. You remember what happened?"

She sat back on her heels. "Of course I do. I argued with her until she took the bird. That's when I decided to be a vet, so I could help animals"

He leaned forward. "No, that's not what happened. What happened was that she said it would cost at least five hundred dollars to treat the bird, and that if you got money from your mother, she would take care of the bird. You said your mother wouldn't pay, so she said she wouldn't help you." He would never forget the absolute determination on Erin's face, or the way she'd clenched her skinny little fists. "You said you'd work for her, and she said you were too young. So, then you said you'd trade your bike."

Erin's eyes widened. "You heard that whole exchange?"

"Hell, yeah. I thought the vet was a bitch for taking your bike. I saw you crying when you handed it over, but you never hesitated. You walked everywhere for the rest of the year." He touched her cheek softly. "You were a rich kid whose parents refused to give you a new bike. You knew that would happen, but you gave your bike away anyway to save that little bird. I'd never seen anyone do anything self-less like that in my life. I had no idea that people like you existed." He wrapped a strand of her hair around his finger. "You changed my world-view that day. There were many times in my life, especially during the last four years, when thinking of you was the only damn thing that kept me going. If you think for one second that I'd ever dishonor you by using your body, then I've completely fucked up, because all I want to do is make you understand that there's no one else in this damn world that matters except for you."

She stared at him, her mouth parted slightly, her shirt still only halfway on. She didn't say anything, and he couldn't tell what she was thinking.

"Don't you get it?" He shook his head, struggling with how to make her understand how much he valued her. "My mother ditched me at my dad's when I was twelve. She'd promised she was going to come back, like she always had before, but this time, she never did. She just disappeared. I didn't belong with my brothers, because they'd grown up there. I believed in her, and she abandoned me to a bastard who kicked the shit out of me. My brothers were almost strangers. I rode horses and played football, trying to be so impressive that I didn't need anyone. And then you showed me that sometimes, people are just kind for no reason at all. Do you understand what you gave me? What you showed me?" He spread his hands, showing all the scars on his knuckles from his father, from sports, and from horses. "This is my life, and yet you make me forget about it all."

He hadn't planned to tell her that she was the foundation that had kept him going his entire life. He knew he hadn't explained it adequately, but he didn't have better words to describe it.

Erin finished pulling her shirt on, then scooted over to him. She sat in front of him, searching his face. "You were the only person who ever, *ever* looked at me like I was special. I didn't know that you saw that thing with the bird, but the expression on your face every time you looked at me was an incredible gift. You're the reason I'm a vet and not a famous doctor. You made me feel like I was worth something just by being me. You never wanted anything from me. Ever. You just smiled at me with kindness."

He framed her face with his hands, the tight ache in his heart easing. "That's all I want," he said softly. "For you to realize how amazing you are. If I can give you that, then I now understand why it wasn't my time to die in that hospital."

Tears filled her eyes. "Why don't you care what happens after ten days? Why doesn't it bother you I'm going to leave? Why don't you want to ask me to stay?"

He closed his eyes against the urge to ask her exactly the same question. Why did she want to leave? Why did she want to return to the world that had treated her so badly? The need to drag her into his world was almost overwhelming, and he had to fight not to do it. Finally, he opened his eyes. She was staring at him, her eyes wide, waiting for his answer.

"I'll break you, if you stay with me," he said finally.

She frowned. "What? What does that mean?"

He brushed the hair back from her face. "My secrets are very bad, Erin. You won't be able to look at me the same way once you know them, and you won't be able to live with them."

She raised her brows. "Why don't you let me make that choice?"

"Because I wouldn't be able to handle it if you looked at me like I was a monster," he said quietly. "The way you look at me is all that gets me through each day. I can't afford to lose that. I can't afford for you to see me the way the rest of the world does. If you stay, you'll find out, and I don't want that."

She bit her lip, searching his face. "You're judging me," she said softly. "You think I can't see past it. That's not believing in me."

"No, it's because I do believe in you." He took her hands. "You deserve more than I could ever give you, and you would realize it. You burn for me because you've never been loved and desired this way. Once you get used to it, you'll be ready for more, for a man who can offer you more than his insatiable need for your body and your soul. I won't trap you in my life." He traced his finger over her mouth. "Sometimes the people who come into your life are supposed to stay in it forever. Other times, their impact on you is what lasts, and they're meant to become a part of your life story, and your past."

Tears brimmed in her eyes, but she pulled back, out of his reach. "I'll never force myself on someone, including you" she said stiffly. "I deserve more. I deserve someone who wants me."

He nodded. "Yeah, you do." He wanted to tell her that *he* was that guy, the one who wanted her with every fiber of his soul, but he didn't.

He had to let her go. *He had to.* So he didn't move as she retrieved the rest of her clothes, watching as all that skin disappeared under layers of cotton, designed to shut him out. She climbed down from the rock to get her boots, not even looking at him.

He knew that he was losing her, but he didn't speak up. She needed to be strong enough to walk away from something that wasn't enough for her, so he wasn't going to stop her, but at the same time, he hated the fact that she was walking away hurt. He couldn't stand knowing that he'd hurt her, but as hell was his witness, he didn't want to tell her the truth. He couldn't risk it.

But as she untied her horse and swung up into the saddle, he couldn't stop thinking about whether he could risk not telling her the truth. What if she did understand? What if she was able to see past it? Then, she would understand why he couldn't be with her, and maybe they could part without her being hurt...and maybe, just maybe...she would still look at him the same way, even knowing exactly who he was. What were the odds? Slim? None? He couldn't risk it. But at the same time, would he ever forgive himself for not trying?

CHAPTER TWELVE

ERIN PUSHED her horse hard on the way back to the ranch. She buried her hurt in the wind tearing through her hair, and in the sound of Stormy's hooves thundering on the parched ground. She let the strength of the animal fill her, and she let the speed tear a lifetime of vulnerability from her. She hated herself for letting Steen hurt her. She hated Steen for hiding secrets from her. Withholding his truth felt almost as bad as when Louis had withheld physical affection from her, because she'd believed in the connection she and Steen had.

She screamed her frustration as they galloped across the meadow, furious at herself for being so pathetic that she let so many people hurt her and manipulate her. She'd run away from her life and her job to hide out in Wyoming, and yet, she was the same person she'd been in Virginia. She was still afraid to fight for what she wanted. She still let people cut her out. She still cried silent tears when she was hurt.

She didn't want to be like this anymore.

The wind blew the tears from her cheeks as she urged the horse onward, trusting the animal to know the way home.

She was still riding hard when the ranch came into view. She was so startled by the vista that she reined Stormy in so she could get a better look. When they'd ridden away earlier, she hadn't looked back and gotten a good view. But now...it was breathtaking. The ranch house was a picturesque expanse of glass and windows, stretching across the crest of the hill. She could imagine how incredible the view was at sunset, looking out across the land, which seemed to stretch on forever.

The house looked over the three barns, which were all well-kept and impressive. A sizeable bunkhouse sat behind the barns, sunk lower behind a hill. It had no scenic view, except of the immediate area, but she still felt the immense peace of the place. In the distance, she could see animals grazing, bound by rustic wooden fences and some wire ones. Beyond the ranch, she could see the driveway leading down toward the road, but from her vantage point, she couldn't see the road. All she could see was land, animals, and the ranch buildings.

She took a deep breath, and she felt the frantic pace of her heart slow, eased by the sheer magnitude of peace that the earth seemed to breathe into her. It was pure simplicity. No fancy cars. No standards to live up to. No one who cared about anything other than taking care of animals and living from the earth.

She inhaled again, and this time, for the first time in what felt like years, she felt her lungs expand fully, taking in air that she'd never had room for.

Behind her came the steady rhythm of hoof beats, but she didn't turn around. She also didn't try to run away.

Steen rode up beside her, and reined in to a halt beside her. He said nothing, but sat astride, surveying the same vista that she was looking at it.

"It's beautiful," she said finally. "I can't believe you live here. I can feel all my stress melting away."

"The bunkhouse is just temporary," he said. "This hill we're on is my hill. If I want to build a house here, this is my spot."

She looked over at him, surprised by his comment. "*If* you want to build here? Why wouldn't you?"

He said nothing for a long moment, still staring across the field. "Because I don't belong. This is my brother's place."

She frowned. "He doesn't want you to live here?"

"No, he does. He wants all the Stockton brothers to set up home-steads. He wants us all to live together as a happy family."

She couldn't decipher the inflection of his words, and she studied his face, trying to understand what he wasn't saying. "You don't want to?"

He finally looked at her. "I didn't grow up with them. I was never a part of the group. Chase has always reached out to me, and I trust him, but I don't know the others. It's not my right to live here."

The defensive shield she'd erected so quickly around her heart seemed to weaken at his words. "It seems to me if Chase believes you have a right to live here, then you might."

"No." He took a deep breath. "I need to stay away from them for the same reason I need to stay away from you. I'm not a good guy."

She turned her horse so she could face him, her heart starting to pound. "And why do you say that?"

He met her gaze, and she saw the tension in his jaw. "My goal was to rebuild you, not hurt you, Erin. That's all that matters to me. If my withholding of the truth hurts you, then it's not the right decision." He took a deep breath, and she knew suddenly that he was going to tell her. He didn't want to, but he was going to.

And that was enough.

She held up her hand to stop him. "It's okay, Steen. I don't need to know."

His brow furrowed. "You do need to know—"

"No, I don't." She urged her horse over to him. "I know how much you don't want to tell me, but you're willing to do it to make me feel better." She put her hand on his cheek, wanting to take away all the pain in his eyes. "Am I so pathetic that I need to torment you just so I can feel better?" As she said the words, she felt a rising strength within her, a self-confidence she hadn't felt in a very long time, if ever. "I know how you feel about me. I don't need a secret to believe in you." And she knew she was right. Steen was who he was, and she believed in him. "You don't ask me to be who I'm not, so I'm not going to ask you to betray yourself."

His eyes narrowed. "You're leaving, aren't you? You're not staying tonight."

"I'm leaving in ten days."

"I meant with me. You're not staying with me, tonight. That's why you're letting me off the hook. Because you've already walked away emotionally."

"Steen—"

"I was in prison, Erin. I was in prison for four years."

Her stomach dropped and her blood ran cold. "What?"

"The day I ran into you when your car broke down, Chase had just picked me up from prison." He gestured at the blue sky. "I haven't seen the sky in four years. I hadn't been able to make my own choice about where I go, what I eat, or when I sleep for four years. I'm on parole. I'm still not free. I can't leave the state. I have to get a job and report in, like a fucking kid who might get in trouble if he's not kept busy." His eyes were blazing. "I'm an ex-con, Erin, and I always will be."

She felt like she was going to throw up. Steen had been in prison? "For what? Why were you in there?" There had to be an explanation. Something that made sense.

"Attempted murder."

～

STEEN STEELED himself as he watched Erin's face blanch in response to his undiplomatic announcement. She looked like she was going to pass out. Shit. He really wished he'd learned tact at some point in his life.

"Attempted murder?" she echoed, her voice faint. "Who?"

He gritted his teeth, but he was committed now. "You remember Rachel?" God, he hated to say the words. He hated to relive that moment. But it would haunt him forever. He'd relived it every day for the last four years. Saying it aloud wouldn't bring back the memories. The memories were always there, at the front of his mind. But saying it aloud would reveal it to Erin, and that...shit...that just felt really, really bad.

Her jaw dropped open. "You tried to murder *her*?"

Shocked ripped through him. "Shit, no. Is that what you think of me? You think I'd try to murder a woman?"

Her eyes widened. "No, of course not, but you just said—"

"Her husband," he clarified. This was unraveling fast. Shit. He had no idea how to handle this. "You remember when I said that her husband caught us?"

She nodded mutely, her eyes wide.

"Well, when he walked into the hotel room and found us together, he was pissed, drunk, and carrying a knife." Hell, he remembered every detail of that night.

Erin's hand went to her heart. "A knife? What kind of knife?"

"The kind you use if you're some commando wannabe who thinks he's a badass." He could still remember the size of the blade as it slashed toward him. He'd never forget the drunken howl of rage as the bastard took a swipe, or the feel of the metal plunging into his shoulder as he ducked. "He went right for my throat. I dodged it, but he hit my shoulder." He instinctively touched the scar, a visceral reminder of how stupid he'd been to trust Rachel when she'd invited him back to her room. He'd been so unaware of what was about to happen, completely clueless that she'd left the door open for the sole reason of getting caught by her husband, just to pay him back for cheating on her. He'd been used, and he'd had no fucking idea until it was too late. "He came after me again, but when I deflected the blow, I knocked him down. His knife hit his neck and sliced *his* jugular." He would never forget the scent of blood, or how bright red it was. There had been so much blood. The screams of Rachel, and the way her husband's breath had started to gurgle—

"Steen." Erin touched his arm, jerking him back to the present. "Are you okay?"

He stared at her hand on his arm. She was touching him. On purpose. Even though she knew what he'd done. He dragged his gaze off her hand and looked at her. "They said I had attacked him. Rachel said I tricked her into letting me into the hotel room, and that I was sexually assaulting her. She claimed her husband heard me in the hall, and he broke in to save his wife. They said it was my knife, and I attacked him without provocation. They both testified that I went to her room to punish her for rejecting me at the bar earlier that evening. It was their testimony that made the jury not believe my self-defense plea. Four years in prison."

And that was it. The truth. The entire, ugly truth.

Erin removed her hand from his. "How did you get stabbed this last time? That happened in prison, right?"

He frowned, trying to follow her questioning. Why had she changed the subject? Why wasn't she peppering him with questions, challenging his slant of the story? He shrugged noncommittally. "I stepped in front of a knife. Bad timing."

She cocked her head, studying him. "What really happened, Steen?"

He gritted his jaw. "A new kid was targeted. It was his first day, and I knew he had no defense. I was getting out soon, and I didn't give a shit if I died. So, I took the hit for him."

Her eyes widened. "You stepped in front of the knife and let the guy stab you?"

He shrugged. "Yeah, well, someone had to help the kid."

"No, no one had to. You just did." She took a breath, and let it out. "Okay."

He frowned. "Okay, what?"

"I'll stay with you tonight."

It took a full minute for her words to register. "What?"

She managed a half-smile, though her eyes were still wary. "I believe it was self-defense with Rachel's husband, Steen. I was on the receiving end of her barbs enough times to know she very well could be the kind of person to lie on a witness stand to exonerate herself, so the conviction means nothing to me. I believe *you*. I'm so incredibly sorry that she betrayed you like that, and then left you to rot in prison. It's not fair. It's wrong. I know nothing I say can change the fact you had to endure it, but it's still wrong."

He felt something tighten in his chest, and for a minute, he had trouble breathing. There was no acrimony or judgement in her words, and her hand was still on his arm. She knew he was an ex-con, imprisoned for attempted murder, and *she was still touching him*. "You don't care?"

"Of course I care." She moved her horse closer. "I am so sorry that you endured that. And I'm so sorry you almost died. But I'm so glad that you were able to save the life of that man, whose family is probably very happy they didn't get a phone call that someone they loved died that day. Maybe you were meant to be there. Maybe you had to be in prison because he had to be saved. He's a good guy, isn't he? The man you saved?"

Somehow, it didn't surprise him that Erin would assume a prison inmate might be a "good guy." And she was right. "Yeah, he is." He thought of the kid's dad. "His family was glad he was okay," he admitted, mulling over her words. He'd never thought of it that way. He'd never considered the fact that Pointer would be dead now if he hadn't been in prison. It was weird to consider that, although he didn't exactly buy into the fact that he had been destined to save him all along.

Erin smiled then, and wrapped her arms around his neck. "I believe in you, Steen. Build your house here. Make a home. You deserve it."

Build your house here. God, the words were too much. She actually believed he belonged here, that he deserved to call this place home. "Erin." Her name was a throaty whisper as he wrapped his arm around her waist and dragged her off her horse onto his lap. She snuggled into him immediately. Her body was soft and warm against his, and she felt so damn right in his arms. "You have to go home," he said, even as he threaded his fingers through her hair, pressing his face into the curve of her shoulder, inhaling the scent he would always associate with her: that delicate flowery scent that was too elusive to identify. "You would never fit in here."

She lifted her face to his. "I'm a vet, Steen. I do animals. Isn't a ranch exactly where I might fit?"

Something seemed to stick in his chest, a memory of so long ago when his mother had made a promise to always be there, and then she'd disappeared. A familiar shield tightened around his chest. "Don't make promises, Erin. We both know we're a couple of broken people right now, and we're helping each other. But that's short term. When you heal, and you realize how amazing you are, life with an ex-con isn't going to sound so good."

Her brow furrowed. "Steen—"

"No." He put his finger over her lips. "Don't make any promises." He'd believed in Rachel when they were in high school, and he'd sure as hell believed in her when he'd run into her five years ago. He didn't want promises from Erin, because they hurt when they were broken. Erin wouldn't mean to break her promise, but she would, because there was no way she would be able to live his life, with the stigma he'd carry forever. "Just make it about today. That's all I want."

She studied him for a long moment, then nodded. "Okay. Today then." She draped her arms around his neck. "I have to go get my stuff. I'll be back early evening. Sound good?"

Good? A warmth began to spread through him, a deep satisfaction he hadn't felt in a very long time. "Yeah. It does." He kissed her again, not a long one, just enough to make a statement.

A statement that he was going to keep her, for as long as she was willing to stay.

And then, he was going to let her go, even if it was the most difficult thing he'd ever done in his life.

CHAPTER THIRTEEN

"WE'RE GOING ON A DATE."

At Steen's announcement, Erin looked up from filing the last notes from the day's patients in Josie's antiquated filing cabinets. There were no electronic files here, which Erin actually found sort of refreshing. She was so accustomed to a life of gleaming medical equipment and patients worth hundreds of thousands of dollars. It was such a shift to be dealing with animals who simply lived with the people who owned them, animals who mattered for reasons other than as a million dollar investment. She'd spent the morning driving to assorted ranches, and the afternoon had been spent in office hours. She'd seen three large mixed-breed dogs, a Chihuahua, a gecko, and sixteen cats, the latter of which had all been owned by the same woman. She was really hoping the cat lady wasn't a warning from the universe about what her future held now that she was divorced and hopelessly infatuated with a man who had absolutely zero interest in pursuing anything long term.

She and Steen had talked deeply over the last few days about his past and hers, but he'd continuously made it apparent that he believed their time together had to end when her stint as Josie's replacement was over. He'd erected a wall between them that she couldn't break through. She was incredibly frustrated with him. Why did he think she cared that he had been in prison? He was innocent, and she didn't need a pardon from the governor to know that.

But Steen was stubborn, and twice he'd actually walked out when she'd pushed too hard.

But now, he was here, at her office, looking like a civilized, incredibly handsome fantasy man as he lounged in the doorway of the clinic's business office. He was still wearing his battered cowboy hat, but his dark blue jeans looked brand new, as did his blue plaid shirt that made his eyes vibrant. Even his well-creased cowboy boots had clearly been polished up for the night. His jeans were low on his hips, showcasing his lean physique and his broad shoulders. He was almost clean-shaven, with a hint of whiskered shadow on his face, as if he couldn't quite eliminate it. In the short time since she'd reconnected with him, he'd already put on weight, and his stamina had improved. He was healing quickly, and he no longer looked like a man who'd almost died recently. He looked, in fact, like a dangerous predator ready to eat her up... which was a really, really tantalizing thought. She couldn't keep the anticipation from fluttering through her as she watched him lounge against the doorframe, looking so deliciously masculine that she was pretty sure he would be illegal in certain states.

Yes, indeed, there was nothing weak about him anymore. He'd been putting on serious muscle, which she knew from the last few nights in his bed, learning exactly how amazing it was to be truly desired by a man. The fact that Steen was tireless in his dedication to finding out exactly what she liked and what she didn't had made for some very late nights and some incredible discoveries.

It had been the best days of her life...and she was all too aware the clock was ticking. There were only six days left until she had to leave. Six days until he would gently, but firmly, kick her out the door and back to her life.

Her throat constricted, but she lifted her chin. No. She wasn't going to think about that.

If he could keep his distance, then so could she. She leaned back in her chair and laced her fingers through her hair. "Maybe I don't want to go on a date with you. Did you think of asking, instead of demanding?"

"I considered it, but I didn't want to give you the opportunity to say no." He produced a bouquet of roses from behind his back and held them out. "For you."

She stared at the flowers, too surprised to react. "No one has ever brought me flowers before." Damn him. The moment she resolved to pull back from him, he had to give her *flowers.* With a resigned sigh, she shook her head, knowing full well that if six more days were all she could have with him, then she'd take those six days and imprint every last second in her memory.

"Then you, my dear, have led a deprived life in which you've been surrounded by idiots." He levered himself off the doorframe and strode across the small office toward her. She couldn't help the shiver of anticipation as he walked around the desk toward her. He plucked the pen out of her hand, clasped her wrist, and pulled her to her feet with just enough force to send her tumbling against his chest.

Then he wrapped his arm around her waist, locking her against him, and kissed her. She should have been accustomed to being kissed by him, but even after several days of constant attention, she still felt her heart leap every time his mouth descended upon hers. Sometimes his kiss was gentle. Sometimes it was demanding and rough. Sometimes it was flirty and mischievous. And other times, like this, it was a sensual kiss that promised an eternity.

This was her favorite kiss.

With a sigh of pure contentment, she draped her arms around his neck and leaned into him, kissing him back, thoroughly enjoying the prickle of his whiskers against her face, and the feel of his lips against hers. He was pure, dangerous seduction, and she'd never felt so alive.

Just as the kiss began to change into something that was going to lead to naked-office-time, he pulled back, but he didn't release her. "That's for later. Right now, I want to take you out."

She lightly grasped the front of his shirt and tugged him gently. "You don't need to court me, Steen. I know you don't have any money, and I'm a sure thing tonight anyway."

Darkness flickered in his eyes, but it wasn't seduction. It was anger, and she realized she shouldn't have mentioned the money. "I can afford to take you to dinner," he said, his voice on edge. "I'm not that pathetic."

"I didn't mean—"

He shoved the flowers in her hand. "I'll be outside if you want to come. If you don't, that's fine." He turned and walked out without another word, leaving her holding the most beautiful flowers she'd ever received...well, the only flowers she'd ever received from a man, standing there in her dirty jeans, muddy hiking boots, and "didn't bother to shower this morning" hair.

She should have known better than to bring up the finances. No man wanted to feel like he couldn't support a woman. Dammit. Frustrated, she grabbed her purse and followed him out of the building.

He was leaning against the front fender of one of the ranch's pickup trucks, his arms folded over his chest. His hat was tipped low over his forehead, but she felt his gaze the moment she stepped outside.

After locking the door, she walked over to him and stopped just in front of him.

He didn't move.

She sighed and flicked his hat back so she could see his face. "Stop it."

He narrowed his eyes. "Stop what?"

"Being a shit."

His eyebrows nearly shot off his forehead. "Did you just swear at me? You never curse."

"I reserve them for appropriate moments, like this one." She set her hands on her hips. "Listen, Steen. I get that you have baggage. Between your mom ditching you, your loser dad, and your lack of bond with your brothers, I understand you have no comprehension of how much you have to offer. I realize the impact that a prison record could have on your future. I understand all that, but I'll be honest, at some point, you have to get over it. Move on." She held out her arms and gestured at herself. "Look at what's right in front of you, and appreciate it, because before you know it, it will be gone."

He stared at her for a long moment, and then sighed. "I'm sorry."

"For what?"

"For being a shit." The corner of his mouth quirked. "You're right. I know you better than that, and I know that you didn't mean it as an insult when you questioned my ability to pay for dinner. Just because I expect to be judged by people in general doesn't make it fair that I reacted that way to you." He held out his hand. "May I have a second chance, fair maiden? I'd like to take you out on the town tonight, on my dime, of which I am sure I can scrape up a sufficient number to pay for dinner, and I promise I won't take offense at any prison jokes you might make. Deal?"

Her irritation fled, and she shook his hand. "Deal."

He grinned. "Then we have a date."

A date. Her first official date with Steen, more than a decade since she'd first seen him.

Hot damn.

~

STEEN REALLY DIDN'T CARE about the menu. He'd barely glanced at the wine list before ordering one. And he hadn't even bothered to try the bread that the waiter had left on the table.

It was all about Erin tonight. That was it. Just Erin. She was the only thing he wanted to notice, the only thing he *could* notice. She simply outshone every other damn thing in existence.

Her eyes were sparkling, and she was sexy as hell in her jeans and tee shirt. She'd complained about going to dinner in her work clothes, but he hadn't let her go home to change. He preferred her this way: natural, casual, and happy. Plus, he'd been half-afraid she'd change her mind about going out if she got home. Another part of him had also been concerned that she might put on some fancy outfit for dinner, reminding them both that she was out of his league. As a rural vet in her jeans and tee shirt, she was accessible, vulnerable, and reachable. She was a real person, and he was able to simply be with *her*. He knew, however, that simple and casual weren't her real life, and if she got dressed up, it would be a constant reminder that she belonged somewhere else. Yeah, he knew she did, but tonight, he wanted it to be just about them. Besides, he liked her this way. He'd told her she looked beautiful exactly as she was and he'd meant every word of it.

The last four days of making love to her in his bunkhouse every night had been incredible. He couldn't believe how responsive she was to him, how completely she trusted him. It was surreal and amazing. He knew that this time with her would somehow sustain him for the rest of his life when the reality of his existence descended after her departure.

He knew she would have been perfectly fine with another night over the grill behind the bunkhouse, but he wanted more for her. He wanted her to know what it felt like to be taken out for a nice dinner. He wanted her to know that he was proud to be with her. It was important to him that she understand that, so he'd made the decision to venture out into town for the first time since his release from prison.

He'd chosen a classy restaurant in the adjoining town, hoping that he wouldn't run into anyone who would know him and where he'd been for four years. In the town where he'd once been a superstar, the big man on campus, he now wanted nothing more than to be anonymous, so he could treat Erin to the night she deserved. He wanted her to enjoy herself, not be burdened by the history of the man she was with.

Steen was aware the place wasn't as fancy as she was used to, but it was about as high class as he was going to find in the area. The wine glasses looked appropriately sparkly. He figured the white tablecloths were up to standard, and even he had to admit the candlelight was romantic. He didn't consider himself a romantic. As a general rule, he saw candles as potential fire hazards and a waste of a good flame, but for the first time in his life, they made him think of the softness of her skin, and the way her hair felt beneath his fingers.

Erin leaned back in her chair, surveying the small restaurant. "It's amazing. Thank you."

He shrugged as the waiter approached with their wine. "It's what you deserve. I want you to know that I'm proud to be with you."

She grinned at him, and leaned forward, her fingers brushing against his in a public display of affection that made something inside him shift. She wasn't afraid to acknowledge she was with him. He'd half-thought she wouldn't want to be seen in public with an ex-con, but not only had she agreed to come to dinner, but she was *touching* him. The thought shook him to his core as he looked down at her fingers tapping the back of his hand.

"Thank you," she said. "I'm having a great time."

He considered moving his hand away for her own protection, but he couldn't make himself do it. Instead, he flipped his hand over and wrapped his fingers around hers. "You're welcome." He grinned at her, and she smiled back, an intimate exchange that was only about them, and their connection. He leaned forward, lowering his voice. "Erin—"

"Steen Stockton? Is that you?"

Steen's entire body tensed as his name was called from across the room, and he quickly pulled his hand away from Erin's. He saw the look of surprise on her face, but he didn't have time to apologize as he turned toward the door. When he saw the man striding toward him, his gut dropped down to his boots. Shit. He was sunk.

Swearing under his breath, he rose to his feet and shook hands with Walt Parker, one of the Rogue Valley High School alums who had funded much of the football team's expenses when Steen had been playing for them. He knew Walt well, or he had, back before his life had imploded.

Walt thudded his hand on Steen's shoulder, then pulled back to inspect him. The older man's face was leathery from years in the sun, but he was as fit and lean as ever, easily recognizable as the man who'd held the passing record at the school for a decade until Steen had broken it. "Good to see you, Steen. It's been too long."

Steen glanced at Erin, who was watching with interest. "Um, yeah, I've been busy." He wasn't sure whether Walt knew what had happened with Rachel. God help him, he didn't want Erin to endure the stigma he'd carry for the rest of his life.

"You come by to see the display, in honor of the school's fiftieth anniversary?" Walt asked.

Steen frowned. "What display?"

"You didn't recognize the table by the front door when you came in? Or the chair you're sitting in?" Walt's eyebrows shot up. "Or the buffet where the wine display is set up?"

Steen's gaze shot to the chair that his hand was still on. He recognized the design immediately. He glanced at the wine display, and remembered all too well the hours he'd spent in that crappy basement carving the table by hand. It looked good, weathered properly. Behind him, was the dining room table he'd made to seat all his brothers after their dad had busted up their table in one of his rages. All his work, furniture he'd labored over as a teenager, back when spending hours building furniture had been his only respite from the life that stalked him. "Where did you get those?"

"Your stuff is all over the area. I buy 'em up when I see 'em." He grinned. "I have to support my fellow ball players, right, my man?" He pointed to a painting by the front door. "That's from Don Simms, a wide receiver who was a few years ahead of you." He winked. "Between you and me, he wasn't all that talented, but he's one of us, so his stuff hangs."

Steen frowned, still trying to process what he'd inadvertently stumbled into, an apparent shrine to his high school football team. "You own this place? What about the winery you were running?"

"I still own it, but I decided I wanted to teach people about the beauty of pairing fine wine with good food." Walt grinned. "Tonight's dinner is on me." He bowed at Erin. "Any woman accompanying a former RVHS football player dines on the house. Welcome, my dear. My treat tonight." He shook Steen's hand again and then headed off to another table, waxing poetically about the wine.

Steen sat back down to find Erin staring at him. "You build furniture?"

"I used to. I built furniture for my mom and me because we couldn't afford to buy it. I liked doing it, and so I built some stuff to sell." He scowled, staring at his wine, irritated that he'd managed to choose the only restaurant in the area where he would know the damned owner. At the same time, he felt an immense sense of relief that his past hadn't come up, though now that he'd been identified, it was possible that his veil of invisibility could slide off at any moment. "Once my mom left me with my dad, I kept building stuff, trying to save enough money so when she came back for me, I could take care of her. In the end, the old man found my stash of cash when I was at a game and he used it on a prostitute—"

He paused when Erin got up and walked away from the table toward the buffet behind him.

He twisted around to watch as she approached the buffet, tensing as she crouched beside it and ran her hand down the leg. He remembered the mistake he'd made on that one, taking a divot out of the inside. It figured that would be the one she'd choose to inspect.

She spent several minutes at the buffet, then walked over to the table by the door. Steen shifted restlessly, uncomfortably with her close inspections, but at the same time, he was sort of...well...he wasn't sure what he thought of her interest.

After a few minutes, she came and sat back down across from him. She folded her arms over her chest and studied him.

He waited.

She didn't say anything.

Finally, he couldn't stand it anymore. "Well?"

"You have a gift."

Stupidly, he felt like grinning. He knew that the furniture was decent. It was the only thing besides football and horses that he was any good at, and her response felt really good. But he simply shrugged, pretending it wasn't a big deal. "It's been a long time."

"It's not furniture. It's art." She leaned forward. "What other art have you done?"

He shifted. "Nothing."

"Do you draw? Paint? Make mosaics out of horse manure?"

He grinned that time. "No, just the furniture, but if I can't find a job, I'll be sure and consider the horse manure as a possible career choice."

She didn't smile. "I'm serious, Steen. Do you like making furniture?"

He shrugged again. "I don't know. I just did it. Like I said, it's been a long time." He picked up his glass, letting the red wine glisten beneath the dim lights. "Tonight is about you, not furniture. I raise my glass to the most incredible woman I've ever met in my life, whose soul lights my way and has since the day I first saw her."

Erin's face softened, and she smiled. "That's beautiful. Thank you." She grinned at him, her eyes teasing. "But I know you're avoiding the topic. Why don't you want to talk about the furniture?"

He put the glass down. "Because it's from a long time ago. I can't make a living at it, and I can't take it with me when I move on."

"Move on?" She frowned. "To where? You've decided not to stay at the ranch?"

"I don't belong there. I never did."

She leaned forward. "Do you *want* to stay?"

He met her gaze, and suddenly, he wanted to say yes. He wanted to stay with her on that damned ranch and do nothing else but lose himself in her for the rest of his life. But that wasn't reality. Making love to her all day wouldn't feed them or give them a life. And he wasn't going to live off the pity of half-brothers who didn't need his shit. "I need to go. I don't belong there."

When she opened her mouth to protest, he put his hand over hers. "I don't want to talk about it, Erin. I just want this to be about you."

She wrinkled her nose at him. "You're being a toad."

He grinned. "A toad? Really? How's that?"

"I'm a woman. I don't like to be ignored when I have something to say."

He sighed and leaned back in his seat. The last thing he wanted to do was disempower her. Shit. He didn't know how to do this supportive guy thing. "Okay, talk."

Her faced softened. "Really?"

The vulnerability in her expression severed the last bit of resistance he had. He leaned forward, lowering his voice. "Erin, listen to me. Yeah, I don't want to talk about my relationship with my half-brothers, or my life. I'm a mess. I get that. There's no way to fix it or to change what my life has been, or to erase all the black marks on my past. I think you're the kindest, most optimistic woman on the face of the planet because you actually care enough to want to fix it. It matters to me what you think. If you have something you want to say, then I'll sit here and listen to every word until you're finished."

She studied him for a long moment. "You don't have to be defined by your past," she finally said.

He sighed, realizing she wasn't going to take his thinly veiled suggestion to talk about sunsets and nakedness instead of his life. "I agree. It doesn't define me, but at the same time, it's a part of who I am."

She cocked her head, studying him. "You don't want to be here, do you?"

He frowned. "Of course I do. I want to take you to a nice dinner."

"But not here." She gestured at the tablecloth. "This isn't your kind of place, is it?"

Well, there was no way to deny that truth, so he shrugged one shoulder. "I wanted to do something nice for you."

"Which I appreciate very much." She reached across the table and took his hand. "Here's the thing, Steen. I haven't thought of you every day for the last decade because you're the kind of guy who will take me out for dinner at a restaurant with linen napkins. The man who matters to me is the one who grew up dirt poor and came to school with holes in his jeans. He's the one who was willing to fight the bullies and get black eyes if he had to. The man who would work all day under the broiling sun to help a horse." She leaned forward. "I came back here to get away from white tablecloths, Steen. That's not what I want. I want *you,* exactly the way you are. So, if tonight was about you, where would we be eating? Where would the real Steen choose for his first night out in four years?"

Heat seemed to pour through him at her words. For a moment, he could only stare at her as her words tumbled through him, igniting a fire that seemed to burn right through his belly. She was absolutely right. He didn't want to be here. He wanted to be somewhere where the very pulse of life beat through him and called to him. For four years, he'd lived in a world that left his soul silent and empty. He didn't want to be there anymore. He wanted to be alive.

Silently, he tossed cash on the table to pay for their untouched wine, stood up, and held out his hand to her.

Her face lit up, and she put her hand into his. "Where are we off to, cowboy?"

He locked his arm around her back and dragged her up against him. He knew it wasn't proper, but in that moment, he didn't give a damn. He kissed her anyway, hot, wet, and with all the raging passion she'd just unleashed inside him. She melted into his body, kissing him back with every bit of the same need that he'd poured into her.

Swearing, he broke the kiss. "I want to rip your clothes off," he whispered. "But first, I want to take you somewhere."

She smiled. "It's about time."

CHAPTER FOURTEEN

ERIN FELT her entire body relax when she walked into the Saddle Rack Tavern with Steen. The crowded bar was low lit, with unfinished wood beams, chandeliers made of battered wagon wheels, and tables that looked like they'd been recycled from old barns. There was a band on the low corner stage, four twenty-something guys in cowboy hats and blue jeans, winking at the audience with such charm she almost wanted to swoon herself.

The place was rowdy with the rumble of good-natured conversation. Almost every man had a cowboy hat on, and Wranglers were on just about every person she saw. The women came in all types: some who looked like they could wrangle a steer as well as any man, but there were also ones who weren't afraid to show they were a woman who could clean up just fine. There wasn't a single suit in sight, and no diamond earring studs flashing in the dim lighting.

It was real, without airs, and it felt like the home she'd never had.

She slid her hand into Steen's and leaned against his arm. "It's perfect."

He grinned down at her, a smile so genuine and full that she felt her heart flutter. Despite all the time she'd spent with him over the last few days, she'd always felt a sense of distance from him. It had felt as if he'd been holding back, and now that she saw the light dancing in his eyes, she realized she'd been right.

She hadn't seen the real Steen until now. Well, she's seen parts of his true self, but he'd been guarded, unwilling to let her truly see who he was. Right now, though, he looked...happy. Comfortable. Like he belonged. "It's been a long time since I've been here," he said, his dark eyes sparkling. "Any interest in a quick spin on the dance floor before we eat?"

"Dance?" She hadn't danced in years. The thought of having Steen's strong arms wrapped around her on the dance floor made excitement rush through her. How awesome did that sound? There was something so magical about being held in a man's arms while the music wove through her soul. "I'd love to dance. Really?"

"You bet." He led the way through the crowd, threading easily across the room to a dark corner of the sparsely populated dance floor. There were hardly any people dancing, but Steen didn't appear to care. The moment they reached the spot he'd apparently wanted, he turned toward her and pulled her into his arms.

The song was upbeat with a contagious rhythm, but Steen locked her against him anyway. He put one hand on her lower back, took her hand, and then began to move her around the dance floor. His dancing was effortless, in perfect time to the beat, and he moved his hips like he was made for music, sweeping her with him. He grinned at her as he spun her around, keeping her so tight against him it was as if they were moving as a single unit. Laughter bubbled up through her as they danced. The music seemed to come alive inside her, and her heart felt lighter than it ever had.

"God, you're gorgeous." He pulled her closer, so close that their knees bumped. He immediately slid his knee between hers, and suddenly, they were moving even more tightly together, their bodies moving in perfect unison, threaded together from shoulder to knee. He directed her with both the pressure of his hand on her lower back, and the unspoken commands of his body, turning her with his hips, his shoulders, and his torso.

She realized he was singing to her as they danced, the words to the song whispered in her ear in perfect tune as he whirled her around. His voice was beautiful, so melodic and deep she knew he could easily be on stage instead of on the dance floor. Music flowed through him as if it were a part of him, and he brought her into that magical circle, moving her with such indefinable grace and musicality that she felt as if she were being whirled around by a breeze on a perfect spring day.

Except it wasn't a breeze. It was the raw, untamed strength of his body that was moving her, and she was locked against him by his hand on her back, and the angle he was holding her. He was leaning forward slightly, using his body as a shield to tuck her against him. She felt as though she were completely protected from everything, cradled by the strength of his presence while still being swept away by the grace of his dancing.

She was so aware of every place their bodies touched. Her skin seemed to tingle everywhere, and she wanted to laugh aloud with happiness. She'd never felt so free, so adored, or so graceful.

The song ended, but he didn't even hesitate, never breaking stride as he merged their dance into the next song, effortlessly adjusting their steps to the new beat. She was astounded by what a wonderful dancer he was, so hopelessly out of her class.

"Just let me lead you," he whispered to her, his voice so deep and sexy that heat seemed to ignite deep in her belly. "Feel the music in your soul and let it fill you. Feel my body against yours, and let yourself connect with me. Follow me, sweetheart. I won't let you fall." He pressed a kiss to her earlobe, still keeping her tucked up against him as he spun them across the floor. "Just feel my soul touching yours, and you'll be with me."

Her throat constricted with sudden emotion, but she closed her eyes, focusing her entire being on Steen. She felt the heat of his body through her clothes, and the sheer hardness of his frame against her. Yet, at the same time, she became aware of the fluidity of his hips, moving against hers. She focused on the movement of his body, softening her muscles, relaxing into him. The moment she did so, she felt herself melt into him, and suddenly, she was completely in sync with him.

Her body seemed to know exactly what Steen wanted from her, and it became effortless to move in unison with him. Her thigh was between his, but she never tripped over his feet or even moved the opposite way of him. The dance became true beauty, filling her with the sheer presence of Steen, and the magic of the music uplifting her.

"You've got it," Steen whispered against her ear as they whirled across the floor. "We're completely connected. God, you're hot. I could dance with you every second for the rest of my life, and it still wouldn't be enough."

Sheer delight bubbled up through her. "You're an incredible dancer."

"Inspired by you," he replied, pressing a kiss to the side of her neck without losing the beat. "I only dance when I'm at peace inside, otherwise I can't feel the music at all. You need to have a completely quiet soul to hear the music. It's like working with troubled horses. The magic happens in the inner silence of the soul."

His words were so heartfelt, she felt her throat tighten. This was the man who thought he wasn't good enough for his brothers? Or to take his place in his family? God, he was beautiful, and not just his face. His soul was pure and beautiful, just as she'd always known. She knew she was catching a precious glimpse that he never shared, an inside peek at the man he tried so hard to hide.

Instinctively, she tightened her grip on his shoulder. "That was beautiful," she said. "Kiss me."

He lifted his head from where he'd had it tucked against the side of hers. His eyes were dark and beautiful, peaceful for the first time she could remember. He searched her face for a moment, and then he kissed her.

The kiss was different than it had ever been before. It was sensual and demanding, as always, but this time, there was something else. An emotion. A need. A connection. She realized it was the first time Steen had kissed her with all of himself, instead of holding back and giving her only the part of himself he was willing to give.

There was a tenderness to his kiss now. A softness. A realness. It was a kiss that touched her heart in a way that it had never been touched.

Steen cradled her face as he kissed her, his touch so gentle she felt as though she could be made of the most fragile china and she would still be safe in his arms. She wrapped her fingers around his wrists, kissing him back until she felt like her heart was going to explode.

It wasn't until she heard the catcalls and the whistles that she realized the music had stopped.

Heat flooded her cheeks as she pulled back, but Steen didn't let her retreat. He kissed her again, longer, and her heart seemed to soar when she realized he didn't care about the whistles or the attention. He wasn't finished kissing her, and he had no plans to stop until he was done.

With a happy sigh, she melted back into him and enjoyed every last moment of the kiss until he finally pulled back, just enough to break the kiss, but his body was still against hers, and his hands still cradled her face.

He grinned at her, and kissed the tip of her nose. "Hey."

She smiled back. "Hi."

"That was fun."

She giggled at his understatement. "Yes, it was."

"Want to dance again when the band comes back on stage?"

She rolled her eyes. "What do you think?"

He kissed the tip of her nose. "I'll take that as a yes." He kissed her one last time, a deep, delicious kiss of connection, and then swung his arm over her shoulder, tucking her up against him as he escorted her off the dance floor. "This place makes great burgers. You up for that?"

"Of course." It felt so natural to be nestled against him, and she wasn't blind to the appreciative glances of the other women as they walked toward an empty table. She also noticed that Steen didn't even noticed the women gawking at him. He was drop-dead gorgeous, yet he had no awareness of it whatsoever. He was simply watching her. After having her husband leave her for another woman, the fact that Steen was literally unaware of the feminine adoration he was receiving was so amazing.

It was incredible to be the focus of his attention. She was so accustomed to being barely seen, that to have Steen entirely focused on her was almost surreal. It felt incredible. She grinned at him. "You make me feel amazing. Thank you."

"Hey." He paused at an empty table and pulled her against him.

"You're the one who deserves the thanks. I forgot what it felt like to be alive. You've changed everything for me."

"Mutual benefit, then." She couldn't keep the smile off her face as he pulled out the chair for her. "Thanks."

"You bet." He eased into the seat adjacent to hers, immediately resting his hand on the back of her chair. There was no doubt about the fact that he was claiming her, and she loved it. He made her feel like she was the most special woman in the entire world, and it felt incredible.

She didn't want to go back home to her life. She wanted to stay with Steen, to feel every moment of the way he made her feel. The depth of her need stunned her, and she realized that if he asked her right now, she would stay.

The realization was shocking, and terrifying. Would she really give up everything she'd worked so hard to achieve for a man who made her feel alive? She had spent her entire life dedicating every last inch of herself to what she'd finally managed to achieve professionally. She'd developed self-worth through her work accomplishments, because she hadn't been able to earn it in her personal life. Steen thought she was a simple vet, but she wasn't. She was a highly specialized equine orthopedic surgeon, specializing in elite, expensive athletes, and she could never do here what she did in her real life. In this area, there weren't many horses of that extreme caliber, the surgery facilities didn't exist, and most potential clients didn't have the money to pay for that kind of work. If she walked away from what she'd accomplished and put herself entirely in the hands of Steen, what would she have left for herself? What would she have to fall back upon when he realized he wanted something else, someone else? Her chest tightened, and suddenly she felt sick to her stomach. Would she really consider giving all that up for him, if he asked? She'd given everything to try to impress her husband and her parents. Was she actually willing to give it all up for another man?

His eyes narrowed. "What?"

She blinked. "What?"

"You were just thinking something serious. I saw it in your eyes. What's up?"

She shook her head, trying to erase the thoughts from her head. She didn't want to ruin this moment with real life. "Nothing."

He cocked an eyebrow. "Don't lie to me. I know it's not nothing."

She sighed, wrinkling her nose at him in exasperation. "Okay, fine. I was thinking something, but I don't want to tell you."

He eyed her speculatively, and she knew he was considering whether to force it out of her. The last thing she wanted was to talk about how they had no future together, or to even tell him what she'd been thinking. He didn't want a future with her, and to offer him her own future would be against everything she'd worked so hard to achieve.

So, instead, she turned the tables on him. "When you compared dancing to communicating with horses, it made me think about your incredible talent with horses. Don't you have any interest in working with them anymore? You could do that at the ranch." He opened his mouth to protest, and she rushed on. "None of your brothers have your gift. You're the only one who could bring that to the ranch. How can you think you don't add value?"

He said nothing for a long moment, leaning back as a waitress stopped by to take their order. Erin knew he was aware of her attempt to change the subject and he was contemplating whether to let her go ahead with it, or force her back to what he wanted to talk about.

After the waitress was gone, however, Steen answered her question. "Horses aren't my thing anymore."

"Why not?"

"I gave it up to play football."

"But you don't play anymore." She knew she hadn't mistaken the depth of emotion when he'd spoken about the horses. It hadn't been there when he'd talked about the furniture, and it hadn't been there when he'd talked about the football days with Walt, but there had been no mistaking it when he'd mentioned the horses. "Why are you resisting the ranch? Help me understand."

"I quit horses because there was no future. No one respected people who deal with horses. I wanted to get the hell out of my life and be someone, and football was the answer, so that's what I did." Steen let out his breath, looking across the bar. Finally, he looked back at her. "My knee healed after I graduated high school, and I was able to get to college on a full ride. It was my only chance out of my hell. I played three seasons, and then I blew out my knee again, this time for good. I had put everything into football, and I had no backup plan. So, I started riding dirt bikes. It was a rush of adrenaline, a way to outrun the reality of my life, like the fact that my job was pumping gas in a crappy station that was so filthy that even the cockroaches wouldn't rob it."

Erin leaned forward, listening intently. "Did you race the dirt bikes?"

"Yeah. I crashed. I severed my spine." His voice was neutral, but she felt the sudden withdrawal of his energy, as if he were battling memories he didn't want to deal with. "The doctors told me I'd never walk again. They said I was paralyzed for life." He looked at her, and she saw the stark anguish in his eyes. "I was twenty-one years old. The only thing I knew was sports. I had nothing, Erin. Absolutely nothing. It was the scariest moment of my entire life."

Her heart tightened. "But you walk now."

"I fought back with everything I had. I had no insurance to pay for fancy physical therapy. It was all me, and I got my legs working again. I won, and then I lost it all again, and again. Everything I tried, I lost, until I ended up in prison for attempted murder." He leaned forward, his voice low. "But I am scared out of my mind that I'll hurt my back again. If I fall off a horse the wrong way, I'm done. My entire horse career was helping the ones that no one else could handle. I have no interest in shoveling manure for the rest of my life or hauling hay bales around. The only thing I'd want to do on this ranch is deal with the horses that no one else can help, and those are the animals that just might send me back into the worst hell you can ever imagine."

She understood then. She understood everything that drove him. He was afraid, the kind of soul-deep terror that could destroy a life forever. She knew, because she'd lived with that every day of her life. Not the fear of being paralyzed, but the fear of never being loved the way she needed to be loved as a human being. Everything she'd ever done had been driven by that fear. She understood what was driving him, and if she were him, she wasn't sure she'd ever get on a horse again either, not at that risk. "You rode with me."

"The horse wasn't a risk. We had a conversation."

She almost smiled at his answer. He had a conversation with the horse? And he was going to walk away from that? "So, you're going to live in fear your whole life, then?"

He met her gaze. "No. I'm going to live with the memory of our time together. That's what's going to carry me."

She suddenly felt tired, like the weight of the world was on her shoulders. "You're an idiot. Why would you do that? You have a family that wants you to be a part of it. Do you know what I'd do if my family wanted me? I'd never leave their side."

Regret flickered over his handsome face. "Shit, Erin, it's not like that. I'm sorry you have a crappy family. But this is different. They aren't my family. Yeah, I'm related to my half-brothers through our dad, but I don't belong. I can't take charity from them and park myself in the middle of the family ranch that Chase is trying to create." He leaned forward. "*I don't belong there.*"

She could tell he meant it, and she didn't know what to say. Maybe he was right. She didn't know. "Come to Virginia," she said suddenly. "Come back with me."

He stared at her, and her invite fell into the heavy silence.

Oh, God. What had she just done?

~

"MOVE TO VIRGINIA?" Steen repeated softly, his voice low with emotion that seemed to thicken the air around them. "With you?"

"Well, I mean, why not? If you're not going to stay here, and then, well, I don't know. We could..." She shrugged, suddenly embarrassed. "I mean, it's not cowboy country or anything, but there are tons of horses. Or you could build furniture. I have a house in the country, and it has a big workshop out back that I've never used." Excitement began to build. "Seriously, why not?"

He didn't take his gaze off her, and his face was utterly expressionless. She couldn't tell what he was thinking, and suddenly she felt

313

horribly vulnerable and exposed. "Never mind," she muttered. "It was just an idea." God, what had she been thinking? Inviting Steen to move in with her?

Steen leaned forward. "Erin."

The urgency of his tone drew her attention to him, and she looked up, her heart skipping a beat with sudden hope. "What?"

"First of all, I'm pretty much overwhelmed you would offer that. It's a huge statement of trust, and I am honored. But there's no way I would ever allow you to support me."

She spun her fork in her fingers, restless and unsettled. "Maybe money isn't what I need from you. Maybe it's something else." She met his gaze. "Like being loved." She held her breath after she said it. Love? Had she really just said love to him?

His eyes darkened, and electricity seemed to leap between them. "Do you love me?" he asked softly.

She bit her lip and shrugged.

He closed his eyes for a long moment, and she thought she saw his hands tremble. Then he took a breath and leaned forward, staring into her eyes. "Look at me, Erin. I want you to really look at me."

She met his gaze, searching the face that was so familiar to her. His hair was slightly longer than it had been, and his face was less gaunt. She knew his lips so intimately, and could easily envision what it felt like to touch his cheeks. He was so human, so strong, and so vulnerable. "I see a man who was dealt a bad hand in life, and somehow, he has emerged with a pure heart and a good soul. That's what I see."

His face softened, and for a moment, he looked ten years younger. The lines on his face seemed to drop away, and the tension he always carried with him vanished. He bent forward and kissed her, a tender beautiful kiss that made her heart soar. He broke the kiss too soon and rested his forehead against hers. "My sweet Erin," he said quietly. "I don't have a job, or any source of income. As I already told you, I can't even leave the state without the permission of my parole officer. I won't be free of those constraints for at least five years. Don't you see that? I'm an ex-con convicted of a serious, serious crime. I have nothing to offer you, sweetheart, nothing that is remotely worthy of you."

She heard the finality of his words, and her heart sank. She pulled back, searching his face. "You know I don't care about you being in prison, right? You know that I see you for who you are?"

"I know you do." He trailed his fingers in her hair. "And I can't even express how much that means to me." He sighed. "I wish life was different, sweetheart. I wish that on the day when you traded your bike, I'd walked up to you and offered to escort you home. If I'd met you back then, before all this shit happened, everything would have been totally different."

She bit her lip, thinking of how close they'd come back then. She'd had no idea he'd been as aware of her as she'd been of him. All it would have taken was a simple hello, one of them being brave enough to close the gap, and their lives would have been completely different. "Is it really too late for us? Really?"

"Erin, I—" His gaze flicked past her shoulder, and he went sheet white for a split second.

She whirled around, searching for what he'd seen. At first, she saw only crowds of people, and then she saw a woman in a bright red sparkly top heading right for them, her gaze boring into Steen with raw hatred. A woman with gorgeous auburn hair, an amazing body, and a face that promised hell. Erin recognized her immediately, despite all the years that had passed since the last time she'd seen her.

It was Rachel, the woman who sent Steen to prison and left him there to rot, and she was heading right for them.

CHAPTER FIFTEEN

STEEN FELT his entire world closing down upon him as he watched Rachel approach. Every muscle in his body tensed, and his lungs felt like a vice was crushing them. He had no time to escape, nowhere to go. All he could do was sit there and watch her bear down on him, his mind racing frantically as he swept the bar, looking for exits, and finding none close enough. Sweat broke out over his brow as the memories came tumbling back of how she'd set him up. She'd tricked him, and he'd paid for it brutally. Was she going to try again?

Erin moved closer to him, jerking his attention off Rachel. *Jesus.* Erin was in the line of fire now. Erin could be a target. No way in hell could he allow that to happen. He surged to his feet, moving in front of Erin to cut off Rachel as she neared the table.

She stopped a few feet from him, her face a cool mask of thinly veiled disgust. "I heard you were out."

He said nothing, every sense on hyperalert, waiting for her to strike. He would never trust her again, never let her get close enough to destroy him, or anyone that mattered to him.

"You have nothing to say to me?" she asked.

He shook his head once. He sensed Erin stand up behind him, and he shifted his position to block her from Rachel's view. She looked past him, however, her eyes narrowing. "You have a new woman already? Didn't you learn anything?"

He ground his jaw, his pulse thundering in his head. Anger surged through him, fury so thick he felt like it was pouring out of his flesh in black, angry waves. "We have nothing to say to each other," he said neutrally. He became aware that the people near them had stopped talking and were watching them. He realized suddenly that the moment he'd walked into the bar, everyone had known who he was. He'd been so caught up in Erin that he hadn't even noticed. *Shit.*

"We *do* have something to say to each other." Rachel moved closer, so close that her breasts were almost touching his chest, so close that he could smell the alcohol on her breath. He wanted to push her away, but he kept his hands hanging loosely by his side, refusing to be goaded into any contact. He didn't step back, however. There was no way he was going to let her force him to retreat. She might have landed him in prison, but she didn't own him, and he was never going to back down from her again.

"You need to leave," he said, still keeping his voice neutral. "You've been drinking. Go sleep it off."

"You bastard." She slapped his face, and he clenched his jaw, refusing to respond. "You broke your stupid knee, leaving me to find another way out of my life. How dare you fail? I invested years in you, and you failed!"

"Leave him alone." Erin suddenly stepped between them, forcing Rachel to take a step back.

Fear tore through Steen, and he clasped Erin's arm, every nerve ending on fire. He wanted to grab and rush her out the back door, getting her away from Rachel before the viper could strike, but he was frozen in terror, afraid to make one move that could get him thrown back in prison. "Don't get involved," he said quietly, for Erin's ears only. "You have no idea what she's capable of."

But Erin didn't move away. Instead, she put her hands on her hips, and glared at the woman trying to burn him. "Rachel, we all know what happened that night in your hotel room," Erin announced, loudly enough for everyone near them to hear her clearly. "Everyone knows Steen is innocent, and that you set him up to mess with your husband.

The truth will damn you, and if you ever come near Steen again, I will make sure the truth comes out."

Steen swore under his breath as Rachel's face contorted with rage. He tightened his grip on Erin's arm, his heart thundering in fear for her safety. He wasn't free to step in and defend her. He was caught, trapped by Rachel's ability to get his ass thrown back in prison. "Get back," he whispered under his breath, pressing his fingers against her arm to pull her back.

She ignored him.

"You bitch," Rachel snapped at Erin. "Don't threaten me. My father is the District Attorney, and he can crush you both. It will take only one phone call from me to land Steen back in prison, so don't mess with me."

Jesus. Steen went cold at the threat, but at the same time, he knew there was no way he could allow Rachel to bring Erin into this situation. Fury roiling through him, he pulled Erin behind him and used his body to shield her. Rage and fear were thundering through him, but he kept his voice calm and his expression stoic as he faced down the woman who'd destroyed him.

"Rachel," he said evenly, using self-discipline he'd never possessed until prison had taught him that it could save his life. "It's over. The courts settled it. Let it go." He didn't want her to notice Erin too closely and figure out who she was. As much as he didn't want to wind up back in prison, he'd do whatever it took to keep Rachel from turning her sights onto Erin. He was well aware that the night Rachel had approached him five years ago that he'd been dancing with another woman, and he'd always wondered if it had been jealousy that had spurred it. If she'd seen the way he'd been all over Erin, she wouldn't stop until she'd plunged her venom deep into both of them. She'd wanted to use Steen as her ticket out of her life, and she needed to punish him for his failure.

Sure enough, her eyes flashed to the woman he was trying to protect as Erin shoved Steen in the shoulder and came to stand next to him again. *Jesus.* Did she have no sense of self-preservation at all?

"Your new girlfriend?" Rachel spat the words with poison that made adrenaline surge through him.

"No." He didn't even look at Erin. "She's not my type, and you know it. Don't waste your time with her."

Rachel's gaze slithered over Erin in her jeans and tee shirt, and then appeared satisfied. Without another word, she spun on her stiletto heel and marched away, weaving slightly as she made her way across the crowded floor.

Steen glanced around and saw dozens of people watching him with the avid interest of paparazzi salivating for a story. He swore under his breath. Had he really thought there was any way to escape his past? He was a fool, and he'd brought Erin into it now. He didn't even look at her. "Come on. We need to leave." Under normal circumstances, he'd park himself right back at his table and refuse to be driven out, but the circumstances were far from normal. He didn't want to hang around and give Rachel the chance to hatch some plot to take him down again, or worse, hurt Erin. So, he grabbed Erin's purse and handed it to her.

She took it silently, and didn't argue when he put his hand on her lower back and guided her through the crowd that fell silent as they passed. He felt the weight of a thousand eyes on them, and quickly removed his hand from Erin's back, dropping back to several feet behind her as she led the way out of the bar, refusing to mark her as his anymore.

It had been a terrible, selfish mistake to mark Erin as his. He was done lying to himself that he could do this with her. It was over. It *had* to be over. Right now. Forever.

End of story.

~

STEEN DIDN'T SAY a word to Erin once they were in his truck, and she realized almost instantly that he was taking her back toward Josie's house, where she hadn't slept in days. He wasn't taking her back to his bunkhouse.

"This is it, then?" she asked, watching the houses flash by as he headed back into town, where Josie lived in an apartment over her vet clinic. "You're dropping me off, and that's it?"

He didn't look at her. "What if she comes after you?"

Erin bit her lip, gazing out the window. Rachel's hatred had been so evident, and she'd had no mercy about sending Steen to prison for attempted murder four years ago. Erin had never met anyone like that before. Her parents had ignored her, and Louis had withheld any sort of affection and then betrayed her, but she understood now that her traumas in life that she'd struggled so hard to deal with were nothing compared to what Steen had endured.

Prison.

Prison.

A mother who had abandoned him.

An abusive father.

A woman he loved, whose betrayal had been setting him up for attempted murder.

God, how was it possible that his heart was still so pure, and he could still live with such honor? Because she knew that despite all he'd endured, he was the kindest, most honorable human being she'd ever known.

But she could see what his life was. All he had now was a ranch he refused to belong to, and half-brothers he wouldn't accept. She looked over at him as he drove, watching the torment in his handsome features. He was completely alone. It was ugly, his life. It was dirty. It was isolated. It was rough. And it was tainted. She understood now why he would never let her into his life, and why he'd never come to Virginia.

And did she want his life? Did she want to spend her life looking over her shoulder for Rachel to come after him? But even as she thought it, her heart bled for him. He was such a good man, who had spent his life trying to dig out of the quicksand that he'd been born into. He'd survived. He'd defeated it, because he'd stayed a good person, but the external factors would always be there, haunting him, making it impossible for him to ever step out from the shadows.

He silently turned into her driveway and pulled up to the front of the clinic, beside the side door that led to the second floor apartment.

Erin didn't move to get out of the car, and Steen rested his forearms on the steering wheel, staring out the windshield at the darkness.

Finally, he shoved open his door, walked around to her side, and pulled hers open. He leaned against the doorframe moodily, his cowboy hat low over his forehead. "You should go," he said softly.

She unfastened her seatbelt and turned sideways in the seat so she was facing him, her feet resting on the running board. She didn't move to get out, though. The truck was high enough that she was almost at eye-level with him. "I know you think you're worthless," she said quietly, "but you're wrong."

He shook his head. "I don't think I'm worthless. I just know what hand I've been dealt, and how I have to play the cards." He reached for her then, his fingers trailing over the ends of her hair in a touch so gentle that her heart skipped. "I know you're the greatest treasure of my life," he said. "But it's not my right to hold onto you."

Tears filled her eyes and she held out her arms. "Kiss me."

He shook his head. "No. I can't do that to you anymore." His thumb brushed over her lower lip. "It's time, Erin. It's time for you to go back and kick some ass in your life. Find the guy you deserve."

She scooted to the edge of the seat and grabbed the front of his shirt, her fingers digging in when he resisted. "I'm going to go back to Virginia," she said. "But before I do, there's something you need to know."

His jaw flexed, but he still didn't let her pull him toward her. "What's that?"

"I was there tonight, Steen. I saw firsthand what you are going to have to deal with for the rest of your life. I know your past. I know everything about your miserable life and brutal past, and I know that you have blood on your hands, even though it's not your fault. I know every dark secret you have, but I also know your heart." She put her hand on his chest. "I had a crush on you in high school, but not anymore."

He stiffened. "Smart woman."

"I don't have a silly schoolgirl crush anymore," she said, her fingertips digging into his chest. "Because it's all changed for me." She looked at him, barely able to see his eyes in the shadows beneath his hat. "Because now, I see you from the perspective of a woman who doesn't care about hot football players or swagger. I care about the man inside, and it's for that reason, that I have fallen deeply, truly in love with you."

He didn't move.

He didn't even react.

He simply went utterly still, so still that she could hear every night sound. The hoot of a nearby owl. The sound of a car passing in the distance. But not a word from him.

She tapped his chest lightly. "I know you don't think you're worthy, and you're probably trying to figure out how to make me stop loving you, but you don't get to choose who loves you. Your brothers love you, or at least Chase does. And I love you. You can reject me and your brothers, but that doesn't mean you get to make any of us stop loving you—"

He cut her off with a kiss so deep and passionate that it seemed to merge souls into one. She flung her arms around his neck as he dragged her against him. He grabbed her thighs and wrapped her legs around his hips. She locked herself around him as he carried her across the driveway, one hand on her butt and the other one supporting her back as he kissed her frantically, with a desperation that she could taste in every kiss.

He grabbed the key from its hiding place by the door, and within a split second, he was taking the stairs two at a time, still kissing her relentlessly. He burst into the upstairs hallway, heading unerringly toward the guest bedroom she'd been sleeping in, clearly having taken note of the layout when they'd stopped by several days ago to pick up more of her clothes.

Her heart leapt as he settled her on the bed, dragging off her shirt and bra in a seamless move as he moved over her, using his body to rock her onto her back, breaking the kiss only enough to get his shirt off as well. The moment she felt his bare chest beneath her hands, a part of her soul wanted to cry. Somehow, she knew it would be the last time she'd ever be with him, the last time she'd ever hold this wonderful man in her arms.

"Don't cry, sweetheart." Steen kissed the tears from her cheeks as he framed her face with his hands. "I don't want you to cry."

She clasped his wrists, refusing to let him go. "Sometimes tears are okay, Steen. Sometimes you have to let your heart bleed or you'll never live. I'd rather cry, than to never love enough to feel that kind of pain. I don't want my heart to be hard anymore, no matter how much it hurts to love."

His face softened as he searched her face. "I'm so far from where you are emotionally," he said.

"No, you're not." She managed a smile through her tears. "You're right here with me, whether you can see it or not." She locked her hands behind his neck. "Make love to me, Steen. Please, make love to me with every last bit of your soul. Just this once, this one time in your life, don't hold anything back from me. That's the gift you can give me."

For a moment, he said nothing, searching her face so intently she felt like he was trying to discern every last scar on her soul and heal every last one by the sheer force of his will. Then, he kissed her, a kiss that was so achingly, mournfully beautiful that she felt as if the lonesome, haunting howl of the wolf had come alive in the kiss.

He broke the kiss and rolled off her, standing beside the bed as he kicked off his boots and shed his jeans and boxer briefs. He didn't let her take hers off, instead sliding them off her body in the most sensual and tender seduction, showering her body with kisses as he exposed her skin.

By the time he'd finally removed the last pieces of her clothing, her body was aching and restless for more. He moved over her, kissing his way up her body before he settled his weight on her. His skin was hot against hers, his body like steel cords of muscle, his kiss the most beautiful seduction. His fingers slid through her hair, caressing her with soulful tenderness.

She wrapped her legs around his hips, her body tightening as his hips moved against hers, his cock sliding over her wetness in a tease that was almost more than she could endure. "Make love to me," she whispered against his mouth. "I want us to be connected forever."

He said nothing, but suddenly everything shifted from sweet seduction to carnal possession and need. It became about lips and tongues, touching and need. It became a desperate attempt for both of them to unleash every last bit of their souls into each other, enough to sustain them forever. His teeth grazed over her nipple, making her body clench. She loved every touch, every kiss, every intimacy. She knew he would never let himself love her, or at least admit it even to himself, but that this moment, the kisses, and the touches, were the words and the emotions he'd never share or acknowledge.

Each kiss was a whisper of his love, of his heart, of his soul, offered to her and no one else, and she treasured every one of them. Louis had said he loved her, but he'd never made her feel loved. Steen had never said he loved her, but she knew she'd never feel as loved as she was in this moment.

His fingers slipped inside her, and she gasped at the invasion, her body begging for more. She was ready for him, so completely, and he knew it. She didn't want any more foreplay. She wanted him inside her. She wanted him to be with her the way that it would never be with anyone else.

As if sensing her need, Steen shifted his position so his cock was pressing against her. Excitement raced through her as she locked her legs around his hips, trapping him. He moved his hips slightly, teasing her, nudging at her entrance.

She couldn't help the groan that escaped her, and he grinned as he caught it in a searing kiss, even as he slid a tiny bit deeper. "You want me?" he whispered.

"God, yes." She gripped his shoulders, shifting restlessly beneath him. "I will always want you, Steen. Just you. No one else." She opened her eyes and stared into his face. She saw the vulnerability in his eyes, and she knew what he needed to hear. Her big, strong man who had survived hell to be here with her needed to hear her say it, despite all his claims to the contrary. "I love you, Steen. With all my heart."

Relief flooded his features, and he thrust deep, plunging into her. He gripped her hair almost desperately, searching her face. "You really love me, don't you?"

"I do." She smiled, even as her body clenched in response to another thrust. "For always."

"You're so incredible." There was a sadness to his words, but he kissed her before she could say anything. From that moment on, there were no more words. Just Steen showing her with his body, his touch, and his kisses how he felt about her. She heard his unspoken words, and she accepted what he offered, the emotions spiraling around them in a rising intensity as the lovemaking became more frantic, until all that was left was the two of them and a need so great that she knew they would never outrun it.

He thrust one final time, and the orgasm flooded her, a magnificent explosion of fireworks that filled her soul with more love than she ever thought possible.

"God, Erin," Steen whispered as the orgasm took him as well. "You're my everything."

It was all he said, the only words he uttered until she fell asleep in his arms, but it was enough.

CHAPTER SIXTEEN

"YOU SURE you don't want me to come in?" Steen reached into the bed of his truck and pulled out Erin's two powder blue suitcases. The airport was bustling and busy, with the energy of a place on the move.

She shook her head, her chin held high. She was still wearing jeans, but her shirt was dressier than she'd been wearing in Wyoming, and she was wearing low heels and makeup. Still the Erin he knew, but with hints of the Erin she really was: independent, successful, and on her way back to the life she deserved. "Nope," she said. "I can handle my bags. They aren't heavy."

"I know you can handle them. I just thought..." Shit. He thought what? That he could follow her into the airport and something would change? Something that would make it so he didn't have to stand back and let her walk out of his life? He'd been so certain that letting her go was the right thing to do, but now that he was standing beside her at the curb at the airport, his instincts were screaming at him to stop being an ass and to claim her right then, right there, for all time.

He hadn't seen her for the last several days, since they'd made love after their date. He hadn't planned to drive her to the airport, but this morning, he'd decided he had to see her again, so he'd driven to the clinic to pick her up for the airport.

He hadn't called ahead. He hadn't asked permission. He'd simply waited outside for two hours until she'd finally emerged, with her suitcases in hand. For a long moment, she'd stared at him, and he'd thought that she wasn't going to let him drive her, then she'd handed him her bags and climbed into the cab of his truck.

The relief he'd felt when she'd accepted his offer of a ride had been almost overwhelming, but it had quickly dissipated when awkwardness had arisen between them. On the entire drive to the airport, there had been only casual, meaningless conversation. He didn't know what he'd wanted to say, or how he'd wanted his last moments with her to be, but he knew it wasn't a car ride filled with empty dialogue.

And now, his time was almost out.

He tipped his cowboy hat back on his head, restless and unsettled, searching for answers he couldn't find. "Don't ever forget how amazing you are," he finally said. It felt lame, but he meant it. He didn't know what else to say.

She cocked her head, studying him. "You have to come get me," she said.

He frowned, confused by her comment. "Come get you from where? When?"

"When you decide you're ready for me. The ball's in your court. You have to be the one to make the next move. You know I love you. The next step is yours."

He ground his jaw, fighting against the sudden surge of hope, disbelief, and denial. The need to grab her around the waist, haul her against him, and claim her forever, was almost insurmountable. Every part of him wanted to be with her, but he fisted his hands, summoning iron-clad self-control to keep himself from reaching for her. He didn't know what to say, how to express what he was feeling. "Erin—"

She held up her hand, silencing him. "There's nothing else to say. I'm going home." She took the bags from him, careful not to brush his hand with her fingers, a rejection that bit deep, so damned deep. She met his gaze. "I don't know that I could live here," she said, her gaze steady. "I don't know that I would give up my career to move out here. I don't know if I'd say yes if you came after me. But that shouldn't stop you from trying, if that's what you want to do."

He searched her face, and saw the truth in her eyes. "You really still love me?"

"Yes, I do. Just as how I'm still your everything." She smiled then, that same mesmerizing smile that he'd first seen so long ago, when she'd succeeded in talking that vet into taking the bird. She cocked her head. "I have one question, before I go."

Hope leapt through him. Hope for what, he didn't know, but definitely hope. "What's that?"

"Did you ever look for her?"

He frowned. "For who?"

"Your mom. When you got older, did you ever try to find out what happened to her? Did you ever find out why she didn't come back when she'd promised she would?"

He shrugged, his muscles tensing. "I tried. I couldn't find anything. She just took off, I guess."

She studied him. "Someone knows what happened to her. You should find out. Sometimes life isn't as hopeless as you believe it must be." She stood on her tiptoes and pressed a quick kiss to his cheek. "Good luck, Steen, with everything." She winked. "And stay out of prison, you hear?"

"Yeah, okay, for you, I'll stay clean." A brief smile flashed across his face. "Promise me, you'll beat the hell out of any man who tells you you're not good enough."

"You bet." She gave him a small salute, and then turned away. He watched her until she faded into the crowd, but she never looked back, not even once. Still, he didn't move. He waited another fifteen minutes, half-expecting to see her running back toward him through the crowds, her arms held out to him.

She didn't come, and eventually, he got back in the truck. He sat there for a few minutes, still watching the door, but she didn't appear. Grimly, he realized that she had truly walked away, without a single glance back. It was what he'd wanted, but it sucked, far more than he had ever expected. His entire soul felt heavy, as if it were being sucked into ever-deepening quicksand, and he felt exhausted, his muscles too drained to even turn the key in the ignition.

Until now, the moment he'd been declared guilty in that courtroom had been the worst moment of his life. He'd been unable to breathe, shocked that he had just been convicted of attempted murder. His entire world had started spinning, totally out of control, and only his tight grip on his chair had kept his hands from shaking violently.

But watching Erin walk away had been a thousand times worse. He felt like his soul simply withered up and died, leaving him with nothing but memories of a time when he'd once been alive. Jesus. How in the hell was he going to go on from this? What did a man do next, when the weight on his soul was too heavy to bear, and he had nowhere better to go, no hope to hang onto, and no dream to pursue?

After a long while, he numbly started the engine, and glanced back at the door one more time. A well-dressed man with silver hair walked out, and for a split-second, he thought it was Pointer's dad, who had greeted him that day when he'd gotten out of prison to thank him for saving his son's life. He realized almost immediately that he wasn't. Of course not. No one was going to walk out those doors for him today.

He started the engine and began to drive, away from the airport, away from the only woman who had ever mattered to him, except his mother.

His mother.

Erin's words about finding out what happened to her flashed through his mind, and for the first time in years, he wondered about the answers he'd never gotten. He gritted his jaw, reminding himself that it was in the past, and it didn't matter anymore.

But he could still see Erin's steady gaze as she'd told him to ask one more time. Shit. He'd wanted to prove to her that she was worthy, not to give up, but it hadn't turned out that way. She was the one who believed in him. He knew she was wrong to think he was such a great guy, but suddenly, he wanted to be the man she believed in. He wanted to make her proud, in at least one small way.

Swearing under his breath as he eased the truck to a stop at a red light, he looked down at his phone, sitting on the console beside him. After a long moment, he picked it up, and then scrolled through and found the number for Thomas Smith, Pointer's dad. He hesitated briefly, and then he pressed "Send."

A cultured woman's voice answered on the first ring. "May I assist you?"

Her voice was so refined and cultured that Steen almost hung up. He didn't belong in that world. Then he thought of Erin, and resolution flooded him. "My name is Steen Stockton. I'm looking for Thomas Smith."

"Steen Stockton? The man who saved Pointer's life?" The woman's voice changed instantly from cool and reserved to warm and inviting.

Steen shrugged. "Yeah, well, I was there—"

"My name is Betsy Smith. That's my son whose life you saved," she said. "I will never be able to express in words how grateful I am to you. I know Pointer made a mistake that got him sent prison, but you gave him the opportunity for a second chance. He's already making plans for when he gets out. He's learned his lesson, and it's because of you, so thank you, from the bottom of my heart."

Steen leaned his head back against the seat, watching the cars cross the intersection. "You don't care that he broke the law?"

"Of course I care, but I still love him with every last bit of my heart, and I'll hug him until the end of time when he gets home again. He's my son. You never stop loving your children, no matter what. And now you're in my heart as well, forever and ever."

His throat tightening unexpectedly at the kind words, Steen drummed his fingers on the dashboard, unsettled by the discussion, and by the warmth of this woman he'd never met. He thought of his mother, who had walked out without looking back. He had to accomplish his task and then get off the phone. He wasn't used to this kind of conversation. "Is um, Thomas there, by any chance?"

"He's not, Steen, I'm so sorry. He went golfing today, and left his phone here. I thought this might be him trying to find it. I'm sure the man thinks it's lost forever. He never keeps track of this thing. Honestly, he's hopeless." Despite her words, Betsy's voice was warm with affection that made Steen think of Erin and how he felt about her. "What do you need, Steen? I might be able to help."

Suddenly, he felt stupid. What kind of person called a random stranger to ask for help? "Nothing. I was just checking to see how Pointer's doing."

"He's great, but that's not why you called," Betsy said. "I've been married for too many years, and I've raised four boys. I know what it sounds like when a man needs something and is too damned stubborn to ask for help. What do you want? I know it's not money, but we still owe you, so tell me."

The stoplight ahead of him turned green, but Steen didn't drive. Instead, he said the words he never thought he'd say. "I need some help finding someone. I don't have the resources or the contacts, but I thought maybe—"

"Thomas knows people," she said briskly. He could hear paper rustling as if she were preparing to write it down. "Who do you want to find?"

A car behind him honked, but he ignored it, his fingers tightening around the phone. "Her name is Alice Marie Rivers." He took a deep breath. "She's my mother."

～

"Great job today, Dr. Chambers."

"Thanks, Molly." Erin wearily summoned a smile at the surgical assistant passing through the locker room as she was finishing changing after surgery. "I appreciate your help." She was tired, so tired, after the seven-hour surgery. Long surgeries were always draining, but this time, it was worse. She felt as though it had sucked every last bit of her reserves from her. It was all she could do not to simply sink down on the floor and not move ever again. It was her first surgery since her trip to Wyoming. The goal of the trip had been to rejuvenate her, giving her back the zest for life, and for *her* life in particular, but it hadn't. Despite the success of the operation, she felt the same lack of satisfaction that she'd felt before she'd left. Actually, it wasn't the *same* lack of satisfaction as before. Now, it was more like a gaping sense of meaningless misery, which was definitely not the step up she'd been hoping for.

Being away hadn't made her life better. It had made it worse, so much worse, because now she had something to compare it to: the freedom, the independence, the romance, and the realness of Wyoming. And, of course, Steen.

Now, her beautiful home on the tree-lined street felt empty and silent without Steen there to grab her hips and molest her while she was trying to make coffee. The air felt barren and arid without the scent of horses and ranch rolling through her windows. Her patient today had been under anesthesia from the first moment to the last, so she'd never had the chance to "have a chat with it" as Steen would have done so well. It had simply been a clinical procedure, and she felt like she hadn't made any kind of meaningful difference at all, except to the wealthy owners who were hoping she could save their horse so they could continue to make money off him.

She'd been home for almost three days, and she hadn't been able to stop thinking about Steen, her phone clutched in her hand constantly, waiting for him to call and say he was on his way from the airport.

But she hadn't heard from him. Not a call, not a text, and not an email. *You are my everything.* She knew she was, which is why she hadn't really believed that he would let her walk away. When she'd told him to come after her, she'd truly thought he would.

But he hadn't.

He'd let her go, just as Louis had, and her parents. It had hurt when Louis had left. It had been devastating to grow up with parents who simply didn't care about her. But knowing that Steen was going to let her go...it hurt so deeply she felt like her heart would never again be whole.

She sighed, too tired to think. She just wanted to go home and crawl into bed. Maybe she would cancel her surgery for tomorrow. It wasn't as if she was in any shape to concentrate—

"It's my honor to assist you," Molly said cheerfully, dragging her back into the present. "Congratulations on Rising Star. It's incredible, what you did."

Erin rubbed her temples, trying not to think about how much her head was hurting. "Rising Star?" The name sounded vaguely familiar, but she was too tired to care or think. She just wanted to go home and figure out how she had gone so wrong.

Molly's eyes widened. "You didn't hear? He won the Kentucky

Derby today. His career was over before you operated on him, and now he won. The procedure you did saved his career. You're going to be famous now, even more than you already are."

Erin stared at Molly, processing what she'd just said. She recalled very clearly the procedure Molly had mentioned. It had been controversial and risky, but the owner of the horse had been willing to try anything to save his investment and give the animal a chance to live up to his bloodlines. The horse had survived the surgery and recovered, but then she'd lost track of him. He'd turned out to be the winner of the Kentucky Derby, one of the most significant races around? *Wow.* "Really? When did this happen?"

"Earlier today. The owner told the press all about the surgery and how well it worked. He gave you full credit." Molly grinned. "You're going to have to open your own surgery center, Doc. There won't be space for all your cases here."

"Wow." Erin sank down onto a bench, her legs starting to tremble from exhaustion. "He told people?" She wasn't used to that. She wasn't used to anyone being proud of her. Well, anyone except Steen, who'd been proud of her simply for saving a bird. "Really?"

"Watch the news. You'll see." Molly paused with her hand on the doorknob. "You want to come out for a drink with us? To celebrate?"

Erin's heart tightened at the invitation. It was the first time she'd ever been invited by her staff. A part of her wanted to go, but at the same time, she knew she didn't belong. They were all so much younger, single, and from a different life than she was. But still, the invitation felt good. Really good. "No, thanks. Not today. Jet lag. I need to sleep. But try again next time?" Maybe next time she'd be ready to step out and try. Just not tonight. Tonight, she was still under the spell of Wyoming, Steen, and the kind of love she'd always dreamed of.

Molly's grin widened. "You bet. Have a great night." She waved as she ducked out the door, leaving Erin alone.

Wearily, Erin stood up and walked over to the sink. She rested her hands on the counter and stared at herself in the mirror, studying the bags under her eyes and the lines around the corners of her mouth. Her hair was matted from the surgical cap, hanging limply around her. God, she looked haggard and bone-weary, not like a veterinarian who had just made history. Was she really the woman who'd innovated a new procedure for racehorses who had broken bones? She didn't feel special. She just felt ordinary and empty, like something so important had slipped out of her grasp and she had no idea how to retrieve it.

She noticed little lines around the corners of her eyes. Laugh lines? She doubted it. More like self-pity crow's feet. She looked older than she remembered seeing, but as she studied herself more closely, she began to notice other changes. Her skin was flushed, not as pale as usual, with maybe a hint of tan. Her hair had light brown streaks around the temples from being outside so much visiting the farms. Her hair was less perfect, even shaggy. She looked more outdoorsy, just the tiniest bit, than she used to be. And she'd opted to put on jeans after the surgery, instead of the pleated pants she usually wore.

So, a little different...but also, in a way worse. She looked even more tired than she had before her vacation, and she felt a thousand times emptier. She felt like the blue jeans and the streaks in her hair were teasers of the brief moments of happiness she'd had with Steen and the animals, already a part of her past.

She thought of the animals she'd met in Wyoming. She'd been bitten, stepped on, and kicked. But she'd also been licked, snuggled, and gently nibbled by the furry creatures she'd worked on. Watching Steen connect with his horse that first time they'd gone riding had been so beautiful. She might know how to heal their bones, but he could heal their hearts, if only he would try. During her short vacation, she'd cried over Steen, she'd discovered passion, and she'd hugged animals who were scared of her. It had been dirty and real, completely unplanned and unpredictable...and now she was back to a life that was as sterile as her operating room.

That wasn't supposed to happen. The trip to Wyoming had been to restore her and revitalize her so she could return to her life with fresh energy and excitement. Instead, she hated being here. "Damn you, Steen," she whispered. "You showed me what my life could be like, and then you walked away."

Her phone rang. Excitement leapt through her. Had Steen seen the news and called her? She grabbed her purse and dug her phone out of it. One glance at the screen, and her heart congealed in her chest. It wasn't Steen. It was *Louis.* Her ex-husband hadn't called her since they'd finished their negotiations and finalized their divorce, except to tell her that he was coming to her family's Christmas party with his new girlfriend and he hoped she'd be okay with it.

She'd skipped the dinner.

The phone buzzed again, and she hit decline to send it to voicemail. Never again would she let him into her life.

She set the phone down and grabbed her bag to head out. As she was reaching for her purse, her cell rang again. This time, she wasn't foolish enough to have hope that it was Steen. She glanced at the screen as she was about to drop it into her purse, then stopped when she saw her dad's name on the screen.

She stared in shock at it. Her dad never called her. *Ever.* Not since the divorce, when she'd failed to hang onto her worthy husband. Her heart suddenly tightened. First Louis and then her dad? Had something happened to her mother? She grabbed the phone and answered. "Dad?"

"I think congratulations are in order." His voice boomed over the phone. "The *New York Times* has already called to talk to you. You've revolutionized equine surgery, my dear. Louis is with me, and he's been doing the interviews for you until you could get here. We're so impressed. Come to the house. We're hosting reporters here. We'll see you in ten minutes?"

"What?" She gripped the phone, trying to process. The *Times* was really interested in *her*? "Are you serious?"

"Dead serious." His voice dropped to a whisper. "Why didn't you tell me that you modified my approach to use on the horses? It was brilliant, Erin. *Brilliant*. There is huge money involved in racehorses, and you just cornered the market. Well done, my dear, *well done*. Hang on a sec. Louis wants to talk to you."

"Louis?" Her fingers tightened on the phone. Had her dad really just said *"well done"* to her? "I don't want to—"

"Erin?" Her ex-husband's slick voice made her stomach congeal. "Hey, congratulations. Great job today. I'm at your parents' house. I'd love to take you to dinner after the press conference. I want to learn

335

more about your procedure. It's incredibly innovative and bold. I had no idea you were working on that. I'm so proud of you."

I'm so proud of you.

The words she'd been longing to hear her entire life, and now she had it. From her dad, from Louis, from everyone she'd been trying to impress for so long. She was too shocked to say anything. All she could do was hold onto the phone. It had taken public accolades and a legion of reporters, but she'd done it. She'd finally proved herself worthy.

"Erin?" Her dad came back on the line. "You coming over? I have more reporters coming. Can you be here in ten minutes? You did it, babe. *You did it.*"

She'd done it. "Okay," she finally said. "I'll be over in ten minutes."

CHAPTER SEVENTEEN

STEEN'S COWBOY boots thudded on the wood as he walked up the front steps of Chase's ranch house. His brother had been home for half a day with his fiancée, just enough time for Steen to pack up his belongings. He was ready to go. Where, he didn't know, but he had to leave. The bunkhouse was filled with too many memories of Erin, and he couldn't stay there any longer.

He missed her so damn much that he couldn't even breathe. He'd lasted ten minutes in the bed they'd shared, and had spent the rest of the nights sleeping on a horse blanket on the floor of the bunkhouse. His back hurt like hell, which brought back memories of the fear he'd lived in when he'd first broken it, which really wasn't helping his mood.

He had to leave, and he had to leave now.

The front door of the house was open, and he could hear voices from the living room. He rapped his knuckles on the doorframe. "Chase? You around?"

"In here." His brother's voice echoed out from the living room.

Steen stepped into the ranch house with its glistening wood floors. He remembered the first time he'd been invited inside for grub, back when the ranch had been owned by Old Skip, who seemed to have made it his mission to give the Stockton boys a place to work. He was the one who'd taught Steen about horses, the one who'd shown Steen exactly how special his gift with them was. Back then, the ranch house had been falling down and worn out, but Chase had fixed it up. It looked good, good enough even for a woman like Erin.

Not that it was his house to offer her. It was Chase's.

Steen stopped in the doorway. Chase was sitting on the edge of the couch, with Mira perched next to him. They were both leaning forward, watching the television. Mira was leaning against Chase, and his hand was on her belly, as if he were staking ownership of the baby she carried. It was a scene of domesticity, one that Steen was pretty sure he'd never seen up close before.

For a moment, he imagined it was Erin sitting there, and he was parked next to her. What would that be like, to have a forever with someone? To have a kid on the way? He waited for the roil of bile in his stomach at the idea...but there wasn't any. Not even fear. He just felt...lost.

Shit. He had no room for this.

He cleared his throat and pulled his shoulders back. "You got a sec?"

Chase looked over his shoulder at him, and grinned. "Come on in. We're watching some horse racing. Mira used to watch it with her family, and she wanted to see it."

Mira looked over at him and smiled, patting the couch beside her. "Come on in, Steen."

He pulled his cowboy hat a little further down over his forehead, incredibly uncomfortable with intruding upon them and their domestic scene. "Nah, I'm good. I just wanted to tell you guys I'm leaving."

Chase's eyes narrowed, and he turned to give Steen his full attention. "Leaving where?"

"The ranch. I'm hitting the road. Gotta go somewhere."

Mira and Chase exchanged glances, then Chase stood up and strode over toward him. "Come with me. Let's talk."

Steen's jaw clenched, and he didn't move. He didn't want to get into it with his brother. "Nah, I'm good. Just wanted to say thanks for the hospitality."

Chase halted in front of him and folded his arms across his chest. "Where are you going to go?" he demanded.

"I don't know." Steen shrugged. "I'll find something."

"Working at a gas station again?" There was a challenge in Chase's voice that made Steen stiffen.

"I'll do what I have to do," he said evenly. "I'm not going to live off your charity."

Chase swore under his breath. "Come on, Steen, you think this is charity?" He gestured toward the barn. "I need your help. I have horses in there that are so messed up that I can't help them. I've tried, and they're in just as bad a shape as when they arrived. I have two more coming in tomorrow. I spread the word that you're back, and the owners are sending their animals. These are horses that no one can help, bro. No one but you."

Steen ground his jaw, tension settling in his muscles. He'd seen horses like that before, with their wild, terrified eyes, and panicked breathing. Once he made eye contact with one of them, nothing else mattered except taking away the animal's fear and giving it the chance to reclaim its life. He shifted uncomfortably. He hadn't expected to be faced with troubled horses ever again, and he didn't have his defenses ready. "I never said I was staying."

"No, you didn't, but you want to, and I need your help. I can't run this whole damned place by myself. I'm mortgaged until I'm bleeding debt, and I have thousands of acres of unused land. I bought this place for all of us, including you."

Steen looked away, staring out the window at the vast fields. "You have seven other brothers to help you," he said quietly. "Brothers that you grew up with. You have a bond with them, not me. I came late to the party."

"Shit, Steen, really? What about the fact we all sat around your bed when you were dying in the hospital? Didn't that mean anything to you? We're all a bunch of anti-social bastards with no loyalty to anyone, except our own, and we were there for you. Not just me. Travis, Zane, Ryder, Maddox, and Quintin. Caleb wasn't there because his phone's been disconnected and we can't reach him. Logan showed up the next day, getting there as soon as he could. You got us all, Steen. When are you going to realize it?"

Steen ran his hand through his hair. A part of him wanted to believe Chase, to buy into this brotherhood crap, but he couldn't do it. He'd been down that road too many damn times, counting on people who blew him off. "I appreciate you guys were there. I do, but hell, man, I don't belong."

Chase met his gaze. "You could belong, if you got over your shit and just let us in."

Steen stared at his half-brother, the only one of his brothers who he'd listed as an approved visitor when he'd been in prison. Suddenly, he didn't see Chase as the successful rancher. He saw the teenager who walked out onto the front porch on his third night after his mom had left. Chase had been wearing a white cowboy hat, just like now, and he'd been holding a brown one in his hand. It had been battered and worn, stinking of horse crap and sweat, and Chase had held it out to him. He'd said only one word. "Welcome." And then he'd handed Steen the hat and walked off.

Welcome.

It was the same hat that he was wearing now. Only one he'd ever worn. Only one he'd ever had. He looked at Chase, really looked at him for the first time. He'd never thought of him as a brother, not really. But he was, on some level. Maybe, just maybe—

He suddenly heard Erin's voice, and he spun around, his heart leaping. "Erin?" She wasn't behind him. He heard her talking, and he turned again, searching until he saw her face on the television. He vaulted over the back of the couch and landed beside Mira, leaning forward. Erin was wearing a tee shirt, and her hair was up in a ponytail, just as it had been so many times when she'd been out in Wyoming. She looked the same, exactly the same, and something inside him seemed to skip a beat.

She was smiling, a huge smile that lit up her whole face as she talked. "She looks good, doesn't she?" he said aloud, to no one in particular.

He was vaguely aware of Chase and Mira talking, and he waved at them to be quiet, leaning forward to hear Erin talk. He couldn't believe she was on television. He listened, riveted, as the reporter interviewed her about some surgery she'd done on the Kentucky Derby winner. Pride tightened in his chest. "Yeah," he whispered. "I knew you'd do something big." Maybe she wasn't the CEO of a major company, but this was better. This was her. This was why he didn't belong with her. What if those reporters got a hold of his past? There was no way on this earth that he'd taint her, but shit, seeing her face again, looking into her brown eyes, hearing her voice...it was too much to resist. He knew he would be lost for her forever.

This was his moment. His last hurrah with her. His everything. She was so beyond him, out of his reach, but her heart and her soul would always be a part of him.

A man moved into the camera to stand beside her. Steen narrowed his eyes when the man put his arm around Erin's shoulder, and he didn't miss her sudden tension. The man was in an expensive suit, and he looked rich as hell. The reporter asked him a question, and he started talking in some medical jargon about something, but Steen couldn't take his gaze off the man's fingers and the way they were digging possessively into Erin's shoulder.

She didn't move away from him.

And then, a banner flashed across the bottom of the screen. Doctor Louis Armstrong.

Louis.

Louis.

Her ex-husband, with his arm locked possessively around her shoulder.

Jesus.

Steen felt like his world was falling out from under him. She was back with her ex? With her *husband?* Suddenly, memories of the night with Rachel in the hotel room came flooding back. He recalled Rachel's sworn declarations that she'd never stopped loving him, his shock when a man had stumbled into the bedroom claiming to be her husband, and his numb horror when he'd watched the man fall to the ground, landing on his own knife. And he'd never forget what Rachel had said when the police arrived, pointing her finger at him and saying, *"He tried to kill my husband."*

And there Erin was, smiling into the camera, with her ex-husband's arm around her shoulder. Jesus, he knew he hadn't been good enough for her. He *knew* that, but son of a bitch, he hadn't ever thought she'd lied to him. He stumbled to his feet. "I gotta go." He had to leave. Get away. For a split second, he'd almost been convinced that he should stay, that he belonged, and it had all been a fucking mirage.

"Hey!" Chase grabbed his shoulder and Steen swung around to face him, fury boiling up inside him.

"How do you do it?" Steen snapped. "How do you sit there with Mira and pretend you know how to be family? How can you lie to her and yourself that you know anything about being a father? How can you sit on that damn couch and think you're worthy?" He snarled the words, so pissed off that Chase had the balls to pretend to be good enough. "You're just another one of old man Stockton's bastards, just like the rest of us. What makes you think you deserve that shit?"

Chase's face grew hard. "It took me a long time to think I deserved it," he said quietly, as Mira came to stand beside him, sliding her hand into Chase's callused one. "Yeah, our father was a worthless bastard who drank and beat the hell out of every one of us. Yeah, we have no idea how to be a family, but I don't care." Chase raised his and Mira's clasped hands. "All I know is that Mira believes in me, and that's enough motivation for me to do whatever I have to do to make it happen."

"You're not worthless," Mira said softly. "None of you are."

Steen looked at her, still feeling sick to his stomach. "Did you even see Erin on television? Did you see her with her husband? *Did you see her?*"

Mira looked him right in the eyes. "What I just saw was a woman who was completely uncomfortable and wanted nothing more than to get away from the man who had his arm around her. That's what I saw."

He stared at her, bracing against the sudden surge of hope in his chest. He wasn't a fool. He'd believed before. "She didn't try to get away from him."

"Did you look into her eyes?" Mira challenged.

Steen glanced back at the television screen, but the interview was over. They were showing golf now. Golf. He closed his eyes. "I can't do this again," he muttered. "I won't."

He turned away and walked out the door.

This time, his brother didn't try to stop him. Neither did Mira. They just let him go.

He didn't look back as he walked down the steps, grabbed his bag, slung it over his shoulder, and walked down the driveway.

~

STEEN HAD ALREADY HIKED a good mile when he heard the roar of a truck behind him, coming from the direction of the ranch house. He ground his jaw and didn't turn his head when the pickup slowed down.

"Keep the cell phone so I don't have to keep tracking you down whenever you get a phone call. Stop hiding and talk." Chase tossed the cell phone Steen had left behind at him, without even stopping.

Steen caught the phone instinctively, inhaling dirt as Chase sped up and drove away, leaving him swallowing dust.

For a long moment, he didn't even look at the phone. It had to be Erin. Who else would be calling him? He didn't know what to say. He couldn't listen to her voice and wonder how much of it had been lies, and wonder how much of a fool he'd been.

Slowly, he raised the phone to his ear. "Yeah?"

"Steen?"

It was a man's voice, one he didn't recognize. "Yeah?"

"Thomas Smith here. I took the liberty of calling this number, since this is the one you called my wife on. We didn't have any other way of contacting you. I hope that was all right."

"Thomas Smith?" The cultured voice became clearer, and he remembered Pointer's father. He stood taller. "Yes, sir, that was fine."

"You left a message with my wife. I've been working on it. Got some info for you."

Steen tightened his grip on the phone. "You mean about my mother?" A part of him wanted to hang up the phone right then. He didn't want to know. He really didn't. He'd had enough truth to last him.

"Alice Marie Rivers was a stripper and exotic dancer for ten years. A prostitute by some accounts, though details are sketchy."

Steen gritted his teeth and walked over to the nearby fence. He leaned on the wood, staring out across the dusty plains that now belonged in the Stockton family. "Yes, she was." He'd never forget the hours he'd spent sitting in one dingy motel room after another, waiting for his mother to come back with a bruise she hadn't had before. At the time, he'd been too young to understand exactly what had been going on, but he'd known it was bad, and he'd sworn every night that he'd find a way to provide for them so she didn't have to do it anymore.

He hadn't come through in time, and she'd bailed on him.

"She had one son, Steen Rivers Stockton."

He braced his palms on the fence and bowed his head, listening. "Yeah, that's her." He suddenly didn't want to hear about her life history. He knew about her life. He knew she'd had it shitty, being saddled with a kid. "Where is she now?" His fingers dug into the fence as he waited. Had she gone on to some better life? Found a rich guy who didn't want her bastard kid? Or had she met a grisly death at the hands of some john because he hadn't pulled his shit together in time to get her out of that life? "Tell me."

"She's dead, son."

Steen bowed his head against the sudden wave of grief. His eyes burned. What the hell was wrong with him? He hadn't seen her since he was a kid. That was too long to grieve the mother who'd abandoned him? "How? When?" His voice was thick and raspy, his words forcing themselves out on their own, asking questions he didn't want the answers to.

"Fourteen years ago. July fifth. Car accident. Someone was driving the wrong way on the interstate and killed her in a head-on collision. It wasn't her fault."

His gut dropped and he sucked in his breath. Killed in a car accident by a bastard driving the wrong way on the highway? What the hell? Who died like that? Then the date sank in. That had been two weeks after she'd dropped him off. "What road? Where was she going? Was it at night? Had she been drinking?"

"Late afternoon. She had just left work from her new job as an administrative assistant at a small printing company, and was, apparently, driving toward Rogue Valley."

Rogue Valley was where his father had lived, where she'd left him. She'd been driving toward *him*. Toward her kid. To get him? He closed his eyes against the emotions flooding him. Disbelief. Anger. Sadness. Relief. And...something deeper. It was as if something deep inside him had shattered, leaving him broken and bleeding...and somehow...better. *She'd been coming back for him*. "She had a job as an admin?"

"She'd just gotten it. She'd been working there for two days."

Steen closed his eyes. His mother had been on her way back to him after finding a legit job. *She'd been coming back*. No matter how many times he thought it, it still hit like a sucker punch to the gut. All these years, he'd blamed her for leaving him, and she hadn't been. He owed her an apology, in a major way. "No one told me." His voice was raw and ragged.

"Apparently, no one knew about you. Those who knew her as a stripper didn't know she had a son, and neither did anyone at her new job. She had no other family around, so they just let her go. No one knew you existed, so there was no one to tell." Thomas sounded disgusted. "It really wasn't that hard to make the connection. I'm not impressed. I don't think anyone tried."

Steen gripped the wood, his body shaking with emotion. He had tried, and he had failed. How had he not found this out when he'd searched before? He didn't know. How different would his life have been if he'd known all those years ago that his mother hadn't ditched him? How would that have changed things? At all? Completely? He didn't even know what to think, how to process it. "Thank you, sir." He managed to keep his voice even. "I appreciate it."

"You okay, son?"

Steen lifted his head. "Yeah, fine."

"Would you like me to find out anything else about her?"

"No, that's all I need. Thanks." Steen disconnected the call, and stared across the fields. His mother had tried to come back for him. She'd left him for only two weeks. Not a lifetime. Not forever. Two weeks. She'd gotten a real job, one that he knew probably paid like shit, but she'd done it for him, for them, so they could be normal.

He let out his breath, fighting the emotion that tried to overwhelm him. For fourteen years, he thought she'd left him. She hadn't. She'd died coming back for him. He looked at his shadow on the dirt, and he saw the outline of the hat Chase had gotten him. He'd probably been wearing it the moment his mother had died.

He looked up at the sky, the endless Wyoming sky. White clouds drifted across, shifting shapes like elusive, whispered dreams. "I'm sorry, Mom," he said, his voice almost breaking. "I'm sorry I doubted you," he said, still looking at the sky. "I should have believed you when you said you loved me, instead of doubting you all these years."

There was no reply from the skies, but he felt tightness ease from his chest, as if an invisible hand had brushed across his heart and loosened the clamps that had locked his heart down for so long. He took a deep breath, a breath that seemed to spread through his entire body, gently wiping away fourteen years of torment.

She hadn't lied. She hadn't left. She hadn't betrayed him. His mom had been every bit the woman he'd thought she was.

He rested his forearms on the fence, watching as some horses came into sight in the distance while he thought about his mom, trying to call up memories of their times together. For the first time since he was a kid, the memories didn't hurt. They made him smile, as he remembered the time she'd traded an hour of braiding hair for two ice cream cones. He'd forgotten about coconut ice cream, her favorite. He'd forgotten a lot, and it felt good to let himself remember again.

A loud whinny caught his attention, and Steen focused on the horses in the distance. They were galloping, tails up, ears back, hooves pounding, the ultimate freedom to run. Those days in prison, he never thought he'd be free again. He'd been so sure he was going to die there, and when he'd taken that hit meant for Pointer, he'd been ready to die. He was glad now he hadn't. If he had, he never would have known the truth about his mom.

And he never would have gotten together with Erin. *Erin*. He wanted to call her and tell her about his mom. She would understand why it mattered. She would get it.

The horses circled toward him, the herd spreading out as they ran. Steen gradually became aware that one near the rear was slow, favoring its right foreleg. Instinctively, he let out a sharp whistle. The injured horse's head turned, and she looked right at him.

In an instant, the world seemed to stand still, until it was just him and the horse, like the old days. The mare slowed down, and then stopped, standing in the middle of the plains, still staring at him, while the rest of the herd began to slow down as well.

Steen looked over his shoulder at the long dirt road. He still had miles to go until he reached town. He'd have to keep walking if he wanted to reach it by dark. Then he looked back at the horses, who had all stopped running. They were milling about, grazing, but the injured one continued to stand still, watching him.

Shit. He thought of his mom, who hadn't walked away. He thought of what Erin had said, how he was magic with the horses. Chase had said it too. They'd both said he was needed and welcome at the Stockton ranch. Was he? They were full of shit, he was sure of it.

But then again, he'd also been damned certain that his mother had betrayed him. How much else was he wrong about?

The injured mare nickered at him.

He glared at her. "Don't start with me."

But she didn't look away, and neither did he. Shit. Did he really want to do this? Did he really want to go back to this life? As he stood there, the horse lowered its head and began to walk toward him again, still favoring her right front leg. Steen watched the mare limp toward him. She was injured and wild, and yet she was still coming to him for help.

How could he say no? He was wearing Chase's hat on his head, a welcome that he'd never accepted. Maybe it was time to accept it. Maybe it was time to pay it forward.

The mare was still twenty yards away when he dropped his bag, vaulted over the fence, and walked toward her.

They met each other halfway.

CHAPTER EIGHTEEN

THE NEXT EVENING Erin sat stiffly in the dining room of her parents' country club, her head ringing as she listened to her father and Louis prattle on about her great success in the Kentucky Derby. Her mother was even there, but she was more interested in discussing her own successes than worrying about what Erin had done.

So, she'd won over her dad and Louis, but not her mother.

She was dressed appropriately, in one of the silk dresses she used to wear to assorted functions she had attended with Louis. Her hair was done in a fancy updo, and she was wearing her diamond studs. She looked classy and refined, and she hated every bit of it. She didn't want to be this woman anymore. She *couldn't* be this woman anymore, not for her parents, and certainly not for Louis.

As she looked across the table at her distant mother, something inside her finally let go. The impenetrable shield that she'd held so tightly around her heart finally cracked, and she realized she didn't care anymore. "Mom."

Her mother raised her perfectly plucked eyebrows at her. "Yes, Erin?"

"I don't care if you're proud of me." God, that felt good to say.

Her mom blinked. "What?"

"I don't care." As she said it, she knew it was true. She took a deep breath, and couldn't keep the smile from turning up the corners of her mouth. "I know that you've never been impressed with my career choice." She realized Louis and her father were listening, so she expanded her circle to include them. "I know I've been a disappointment to you all—"

Her father started to interrupt. "Erin, all that has changed—"

She held up her hand. "No, it hasn't." She took a deep breath to fortify herself and looked around at them all. "I don't want to do this anymore. I don't want to be an equine surgeon. I want to be with animals who matter to people, who aren't simply about money."

The three of them stared at her blankly, completely unable to comprehend any speech that dismissed the value of money. "I'm quitting my job," she said, speaking slowly so they could understand. "I'm moving out west."

"To Wyoming?" Louis's disdain dripped from his words.

She paused as the image of Steen flashed in her mind. For a split second, she wanted to say yes. God, how she wanted to say yes. But there was no way she was going to go down that road again. She'd learned her lesson about trying to pry love from someone who didn't want to give it to her. "No, not to Wyoming. Maybe Oregon. Or Washington. Or Texas. I don't know. Somewhere. Just not here." As she said the words, she felt the most amazing sense of freedom and exhilaration. She didn't have to be this woman anymore. She didn't need their approval. A smile began to spread across her face. "I'm going to open my own clinic, in some small town where there's no other vet to take care of the animals."

Her father looked horrified. "But you've finally broken in. You're on the way to the upper echelons. Why would you ever walk away from that? Is it stress? Do you need a prescription? I can write you up a script and—"

"No, I don't need tranquilizers," she interrupted. "There's nothing wrong with me. I just don't want to do this anymore."

"Why would you do this?" Louis was staring at her with his eyes narrowed.

She could practically feel his withdrawal, and it felt brilliant. Never had disdain felt so freeing. Being rejected by people with Louis's values meant she was finally doing something right. She leaned forward so that they could all hear her. "I'm doing it, because it will make me happy."

Their blank, uncomprehending expressions in response to her announcement were all the confirmation she needed. They had absolutely no ability to grasp that simple concept. She was finished here. "I'm going home to pack." She'd given her notice yesterday, and today had been her last day. Her clinic hadn't been happy about the short notice, but that was too bad for them. It was her life, not theirs, and she was finally going to claim it.

"What about the house?" Louis caught her arm. "You're just going to leave it?"

She raised her eyebrows at him. "Do you want to buy it from me?"

"No, I want you to stay so we can work this out," he said urgently. "I made a mistake, Erin. Don't throw away your career just because you're pissed at me." He reached into his pocket and pulled out a ring, an engagement ring twice the size of her old one. "Listen, I made a huge mistake when I left you. I was a bastard, and I know it. I'm not with her anymore. I want you back. Think of what we can accomplish together."

God, how long she'd waited to hear those words, to have him beg to take her back, to see what he'd lost when he'd let her go. And now that she had it, she felt nothing. No, that was wrong. She felt disdain and disgust. "Louis—"

His gaze flicked behind her, and disdain flooded his features.

Instinctively, she turned, and her heart skipped when she saw Steen standing behind her. "Steen!" Her heart leapt at the sight, and suddenly, she couldn't breathe. He was there.

He was wearing his same battered cowboy hat, jeans that fit him just right, and cowboy boots that were still covered in dust. He looked like he'd just walked right in off the ranch, with his unshaven jaw and his plaid shirt unbuttoned at the throat. He looked rugged, dangerous, and incredibly handsome. What was he doing in Virginia? In her parents' country club? How was he even standing there?

His gaze was on Louis, not her. With a sinking heart, she realized he was staring at the engagement ring in Louis's hand. She knew all too well how badly Rachel had betrayed him, and now, here she was, with her ex-husband handing her a diamond ring. "Steen—"

His attention leapt from the ring to her face, and she saw the hesitation in his eyes. God, is that really what he thought of her? That she'd run back to Louis after all the time she'd spent with him?

"And who is this?" Louis put his arm over her shoulders, pulling her against him in a statement of ownership. "Some ranch hand from your trip to Wyoming?"

She stiffened instinctively as anger roiled through her. She opened her mouth to snap at Louis, when Steen's expression stopped her.

He was staring at her so intently she felt as if he'd stripped her soul bare. His gaze flicked to Louis's arm, then to the huge diamond ring, and then back to her face, searching her eyes as if he could ferret out every last secret that she'd hidden inside her. Hope leapt through her, hope that maybe, just maybe, he could see her truth, that she wasn't too good for him, that she would never treat him the way everyone else in his life had treated him.

Time seemed to stand still as she waited for his reaction. She had tried so often to convince him, and finally, she realized he had to decide for himself. So, she didn't defend herself. She said nothing. She simply waited, her heart thundering as she waited for Steen to speak.

Louis stuck out his free hand, still not releasing her shoulders. "I'm Dr. Louis Armstrong, Erin's husband. Who are you?"

Steen looked at Erin. "I'm the guy who loves her."

"You are?" Tears burned in her eyes, and she couldn't keep the huge smile from lighting up her face. "You do?"

Louis's arm tightened around her. "Did you not hear me say I was her husband?"

Steen ignored Louis, instead, staring at Erin, speaking directly to her, as if Louis's arm wasn't around her and he wasn't trying to shove a massive diamond ring onto her hand. "She died," he said. "She didn't leave me. She died coming back to me. My mom."

Erin's heart softened for him. She wanted to hug him, but she didn't move. She still didn't know why he was there, or what he wanted. "Of course she didn't leave you. What woman would ever leave you?"

"You did."

She shook her head. "You let me go. There's a difference. I tried—"

"I know." Steen suddenly reached for her, enfolding her hand in his. "I know you tried. I know you gave me your heart and your soul, but what I didn't know was that I gave mine right back to you."

She pressed her lips together, fighting against the emotions threatening to overtake her. "I knew you did. But it wasn't enough, was it?"

Steen shook his head. "That's where I was wrong." He tugged on her, pulling her away from Louis. Neither one of them acknowledged his sputter of fury as Steen took both her hands in his. "Here's the deal, Erin. My past hasn't changed. I'm still going to be living under that shadow. I can't change that. But I heard what you said about the horses. You're right. They matter to me. I'm going to work with them. It's what I need to do."

She nodded. "I'm so glad. You'll do great things for those horses." She had to ask, ask for the words she knew would never come. "Why are you here? In Virginia? At my parent's country club?"

"There are horses all over the place. Chase asked me to stay on the ranch." He shrugged, and touched the brim of his battered old hat. "I could do it, but I can't stand to be there alone. I need you with me."

Her heart seemed to come alive for the first time in her life, thundering in her chest. "You do?"

"But I won't ask you to give up your career. I saw your interview. I know you're amazing and talented, and I won't ask you to give it up. I can petition the court to move my parole to Virginia—"

"Parole?" Louis interrupted. "*Parole*? You're a convict?"

Steen's gaze flashed to Louis. "I was in prison for attempted murder," he said softly. "Don't push me."

Erin could barely stifle a giggle when she saw Louis turn ashen and hurry away to talk to her parents, who were watching the scene with shocked faces. She was sure they were horrified at the sight of Steen in his cowboy hat and jeans, and she didn't care. She looked back at Steen. "They're going to call the police. You should go."

"I got permission to leave the state. Pointer's dad pulled some strings for me. It turns out, saving his son's life made him like me, and the man has connections." He cradled her hands against his chest, searching her face. "Here's the thing, Erin. I know you're a thousand times more than what I could ever be, and I can't offer you country club dinners, but I can swear on my mother's soul to love you the way you deserve to be loved. I will always stand by you, I will always be proud of you, and I will always be the best man I can be for you. I will always, without fail, love you with every last bit of my heart. I've loved you since you were fourteen years old, and I will love you until the end of time."

This time, she couldn't stop the tears from falling. "I love you, too, Steen."

He went down on one knee, and took her hand in his. "I will be yours in whatever way you'll have me. If you want me to walk away, I will. If you want me to move to Virginia, I'm on it. If you want to live on the ranch with me, I'll build you the best damned house anyone ever lived in."

She knew what her answer was, oh, she knew, but before she answered, she had to ask him. "When did you realize that what you can give me is enough?"

He looked up at her. "When I realized that my mom had died for me. She didn't need to get a real job for me. Just her alone would have been enough. All I wanted was for her to love me. Her love would have been enough for me, which made me realize that maybe, just maybe, my love would be enough for you."

She went down on her knees so she was level with him and framed his handsome face with her hands. "Being loved by the person you love isn't simply enough. It's everything."

For the first time, hope hovered in his eyes, chasing away the shadows that had been haunting them for so long. "You're my every-thing, Erin. I love you."

"You're my everything, Steen. You always have been." Her throat was tight, but she knew she had to get out the words before she was crying too much to talk. "I just told my parents I was quitting my job and moving west to open a regular vet clinic. I need a place to live, and a roommate to split the bills." She wrapped her arms around his neck. "I pick you."

Disbelief swept over his face. "Really? You want to move to the ranch with me?"

She grinned. "Really. If you'll have me."

"Damn woman. I'd have given my soul for another minute with you. To have you with me forever? It's more than I could ever have dreamed. Before you, I didn't even know this existed." He pressed his palm over her heart. "Love, passion, commitment, trust. You showed it to me, and you taught me to believe." He slipped his hands into her hair, gently tugging her closer to him. "I've been waiting for you my whole life, bird girl." Then he kissed her, a kiss that was so private, and so personal, and so beautiful that she knew she had finally found where she belonged: in the arms of the man who had won her heart so many years ago.

CHAPTER NINETEEN

STEEN PAUSED in the doorway of Chase's living room, taking a moment to survey the scene. Mira and Erin were sitting side by side on the couch, going over paint swatches. Mira's belly was enormous now, and Steen half-expected that baby to pop out at any second, though his brother assured him they still had another couple months to go. Chase was leaning back in the easy chair, with a glass of lemonade in his hand, watching the women with the most satisfied expression on his face.

Steen knew that expression, because he felt the same way. So damned happy. He never thought he'd walk into Chase's living room and feel comfortable, but he did. He loved coming in here and knowing that he belonged, that he was slowly building connections he'd never had before.

It would take time, but it felt good. Really damn good. And it was all because of Erin.

It was a familial scene, one with women's laughter and pastel colors for the baby's nursery. There was a fire in the fireplace, and pictures on the mantle. It was a place he never, ever thought he'd be, but with Erin to support him, he was learning how to navigate it.

Granted, his favorite time of the day was retiring to the bunkhouse each evening with Erin, but a few dinners with his brother and Mira weren't so bad. Not bad at all, in fact.

As he stood there with drinks in his hand, Erin looked up. She immediately smiled, the kind of warm, just-for-him smile that always melted his heart. He grinned back and walked into the room. He handed Mira her lemonade, then sat next to Erin and gave her the glass of wine he'd poured for her.

Yeah, there wasn't much space on the couch, but he needed to be beside her. He always needed to be beside her, touching her, talking to her. He wanted her input in the plans for their new house, and for the vet clinic he was going to attach to it. Of course, Josie already had her clinic in town, but she'd been thrilled to have Erin set up shop. Apparently, she hadn't been able to keep up with the demand, and there was plenty of market share.

Erin held up a pale pink color swatch. "What do you think of this?"

He raised his brows. "I thought it was a boy. Not sure he'll be okay with that."

She rolled her eyes. "Not for them. For us."

He stared at her, and his gut suddenly dropped out of his stomach. "For *us*? Are you—" His gaze dropped in shock to her belly, and a thousand emotions rushed through him.

Her face paled. "No. I meant for the waiting room at the clinic."

"Oh." He couldn't stop the crash of disappointment that plummeted through him.

She stared at him. "I thought you wanted to wait until you were done with your parole and were totally free before we got married or had children. Did you want me to be pregnant just then?"

"Shit, yeah. I mean, yeah, to wait. But—" He jerked his gaze to hers. "When you just said...I thought..." He spread his hands. "I don't know. It just...the thought of you being a mom...it felt right."

Her face softened. "And what about you being a dad? How did that feel?"

Steen looked across the room at his brother, feeling helpless. What the hell did he know about being a parent? Chase nodded once, grinning at him "You'll figure it out." As Chase spoke, Mira got up, walked over to him, and snuggled into his lap.

His brother rested his hand possessively on Mira's belly and pressed a kiss to her hair. "It's all good, bro. You'll be fine."

Steen looked back at Erin, who was watching Mira and Chase with a wistful expression on her face. He'd never seen such stark longing, and a part of his gut twisted up. "Erin." He spoke softly, just for her.

She turned back toward him, and the wistfulness was gone, replaced with the same look of tenderness she always reserved just for him. "Yes?"

"I'm so sorry we're not married yet."

The wistfulness came back into her eyes. "Steen. I would marry you in a heartbeat, but I understand that your sense of honor guides you. You want to give me a chance to leave if your past becomes too much." She tucked her feet up beneath her as she slipped her hands around his neck. "You need to understand that you could be on parole for the rest of your life, and I will never leave you." She took his hand and placed it over her heart. "You're my home, Steen. You're my heart. You're my everything. I spent my life waiting for people to look at me with the respect I wanted, and I almost destroyed myself in my effort to impress others. I don't care about that anymore. I just care about the man I love."

Steen's throat tightened, and his eyes suddenly felt like they were burning. "How did I get so lucky to find you?"

She shrugged. "It took kind of a long time. It wasn't exactly easy."

"No, it wasn't." He slipped his finger beneath her chin and kissed her lightly. "It was worth everything I endured, because it made me end up with you." He pushed her hair behind her ears, staring down into the face of the only person in the world who mattered to him, though Chase and Mira were starting to claim their space. None of the other Stocktons had come by yet, and he wasn't sure how he'd feel when they showed up, but he was willing to try. But in the meantime.... "I swear I'll marry you," he said, pressing a kiss to Erin's lips. "I bought the ring." His heart lifted when he saw her face light up. "I'm just waiting until I can give it to you, but I needed to have it." He needed the tangible reality of their future that the ring gave him, but he couldn't give it to her yet. He needed her to be free to leave him, and he couldn't give her the ring until he knew that she would never want to walk away from the baggage he brought with him.

"Don't tell her you bought a ring," Mira protested. "That takes all the surprise out of it. A woman needs romance."

"Like being proposed to in a tree?" Chase teased. "Was that romantic enough for you?"

She giggled at him, and whispered something to Chase that had them both laughing and whispering.

Steen kept his focus on Erin. "When Chase and Mira get married in a few weeks, it might make you uncomfortable, but I don't want you to doubt how I feel about you. I want you to be certain of my intentions." He still couldn't believe all his brothers except Caleb would be coming for the wedding. He wasn't ready to face them yet.

She nodded. "I do know, but I appreciate you telling me. It feels good to hear it aloud." Her eyes sparkled. "Can I peek at the ring?"

He grinned. "No, of course not—"

A heavy knock sounded on the front door, and Steen tensed. "Zane?" he guessed. Zane was the brother most likely to stop by, but he hadn't heard the roar of his motorcycle.

"I don't know. It's late." Chase started to untangle himself from Mira, but Steen stood up. "I'll get it."

He had to face his brothers at some point. He had to learn who they were. He strode across the door and pulled it open.

It wasn't Zane.

It was Thomas Smith, Pointer's dad. He was wearing pressed jeans and a sweater, but his dress shirt was untucked, as if he'd barely managed to pull himself together before heading out. Steen's first thought was of the young man they both knew. "Is Pointer okay? You need something?"

He ignored Steen's questions. "May I come in?" The cultured tones of Thomas's voice no longer felt so threatening to Steen. He knew that Thomas was on his side, and the man was willing to throw considerable weight around for him.

"Of course." He stepped back as Erin and the others stood up. "This is my brother, Chase Stockton, his fiancée Mira Cabot and my..." He met Erin's gaze. "My..." He wanted to say fiancée. Wife. Anything to show how special she was. Girlfriend seemed pathetically inadequate, and he wouldn't say fiancée until she was wearing his ring. So, he simply settled for her name. "Erin Chambers." His fiancée. He wanted to say it, but he didn't dare. It wasn't fair to her. All he could offer was the tone of his voice when he said the words, as if he could somehow inject into her name how deeply he felt about her. He knew it wasn't enough, but he couldn't take more from her, not yet. He instinctively glanced at Erin's face to make sure she was okay with it.

Her smile said she was, as did the way she slipped around the end of the couch and walked over to stand beside him, gently sliding her hand into his. Steen grinned at the man.

Thomas smiled at Erin. "So this is the woman you ran off to Virginia to track down. I guess it paid off."

Steen grinned. "Yeah, it did. She took me back."

"Glad to hear it."

"Thank you, sir. I really appreciate it."

Thomas rolled his eyes. "Don't call me 'sir.' Just Thomas."

Steen nodded. Thomas was a man who had always been so far above him in life, and now he was just Thomas. It felt good, really good. "Can I offer you a drink?"

"Hell, no. I need to get going." Thomas's blue gaze settled on Steen's. "I've been working all my contacts to try to get Pointer's conviction overturned. He's a good kid, and he got caught up in the aftermath of my work. He made a mistake, but it wasn't his fault, and I was willing to do whatever it took to get him out of there."

Hope leapt through Steen. "Is that why you're here? Is Pointer free?"

"He sure is." A broad grin broke over Thomas's face. "I'm on my way now to pick him up."

Steen grinned. "That's fantastic."

"Yes, it is." Thomas's smile faded. "But if you hadn't saved his life, it would have been too late. I owe you."

Steen put his arm around Erin and pulled her against him. "No, you don't. We're even. I got the girl. We both got the one we loved. We're more than even."

"Not yet." Thomas held out a folded paper. "When I had my team researching your mother, we uncovered a lot more about you. The truth."

Steen frowned as he took the paper. "What are you talking about?"

"You didn't try to murder anyone. You know it, the lying bastard knows it, and now the governor knows it."

"What?" Steen stared at the older man. "What are you talking about?"

Thomas just nodded at the paper. "Open it."

Steen slowly, disbelievingly, unfolded the paper. Erin leaned over his arm, reading with him. He saw the letterhead. He saw his name. He saw the word *pardoned*. And the word *innocent*. Erin made a small noise of disbelief, and Steen felt his whole body begin to shake. He stared at Thomas. "What is this?"

"You're a free man, Steen. You've been pardoned. It's over." He met his gaze. "I could have asked for a retrial, but those take time and anything can happen. I wanted it over. The governor pardoned you based on several private, off-the-record, confessions to the governor at his home that I...facilitated." He winked, leaving no doubt that those private confessions had not been obtained easily. "The other parties involved are now being investigated for perjury, but I wouldn't hold my breath. Her father has considerable influence." Thomas grinned. "Not as much as I have, though."

Steen felt like his head was spinning, and his hand was shaking. He'd been pardoned. His record expunged. No parole. No conviction. Nothing. Just a new life of complete freedom. "I don't know what to say—"

"There's nothing to say," Thomas said. "It still doesn't repay my debt to you." He nodded at the others. "I have to go get my kid," he said. He held out his hand. "It would be my honor to consider you a friend, Steen."

Steen didn't hesitate. He shook Thomas's hand. "The honor is mine, sir... Thomas."

Thomas said his farewells to the rest of the crew, and then jogged down the stairs to a black Mercedes idling in the driveway.

Steen didn't even bother to close the front door. He simply turned to Erin, took her hand, and went down on one knee. "Will you marry me?" He wanted to say a million things, to tell her how much he loved her, to shout to the world the gift that Thomas had just given him, but in that moment, he wanted only one thing, for Erin to be his wife, so he could hold onto her forever.

Her eyes shimmered with unshed tears. "Of course I will. You didn't need to be pardoned for me to marry you."

"I know I didn't, but I needed to be the man you deserve." He dug into his front pocket and held up the diamond ring he'd bought on his way to Virginia. He'd had it in his pocket since that day, always prepared to show it to her if she began to doubt his intentions. Never in a million years had he thought he'd have the chance to give it to her so soon. "I know it's not as big as the one Louis gave you—"

"It's perfect." Her whisper was so full of emotion and love, that he knew it was. She held out her hand, and he slipped the ring onto her finger. The diamond glittered like the stars on a summer night, and he pressed a kiss to the sparkling stone.

She held out her arms to him, and he rose to his feet, pulling her into the fold of his body. He kissed her, their first kiss as an engaged couple, and it was a thousand times more perfect than all the other perfect ones they'd shared. Her body felt amazing, incredible, and perfect against his. He broke the kiss, whispering in her ear. "Let me take you back home. I need to make love to my fiancée," he whispered.

She beamed up at him, her face glowing with happiness. "Yes, please do."

He looked over her shoulder at Chase and Mira, who were beaming at them. "I think we're going to head out. Thanks for dinner."

"Not yet." Chase held up his hand, exchanging glances with Mira, who nodded. Then both of them looked at Steen and Erin. "We'd be honored if you guys wanted to do a double wedding with us. I know it's soon, but not really. It's been a long time for you guys. No pressure, but the invite's open."

Rightness roared through Steen, and he knew that he wanted nothing more than to marry Erin as soon as possible. He looked down at her, and his heart softened when he saw the expression on her face.

He took her hand and pressed a kiss to her palm. "I've been waiting for you for years," he said softly. He'd been willing to wait for as long as it took to make himself worthy of her, but now that Thomas has purged his past, now that he had the opportunity, his entire soul was burning for her, to make her his, forever. "I'd marry you tonight, if I could. I know that you probably want your own wedding, and that's cool. I'll wait as long as it takes, but—"

"Yes."

He broke into a grin. "Yes? Yes, to the double wedding?"

She grinned. "Of course, yes. I think we've waited enough years, don't you?"

"Hell, yeah." He let out a whoop and swung her in his arms, unable to wipe the grin off his face. He grinned stupidly at his brother and Mira. "You guys sure? I mean—"

"Family, man." Chase walked over. "It's all about family." Then his big brother dragged Steen into a bear hug. For a split second, Steen hesitated, then he felt Mira's arms go around him and Chase, locking them together. Steen wrapped one arm around his soon-to-be sister-in-law, and then held out his other arm to Erin.

She came willingly, sliding into his embrace and into the circle of the family that he was no longer willing to run away from. He couldn't turn them away. It just felt too damn good to be a part of it, and he knew that it was Erin who had given him the strength to reach out and be willing to try.

"I love you," he whispered to her.

She smiled up at him. "I love you, too, cowboy. Always and forever."

The best damn words he'd ever heard.

∾

Did you enjoy Steen and Erin's story? If so, please consider leaving a short review on the eTailer and/or Goodreads. Reviews make a huge difference for authors!

∾

Do you want to know when Stephanie has a new book out, is running a sale, or giving away prizes? Sign up for her private newsletter here!

~

Keep reading for the next Wyoming Rebels book!

Stephanie ROWE

A Real Cowboy Rides a Motorcycle

WYOMING REBELS

COPYRIGHT

For Donna Bossert. Thank you for all your support and friendship. I treasure you!

CHAPTER ONE

TAYLOR SHAW PEERED through the torrential rain hammering her windshield, inspecting the somewhat grand ranch house stretched out in front of her. It was a single story, but the huge porch and the massive picture windows gave the impression of grandeur and luxury that made her smile. This was the home of her best friend, Mira Cabot, and it was perfect.

For a brief moment, tears burned in her eyes and her throat tightened, as she recalled how hard Mira's path had been for so long. And now...she'd found her place. *You go, girl.*

God, she couldn't wait to hug Mira, and to hear about the life she'd been brave enough to tackle. Taylor knew she'd never have been as courageous as Mira, and she was so damn proud of her. Unable to keep the grin off her face, Taylor shoved open the door of the tiny rental car she'd managed to procure at the airport and almost dove out of the car in her eagerness to see Mira.

Dodging the flood of raindrops pummeling the Wyoming ranch, Taylor bolted across the muddy driveway, and vaulted up the steps to the front door. She rang the doorbell, and hopped back and forth, trying to keep warm as she waited for Mira to open the door.

She was drenched within seconds, but she didn't care one bit that she'd left her coat in the car. Who needed a coat when she was going to be hugging her best friend after months of being apart? She waited eagerly, barely even noticing how the rain was driving the coldness right through to her bones. In seconds, she would be hugging Mira. *Seconds!*

Footsteps thudded inside, and she grinned wider as she saw the door begin to open. She flung out her arms with a squeal. "Surprise—!" She cut herself off, startled to see a tall, well-muscled cowboy staring at her like she was some crazed, bedraggled freak. His blue plaid shirt was unbuttoned, revealing an amazing chest, and his dark hair was tousled, as if he'd been climbing into bed just before she'd rung the doorbell.

Whoops. She immediately dropped her arms and tried to appear harmless and sane. "Oh, sorry. I thought Mira would answer. Is she here?" She tried to peek past him, but he was big and muscular, blocking the door.

"She's asleep." He looked her up and down. "Can I help you?"

"Asleep?" She stared at him, horrified at his comment. "What time is it? Is it late?" She knew she'd gotten lost a couple times on the way there, but it couldn't be that late, could it?

"It's nine o'clock, but she gets tired easily." He narrowed his eyes, and there was no doubt of his protectiveness of Mira, which, of course Taylor appreciated, except for the fact that Mira didn't need protection from her.

There was only one man who would defend her friend so determinedly, and that would be the man who Mira had traveled cross-country to shack up with, Chase Stockton. Taylor smiled and held out her hand to shake his, realizing belatedly that introductions would probably be appropriate before barging into his house. He couldn't be expected to know how to handle their typical interactions. "You must be Chase. I'm Taylor Shaw, Mira's best friend from home."

"Taylor!" His frown disappeared into a welcoming smile that made him devastatingly handsome, and he swung the door open. "Come on in. I didn't know you were coming today. I thought it was next week. The wedding isn't for ten days."

"Thanks." Ah, yes, being invited indoors was way better than having her path blocked. Inside was definitely preferable to standing in a torrential downpour. "I wanted to surprise her, so I didn't call ahead. We like to do that to each other sometimes." She didn't mention that she'd also been desperate to escape from work. It was sucking the life out of her, and she needed to regroup and figure out what to do. What better place to regroup than with her best friend and a pint of ice cream, like they'd done countless times over the years?

As uninspiring as her work was, the problem wasn't that simple. As it turned out, having Edward become her ex-boyfriend, while still being her boss, was making work almost intolerable. Every time she saw him, a thousand emotions came flooding back, none of which were ones that made her want to jump for joy and dance on top of her desk in celebration.

So, she'd come here to support Mira in her upcoming wedding, as planned, but she'd come early because she needed her friend's advice and support. She and Mira had always been there for each other, especially when neither of them had anyone else to turn to, which had been the situation for both of them for a long time.

"Well, come on in," Chase said, gesturing her inside. "Get out of the rain."

Whoops. She'd forgotten to actually accept his invitation and go indoors. Oy. She was more stressed than she'd even realized. "Right. I'm on it." She stepped inside, and her flats squelched on the floor. They both looked down at the pool of muddy water spreading out from her feet and across the gorgeous stone floor. Heat flooded her cheeks. "Oh... I'll just wait outside—"

Chase snorted. "It's a ranch, Taylor. It's made for mud."

"Yes, but it's a really lovely ranch." The entry was paved with stone, but gleaming hardwood floors stretched across the rest of the house. She could see into a sleek modern kitchen, and a comfortable, rustic living room was just off to the right. The house was beautiful and homey, and a little bit of envy trickled through her when she thought of the stark apartment that she slept in on the rare occasion she wasn't traveling for work.

He grinned. "Thanks. We've put a lot of work into it." The pride was evident in his voice, making Taylor smile. She could tell already that Chase was a good man. Mira had been right to believe in him.

"I'll go see if she's awake. Help yourself to anything in the kitchen. I'll be right back." Chase indicated the kitchen, and then strode down the hallway, his cowboy boots clicking on the beautiful floor, his Wranglers faded like a real cowboy's should be. There was no doubt Mira had found herself a genuine cowboy, one that was every bit the man Mira had thought he was.

He disappeared through a closed door at the end of the hall, leaving Taylor alone. She let out a sigh as her stomach rumbled with hunger. She glanced longingly at the kitchen, but made no move toward it. Normally, she wouldn't hesitate to raid Mira's cabinets in search of sustenance, but this was Chase's house, and she was a stranger.

She shifted restlessly, afraid to walk around and drip all over everything. Hugging herself against the encroaching chill while she waited, she heard low, intimate murmurings from down the hall, whispers that weren't for her, whispers that she'd expected to be a part of when she'd decided to come here.

Wow. Right. She wasn't Mira's number one anymore. She hadn't thought of that.

She took a deep breath. That was okay. She was ecstatic Mira had found Chase. There was still room for best friends even when a man was in the picture.

"Taylor?" Mira's sleepy voice echoed down the hall, and Taylor's heart leapt.

She spun toward her friend, and then her mouth dropped open when she saw Mira waddling toward her, her massive belly barely covered by her pale pink robe. Her dark blond curls were longer now, and she was no longer sporting the too-skinny look that had worried Taylor for the last few years. Her breasts had tripled in size, and she looked radiant, gorgeous, and healthy, everything Taylor had hoped for with all her heart, everything that Taylor had never been able to do for her. "Wow. You're huge, girl. It's like you have half the kitchen tucked up under there." Of course she'd known her friend was pregnant, but seeing her that way was a shocking reality. Chase was walking beside her, his arm over her shoulders, as if he couldn't bear not to be touching her, and Taylor's sense of exclusion grew stronger.

Mira grinned and put her hand on her belly. "Only a few more weeks until you can call me mama."

"I call her mama already." Chase's voice was affectionate and warm, and he looked at Mira as if she was his entire world.

It was so intimate between them, with no room for a third party. Taylor stepped back, her hands falling down to her sides as she abandoned her hug. What had she done coming here? Why had she thought nothing would change now that Mira had found Chase?

But Mira didn't hesitate, throwing her arms around Taylor and hugging her just as tightly as she ever had.

Tears filled Taylor's eyes and she hugged Mira back just as fiercely, all her fears melting away. "I missed you," she whispered, her throat tightening up. God, she hadn't realized how lonely she'd been since Mira had moved away, but being with her friend again made her viscerally aware of how empty her life was when she wasn't burying herself in her work.

"I missed you, too, Taylor," Mira replied, pulling back.

Reluctantly, Taylor released her. "How are you doing? You feeling okay?" She glanced at Chase. "Is he being good to you?" she asked in a mock stage whisper.

Mira laughed, her eyes lighting up with happiness. "Everything is great. What about you?"

Taylor glanced at Chase with his arm around Mira again, and she knew now wasn't the time for her to start crying on Mira's shoulder. So, she managed a flippant smile. "Everything is awesome. I finished my latest assignment early, so I wanted to come early to help out. I figured you could use another hand getting things ready for the wedding and the baby."

"Of course! You're always welcome." The genuine warmth in Mira's voice eased some of Taylor's rising tension and sense of isolation. "I'll put you to work in the morning. Where are you staying?"

"Where am I—?" Taylor felt heat rush to her cheeks. It hadn't even occurred to her to find a hotel. She'd just assumed that she'd stay here, but she quickly realized what a mistake that had been. "I—"

"Oh, stay with us," Mira said quickly, her face softening as she astutely picked up on Taylor's situation. "Our basement guest room is full of boxes we retrieved from my parent's house and haven't unpacked yet, and the first floor bedroom now has a crib in it, but you could sleep in the living room."

Taylor felt her heart sinking. Sleep on the couch? In their space? She knew she'd feel like she was intruding every second she was there. "That's okay. I'll just—"

"Or the bunkhouse," Mira interrupted, her face brightening as she thought of it. She and Chase exchanged a special smile that once again made Taylor feel like she was standing on the periphery. "Is it ready for her, Chase?"

He nodded. "I had it cleaned after Steen and Erin moved out. It's all set."

Taylor frowned, trying to follow the conversation. "Steen and Erin? Who are they?"

"Oh, you'll love them," Mira said, her eyes sparkling with happiness. "Steen is Chase's brother, and Erin is his fiancée. They're building a house and a vet clinic on the south side of the property. They were living in the bunkhouse, but they moved to a trailer home next to their house so they have a little privacy while it's being built. Erin is such a doll. You'll love her."

"Oh." Taylor cleared her throat at the obvious affection in Mira's voice. Clearly, she and Erin had become close friends, and they were almost sisters now if Erin was engaged to Chase's brother. Taylor clasped her hands behind her head, suddenly wishing that she'd arranged for a hotel room. This wasn't what she'd envisioned at all. "I'm sure we'll get along great," she managed.

"Of course you will." Mira yawned, and Taylor realized she was overstaying her welcome.

"So, I'll just let you guys do your thing," she said, taking her cue to leave. "If you can point me to the bunkhouse, I'll go set up there."

"I'll take your bags down there," Chase said, reaching for a weather-beaten trench coat that looked like it was built for storms like the one howling outside.

"Oh, no. I'm all set. I don't have much—"

"You're not going out alone," Chase said, his voice mellow but unyielding. "I've got you covered."

Taylor's throat suddenly tightened, and she had to look away and blink several times. God, how long had it been since someone had done something as simple as heading outside in a driving rainstorm to help her with her bags? She didn't even know Chase, but he made her feel like she mattered. How had Mira found someone this wonderful? She hadn't even realized men like Chase existed.

"Do you want to snag some food to take with you?" Mira asked. "I don't think there's anything there." Before Taylor could answer, she was already heading to the kitchen. "I think I have some coffee you'll like," she called out as she opened cabinets. "And of course, your oatmeal for breakfast. And I have some leftover chicken that Chase grilled tonight," she said, yawning again. "I'm so sorry that I can't stay up with you. I just get so tired."

"It's totally fine," Taylor said. "I should have called first." God, she should have called. She'd had visions of sitting up on the couch for hours with ice cream and hot chocolate while they caught up. She hadn't thought about how things would be different, and she should have.

Chase shoved a cowboy hat on his head while Mira handed Taylor a grocery bag. She hugged Taylor again, a fierce hug that soothed some of Taylor's tension. "I'm *so* glad you're here, Taylor."

"Me, too." The tightness around her chest loosened slightly at Mira's sincerity. "I'll see you in the morning. You can come grab me when you're ready for company, okay? I don't want to barge in on you twice."

Mira smiled. "Deal."

Chase walked over to Mira, locked his arm around her waist, and pulled her close for an almost unbearably sweet kiss. "I'll be right back. Don't have the baby while I'm gone."

Mira laughed and lightly swatted his chest. "You'll have to take it up with the baby, not me."

He leaned forward and put his ear to her belly, as if he were listening. Then he nodded. "The baby says that I'm in charge. He says he'll wait."

Mira's eyebrows shot up. "*She'll* do what *she* wants."

He shot her a cocky look. "We'll see."

A part of Taylor wanted to put her ear to Mira's belly and listen to the baby as well, but another part of her wanted to slink away from the intimacies that she wasn't a part of and hop on the next plane out of town. She did neither. She was too tired to leave, and too uncertain to reach out and slap her palm across her best friend's belly. So she just smiled. "See you in the morning, Mira."

"You bet!" At Mira's wave, Taylor ducked out into the rain, no longer caring that she was soaked and covered in mud. She just wanted a moment to regroup and figure out where she could fit into her best friend's new life.

There had to be a place, right? Because if there wasn't, she had no one else.

God, that was a great thought. Surely she could muster up a more positive attitude. She could get a cat. Or a goldfish. A fish would be a good listener, right?

But as she slogged through the mud, following Chase to her car, she knew there was no way to deny the truth: fish were slimy, and if she had to rely on one to be her dearest friend...well...that was just not a good solution.

She shook her head, unable to shake the isolation that was beginning to grip her. What was she going to do?

HE WAS TIRED.

He was cranky.

He was wet.

Zane Stockton idled his motorcycle outside his brother's ranch house, narrowing his eyes at the darkened windows. Gone was the time when he'd let himself in and crash. There was a woman in there now, and that changed all the rules, especially when it was two in the morning.

He probably shouldn't have come tonight, but he was here, and he was done being on the road for now. Rain had been thundering down on him for hours, and he was drenched. He just wanted to sleep and forget about all the crap that had gone down today. Grief was gnawing at him, the kind of grief that he had to escape, the kind that would destroy him if he let it.

Which was why he'd come to the ranch. It was the only place in his life, besides the open road, where the noise in his head quieted long enough for him to think.

Trying not to rev the engine too much, he eased his bike down the driveway and turned right into the lean-to beside the bunkhouse. He settled his bike and whipped out a couple towels to clean it off, making sure it was mud-free before calling it a night.

Task accomplished, he grabbed his bag from the back of the bike, scowling when he realized it had gotten wet. Not that it mattered. Nothing mattered now except crashing. He sloshed through the puddles toward the front door of the bunkhouse, retrieved the key from the doorframe, and pried the thing open.

It was pitch dark inside, but he knew his way around and didn't bother with a light. He dropped the bag, kicked off his boots and his drenched clothes, then headed for the only bed that was still set up in the place after Steen and Erin's brief occupation of it. Zane was damn glad they'd upgraded their lodgings to a temporary mobile home so the bunkhouse was now available again for use by the family vagrant.

Zane jerked back the covers and collapsed onto the bed. The minute he landed, he felt the soft, very real feel of a body beneath him, including the swell of a woman's breast beneath his forearm. Shit! "What the hell?" He leapt to his feet just as a woman shrieked and slammed a pillow into the side of his head.

"Hey, I'm not going to hurt you! I'm Chase's brother!" He grabbed the pillow as it clocked him in the side of the head again. "Stop!"

There was a moment of silence, and all he could hear was heavy breathing. Then she spoke. "You're Chase's brother?" Her voice was breathless, and throaty, as if he'd awakened her out of a deep sleep, which he probably had. It sounded sexy as hell, and he was shocked to feel a rush of desire catapult through him.

Shit. He hadn't responded physically to a woman in a *long* time, and now he'd run into a woman who could turn him on simply by *speaking* to him? Who the hell was she? "Yeah," he said, sounding crankier than he intended. "Who are you?"

"You're Steen?" He heard her fumbling for something, and he wondered if she was searching for a baseball bat, pepper spray, or something that indicated she hadn't been nearly as turned on by his voice as he'd been by hers.

"No, a different brother," he replied, his head spinning as he tried to figure what was going on, and why he was reacting to her so intensely. "I'm Zane. Harmless. Good guy. No need to decapitate me."

There was a pause in her movements. "I wasn't going to decapitate you. I was looking for my shirt."

"Your shirt?" he echoed blankly. "You're not wearing a shirt?" He hadn't noticed that much bare skin for that brief moment he'd been on top of her. How had he missed it?

"I'm wearing a camisole, but it's not exactly decent. Give me a sec." A small laugh drifted through the darkness. "You're such a guy. Of course you'd fixate on the possibility of me being naked. Do all men think only of sex?"

He grinned, relaxing. He'd startled her, but she'd regrouped quickly, and he liked that. She wasn't a wimp who was running to the door screaming. "What's your name?" he asked.

"Taylor Shaw. I'm Mira's best friend from home. I surprised her for a visit, but it turns out, there's no space in the house."

"Nope. Not anymore. I'm displaced too." He suddenly wanted to see her. "You decent yet?"

"Yes, but barely—"

He reached over and flicked on the small light by the bed. The soft yellow glow was less harsh than the overhead light, but it still took his eyes a moment to adjust to the brightness. When they did, he saw Taylor sitting on the bed, curly blond hair tumbling around her shoulders in a disheveled mess that made her look completely adorable. Her eyes were a deep blue, fixed on him as she squinted against the sudden light. He could see the curve of her shoulders beneath her light pink, long-sleeved shirt. The faint outline of a white camisole was evident beneath her shirt, not quite obscuring the fact that she wasn't wearing a bra. Her gray yoga pants were frayed at the knee and cuff, but they fit her hips with perfection. She looked like she'd just tumbled right out of a bed, and she was sexy as hell.

But it was her face that caught his attention. Her gaze was wary, but there was a vulnerability in it that made him want to protect her. He had zero protective instincts when it came to women...until now, until he'd met this woman who'd tried to defend herself with a pillow.

Then her gaze slid down his body, and his entire body went into heated overdrive. It wasn't until her eyes widened in surprise when her gaze was at hip level that he remembered something very important.

He was naked.

CHAPTER TWO

TAYLOR BLINKED in surprise as her gaze stopped just below Zane's navel. He was *naked*.

"Shit. Sorry." Zane grabbed the pillow she'd used on his head and slammed it in front of his crotch a split second before she managed to get a full eyeful. "I forgot."

She jerked her attention off his muscular body, and back to his face, horrified that he'd caught her staring at him. She hadn't *meant* to check him out. It was just that he was standing there, and he had amazing shoulders and her gaze had wandered, because what woman's wouldn't have, right? "It's okay," she said quickly. "Not a big deal." Not a big deal. It wasn't, of course, in the grand scheme of things. A naked man was a naked man, right? They all had the same body parts.

Except that Zane Stockton had taken the definition of man to an entirely new level. He was rippling with muscle, there were criss-crossed scars across the front of his right shoulder, and the dark hair on his chest angled down to a V where his hips narrowed. He was sculpted masculinity, and there was no way for her to lie to herself and pretend she hadn't noticed.

"No?" He cocked a dark eyebrow at her. "Not even a little bit of a big deal?"

"Of course not." She tried to keep her voice even, and her eyes on his face, but it was difficult. She'd never been around a man who exuded so much maleness. She could easily believe he was Chase's brother after seeing how utterly masculine Chase had been. Unlike Chase, however, Zane felt dangerous and wild, a man who had never sat behind a desk or in a boardroom. The wolf tattoo on his right biceps looked like it had come from within him, instead of being penned on by someone else.

"Then you can have your pillow back." He tossed it at her, and she caught it as he sauntered across the room toward a duffel bag on the floor.

She tried, she really *tried*, not to notice the way his back rippled with muscles as he walked away from her, and she *really* tried not to check out his butt. She almost succeeded, managing to sneak only a quick glance before finding a place on the wall to stare at blankly.

"I don't care if you stare." There was definite amusement in his voice as he grabbed a pair of boxer briefs from his duffel.

"I'd care if you were staring at me naked," she pointed out, trying to justify her laser-like focus on the knot in the wall.

"Interesting thought." His voice was low and husky, shivering across her skin like an invisible caress.

She shot an annoyed glare at him, and then relaxed when she saw that he was wearing his boxer briefs. The dark blue hid enough detail that she could face him. "Clearly, I have more manners than you do."

Zane walked over to her, and she scrambled to her feet as he neared. He was barely dressed, and she didn't want to be sprawled on the bed as he approached. "I have no manners at all," he said. "I was raised in a shit hole, and I don't clean up well."

His tone was hard, daring her to challenge him, but she saw a spark of defiance in his dark eyes that made her heart soften. She had no doubt that he was raised exactly as he'd just claimed. "I'm sorry."

He narrowed his eyes. "Sorry for what?"

"That you were raised in a shit hole. No one deserves that."

He stared at her for a long moment, so long that she wanted to squirm. She didn't, however. Instead, she simply raised her chin.

Silence hung between them, suspended in the dimly lit cabin. Finally, he shrugged. "You want the wall side?"

She blinked. "What?"

He gestured at the bed. "Which side you do want?"

Her gaze snapped to the double bed, which was far smaller than the queen-size bed she had at home, or the king-size beds she always requested in her hotel rooms. "You're going to sleep with me?"

"Yeah."

She let out her breath, ignoring the warring factions inside her of joy and delight versus outrage and fury. "Why would you think that is a good choice?" Wow. She was impressed with how diplomatic she'd managed to sound. One might think she had years of experience with hellish bosses and nightmarish clients. Oh, wait, she had.

He ran his hand through his hair impatiently, drawing her attention to how damp it was. The dark hair was curling around the base of his neck, too long to be a cowboy or a corporate exec, but just long enough to belong to a troublemaker or a rebel. "Because I've been riding for hours. I'm wet. I'm tired. This is the only bed left in the bunkhouse or anywhere on the ranch. I'm getting in it, and you can sleep on the hard floor by yourself, or with me in the bed."

And with that, he moved past her, flipped back the covers, and dropped onto the mattress.

For a moment, she stood there in shock, staring at him as he made himself comfortable in the bed she'd been occupying only moments before. "You're kidding, right?"

"I don't have a sense of humor." He rolled onto his side, facing her. The bed seemed to have shrunk to half the size now that he was in it. His shoulders were broader than she'd realized, and he seemed to literally possess the area he was in. His eyes were dark and unfathomable, so intense she felt as though he were prying away all her haughty facades and seeing her for the broken, exhausted woman she really was. "I'm not a good guy, but I have a sense of honor I'd never break. We could both be naked in this bed, and I'd never touch you unless you asked me to. You're safe with me."

He never broke eye contact when he spoke, and Taylor knew he meant every word. "You're a cowboy? Like Chase?" She knew it was silly, but she'd always associated cowboys with a sense of honor and morality. They were the men who knew how to be polite to a woman, who wouldn't hesitate to defend his girl, no matter who came after her.

Zane, however, didn't offer himself up as her fantasy man. "I was once. Not anymore." He offered no further explanation. Instead, he rolled onto his back and draped his arm over his face, shielding his eyes. "Turn out the light when you decide where you're sleeping. The floor sucks, though."

Taylor glanced around the bunkhouse. There was a small kitchen area, the door to the tiny bathroom, and the bed. Nothing else except another door tucked against the far wall. "What's in there?"

"Everything that Steen and Erin rejected." He didn't move his arm from his face. "Chase used to have this place set up with a bunch of bunks so that he could accommodate all the vagrants who showed up to stay, but we never came, and Erin and Steen redecorated. Now we have one bed."

Taylor quickly walked across the room and opened the door. It was pitch-black inside, but she found a light switch by the door. Piled from floor to ceiling were bunk bed frames and mattresses, packed in the tiny room. No bedding, and the room smelled musty and old. There was no way anyone was going to sleep in there tonight. It would take days to get it cleared out.

Grimly, she pulled the door shut and leaned against it, staring at the bed. Zane was stretched out across it, taking up almost the whole thing, except for a small area against the wall. She'd have to climb over him to get to the free space. With a sigh, she ran her hand through her hair. How could she kick him out? She could hear the rain hammering on the roof, and she knew there was no space up at the main house.

But how could she just climb in there with him? She didn't know him, he was mostly naked, and he was...well...a man. Not just a man, but a man she was viscerally aware of as a woman. She'd spent a long time convincing herself that she didn't need a man, but there was something about Zane that had awakened a part of her that had been long dormant. Yes, of course, seeing him in the flesh was riveting, but there was something more to him, something that called to a part of her that had been broken so badly that she'd never thought it would work again. She'd never wanted it to work again, because to feel things meant heartbreak she wouldn't survive. Somehow, Zane had touched those chords inside her, and she didn't want them to wake up.

He moved his arm off his face and lifted his head to study her.

She lifted her chin, folding her arms to ward off the chilly, damp air that was beginning to settle in her bones. "I can't share a bed with you. I don't even know you."

He said nothing. He simply held out his hand to her.

She stared at his hand, and part of her wanted to just take what he offered and crawl into bed with him, to fall asleep hearing someone else's breathing for the first time in a very long time. The other part of her wanted to grab her bags, run back to the airport, and get on the first plane back to the life she was used to...the one that was slowly killing her.

"You're tired," he said. "I'm tired. Come on."

She sighed, fighting the urge to capitulate, even as her teeth began to chatter. Her feet were ice cold, and she was shivering. "I don't think—"

"The heat's not working in this place anymore," he said. "Unless you have an electric blanket, you're going to need me anyway."

She barely stifled a giggle. "You're trying to convince me by presenting yourself as an electric blanket?"

"For hell's sake, woman, get your ass in this bed before I make you." He held up the blanket to make space for her to slide in with him. "Martyrs are fools, and I can't stand fools. Are you going to wimp out and spend the night freezing, or are you going to get your ass in here?"

"I'm not a wimp," she snapped, even as she gave in. She wanted to be in that bed with him, and there was no way to deny it. With a sigh of resignation, she darted across the room to the bed. He was still on the outer edge, and he didn't move over.

His eyebrows rose in a challenge, and she thought she saw the smallest hint of amusement twitching at the corner of his mouth.

"Oh, for heaven's sake." She yanked the blanket out of his hand and climbed across him. There was no way to avoid touching him, and her belly tightened at the feel of his body beneath hers as she crawled over him. It just felt good, so crazy good, to feel another human being's body against hers.

As she settled into her corner of the bed, she realized that she'd had no idea how much she'd missed physical contact. Just being beside Zane made her want to burrow up against him and breathe deeply.

Zane moved beside her, and she heard him click off the light on the nightstand, plunging them into total darkness. He shifted again, and the bed creaked beneath his weight as he settled into the mattress, pulling the covers up over both of them.

"You think this bed will hold both of us?" she asked. She knew it would, but she felt awkward lying in the silent darkness with him, a stranger. She needed to connect with him so it wouldn't feel so weird.

"Given what Steen and Erin probably did here, I'd say it's plenty strong for sleeping."

Awareness swirled through her at the implications of his words. "It's always about sex with guys, isn't it?" They weren't touching, but she could feel the heat from his body filling the space they shared beneath the blankets. He was such a strong presence, he made her feel warm and safe. She liked the fact he was between her and the rest of the room. If anyone came in, they'd have to go through Zane to get to her, and she suspected that wouldn't be an easy task.

He laughed softly at her question. "Darlin', it's never about sex with me. Been there, done that. I got no time for that these days."

She snorted. "Give me a break. Every remark you've made tonight has had sexual innuendoes." Well, maybe not *every* one, but it had been a high percentage for sure...then, as she thought about it, she realized that maybe he hadn't actually made any sexual references. Maybe she'd just interpreted them that way because *she* was the one with sex on the brain? She felt her cheeks begin to heat up with embarrassment, and she wanted to sink into the mattress.

"Is that so?" Zane sounded thoughtful. "You might be right. If you are, then I'd have to revise my answer and say that it's never about sex with me anymore, unless a certain Taylor Shaw is in my bed."

His answer seemed to ignite the darkness, and Taylor caught her breath. So, the chemistry humming between them wasn't just her being delusional? It was mutual. Oh, *wow.* "You don't even know me," she whispered, rolling onto her side to face him. Of course, she couldn't see him at all, just darkness. She wanted to reach out and touch him, just to see where he was, but she didn't. How could she? This weird, middle-of-the-night intimacy wasn't about getting real with actual touching.

"Nope, I don't, but I got some things figured out already." The bed shifted as Zane turned, and she wondered if he was facing her. "I know you're a little scared of being in this bed with me, but you did it anyway. Not only is that endearing as hell, but I also appreciate the fact you didn't tell me to get my ass out into the rain so you could have your privacy. You hit me in the head with a pillow to protect yourself. What guy doesn't admire that kind of attitude? Vulnerable, empathetic, and a little bit bad ass? And you surprised your best friend with a visit, but didn't say one bad thing about the fact you got booted to the bunkhouse upon your arrival. That says loyalty to me, and loyalty is damned important. Plus, you look smoking hot in that getup you've got on, so yeah, you got me thinking about things I haven't had time for in a long time."

Her heart began to race, and desire curled through her. A part of her wanted him to reach for her and draw her into his arms. Somehow, in this darkness, in this intimacy, it felt like she could do things that she'd never do in real life...like get naked with a man she didn't even know?

Oh, God. Really? She rolled onto her back, clutching the blankets to her chest. What was she thinking? Just because Zane was the brother of the man her best friend was going to marry didn't change the fact he was a complete stranger.

"And what man wouldn't fall for that look of absolute vulnerability in those eyes of yours? So bold, and yet soft at the same time. It's compelling." Zane said softly, almost so quietly that she didn't hear it. But she did, and she knew she was meant to.

"Are you trying to seduce me?" she asked, her voice equally as quiet.

He was silent for a moment. "Would it work?"

"It might," she said honestly. "There's something about you."

"Yeah. I know what you mean."

Again, neither of them spoke for a moment, and she waited, nervous, afraid he would break his promise and try to seduce her, afraid that she would say yes. She'd never had a one-night stand in her entire life. She wasn't cut out for it emotionally, and she didn't like sex enough to need a quick fix of hot and sweaty to get through the day. But with Zane...something seemed to come alive inside her, something that was powerful and dangerous and made her tread too close to an edge she'd battled against for so long.

"You dating anyone?" he asked, his voice startling her when he spoke.

"No. You?"

"No."

Again silence, then he spoke again. "I don't get involved with women," he said. "I don't have time for a girlfriend or anything serious. You should know that about me. I don't want you to think I'm something I'm not. I'm in town to run the ranch while Mira and Chase have the kid, then I'm out of here. I'm not sticking around."

She bit her lip and closed her eyes. "You're not a family guy? No dreams of a white picket fence and little munchkins running around the yard?"

He stiffened beside her, as if she'd just tried to shoot him in the head with a gun. "Shit, no. You've got to be kidding."

She heard the absolute truth of his words, and her entire body shuddered with relief. Zane wasn't lying to her. He wasn't a family guy...which meant he was safe.

"Why?" His voice was wary now. "Is that what you're looking for?"

She shook her head, giving the answer she always gave now, the one that she had almost convinced herself was the truth. "Absolutely not. Settling down isn't in my nature."

He moved then, and suddenly, she felt his breath warm against the side of her neck. "No?" he whispered.

She went still, afraid to move, afraid to face him, afraid that if she turned toward him, if her lips accidentally brushed his in the dark, that it would start a cascade of chain-reactions she wasn't prepared for. "No," she said.

"How long are you here for?" His words sent shivers down her spine. "In town?"

She could barely breathe through the tightness in her lungs. "Until the wedding, and the baby. Two weeks, probably."

"Two weeks." He said the words like a seduction that caressed along her spine. "Could be an interesting two weeks, Taylor."

She swallowed hard. "Go away, Zane. I need to sleep."

He laughed softly, a deep rumble that seemed to echo through her body and settle low in her belly. "Good night, darlin'. I'll see you in the morning. Let me know if you get cold." He moved away, back to his own side of the bed, which was still dangerously close to her.

Taylor let out her breath in a shuddering exhale. She was still cold, and she knew he was well aware of it. Not that she would *ever* ask him to warm her up. She wasn't that foolish. Or brave. Or whatever you wanted to call it.

She might have climbed into bed with him, but that was as far as it was going, end of story.

CHAPTER THREE

ZANE AWOKE to the scent of a woman. It drifted through him, enveloping him in a sense of primal satisfaction he hadn't felt in a long time. Then, he became aware of not only the scent of a woman, but the feel of one wrapped intimately around him.

His eyes snapped open, and he lifted his head. In the dim light of morning, he could see the woman from what he'd thought were his dreams wrapped around him. It hadn't been a dream. *She was real.*

Taylor was using his chest as a pillow, and her blond curls were tumbling across his bare skin. Her feet were tangled with his, and his arm was wrapped around her shoulders, holding her close against him. Her belly was snug against his hip, and her thigh was resting directly on top of his cock, which was hard as rock.

But what he noticed most of all was that her fingers were wrapped around his wrist, holding on tightly to him in her sleep, as if she were afraid he would leave her. He stared at her hand, amazed by how delicate it looked compared to his wrist. She was all woman, with curves that made him hunger for more.

He let his head drop back to the pillow, contemplating. He couldn't remember the last time he'd slept with a woman. Yeah, he'd had a few nights of fun, but he always made sure that when it came time for sleeping, he was alone. He didn't like people in his space, and he certainly didn't want to wake up in the morning and owe someone else his time and energy, or even coffee.

And yet, here he was, so tangled up with Taylor that there was no way he'd be able to extricate himself without waking her up. He was completely trapped by her, and it should feel like a noose was around his throat.

But it didn't.

He was actually damned comfortable right where he was. He liked having her against him, and he really liked the way she was gripping his wrist in her sleep. Was it because he hadn't had sex with her? He owed her nothing, and she would expect nothing, so there was no pressure to be anything other than who he was. Hell, he'd already made it clear that he had no manners, right?

A small smile played across his lips as he tightened his arm around her, tucking her even more securely against his side. His hand was on her hip, and he left it there. He had a sudden urge to trace circles on her hip, to tease his fingers across her skin, but he didn't move.

Staying where he already was felt like it was within the parameters of acceptable. Doing something else, like running his hand over her thigh where it was draped across his cock, was not, but there was no way to deny he was thinking about it.

He thought back to how she'd whacked him in the head with a pillow, and his grin widened. She had spunk, and she hadn't wanted anything from him. He was used to women wanting him for his body or his name, and it was damned refreshing to have Taylor see him completely naked, but then not want to have sex with him. She'd treated him like he was a regular human being, and he liked it. A lot.

She stirred against him, mumbling something in her sleep, and he went still, trying not to wake her up. He wasn't ready for reality to intrude. He wasn't ready for the yelp of horror or an insulting accusation that he'd tried to assault her during the night. He wasn't ready for that predatory gleam in her eyes when she realized that the man she'd spent the night with wasn't only the brother of her best friend, but a man who many women had tried to claim.

His good mood faded, and he tensed, waiting for that same crappy experience of being recognized as the three-time bull riding world champion and all the shit that came with it.

She yawned, and nestled closer against him, tucking herself against his side so intimately that his jaw clenched. It felt fantastic, like the calm before the storm. He probably should get up, shove her aside, and hit the road before she realized her good fortune in who she'd slept with, but he didn't.

He waited.

For some stupid-ass reason, he waited.

It didn't take long. He knew the moment she woke up and realized where she was. Her body tensed against his, and her breathing changed. She didn't move for a long moment, and he knew that she was trying to figure out whether he was awake. He realized, then, that he should probably have moved his hand off her hip. Now that he was awake, there was no excuse for leaving it there.

Shit. What was she going to pull on him? Was she going to accuse him of manhandling her? He should have gotten up the minute he'd woken up, and at least given himself a chance to get out of bed before she realized what position they'd ended up in.

"Zane?" Her voice was thick with sleep, and desire raced through him.

He gritted his teeth, debating whether to pretend he was asleep, but he quickly dismissed it. He'd never run away from anything, and he wasn't going to now. "Yeah?" He waited for the words, for the challenge, for the accusation, for whatever would be coming.

She yawned again, making him wait for her response. "Thanks for not getting up," she finally mumbled.

He frowned, trying to process what she'd just said. "What?"

"You didn't get up." To his shock, she burrowed even more tightly against his side. She didn't jerk her leg off his cock, but she also didn't try to grind it against him either. She made no reference to the sexual potency of their position at all. "I haven't woken up with someone in a long, long time, and I forgot how good it feels."

He thought about it, waiting for the next words, the ones that would condemn him. "But?"

"No buts. It's just nice." She sighed again, a deep sigh of such contentment that he started to relax. "There's no baggage, you know? Since we don't know each other and didn't have sex or anything. It's just...nice. No pressure. Just nice."

The tension vanished from his body, and he tightened his arm around her. "Yeah, I know what you mean." He hesitated, and then brushed his finger over her hair. He'd been dying to touch it, but he hadn't dared.

She didn't object, and he moved his hand, trailing it down her head and over her hair.

"That feels good," she said softly. "I haven't been touched like that in a long time."

He relaxed further, tangling his fingers in her hair. He couldn't remember the last time he'd touched a woman without having to watch his back. He was always moderating his comments and his actions, unwilling to do or say anything that could get him into trouble or make her think he was promising things he wasn't, so he never had the luxury of simply experiencing the moment. "Why not? Seems like you'd have a posse of guys after you."

She shrugged, and released his wrist to splay her fingers across his chest. Her touch was so soft that his gut clenched. He was used to women who touched him with the purpose of seduction, but Taylor's touch was simple and innocent, and completely erotic. "Dating men is so complicated," she said. "I've been taking a break for a while. I don't mind being alone." She drew a circle on his chest. "I forgot about this kind of intimacy, though," she said. "Just being held, you know?"

"Yeah." On a whim, he lifted his head and pressed a kiss to the top of her head. She sighed with contentment, making him grin. "I haven't been in a relationship in a long time. I don't have the time or energy for it. Women..." He paused, not wanting to insult her gender.

"Women what?" She yawned again, still tracing lazy circles across his chest. She didn't sound like she was about to take offense, so he decided to answer the question.

"Women can be mercenary."

She laughed softly. "Yes, they can." She looked up at him, her blue eyes clear now. He was shocked by how blue they were. In the night, he hadn't had a sense of exactly how vibrant they were, but now...they were vivid and intelligent, and absolutely riveting. "Tell me, Zane, what do they want from you? Is it because you're hot?"

He grinned. "Am I hot?"

She smiled back at him, and lightly punched his chest. "You know you are. I can see it in your eyes."

His smile faded, and he realized that she had no idea about his past. He didn't want to tell her. He liked that she looked at him like he was just a guy. He lived in a world where he hadn't been just a guy for a long time, perhaps ever. He'd once been the troublemaker from the wrong side of the tracks, and then he'd become the tour's most eligible bachelor, and all of it had sucked. So, he just shook his head. "It's nothing—"

There was a sudden sound from the front door, but neither of them had time to move before the door flew open and Mira walked in. She took one look at the two of them in the bed, and her jaw dropped. "Zane? Taylor? What's going on?"

Zane's first instinct was to haul ass out of the bed and explain that nothing had happened, to establish that he and Taylor were not together...but he didn't. He actually, without meaning to, slid his fingers around to the back of Taylor's neck and lightly clasped her. "Good morning, Mira. The house was dark when I arrived, so I didn't want to bother you. I crashed here."

"But—"

"Oh, stop, Mira." Taylor patted his chest affectionately, and then sat up, her long-sleeved shirt sliding off one shoulder in a dangerously sexy move. "You know perfectly well nothing happened here. Zane barged in, completely soaked, and claimed half the bed."

Zane realized that all hell wasn't going to break loose. Taylor wasn't going to fall over herself trying to pretend that they'd had sex, and she wasn't going to freak out and dive out of the bed. She was relaxed, and utterly unconcerned. Slowly, he clasped his hands behind his head, amusement beginning to build deep inside him as he watched the interplay between the two women. He liked the fact Taylor was in his bed and not getting up. Yeah, he liked it a lot.

Mira's gaze slipped to Zane. "He's naked. And in bed with you."

Taylor's smile slipped. "You really think I had sex with him?" Her voice was hurt, and she sounded confused. "Why would you think that?"

Zane was surprised at the question. Why *wouldn't* Mira think that? She'd walked in while they were entwined around each other in bed, and, as far as she knew, he was naked.

But when Mira looked at Taylor, her face softened. Then she smiled, her face so full of warmth that jealousy actually twitched inside Zane. "I'm sorry. You're right. I know you better than that." She walked across the room and sat down on the bed, next to Zane. "I missed you, Taylor."

"I missed you, too." The women reached across him and hugged each other, and Zane's ease with the situation vanished. He wasn't into hugs and tears and all that stuff. He held up his hands, not sure where to put them with the women hugging across him the way they were. "Okay, ladies, I'm generally up for threesomes, but when one of the women is pregnant and about to marry my brother, I draw the line."

The women broke apart with a burst of laughter, and Zane used the opening to extricate himself from the covers, whipping his feet around Mira and hitting the floor. He grabbed his still-damp jeans and a shirt, yanked them on, and pulled on his boots, all in about five seconds. He grabbed his duffel. "I'm going to dry my clothes—" He realized then what he'd said. "I mean, is it okay with you if I use your dryer, Mira?" Shit, it annoyed him that he had to ask that. This ranch was for the Stockton men, not for the women. He knew it had changed, but that didn't mean he had to like it.

She smiled, that same warm smile she'd always given him, as if she didn't care one bit that he didn't like her there. "Zane, you don't have to ask. You're always welcome. Breakfast will be ready in ten minutes, if you want to join us."

"Yeah, maybe, thanks." He ducked out of the bunkhouse, leaving behind the sound of the women's laughter. He wondered how long it would take for them to start talking about him, and irritation slid down his spine. Mira would tell Taylor all about him, and the next time Taylor looked at him, she'd see what everyone else saw.

He felt like snarling as he stepped out into the bright sunlight, squinting against the light. With a low growl, he walked over to his bike and opened the case on the back. Inside was his cowboy hat. He never wore the damn thing anymore, but if he was running around the ranch for two weeks, he'd need it. He pulled the old thing out and jammed it on his head.

It felt weird, and he didn't like it, but at the same time... something about it called to him. He ran his finger over the brim, instinctively wiping off the bit of dust that had tried to claim it. He brushed his hand over the soft leather of his bike seat, so slick compared to the feel of his hat. The urge to climb onto his bike and leave was so strong, he actually wrapped his fingers around the cool metal handlebars. He'd never stayed here more than one night at a time. He never stayed anywhere for long.

But he'd made a promise to his brother, and he wasn't going to let him down. He was going to stay to help with the ranch until the baby was born. His brother had never asked him for help before, and Zane wasn't going to turn him down. That's what Stockton men did: they always, *always*, stood by each other, no matter what.

With a grim sigh, he turned away from his bike, and headed for the barn. But as he walked, he couldn't help but glance over his shoulder at the bunkhouse. The small, flat-roofed building looked like nothing, but he could still hear the whisper of women's voices. He paused for a moment, trying to separate Taylor's voice, but he was too far away.

The moment with her was over.

It was what it was, and he was moving on.

But as he headed down the dirt driveway toward the barn to do a quick assessment of his responsibilities before breakfast, he couldn't help but think about the fact that both he and Taylor were going to be on the ranch for the next two weeks.

Two weeks was a long, damned time. Long enough that he'd considered it a rare, specialized torture designed just for him...until he'd met Taylor. Now, two weeks was still a long, damned time...long enough that interesting things could happen. Really interesting. With a slow smile, his irritation faded, and by the time he'd reached the barn, he was whistling.

CHAPTER FOUR

"WHEN WAS the last time you had sex?"

Taylor grinned at Mira's question, shouted unabashedly from the other side of the bathroom door. She turned off the hairdryer, amused that Mira had managed to restrain herself that long before interrogating her. It felt so good to be harassed by Mira again. She'd missed having her privacy invaded by her. "It's been a while," she admitted, running a brush through her still-damp hair.

"Tony? Was it Tony?"

Taylor's smile faded, and that familiar ache settled in her heart, the ache that she was beginning to think would never fully go away. "I've dated since my ex-husband," she said.

"Have you? I mean, really?" The door opened, and Mira stuck her head in the bathroom. Her brow was scrunched in worry.

Taylor picked up her foundation and opened it. With Zane wandering around the ranch, a part of her was tempted to put on makeup and turn herself into the corporate Taylor who never showed her flaws. She studied herself in the mirror, at the face she always covered up with makeup when she was at work. She was so used to wearing foundation and smoothing over her skin so she was always perfect. But today, her cheeks were flushed, and she looked...alive.

Suddenly, she didn't want to plaster foundation over her face, and she didn't want to shove her hair up in a tight bun. She dropped the foundation and picked up her mascara instead. A brush over her lashes was all she felt like doing, and it was liberating. "I dated Edward for six months."

Mira leaned against the doorway, her arms folded over her chest. "Your boss? That Edward?" She frowned, looking confused, for good reason, since Taylor had never told her.

Taylor glanced at her. "Yeah, but he wasn't my boss when we started dating."

Her friend's mouth dropped open. "You never told me about him. How could you not tell me about him?"

Taylor turned to face her. "Mira, you were so buried in taking care of your mother, I was afraid to tell you. I didn't want you to feel bad that I had someone and you didn't. You were struggling so much, and I just couldn't do that to you."

Mira's eyebrows shot up. "*And* you didn't want me to interfere."

Taylor smiled. "Yeah, well, you do like to stick your nose in my social life." She turned back to the mirror and finished up with the mascara. "It doesn't matter. It's over."

"When did it end?"

Taylor bit her lip. "A while ago. Once he became my boss, it got awkward. You know, he got more responsibility and had different priorities."

Mira said nothing, and Taylor glanced over at her. Her heart tightened when she saw the knowing look on her friend's face. "Don't say it."

"He wanted to settle down with you, didn't he? He wanted more from the relationship?"

Taylor didn't answer right away, busying herself with putting her makeup back into her travel bag. "It just wasn't a fit," she finally hedged.

"So, that's why you like Zane, right? Because he's a perennial vagabond, and you know he'll never want to settle down with you. He's as afraid of commitment as you are."

Taylor glared at her friend. "I'm not afraid of commitment. It just wasn't right with Edward."

Mira put her hands on her hips. "Did you love Edward?"

"I don't know. I—"

"Did he ask you to marry him?"

"No. Not in so many words, exactly." Taylor pushed past Mira and walked back into the main room of the bunkhouse. Her bag was on the floor against the wall, and she grabbed a pair of jeans from it.

"Did he ask you to move in with him?" Mira pressed.

Taylor yanked on her jeans. "Maybe, but just because I didn't want to move in with him doesn't mean I have commitment issues—"

"It's been six years, Taylor. You can't keep hiding from men—"

"I'm not hiding," she snapped as she grabbed a long sleeved tee shirt and yanked it over her head. "I work hard. My career is important to me, and I don't have extra time to give to a guy who wants more from me." She sat down on the bed to pull her socks on, and she made the mistake of looking at Mira.

Her friend's face was filled with sadness, making Taylor's heart ache. "Don't look at me like that, Mira," she whispered. "I'm okay."

Mira walked over and knelt in front of her, putting her hands on Taylor's knees. "I didn't think I had time for anyone either," she said softly, "but Chase has accepted me for who I am. He doesn't want anything, except what I can give him."

Tears suddenly burned in Taylor's eyes, but she blinked them away. "I'm happy for you, Mira. I can't even tell you how happy that makes me. You deserve it."

"But I didn't want to try either, any more than you do. I was forced to put myself out there, and I never would have if I hadn't had to. You and I have been hiding for years. It's time to stop. It's really, really good out in the sunshine."

Taylor managed a smile. "But you're amazing, sweetie. Chase would be an idiot not to love you."

"And you're not amazing, too?"

Her smile faded. "We both know what I am." There was no need to spell it out. Her best friend knew all her secrets.

Mira's chin jutted out, refusing to accept Taylor's claim. "The right guy won't care."

"He won't care, until he does." She met Mira's gaze. "They always eventually care, and I'm not going to wait around for him to realize it. My work gives me the independence to live my life the way I want. I fit in relationships when I can, and get out in time."

"That's no way to live." Mira sighed. "Don't go down this road with Zane. It has no future. He's not the kind of guy who even has the capacity to realize how amazing you are, let alone decide you're worth investing in."

A little part of Taylor ached at Mira's words, a longing that she worked so hard to keep buried. "Then he's perfect for me, right? Some fun for a couple weeks, and then back to the grind for both of us."

"No." Mira's fingers tightened on Taylor's knees. "Don't sell yourself short. At least pick a guy who might be able to step up. Choose someone who at least has the chance of surprising you."

"In my experience, the surprises that men have to offer are never, ever good." Taylor sighed. "Listen, sweetie, this isn't about me. This is your time. I'm here to help you get ready for the wedding, or do your laundry or whatever you need." She nodded at Mira's massive belly. "You should be sitting around with your feet up, not worrying about me."

Mira raised her brows. "I live on a ranch. No one sits around with their feet up. There's work to be done, my friend."

Taylor finished tying her boots and stood up. "Then show me what to do. I'm ready to get busy." She held out her hand. Mira grasped it, and she hauled Mira to her feet. "Damn, girl, you're getting heavy. What do you have in there? A set of gym weights?"

Mira laughed, her voice lifted in genuine happiness. "Feels like it sometimes. You want breakfast? I made muffins."

"Your famous blueberry ones?" Taylor's mouth started to water.

"One and the same."

"I'm in." Taylor tucked her arm through Mira's as they walked toward the door. Despite their heavy conversation, her heart was lighter now than it had been. Even if Mira was about to become a wife and a mom, their bond was still the same. The only difference now was that Taylor didn't have to worry about Mira whenever she was traveling.

And of course, there was the fact that whenever she went home, Mira was no longer there. She lived in Wyoming now, a thousand miles away from the town where Taylor called home. That was another difference, a huge one.

This time with Mira wasn't real life anymore. This was just a quick vacation. No more girls' nights together, just brief visits that would be all they had to maintain their bond.

Mira looked over at her as she pulled open the screen door. "What's wrong?"

Taylor managed a smile. "Nothing at all. I'm good." She stepped back to allow Mira to waddle through, refusing to acknowledge her sadness about leaving the ranch. She was here for two weeks, and she was going to enjoy every minute of it, not worry about a future that wasn't here yet.

And, as she followed Mira outside, she couldn't help but look around for Zane, to no avail. He was nowhere to be seen. She sighed, all too aware of the flash of disappointment that he wasn't around. Yes, she knew he wasn't the kind of man a girl would build a future with, but that was why she liked him. Zane was safe, as safe as a man could ever be for her. She knew that was why she was attracted to him, but she didn't care.

It had been a long time since she'd had a morning as nice as the one she'd had, waking up in his arms.

"Do me one favor?" Mira said as they headed toward the house.

"You bet. What's that?" Taylor noticed a huge motorcycle tucked up next to the bunkhouse. Was that Zane's? Was he a biker? A biker cowboy? Wow. That was like a double dose of testosterone right there.

"Just don't have sex with him."

Her gaze jerked back to Mira. "What?"

"With Zane. Sex complicates things. You're a woman, and no matter how much you deny it, if you have sex with him, it's going to complicate things. You're not made of steel, Taylor, no matter how much you wish you were." Mira raised her brows. "Promise me, Taylor."

The promise was easy. "Of course I won't have sex with him." Attraction and innocent snuggling was one thing. Sex? That was different. Mira knew her too well. "I promise not to have sex with Zane. Ever." And she meant it.

~

SHE WASN'T GOING to have sex with him? Ever?

Zane stopped dead in his tracks, his hand suspended in the air just above Taylor's shoulder, her words stopping him in mid-motion. Sex? She and Mira were talking about whether she was going to have *sex* with him?

Yeah, he thought she was appealing and intriguing, and he'd thought more than once about what it had felt like to have his hand on her hip while he'd been at the barn, but to be discussing it in broad daylight took all the spontaneity out of it.

Plus, she'd said *no*.

His brother's low chuckle jerked him out of his stupor, and he glared at Chase, who had stopped next to him. "Shut up," he growled.

"Don't mess with my fiancée's best friend," Chase said in a low voice, as the women kept walking, so caught up in their discussion that they hadn't even noticed the men approach from behind. "She wants your hands off Taylor, so keep them that way."

Zane shoved his hands in his pockets. "Since when do women define the rules between us, bro?"

Chase's eyes narrowed. "Don't try to bring Mira between us. It's about basic human respect. This place is yours, and you know it. You've got a hundred and twenty acres waiting for you any time you want to claim it."

Zane watched Taylor walk up the driveway. Her jeans were snug and fit her curves just right, and she looked like sin and temptation in her hiking boots. In his youth, cowboy boots would have been even hotter, but he'd had enough of women in cowboy boots. "I'm not staying around," he said. "Give that part of the ranch to someone else."

"Everyone has a part. That one's yours." Chase slammed a hand down on his shoulder. "Someday, you need to give me a different answer, and tell me you're staying."

Zane jerked his eyes off Taylor and looked at his brother. "You got it all now. You got a woman and a kid, you've got Steen and Erin setting up roots. You don't need me or any of the rest of us here. Let go of the fantasy."

Chase met his gaze. "We went through hell as kids. The only thing that got us through it was each other. Those roots are important. Life is going to get shitty again sometime, for all of us, and it matters to me that we can count on each other. This place is the Stockton ranch, which includes all the brothers, even you."

"You want to know why I don't come around more?" Zane's bad mood from yesterday came back with a vengeance. He'd come to the ranch to get away from stuff he didn't want to deal with, but he was right back into the full pressure situation with Chase. "Because every time I set foot on this property, you ride my ass to move back here. I'm not coming back. I haven't lived with you guys since I was a baby. It's not my thing. Stop pushing it on me, or at some point, I'm not going to come back at all. Just back the hell off. This is what I am. Nothing more. I can't play house with you and the rest of them. It's just not my thing, so let it go."

Chase dropped his hand from Zane's shoulder. His jaw tightened, but he inclined his head. "Understood. I won't ask again. You know the deal, if you ever change your mind."

"Yeah, I know it." Relief settled through Zane at Chase's capitulation. No more pressure from Chase about setting up shop at the ranch.

Silence settled between the brothers for a moment, and Zane felt a twinge of guilt at shutting his brother down. But at the same time, he couldn't go there, and he knew it. "We good?" He held out his hand.

Chase grabbed and shook it. "We're good." He yanked Zane over for a brotherly hug that Zane managed to endure, and then released him. "You want some grub? We have a lot to do today. I want to ride out to the far pastures and show you some fence work that needs to be done."

"Yeah, you got it." Zane fell in beside Chase as they headed up toward the ranch house. As they walked, he couldn't help but contemplate the fact that Mira and Taylor had disappeared through the front door a few moments ago. He didn't like women in his space or on the ranch, but having Taylor at the breakfast table made it a hell of a lot more interesting. He was actually kind of looking forward to it.

"I don't think she's going to make it to the wedding," Chase said as they neared the house.

Zane shot a sharp glance at his brother. "What are you talking about?" Did he think Mira was going to bail on him?

"The baby. I think he's going to come early. I'm going to be counting on you to hold down this ranch while we're at the hospital, and the first few days." Chase looked at him. "I want to be a good dad. A real dad. I want to be there from the first minute. I don't want to be running out to deal with a sick horse when my kid needs something. I want to be there."

Zane tipped his cowboy hat at his brother. "I got you covered. I'll take care of everything until you're ready."

Chase nodded, tension flexed in his jaw as he looked toward the house again. "It scares the shit out of me that this kid is going to count on me," he said softly. "What do I know about being a good dad? Or a good husband? All I know is hell."

Zane didn't have a lot of words of advice for his brother. He knew exactly what Chase's childhood had been like, what all their childhoods had been like. But Chase was waiting, and he had to say something. "You took care of all of us as kids. Just do the same thing and it'll be good."

Chase glanced at him. "Same thing? That's it?"

"Same thing, bro. You did good."

"I can do that, I guess." Chase let out a deep breath that Zane hadn't realized he'd been holding. "Okay, let's go eat."

"You got it." As Zane followed Chase up the stairs, he considered Chase's confession. He'd never really thought about being a dad or a husband. It was so far from his realm of possibility, that he'd never bothered to waste a thought on it. But Chase was facing it now, and Zane had to admit that if he were in Chase's boots, he'd be pretty damn terrified too.

In a way, he already was in Chase's boots, and he'd already failed, and the funeral he had to attend in three days was damning proof of it.

CHAPTER FIVE

Taylor had never realized exactly how pathetic she was until spending a day with her hugely pregnant friend, who had completely shamed her with energy and cheerfulness. Taylor was fit, healthy, and wasn't packing around a watermelon under her sweatshirt, and she hadn't been remotely capable of keeping up with Mira's frenzied activity. By the time dinner was over, she was toast.

With a groan, Taylor flopped face-first onto the bed in the bunkhouse, not even bothering to take off her boots. She'd always known Mira was tireless as a caretaker when her mother was so sick for so long, but she'd had no idea exactly what a powerhouse she was.

The woman was weeks away from giving birth, and it hadn't slowed her down one bit. She'd been on a relentless mission in the basement, unpacking all the boxes of stuff she'd brought back from home. Mira had unpacked like a woman possessed, claiming it was the nesting instinct of a pregnant woman. Whatever it was, it had turned the day into a whirlwind of heavy lifting that had made every muscle in Taylor's body ache.

"I think I liked her better when she sat around on the couch and ate ice cream with me," she muttered to herself, not even bothering to open her eyes. It was only nine o'clock, but she was completely done for the night. She was pretty sure she was going to fall asleep in her boots. Even the mere thought of peeling them off her feet was exhausting.

She'd hoped to catch glimpses of her favorite eye-candy on the ranch, but she'd been buried in the basement all day and seen nothing but boxes, family heirlooms of dubious value, and Mira. According to Mira, Chase and Zane had been riding the pasture fences all day and had taken lunch with them. The men hadn't even appeared for dinner, which, in retrospect, was probably a good thing.

A day with Mira had reminded her that she was here to support her friend, not to indulge in stupid fantasies with short-term men. She'd met Erin, Steen's fiancée, briefly when she'd stopped by to steal some coffee filters, and Taylor had liked her immediately. She'd been a little jealous of the apparent friendship between Mira and Erin, a bond that had once included only Taylor and Mira, but Erin had been so lovely that Taylor hadn't been able to stay cranky and feeling sorry for herself.

Steen and Erin were apparently wrapped up in the construction of their new home and Erin's vet clinic on the south side of the ranch, but she'd invited Taylor by to see the progress. She'd been glowing with happiness, just like Mira, and their excitement had been contagious, but it had also made Taylor feel like a crotchety spinster aunt.

Either way, she was glad for the privacy of the tiny bunkhouse and a night off from having to socialize in a world she didn't quite fit in.

"Nice view." Zane's low voice slid over her as the door creaked open. "Is that an invitation?"

Excitement rushed over her, and she scrambled to a sitting position, depriving Zane of the view of her backside sprawled across the bed. As she righted herself, Zane strode into the tiny bunkhouse, using the heel of his boot to kick the door shut. He was covered in dust and grime, and he was wearing leather chaps over his faded jeans. His cowboy hat was tipped back, and his cowboy boots thudded on the wooden floor. Whiskers shadowed his jaw, and he looked every bit the rugged frontier cowboy, and *nothing* like the clean-cut starched-shirt businessmen she worked with every day. Zane was dangerous, elemental male, and just the sight of him made her stomach do flip-flops. "Of course it's not an invitation," she said, "I didn't think you were coming back here."

He unfastened his chaps and hung them on a hook by the door, showcasing exactly how well his jeans fit over his narrow hips. "Where else am I going to stay? The house is full, my bike isn't great for sleeping, and I'm too old to sleep in the barn with the horses."

"You're sleeping here? Again? With me?"

Zane looked over at her, his eyes dark and moody as he took off his hat and hung it on the wall. He ran his fingers through his hair, fluffing the indent from his hat as he strode across the room toward her.

Taylor stiffened as he bent over her, setting one hand on either side of her hips. His face was inches from hers, and the scent of leather and man slid through her like an intimate caress. "Darlin', I've spent the entire day working on a ranch doing things I swore I'd never do again, and all day, the only thing that's kept me going was the thought of wrapping myself around you in that bed all damned night. So, yeah, I'm sleeping in that bed, and if you drag out one of those old mattresses from the back room, I'm going to burn the damn thing up so you have nowhere else to sleep."

Her heart leapt, and she lifted her face to his. "Nothing's going to happen if you sleep here," she said. "I'm not going to have sex with you."

A lazy, dangerous smile drifted across his face. "I know you're not. I heard you guys talking. But you never said a damn thing about wrapping that fine little body of yours around me all night."

She blinked at the image of being wrapped around him all night, and tried to force it out of her head. "You heard us talking?" She quickly replayed their conversations from the day, trying to figure out what else he might have heard. "When?"

He winked at her as he stood up and began unbuttoning his faded plaid shirt. "Can't remember." He stripped off the shirt, revealing a tight, black tee shirt that showcased biceps and pecs that strained against the fabric. "But I remember admiring your butt in those jeans." He tossed the shirt on his duffel bag, and then ripped off his tee shirt.

She knew she should avert her gaze, not simply because he was trying to get her to look at him, but also because, well, she *wasn't* going to do anything about the fact that she was completely captivated by everything about him. She tried, she *really* tried not to gawk, but when he walked over to the bed and stood in front of her, there really wasn't anywhere else to look except at him.

She cleared her throat and pinned her gaze to his face, trying not to gape at his bare chest or the washboard abs, or the scar on the front of his right biceps. "What?"

He narrowed his eyes, and said nothing. It was as if he were waiting for something.

She held up her hands in a gesture of confusion. "I'm sorry, Zane, but you're kind of like a dog, staring at me like you want something and expect me to read your mind. You want a walk? A bone? What?"

The corner of his mouth twitched. "That's it? That's all you have to say?"

Did he have a dimple? He almost had a dimple. How could a rugged cowboy biker with five o'clock shadow and layers of ranch dust have a dimple? That was just too endearing for a man like him. "I have a lot to say as a general rule. I just have no clue what it is that you're expecting me to say."

"She didn't tell you?"

"Who didn't tell me what?"

"Mira didn't tell you who I am?"

She frowned. "Aren't you Chase's brother?"

"Yeah, not that." He gestured impatiently. "The whole bull riding thing. That."

"You ride bulls?" Wow. He'd just gone from rugged to hardcore. "Is that what the scar on your arm is from?"

"I used to ride. Not anymore." He narrowed his eyes. "I was the world champion for three years in a row."

"Um...congratulations? Is that what you want from me?" Tension was vibrating fiercely through his body, making his muscles strain beneath his taut flesh, making her pretty sure that kudos wasn't what he was waiting for. "Seriously, Zane, I'll be honest, I have no clue where you're going with this, and I'm too tired to guess. I can tell you're upset, but I'm totally clueless about what's going on. So, great job on the championship. I'm impressed." She held out her hands in a gesture of surrender. "Or...should I ask to see your trophy? I don't know what you're getting at, or why you look so angry with me." She supposed she should be nervous with all his simmering hostility, but she wasn't afraid of him at all. She somehow knew he'd never hurt her. She *was* confused, however.

He stared more intently at her. "You don't care," he said softly. "You don't care, do you?"

She sat up straighter. "That's a little harsh, don't you think? I mean, yes, I barely know you, but I'm not callous enough not to care when someone accomplishes their dream. Seriously, what do you think I am—"

"No." He crouched in front of her, his hands on her knees. It was the exact same position that Mira had been in with her, but it was a completely different experience when Zane did it. He seemed to take over the space between them, trapping her. She didn't want to run, though. He was dangerous and irritated about something, but she wanted to stay right where she was. The same feeling of rightness filled her, that same wonderful sensation of awakening in his arms. There was simply something about him that made her want to stop running and stand still, not forever, but for a little bit. "You still see me, don't you?" he said softly.

She narrowed her eyes, searching his face as she tried to understand what he was saying. His eyes were turbulent, and his jaw was tense. His hands were warm on her knees, dwarfing her leg. "Yes," she said slowly, trying to figure out the issue.

He moved closer to her. "I want to have sex with you tonight," he said, his voice a low rumble that seemed to ignite everything inside her. "I want to kiss every inch of your body, and give you the best damned night of your life."

Heat flooded between her legs, and her heart started to pound at the completely unexpected change in topic. "Seriously?"

"Yeah." He slid his hand behind the nape of her neck. His touch was seductive and amazing, sending chills down her arms. "Kiss me, Taylor. Just one kiss."

Oh, God. This was way out of control, especially given the fact that she wanted desperately to say yes and lose herself to him. But there was no way. She'd made a promise to Mira, and it had been the right promise. "I can't." She put her hand on his chest to push him back. "Don't get me wrong. I think you're...um...well, you tempt me and no one else has tempted me for a long time, but I can't do that with you."

He didn't back up, or let her go. "One kiss, Taylor. Just one." He moved closer, and for a split second, she considered letting him kiss her. It would be so incredible to be kissed by a man she was so entranced by. How wonderful would it be to once, just once, let herself go with a man and not worry about the consequences.

Except there were always consequences. "I can't." She pulled her legs back from between his knees, swung them to the side, and vaulted off the bed. By the time she'd landed on her feet and managed to get her hands in a position of sufficient defiance on her hips, Zane was standing as well, staring at her with an expression of absolute disbelief.

His shocked expression irritated her. "What? Are you that surprised that I could turn down a bull riding champion? Did you think that just because you're some famous hottie that all the women want, that I'd fall for it too? That's why you told me, wasn't it? So I'd have sex with you?" God, she was so disappointed. She hadn't expected that of him at all. "I can't believe you used that ploy with me." She pointed at the door to the back room. "You can get yourself an old musty mattress, because there's no space in that bed tonight." Suddenly, she didn't feel safe with him. Last night had been perfect, and he'd made no move to seduce her. She hadn't expected that to change, and now that it had, she felt uncomfortable. She was also kind of crushed. He'd seemed like such a good guy, dangerous and sexy, but honorable. And now he'd tried to use his bull riding thing to get her to have sex with him? She was so bummed. She'd totally misjudged him, as well as her ability to see who she should have faith in. "Or sleep on your bike. Not here."

"Hey." He caught her shoulders as she tried to spin away. "Wait a sec."

She tried to knock his hand away. "Let me go, Zane. Seriously. You crossed a line there, and—"

"I had to see," he said, his voice urgent. "Let me explain."

There was something about the tone of his voice that got her attention. She paused, eyeing him warily. "What?" She seriously doubted there was a reasonable explanation, but for some inexplicable reason, she wanted him to have one. Until now, he'd made her feel safe. She'd trusted him. It had felt good, and she wanted it back.

"When I was on the tour, women were always all over me," he said, not releasing his grip on her shoulders, forcing her to stand and listen. "They wanted a chance to be with the superstar. I had one woman claim that I'd gotten her pregnant, even though I'd never even had sex with her."

Taylor blinked, startled by the unexpected revelation. "Really?"

"Yeah. Her friends all swore she'd gone back to my hotel room with me. The only thing that saved me was a video in the hall outside my room that showed me going in there alone that night. These women were the type who hadn't given me the time of day when I was a dirt-poor kid with no home. Now that I was famous, they all wanted to have sex with me. I had to know if you were like that. I thought—" He shrugged. "I heard you tell Mira how there was no chance you were going to have sex with me. I needed to know if that would change once you knew who I was." He searched her face. "I'm sorry," he said softly. "I just can't deal with women like that anymore. I didn't want to get in that bed with you tonight if you were going to twist it to your advantage in the morning, regardless of what actually happened."

He didn't try to hide his exhaustion, and her heart tightened. She could tell he was being honest, and she doubted he was a guy who revealed his vulnerabilities very often, if ever. His explanation made sense. Her fear and distrust of him dissipated, but at the same time, she felt a vague sense of disappointment. "So, you actually have no interest in getting me naked? Is that what you're saying?"

He stared at her, and then a slow grin appeared. "I gotta be honest, Taylor, getting you naked has been on my mind since last night."

Heat coiled around her. "So what would you have done if I'd said yes?"

"I would have walked away." His response was so automatic that she knew he spoke the truth. As much as he wanted her, his emotional baggage was so heavy that he would have gotten out of the bed and left if she'd been the type of woman he was accustomed to.

She lifted her chin. "So, you want me only as long as you can't have me. Is that what you're saying?" She met his gaze. "I hate games, Zane. I really do."

"No, that's not what I'm saying." He released her shoulder and lightly clasped her chin. "I'm attracted to you. But my aversion to being used trumps everything else. But since we have that cleared up, I can now go about trying to seduce you and actually mean it."

Her heart began to hammer again, just like it had on the bed. "Don't kiss me. I mean it. I can't climb in that bed with you if I'm going to have to worry about what might happen once you get in there." She searched his eyes. "I'm not a one-night stand, Zane. Don't treat me like one."

He paused, his tempting lips only inches from her mouth. "You said you don't like commitment."

"I know, but...I mean..." God, how did she put it into words? "I don't do sex without commitment, but I don't want commitment." As she said the words, she realized how stark it made her sound, how empty it made her life sound. "I just—" She touched his chest. "Last night was wonderful," she said softly. "I didn't worry about anything. It was just us, and it was safe and sensual and..."

"You felt safe with me?" He sounded surprised.

She nodded, sort of embarrassed by her comment. "I mean—"

"No. It's perfect. I want to give that to you." He lightly pressed a kiss to her forehead. "You don't need to say anything else. Go to bed. I'll be there in a few minutes. I just need to shower." He pulled back and winked at her. "Unless you want to join me in the shower?"

She had a sudden image of water cascading over his chest. "Stop."

He grinned. "Harmless teasing, darlin'. I'm not going to do a single thing to that sexy body of yours until you beg me to." He turned away and headed toward the bathroom, unfastening his belt as he walked. "I'll leave the door unlocked in case you change your mind, though." He gave her a cheeky grin, then toed the door shut, leaving it ajar ever so slightly.

Taylor let out a breath and leaned against the kitchenette stove. Zane was trouble. She had no doubt about that whatsoever. He was sexy as sin, and he knew it. But at the same time, his vulnerability about being used for his fame had been genuine and endearing. He was still fit and strong, clearly in condition to be riding bulls, but he'd referred to it in the past tense. Why had he walked away when he was at the top of the game?

The shower turned on, drawing her attention back to the present. She stared at the wooden door, sort of shocked by how tempted she was to take him up on his offer. She needed a shower, too. It had been a long time since she'd showered with a man. Bathing with a guy wasn't just about sex. It was more intimate than sex, a sharing of personal space, kind of like how snuggling in bed had been, only with nakedness and streams of water cascading over bare flesh.

She closed her eyes. Why was he tempting her so much? As she'd told Mira earlier, she was fine being alone. She didn't miss having a man in her life, and she didn't need someone else to love her in order to feel complete. But Zane, with his vulnerability, his cockiness, his potent sexuality, and his tenderness, was making her crave the kind of physical and emotional intimacy that she'd worked so hard not to need.

She wanted him to make love to her. There was no way to deny it. If he tried tonight, she didn't know if she could say no. But Mira was right. If she had sex with him, it would complicate things for her emotionally, and she couldn't go through that again. She would regret it in the morning if she gave in tonight.

With a sigh, she walked across the room to her suitcase, which was tucked in the corner. After making sure the shower was still running, she quickly stripped out of her boots and clothes. She pulled on the same camisole and leggings she'd slept in last night, but paused with her long-sleeved tee shirt in her hand. If she were sleeping alone, she wouldn't be wearing it. But it made her feel safer, not from Zane, but from herself.

The shower went off, and she jumped, quickly dragging the shirt over her head. By the time Zane walked out of the bathroom, wearing nothing but a pair of boxer briefs, she was waiting by the door, toothbrush in hand, fully covered from her neck to her ankles.

But when Zane walked out and his gaze burned over her, she suddenly felt like she had absolutely nothing on whatsoever.

"Love those stretch pants," he said, his voice just the tiniest bit rough.

She swallowed. "They're comfortable."

His gaze went to her tee shirt. "You going to be hot in that, darlin'?"

"Probably. Are you going to be cold wearing only your underwear?" She couldn't fail to notice that he had an erection, and the realization made heat pool between her legs, but she refused to look anywhere but into his eyes, which were smoldering with so much heat that it didn't really help matters.

He grinned. "No chance of that. Body heat is a powerful thing. I promised no sex, but I also promise you that I'll be wrapped around you all night long." He cocked an eyebrow. "If that's okay?"

She smiled, touched by his hesitation. "Yes, that's okay."

His grin widened. "Well, then, brush those pearly whites and get that hot little ass of yours into my bed soon, will you?"

She laughed, and poked him in the chest with her toothbrush. "I was here first. It's my bed."

He caught her hand and pressed a searing kiss to her knuckles. "Our bed, then. Be quick. I miss your body." His gaze was burning into her. "And I mean that."

She swallowed. "I can tell."

Neither of them moved, his hand still wrapped around hers. For a moment, she thought he was going to kiss her, then he dropped his hand and turned away, releasing her.

She took a deep breath and fled into the bathroom, but it took several minutes for her heart to stop pounding. How on earth was she going to sleep with him all night and keep saying no?

But she had to. She knew she did.

CHAPTER SIX

HER HAND WAS on his cock, and his self-control was just about at its limit.

Zane clasped his fingers more tightly behind his head, his biceps taut as he stared at the ceiling of the bunkhouse. The faint light of the moon illuminated the knots in the ceiling as he counted the small wooden circles, trying to think about anything other than the woman sleeping on top of him.

He'd woken up an hour ago in the middle of the most erotic dream he could recall having, one that involved him, Taylor, and a whole lot of nakedness. He'd found himself on top of Taylor, his cock hard as rock, his face buried in the curve of her neck. Her hands had been tangled in his hair, and her nipples had been hard against his chest, but her steady breathing had told him that she was still deeply asleep. Her body had been soft and incredible beneath his, and it had taken several moments for him to wake up enough to realize what was going on.

When he'd figured it out, he'd rolled off her immediately like a good guy. Unfortunately, she'd followed him all the way across to his side of the bed. Still dead asleep, she'd wrapped herself around him, somehow slid her hand underneath his shorts and wrapped her fingers around his cock, as if he were her security blanket and she needed him for comfort.

And there she'd stayed for the last hour, her steady breathing against his neck like a hot wind of desire on his flesh. His entire body was rigid with need, and his cock was hurting from being so hard for so long. He'd sworn off women a long time ago, and it hadn't been diffi- cult, because he'd had no interest in breaking his vow. All the shit he'd dealt with as a bull rider had been enough to cure him of the need to sink himself into a woman, unlike most of the other guys who seemed to think that the more women they could nail, the better life was.

And yet, Taylor had shredded every last resolution. He hadn't even kissed her yet, but his need for her was growing exponentially by the hour. He didn't like sleeping with women, but all day long while he'd been out on the range dealing with broken fences and learning about the horses Chase had on the ranch, he'd been thinking about the moment that he was going to crawl into bed with her tonight. While Chase had been talking horses, Zane had been fantasizing about how it would feel to have her body wrapped around his. Yeah, he'd been thinking about sex, but he knew sex was a long shot, and he'd been okay with that. He'd just wanted to be with her.

But now, with her fingers encircling his cock and her body so relaxed and soft against his, the stakes had changed.

She moved slightly, nestling deeper against him, and her fingers tightened on his cock. *Shit.* He grimaced and stared more intently at the ceiling, trying to find more knots in the wood to count. He clamped his fingers behind his head so tightly that they were beginning to ache. "Seventy-six," he muttered, trying to distract himself with his own voice. "Seventy-seven." There was another one in the corner, a small one, he hadn't seen yet. "Seventy-eight."

But it didn't help. Nothing was helping. His penis was like a steel rod, and the nerves ignited each time she adjusted her grip on him. Her tee shirt had slid upward, which meant her bare stomach was against his side. She'd thrown her thigh over his so that her knee was between his legs, and she'd slipped her foot underneath his thigh, tucking herself in. She smelled faintly of something flowery and feminine, but it was so subtle, layers deep beneath the simple scent of woman, of her, of promise and seduction.

He was half-tempted to get out of bed and head to the bathroom to give himself a little release. Normally, he'd do that in a heartbeat, but he didn't want to move. As painful as it was to lie there and not be able to do anything about the need amassing inside him, he didn't want to move. He liked having Taylor on top of him. He liked the way she trusted him enough that in her sleep, she didn't feel the need to protect herself from him. He wasn't going to lie, it was sexy as hell that when her inhibitions were erased by sleep, that her instinct was to wrap her hand around his cock. Despite her protests, there was something hot between them, and it was definitely mutual.

If he got up, she might slide back to her side of the bed for the rest of the night. Yeah, he could go after her and wrap himself around her, but having *her* being the aggressor changed everything. She wanted him. She trusted him. She needed to touch him. That shit felt really good, and he wasn't going to screw up by his need to get relief.

So, he didn't move.

She didn't either.

When dawn finally began to streak its golden rays through the small windows, Zane hadn't slept for even a minute, his cock hurt like hell from being hard for so long, and his entire body ached from holding so much tension in it.

He was pretty sure it was the best damn night of his life, and he was never going to forget it.

SHE WAS in over her head. She knew it.

Taylor strode toward the ranch house, keeping her head high and refusing to look around as she walked. Refusing, specifically, to look for Zane. She'd awoken slightly several times in the night just enough to snuggle deeper into the heat of his body and bask in the feel of his body against hers. Each time, the best feeling of contentment had filled her, and she'd fallen back asleep.

But this morning? She'd woken up to an empty bed.

No note. Nothing. Just alone.

She was used to waking up alone, but this morning, she'd felt so achingly empty to find Zane gone.

That kind of reaction to his absence wasn't good. Not good at all. Of course he'd be gone already. They were on a ranch, and he'd probably been out the door before dawn to ride with Chase. There was absolutely no reason to expect him to lounge in bed with her, or to have left her some sweet note, and yet she'd been sort of crushed anyway.

She couldn't afford to need him, or anyone. Her survival depended on her being okay with a solo life, but Zane was breaking through her resolves at warp speed, even though she hadn't even kissed him.

This had to end. No more sleeping in the bunkhouse. She'd get a hotel room, or something. But even the mere thought of moving to a hotel made her sad, not just because of Zane, but because she'd come out here to be with Mira, not to cloister herself in a hotel room, like she did almost every other night of her life.

Resolutely, she lifted her chin as she neared the house. She was not going to let Zane drive her away. She was here for Mira, and no man was going to interfere with that. She'd just drag one of those dusty mattresses out and sleep on that. Situation solved.

She smiled, feeling better as she pulled open the front door, looking forward to breakfast with Mira. Some girl time would be great. She could talk to Mira about Zane and—

Conversation stopped, and five faces turned toward her as she stepped inside. At the kitchen table, visible from the front door, were Mira, Chase, Erin, Zane, and a man who looked enough like Zane and Chase that she was willing to bet it was Steen. The table was littered with nearly-empty serving plates, and the scent of bacon and fresh bread filled the air. It looked like a genuine down-home breakfast, filled with warmth, camaraderie, and family. Longing swept over her, quickly followed by a discomfort and awkwardness. There was so much intimacy in the room, and she wasn't a part of it.

Mira waved at her, not getting up from her seat between Chase and Erin. "Hey, girl! You just made it! We saved a couple pieces of bacon for you. Pull up a chair."

"I'll get one for her." Zane stood up quickly, flashed her a smile that eased a little bit of the tension in her body, and then he disappeared around the corner.

"Um, okay." She walked into the kitchen, aware that conversation had stopped, as if her presence had derailed it. She managed a smile at the man she didn't know. "You must be Steen."

He stood up immediately and leaned across the table to shake her hand, his face creasing into a warm smile. He was wearing jeans, cowboy boots, and a crisp plaid shirt. "Steen Stockton. It's great to meet you, Taylor. Mira has been so excited about you coming."

"Thanks." His grip was warm and strong, his hands slightly roughened from all the work he'd been doing on the house. His eyes were a brilliant blue, just like Chase's, and he had the same angular jaw as his brothers. "It's great to be here."

"I got a chair." Zane walked back into the room, carrying what looked like a hand-made wooden chair. Had one of the brothers made it?

"Put it there." Mira pointed to a spot between Chase and Steen, close to where Zane was standing.

He obediently set it down, holding it out for her. He gave her a private smile as she sat down, and her heart fluttered in response. "Thanks."

He nodded, and retreated back to his seat on the other side of the table.

Taylor helped herself to some cold eggs, a couple pieces of bacon, and half a muffin. Everything was cold, and everyone's plates were empty, making her realize that breakfast had been going on for quite a while. Why hadn't anyone come to get her? She bit her lip as she started to eat. The conversation swelled again, a rapid-fire exchange as everyone made plans for the day.

"Chase and I are headed into town to do some shopping," Mira announced. "We really need to finish furnishing the baby's room."

"Steen and I are heading into town too," Erin said. "We're picking up more stuff for the house and the clinic. You want to meet for lunch?"

"Totally." Mira grinned at her. "Maybe we could go shopping for clothes after lunch?" She patted her belly. "I need a couple more tops. I can't fit anything over my belly anymore." She beamed at Chase. "You and Steen can do some man stuff."

He smiled and put his arm around her. "You know I'm happy to shop with you. I'll go with you."

Taylor bit her lip, listening to the exchange. "Um, you need any help from me?" She wanted to be the one buying clothes with Mira, but she wasn't sure she was invited.

"Oh, no," Mira laughed. "You take the day off. We have it covered. We'll get back to work on the basement tomorrow."

"You sure? I mean, I'm here to help you—"

Mira rolled her eyes. "You've done so much, Taylor. Take a day off and relax. You never do that."

Taylor let out her breath. Yes, that was true, she never relaxed, but she had no clue what she was supposed to do for fun, especially here. She hadn't come here to relax. She'd come here to help Mira, and now it seemed like Mira didn't need her help.

Before Mira had met Chase, she and Mira had been the primary support for each other. They'd both gone through some tough times, and they'd always picked each other up. Mira had more people to count on now, which was great for her, but Taylor's life was the same as it always had been. The one place she'd fit, that she'd always belonged, no longer had as much room or need for her. "I don't mind. I can work in the basement while you're gone. Just tell me what to do."

"No." Mira leaned forward, her familiar eyes soft. "Seriously, Taylor, this is a beautiful ranch. Breathe it in. Let it fill your heart. Let yourself get off the treadmill for one day. You might find you like it."

Taylor's cheeks heated up when she realized everyone was looking at her. Suddenly, she felt like a charity project, like Mira had invited her here to save her, not because she'd needed help. "Oh, I'll be all set," she said brightly. "You go and have a good day. I have lots to do."

"No." Mira shook her head. "Don't do. Just be."

Just *be*. What did that mean? Taylor managed a smile. "Right, okay, I got it. I'll be fine."

But it was a total lie. She didn't even know what fine meant anymore...especially not with the way Zane was watching her so intently, and not saying a single word.

ZANE WATCHED Taylor carefully as she discussed the day's plans with Mira. Her smile was as gorgeous as ever, but he already knew her well enough to notice it wasn't reaching her eyes. She was holding her fork a little too tightly, and her shoulders were stiff. She was clearly feeling uncomfortable and out of place, and he knew it, because he felt the same way.

Walking into that cozy little scene at the breakfast table had been his idea of hell. He'd been hungry, and he'd smelled food, but he hadn't expected Steen and Erin to be there as well. The foursome was in high gear when he'd walked in, and he'd turned to walk right back out the door, until Chase had seen him and roped him in.

The family scene wasn't his style, not in any way. It was harder than he'd thought, being back here, being a part of this group that claimed him as family, but it didn't fit him at all. But, they were all he had when it came to belonging anywhere. So, he was here, but he didn't want to have to play nice. He didn't even know how to play nice.

It was a major relief that everyone was taking off for the day. "You need me today?" Zane asked, lounging back against his chair. His arm was stretched over the back of Steen's chair, his body language lazy and relaxed, putting on the same facade of nonchalance he'd perfected as a teen when he'd learned to pretend he didn't give a shit what anyone thought of him.

"No, we already got stuff done for the morning. I'm all set today." Chase raised his brows, his brown gaze too knowing. "Take some space, bro. I know you need it."

Zane nodded. "I'll be back tomorrow, then." Taylor's gaze snapped to his, and he saw the surprise in her eyes that he was leaving for the night.

Regret thudded through his gut. Did he really want to miss a night with her? No, not really. But hell, he needed to get out of here.

Tomorrow was going to be a rough day, and having tonight off from trying to play the dedicated brother was a good thing.

"Sounds good." Chase met his gaze. "Keep your phone on, though."

Mira laughed softly and whacked his arm. "Oh, come on, Chase. The baby isn't coming tonight. You need to stop worrying."

"I'm not worrying," he said, but his eyes held volumes of concern that Zane had never seen on his brother's face before. "I'm just making sure we have everything covered."

"It's all good, Chase. We've got your back." Steen stood up, gathering his plates. "Okay, so we'll see you guys in town."

Erin hopped up, grabbing more debris from the table. "Steen and I will get this cleaned up in two minutes. You guys cooked, so we'll clean."

"Oh, that's okay. We'll do it together. It'll go super-fast." Mira and Chase got up, and Zane watched as Taylor started to stand, her half-eaten plate of food in her hand.

"Oh, no, sweetie, you keep eating. We've got this one." Mira waved her off, and Taylor sank slowly back down to her seat.

Zane didn't move, watching Taylor wage some internal battle. He could tell she wanted to help, but her assistance had been summarily rejected. Plus, it was true she hadn't eaten yet. She glanced across the table at him, and vulnerability flashed across her face, so much vulnerability that his chest constricted.

She didn't belong here anymore than he did, and she knew it. "You want to go with me?" The question was out before he could stop it.

Shit. Had he really just asked that? He needed space, not a woman.

She stared at him, a sliver of hope flashing across her face. "What? Go where?"

It was that flash of hope, that momentary whisper of need for help, for someone to notice and care, that got him. He knew what that felt like, and he knew that it hurt like hell. And he wasn't going to lie. He wasn't looking forward to the next twenty-four hours, and the thought of having Taylor along felt like a breath of relief in the darkness that had been trying to suffocate him. As a rule, being around people made him feel crowded, but Taylor was an exception. She brought him peace. Maybe it was because she didn't want anything from him, at least nothing that he wasn't willing to give. She was leaving town soon, so there was no future to worry about. Just a present that made his day better.

So, yeah, he'd rather have her along than go by himself. "I have to go to a funeral." He said it quietly, for her ears only. He didn't want to get into it with his brothers. He didn't want to get into it with anyone, but somehow, it felt right to bring her along. It was going to be a dark twenty-four hours, and Taylor was the only thing that had brought him relief in a long time. He wanted her with him.

She glanced over at the others, and then back at him, clearly realizing that he didn't want anyone else to know. "Okay."

Just one word. Okay. She didn't ask questions that he didn't want to answer right now. She didn't press for details. She gave him exactly what he needed. Space. Privacy. And the answer that he'd wanted. *Yes.*

He nodded, taking a deeper breath into his lungs than he'd been able to take since the world had gone dark five days ago. "Can you be ready in a half hour?"

"Sure." Her gaze searched his, and suddenly, it felt like the two of them were the only ones in the room. The clank of dishes being loaded into the dishwasher vanished. The murmur of animated conversation faded. The presence of too many bodies faded. All that remained was his intense awareness of her, as a woman, but also, as his anchor.

He'd never had an anchor. He'd never had anything to hold onto when the shit tried to come down on him. Chase had created a solid foundation for the Stockton's, fostering a connection that Zane always came back to, but he'd returned to the ranch like a moth circling a light bulb, receiving the light but never touching.

Taylor was different. It felt like she was his, an anchor that would dig into him and lock him down when he started to slide. He knew he should be walking away, running, retreating into the solo existence that he'd carved out for himself, but he didn't want to.

He wanted her, on his bike, holding onto him, refusing to let go. "Pack light."

Her eyes widened. "You want me to ride on your bike with you?"

His gut clenched. Of course Taylor wasn't a motorcycle kind of girl. Shit. "We can take your rental."

"No," she said softly, a thoughtful gleam growing in her eyes. "I've never been on a motorcycle. Let's do that."

He grinned, satisfaction pulsing through him. "You'll have to hold onto me. Tight."

Her eyebrows went up. "Okay."

"Okay." He grinned, and she grinned back, and suddenly, the next twenty-four hours held a promise they hadn't held before.

CHAPTER SEVEN

TAYLOR LIKED MOTORCYCLES.

It was a surprising discovery, especially given that she'd spent her life ridiculing those who were foolish enough to utilize such a high-risk mode of transportation, but she certainly understood the appeal now. She laughed with delight as Zane sped around a bend on the isolated stretch of highway, and she leaned with him, her knee only inches from the pavement.

She supposed she should be scared, but it was the most exhilarating experience of her life. She was pressed up against Zane's back as if she were attached to him, and her arms were locked around his waist. He was solid muscle, a sheer immovable force that anchored her to the seat. She felt completely secure holding onto him, and she loved the strength he gave her. Her inner thighs were flanking his hips and legs, and the leather seat vibrated beneath her. She couldn't believe how amazing it felt to have the wind whipping past her. She loved breathing the fresh air, basking in the sun as it beat down on her shoulders. The sensation of speed was incredible, and she felt freer than she ever had before.

They'd been on the bike for almost three hours, and she still wasn't tired of it. Breakfast had been tough for her, and she'd been so relieved when Zane had invited her to tag along. But despite the fun of the bike ride, she couldn't help thinking about the pain in his eyes when he'd told her he had to go to a funeral. Who had died? She could tell he didn't want to talk about it, so she hadn't asked, but it was on her mind. Losing someone you loved sucked, and she imagined it was even more difficult for a man like Zane who held his emotions so tightly in check.

"You hungry?" Zane asked, his voice easily audible over the built-in headset in the helmet.

She smiled. He'd asked her that every half hour for the last three hours, always checking in to make sure she was okay. "Maybe a little."

"Great. I love this place up ahead." The roar of the engine eased, and he pulled off the highway. They drove down a dirt road for about five minutes, and then he eased into the dirt parking lot of a small building that looked like it had been a railway car a hundred years ago. An old wooden sign declared it was "Casey's Place."

Behind the building stretched plains of grass that went on forever, and above her head was an endless blue sky, dotted with a few puffy white clouds. She couldn't believe how small she felt, and how huge the sky was. No conference rooms, crowded airports, computers, or rental cars. There was nothing but trees, shrubs, and untouched land extending in all directions. She couldn't see the highway anymore, and she felt like they were the only ones alive on the entire planet.

All her tension melted away, and her life seemed like a distant memory. "It's magical, being out here," she said.

"I know. I love the open road." Zane pulled off his helmet, and grinned at her as he swung his leg over the bike and stood up. His sunglasses hid his eyes, giving him a mysterious aura that merely added to his sexiness. His jeans were low on his hips, and his leather jacket made his already muscular shoulders even bigger. He was primal male, the ultimate bad boy, everything she'd never been attracted to in a man. He was nothing that she wanted, and yet she was completely drawn to him, in every way.

She'd always gravitated toward men in ties and dress shoes, the ones who kept their hair short and their faces shaved. Zane had two days of whiskers on his jaw, his hair curled over the collar of his jacket, and his entire demeanor told everyone to stay away from him, everyone except her.

There was no mistaking that the go-away vibe was not being sent in her direction at all, which she had to admit was incredibly sexy. To be the only one who was allowed in his personal space made her feel special, like some red carpet had been laid out just for her.

She unfastened her helmet and took it off. She shook out her hair and closed her eyes, letting the sun beat down on her face. It was a beautiful day, the perfect temperature with a slight breeze.

"Helmet head." Zane's voice was affectionate as he ruffled her hair, fluffing it up.

She self-consciously touched her hair, her fingers brushing against Zane's. She was the queen of always looking put together, but she hadn't bothered today. No bun, no curling iron, just a quick shower and blow dry. "I must look terrible."

"No." Zane's fingers closed around hers, stilling her attempt to smooth her hair. "You look gorgeous. I like being able to see the real you. I've seen enough women with so much makeup and hairspray they're practically made of plastic. Unlike you. You're just you. It's hot." His voice was low and throaty, and she felt heat rise in her cheeks.

"Really?"

"Yeah." He moved closer, and suddenly, the bike felt confining between her legs. She had nowhere to retreat to, unless she swung her leg over the massive machine in some awkward and obvious attempt at avoidance.

She swallowed, as his hand slid from her hair to her jaw, his fingers so light as they drifted across her skin. "Zane—"

"All the women on the tour get all fancied up, thinking that if they wear enough makeup and hairspray, that they'll get laid. It's all fake shit out there." He was so close now that his thigh bumped her knee. He didn't back up, and she didn't move away, but her heart was hammering now. "Unlike you."

"I dress up to go to work," she whispered. Was he going to kiss her? She wanted him to so much, but at the same time, she was terrified. She was starting to like him already, more than she could deal with. "I wear my hair in a bun, and I use hairspray." She was babbling now, trying desperately to make him see that she wasn't really the woman sitting on his bike. "I'm kind of a workaholic, and I don't do things like ride motorcycles—"

"Shut up," he said softly, the irresistible dimple appearing in his cheek as he smiled. "I know who you are, and I like it just fine." His mouth was a breath from hers now. "The last few hours of having you wrapped around me has been killing me. I need to kiss you, right now. It's not my style to ask first like I'm a good guy, but I made you a promise. So, say yes." His fingers slid along her jaw and down the side of her neck, sending chills ricocheting down her spine. "Ask me to kiss you," he whispered, his voice rough across her skin. "Beg me."

Heat flared in her cheeks, and her knee was burning where his thigh was pressed up against it. "Beg you?"

"I made the dumbass promise that I wouldn't touch you until you begged me. I won't make you feel unsafe, so you have to beg." His lips were almost on hers, his voice throaty and low, rippling with a carnal desire that made heat pool between her legs. "I trapped myself, darlin', and it's up to you to cut me loose."

She wanted him to kiss her desperately, but *asking* him to kiss her was such a statement. It forced her to make a choice instead of simply allowing it to happen. But, God, she wanted to feel his mouth on hers, so badly. What harm would it do? It wasn't like it could go too far, given that they were in the dirt parking lot of a diner at noon. She was leaving, too, right? So, it would just be a kiss with a man who made her feel alive for the first time in a very long time. She wanted the kiss. She wanted *his* kiss. She wanted *him*. So, she nodded once. "Okay."

He grinned, and brushed his lips past hers, not quite touching. "Okay doesn't cut it, darlin'. You need to be explicit in your instructions."

She rolled her eyes and pulled back, setting her hands on her hips. "Really?" She couldn't keep the exasperation out of her voice. "You want me to beg? Can't you just accept the unspoken body language and the implications of the word 'okay' and do your man thing and sweep me into your arms for a kiss that will rock my world? Seriously, Zane. A woman should not have to beg for her first kiss with a guy. There's just nothing remotely romantic about that—"

He locked his arm around her, yanked her up against him, and kissed her.

The kiss wasn't gentle or tentative, and there was nothing gentlemanly or uptight about it. It was sizzling, unadulterated heat, a searing demand that ignited every part of her body. It was a kiss of relentless need, as if he were pouring every broken fragment of his soul into the kiss and into her hands.

Her heart tightened, and she dropped the helmet to wrap her arms around his neck. He dragged her off the bike so their bodies were flush against each other. Her breasts were crushed against his chest, her nipples aching with need as he palmed her hips, locking her against him. His cock was hard, pressing against her belly, and the kiss was beyond hot, beyond scorching, beyond anything she'd ever experienced, and she loved it.

She was used to polite, perfunctory sex. None of this raging inferno that seemed like it was going to melt the clothes from her body. She'd had no idea that this kind of heat even existed, but it was perfection, it was everything she needed, it was everything she wanted, even though she hadn't known it until this moment.

His hand slid through her hair, tangling in the strands as he angled her head for a deeper kiss. His tongue was demanding, finessing her with such intoxicating passion that she felt her entire body explode into uncontrollable desire. Never had she wanted anyone the way she wanted Zane. She wanted his kiss, his touch, his soul, and his body. She wanted him to make love to her until they were both so spent that they couldn't move even an inch, and then she wanted him to make love to her again.

He tasted sultry, with something faintly sweet beneath the surface. Vanilla from his morning coffee? She wasn't sure, but she knew she wanted more. He was addictive, a force larger than she could imagine, blowing into her life like a hurricane, stripping her of every careful control set around her, and her entire being burned for more.

His hand slid up beneath her jacket, and cupped her breast. She couldn't contain the gasp of pleasure as he thumbed her nipple, sending heat cascading down her trembling legs. He swallowed her gasp with his kiss, a devastating assault that made her heart tumble. How could one man affect her like this? She could barely think over the roar of need sweeping through her, and she tightened her grip on him, pressing her body against his as he deepened the kiss—

A horn honked next to her, and she jumped, letting out an involuntary yelp. Zane caught her as she stumbled over the bike, holding her upright as a pickup truck with two men in it honked again, hooting and hollering as they waved their cowboy hats at them.

Zane grinned at her, and gave the truck a wave as it pulled into a spot on the other side of the parking lot. "Well, shit," he said, turning back to her. "That was the best first kiss I've ever had."

Lightness filled her heart, and she couldn't help but grin back at him. "It wasn't bad, I'll admit—"

"Not bad?" He grabbed her wrist and yanked her against him, his eyes still hidden behind those dark sunglasses. "You better admit I'm the best damned kisser you ever had, or I'm going to maul you out here in the middle of this parking lot for all the world to see until you come clean." His hand slipped to her butt. "'Fess up, corporate girl. I'm the best you've ever had. Say it."

She grinned, letting herself melt into him. God, it felt amazing to feel the hardness of his frame against hers. "Is that like ordering me to beg you?" she teased. "Don't you know it takes all the romance out of it if you have to command a compliment? Wasn't it obvious from the way I responded?"

He studied her for a moment, and then a small smile curved the corner of his mouth. "You don't usually kiss like that?"

She gripped the front of his jacket, and tugged lightly. "Zane, I've *never* kissed like that in my life. I'm not really that passionate. I'm controlled, contained, and deeply protective of myself when it comes to men. Kissing like that...it's not me."

His hands softened on her hips, and he shoved his sunglasses on top of his head. His gaze searched hers, and she felt her heart tighten at the understanding on his face. "Does it scare you?" he asked. "The way you react to me?"

She shrugged. "It should, and it might later, but right now, it just...I just feel well...I feel alive for the first time in a really long time."

His grin widened, lighting up his eyes. "Me, too."

She smiled, then. "But I'm still not going to have sex with you tonight. That's a different line to cross." But even as she said the words, she knew she sounded just a little too desperate. If they'd been alone, there was no way that kiss would have ended before full nakedness had occurred. "Two rooms tonight?"

He shook his head. "Sorry, darlin', but my place has only one bed. You're stuck with me."

"Your place?" She was surprised by his comment. She doubted Zane was the type of man who let anyone into his private domain. "We're going to your place?"

"Yeah." He shoved his sunglasses back down over his eyes, cutting off his emotions from her view. "It's a pit. You'll hate me after you see it." He put his arm around her. "Come on. This place has the best burgers for a hundred miles. I'm starved."

He made no more comments about his place as they walked inside, but he'd said enough. She'd heard the edge to his voice, and she knew he was dead serious when he'd said she'd hate him once she saw his place. If he was so sure of that, why was he taking her there? Another test? Or maybe, he was as afraid as she was of the direction this thing between them was going. If she hated him after she saw his place, then neither of them would have to worry about what was happening.

She kind of hoped she hated it.

And she really hoped she didn't.

CHAPTER EIGHT

ZANE SLOWED the bike as he neared the old warehouse on the outskirts of town. When he saw the familiar sight that he'd been so proud of, he felt something sink deep in his gut, and regret and failure dug into his heart.

He paused the bike in the middle of the road. For the first time in the two years since the place opened, he didn't want to go in there. How the hell could he walk in there again?

"Is everything okay?" Taylor rested her chin on his shoulder, looking past him, her arms still tight around his waist.

Her voice wrapped around him, jerking him back to the present. He looked down at her hands locked around his waist. Her fingernails were painted a pale pink, so light he could barely see it. She was wearing a ring on her right ring finger, an antique-looking design with a pale blue stone in the middle. It looked like something she'd picked up in a thrift store, not at a fancy department store counter, but he was willing to bet it was real, not some fake shit that was supposed to look like it cost thousands when it was actually worthless.

She squeezed him lightly. "Zane?"

"Anyone you know ever die?" he asked, still not driving forward.

"Yes," she answered without hesitation. "Mira's parents were very

433

dear to me, especially her dad. My parents weren't around much, but her dad took care of me. I was devastated when he was killed in a car accident." Her voice was soft, but steady. "It's horrible when you lose someone you love."

"Yeah." He took a breath. "You ever fail anyone?"

She was silent for a moment. "Yes."

"Who?"

"My ex-husband."

She'd been married? Jealousy surged through him, a sudden, inexplicable hate toward the man who'd once been lucky enough to see his ring on her finger. "I doubt you failed him," he said, his voice harsher than he'd intended.

"I did." She shifted behind him, and he felt her lean her forehead against the middle of his back between his shoulder blades, like she was trying to hide from the memories. "It sucks."

"Yeah, it does." Suddenly, going into that building didn't feel so overwhelming. He wasn't the only who'd failed someone. Taylor understood. He was suddenly damn glad she was there with him. He revved the engine, and rode forward, turning into the parking lot behind the metal building.

He parked on the far side, not in his usual spot, then swung his leg off the bike. Taylor was still sitting on the bike, watching him. The ends of her hair were peeking out from the bottom of the helmet, and he could see a thin gold necklace resting on her collarbones, just visible under the edge of her jacket. The big helmet made her look tiny, and utterly feminine. Shit, he liked seeing her on his bike, which was weird, because he didn't let anyone near his bike. "You want to come in with me?" He hadn't intended to bring her inside, but now that he was here, he didn't want to go in alone.

She unfastened the helmet and pulled it off, glancing at the weary-looking warehouse. "What is it?"

"A place." He took the helmet from her and hung it from the handlebars. "No one will bother it here. They know my stuff."

"A place?" She swung her leg off the bike. "Did anyone ever tell you how uncommunicative you are? I mean, seriously. A place? What kind of answer is that?"

He caught her wrist and pulled her over to him, framing her face with his hands. "I need to kiss you." That was the only warning he gave her before he kissed her. He didn't ask this time, because he couldn't afford to give her the chance to say no. He did need to kiss her, more than he could ever articulate. He needed to feel her against him, and he had to taste her, to lose himself in her kiss, before he faced what was inside that building.

She responded without hesitation, her body melting against his as her arms slipped around his neck. Her lips were as silky soft as they'd been the first time he'd kissed her, and it felt like his entire soul stilled the moment he tasted her. Her body felt surreal against his, warm, pliable, and curvy in every place he could have dreamed of. He slipped one hand under her jacket, sliding up her spine to her shoulder blades. She wasn't bone-skinny, like some of the women he was used to avoiding. She had a real body, with actual curves, and her breasts were the right size for her frame, not a pair of huge knockers that would give a man a black eye if he wasn't careful.

Maybe she was used to a life on airplanes and shit like that, but she was more real than any person he'd met in a long time. Kissing her seemed to chase away the darkness that had haunted him for so long, because he knew she was kissing the man she'd just met, a man she knew only in the present. She had no idea who he'd been his whole life. She simply saw him for who she'd seen these last few days, and he liked that. He liked that a lot.

He liked the fact that she didn't date, and he liked being the one who'd broken through her walls. Shit. He liked everything about her, including having her tongue tangled up with his, and her nipples crushed against his chest.

Keeping one hand splayed over her upper back, he slipped his other hand into her hair, weaving his fingers in the soft strands, tugging lightly as he deepened the kiss. A need to claim her began to build inside him, a need to declare that she was his, to trap her against him so that he never had to worry that he'd look over and find her missing.

"Zane!" A familiar voice broke through the haze of the kiss, and he swore, jerking his hand out from under her jacket.

He kept his arm around her, however, as he turned toward the building. Approaching them was a familiar guy in faded jeans, old cowboy boots, and a cowboy hat that had seen better days. Just seeing the old man made Zane's jaw tighten. Jesus. He didn't know if he could do this. "Ross." He inclined his head.

"You heard?"

"Yeah." Of course he'd heard. That's why he hadn't been back. "Sucks."

"Yeah." Ross searched his face. "You okay? This happens sometimes. You can't blame yourself. We do everything we can."

Zane cleared his throat. "Yeah, well, I take responsibility."

Ross sighed. "Zane—"

"This is Taylor Shaw," he interrupted, not wanting to have that conversation. "Taylor, this is Ross Stevens. She's from out of town."

Ross tipped his hat to her. "Nice to meet you, Miss Shaw."

She smiled at him, warm and genuine. "Taylor," she corrected. "Just call me Taylor."

He grinned. "Then you need to call me Ross, young lady."

Taylor smiled wider, and Zane tightened his arm around her shoulders. "Ross it is, then," she said. "What is this place?"

Ross glanced at Zane. "He didn't tell you?"

"No, he's being completely uncommunicative, as usual. You know how he can be." She said it cheerfully and intimately, as if she'd known Zane forever, not just a couple days. But she was right on target, which made Zane grin.

Ross laughed. "Yeah, I do." He held out his arm. "Would you like a tour, Taylor? I'll show you everything Zane has never told you about himself, the shit he should have known I'd spill if he brought you here."

Taylor glanced at Zane, and he realized that, somehow, she understood that something was going on, something that was affecting him, and she was checking to make sure it was okay if she accepted Ross's offer. She was putting him first. Shit. He didn't even know what to say, so he just shrugged.

She smiled, then turned to Ross. "Give me a tour, then, Ross. I'm in." She took his arm, and then held out her other hand to Zane. "I want both of you to escort me. It will fulfill my childhood fantasy of feeling like a queen." There was laughter in her eyes, and Zane couldn't help but grin as he walked up and held out his arm for her.

She slipped her hand into the crook of his elbow, and let the two men escort her toward the building. "I could so get used to this," she announced. "Two devastatingly handsome cowboys all to myself."

Ross grinned, his leathery face creasing. "If Zane ever treats you badly, you come knockin' on my door, and I'll beat the hell out of him."

She laughed, her delight making Zane grin despite the foreboding pressing down upon him. "I'm sure you could take him down, Ross," she said. "But I don't think I need to worry about that." She glanced at Zane. "Zane's a far better man than he thinks he is."

He could tell she meant it. Something shifted inside him at her words, and his smile was real as they walked into the building.

TAYLOR WASN'T sure what she'd expected to see inside the decrepit warehouse, but a gleaming new, full-sized basketball court, a computer center, extensive free weights, and a library complete with couches and a dozen bookshelves weren't top on the list. She was even more surprised to see the cavernous space being used by an assortment of boys, ranging from scrawny six-year-olds to beefy older teens who were well over six feet tall, and who looked more than a little dangerous. She saw tattoos, earrings, scraggly facial hair, and tee shirts packed with more attitude than she'd encountered her entire life. They were bold, arrogant, and absolutely lost at the same time.

For a moment, she stared in shock at the boys, then tears sprung to her eyes before she could catch herself. She jerked her eyes off the kids and looked at the ceiling, clamping down on sudden onslaught of grief, longing, and sadness. Dammit. Usually, she was okay with kids if she knew she was going to encounter them, but she hadn't prepared for children, especially not ones who were so obviously in need of someone to care. She bit her lip, fighting back emotion. God, she had to pull herself together. It was just the sight of a few kids. She was way overreacting, even for her, at least given how much time had passed since the days of her broken dreams.

"Welcome to the Garage." Ross swept his hand out. "This place used to build and service farm equipment, but now we try to keep kids out of trouble. There's not a lot to do in these parts, so we try to give them a chance."

Taylor took a deep breath and focused on Ross and Zane. This was about them, not her. "This is what you do when you're not at the ranch?" She asked Zane, and then her heart seemed to freeze when she saw the look of raw anguish on his face as he stared across the warehouse. The pain in his eyes jerked her out of her own melodrama and twisted at her heart. Instinctively, she wrapped her hand around his arm, trying to support him. "Zane? What's wrong?"

He didn't answer, and she tore her gaze off him to try to ascertain what had caught his attention so ruthlessly. On the other side of the basketball court, a boy was leaning against the wall, staring at Zane. He looked about fourteen years old, all bones and ratty, baggy clothes. His eyes were big and dark, sunken into the shadows on his face and his arms were folded across his chest. His dark hair was a little long, and even the light brown tint to his skin couldn't hide how pale he looked. He looked lost and so much younger than his years.

"Shit," Zane muttered under his breath.

"Talk to him," Ross said. "You have to do it. He needs you to do it."

The other kids saw Zane, and he got some shouts and waves that were clearly very enthusiastic, and he acknowledged them, but he never took his gaze off the boy by the wall. "I don't know what to say," he said, his voice strained.

"It doesn't matter. He just needs to hear something from you."

Zane's face was pale, but he nodded. He glanced at Taylor. "I'll be right back."

"Okay." She squeezed his hand, her fingers drifting off his as he walked away. The basketball game stopped as he neared the court. The boys swarmed him, all of them talking over each other in their attempts to get Zane's attention. He took the time to acknowledge all of them, but the boy on the other side of the court continued to stand silently, waiting. "What's going on?" she asked Ross.

Ross sighed. "One of the kids Zane had been working with died a few days ago. He got in trouble with some kids, some shit went down, and he wound up dead. Zane had been trying to get him to spend more time here, but he wasn't interested. This place wasn't his thing, but Zane thought he could help him."

"Oh, no. How awful." Now she understood Zane's earlier question about whether she had ever failed anyone, and she knew who the funeral was for. He blamed himself for the death of that boy, a devastating burden that he was carrying silently. Her throat tightened, and tears burned at the back of her eyes. Her own trip down self-pity lane seemed so pathetic now, in comparison to what Zane was going through. "And the boy over there?"

"Luke? It was his older brother, Brad, who was killed."

"Oh, God." As she watched, Zane made his way over to the boy. Luke turned his back on Zane and walked away. Zane's hands clenched, and for a moment, he hesitated, then he followed the boy, clearly talking to him. Luke stopped, his arms still folded across his chest, his back toward Zane. He cocked his head, however, clearly listening to Zane, even though he wasn't facing him.

"Zane started coming by a year ago," Ross said. "He's made a big difference for the kids. Zane's not some big star trying to throw some charity their way for PR purposes. He *was* them, when he was younger. He lived their life. They know that, so they listen. Zane paid for the basketball court to be built indoors. He wanted them to be able to play even during the winter. Before that, they just played in the dirt parking lot."

Taylor's throat tightened as she watched Zane and Luke. There was so much tension in both their bodies, so much distance between them. "Zane was homeless? Poor?" She'd seen only evidence of family and love on the Stockton ranch. What else did she not know about him?

Ross glanced over at her. "That's for Zane to tell you, not me. Ask him."

She nodded, tears burning in her eyes as Luke finally turned around to face Zane. His jaw was thrust out, and he looked hostile and angry, but his earnest gaze was riveted on Zane's face, as if he were inhaling every word Zane spoke.

It was clear there was a deep connection between the two, and this time, Taylor didn't need to turn away to protect herself from her own emotions. She watched them, her heart aching for the depth of caring so evident in the way Zane was talking to Luke. He was such a good man, so caring, so different from how he pretended to be. "It looks like they're talking. They might be a while," she said, hoping she was right. She had a feeling Luke needed Zane in a big way. "How about a tour while we wait?"

Ross smiled back, and in his eyes, she saw decades of wisdom, kindness, and understanding, the kind of patient man it would take to work with kids who carried trouble on their backs. Suddenly, all the lies she'd been telling herself about the importance of her work were shattered. Ross and Zane were the ones making a difference. They were the ones giving hope and opportunity to kids who had no one else. She did what? Sat in boardrooms talking about how a company could earn more money? God, no, she couldn't think like that. She had to live her life. She couldn't see it for what it was, or she'd never survive it.

"Sure thing, Taylor," Ross said, jerking her back to the present. "It's not much, but we do what we can." He led the way, and she hurried across the cement floor, glancing back just in time to see Zane hug Luke.

Her throat tightened, and she turned away. Zane wasn't the man she'd thought he was, an isolated loner who didn't connect with anyone. He wasn't the man he'd claimed he was, either. He was the man she'd feared he might be, the kind of man who could never accept her for who she was. He was the kind of man she could really fall for...and lose.

She had to let him go. *She had to.* She couldn't play this temporary game with him anymore, not now that she'd seen the side of him he'd kept hidden so well.

But as she followed Ross up a set of narrow, metal stairs, she realized she didn't want to let him go. It was too late. *It was too late.*

CHAPTER NINE

ZANE KNEW HE WAS CRANKY. He knew he wasn't in the right frame of mind to have any kind of constructive discussion, but by the time he and Taylor walked into his apartment, he was too pissed to hold it in.

He shoved the door open, no longer caring about how small his place would look to Taylor. He didn't give a shit about the peeling paint on the walls or the mismatched chairs and kitchen table that had come with the place. He'd gotten the place to prove a point, even though he could have bought a damned ranch with the money from his earnings. He'd felt the need to be in this kind of place after he'd walked away from the spotlight. He'd been prepared for Taylor to hate it and walk out, and he'd been planning to let her, but now, he didn't even care what she thought of it. They were way past that.

He slammed the door shut behind her and leaned against it, folding his arms, anger building inside him as he watched her walk into the middle of the one bedroom apartment, slowly turning around as she inspected it. "It's not exactly high fashion," she said, "but I'm impressed with how clean it is. I was expecting some typical bachelor pad, but it's immaculate." She turned toward him. "What exactly was I supposed to hate about it?"

"What's going on?" He didn't mean to snap the question, but he was tired and felt like shit from going to the Garage today. "You've shut down ever since the Garage. Dinner was like trying to twist answers from you. I'm tired, and I don't want to deal with this. You don't like the kids? You think they're shit just because they don't have money? You think it's a waste of time to try to help them? That they'll all end up like Brad, dead after some bad choice, because they have no parents to guide them? A waste of the earth's resources?"

He spat the words that he'd heard so many times, unable to keep the venom out of his voice. He wasn't a kid anymore, but he'd never stop being one of *those* kids, and the words still felt like a personal insult every time he heard them, because they were. He didn't have to take that kind of shit anymore, and he didn't, but as hell was his witness, he never thought Taylor was the type who'd say them. Some people, he expected to feel that way, and he wasn't disappointed when they proved him wrong.

He realized, too late, that he'd had faith in Taylor, and he was shocked that she was like the others. It pissed him off that he was wrong about her. He felt like she'd betrayed him, and that made him even more angry. Not that she'd betrayed him, but that he'd let himself trust enough that she could make him feel like this.

Her eyes widened, and she stared at him. "What?"

"Just say it." He shoved himself off the door and tossed his bag on the ratty couch. "Just admit what you were thinking when you walked in there. The minute we got in there, you shut down." He stalked over to her. He couldn't believe how pissed he was. He hadn't expected her to be like that. He hadn't even considered it as a possibility, but he shouldn't have been surprised. He knew what to expect from people, and her nice rental and well-mannered ways should have told him what she was like. She'd just been so real. He'd believed in her, and he didn't believe in many people. "I'm surprised you didn't demand I take you to a hotel tonight, although you can probably guess there aren't a lot of luxury accommodations in this town."

"Hey." She narrowed her eyes at him. "I completely understand that you're going through something really difficult right now, but it's not fair to strike out at me—"

"Strike out?" He ran his hand through his hair. "I know what it's like when a man strikes out, and I've had the broken bones to prove it. I'm not lashing out. I'm pissed, and I'm calling it like it is. I have no time for this crap."

"What crap?" She put her hands on her hips, her eyes flashing with anger. "You think I looked down on those boys because they're poor, and come from broken homes? Is that what you really think of me?"

"Yeah, I—" He stopped mid-sentence at the expression on her face. There was something about the outrage in her eyes that made him pause. It wasn't indignant anger. There was something else there. Hurt? Vulnerability? "Isn't that what's going on?" he asked, hesitating ever so slightly. "You shut down. I know you did." He searched his mind for anything else that had happened, but he couldn't think of any other explanation. "You were fine, completely wrapped around me before we went in, and after I talked with Luke, you put up a wall so fast I couldn't have gotten through it with a jackhammer. If it's not the boys, what is it?"

"It's not—" She paused, her face stricken.

A cold chunk of ice settled in his gut at her refusal to answer. "It *was* the boys, wasn't it?" He couldn't keep the bitterness out of his voice. "You think they're dangerous and should be in juvie instead of someone giving them computers, don't you?"

Wordlessly, she shook her head, and suddenly he saw tears shimmering in her eyes. His anger stalled out instantly, and he stopped, staring at her, his heart clenching at the pain in her eyes. Shit. What was going on? "What? Tell me what it is."

She let out her breath, staring past him at a spot on the wall. "My whole life, I've loved kids," she said softly. "All I ever wanted was to be a teacher, and I wanted a dozen kids of my own. I'm an only child, and my mom died when I was little, and my dad was always working, so I grew up in a quiet house. I hated it. It felt so lonely, which is why I wound up hanging out at Mira's all the time."

Zane's fists unclenched, and he rocked back on his heels, trying to wrap his mind around the story she was telling. "You didn't have a mom?" He'd figured her for a perfect childhood, not a one-parent household like he'd had. Well, he'd had more like a sliver of one parent, and that was on his mom's good days. He'd hadn't spent much time at the Stockton hellhole once his mom had ditched the old man, but he'd been screwed no matter which parent he was with.

"No." Taylor dropped her bag on the floor. It landed with a soft thump, and she walked over to the window, staring out at the landing of his apartment. Her only view was the parking lot and another tenement apartment building across the street, but that didn't seem to bother her. "I got married a week after I graduated from college. Dan Parker. He wanted a family as much as I did. We got jobs as teachers in the same school district. It was perfect."

Dan Parker. The name of the man she'd given herself to. Zane took a deep breath, trying to let go of the sudden surge of jealousy. Taylor wasn't his, and he had no claim on her, not her present, not her future, and certainly not her past. "What happened?"

She looked back at him, and there was a single tear trickling down her cheek. "I can't have children. I had an infection when I was a little girl." She shrugged. "I didn't know. Dan was mad. He said I should have known, and that I misled him."

Zane swore softly. "Bastard."

His reply made her laugh, a teary, heart-wrenching laugh that hurt to hear. "We talked about adopting. He said he'd be okay with it." She shrugged again, a casual gesture that was a total lie. "And then he got one of the other teachers pregnant, and he left me for her. He said he could never love a woman who was broken."

"Broken?" Outrage began to pour through him. "He said you were *broken?*"

She held out her hands. "I am," she said quietly. "Everyone at the school knew what had happened. I...couldn't stay there. I left the school. I couldn't be a teacher and look at all those children I could never have. I found a corporate job, and I got away."

He stalked across the room and grasped her shoulders. "He's an idiot," he said. "And a scumbag."

She met his gaze, ignoring his comment. "Since then, I've kept it light. I didn't get serious with guys, not enough to talk about the long term. But there was one man who got under my skin. We started to get serious. I was falling in love with him, and he said he was, too. He was talking about getting married, so I had to tell him. He said it was fine, that he didn't care, that we could adopt or not have kids. I was so happy." She managed a half-smile. "Then a couple months later, one of his friends had a baby, and he said it made him realize that he wasn't willing to give up on the chance for a biological family. He was too young to settle. If he didn't find anyone in a few years, then maybe we could try again." She looked at him. "Do you know how much that hurts, Zane? To be told by the man I loved that I should try him again in a few years and if he was desperate enough, maybe he'd be willing to settle for me?" She shook her head. "I believed in him, and I was so wrong."

His fingers tightened on her arms. "You have shitty luck to find two guys who believe that. Not all men are like that—"

"In their hearts they are. It's human nature." She met his gaze. "I won't take that future away from a man, because someday he'll resent it, and he'll hate me for it." There were tears shimmering in her eyes. "I wasn't expecting to see all the kids there today. I wasn't prepared. Sometimes it hits me hard, you know? I've worked really hard to create a great career and a fulfilling life, and it's enough for me, but some-times..." She shrugged. "I'm sorry. I just let it get to me." She met his gaze. "Those boys are beautiful," she whispered. "Every single one of them deserves the world."

He saw the honesty in her eyes, and her voice was soft with the kind of genuine passion that could never be faked, and he knew she was telling the truth. She believed in those boys as much as he did, but he'd misinterpreted her response completely. He'd judged her the way he *hated* to be judged by others. He swore at himself, disgusted by how he'd treated her. "I'm such a bastard," he said softly. "I'm so sorry for what I said to you. I had no idea—"

She shook her head, putting her finger across his lips. "No, no apologies. How would you have known?"

He wrapped his hand around hers and pressed a kiss to her fingertips. "I have a huge chip on my shoulder when it comes to being poor and from the undesirable part of society," he said. "I shouldn't have judged you like that just because I have issues. I'm sorry. Really."

She smiled, watching him trail kisses across her palm, tears still glistening on her cheeks. "You and me," she said softly. "No wonder we connect. We're both a mess."

"You're not a mess." He slipped his hands around her waist and tugged her against him. His body relaxed when he felt the heat of her body against his. "But I'm not going to deny that I'm an insensitive, judgmental bastard."

A small, tearful laugh escaped her, and she laced her fingers behind his neck, gazing up at him. "If you could have seen the way you were interacting with those boys today, you would never be able to call yourself an insensitive, judgmental bastard. It was beautiful." Her blue eyes shined with warmth that seemed to wrap around him.

No one had ever said anything like that to him. Ever. They'd praised his skill with the bulls. They'd coveted his bank account. They'd ogled his body. And before that, they'd ridiculed his old clothes and boots. They'd scorned everything about him, and the girls had wanted him only to shock their families or make their boyfriends jealous. No one had ever, *ever,* looked at him and seen anything real that was worth saving.

Until Taylor.

"Thank you." He bent his head and kissed her, brushing his lips over hers in the only way he knew how to tell her what it meant.

She sighed and leaned into him, welcoming the kiss. Her lips were responsive and warm, encircling him with a sense of belonging he wasn't accustomed to having. With a low growl, he tightened his arms around her and deepened the kiss. Her breasts were crushed against his chest, and his palms were tight on her hips. Still kissing her, he ran his hands over the curve of her ass, jamming his hands in the back pockets of her jeans and pressing her against him.

She tasted amazing. Pure, fresh, with a hint of something darker and sexier.

They were alone now.

No one was going to walk in.

No one was going to stop them.

He broke the kiss, his lips whispering against her ear. "I want to take you to bed," he whispered. "My bed. No rules. Just us."

She didn't answer, but she pressed a kiss to his throat, and tightened her arms around his neck. He smiled to himself as he scooped her up, wrapping her legs around his hips as he carried her across the small room to the tiny bedroom off the back. "Sometime," he said between kisses, "I want you to actually tell me that you want me with your words. I can read between the lines with you now, but it's okay to admit you want this, you know?"

"No, it's not." She pulled back to look at him, her hands still loosely linked behind his neck as he carried her. "If I say I want it, then it's harder to deny that it matters to me. I need to protect myself, Zane."

His heart tightened at the pain in her voice as he lowered her to the bed. She fell back into the pillows, and he lowered himself on top of her before she could scoot away, using his weight to pin her to the bed. "You don't need to protect yourself from me, Taylor." Damn, it felt good to have her beneath him. Kissing her in a vertical position had been good, but there was nothing like the sensation of being tangled up with her along the entire length of their bodies.

She laid her hand on his cheek, her eyes searching his. It was dark out, but the streetlights gave just enough illumination for him to see her. "But I do, Zane. You affect me in a way that makes me vulnerable to you."

Satisfaction pulsed through him, and he turned his head into her hand, pressing a kiss to her palm. "I'm not going to lie to you, darlin'," he said, as he kissed the inside of her wrist. "I don't want anything from any woman, and I don't want a relationship, but I can't help it that I absolutely fucking love the fact I affect you." He caught her lips in his before she could answer.

He didn't want to say anything more. He didn't want to make promises, or ask for something which would never fit into his life. He didn't want her vulnerability to bring out some delusional knight-in-shining-armor side of him that he could never deliver on. She'd run into enough bastards, and she didn't need him adding to it by making promises he could never keep.

But he needed her. He needed her kiss, her companionship, and her support.

She broke the kiss. "I'm not staying forever, Zane. We don't have a future." Her voice was desperate, as if she were trying to remind herself of that, not just him.

"No one really has a future," he said. "No one knows whether they have a tomorrow." He tangled his fingers in her hair. "You're the first woman who has mattered to me in a long time," he said. "Maybe ever. You're sure as hell the first one I've ever trusted, so, yeah, I don't really care what might or might not happen someday. I just don't want to miss out on this moment with you, the one we have right now."

She searched his face. "I don't know how to do that. I don't know how to let go of the forever and the future. I just worry that I'll get my heart broken, or that I'll let you down, or that it will be too hard to leave, or that—"

He kissed her, hard, deeply, cutting off her words. He had long ago given up any thoughts of a future, because every one that he could envision sucked. It was better to just be in the present and take it day by day, because then he had a chance to breathe. Anything was endurable in the present. It was when he thought of doing it for a life-time that it became too much.

He didn't want to think about the future with Taylor, because the future was like trying to hold sand between his fingers. It just slid out of reach, every time, with steady, relentless ruthlessness. But this moment, her kiss, her body...it was real. It was something he could hold onto for the rest of his life.

With a sigh, Taylor wrapped her arms around his neck. He could tell the moment she gave up resisting. Her body softened, and her kiss became more fluid, a searing, heated interplay of lips and tongues.

"I need skin," he whispered, rolling off her long enough to jerk off his jacket and shirt. He was back on top of her before she'd even reached for the hem of her shirt. "Let me." He pulled her up to a sitting position, then slid her jacket off her shoulders, kissing her collarbone as he did so.

"That feels amazing," she whispered, leaning her head against his as he pulled her hands free.

"You ain't seen nothin' yet, darlin'." He slid his hands down her arms to her wrists, then raised her arms, clasping them together over her head. For a moment, he held her there while he kissed her, a deeper, more penetrating kiss than before, one of mounting anticipation. He'd never seen her naked, never kissed her in all the places he wanted to, but he knew it was going to happen tonight. He wanted to tear his clothes off and attack her, but at the same time, now that he knew where this was going, he felt a sense of patience utterly foreign to him. He wanted to take his time and savor every moment, to slow time to a crawl so he could make it last as long as possible.

His cock was already hard and ready, straining against the front of his jeans as he grasped the hem of her shirt and slipped it upwards, his thumbs skimming along her skin as he pulled the fabric along her body, over her arms, and off.

He leaned back, his hands sliding down her arms again as he ran his gaze over her body for the first time. Her bra was pale blue, with just the faintest bit of lace around the edges. Demure, but sinfully sexy. So much better than the black and red overstated and overfilled bras that women used to show him when they'd corner him on the way back to his hotel. "Perfect," he whispered, lowering his head to press a kiss to the swell of her left breast.

She sighed, her fingers sliding through his hair as he kissed his way across her chest to her right breast. "You know what?"

"What?" He hooked his finger over the lace of her bra and tugged it down, exposing her nipple. It was hard and erect as he took the nub into his mouth, swirling his tongue over it as he sucked on it.

She made a small noise that made him grin, as she shifted her hips. "I've been kind of neurotic about sex since Dan left me. Insecure. Uptight, you know? But—"

He bit her nipple, grinning when she yelped and grabbed his shoulders. "But what?" He blew on the taut peak, easing the burn.

"Um...yeah..." She twisted restlessly under him as he lightly tweaked her other nipple between his thumb and forefinger. "With you...I just want more. It just...it's just right, you know? I mean..."

Feeling her gaze on him, he looked up at her. She was staring down at him, her fingers trailing through his hair.

He pressed a light kiss to her mouth. "What is it, Taylor?"

She ran her fingertips across his whiskers. "You make me want to forget all the noise in my life, and just be here. I can't even tell you how amazing it is to be in your arms. I don't want to be anywhere else, but there's so much to consider—"

"Shh." He kissed away her protest. It wasn't until she began to kiss him back that he broke the kiss, stroking her hair back from her face. "I know you want the marriage and kid thing, Taylor, and you deserve it. I'm not going to lie and mislead you. I can't do that. I don't know anything about creating a family, and I don't even know how to stay in the same place for more than a couple nights. If I wanted kids, though, I'd be perfect for you, because I don't give a shit about kids being biologically related to me. My parents were biologically mine, and they sucked beyond words. Biology doesn't create a family or love, or anything good, and I've lived that. I'm not the only man in the world who knows that, either." He cupped her breast. "You're amazing, not broken, and I want to make love to you until neither of us can move, but I have to be honest with you. I'll never be able to be that devoted husband you deserve. I can be your today, but for me, that's all there is anyway. That's what matters, that's where the living is done, so to me, that's everything. My today is my everything, and that's what I can give you."

He kissed her again, deeply, pouring every last bit of who he was into the kiss. He didn't have much to offer her. Shit, he had nothing to offer her. He was the one who was broken, lying in scattered fragments in his past, fragments that could never be rebuilt into anything whole or decent. "I'm not worthy of you," he whispered. "But I'll give you everything I have to give."

She pulled back, searching his face, and for a moment, time seemed to freeze inside his heart. He'd said too much. He never talked like that. He never said words like that. What the hell had he been thinking? He kept things clean, simple, and detached. That was how he lived. That was—

Then she smiled, wrapped her arms around his neck, and kissed him. "Make love to me, Zane," she whispered between kisses. "I'm begging you."

CHAPTER TEN

THE WAY ZANE kissed Taylor took her breath away. His kiss seemed to sear every cell in her body, burning away all the tension and stress, leaving nothing behind but relentless, untainted need for him. She felt more alive than she had in so long, maybe ever.

His hands were like magic where they roamed her body, gliding over her skin as if she were made of the most beautiful, fragile porcelain, as if he believed he was the luckiest man on earth to be able to touch her.

The kiss was sensual and tempting, a slow, decadent seduction. It wasn't carnal heat, but something deeper and more powerful.

She'd never lived in the present. She was always trying to fix today to make tomorrow better, constantly looking ahead to where she was going, or looking behind her to make sure she didn't wind up in the same place she'd once been. But Zane's words had entranced her, making her want to crawl into his arms and never move, to simply be with him in the moment.

He slid down her body, trailing his lips along her throat, her collarbone, and to the swell of her breasts. His hands spanned her hips, his thumbs sliding below the waistband of her jeans in slow, tantalizing circles. Desire began to roll through her more intensely, and she shifted her hips restlessly. She clasped his shoulders, her fingers digging into his muscles.

She loved having his body against her. The feel of his skin sliding over hers was amazing. So much intimacy, so much sensation. She'd missed this kind of connection. She'd missed it far more than she'd realized. Or maybe, it wasn't simply that she'd missed it. Maybe it was that being touched by Zane was what she'd been waiting for all this time.

He lightly bit her nipple, and she gasped at the flood of desire... then he unfastened the button on her jeans. She tensed. Was she really going to do this? Was she really going to let him get her naked? Because she knew where it was going to lead. The need between them was too great. Nothing was going to stop them once they crossed that line. She closed her eyes, her fingers sliding through his hair as he kissed his way down her belly, pausing to lave her belly button as he unzipped her jeans.

Oh, God, really? She focused on his touch as he gripped the waistband of her jeans and began to tug them down her hips, his mouth trailing kisses lower and lower as he pulled her jeans down. Instinctively, she lifted her hips, helping him. That was all he needed, and within a second, her jeans were gone. He'd left her underwear on, but he was already raining kisses over the soft fabric that provided no useful barrier between them.

He pressed a kiss to her swollen nub, and she gasped, twisting beneath him. His fingers traced circles along the edges of her underwear, brushing over the lace, making her want to beg for him to tear it off her. But she didn't. There was something about the teasing that was amazing, making her feel he wanted to savor every last second.

She'd never been savored before. She had to admit that she really liked it.

"I want to take my jeans off," he whispered. "Is that okay with you?"

She opened her eyes to look at him. He was stretched out between her legs, an arm wrapped round each of her thighs, his gaze searing into her as he waited for her to reply. She could see the muscles rippling in his back and shoulders, along with a few faded scars she assumed were from his bull riding days. He was rugged and raw, far from perfection, and her entire body clenched with the need for him. She nodded. "Take 'em off, cowboy."

He flashed her a grin, showcasing that dimple of his that made her want to melt, and then he eased himself off her. He stripped off his boots quickly, and she rolled onto her side, riveted as his muscles flexed while he disrobed. She couldn't help the sigh of anticipation as he stood and began to unfasten his jeans.

"You have a six pack," she said, her gaze trailing over the smattering of hair on his chest and his abs. "I didn't think real guys actually had them. I thought it was a myth created by skilled photo editing."

His fingers stilled on the bottom of his jeans, and he looked over at her. "Darlin', this here is all real, and it's all yours." He took his hands off his jeans. "You want the honors?"

She let out a choked laugh of embarrassment. "No, that's okay. I like to watch."

He sauntered over to the bed and leaned over, his palms sinking into the covers. "Go ahead," he said softly. "Indulge yourself. I want you to."

She had to admit, the idea of taking charge was a little intoxicating, especially when it came to a man who was twice her size and had enough muscle to dominate her easily if he chose to. He was so much stronger than she was, but right now, in his bedroom, she felt like she was the one with the power. She couldn't keep the grin off her face. "Okay."

"That's my girl." He stepped back and clasped his hands behind his head, his biceps flexing so ridiculously much that she felt like she had to be imagining things. Was this man really here for her, and just her? Had he really said that she was the first woman he'd ever trusted, in his entire life? Was it really possible that she was special to *him,* a man who was not only a physical specimen, but also who had a beautiful heart and so much vulnerability?

She swung her feet over the edge of the bed, and stood up. The moment she did, his eyes raked over her, burning her from head to toe. She was no svelte, gorgeous model, and couldn't even pass off her body as an athletic build. She wasn't even on the same scale as he was when it came to physical beauty, but the appreciation in his eyes made her feel like the most beautiful woman in the world.

Her nipples tightened, and she walked over to him. His eyes darkened as she neared, but he kept his hands laced behind his head. A part of her wanted to go right for his jeans like he'd invited her to do, but another part of her wanted to savor the moment, the way he'd done to her.

She splayed her hands on his chest, feeling the softness of his chest hair, and the hardness of the muscles beneath. His jaw tightened, as she slid her hands upward to his shoulders, and then across and down his arms. His skin was hot to the touch, and so incredibly sexy. Need pooled in her belly when she saw the desire darkening his eyes. "I like your body," she said.

"I'm glad. Feel free to make it yours." His voice was low and rough, curling through her like a private seduction.

"Mine? Hmm..." She smiled, and put her hands back on his chest, running them over the ridges of his torso as she moved them downward. He sucked his stomach in as she touched it, the muscles quivering beneath her fingers. Resting her fingers on his waistband, she stood on her tiptoes to kiss him.

His kiss was ravenous, immediately taking control, pouring such desire into her that her entire body began to melt into a boiling pool of need. He kept his hands clasped behind his head, though, still giving her the power, even while he stripped her soul bare with the intensity of his kiss.

She pressed her breasts against his chest, loving the feel of his skin against her nipples while he kissed her. Allowing her fingers to dance over the waistband of his jeans, she unfastened the button and then unzipped his fly. His erection was straining against the front of his jeans, and she couldn't help the shiver of anticipation. She couldn't remember the last time any man had wanted her this much, let alone the last time that she'd responded so intensely.

She hooked her thumbs over the waistband of his jeans, and tugged downward. She realized almost immediately that she'd accidentally grabbed his boxer briefs as well as his pants. She paused, hesitating.

Did she really want this? This moment, this man, this magical experience?

He stopped the kiss, as if sensing her hesitation. He waited in silence, his lips resting against hers, giving her the chance to make her choice. Time seemed suspended as she waited, struggling with need and her own sense of self-preservation. A part of her wanted him to take charge, to be the one to rip off their clothes, to be the one taking ownership of what happened between them, as if that would somehow safeguard her heart, if she didn't actually admit to herself that she wanted this.

She pulled back to look at him. His dark eyes were hooded with desire, his gaze steady. Somehow, seeing his eyes made everything settle. This was Zane she was with, not some ridiculously hot stranger who meant nothing to her. Whatever happened in their future, she knew that this moment mattered deeply to both of them. Maybe it was the most either of them could give, maybe this was the pinnacle of what could ever be between them, but it didn't change that this moment was special, extraordinary even, a gift that she didn't have to fear.

She smiled, tightened her grip on his jeans and boxer briefs, and then tugged them down over his hips. His cock sprang free as his pants hit the floor, and she wrapped her hand around it as she stood up. The skin was velvet soft over the hardness, and her stomach fluttered in anticipation as Zane sucked in his breath.

"Nice," he whispered. "Did you know the second night we slept together, you were doing that to me? Holding me just like that?"

Heat flared in her cheeks. "What? I wouldn't have." She started to let go, but he grabbed her hand and held it where it was.

"You were asleep," he said, his voice rough with desire. "I thought it was awesome that you felt safe enough in your sleep to do that. A hell of a turn-on, too, I have to admit." He palmed her lower back with his free hand, lowering his head to nip at her earlobe. "I have never stayed so still for so long in my entire life, desperate not to disturb your sleep."

She let out a giggle, imagining Zane frozen for hours, afraid to dislodge her hand. "You're such a dork."

"Nah." He locked his arm around her waist and dragged her up against him, so his erection was against her belly, her hand trapped between their bodies. "I'm just a hot-blooded guy who knows when the right woman is in his bed. Speaking of which..." He scooped her up in his arms and tossed her into the middle of his mattress.

She'd just barely landed when he lunged after her. A scream of laughter burst from her as she scrambled up the pillows away from him, but he caught her ankles and dragged her back down toward him. She had no time to escape before he was on top of her, pinning her mercilessly to the bed with the weight of his body.

"And now, you're mine, my precious," he teased, sounding like some evil wizard who'd trapped her in a dungeon. He kissed her hard, deeply, mercilessly, claiming her in a kiss so searing she was pretty sure steam would soon be rising from her body.

He broke the kiss and lightly bit her ear, and then began working his way in small nibbles and licks down the side of her neck. "You're at my mercy," he continued in his mock evil voice, "to do whatever I wish. I warn you, my darlin', the fantasies I have about your naked body will shock you."

She giggled again, sliding her fingers through his hair as he worked his way down toward her breasts. It felt totally different having them both naked, except for the wisp of her underwear. So much skin, so much heat, so much intimacy, and so much trust. "I'm too innocent for a bad boy," she teased. "I think you should let me go."

"Never." He grabbed her wrists and pinned them above her head, his hips pressing down against hers. His eyes were dark, and impenetrable. "You're mine, darlin', and I intend to keep you."

She knew he meant his words in play, and that he was referring just to this moment, but that didn't keep her heart from constricting. *I intend to keep you.* How amazing did those words sound? She wanted to be kept, to be fought for, and to be treasured beyond all words. Maybe there was no future for them, but in this moment, she felt like she had everything she wanted. "I don't think I can keep up with you." She grinned, tugging at her wrists just to see if he'd let her go.

He didn't. "I'll teach you everything you need to know." He paused at her breast, drawing her nipple into his mouth, using his tongue, his teeth, and his lips to torment her. Desire spiraled out in all directions, and she couldn't help but move her hips restlessly, needing more, already under his spell even though he'd barely begun to touch her.

"Like what?" She couldn't keep the breathlessness out of her voice.

"Like telling me what you want." He moved up again, and captured her mouth in a devastating kiss. "Take ownership of your body, Taylor," he whispered between kisses. "Claim me. Direct me. Make me your fantasy." He moved his hips, tempting her. "What do you want, darlin'? I want to give it to you."

"Kiss me," she whispered. "Kiss me."

"Like this?" He immediately captured her mouth in a kiss that plunged right to her soul. His tongue claimed hers, his mouth a sinful tool of seduction. She tried to get her hands free to wrap them around his neck, but his grip on her wrists tightened.

Excitement began to pulse through her at his refusal to free her. She liked the dichotomy of his relentless, bossy strength, combined with the fact he was demanding she take control. Power and submission combined into a heady place. "Let me go," she whispered, testing him.

"Not yet." He shifted his grip so both her wrists were in his left hand, and then slid his right hand over her breasts and down her belly. "What else do you want me to do, darlin'?" His breath was hot against her mouth, a temptation that was just out of her reach.

"Touch me."

He grinned, his dark eyes smoldering. "Here?" He put his hand on her elbow.

"You're a jerk."

He laughed. "That's not what you want? How about here?" He cupped her breasts, his finger flicking over her nipple.

She shifted under his touch. "Better."

"Where else?" he whispered, between kisses.

"Lower."

"Here?" He cupped her knee, making her laugh.

"You're such a pain," she said with a giggle.

"I just want you to feel the power of telling me what you want." He kissed her again, an intoxicating assault on all her senses, while his thumb drew circles on the inside of her knee. Okay, so she hadn't *thought* she wanted him fondling her knee, but the way his thumb was sliding over the skin on the inside of her knee was sending tendrils of desire though her body.

"A little higher," she whispered into the kiss.

He moved his hand to her thigh, his fingers tracing designs on the skin, making chills race down her leg and up her spine. "Here?"

"To the left."

His hand slid to the inside of her thigh, still tracing designs on her skin. "Here?" He kissed her again, taking her breath away before she could answer. The kiss was so amazing she could barely think, and her hips shifted even more restlessly, moving of their own accord, as if she could force his hand to go where she wanted just by sheer force of will.

"Higher," she whispered.

He moved his hand upward, until his fingers were brushing over the delicate fabric of her underwear, tantalizing her with the soft, barely-there touch as he glided across her body. "Nice," he whispered, as he ran his tongue down the side of her neck.

She shifted beneath him again. "Take it off."

"Take what off?" He pressed his palm to her folds, igniting a rush of desire, even through her underwear.

She groaned. "You're so impossible. Just take off my damned underwear and make love to me."

He laughed softly and kissed her, a kiss so penetrating that her body clenched in response. "You're so bossy." He finally released her wrists to drag her underwear over her thighs, trailing kisses down her leg as he slid the scrap of material off.

When she was finally naked, she had a brief second where she felt utterly exposed and vulnerable. There was nothing between them now. *Nothing.*

Then he kissed her toe, making her giggle. "You have such a sexy toe," he murmured as he kissed the arch of her foot. "And under here. I've been dying to kiss this very spot." His hand was warm where he'd wrapped it around her ankle, trapping her just as he'd immobilized her wrists. He kissed her anklebone, and then the front of her shin.

She swallowed, watching him as he worked his way up her leg. His eyes were on her, his dark gaze swallowing her up in its heat. He kissed her kneecap, and then the inside of her knee. And then he began working his way up the inside of her thigh, never taking his gaze off her face.

He hooked his arm under her right thigh, moving her leg to the side as he kissed higher, and then locked his other arm across her hips, pinning her to the mattress.

She didn't think she would ever tire of his strength. "You like to do that, don't you? Trap me."

"Yeah, I do. You mind?"

She shook her head, her body taut with anticipation as he moved her legs further apart. He met her gaze, his mouth inches from her most private parts. "What do you want now, darlin'? Tell me."

"Kiss me. Touch me. Do everything you've fantasized about." Her voice was breathless, and her heart seemed to skip a beat when a slow, dangerous grin spread across his face.

"Be careful what you wish for," he said. "You have no idea what I'm capable of imagining."

"No one has ever fantasized about me before," she whispered. "Show me."

"You're in trouble now," he said. "Big trouble. Cowboy trouble." Then he swept his tongue across her folds in a single bold swipe that made her entire body clench. He gave her no respite, still pinning her to the bed with his forearm as he invaded her body with his mouth, his tongue, and even a few light nips with his teeth. Sensations cascaded through her like fireworks in her blood. Her hips bucked under his sensual assault, but each time she tried to move, he simply exerted more force with his arm, holding her in place effortlessly.

She loved how he held her down. It was incredibly sexy, especially since she knew that if she ever asked him to release her, he would in a heartbeat. It was the illusion of being trapped that was so intoxicating, plus the way his muscles flexed to resist her was completely sexy as well.

He released his tight grip on her leg, and slid his fingers inside her. She gasped at the invasion, suddenly no longer able to focus on anything but his touch, and the way it felt to have him inside her. He didn't let up on his assault with his mouth, his tongue swirling over her folds as his fingers slid deeper inside her, unfurling a cataclysm of need inside her.

She gripped his shoulders, gasping as her body burned with need. She could feel an orgasm building inside her, getting tighter and tighter until she thought she'd burst. "Stop," she gasped. "Make love to me. Now."

He responded instantly, crawling up her body to take her mouth in a devastating kiss as he kneed her thighs apart. She felt his erection pressing against her, and she wrapped her legs across his hips, trying to draw him into her. He didn't give in. Instead, he broke the kiss and framed her face with his hands. "I don't have any condoms." His voice was rough. "I haven't done this in a while, and I wasn't prepared. I was so pissed this afternoon that it didn't even occur to me this would happen."

A little part of her died at what she had to say. "It's okay. I can't get pregnant. It doesn't matter."

"I got tested a year ago," he said, not even appearing to notice her comment. "I wanted to know if I had paid the price for any of the shit I'd done. I'm clean, and I haven't been with anyone since."

She nodded, some of the tension easing from her body at his utter nonchalance about her confession. She realized that it truly didn't bother him in the least. He didn't see her as flawed or broken or anything. She smiled, her heart suddenly a thousand times lighter than it had ever felt. "My last boyfriend and I did the testing thing. He didn't want to use a condom if he didn't have to. I'm good."

His eyes darkened. "I don't like it when you talk about your last boyfriend." He moved his hips against her, his cock straining at her entrance. "I want this about us. Me. You."

Her breath caught at the sensation of his body pressing against hers, so close, so tempting. "It's only about you, Zane. I feel like..." God, could she say it? Wouldn't it make her too vulnerable? But she wanted to say it. She felt, somehow, that they both needed to hear it. "I feel like I need this with you. I need *you*. I thought I came here for Mira, but really, it was because I needed to meet you."

He didn't ridicule her or pull away. He simply nodded. "I feel the same way." His fingers tightened where he was framing her face, and he kissed her again. There was something else in the kiss this time. Something new. A tenderness. A vulnerability. She wasn't sure, but it made tears burn and her throat tighten. She felt utterly and completely cherished, treasured beyond words, despite all he was.

Zane pulled back to look at her, his eyes boring into hers. "You're mine," he said, his voice rough. "Mine."

Her throat tightened even more, and she nodded, not quite able to speak.

His eyes still boring into hers, he moved his hips, sliding his cock past her barriers and plunging deep inside her. She gasped, her heart tightening at the feel of him buried inside her. "It feels so right, doesn't it?"

"Yeah." Still not taking his gaze off her, he withdrew, and then thrust again, deeper this time, making her body ache for more. "It does. You do. We do." He braced his hands beside her head, looming over her on the bed. "I give you my everything, Taylor Shaw. It's not much, and you deserve more, but it's my all."

Tears filled her eyes, but before she could answer, he kissed her, a devastating, sensual kiss that seemed to carve a path through the aching loneliness in her heart. She wrapped her legs more securely around his hips, locking him against her as he drove deeper again and again, each thrust coiling desire more and more tightly through her, until she felt as if her entire body was going to explode.

She met his gaze, unable to drag her focus off his face. He was watching her so intently, as if he were trying to memorize her every feature so he could hold it in his memory forever. He was so present in this moment with her, making her feel like it was only about them, that this moment had meaning because it was the two of them coming together.

He cupped the back of her head and kissed her again, a feverish dominating kiss that tore through her like a fire that would never be stopped. Her entire body coiled, and she gripped his shoulders, gasping at the tension amassing inside her. This was her moment, her man, her everything.

"I'm yours, forever yours," he whispered, and then he took one final plunge that thrust her over the edge into an abyss of sensation.

"Zane." She clung to him as the orgasm raked through her. He bucked against her, and she knew the moment he surrendered. His entire body went taut, his muscles became rock hard beneath her hands, and then he shouted her name, driving deep inside her as the orgasm took him, sending him over the same precipice as she, until there was nothing left to hold onto but each other.

CHAPTER ELEVEN

ZANE WANTED to stay right where he was and never move...for at least ten minutes, until he recovered, and then he wanted to make love to Taylor again. And *then*, never move again. Until he recovered, and then—

"Wow." Her sigh of contentment interrupted his fantasies, making him smile.

He grinned as Taylor nestled against him, her hair tickling his chest. "Yeah, it was."

She splayed her hands over his stomach, tracing designs on his skin. "You're going to make it hard for me to go back to my real life," she said.

His amusement faded, and his arm tightened around her instinctively. "When are you leaving?"

She shrugged. "I promised Mira I'd stay 'til after the baby is born and help out. I have about six weeks of vacation accumulated, but I doubt I can take them all. They need me."

Six weeks. Or a week. He wasn't a long-term guy in any way, but the thought of Taylor getting on an airplane didn't sit well with him. But shit. What did he have to offer her? Nothing.

"Can I ask you something?" Her voice was slurred with contentment, making something inside him warm.

He liked that she was relaxed. He liked that he was the one she was relaxing with. "Yeah, sure. Ask away." Anything was better than dragging himself down about her leaving.

"Why did you quit bull riding?"

A cold wind swept through him, and he stiffened.

Taylor lifted her head to look at him, her brow furrowed. "What's wrong?" Her guileless gaze was fastened on him, utterly devoid of ulterior motive. He realized her question was genuine, not some tabloid wannabe trying to get the scoop on him.

Shit. He had to chill. Taylor was different. She wasn't like the others.

With a sigh, he stretched out on his back, staring at the cracked ceiling as he ran his fingers along her spine. He never talked about his past, not to anyone, but for some reason, he wanted Taylor to know. She'd trusted him with her deepest secret, and he owed her that much. "Before I was born, my mom shacked up with my father. They never got married, but he knocked her up. We lived with him for a while, and then moved out." He concentrated on the feel of her skin beneath his hand, trying to distance himself from the story he was telling. "She never held a job. She just hooked up with assorted men and slept with them in exchange for being able to live with each of them and have him support us, until she got tired of him and moved on."

Taylor frowned, and propped herself up on her elbow to look at him.

He didn't look at her. He didn't want to see what she was thinking. Instead, he kept his gaze on the ceiling. "Most of the men she was with were bastards. I learned fast to vacate when her boyfriends were around. By the time I was five, I was spending my days on the streets. I was already trouble, I'll admit that."

Taylor scooted on top of him, so she was laying on his chest, her chin resting on her palms, while she watched him.

Zane scowled at her for interfering with his attempt not to make eye contact, but she smiled gently. "It's okay, Zane. I already knew you grew up poor, and you told me you were like those boys. I knew that before I slept with you. I'm not going anywhere."

At her words, something inside him eased, a tight knot that had been there for as long as he could remember. She knew who he was, and she wasn't going to leave him. With a sigh, he lifted her hair off the back of her neck and let it slide through his fingers. "When I was six, I ran into Chase. He took one look at me, and he said I looked too much like a Stockton not to be his brother. I asked my mom, and she said yes. I was psyched, you know? I had brothers. I had family. I belonged somewhere."

She smiled. "Chase seems like a good guy."

"He's a great guy." Zane couldn't keep the faint smile off his face. "He dragged me out to the ranch, which was owned by some old guy named Skip back then. Chase and his brothers, my brothers, used to go out there all the time and take care of the horses, and I got to tag along. The ranch wound up being my salvation. I had a talent for riding, and I loved it. Dealing with those bulls gave me a place for my anger and aggression." He picked up her hand and pressed a kiss to her palm, needing to ground himself in her presence. "I was poor, my mother was a slut, and everyone thought I was worthless, until I met Chase and started riding bulls. I had a major chip on my shoulder, and if it wasn't for the bulls, I would have wound up in prison for life."

She smiled. "So, you found your place?"

"Not really." He sighed. "My brothers had mostly grown up together. They had a closeness I never quite broke into. Yeah, I was one of them, but at the end of the day, I went back to whatever shit hole we were living in at the time, and they went home together. I hated being an outsider, both with my own brothers and in society. I figured if I became a star bull rider, I'd matter. I'd belong."

She cocked her head, her eyes sharper than he'd expected. "It didn't change anything, did it? The money? The fame?"

"I tried. I filled my life with women and parties and big trucks. I thought I was the man." He twisted her hair around his index finger. "I found a woman I thought was right. We were engaged. I was on top of the world."

"And then?" Her voice was soft, non-judgmental, and he found himself looking at her, wanting to see her, needing to connect with her.

"We were leaving a bar late one night with some other riders. There were some boys hanging around outside, kids like the ones you saw today, kids like I used to be. They wanted autographs, but a couple of the guys told 'em to take a hike." He gritted his jaw, that same anger returning. "They treated those kids like shit. My fiancée actually called them filth. *Filth.*" He met her gaze. "I'd once been one of those kids, Taylor. The people I called my friends treated them the same way that all those people had treated me as a kid. I felt like I'd betrayed who I was, and that my friends had betrayed me. How had I become the kind of person whose friends were like all the bastards who treated me like shit when I was poor? They liked me now, because I was rich and famous. It was just...it was crap." The same fury and self-loathing boiled through him. "I quit at the end of that season. I was done. I didn't want to live that life or be with those people."

She was still watching him. "But bull riding is all you know," she said, far too observant. "It's your identity, isn't it? Without it, you don't know what to do."

He shrugged. "I don't belong anywhere. I don't belong with any people. Which is fine. I don't care. I live my life, and I'm free to go where I want. No one counts on me, and I don't count on anyone. It works."

She was still resting her chin in her hands, studying him. "I count on you," she said softly.

His hands stilled in her hair, and something shifted in his chest. "Shit, Taylor, I told you—"

She put her finger on his lips to silence him. "I didn't mean that I'm counting on you to marry me. I just meant that I count on you to be the man I trust, the one that makes me feel like I matter. I don't belong anywhere either, Zane. My parents are long gone. I travel so much that I don't even know if my fridge actually works. Mira is my only connection, and now I've lost her too, in a way. But when I'm with you, I feel like..." She paused, as if she were trying to find the words. "I feel like my soul can stop fluttering around, and it can just rest in your arms and breathe."

He stared at her, shocked by her words, by the way she'd articulated exactly how he felt when he was with her. He wouldn't have been able to explain it, but the moment she'd said it, he'd known she was right. "That's how I feel."

She smiled, a gentle, genuine smile that seemed to light up her eyes. "I'm glad. You deserve to feel like that, but you know, I get the feeling that Chase and Steen would be willing for you to land there, on the ranch."

"I know." He started trailing his hands through her hair again. "But it's not my thing. I'm not that kind of guy who connects like that. Trying to put down roots is a trap. It makes you blind."

"Like when you didn't see the true nature of your friends and fiancée?"

He nodded. "Exactly like that. I won't make that mistake again. I like my brothers, and I've got their backs, but I don't fit with them, not on a permanent basis." He lifted his head to kiss her, needing to feel the softness of her lips against his.

She melted against him, returning the kiss with such warmth that his gut seemed to twist inside him. Suddenly, he didn't want to talk anymore. He just wanted to lose himself in Taylor, in her kiss, and in her body.

In a single swift move, he rolled over, flipping her beneath him without even breaking the kiss. She slipped her arms around his neck, kissing him back as he moved his knee between her thighs. He was already hard, needing to be inside her. After working so hard to create a solid, immovable foundation under him that no one could derail, he suddenly felt like he was standing on quicksand, and everything he knew was slithering out of his grasp.

He nudged his cock at her entrance, and found she was ready for him. Heat roared through him, and he sheathed himself inside her, desperate to ground himself in her, needing her to be his rock.

She whispered his name, wrapping her legs around his waist as he withdrew and then slid even deeper. As he made love to her, he pulled back, searching her face for the answers to questions he couldn't articulate.

Her fingers laced behind his neck, and she smiled at him. No words, just that private smile that seemed to unleash a thunder inside him.

Suddenly, he felt lost, so unbearably lost, like he was a four-year-old kid, standing on his front porch, trying to understand where he was supposed to go, and how he was supposed to survive. "Taylor." Her name tore from him with a rawness he hadn't intended, and he captured her mouth in a desperate kiss.

He didn't know what he wanted, all he knew was that it was Taylor he needed. Her kiss, her touch, and her voice. Somehow, she filled a void inside him that he hadn't even known was there, but at the same time, being with her created a restlessness inside him that he didn't know how to fix. He plunged deep inside her, and he felt her muscles contract as the orgasm took her. He didn't hesitate, abandoning all vestiges of control so that he tumbled into the orgasm with her, holding her more tightly than he'd ever held anything, or anyone, in his life.

And he still felt like his grip on her was slipping...

TAYLOR AWOKE to the shrill ring of her phone. It was the ringtone she'd assigned to Edward, back when he'd been her boyfriend as well as her boss. He'd promised to allow her an actual vacation, but apparently, he was a liar. Too asleep to open her eyes, her hand shot toward her nightstand.

When she didn't find her phone, or even a nightstand, she became aware of Zane wrapped around her, his arms tucking her securely against him. She smiled sleepily, and nestled more deeply into his embrace, as she recalled the previous night. She, the queen of being attached to her phone, had actually left it in her purse when she'd been distracted by an entire night of loving with Zane. She ran her hand over his bare shoulder, and smiled. Her body ached in a thousand places, and all of it was perfect.

Her phone rang again, jerking her back to the present. Her smile fading, she started to slide out from under the covers to retrieve her phone, but Zane's arm snaked out and locked around her waist. He dragged her mercilessly back into the bed without any apparent effort. "Don't answer it," he mumbled, sounding half-asleep.

"It's my boss. I have to." She tried to wiggle out from under his arm, but he gripped her more tightly.

"You're on vacation," he muttered. "In my bed. No phones allowed."

The phone rang again, an incessant beckoning she couldn't ignore. "Zane. It might be important. Let me go." She tried to roll away from him again, but this time, he dragged her all the way into the middle of the mattress, lifted himself up just enough to scoot her beneath him, and then lowered himself on top of her, pinning her to the mattress as he buried his face in the crook of her neck.

"Love this," he said, his voice muffled. "Waking up with you."

The sleepy honesty of his voice chased away her irritation at being banned from her phone, and she sighed, relaxing back into the sheets. It felt absolutely decadent to have him wrapped around her. She felt like she was waking up in a cocoon of love...well...not *love,* but love. "Zane." She wrapped her arms around his neck and tangled her feet over his calves, feeling her whole body shudder with relief as she allowed herself to focus on him.

He was right. This was where she wanted to be. With him.

Her phone buzzed that Edward had left a message, and she grimaced. "I should at least check the message—"

He shut her up with a kiss designed to distract her completely from anything but the feel of his body.

It worked.

Yes, real life was hovering in the background, but Zane was right. She was on vacation, in his bed, being kissed most deliciously by a naked cowboy with a heart the size of Wyoming.

Why in heaven's name would she answer her phone?

She wouldn't.

Forget the phone.

For now.

$\sim$

THE TIGHTNESS of Zane's grip on her hand told Taylor all she needed to know about the emotional state of the cowboy sauntering into the funeral as if he owned the place. He was wearing dark blue jeans, a collared shirt, and he'd even shaved. She noticed that he'd selected cowboy boots, despite his avowed aversion to the cowboy identity anymore. He looked incredibly handsome, but at the same time, there was a vulnerability and pain in his eyes that he couldn't hide from her, and his grip on her hand was relentless, as if he were afraid she'd walk away and leave him to face it alone.

He'd sat on his bike for ten minutes down the street from the church, watching everyone walk in, his hands so tight around the handlebars that it was as if they'd become fused to the bike. It had taken him so long to move that she'd begun to think he wasn't going to attend when he'd finally started the bike rolling forward again, sliding it up beside the dumpster on the far side of the lot.

"Zane!" The boy he'd spoken to yesterday at the Garage ran up as they entered the church, throwing his arms around Zane.

Zane swore under his breath, but he wrapped his free arm around the youth, despite the death grip he still had on Taylor's hand. "I'm sorry, Luke." His voice was rough and harsh. "It's my fault."

Luke's brow furrowed as he pulled back to look at Zane. "How is it your fault?"

"I should have been there. I should have found a way. I—"

Taylor squeezed his hand gently, and he looked over at her, pain etched on his face. "You did more for him than anyone else ever did, I would bet," she said softly. "Didn't you?"

He stared at her for a second, then shrugged.

"Zane," Luke said, gripping Zane's arm tightly. "Will you be at the Garage today?" His young face was eager, almost desperate. "I'll shoot hoops with you."

Zane sighed and shook his head. "I told you about my brother, right? The one with the ranch?"

Luke frowned. "Yeah."

"He's about to get married and have a kid. I told him I'd help him out. I have to go to the ranch for a couple weeks. I'll be back soon, though, okay?"

Luke nodded, but there was no mistaking his crestfallen face. "Okay. Sure. Whatever."

"Hey." Zane caught his arm as the boy turned away.

Luke looked back at him. "What?"

"I *will* be back. I'm not abandoning you. You can count on me." His voice was fierce, almost angry, but Luke didn't look scared. On the contrary, he looked relieved.

Luke nodded. "Okay." This time, however, he was smiling.

"Okay." Zane held his arm for one more second, and then released the youth. Zane didn't take his eyes off Luke as he walked across the church toward the front pew, joining Ross, the manager of the Garage, two other women, and a young boy maybe four years old, who was leaning on the back of the pew, watching Zane with wide eyes.

"Is that Luke's family?"

"That's his kid brother, Toby, but they don't have any other family. They're foster kids. His mom's in prison for drugs, and his dad is some deadbeat that no one can find. Ross footed the bill for the funeral, since his brother came to our place." His gaze was moody as he watched Luke put his arm around Toby. "They have no chance," he said softly. "It's a no win for them. They have nothing."

Taylor's heart tightened. "What about aunts or uncles?"

Zane looked over at her. "You got any of those?"

She shook her head.

"Neither do they. Most of the people here didn't know Brad. They're just coming because it's at their church." The anger in his eyes burned, and her heart turned over at the depth of his emotions. But before she could say anything, another boy came up. She recognized him as Luke's little brother, Toby. He slid his hand into Zane's, and Zane immediately crouched down to eye level, engaging in a whispered conversation that she couldn't overhear.

She let out her breath and looked around. The service was sparsely attended, but there were a few adults and some kids, mostly boys. The church was simple, but well-kept, and it had the aura of a place that was pulsing with life and vitality. She was glad that Ross had arranged for the funeral to be held in the church. Maybe the people in attendance hadn't known the boy, but they were there for him.

Toby ran back to the front of the church and climbed up next to Luke in the front pew. Zane had moved away from Taylor, talking in low tones to a woman wearing a navy suit and sensible heels. She looked like she could be a social worker, or a teacher, there to take note of the proceedings. As she watched, another boy tugged on Zane's hand, and he broke off the conversation to talk to the boy, crouching down to give him his full attention.

Her heart began to tighten as she watched Zane interact with the boys. He treated every one of them as if they were the most important conversation he'd had all day, and she could see in their eyes how much his respect meant. He was a natural with them, his soft heart obvious.

He might not want children of his own, but he had enough of a heart to encompass the world.

Tears burned in her eyes, and she had to look away, taking a deep breath to combat the sudden sense of loss. Zane might think he was broken and isolated, but he lived with his full heart and soul more than anyone she'd ever met. He cared, and he used his time to matter. What did she do? All she did was run around with a smartphone and laptop, making sure the hotel had pressed her suits in time for her next meeting.

She couldn't remember ever having the kind of community that Zane was clearly surrounded by.

The music began to play, and Zane walked back over to her. "Hey." His face was taut, and the muscles in his jaw were tense. He grabbed her hand, gripping her tightly as he pulled her toward him.

She realized that despite the show of ease he was putting on, and the connection he had with so many of these kids, in truth, he was nearly undone by the situation. The loneliness she'd felt drifted away, replaced by a need to be there for him. "Let's sit." She led him to a nearby pew, one that was empty.

He sat next to her, so close that his shoulder was against hers. He leaned forward, bracing his forearms on his thighs. His shoulders were bunched, and his head was down, and he'd sandwiched her hand between his. The tension radiating from him was palpable, and she leaned forward, resting her face against his. "Do you want to leave?"

He nodded. "But I have to stay."

"Okay." She leaned against him as the minister began to talk about the value of life, and honoring those who are no longer with us.

Zane's grip tightened on her hand. "This shouldn't have happened," he whispered. "I couldn't get him to come to the Garage. He thought it was a bunch of crap. I tried. I fucking tried, but not enough. I let him go. I figured he'd find his way. *Shit.*"

Her heart twisted at the depths of his self-recrimination. "Everyone chooses their own path, Zane." She kept her voice low, quietly speaking just to him. "You couldn't force him. All these other kids respond to you. You're doing a lot right. Don't let this make you doubt yourself."

He looked over at her, the desolation stark on his face. "When I was fifteen, my best friend wanted to steal a car. I had a rodeo to go to. I went to the rodeo. He crashed the car and died. If it weren't for the bulls, I'd be dead. Chase gave that to me, but I couldn't give it to the one kid who needed it."

She had no words to ease the torment on his face. "I'm sorry, Zane."

He nodded, crushing her hand between his as he faced forward again, but he was still hunched over, his arms on his thighs, and his head bowed. He wasn't moving, and appeared to be deep in thought, but the death grip he had on her hand told her the truth that he wasn't letting anyone else see: that he was barely hanging on.

She moved closer to him, resting her shoulder against his, giving him the only comfort she could give, which was the knowledge that he wasn't alone. With her, he didn't have to pretend to be anything other than who he was.

It wasn't much, but she knew that it was all he wanted from her, and she would give it to him.

CHAPTER TWELVE

BEING on his bike had never felt so good.

Zane gripped the handlebars more fiercely as he sped along the winding roads. He'd skipped the highway, needing the silence and solace of nature to cleanse the funeral from his system. What the hell had he been thinking, going there? He didn't belong there. Luke's face. Hell. The kid's face had been devastated when Zane had told him he was leaving.

How had that kid come to count on him? When had that happened? He'd shown them all what happened when he got involved with those kids. They died. So why had Luke and Toby looked at him like he could fix everything for them?

Shit.

He kicked up the heat, flying through the winding roads.

"Zane?" Taylor's voice echoed in his helmet.

He swore at the sound of her voice, his gut lurching. He couldn't believe he'd lost his shit in front of her. He was embarrassed as hell at the way he'd clung to her, like some pansy. But at the same time, he wasn't going to lie that if she hadn't been there, he would have walked out. She was the only reason he'd managed to stay. "Yeah?"

"You're scaring me."

He gritted his jaw. Just because he'd been silent and uncommunicative, she was getting upset? See? That was the problem when he got close to people. They wanted more from him when he had nothing more to give.

"Can you slow down?"

"Slow down?" He glanced at the speedometer, and swore when he saw how fast he was driving. He immediately eased off the gas. "That's why you're scared? Because of my speed?" Not because he'd been moody. Because he'd been driving too fast. *Hell.* He noticed suddenly how tightly she was gripping him. Her knuckles where white from holding so hard, and her thighs were clenched around his hips.

"I'm sorry," she said. "I know you needed to go fast, but it's just too much around those curves."

Shit. He was an ass for not noticing she was worried. "Sorry." He slowed even further, and he felt her take a shuddering breath and lean her head against his back.

"Thanks. I just need a minute." Her grip on his waist hadn't lessened, even though they were at a crawl now. "I'm really sorry. I don't want to interfere."

"It's okay." His irritation at her disappeared, replaced by guilt about failing to notice what he was doing to her. He burned for the adrenaline rush of speed and danger. Since he couldn't get it from the bulls anymore, he got it from the bike. He'd been an insensitive ass not to be aware that she might not feel the same way. "Let's take a break." He pulled the bike off the road, driving a few yards off the main road into a cluster of trees. He stopped the bike and turned it off.

Taylor sagged against him, her entire upper body limp against his back. She peeled her hands off his waist. As she moved them, he saw they were trembling. Guilt hammered hard and he took her hand in his, pressing a kiss to her palm. "I'm sorry," he said. "I'm really, really sorry."

"You're upset. It's okay."

"No, it's not." He swung his leg off the bike and jerked his helmet off. Taylor already had hers off. Her face was pale, and her hair was a mess. A sexy-as-hell mess that he wanted to bury himself in and forget all the crap. Except he couldn't. He'd betrayed her by scaring her. "Lis-

475

ten." He ran his hand through his hair, wishing he was anywhere but where he was, and living any life except the one he was living. "It was a complete asshole move to drive that fast. I didn't even realize you were scared. *Shit.*" Unable to take the steadiness of her gaze, he moved away, his boots kicking up dust from the parched ground.

He heard Taylor sigh behind him, and his jaw tightened. Maybe this was for the best, a steady reminder for both of them that he wasn't a man she should count on. Even if he wanted to be the kind of guy people could depend on, he couldn't do it. Better that they both remembered.

He hopped up onto a six-foot boulder, sat down, and draped his arms over his knees, glaring at the foothills in the distance. How was he going to go back to the ranch right now? How was he going to keep sleeping with Taylor? This was why he never committed to a place. If no one expected anything from him, he could take off when he wanted. Right now, he just wanted to ride until he was so far away from everything that it felt like he never had to go back.

Taylor's boots scraped on the rock, and he tensed, listening to her as she climbed up beside him. His fists bunched, but he didn't look at her as she sat next to him, mimicking his pose.

He ground his jaw, waiting for the recriminations that he knew would come. Which would she start with? His antisocial behavior at the funeral? The fact he'd scared her on the bike? It didn't matter. He'd already apologized. There was nothing more he could do.

"After Dan left me for that other teacher, I left town for six weeks," she said quietly.

He didn't look at her, but his jaw tightened at the reminder of the man she'd given her heart to. He wasn't worthy of her, and he didn't want the obligations of a relationship, but the thought of her with anyone else hurt like hell.

"I just got in my car and drove over seven thousand miles."

He glanced over at her then, but she wasn't looking at him. She was staring across the parched plains, hugging her knees to her chest and resting her chin on them. She looked vulnerable and small, and he wanted to drag her into his arms and protect her. Why did he have the hero complex with her? He wasn't meant for that role.

She continued, apparently ignoring his turmoil. "I was trying to find a place to settle down. I drove through so many small towns, looking for the place that called to me, but, as you might expect, there were children and men everywhere I went."

A small laugh escaped him. "Bastards."

She managed a half-smile, but she didn't pick her chin up from her knees. "I finally realized that any kind of home would make the loss too great. So, I got a job that required me to travel almost all the time, and that was it. I basically gave up a home and connections. Mira is the only friend I still have who's not a part of my work, and my work friends are just colleagues."

He frowned, listening carefully now. "So, you're like me, only you use a plane and I use a bike."

"Yep. That's why I knew what you were doing today." She finally looked over at him. "Here's the thing, Zane. You might think you're not worthy or you don't belong, but you're wrong. The reason Luke and those boys look up to you is because they know you respect them and would do anything to help them." She smiled when he started to feel mutinous again. "Your brothers want you home, too. You have so many people who care—"

"I didn't ask them to care."

"I know, but they do." She turned to face him. "They all know the real you, and your background, and they see value in you anyway. Believe them when they say you're worthy."

He ground his jaw. "I know I'm a decent guy. I just don't want to owe anyone anything. When people count on you, you're going to fail them."

"Like how your mom failed you?"

He shrugged. "My mom sucked. She's not worth talking about." His dad was a bastard too. A perfect team. At least his mom had moved out of the Stockton house before his dad had started beating him, unlike his brothers.

"Maybe you're more worried about people failing you, than you are about failing them."

Okay, that was enough. He wasn't interested in this kind of discussion. He stood up to vault off the rock. "Let's get going—"

"I'm scared that people are going to fail me," she said softly, not moving. She was staring out across the plains again. "I didn't realize it until I met you. You made me see that I was living in a cocoon. When I got here, and I was shut out by Mira, I wanted to leave. Yesterday morning, I wanted to leave, too. When everyone was sitting around the table, I felt like I didn't belong."

He got that sentiment. He wanted to leave right now. But he was rooted to the spot, unable to drag himself away from her. He needed to hear what she was saying.

She looked up at him, her eyes shimmering with emotion. "In the last few days, you've made me laugh. You've made me feel joy, sadness, love, and connection. You've given me the best love making of my life. You brought me to life. I didn't want it. I wanted to stay in my shell, but today with you has been the best day of my life, I'm pretty sure."

He stared at her, barely able to process her words. He'd been an ass. He'd scared her. He'd come clean about what a mess he was. She'd seen the real him on every level, and that had been a *good* day for her? "I don't understand." He knew he sounded like an idiot, but he was absolutely confused about how she could say those things after how he had been.

She smiled, a tender smile full of such warmth that he slid to his knees before her, unable to keep the distance between them anymore. She touched his cheek, a gentle caress that made him want to close his eyes and lean into it. But he didn't. He just waited, not even sure what he was waiting for. He just knew that she had something he needed, something he was desperately craving, even though he had no idea what it was.

Taylor laced her fingers behind his neck, resting her wrists on his shoulders. "Just you," she said softly. "You're enough, just the way you are. If you were different, you wouldn't be what I needed so badly."

He wrapped his fingers around her wrists. "You deserve a man who will be there for you. You want the picket fence and babies. I can't do that—"

She shook her head. "The picket fence dream is long gone," she said, with a conviction that made something in his gut ache.

He didn't want her to give up on that dream. It pissed him off that she could even say it, because he knew how much she craved it in her soul. "Don't say that—"

She pressed a finger to his lips. "I wouldn't trust a picket fence even if it came knocking at my door. The reason I can relax with you is because that life is off the table. I needed you, just you, to bring me back to life. I see your greatness, Zane, and maybe it's because of your refusal to see it in yourself that I see it so clearly. Maybe it's because I need to see someone worth believing in, because I haven't had a lot of people in my life to believe in."

He swore under his breath. A part of him wanted to stand up and announce that he'd never, ever let her down, that he could be the guy that she could believe in, but there was a dead kid who would prove that was a lie. "Don't believe in me." He hated to say the words. If there was one person on the planet that he'd want to be worthy of, it was Taylor. He didn't want to drive her away, even though he knew he had to.

"You know what I think?" she asked, ignoring his orders, much to his selfish relief.

"What?"

"I think you should take your portion of the ranch, and create a place for kids to come and learn about horses, the way you did. Brad didn't want to play basketball or use computers, but maybe horses would have reached him, the way they did you."

For a split second, he stared at her, shocked by the idea. A part of him ignited with fire at the idea...and then he shook his head. "That would require me to commit to them. I can't do that. I don't know how to stay in one place."

She cocked her head. "That's a bunch of crap, Zane. You know it. You're just scared, but you know what? You're a bull rider. You, of anyone, should know how to overcome fear."

"It's not fear. It's reality. I know how much it sucks when someone lets you down, and I know myself well enough to know that I'll screw up eventually."

"Of course you will. Everyone does. That's okay."

"No, it's not. Not when people are counting on you." He sighed and ran his hand through her hair. "You're such an idealist," he said softly. "How do you see so much good in the world?"

"I don't. You made me."

He saw the truth in her eyes, and something inside him shifted. Was it really possible that he'd done something decent in his life, something that mattered? Because if he'd made a difference to Taylor, then, yeah, that was worth doing. He slipped his hand into her hair and kissed her, his lips gliding over her softer ones.

She responded instantly, telling him without words that she wasn't mad, that she didn't judge him. She truly accepted him, and wanted nothing from him except whatever it was he felt like giving her. A part of him didn't like that, because he wanted her to demand the world from him and anyone she trusted, but at the same time, it was a tremendous relief, the knowledge that he didn't have to be more than he was.

He cradled her face, kissing her more deeply, needing the connection with her. He loved the taste of her mouth, the feel of her lips, and the softness of her skin. He could lose himself forever in her and never want to go back to the world he inhabited.

She made a small sound of pleasure, and wrapped her arms around his neck. He pulled her against him, using his weight to keep their balance so they didn't tumble off the rock. They were exposed to the world in all directions, perched on their pedestal, but he didn't care. He just wanted her.

In the distance, he heard her phone ring, and she tensed slightly in his arms. "Work?" he asked between kisses.

"Yes. That's the ring I have for my boss."

"He gets his own ringtone?" Damn. He wanted her to assign a ringtone to him. The phone rang again, and he felt her attention wander toward it.

No. This was *his* moment with her. No one else got to intrude.

Zane angled his head, deepening the kiss, dragging her attention back to him. When she sighed and wrapped her arms more tightly around his neck, he felt a primal sense of satisfaction. He knew how much her work meant to her, and she'd chosen him. He didn't want her to invest in him, but at the same time, he wanted her to choose him, give him his own ringtone, and park herself in his life and never leave—

His phone rang next, echoing across the parched earth from where he had it stashed in his bike.

"Who is it?" she asked.

"I don't know. Everyone gets the same ringtone on my phone." He caught her mouth in a kiss again, whispering against her lips. "The only person I want to talk to is right here, so I'm not answering."

She smiled. "You do realize when you say things like that, it makes me melt for you, don't you?"

He grinned and dragged her into his arms, his cock rock hard. "You're at my mercy, woman. I love that." He cupped her breast as he nipped her earlobe.

She gripped his upper arm. "We're in plain view, Zane. Don't—"

He cut off her protests with a kiss. He didn't care where they were. He just wanted her now. He had so much emotion swirling inside him, and Taylor seemed to take away all the shit and leave behind relief.

She sighed and kissed him back, arching into him as he slipped his hand beneath her shirt and pinched her nipple—

Her phone rang again, and this time it was a different ringtone.

She stiffened again, breaking the kiss "That's Mira's ringtone."

"When do I get my own ringtone?" He didn't stop kissing her.

"I don't even have your phone number." She put her fingers over his mouth, seriously impeding his seduction skills. "What if the baby's coming?"

Zane shook his head. "She said it wasn't coming for a while—" Then he cut himself off, remembering the call that had just come in on his phone. He didn't get many calls. What if that had been about the baby? Sudden tension poured through him. He leapt down off the rock and sprinted over to his bike. He unearthed his phone as Taylor climbed down from the rock.

He had a missed call from Chase. Swearing, he called his brother as Taylor ran over.

Chase answered on the first ring. "The baby's coming. Something's wrong. We're at the hospital. Can you take over at the ranch?"

Taylor grabbed the phone from him. "Chase? What's happening? I want to talk to Mira!"

"We don't know what's going on yet. Mira can't talk to you right now. I was using her phone to call you because I didn't have your number. If you guys can go back to the ranch and take care of the animals, we'll call—"

"No!" Tears glistened in Taylor's eyes. "I'm not going to the ranch. I'm coming to Mira. Where are you?"

Chase swore. "Listen, there's nothing you can do—"

"She's my best friend," Taylor interrupted fiercely. "You don't get to send me away. Where are you?"

Zane held out his hand for the phone. Wordlessly, Taylor set it in his hand. Zane held it to his ear, while Taylor pressed her head next to his to listen. "Bro, shut the hell up. I'll find someone to do evening feed at the barn. You don't get to play solo on this one, and you know Mira would want Taylor there if you'd just ask her. Their bond is like ours. We're coming. Got it?"

He felt Chase's relief over the phone. "Yeah, okay, thanks. It's rough, man. I could use you, as long as the animals are okay."

"They'll be fine. You're at the regional hospital?" He'd been there many times, after assorted bull riding accidents when he was growing up.

"Yeah." Chase lowered his voice. "I'm scared, man. Mira and this kid are my life."

"We're on our way." Zane hung up, and jammed his phone in his bag. Taylor was already reaching for her helmet, and her face was ashen. The helmet slipped out of her fingers and thudded to the ground.

Zane retrieved it for her, and set it on her head. Her hands were shaking so much she couldn't even grab the chinstrap. He folded his hands in hers, squeezing gently. "She's in a great place," he said. "It's a great hospital."

"Just go," she said, pushing him toward the bike. "We need to go—"

"Hey." He grasped her shoulders, forcing her to look at him. Her blue eyes were wide, her forehead furrowed with anguish. "Listen to me, Taylor. Mira is in good hands. They'll do everything possible for her, and Chase will make sure of it."

She gripped his wrists, her hands trembling violently. "She's all I have in my life, Zane. She's it. If I lose her—"

"You have me, too. I've got your back, for whatever you need. Understand?"

She stared at him. "But you said—"

"I'm made for crisis situations. I'm not going anywhere. Lean on me. I'll catch you. Got it?" Strength poured through him, an absolute determination to carry her through this, as well as Chase and Mira. This was why he'd hung around all these years, keeping his tenuous connection with his brothers. Because sometimes, all hell broke loose. He wasn't the nightly dinner kind of guy, but when the shit hit the fan, it was his party.

She nodded, tears filling her eyes. "Thank you."

"You got it." He caught her chin and kissed her, a kiss meant to reassure her that she could count on him. As he'd hoped, she gripped the front of his jacket fiercely, dragging him against her as she kissed him back, pouring all her fear and worry into her connection with him.

He locked his arm around her back and kissed her hard and deep, taking all her worry and accepting it as his own, offering her his strength.

After a long moment, she broke the kiss, and buried her face in his neck. He wrapped his arms around her and held her tight. He loved the feeling of her body pressed against his, of the way she was leaning on him for comfort and strength. He knew he wasn't a long-term guy, but in this moment, he could see the appeal of doing this for the rest of his life. Being the strong guy, the source of comfort, the one who could make her day better, felt damn good. He pressed a kiss to her hair. "Ready?"

She nodded and pulled back, her eyes searching his. "You think she'll be okay?"

He wasn't going to lie to her. He had no idea what was going on at the hospital. "Whatever happens, we're going to handle it. I promise you that."

She nodded once, biting her lower lip. "Okay." She didn't take her gaze off his as he finished strapping her helmet on. He brushed his finger over a tear sliding down her cheek. "You can do this, sweetheart. Mira needs you to be strong for her and believe in her, but you can be as scared as you want when you're with me. I've got you. Lean on me."

She nodded again. "Thank you," she whispered. "Thank you for being here with me."

"I wouldn't want to be anywhere else." He swung his leg over the bike as she climbed on behind him. As she wrapped her arms around his waist and pressed herself against him, he squeezed her hand. "I'll keep the speed reasonable."

"No. Don't. Please hurry."

He hit the ignition and the bike roared to life. "You got it." Yeah, he'd go fast, but he wasn't going to take the kind of chances he'd take when he was alone. He'd learned his lesson on that one. Taylor's safety mattered more than any kind of speed, no matter what the reason, including running away from the life he didn't want to live. "Hang on, sweetheart."

Her arms tightened around his waist, and he eased the bike forward, swinging it around to head back to the main road. The moment the tires hit the pavement, he opened it up. The wind hit hard, just as he loved, but for the first time in his life, his bike wasn't about an adrenaline rush or a chance to be alone. This time, his bike was about something more. It was his chance to do something for someone else, and it felt good.

Damn good.

CHAPTER THIRTEEN

TAYLOR FELT like her entire world was crumbling. The waiting room was tense and silent. Zane was sitting beside her on the couch, his arm around her. Steen and Erin were sitting beside each other on another vinyl couch, and Chase was pacing restlessly. The hospital smelled of antiseptic and broken dreams, and the white walls were unbearably stark. Nurses and other patients bustled past, a blur of activity that didn't matter, that barely registered.

Only Mira and the baby mattered, but there had been no news for too long.

"They should know by now," Chase said. His face was ash white, and he looked like he was on the verge of passing out. He sank down next to Zane, his face in his hands. "I can't lose them," he whispered. "They're my world."

Zane leaned forward, his head beside his brother's as they exchanged quiet words. Steen stood up and came over. He sat on the edge of the coffee table, leaning forward to join the conversation between the brothers.

The three men sat with their heads together, talking quietly. The intensity of the bond between the brothers was evident, and Taylor's throat tightened. This was Mira's world now, surrounded by people

485

who loved each other and cared so deeply. She was so happy for her friend. After having to support others for so long, Mira had found a family who would never walk away from her. She'd found Chase, and acquired a posse.

"She's going to be okay," Erin said. "They both are."

Startled, Taylor looked over at Erin, who was also leaning forward, her hands clasped together. She was looking at Taylor, addressing her, bringing her into the circle that she didn't fit in. "You think so?"

Erin nodded. "She's an incredible woman, and she's so protective of her baby. There's no way she's going to give up."

Tears filled Taylor's eyes. "I know how strong she is, but—"

"No buts." Erin's eyes were glittering with unshed tears. "You can't think that way."

Taylor took a deep breath, and nodded. "Okay. They'll be fine, right?"

Erin nodded. "Of course they will—"

"Chase Stockton?" A nurse appeared in the doorway. "Come with me, please."

Chase leapt to his feet so fast he almost knocked over Steen, who had to scramble to get out of his way. "Are they okay?"

"Come meet your son. He's completely healthy."

"My son?" Chase's face paled. "And Mira? What about Mira?"

"She's still in surgery. Come on." She nodded at the others as Chase followed her. The two of them disappeared down the hall, leaving the others sitting there.

Taylor felt like she couldn't breathe. She looked around, and saw the others were equally grim. They should all be elated that there was a healthy baby boy, but with Mira's fate uncertain, there was no room for celebration. Zane pulled her against him. She sagged into his side, barely able to hold herself together.

Steen went to sit with Erin, and she nestled into his side exactly as Taylor was doing with Zane. She couldn't remember the last time she'd looked at a couple and not felt a deep pang of envy in her heart, but right now, when she looked at Steen and Erin, she just felt camaraderie. With Zane holding her, his warmth wrapping around her, even though she was facing the scariest moment of her life, she felt the safest she'd ever felt.

"How do you like living on the ranch?" Zane asked, his gaze steady on his brother.

It felt weird to have him ask a question like that when Mira's life was so precarious, but she knew he was trying to distract them from the uncertain fate trying to crush them.

Steen looked at him in surprise. "I like it. I'm psyched about the house, and Erin's vet clinic is shaping up well." He shrugged. "I like being back with the horses. I didn't realize how much I missed them." He grinned. "There's nothing like connecting with a horse that no one else can reach. That moment when trust happens is amazing. There's nothing else like it." He looked steadily at Zane. "You need to get back in the game, bro. It's in your blood. You won't be complete until you're around the ranch. Stop fighting it. Get off the bike and get back on the bulls."

Zane stiffened, a move so imperceptible she knew that she was the only one who could tell, because she was leaning against him. "It's not my thing anymore."

Steen regarded him without flinching. "It *is* your thing. It's in your blood. The reason you can't stay still anywhere is because you're not where you should be. Live, bro. You only get one chance at life."

Taylor glanced at Zane. His face was stoic, not inviting further comment.

Erin didn't seem phased by Zane's body language. She just nodded her agreement. "You should see Steen with the animals. He literally comes alive."

He grinned at her. "I never would have tried it again if not for you."

She smiled at him, a private adoring smile filled with love. "And I'm so glad you did." She grinned at Zane and Taylor. "He comes on my rounds with me when I have an animal I know is going to be difficult. He can calm any animal. He's really amazing. And my clinic is going to be wonderful. We're going to have a full equine surgical center, the only one within a thousand miles." She laced her fingers with Steen's. "That's my specialty, you know. I mean, I love all animals, but equine surgery is my thing. I didn't think I'd be able to keep doing it out here, but there are so many horses. Steen and I combined our funds to make it happen." She squeezed Steen's hand. "He made my dreams come true. I couldn't have done it by myself."

He put his arm around her, and smiled at her, a smile so tender that it seemed to light up the entire room. "You should see her operate," he said to Taylor and Zane. "She's gifted."

Erin was beaming now. "You guys really need to come see the clinic. It's just amazing."

Zane made a non-committal grunt, but Taylor couldn't resist. "I'd love to see it." How could she not? Erin's passion for her work was contagious, and she wanted to be a part of it, to see what it was like when someone lived a life that illuminated them so much. The happiness of the other couple was evident. It was clear they were very much in love, and that they were also following their dreams.

Taylor remembered being that excited the day she'd first walked into her own classroom. She'd forgotten what it was like to be so excited about life. She'd forgotten about being willing to love someone and be loved back. She'd forgotten about it all, until Zane had reminded her. She and Zane were exactly the same. Both of them walking away from what they loved because the baggage around it was too painful. She'd thought it was better to play it safe, but seeing how happy Steen and Erin were made her wonder if she'd been wrong all this time.

Chase appeared in the doorway, his face haggard and drawn. They all bolted to their feet, silence descending upon the small group.

Taylor gripped Zane's hand, her heart pounding as they all waited.

"She—" Chase's voice broke, and he cleared his throat.

Taylor felt the blood drain from her face, and she started to sway. Zane tightened his arm around her, keeping her on her feet.

"She's okay," Chase finally managed. "She's going to be okay. Everything is going to be okay." He looked at them all. "We have a son," he said, his voice raw with wonder. "A baby boy."

The waiting room erupted with congratulations, relief, and tears of joy. Taylor found herself swept into a circle of hugs, not just from Zane, but from everyone, the family that had taken in her best friend. She

might have felt like an outsider at breakfast, but in this moment, she
knew she belonged, and it was perfect.

~

"HE'S SO BEAUTIFUL." Taylor held the tiny baby in her arms, terrified
she would drop him. He was so small, so vulnerable, and so perfect as
he slept in her arms. She couldn't believe how much love she felt for
such a tiny bundle. Her heart felt like it was going to explode. "I can't
believe you're a mom."

Mira smiled at her, her face pale but radiant as she lay among the
pillows. "Me, either. I never would have thought I was ready, but here
I am."

"You'll be a great mom." Taylor leaned forward, to press a kiss to
his tiny forehead. "You listen to your Aunt Taylor," she told him.
"Appreciate your mom, because she's the best."

Mira grinned. "Keep telling him that. I'm sure he'll need reminding
if we're going to brainwash him sufficiently to listen to everything I tell
him to do."

"I'll be happy to brainwash him." Taylor grinned at her best friend.
"Can't you at least tell me what names you guys are considering?"

"Chase swore me to secrecy. He's afraid we'll be harassed by you
and his brothers to pick a certain one, so I'm not allowed to tell."

Taylor wrinkled her nose. "I would never try to influence you."

"No?" Mira raised her brows. "I doubt that." She cocked her head,
a new gleam in her eyes. "What's going on with you and Zane? What
happened on your trip?"

Taylor glanced toward the door, but the men weren't back yet.
They'd been down in the cafeteria getting food when the nurse had let
Taylor in, so she'd had a chance to meet the baby first. "He's a great
guy," she hedged.

Mira didn't let her off the hook. "Did you sleep with him?"

Taylor couldn't keep the goofy, deliriously happy grin off her face,
and Mira clapped. "I love that smile, sweetie. You look so happy."

She shrugged, trying not to smile, but totally failing. "He's such a
good man, Mira. He really is. We get each other, you know?"

Mira raised her eyebrows. "So...maybe you'll stay in town, then?"

Taylor's smile faltered. "What?"

"Listen, I didn't want to say anything or pressure you, but I miss you."

A lump formed in Taylor's throat. "You do? I miss you, too. So much it hurts," she admitted softly.

Mira nodded. "I love my new family, but you're in my heart, too. I can't imagine my child growing up and not knowing his Auntie Taylor. I know you don't love your job. Maybe it's time to quit. Start being a teacher again. Move here." Mira cocked her head thoughtfully. "Hang out with Zane. Maybe he's the guy for you."

Taylor cradled the infant against her chest, her fingers brushing lightly over the soft fuzz on his head. Tears burned in her eyes, and she fought not to cry. "I miss you so much," she whispered, "but I can't move here."

"Why not?"

"I have my job—"

"Which you don't like. Who wants to work for an ex-boyfriend? It's been a nightmare and you know it. And there's Zane—"

"Zane and I connect because I'm leaving. We have an understanding that it's a short term thing—"

"Chase said it doesn't look like that," Mira interrupted. "He said Zane couldn't keep his hands off you, out there in the waiting room." She met Taylor's gaze, deep understanding in her blue eyes. "These Stockton men have had really tough lives. They don't trust anyone. They don't believe that life can bring them good things. It takes a special woman to reach them, and you've done that with Zane. They don't love lightly, but when they love, it's forever."

Taylor stared at her in shock. "He doesn't love me." Did he? He didn't. He couldn't. He wasn't made that way. Love was just...there was no room for love.

Mira raised her brows. "Do you love him?"

"No," she said quickly, too quickly. The moment she denied it, she felt something constrict in her chest. She looked desperately at Mira, who had a sympathetic expression on her face. *Did* she love him? Was it possible? "Well, I mean, I do, as a human being. How could I not? He's such a good man. But that's different than romantic love—"

"Is it?" Mira challenged. "Can you really tell me that you haven't fallen completely in love with him, not simply as a human being, but as a man? I can see it in your eyes, Taylor. I know you do."

"I can't. I can't go there again," she whispered, staring in horror at her friend. Her stomach felt like there were a thousand butterflies spinning around in it.

"You can. You need to learn to trust just like he does." Mira smiled gently. "You're an amazing woman, Taylor. It was only a matter of time until a great guy noticed."

"But—"

A light knock sounded on the door, and Taylor snapped her mouth shut. She glanced toward the door, and heat flared in her cheeks when she saw the three Stockton brothers in the doorway, along with Erin.

Chase looked back and forth between the women. "Are we interrupting?"

"Yes," Mira said, at the same moment that Taylor said, "No." She was so grateful for the interruption. She just didn't want to go where Mira had been trying to take her.

Chase grinned, and walked into the room. "It doesn't really matter. I want to show off my son." He held out his arms for the baby, and Taylor reluctantly handed him over. The moment the baby was out of her arms, she felt a sudden sense of sadness, a gaping loneliness she hadn't felt in so long.

She sank back in her chair as she watched Chase turn toward his brothers, the baby so very tiny against his broad chest and muscular shoulders. Zane was hanging back, looking uncomfortable as Steen and Erin fawned over the newborn.

Taylor's loneliness faded as she watched Zane step awkwardly around the cooing threesome, heading across the room toward her. She might want a baby more than her heart could manage, but Zane clearly wasn't suffering from the same angst. It was apparent by his discomfort that he didn't have the baby gene. He hadn't lied to her when he said he wasn't a baby guy. Was it possible that he truly didn't have the instinct to be a father? That there was a chance that he would really be fine with who she was? So maybe, just maybe, if she did love him, it would be okay?

Her heart started to hammer in her chest, and she had to fight to breathe as he reached her. His fingers wrapped around hers as he sat down on the arm of her chair, sliding his other hand over her back. "You okay?" he asked softly, nodding toward the baby, as if he understood it might be hard for her.

She smiled at him, the emptiness fading from her heart as he settled in next to her. She nodded. "I'm good." Was Mira right? Was she falling in love with Zane? Was it really possible he was the right guy for her? What if she did give up her job? Could she be happy as a teacher if she had a man who loved her for who she was?

492

CHAPTER FOURTEEN

HER PHONE RANG, and she sighed, recognizing the ring. It was the fifth time Edward had called, and she hadn't answered once. Yes, she was on vacation, but he wouldn't be trying to reach her so much if something wasn't going on. She reached into her pocket and pulled out her phone, but Zane's hand closed over hers. "No cell phones in the hospital," he said.

She frowned up at him. "Since when do you care about the rules?"

His eyes narrowed, and for a moment, she thought he was going to say something, but he didn't. He just shrugged, and took her phone, folding his hand over it before tucking it back in her pocket.

"Zane." They both looked up as Chase walked over, holding the baby. "Here. Hold him."

"No." Zane didn't hesitate, folding his arms across the chest. "I'll take the kid on my bike when he's sixteen, but I don't want to—" He swore as Chase set the kid on his chest. He had no choice but to take the baby as Chase stepped back.

Taylor couldn't help but laugh at the horrified expression on Zane's face. "Here. You have to support his head." She helped rearrange the baby in Zane's arm, so that he was tucked up against Zane's chest, his little head leaning against him.

Zane grimaced, staring down at the child as if it might leap up and bite his head off.

The room filled with laughter, and even Taylor giggled.

Zane looked up at Chase, his face desperate. "He blinked. I think he's waking up. You better take him."

Chase folded his arms over his chest, a broad grin making his eyes dance with happiness. "Nope. He's all yours."

Taylor leaned over Zane's shoulder, watching as the baby's eyes flickered open. His radiant blue eyes seemed to focus on Zane's face, and her breath caught as he wiggled his little hand at Zane. "Let him grab your finger, Zane."

"Seriously?" Zane looked like he was in pain as he shifted his position and poked his index finger awkwardly at the baby. The tiny fingers wrapped around Zane's finger, holding him still.

Zane frowned, staring at the baby. "Strong grip."

"Good for bull riding," Chase said.

Mira threw a pillow at him. "My son will not be a bull rider! It's too dangerous."

"Honey, he's going to be a cowboy. There's no way around it." Chase settled down on the bed, wrapping his arm around Mira and pressing a kiss to her head, leaving Zane unattended with the baby.

Taylor expected Zane to panic, but he didn't look up. He was still studying the baby.

She glanced at him, and her heart seemed to flutter when she saw the look of pure awe on his face. His head was bent over the baby, and he was whispering something to him about bull riding, his finger still trapped in the baby's tiny hand.

Taylor sat back in the chair, unable to take her gaze off Zane's face. The wonder and emotion was evident in his expression. She realized with a ripple of shock that he'd fallen in love with his nephew. She could see it on every line of his face, in the protective way he'd tucked the baby against his chest, in the softness of his expression. He no longer looked like an awkward uncle. He looked like a guy who would lay down his life for the child in his arms.

She glanced around the room to see if anyone else noticed, and she saw everyone in the room watching Zane with the same expressions of awe and delight on their faces. They all knew he'd fallen in love with the baby. It had taken less than a minute, and Zane had become a baby person.

He looked up, his gaze meeting Taylor's. His eyes were bright, filled with more warmth than she'd ever seen. "He's perfect, isn't he?"

She nodded once, unable to speak over the lump in her throat.

"I had no idea." Zane held the baby up so he was eye level with him. "Listen, little man, I want you to know that your dad's a great guy, but I am definitely going to be your coolest uncle. Anytime your parents drive you crazy, you give your Uncle Zane a call, and I'll straighten them out. Got it?"

"You know," Chase said, his voice so deceptively casual that Taylor looked over at him. "You could move onto the ranch, and then he could just run over to your place and not waste time calling you. Steen will probably be his favorite uncle if he's the only one he sees on a regular basis."

Zane looked at Chase sharply, but instead of snapping back with his customary refusal to move to the ranch, he said nothing. Chase's eyebrows shot up in surprise at Zane's lack of resistance, and the room fell silent. Taylor's heart froze in her chest. After all his rejection of the ranch, it was the idea of being around for his nephew that made Zane pause long enough to consider breaking all his rules and moving onto the ranch.

A baby. He was willing to uproot his life for a baby, for his nephew.

At that moment, she knew the truth, the truth she couldn't deny, no matter how much she wanted to. Deep in the recesses of his scarred and broken heart was a man who would be a great dad, who had that protector, father gene deep in his soul, a man who would love his babies with every last bit of his heart. Zane was going to want children.

She let out her breath, barely able to breathe over the ache in her chest. The depth of the anguish crushing her told her all she needed to know. Too late, she realized that Mira was right. She *had* fallen in love with him. She had somehow, someway, let herself believe that this was more than a short-term fling. Her heart belonged to him, and so did her trust.

She'd been wrong to think she could keep from loving him, and wrong to believe he didn't want kids. Now her heart felt like it was shattering piece by piece as she sat there watching the man she loved falling in love with his nephew.

Not that he'd lied to her about whether he wanted to have babies, because she knew he'd spoken the truth at the time. There was no way he would have predicted his response to his nephew, but she should have known, based on how deeply he cared for the boys at the Garage.

Zane was not a man who would be content with a woman who couldn't give him children. Not anymore. No matter what he said today, eventually, there would be a time when he'd wish he'd made a different choice.

The baby started to cry, and Zane got a comically horrified expression on his face. "What do I do?"

And there it was. *What do I do?* He didn't try to hand the baby back to Chase and bolt from the scene. He asked what to do, so he could manage it himself. He wasn't even afraid of a crying baby. Just like that, his world had changed, and he was on board with it.

Chase grinned and hopped off the bed. "Unless you want to whip out a breast for him, I think this one's on Mira."

Zane laughed and handed the baby over, his fingers drifting over the baby's head as Chase took him. "Yeah, I'll pass on that one."

He sat back down beside Taylor, taking her hand in his as he grinned at her. "Did you see him? Are all babies that small?" He held up his hand. "He practically fit in my palm, but he was a real person."

She managed a smile. "Yes, they're all that small. He's beautiful." As she watched the expression of wonder on Zane's face, she felt herself falling even more in love with him. What woman wouldn't fall for a man who could love like that?

Her phone rang again, and she glanced down. It was Edward again, and for the first time since she'd arrived in Wyoming, she wanted to take the call. "I really need to get this. He's been calling for days."

Zane frowned, but she slipped out of his grasp before he could stop her. She waved her phone at the room. "I need to run outside to take this call. I'll be back in a minute." No one even really noticed as she ducked out, all of them too riveted by the miracle of life.

She let the call go into voicemail as she walked quickly down the hall. Her heart was hammering and she wanted nothing more than to get outside and breathe fresh air. She reached the stairs and jogged down them, following the signs to the nearest exit. She didn't even care where it was. She just wanted out.

By the time she reached the steel exit door at the base of the stairs, her heart felt like it had broken into a thousand pieces. Why had Mira tried to convince her to stay? For a split second, Taylor had taken the bait and imagined that future. Living on the ranch with Zane, Mira, and the others. Being a part of a family that stood beside each other no matter what, no matter how difficult things were. It had been only a moment, but it had been enough to awaken her heart...just in time for it to be broken.

She shouldered the door open and stepped outside into the dirt parking lot behind the hospital. There were plains stretching out in front of her, and that same vast expanse of sky that looked so different over Wyoming than it did from the window of an airplane. She'd never noticed the blue before, and she'd never felt this kind of awe for the grandeur and beauty of nature.

She wanted to be here. This was the place she wanted to call home. But how could she possibly do it? She knew it would never work with Zane. So, where did that leave her? Watching him fall in love with someone else, while she played Aunt Taylor to a baby she wasn't even actually related to, trying to live vicariously through a family that wasn't really hers?

Her legs feeling like heavy weights, she walked across the dirt and sat down on a patch of grass, pulling her knees to her chest.

Her phone beeped and she looked down, surprised to see a text from Edward. As she read the words, a cold feeling seeped into her body. *Taylor. Have you even listened to my voicemails? Call me back. I've accepted a promotion. My current position is open, and it's yours. I've been trying to reach you to make an official offer. I need an answer tomorrow. Congrats on the promotion. You deserve it. Now call me!*

She stared at the phone, rereading the words over and over again. Edward was leaving. No more working for her ex-boyfriend. And he was offering her a promotion. A raise. More travel. She pressed the phone to her heart, tears falling silently down her cheeks.

Before she'd come to Wyoming, she would have been thrilled. It was everything she'd been working so hard to achieve. But now? The thought of getting on a plane and going back to that life of hotels and airports felt like it would crack her soul in half. But what was worse? Staying here and having her heart bleed every time she saw Zane or the baby?

The door to the building opened, and Zane stuck his head out the door. His brow was furrowed, and he looked so concerned that the tears started again. "Hey, babe," he said, stepping out into the parking lot. "I thought you might not be okay."

She lifted her chin and wiped the tears off her cheeks. "I'm fine. Just needed some air."

"I know." The rocks crunched under his boots as he walked across the parking lot and crouched in front of her, his forearms resting on her knees. "We need to get back to the ranch to take care of the animals."

"We? What do I know about the animals? You don't need me there." She couldn't quite keep the bitterness out of her voice.

His eyebrows shot up. "I assume you have the capability to listen to instructions, right? You seem intelligent enough to learn new skills."

She bit her lower lip and shrugged. "I guess."

He rubbed his hands over her thighs, a touch meant to comfort, not seduce, but all it did was make her tears want to fall even more. "You want to talk about it? The baby?"

"God, no." She took a deep breath. "It's fine. I'm really happy for them." How could she tell him that it wasn't the baby that had made her cry, but the fact she'd lost Zane to the baby?

He narrowed his eyes, still rubbing her thighs. "So, what's the problem then? Something wrong at work?"

"Work?" The question made her laugh, a laugh that had no joy in it. "No, that's fine." She handed him her phone with the text message on display.

Zane read the message, staring at the phone for what felt like an eternity. She frowned. How many times did he need to read it to understand what it said? "I got a promotion," she said, wondering if he'd failed to understand what Edward had written.

"I can see that." He finally looked up, an unreadable expression on his face. "Are you going to take it?"

She paused at his question. He hadn't said congratulations. He'd asked if she was going to take it. What did that mean? Was there even an option of not taking it? Was he thinking more than a few weeks with her as well? But even as she thought it, she realized it didn't matter. Falling in love with Zane would break her heart. He might not realize that he'd changed his mind about babies, but she did. "I don't know. I need to talk to Edward and get the details." She shrugged. "It's a great opportunity."

"What about teaching?" The question was blunt and without apology.

She narrowed her eyes. "I don't teach anymore."

"You could."

Frustration rolled through her. "Why are you pushing the teaching? You know I can't do it anymore. I walked away from that."

"It's your passion. Why would you reject something which makes you feel alive, and accept a safe route that drains your soul?"

His words bit deep, true words that made her angry. "Really? Isn't bull riding your passion? You rejected it because you didn't like that it put you into contact with people who don't like poor kids who tread the edges of society. Instead, you run around on that bike, not even letting yourself help the kids you want to defend."

He dropped his hand from her leg, his face going stoic. "That's my business—"

"Is it?" She stood up, suddenly so angry. "Why do you judge me, when you're just as guilty? You say you defend those kids, but even after losing one who couldn't connect to basketball in a warehouse, you still refuse to look at other options. You talk about how the horses and bull riding saved you, but you won't give those other kids the chance you had. What are you going to do with all that money you won? Let it rot in a bank account somewhere because you've convinced yourself you're worth nothing?"

He stood up slowly, his eyes narrowed. "Why are you going off on me?" His voice was even and calm, but she knew him too well not to notice how angry he was.

"Because I'm tired of being made to feel like I'm not good enough!"

He raised his eyebrows, studying her intently, as if he didn't believe her. "You are good enough. You just don't realize it."

"Really? If I'm so good, why am I not enough for a man like you? Why is it that you fall in love with a baby and not me?" Oh...crud. Had she really just said that?

Zane's eyes widened. "What?"

"Nothing." Horrified, she shoved her phone in her pocket. "I have to go." She ducked past him and raced back to the building. She grabbed the door handle and pulled...and it didn't move. She yanked again, harder, and still it didn't move.

"It's locked from the inside," he said, still standing where she'd left him.

"I can see that!" She whirled around and started stalking around the building, in what she hoped was the general direction of the front door. "You go back to the ranch. I'll catch a ride with Steen and Erin later." She pointed in the other direction. "I think you left the bike that way," she lied.

He ignored her, broke into a jog, and settled in beside her. "Taylor—"

"I don't want to talk about it. I didn't mean to say that, and I meant nothing by it, so let it go." She knew she sounded snappy, but she was just so embarrassed by what she'd blurted out. Between the baby and her job, she felt so overwhelmed right now she couldn't even think straight.

"I was just going to say that I need your help at the ranch. You promised Mira you'd help her, and this is what she needs. Erin has some critical cases she needs to attend, and one is a dangerous bull that she needs Steen's help with. They'll help out when they get back, but we're the ones that aren't needed anywhere else."

Taylor bit her lip. She *had* promised Mira. That was why she'd come to Wyoming in the first place. So what if she'd managed to fall in love and get her heart broken? That didn't change that she owed her friend. "Fine. But you can sleep on your bike tonight."

He lightly wrapped his fingers around her elbow and leaned in, his breath warm against her ear. "Darlin', I don't know what's gotten into you, but there is no chance in hell I'm sleeping on my bike. I'll give you space for the moment, but we're talking this out tonight, whether you like it or not. Got it?"

"Fine. I'll sleep on your bike." She felt like her soul had fragmented into a thousand pieces, and she'd forgotten how to breathe. She needed space to regroup, to think, to recalibrate. She needed to find the place of equilibrium that had served her so well for so long.

"No chance of that," Zane said.

The certainty in his voice made chills run down her spine. A part of her didn't want him to give up on her. A part of her wanted him to fight for her, to prove that she was wrong for thinking that he didn't love her. But another part of her, the part that had been broken too many times, wanted him to just let her go while she could still get away.

Because right now, all she wanted to do was run.

CHAPTER FIFTEEN

ZANE LEANED against the stall door, watching Taylor as she swept the aisle. They were both sweaty and exhausted, having worked for almost four hours straight to take care of all the animals. The help Zane had called in had fed and watered everyone, but the stalls had needed to be cleaned, horses turned out, and then evening rounds had been done.

Taylor had been tireless, almost relentless in her work, never slowing down long enough to talk, which was fine with him.

He hadn't figured out what to say.

Unaware that he was watching her, Taylor paused and leaned on her broom, resting her head against the handle. Her shoulders were slumped, and she looked exhausted. Her hair was a mess, she was covered in dust and shavings, and she had a smudge of dirt on her right cheek.

She was so beautiful that she made his heart stop in his chest, so vulnerable that he wanted to scoop her up in his arms and protect her forever, and so strong that he wanted to get down on one knee and bow to her. Working with her for the last four hours had reminded him of what it had been like to work on the ranch with his brothers when he was a kid. The ranch was the only time that he'd felt accepted, like he belonged. The animals never judged him, and he was so good at riding that he'd earned the instant respect of his brothers. Plus, his brothers were just as much of a stain on society as he had been, so he'd felt like their equal, not some insult to their existence.

He'd missed the ranch, he realized. He'd missed the animals, the hard work, and the smell of fresh hay and shavings. And, he'd missed the camaraderie that he'd found with Taylor, especially when she'd become too tired to remember she was mad at him.

She was tired now, and the evening had to change direction. "You ready?" he asked.

She startled, looking up at him as she pulled her shoulders back, hiding her exhaustion. "Ready for what?"

"To be finished. We're all set." He levered himself off the stall door and walked over to her, sliding his hands over hers as he took the broom. "You did great."

She didn't protest, instead sinking down on a nearby hay bale. "I'm so beat."

"I know. It was a lot of work tonight." He put the broom away. "I never could have done it without you. Between Chase, Steen, and Erin, there are a lot of animals on this ranch."

"You need help here," she said. "Especially now that Chase and Mira are going to be spending time with the baby."

"Maybe. Help costs money."

She met his gaze. "Not if they're poor kids who need a reason to believe in themselves."

And there it was, that same idea she'd been pushing at him. He sighed and sat down beside her, his shoulder leaning against hers.

She didn't move away, so he rested his forearm on his thigh and held out his hand.

After a moment, she put her hand in his. The moment his fingers wrapped around hers, he felt himself relax. He realized he'd been worried that he'd never get a chance to hold her hand again, after she'd been so mad at him earlier. Stupid thing to worry about, but he had.

"You want to tell me what's going on?" he said. The job. Her job offer. It had been gnawing at him all evening. He couldn't understand why it was bothering him so much. No, he knew why. It was because she should be a teacher, not some corporate exec living in hotels and

503

airplanes. She was more than that. She had the biggest heart he'd ever seen, and he didn't want it killed by a sterile life.

She looked over at him, said nothing, and then shrugged. "I'm tired. I'm going to bed." Then she stood up and started to walk down the aisle.

Zane frowned, jumped up and sprinted after her, grabbing her arm just before she made it to the main doors. "What the hell is going on?"

She glared at him. "Can't you tell I don't want to talk about it? Leave me alone."

"Wow." He stiffened at her rejection, sliding back into the defensive mode he'd lived with for so long. He would not put himself out there for someone who didn't want him. Ever. "Fine." He let go of her arm, and walked away, heading back toward the shed.

Thoughts hammered through him, but he shut them out. He would not let her get to him. She didn't matter. It didn't matter what anyone thought. He reached the door, and kept walking toward his bike. He'd have to take care of the horses in the morning, but tonight was his.

He swung his leg over the bike and fired up the engine. It roared to life, filling him with the same thundering storm it always did...only it didn't work this time. It wasn't enough. He didn't want to get on that bike. He wanted to be in Taylor's arms in that bunkhouse.

Shit.

The tires began to roll, and he swung around toward the driveway, only to swear and slam on the brakes. Taylor was standing in front of him, blocking his path.

"Move," he yelled over the engine.

"No!"

He swore under his breath, backed up, and began to drive around her. She immediately ran in front of the bike again, forcing him to stop. Swearing, he stopped the bike. "Taylor—"

"Turn it off!" she yelled.

He swore and killed the engine, folding his arms over his chest as he glared at her. "What?"

"I'm sorry."

He frowned. "What?"

"I'm sorry." She sighed. "I'm sorry I took my bad mood out on you. It's not fair."

He narrowed his eyes, unwilling to trust the apology. "Doesn't matter. Is that it?"

"No!" She walked up and grabbed the handlebars. "When you turned away from me in the barn, I saw the look on your face. I knew that you thought I'd rejected you, that I'd somehow decided that you weren't good enough."

He ground his jaw. "You're wrong."

"I'm not." She sighed, suddenly looking so tired that his anger dissipated. "Listen, Zane, I'm going to say this once, not because I want anything from you, but because you need to hear it. The reason I was upset in the hospital wasn't because Mira and Chase have a baby and I don't. I was upset because you fell in love with him."

That hadn't been what he'd been expected to hear. "What are you talking about?"

"The baby. I saw the look on your face. Everyone did. You love him."

He shrugged, uncomfortable with the discussion. "He's my nephew. I'm not going to reject the kid."

She shook her head. "It was more than that. You should have seen the expression on your face. I've never seen that kind of love on a man's face. It was beautiful." She held up her hand before he could interrupt. "You've got the dad gene, Zane. You might not know it yet, but you do. Which means..." She took a deep breath.

He waited, every muscle taut in anticipation of what blow she was about to deliver.

She met his gaze. "I've fallen in love with you. So deeply that I feel like I came alive for the very first time."

His heart froze in his chest, and suddenly he couldn't breathe. He'd had countless women scream their love at him during his bull riding tenure, but never had he believed it or cared. Until now. Taylor meant it. She loved him. *She loved him.* How was that possible? She was the most giving, caring person he'd ever met. She knew all his ugly secrets, and somehow, she'd decided he was worth loving? What the hell? He could never live up to that. He could never repay her for that. What was she doing, cheating herself out of life by loving *him*? "I don't want—"

"Stop." She sighed and released the handlebars. "I think I let myself fall in love with you because you were safe. I was leaving, and you definitely wanted nothing to do with kids, so either way, I was protected. But then..." She paused.

He leaned forward, curious despite his instinct to fight back against her declaration. "Then what?" He didn't know what he wanted her to say. All he knew was that he felt his entire being was on the edge of a precipice, waiting for words he couldn't articulate.

"Then I wanted to stay."

"Stay? Where? On the ranch?" *With me?* He didn't ask the last question, because he didn't want to hear her say no. And he didn't want to hear her say yes.

"With you. On the ranch. I wanted to become a part of your amazing family."

Hell. He leaned back, his mind going a thousand miles an hour. He knew he should be telling her to find a new life, a new dream, to walk away, but the words wouldn't come. He couldn't make himself send her away, no matter how much he wanted to. He wanted to hear more.

"But then I saw you with the baby." She sighed, and he saw in her eyes a grim resignation that was heartbreaking. "You would be a great dad. You'll be a great uncle. I couldn't live with myself if I took that chance away from you. Someday, you would resent me. And I know you want your freedom anyway, so..." She shrugged. "I'll take the promotion, then—"

"No." He swung his leg off the bike and grabbed her arm just as she was turning away.

She looked at him, hope and fear gleaming in her beautiful eyes. "No, what?"

"No—" He didn't even know what he wanted to say, what he needed to say. "Just, no."

She laughed softly, that same beautiful laugh that had lifted his heart so many times. "I can't stay, Zane. I can't stay and watch you live a life with someone else—"

"There's no one else. There will never be anyone else." That much he knew was the truth. "I don't like women. I don't want one."

She laughed aloud then. "You will. You'll find someone, and I can't watch it."

"Fuck that." He grabbed her wrist and hauled her against him. He locked his arm around her lower back, keeping her pinned against him. "Do you know what my life plan was after I walked away from bull riding?"

She raised her eyebrow and shook her head.

"I vowed to never trust anyone ever again. My plan was to count on no one, and let no one count on me. I was done with the crap of society. I just wanted to be left alone to hate the world on my own."

Her fingers wrapped around his upper arms. "That's kind of antisocial," she said. "You're worse than I am."

"But that's the thing," he said, searching her face, as if he could find in her eyes the words he couldn't come up with on his own. "That was my plan, and I was cool with it. And then I met you. And you fit me." He didn't know how to explain it any better. "I like us together."

A slow smile formed on her face. "I like us together, too," she said. "But we fit right now. We don't fit forever."

"Why not?" Shit. Had he really just said that? Was he really arguing for a forever with her?

"Because, Zane, I want to get married and be treasured for who I am. You're not ready to go there, but someday, you will realize you want kids, and I won't have you looking back and realizing that you're trapped."

His grip tightened on her arms. "What the hell are you talking about? We're wrong because you want to get married, and I don't, and also because someday, not only will I want to get married, but I will also want kids? Those two excuses are completely contradictory. You're making shit up as an excuse to walk away."

She stiffened. "I'm not making—"

"You're making shit up because you're afraid of being hurt again."

She stared at him, then a single tear spilled down her cheek. "You have the power to shatter my heart," she said softly. "I can't live through that again."

His grip on her arms softened. With a sigh, he enfolded her into his arms. She melted into him, burying her face in his chest as he held her. "I'm sorry, babe," he whispered, as he pressed a kiss to her hair.

"I'm sorry, too," she said, her face still hidden against his chest.

He pressed another kiss to her hair. He didn't even know what to say to her. He didn't know what he wanted to say. He just knew that he didn't want her to walk away from him tonight. "I don't want to hurt you," he said. "Ever."

"I know you don't." She lifted her head to look at him, her eyelashes frosted with tears. "That's why I opened my heart to you, and that's why you could break it."

He wiped his thumb over her eyelashes, brushing away the tears. "Stay with me tonight."

"Tonight?" She nodded at the bike. "I thought you were leaving."

"I don't want to leave." He slipped his fingers through her hair and bent his head, pressing a soft kiss against her mouth. "I need you." He knew he should have bailed when she'd told him she loved him, and he'd been unable to say it back. A responsible guy would step back when she'd confessed that he could hurt her. But he didn't want to let her go. He wanted to hold her in his arms and make love to her until the sun broke across the sky in one of those Wyoming dawns that he never got tired of.

She gripped the waistband of his jeans, closing her eyes as he sprinkled kisses over her cheeks, her nose, her chin, and her lips. "I don't want you to leave, either," she whispered.

Relief rushed through him, and he angled his head, taking her mouth in a real kiss, the kind of kiss that could carry a man through the very darkest of times.

He scooped her up in his arms and carried her back to their bunkhouse. She opened the door, and then he kicked it shut as soon as they were through. He didn't waste time with a shower, even though they were both grimy from working on the ranch. He needed her now, and he needed her in every way.

By the time they reached the bed, their kisses were pure wildfire. He groaned as he lowered her to her feet, sliding her down his body. Her skin was soft as he framed her waist, kissing her hard and deep, pouring everything into the kiss that he could never say. Her arms were wrapped tightly around his neck, kissing him back just as fiercely, as if she were afraid it was the last time they'd ever be together.

It wasn't.

It couldn't be.

He'd never survive without her.

Somehow, they managed to get their clothes off without breaking physical contact. The moment nakedness reigned, he picked her up again. She locked her legs around his waist as he gripped her hips, his fingers digging into her bare flesh as he relocated them onto the bed.

He was inside her before they'd even hit the mattress. He wanted to honor her with a long seduction, with kisses meant to show how incredible she was, but he couldn't do it. There was something inside him that was so desperate to connect with her that he couldn't hold back. He just buried himself inside her, needing that connection, needing to claim her, and make her his.

His kisses were desperate, his hands all over her body, his entire being shouting for her. Taylor didn't let him down. She met every kiss with equal passion, her hips moving in an invitation that ignited his need for her even more. He could feel the orgasm building, tightening around them both. It was too fast, too soon. He wanted more for her but—

The orgasm hit them both at the same time. *"Taylor."* Her name tore from him as he drove inside her, giving her all that he was, while she bucked beneath him, mercilessly caught in the same climax gripping him so hard.

It seemed to last forever, the moment of ecstasy that brought them together as one. He tried to hold onto it. He tried to make the moment last forever...but eventually, it faded, releasing them from its grasp.

Completely drained, he collapsed beside her, dragging her tightly into his arms. He locked his leg over her hips, his arms around her upper body, and buried his face in her hair, needing to get as close to her as possible.

"Zane?" She nestled into his body, tucking herself against him exactly how he wanted.

"Yeah." He pulled her even tighter.

"I love you."

He closed his eyes and pressed a kiss to her hair, his chest tightening at her words. He didn't know what to say to her. Nothing was worthy of what she gave him. "Stay," he finally said. "Don't take the job. Be a teacher."

She didn't answer for a long moment. "And what about us? What happens to us if I stay?"

He wanted to give her the response she craved. He wanted to be that guy for her, the one that would declare his love and honor her. But how could he say that? He knew he could never deliver, and he couldn't make her promises that he would later break, no matter how right it felt at the moment. "I haven't slept in the same bed for more than four nights in a row since I was fifteen," he said. "And those longer stretches were for competitions. If I can't sleep in the same bed, how could I possibly offer you a forever? Or anyone? Including a kid?" She was wrong. He didn't want kids. A nephew was different than having that kid count on you every second of every day for its entire life.

She trailed her fingers over his chest, drawing designs that felt amazing. "I think," she said softly, "that if I were to accept that answer from you and let you trap yourself with me in some sort of off-again on-again relationship with no family in the future, I would be doing you a great disservice, by allowing you to hide from who you truly are."

"Oh, come on." Frustrated now, he rolled her onto her back, pinning her to the bed. "I make my choices, Taylor, and right now, my choice is you. With me. In my bed. Wherever that is." He stopped when he realized what he'd said. Had he just invited her to be a part of his vagrant life? Shit. She deserved more. Scowling, he rolled off her, resting on his back and staring at the ceiling, chastising himself for being so weak that he actually offered her a life that she didn't deserve, just because he couldn't stand the thought of being without her.

She didn't come after him, and the two-inch gulf between them felt like a crevasse that could never be crossed.

"You know," she said, her voice drifting through the darkness. "On some levels, that sounds like the best way ever to spend my life, living on your bike with you, seeing new places every day. These last few days with you have been the best days of my life."

He stiffened, hope suddenly springing through his body. He turned his head to look at her. She was lying on her side, her hands tucked under her chin, and her knees curled up, watching him. She looked vulnerable and beautiful, and his heart softened as he rolled onto his side to face her. "Mine, too," he said.

She smiled, and held out her hand to him. He wrapped his fingers around hers. "What do you really want, Taylor? From life? If you could really have it."

"I don't think like that, Zane. We have to tailor our dreams to fit our reality, or our heart breaks a little bit with every single heartbeat."

Listening to her made his heart break a little bit. She was so brave and courageous, and he wanted her to fight for what she wanted. He wanted her to get married and have those kids and teach until her smile reached her eyes every second of every day.

But at the same time, he wanted her for himself, and those two pictures weren't compatible. Which did he want more? To make himself happy by keeping her and giving her the half-life he could offer her? Or by letting her go so she had the chance of finding that guy who could give her everything?

"What about you?" She asked. "If you could have anything you really wanted, what would it be?"

He didn't hesitate. "You."

Tears filled her eyes. "Zane—"

Before she could finish, her phone rang. Her boss's ringtone. Sudden fear rippled through him. "Don't get it."

"I have to. He needs an answer." She scooted off the bed and ran to her purse. He leapt up after her and grabbed her wrist just as she pulled the phone out.

"Don't. Let's talk—"

She looked at him. "Why, Zane? Why shouldn't I answer it? *Why?*"

He hesitated. Why? What good reason did he have? Just because he didn't want her to go off on the grand adventure of her life, accepting a great job that would propel her to the kind of stardom she deserved, so he could keep her on the back of his bike, living in shit hotels, making her live life as a teacher, just because *he* thought that was a better choice for her? The truth was, *she* was the one with the parent dream. She might not be able to have biological kids, but there were a lot of ways to be a parent. She didn't need a man who didn't want kids. What she needed was a man who wanted kids as much as she did, who didn't give a shit about where they came from.

He didn't give a shit about where kids came from, but being a dad...he couldn't do it. She could find her way back to teaching in a year or two, but if he kept her, she'd never find the man who could heal her heart.

Slowly, he dropped his hand from hers. "Never mind." He turned away and walked back to the bed, leaving her with the chance of her lifetime.

CHAPTER SIXTEEN

TAYLOR'S HEART seemed to crumble into a thousand pieces as she watched Zane walk away from her. Yes, she hadn't truly expected him to declare his love for her when she'd told him she loved him, but when he'd said all those words, something inside her had come to life, hoping so desperately that there was a way to make it work. She didn't want to let him go, and she didn't want him to let her go...

He disappeared into the bathroom. He left the door open, but turned on the shower and got inside, giving her privacy.

The phone rang again. Edward's name flashed across her screen. For a brief second, she remembered how she used to feel when she saw his name, back when they were first dating. Her heart would leap and a huge smile would spring onto her face. But he'd never made her feel the way Zane made her feel. She didn't want his job. She didn't want that life. She didn't want to talk to him.

But at the same time...Zane had made the choice they both knew was right. Maybe that was his role in her life. Maybe his job had been to make her love again, and to teach her to have faith in the goodness of other people. Maybe his role had simply been to heal her, so she could go forward with the life that she was meant to live.

Maybe he was destined to simply be a memory.

Maybe it was time for her to stop running away from what she wanted and start fighting for herself...but what did she want?

A text message flashed across the screen from Edward. *This is the last time I'm going to call, Taylor. Answer the damn phone or the job goes to someone else.* The phone rang again, his name flashing across the screen,.

This time, she answered it. Slowly, her hand shaking, she lifted it to her ear. "Hi, Edward."

ZANE STAYED in the shower until the hot water ran out. And then he stayed in the cold water for as long as he could take it. It wasn't until he was chilled to the bone that he finally turned off the water. Once silence reigned, he waited, listening for the sound of Taylor talking to her boss.

There was no conversation coming from the main room.

Was she asleep? Had she packed her bags and bailed on him? Sudden panic rushed through him, and he jerked the bathroom door open. When he saw her curled up in the bed, her hair spread over the pillow and her hands tucked under her chin, he was so relieved he had to grab the sink to keep from going down to his knees.

Jesus.

How could he let her go? But how could he be the selfish bastard who kept her from what she wanted?

He took a breath and grabbed a towel, carelessly wiping the droplets off his skin, never taking his eyes off her. She was asleep, her chest moving in a slow rhythm, her eyelashes soft against her cheek.

He tossed the towel on the sink, then walked across the room. He knelt beside the bed and bent toward her. "Taylor," he whispered.

She didn't stir.

He brushed her hair back from her face, his fingers drifting over the incredibly soft strands. She was so beautiful and courageous, full of love, warmth, and vulnerability. He kissed her, a soft kiss, the kind of tender, gentle kiss he'd never have the courage to give her if she were awake. "Hey, babe," he whispered, keeping his voice low so as not to

514

wake her, so she wouldn't hear the words that he had to say. "I want you to stay, but I can't take away your dream of being a mom. You'll find the guy who will give you that. I'm the one who can't handle watching you with someone else, because there will never be anyone else for me. You're it. You're my one and only. You're my forever."

He waited for a moment, almost hoping that she'd heard him in her sleep, hoping a foolish hope that she'd wake up and somehow show him a way that it could all work.

But she didn't stir, and her breathing stayed in the deep, even rhythm of sleep.

Which was for the best.

He let out his breath in a deep sigh, then eased the covers back and climbed in beside her. He wrapped her up in his arms and tucked her against him, her back tight against his chest, her hips nestled tightly against his. She felt so good and so right in his arms. He'd never wanted anyone to have a claim on him, but he knew that if he could wake up every single day with her in his arms, he'd have found the life he didn't deserve. But not at the cost of her dreams. He wouldn't do that to her. He pulled her even more tightly against him, knowing without asking that she'd accepted the promotion. Would she leave tomorrow? If not, then would it be the day after, as soon as Mira was settled? Maybe the day after that, but it would come.

The thought that this might be the last night he would ever hold her made something inside him tighten, a raging anger fueled by gaping loneliness he hadn't felt since the night he'd sat alone on his eighth birthday, watching the shadows on his bedroom wall while he listened to his mother screw her new boyfriend, completely forgetting that it had been her son's birthday that day.

She'd never remembered a birthday after that, and he'd learned not to care. He'd learned not to feel. He'd learned to accept what he could from his brothers, and to appreciate his talent as a bull rider. And most importantly, he'd made sure to never let anyone matter to him.

But Taylor mattered. She mattered on a thousand different levels. She mattered so much that he was willing to rip his heart out of his chest and let her get on that airplane and walk out of his life.

An image of an airplane cutting across the Wyoming sky flashed through his mind, and the greatest sense of desolation rolled through him. She would be on that plane soon.

But tonight, he had her.

Tonight wouldn't last forever, but he wasn't going to waste it.

"Taylor." He pressed a kiss to the nape of her neck. "Darlin', wake up."

She mumbled something and snuggled more tightly against him. For a moment, he considered being a good guy and letting her sleep. Then he decided to fuck it. He was being the hero by letting her go. Tonight, he was going to be the selfish jerk, and he was going to use every last second he had with her to fill his soul with enough of her love to sustain him the rest of his miserable, vagrant life. He palmed her belly, and began to nibble on her neck. "Taylor," he whispered. "Wake up."

Again, she mumbled something incoherent, but, even in her sleep, she pushed her hips back into him as he moved his hand lower on her belly. This woman, who trusted no one, had learned to trust him even in her most vulnerable moments.

That was worth everything to him.

Grinning, he rolled her onto her back and moved over her. He kissed her, a slow, tantalizing seduction of lips and tongues while he slid his knee between her thighs and wedged himself where he wanted to be.

He knew the moment she woke up. Her breath changed, and her muscles tightened, but he didn't stop kissing her. There was no way he wanted to give her the chance to talk about the job offer, no way he wanted to give her the chance to steal this last time together that they had.

She didn't try to stop him. Instead, she slipped her arms around his neck and kissed him back, even as she wrapped her legs around his hips, locking her feet together behind his back. "My sweet angel," he whispered, just before he slid inside her.

Neither of them was getting any sleep tonight, no matter what.

∼

WHEN TAYLOR FINALLY WOKE UP, the sun was low in the sky, and Zane was still wrapped around her. He was holding her tightly, tangled around her from head to toe, his face buried in the curve of her neck. He was breathing deeply, finally asleep, after making love to her all night, all morning and most of the day. He'd let her sleep twice, while he'd run out to take care of the animals, but when he'd come back at noon, he'd told her Steen was back and he was taking the rest of the day off. He hadn't left the bed since then, and neither had she.

And now, it had to be close to dinnertime, and she'd spent the whole day in bed with him. She'd thought the other day had been the best day of her life, but it had been topped. If she stayed with Zane, would every day with him keep getting better? What a life that would be to look forward to.

She sighed, trailing her fingers over the dark hairs on his arm where it was locked across her chest, his forearm angled between her breasts as if he was claiming her even in his sleep.

They hadn't talked once about the future. They'd talked about his childhood with his mother, the first time he'd met Chase, and the glories of bull riding. She'd talked about being so sick as a child, and her father's sadness when she'd had the surgery that had taken away her childbearing capability, a sadness she hadn't understood for a long time...until she finally had.

They talked about the boys at the Garage, and the one who had died. Zane had cried for the boy who'd died, for his inability to save him. He'd let Taylor comfort him and take away his grief and guilt, which had been one of the most beautiful moments of her life. She'd never felt so close to anyone, even Mira.

She knew she mattered to him. Zane was a loner, and he'd some-how, someway, found a place with her. Was that enough? Could she take that and hope it would make his life enough? "Zane?"

He grunted and tightened his arms around her.

"Zane." She lightly hit his arm.

"Yeah." His voice was groggy with sleep.

"Do you think..." God, could she really say it? "Do you think..."

His body stiffened almost imperceptibly. "Do I think what?"

"We could...make this work?" She held her breath, her heart pounding. She couldn't believe she'd said it. God, how could she say it? That was so selfish of her. "Never mind. Forget I said it—"

She started to pull away from him, and suddenly she found herself on her back, pinned to the bed by a man who looked surprisingly irritated given that he'd been dead asleep only moments before. "You need to understand something, Taylor." His voice was rough and steady, his gaze burning through her with intensity.

She swallowed. "What?"

"I'm not letting you go because you're right that someday I'll want biological kids and you'll destroy me by taking away that dream."

Tears threatened. "Zane—"

"No." He cut her off. "Listen to me. You know how you said the fact I love my nephew means I'm going to want biological kids someday?"

"Yes." She'd never forget the look on his face.

"In case you forgot, that kid's not my biological nephew. Chase isn't his biological dad."

She stared at him, his words sinking in. She'd totally forgotten. How could she have forgotten? Chase was so in love with Mira and the baby that she hadn't even thought about the bloodlines of the baby.

"I have no blood ties to that baby, and I'd slay a demon for him. Do you understand?"

Slowly, she nodded, her heart starting to pound.

"Here's the thing, sweetheart. My mother was total shit. And so was my dad. They both sucked as parents. Biology doesn't mean anything when it comes to family and love. If I decided I wanted to be a dad, there's a thousand ways to become a dad other than knocking up a woman with my sperm. In the end, all that matters is that you've got a kid who needs a parent who will stand behind them and fight the entire damn world on their behalf. I'd be that dad, and it wouldn't matter one bit if my blood ran in their veins or not. You need to understand that." His voice was fierce and angry, so full of emotion that she could almost feel it.

She realized he was telling the truth, the absolute truth. He didn't care about biology when it came to children. He truly didn't. For the first time in her life, hope flared in her belly, a terrified, faint hope that she'd never dared have in her whole life. "Zane—"

"I'm not the only guy like that. So don't sit there in your prison cell and hide from men. Find the one who won't care."

His words made her heart freeze. "What?" Find the one? Hadn't he just said that he was the one? "But you just said—"

"Taylor." His voice softened as he framed her face. "I can't be a father. I can't do it. I don't want that responsibility, and I can't be the world to some innocent child. It's so far from the realm of who I am, and what I'm capable of. If you were to stay with me, it's *you* who would be giving up on your dreams, not me. I want to keep you, more than you could ever, *ever* know, but if you stay with me, there will be no children, and that's a violation of your soul. I won't do that to you." He put his hand over her heart. "You've spent your life trying to convince yourself you don't want kids. You do. You can have them. You can have a dozen of them. If you give yourself to me, you will lose that dream, and it's not right."

"But—"

"Look into your heart, Taylor. Do you want kids? Do you want to be a mom? Do you want a real family, all sitting around the breakfast table, arguing over who gets the last piece of bacon?"

Tears filled her eyes at the image he presented, and she nodded silently, tears streaming down her cheeks. "I do," she whispered. "I really do." As she said the words, she felt the thick walls around her heart start to shatter, tumbling down as she acknowledged what she really wanted, that she'd been trying to hide from for so long. "I want to be a mom, more than anything. I just thought—"

"You thought that if you crushed your own dreams with enough force that you could destroy them."

She nodded, silently, starting to cry hard. It was terrifying to give up the pretense that she didn't care, but at the same time, she felt like a tremendous weight had been lifted from her shoulders. She could breathe again, truly breathe again. "I didn't believe there would be men who didn't care that I—"

"That you're the most incredible woman ever?" He brushed her hair back from her face, his dark eyes searching hers. "Don't ever sell yourself short again, darlin'. You're so incredible that when you meet the right guy, he'll turn heaven and earth to have you for his own, exactly the way you are. He won't want to change anything about you."

"Like you? Do you want to change anything about me?" She hadn't meant to say it, but the words had tumbled out.

His hand stilled in her hair, and he met her gaze. "No, I don't. I wouldn't change a single thing about you, on any level."

More tears fell, but this time, they were different tears. They were the tears of being loved for who she was. Maybe he hadn't said the words, but she knew that was how he felt.

He wasn't finished, however. "I wish I could change myself, though, and be able to be a dad for you. I wish that there was something inside me that wanted to take on that responsibility, but all I see when I look inside are the losers who spawned me. That part of me broke a long time ago, and it's never going to heal."

She saw the honesty in his eyes, and she heard the truth in his voice. Maybe he wanted kids deep in his soul, on a deeper level than he was aware, but he would never, *ever*, let himself go there. He was too scarred from his own life to ever be willing to take on the responsibility of another human being, one who was innocent and dependent. He was too certain that he would eventually fail a child, and nothing was going to change that conviction, because he didn't want to change. His instinct as a protector was what drove him to protect others from the worst enemy...which was himself.

A great sadness spilled through her, as she realized the truth, that no matter how much she loved him, there was a chasm that could not be crossed. He was right. If she went through life and never had children, a part of her heart would shrivel up and die. But wouldn't a part of her heart always stay behind with him? How could she split her heart like that? "Maybe—"

"There's no maybe." He kissed her, softly, a kiss that felt terrifyingly like good-bye. "I can't be the man I wish I could be, the one you deserve. I just can't. But I can honor who you are by letting you go. I'm not the only man you're capable of loving, Taylor. There's a guy out there who will give you everything you want, and not the incomplete half-life I could give you."

She knew then, that it was over.

There wasn't going to be a tomorrow, or even a tonight.

This was the last moment of their story.

CHAPTER SEVENTEEN

ZANE BENT HIS HEAD, pressing his forehead against the soft fur of the gray mare that had arrived only two days ago. The animal nudged Zane's chest as he ran his hand along the animal's neck. "You feeling better now?" he asked her. "Erin's pretty impressive. I've never seen anyone operate on horses the way she does. You're in good hands."

The mare had been on three legs when she'd been unloaded from the trailer, and thirty-six hours out of surgery, she was already bearing weight on her gimpy leg.

"You really going to let Taylor go?" Chase appeared in the door of the stall, holding his son in his arms.

Zane stiffened, and turned away from the animal to face his brother. "Yeah." He glanced at his nephew, who had officially been named, Joseph John Stockton. The John was for Mira's dad, and Joseph had been the middle name of the kid's biological dad. Everyone was already calling him J.J., which worked just fine. Not a bad name for the kid. Nothing that would get him bullied.

"Why?" Chase tucked the baby more securely against his chest.

"Because she deserves more."

Chase scowled at him. "That's a bunch of crap, bro. She's in my house with Mira and Erin, crying her eyes out because she's leaving here in two hours."

The ache in Zane's chest intensified even more than it already had been. For two weeks, he'd slept in an empty stall while Taylor had occupied the bunkhouse. For two weeks, he'd watched her over dinner in the main house, becoming friends with Erin and his brothers, beginning to fit into ranch life. For two weeks, he'd burned to walk into that bunkhouse and climb into bed with her. He'd wanted to talk to her, to hold her, and to make love to her again and again.

But he hadn't.

He'd kept his distance, because he knew that if he stayed with her, neither of them would do what was right for her. "She'll be fine."

"No, she won't."

Zane looked sharply at his brother. "You don't know what you're talking about."

Chase leaned against the doorjamb. His cowboy hat was tipped back on his head, his jeans were dusty, and his boots were well-worn. Except for the baby in his arms, he looked every bit the cowboy that Zane did, but Zane knew that his cowboy persona would go back in its box when he left here. "I never would have put myself into the role of a parent, Zane. I don't know anything about being a good dad. None of us do. There was no chance I was going there...until I had to. I had nothing to offer Mira, but we made it work." He grinned, the happiest damned grin Zane had ever seen, as he held up the baby. "You see this little person? He's my son. He's counting on me to be there for him, and to get it right."

Zane's gut turned over. "What if you screw up? What if you become like our dad?"

Chase's eyes narrowed. "I'm not going to become like him. I realized that there's no chance of that happening. Yeah, I don't know anything about being a good dad or husband, but Mira's dad was awesome. She said she'd help me, but she also said that she'd never have married me if she didn't think I could do it on my own."

Zane's eyebrows went up. "You haven't married her yet."

Chase grinned. "Actually, I did. I wanted my baby to be born to my wife, not my fiancée, so we got hitched in the hospital. I'm not allowed to tell because Mira still wants her big, fairytale wedding, but yeah, she's mine, and I won't have it any other way."

Zane studied his brother, surprised by how damn happy he was. He'd wanted to get married so badly he'd done it over a hospital bed, and then was going to do it again with the fancy party? "You're whipped, man."

"Finding the right woman is the best thing that could ever happen to a guy. You found yours. Keep her."

Zane jutted his jaw out. "She wants kids. I'm not going there. There's no commonality."

Chase turned John around so that Zane could see the kid's face. His eyes were closed, and he was sleeping peacefully. A deep protectiveness surged through Zane, a need to protect that kid from anything that might ever try to harm him. "You can do the dad thing, Zane. Try it."

"Try it? And if I fail, then what? Leave a string of fucked up kids behind? No way. That's not something you try. You go all in, or you don't. I'm not taking the chance of being the one to screw it up."

Chase sighed. "You won't screw it up."

"How do you know?" Zane challenged. "The three weeks I've been here are the longest I've been in the same place since I was fifteen. How do you start building a family on that? You have to give a kid a forever, not a few weeks here and there."

His brother tucked the sleeping baby against his chest again. "Let me ask you something."

"What?"

"How has it been? Staying here? Have you lost your mind? Gone insane? Developed hives or a weird rash that no one wants to touch?"

Despite his irritation, Zane couldn't help but laugh. "No rashes. It's been okay." He glanced at the horse snoozing behind him. "It's been good to be around the animals again," he admitted.

"So, there you go." John suddenly awoke with a loud wail, and Chase grinned. "He needs his mama. You going to come out to say good-bye to Taylor, or are you going to make the woman you love walk away alone?"

Zane wanted to hide in that stall. He didn't want to face that moment of watching Taylor walk away from him. He wanted to get on his damned bike and take off in the other direction, riding so hard and fast that he could feel nothing but the wind sliding into his flesh.

But this was Taylor. She deserved more. "I'll come."

~

TAYLOR HUGGED MIRA FIERCELY, unable to stop the tears from streaming down her cheeks, even as she forced a smile to her face. "I'll miss you so much," she admitted. "I hate leaving you."

"I'll miss you, too." Mira pulled back, her own eyes rimmed with tears. After a couple weeks of staying low key after her surgery, she was starting to get mobile, which Taylor knew was her signal that it was time to leave. "I don't understand why you're taking this job. You don't want to do it. I can tell. You're even missing my wedding for it."

"I know, but it's not your real wedding." When Mira's eyes widened, Taylor rolled her eyes. "Of course I know you secretly got married in the hospital. Why else would you be willing to move your wedding out for a couple months until you're fully recovered and all Chase's brothers can come? I know you too well, my friend, so don't even bother denying it."

Mira gave her a sheepish smile. "You're not mad I didn't tell you? I was worried that you'd feel I didn't love you if you knew I'd gotten married without you. I know that it's been hard for you, adjusting to sharing me."

"I'm fine with it." Taylor smiled through her tears. "I've finally learned that life and friendship are so much more complicated than things like that. I know you wanted to be married before John was born, and I get it. It's okay." She took a deep breath. "But, despite the fact that I would love to hang around and see you in your lacy white dress, I need to take this job, at least for a little while."

Mira bit her lip. "You're sure?"

"Yes." She was proud of how certain she sounded. She'd thought so much over the last two weeks about staying in Wyoming and trying to find a teaching job. She'd dreamed about it. She'd fantasized about it. She'd even driven by a few schools just to see how she felt, but she'd felt like she was just trying to use teaching to fill the gap left by Zane. She had to heal herself first, and then see where she wanted to be. Staying around for another few weeks with Zane and the baby was just too hard. In addition, with all the Stockton brothers descending upon the ranch for the upcoming wedding, it just wasn't where she could be right now. "I'm not ready to make a career change. I want to see this job through."

Mira wrinkled her nose. "Okay, but you have to stop by here regularly, okay? Sell your house and buy one here, so at least this becomes your home base."

Taylor smiled through her tears. "Maybe."

Erin walked up and wrapped her arms around both of them. The genuineness of her hug made Taylor feel even more desolate. She'd gotten close with Erin quickly, and she felt the real loss of leaving town just as the friendship had begun to solidify.

"I feel like I just got a new friend," Erin said, "And I have to lose you before we've even had a chance to cause enough trouble together."

Taylor laughed and hugged Erin. "I was so scared of you when I first got here. I thought there was no room for me with you and Mira."

Erin's eyebrows went up. "And now?"

"And now I know you're cool. The second sister I never had."

"Because I'm the first sister," Mira declared, tucking her arm through Taylor's. "You know, Erin, if we delay Taylor for another ten minutes, she might miss her flight. Should we do it?"

"Don't," Taylor laughed as she pulled her arm free from Mira's. "I have to go. I get to fly first class now. I'm really looking forward to those hot towels."

"I can make hot towels," Mira said, frowning. "Seriously."

"Stop." Tears threatened again as Taylor picked up her purse. Her bags were already on the front porch. "You guys stay here. I'll cry if I have to say good-bye again." Her heart felt like it was breaking, but it was a good break. She had found a home here, and she would be back. She'd arrived without roots, and she had some now. "Love you both."

The three women hugged again, a fierce, desperate hug that promised a friendship that would last forever. Tears were streaming down her cheeks again as she stepped back. "Okay, no more of that. I'll call you guys." She then turned and hurried out the door, not looking back.

When she got to the porch, her bags were gone. She looked up, and saw Zane loading them into the trunk of her rental car for her. Her heart seemed to freeze when she saw him. He'd come to say good-bye? God, how could she do this? Why hadn't he just let her go?

Chase walked up. "Good luck with your job, Taylor. You know you're welcome here anytime."

"Thanks." She hugged him, and then gave a bit of extra love to little John, snuggled in his daddy's arms. "Don't forget your Auntie Taylor while I'm gone," she told him. "I'm the best, and you need to always remember that."

John, however, seemed unimpressed. Instead of cooing, he wailed at her, his face red and contorted. Chase grinned. "He needs Mira. Travel safe, Taylor."

"I will."

She watched as Chase carried the baby into the house, calling for Mira. Her friend and Chase had come together in the most extraordinary of circumstances, but they'd turned it into something so beautiful. That was what she wanted: a relationship so full of love that the world became a more beautiful place simply by its existence.

"You ready?"

Her heart leapt at the sound of Zane's voice, and she turned toward him. He was standing by her car, his hands on his hips, watching her. His cowboy hat was tipped back, his jeans and cowboy boots were well-worn and sexy, and his shoulders were broad beneath his cotton shirt. He looked every bit the cowboy, and none of the biker, and he was gorgeous.

God, she'd missed him.

Tears tried to come again, but this time, she refused to let them. Instead, she put her sunglasses on, lifted her chin, and marched down the stairs toward her car. He didn't move out of the way, and she finally stopped right in front of him, craning her head back to meet his gaze.

For a long moment, neither of them moved. She felt like her world had come to a standstill, hovering in suspended animation, waiting for him to ask her to stay. She would. In a heartbeat. Just one word. That was all he had to say. One word. She knew he'd be okay with what she had to offer, and in this moment, she felt like foregoing her own dream of being a mother was worth it to never have to say good-bye to him. *Just ask me to stay, Zane. Just ask.*

He raised his hand and brushed his fingers over her jaw. His eyes were dark and inscrutable, a mask she couldn't penetrate. Two weeks ago, he'd cried in her arms over a boy who'd died, and now he had so many walls up, she couldn't see a single whisper of his humanity...but she knew it was there. "I love you, Zane."

Crud. She hadn't meant to say that. She'd promised herself she wouldn't beg for his attention. She was more than that. She deserved someone who would chase her down and offer everything he had to keep her.

"I know you do."

She blinked. "I know? That's how you respond? *I know you do?*" Sudden anger rushed through her, anger that she'd wasted so much emotion on him over the last two weeks, wondering if there was a way to make it work. "Forget it, Zane. I have to leave."

He dropped his hand and stepped back from her without argument. "Be safe."

"Of course." She climbed into the driver's seat and tossed her purse down. Her hands were shaking, and she wasn't sure if it was from anger or the fact her heart was shattering into a thousand pieces. "You, too." She gripped the steering wheel as he shut her door. It closed with a soft thud, and then he stepped back.

She glanced out the window at him. He met her gaze, and in that moment, she saw the depth of his pain, the agony of what he was enduring. Her heart seemed to stop, and she flung the door open. "Zane!" She threw herself into his arms, and he caught her, holding her tight against him.

He kissed her, hard and fierce, his fingers tangling in her hair as if to trap her. She melted into the heat of his body, into the fire of his kiss, losing herself to him on every level. She'd missed him so much, and being in his arms was the only place in the world she wanted to be. "Make love to me, Zane. Take me to the bunkhouse and make love to me."

His arms tightened around her, but he broke the kiss, resting his forehead against hers. "I can't break your soul, Taylor. I love you too much to do that to you."

Her heart seemed to stop. "What?"

He pulled back, his gaze searching hers. "If I didn't love you so much, I would keep you. I'd be willing to take your dreams away so I could have you for myself. But I can't do that, because hurting you would destroy me."

He loved her. She'd known he did, but hearing him say it was different. It was beautiful. Perfect. The most amazing words she'd ever heard in her life. "Maybe being an aunt would be enough—"

"No." He kissed the argument away. "You know it wouldn't. I know it wouldn't."

"Zane!" Chase walked out on the porch, and Zane grimaced at the interruption.

"Later," he said, not taking his gaze off Taylor, and not loosening his grip on her.

"Some guy is on my landline from a garage. He said that Luke and his little brother ran away. He thinks they're headed toward the ranch. Wants to know if they're here. You know what he's talking about?"

Zane's face paled and he spun away from Taylor. He raced over to the house and grabbed the phone from Chase. Taylor hurried after him, but by the time she reached him, he'd already hung up. He turned toward her, his face stricken with fear. "Luke took off in the middle of the night, apparently taking Toby with him. According to one of the other boys at their foster home, Luke's planning to hitchhike all the way here. Do you know what can happen to kids who hitchhike? We have to find them."

"I'll help." She didn't hesitate. She knew she'd miss her flight, but she didn't care. She'd seen him cry over the guilt of Brad's death. There was no way she was leaving him to face this on his own. "We can take my car."

"Okay." He shoved the phone at Chase. "I need to get my cell. Get the car started," he ordered Taylor. He vaulted down the steps and sprinted toward the barn, while she ran for her car. He was back within

529

a minute and a half, and dove into the passenger side of the car as she peeled out.

As she sped down the driveway, he leaned forward, searching through the windshield, scanning the road and the fields. "They could be anywhere along the route," he said, his voice rough and stark. "They'd had enough time to make it here if they got a ride immediately, but they could be two miles from their home if they didn't. Hundreds of miles that could swallow them up. Oh, God." He groaned and dragged his forearm across his brow. "They're just kids."

"Luke's a tough kid," she said. "I'm sure they're okay."

"Don't lie," Zane snapped. "We have no idea if they're safe. Toby is four. Four! Luke took his four-year-old brother!" He was gripping the dashboard, his knuckles white as he searched the road ahead. "They've been in foster care for the last year. I knew their situation was bad, but hell. It can't be bad enough to risk this. The ranch is more than two hundred miles away from the Garage. Why would he come after me?"

"Because you're all he has," she said softly, scanning the fields for two boys as she drove. "He's picked you, Zane. He's picked you to save him."

Zane glanced at her, his eyes panicked. "He's made the wrong choice. His brother's already dead. I can't save anyone."

"No, you're wrong." She shook her head. "You couldn't save Brad, but Luke and Toby are still alive. Kids are smart, Zane. They know how to survive, and it looks like Luke has realized you're his best bet."

"Jesus." Zane bowed his head, and his shoulders shuddered. "What if something happens to them? What if they die coming after me?" He sat back and ran his hands through his hair, his fingers shaking. "I should have realized this was going to happen. I should have seen it. A couple months ago, Luke asked me where the ranch was. He made me show him on a map, and asked me to point out what roads I took when I came here. I should have realized. I should have talked him out of it before I left—"

"Stop it!" She slammed on the brakes, and the car skidded to a stop.

Zane gripped the dashboard, glaring at her. "What are you doing? Drive!"

"I am so damned tired of you blaming yourself for things that aren't your fault! People are responsible for their own choices. You did your best to help Brad, and he still went with his friends to rob that store. His choice, not yours. You're a great man, and a born protector, and Luke knows that. He's willing to do anything to save his little brother, and you're their only chance. Brad's death probably made Luke realize exactly how dire their situation is if he doesn't change it. Their life is probably like yours was, or your brothers. When you were fourteen, if you'd had someone counting on you, you would have done whatever it took to protect them, right? Even if it meant hitchhiking two hundred miles to find the one person in the world you trusted?"

"Of course. I would have travelled a thousand miles if that would have helped." He stared at her, his face ashen. "You think it's as bad as it was with my dad?"

"If it wasn't, would he be dragging his brother down two hundred miles of highway searching for you?"

Zane seemed to pale even more. "I can't—"

"Yes, you can! God, Zane, stop being an idiot! Those boys need you, and you better pull yourself together by the time we find them!" She smacked his shoulder. "They need you, Zane Stockton, and no one else. Just you!"

He bowed his head, and laced his fingers behind his head, his elbows resting on his knees. His shoulders were shaking, and she could hear his ragged breathing.

Her anger dissipated, and she leaned over, putting her hand on his back. "Zane," she said softly, leaning her head against his.

"What?" He didn't look up, his voice hoarse.

"You can do this. You can be what they need. I know you can."

He looked over at her, and she saw that his eyes were bloodshot. "Brad died," he whispered. "*He died.*"

"I know he did. It was tragic and terrible. You can let that destroy you, or you can learn from it. He died because he had no one to hold his hand and guide him. These boys are coming to you, Zane. There's no one else in their lives who can help. Without you, they have nothing. Aren't you better than nothing?"

He stared at her for what seemed like an eternity, then he nodded

STEPHANIE ROWE

once. "I'm better than nothing," he admitted in a barely audible whisper, his voice raw and agonized.

"There you go." She knew he was far better than that, but at least it was progress. "Let's go find them, okay?"

He nodded. "Okay. Drive fast."

"Don't worry. I will."

CHAPTER EIGHTEEN

THE MILES CRAWLED by with agonizing slowness as Taylor raced down the winding, two-lane back road. Zane told Luke he took this road because he liked the curves, but it wasn't the fastest way. Which way would Luke select? Was he wrong that Luke would go as Zane went? What if the kid decided the highway was faster? What if he and Taylor were searching on the wrong road?

No, he was sure Luke would follow his path, both to stay off the main road where the cops might pick him up, and because he'd want to be like Zane.

Shit. *Luke would want to be like him.* How the hell had this happened?

No. It didn't matter how it happened.

All that mattered was that they found them.

They'd been driving for two hours already. Two hours. Still more to go. What if they didn't find them on the road? What if they made it all the way to his foster home and the Garage and didn't find them?

Then they'd go back over it again. And again. Until they found them. He thought of the funeral, and he felt sick. "What if they're dead? What if—"

"Stay focused, Zane. Keep looking." Taylor was steady and calm, as she had been since they'd left the ranch. Without her, he knew he'd have lost his shit by now.

He let out his breath and nodded, his gaze relentlessly sweeping the roadside as they hurtled past the endless fields—

He suddenly saw a dark shadow in the field to his left. He whipped around in his seat, searching the fields, but he didn't see anything.

"What is it?" Taylor eased off the gas.

"Nothing. I don't see anything. Mind tricks."

She looked over at him. "Zane. Do you think you saw something?"

Her unwillingness to dismiss his initial reaction made him think again. Had it been mind tricks, or had he seen something real? He looked at her, then looked back at the field. His gut said it had been them. "Turn around."

She immediately slowed down, then hung a U-turn across the road. He leaned forward in his seat, scanning the grasses. He saw something dark again, and his heart started to speed up. Something was running through the grasses. "Do you see that?"

"Yes. I can't tell what it is." She sped up the car, flying down the highway, closer and closer until—

"It's them!" He could see the two boys racing through the grasses, rushing away from the highway as fast as they could. He shoved open his door, leaping out of the car before Taylor had come to a complete stop. "Luke! Toby! It's me! It's Zane!"

They kept running, frantic and terrified, running away just like he'd done so many times.

"Luke!" He bellowed his name, and broke into a sprint, racing across the field, his heart hammering. "Luke! It's me! It's Zane!"

Suddenly, the taller boy stopped. He whirled around, looking back at Zane, then he screamed Zane's name, picked up his brother, and started running toward Zane, stumbling on the uneven field.

Zane ran faster, his heart pounding when he saw Luke stumble and fall, Toby tumbling out of his skinny arms onto the dirt. "I'm coming! Just wait!"

Luke tried to pick up his brother, dragging himself to his feet as he tried to run toward Zane again. He was so exhausted, he fell again, but again, he grabbed his brother and surged to his feet, refusing to give up.

"Luke!" Zane lunged the last few feet as Luke started to fall a third time, catching both boys in his arms. They fell into him, two skinny kids shivering from cold, even though it wasn't even that cold out.

Zane went to his knees, hauling the boys against him, shaking as hard as the kids were. They were okay. *They were okay.*

Luke flung his arms around Zane's neck, clinging so tightly that Zane couldn't breathe, not that he cared. He pulled the kids tighter against him, holding on as tight as he'd ever held onto anything in his life.

It felt like forever before Luke finally loosened his grip on Zane, who immediately softened his own hold on them, giving them space. Toby kept leaning against Zane's side, staring up at him with big, brown eyes. Zane grinned down at him. "Hey, Toby. You've been on an adventure, huh?"

Toby nodded once, still staring at Zane. "Luke says you'll take care of us. He says we can live with you."

"He did?" A cold fist jammed itself into Zane's stomach, and he looked at Luke, who was staring warily at Zane. "What's going on, Luke?"

Luke still looked scared. "You're not mad? You're not going to yell at us?"

Zane wrapped his arm around Toby and hoisted him up so the kid was on his hip. He didn't answer Luke's question. Instead he asked one of his own. "How bad is it?" He knew Luke would know what he was asking.

The teenager met his gaze. "Bad. It's real bad, Zane."

Zane took a deep breath and nodded. He knew what 'real bad' was to a kid like Luke, who had learned to cope with a lot of bad shit in life. For Luke to say it was real bad...he knew what that meant. "Okay."

"You going to send us back?" Luke looked scared, like a little boy who was terrified of what lay before him, not like a fourteen-year-old who should be thinking he ruled the world.

Suddenly, as Zane stared into Luke's face, he felt his own heart break. Little pieces that he'd kept glued together for so long began to shatter. He couldn't stop the tears, and he didn't bother to try. He just held out his arm to Luke.

For a long moment, Luke didn't move, then the fear left his face and he walked into Zane's embrace. This time, the hug was different. It wasn't relief that the two kids weren't dead. It was a promise, the kind of promise no one had ever made to him when he was a kid, the kind of promise that he'd never thought he'd make...until now.

~

TAYLOR KNOCKED LIGHTLY on the front door of the bunkhouse and poked her head in. Zane was just closing the door to the back room, where he and Taylor had managed to right two cots and make them up with fresh linens when they'd finally gotten back to the ranch. "Are they asleep?"

Zane shook his head. "Toby's waiting for you."

Taylor's heart softened, and she hurried past Zane into the back room. The lights were still blazing, and the boys had crawled into the same tiny bed, with Luke's arm around his little brother. The bed they'd set up for Toby sat empty, abandoned in favor of the security of each other in a world where they'd learned to be afraid.

"Hey," she whispered, walking over to the bed.

Toby rolled over to face her, and he smiled, that adorable smile that she hadn't seen until an hour into their stop at a roadside tavern for dinner and ice cream on the way home. Zane had placed a few calls that had given them permission to take the boys back to the ranch for the night, leveraging his superstar reputation and his hundreds of hours of volunteer work at the Garage to get what he wanted. "How's it going?" she asked.

Toby nodded. "It's good." He held out his hand, and she took it, wrapping it up tightly in hers. Her heart seemed to melt for him, and she had to blink back tears. So much love and innocence still alive in him. He still had a chance.

She looked at Luke, who was watching her silently. "How are you doing?"

He shrugged, warily. "Okay."

"Is there anything I can get you?"

He shook his head.

Toby's fingers relaxed in hers, and she saw that he'd already fallen asleep. Quietly, she tucked his hand against his chest, and brushed her fingers over his tousled hair. When she looked back at Luke, she saw he was still watching her.

"You're nice," he said quietly. "You're not like the others."

She didn't know exactly what others he was referring to, but she could guess. "Yes," she said. "I'm not like the others. I'm like Zane."

His shoulders relaxed, and he took a deep breath. "Okay."

She smiled. "Okay, then." She lightly kissed Toby's forehead, and then looked at Luke, who hadn't taken his gaze off her. "Can I give you one?"

He shrugged again, but not before she saw a flash of yearning in his eyes. She quickly pressed a quick kiss to his head as well, then pulled the covers up around them. "Good night. See you in the morning."

Luke said nothing as he closed his eyes, pulling Toby more tightly against him.

She leaned over the boys, putting her hand on Luke's shoulder. She bent over, lowering her voice for his ears only. "You're safe here," she whispered. "It's okay now."

Luke didn't answer, but she saw the corner of his mouth turn up ever so slightly. She was smiling to herself as she ducked out of the room and pulled the door shut behind her, leaving the lights on for them. She had a feeling it would be a long time until they would be ready to sleep in the dark.

Zane was leaning against the kitchen counter, his arms folded over his chest. His cowboy hat was on the hook by the door, but his boots were still on. He looked exhausted, but there was a fire in his eyes that she hadn't seen before. "I need to talk to you." His voice was tense and clipped.

"Okay." The bed was still the only place to sit, so she walked over and sat on it. She tried not to think of all the times she'd been wrapped up in Zane's arms in that bed, and of all the nights since, when she'd lay there in silence, listening and hoping for his footsteps outside, footsteps that had never come. "What's up?"

Zane didn't join her. Instead, he gripped the counter, his muscles tense. "So, I made some more calls while you were at the main house updating Mira and Chase."

"You did? What kind of calls?" She'd made some calls, too.

"I'm making them mine."

Her heart leapt at his words, but she didn't move. "What do you mean?" she asked carefully, not wanting to jump to conclusions.

"Foster to adopt. They have no one else. I have to do it." His voice broke and he walked across the room, going down to his knees in front of her. He gripped her hips, staring up at her. "They don't have a single living relative," he said. "Do you realize that? I thought their mom was in prison, but apparently she died of a drug overdose not long ago. They're totally and completely alone. No parents, and not a single relative will claim them. Now that Brad's dead, they have *no one.*"

Her heart ached at the pain in his voice, and she nodded. "I figured they had no one else once I heard that they were coming here for you." She touched his jaw, thick with the whiskers of a man who never bothered with society's conscripts to make himself presentable, unless he felt like it. "You're adopting them? Really?"

He nodded. "They've got nothing, Taylor. I'm better than nothing."

She smiled. "You're a lot better than nothing, Zane."

"I'm not." He leaned his head against her stomach, and she wrapped her arms around him, holding him tight. "I don't know what the hell to do with them. I don't know what kids need. I don't have a place for them to live. I—"

"Stop it. You're everything they need. It's not going to be easy. Kids can be challenging, but love is all that they really need. You might not want to admit it, but you love them, and that will be enough. You'll figure the rest out." Her heart ached for his pain, for his inability to see how amazing he was. "You do realize that I would never have fallen in love with you if you weren't the most extraordinary human being I've ever met, right?"

He looked up at her, searching her face. "You believe in me," he whispered.

"Of course I do."

"You're the only reason I told them I'd take them. Because you make me see things in myself I can't see alone."

She smiled. "I'm glad—"

"Adoption is forever," he said. "It's a forever promise. I can't ever take it back."

She cocked her head, studying him. "You don't sound scared," she said.

He shook his head. "I should be, but I'm not. It feels right. Like it's what I'm supposed to do, you know?"

She nodded, her heart swelling for him. "You'll be a great dad, Zane. I know you will, because—"

"Taylor?" He cut her off.

"What?"

He took her hand, sandwiching it between his palms. "I know you want babies. I know that's your dream. I don't want babies. I really don't. But...I've got these boys now. They're not little. They've got scars we'll never be able to see. They're not easy. I don't even know basic stuff about them, like if they eat bacon at breakfast. But, it's a family, kind of, you know? I mean...maybe..."

Her heart started to pound, a frenzied rhythm of hope that she hadn't felt in so long. "What are you trying to say?"

"Would it be enough for you? The boys? Me? I'm thinking I'll set up shop on the ranch. I think the animals would be good for Luke. My brothers would accept them, and the boys would always have a place, so that even if something happened to me, they'd be a part of the place. They'd always have a home, right? So, here is good for them. So, you know, I don't know, what do you think? I mean, you have a great job, and stuff, but—"

Tears filled her eyes. "I quit my job tonight."

He stared at her in disbelief. "What?"

"I called and quit. When I saw the way Luke screamed your name and started running for you, I realized I couldn't do one more day in hotels and airplanes. I believe in children, and I want to help them. But not just being a teacher. I want to help kids like Luke and Toby. I can make a difference. I know I can. I've been caught in this societal tractor beam of biological children, and I realized that it's all just stupidity that has been dragging me away from who I am."

He grinned, a slowly widening grin. "So, you're not afraid of kids like Luke and Toby? They're from the wrong side of the tracks, you know."

She whacked him lightly on the side of the head. "Let go of that wrong side of the tracks thing, Zane. That chip needs to get off your shoulder."

"I'll never get it off my shoulder," he said, his smile fading. "I can try, but it'll never go away. I'm just me."

She sighed. "I know who you are. That's who I love. I didn't mean you have to change for me. I just meant that I want you to realize how amazing you are."

He said nothing, studying her intensely. "Tell me it's okay to ask," he finally said, his voice hoarse. "Tell me it's not selfish. Tell me that I won't ruin your life if I ask."

She went still, her breath suddenly frozen in her chest. "Ask," she whispered. "Ask me."

Silence again, then he cleared his throat. "I know that I'm not what you might have dreamed of. I know I'm not going to bring you babies, but I have a couple kids, you know? And they're going to need help. More than I can give them. And—"

She put her finger over his lips. "Just ask."

"I love you, Taylor. More than you could ever understand." He grasped her wrist, and then kissed the palm of her hand, never taking his gaze off hers. "I want so desperately, with every fiber of my soul, to wake up with you every morning for the rest of my life. I want to hold you all night, every night. I want to learn how to be a parent with you. I want to watch the boys at their first rodeo together. I want to make love to you every night, a dozen times a night, and I want to hold your hand every day until we die."

Tears filled her eyes. "Zane—"

"I need you in my life, Taylor. I can't do it without you. And by 'it', I mean survive, thrive, breathe, or even smile. I need a forever promise from you. I'll give you mine." He took her hands and sandwiched them between his. "I promise I will love, cherish, and protect you forever, if you will please, please, please, agree to marry me." He cut himself off, vulnerability etched on his handsome face as he searched hers. "Be my wife, Taylor. My forever. Our forever. Me and the boys. All of us."

A tear trickled down her cheeks, and she smiled through her tears. "I would have married you without the boys," she said. "I would have kept the boys without you, if I could have. Together? It's everything I could ever dream of. Of course, of course, *of course*, I will marry you, and the boys."

A huge grin spread over his face, and he let out a whoop worthy of the most die-hard cowboy. Then he dragged her into his arms, and he kissed her, the kind of forever kiss that she'd long ago given up hope of ever having.

Until she'd met Zane.

CHAPTER NINETEEN

"LUKE?" Zane finally found him in the last aisle in the barn, leaning over the door, watching the horse inside. "I've been looking for you."

Luke looked at him with sudden fear. "Am I in trouble? Did I forget to do something? I thought I fed everyone. Did I miss a horse?"

"Nah. You're doing great." Zane's heart sank at Luke's instinctive reaction. The boy had been on the ranch for almost two months now, and he was still skittish. Toby had fallen in love with riding almost instantly, but Luke had been unwilling to have anything to do with the horses, aside from doing chores around the barn. He worked hard, too hard, as if he were afraid he'd lose his new home if he wasn't valuable. Zane didn't know how to help him, and it was killing him.

"I wanted to check in with you and make sure you were doing okay." He walked over and leaned on the door beside Luke, studying the animal within.

The bay mare was in bad shape. She was all bones and had a long scar across her hip. Erin had found her on one of her outings, abandoned in a back field. She'd bought the animal on sight and brought her home. The mare had arrived yesterday, but she hadn't eaten a bite yet. She was too skinny to go much longer without getting some nourishment, but she'd refused even the hot bran mash.

"She's not eating," Luke said.

"Nope, she's not," Zane agreed, surprised that Luke had noticed.

"Why not?"

"She's scared. She's had a rough time of it. If an animal is in a constant state of fear, sometimes they can't relax enough to eat."

"She'll die if she doesn't eat. Look how skinny she is." Luke's voice was worried, and he didn't take his gaze off the animal.

Zane thought for a moment, then an idea formed. "You know what she needs?"

Luke shook his head. "What?"

"To feel safe. To feel like someone is going to protect her. She needs to bond with someone. Horses are herd animals, and they're not used to living alone. She doesn't know how to connect with other horses because she's lived alone for so long. She needs someone to be her champion."

Luke said nothing, his arms hooked over the door as he watched her.

"I don't have time," Zane said, choosing his words carefully. "Taylor and I are working on plans to get the cabins built for the summer camp for the kids. Steen's working with the horses that come to the ranch for rehab or training, but this one's not ready for that. Chase and Mira are swamped too." He paused for an extra moment. "We'll have to sell her, and find her a new home. One where someone has time for her."

Luke said nothing, and Zane waited.

Finally, the boy said, "What if they don't take good care of her? What if it's not as nice a place as this one?"

"We'll do our best. We won't let her go somewhere that's not safe."

Luke looked at him. "But how do you know? You never know what's going on inside another place, unless you're living in it."

Zane's heart broke for the lessons that had prompted that observation. "This is true," he said evenly, "but we'll make sure—"

"No." Luke shook his head. "No. I'll take her. I'll take care of her. She needs me."

Zane couldn't stop the grin from spreading over his face, but he quickly wiped it away when Luke looked over at him. "You think you're up for that?" he asked, keeping his expression solemn. "You'll have to gain her trust and get her to eat. When she's ready to be ridden, you'll be the only one she'll want on her back. So, you'll have to be ready for that. You'll have to learn to ride so that you'll be skilled by the time she's ready."

Luke nodded seriously. "I can do that. I'll start right away. Can we do a lesson today?"

Zane couldn't stop the grin this time. "You bet we can." He nodded at the mare. "She needs a name. What are you going to call her?"

"I get to name her?" Luke looked back at the mare, studying her. "Harley," he said decisively. "Her name is Harley. Like your bike. She'll be as fast as your bike when she's better."

Zane grinned. "Harley it is." He put his hand on Luke's shoulder as they both looked in at the mare, who was dozing in the back of the stall. "You'll have to talk to Chase and figure out what to feed her, and how to get her started eating again."

Luke nodded. "I can do that. Chase is a good guy."

"That he is." He pulled open the door. "Go on. Say hi. Introduce yourself."

"Really? Can I?" Luke couldn't keep the eagerness out of his voice, ducking inside the stall even as he asked the question. He walked right up to the mare, who raised her head nervously and backed into the corner at his approach.

Zane watched as the boy instinctively slowed down, and began talking in low undertones to the mare. Harley's ear flicked forward to listen, and slowly, ever so slowly, she lowered her head, still listening.

"Zane—" Taylor appeared beside him, and then fell silent when she saw Luke with the mare. She moved up beside Zane, her hand sliding into his as they watched Luke talk to the mare. Slowly, inch by inch, he moved closer. Harley kept lowering her head more and more as she relaxed, and her ears kept flicking forward, until he was standing right next to her. He leaned in, whispering into her ear, not attempting to touch her. Harley was absolutely still, listening.

Taylor pulled her hand out of Zane's and slipped into the stall. Neither Harley nor Luke noticed her approach, and she slid a carrot into Luke's hand before ducking back out. Zane grinned and put his arm around her as they watched Luke glance down at the carrot. He looked back at Zane, who gave him a nod, and then he held the carrot in front of Harley's nose.

She sniffed it, then turned her head away.

Luke resumed whispering in her ear, still holding the carrot out. Harley cautiously sniffed the carrot again, and then she carefully took it from Luke's hand and crunched it. Luke looked back at Zane and Taylor, a huge smile etched on his face, his light brown eyes dancing with delight.

Zane's heart tightened, and he pulled Taylor closer against him as they both gave him a thumbs up. This was it. This was what being a parent was. This was what being a family was. Sharing moments like this, with the people he loved.

He looked down at Taylor, and he saw her eyes glistening with happiness. "I love you, darlin'," he whispered.

She smiled. "I love you, too."

He kissed her, and then laughed when he heard Luke's groan. "You guys are kissing again? That's so gross."

But when Zane looked over at him, the kid was grinning, watching them as if seeing them together was the best thing he'd ever seen. "If you're done with Harley," Zane said, "the house is here."

Luke's face lit up. "The house? Our house? Really?"

"It's coming up the driveway right now," Taylor said. "I saw it myself."

"I can't believe they moved that old farmhouse," Luke said. "Is it on rollers? A truck? How are they doing it?"

"You'll have to see." Zane had decided the boys couldn't wait a year for a house to be built. Plus, who needed a brand new house, anyway? Together, they'd found a fantastic old farmhouse in the next town, and he'd bought it and paid to have it moved. The foundation was already laid, and it would take only a few days to get the house settled sufficiently for them to move into it. Four bedrooms, three bathrooms, and he was planning to build a serious game room on the back, the kind of game room that would keep the boys at home and not out on the town where they could get into trouble.

He knew what boys did, he knew what it took to keep them out of trouble, and he was going to give them everything he had to keep them safe. He was already figuring out the dad thing, learning how to balance love with rules. Who knew he had it in him? He smiled. Taylor had known. Without her, he'd never be where he was, living the life that he was meant to lead.

"Awesome!" Luke hurried out of the stall, taking time to make sure Harley's door was locked, before taking off in a sprint down the aisle.

Taylor started to go after him, but Zane grabbed her wrist and pulled her back, pinning her against the stall door. "I need one second with you," he whispered, tunneling his hands through her hair. "Sharing that bunkhouse with the boys has seriously cramped my naked time with you."

She melted against him, their bodies fitting together perfectly, as they always did. She wrapped her hands around his neck. "It's been perfect," she said.

He grinned, thinking of how they'd woken up this morning with Toby in bed with them, snuggled up beside Taylor. "Yeah, it has." They'd had to start sleeping with clothes on, but he learned that it was so worth it. "My wife," he said softly. "I'll never get tired of saying that. *Ever.*"

She beamed at him. "Good," she said. "I'm glad to hear it." She grinned. "I'm glad we didn't wait for Mira and Erin's double wedding. Our ceremony was perfect with just us and the boys."

"I couldn't wait, and I didn't want to share." He kissed her forehead, then her cheek. "If you'd said you wanted to wait for the big wedding, I think I would have had to kidnap you."

Her smile faded. "I had the big wedding, Zane. I didn't want another one. I just wanted you and the boys."

"I love you." He kissed her again, a kiss that seemed to melt away every last bit of tension in his body. Holding her in his arms was a gift he'd never dreamed of...until he'd met her. "I love everything about you, just the way you are."

She smiled. "I know you do, and I feel the same—"

He cut her off with a kiss, the kind of kiss that still shook them both to their cores, a kiss of forever, of commitment, and of a passion that would never die. With a deep sigh, she wrapped her arms around him, kissing him back just as fiercely.

His cock growing hard, he grabbed her legs and lifted them around his hips. There had to be an empty stall around—

"Mommy! Daddy!"

He swore and set Taylor down as Toby came hurtling around the corner, his little legs pumping as fast as he could go. "You have to come see the house! It's even bigger than I remember! Come see! Come see!" He grabbed Taylor's hand and started dragging her toward the door.

Taylor laughed, tossing a smile back at Zane as she let Toby lead her out. He grinned, laughter bubbling up deep in his chest as he followed them.

Yeah, this was good. Really, really good.

~

Want more Stocktons? When single mom Lissa McIntyre enlists the help of a handsome stranger during a busy lunch at her Wyoming Café, she has no idea she's just conscripted a world-famous country music star to be her busboy. Check out *A Real Cowboy Never Walks Away* to see what happens when Travis Stockton reluctantly returns to his hometown for a single, emotional performance that will change his life.

~

Keep reading for a Rodeo Knights novella and sneak peeks of the next Wyoming Rebels novels and other Stephanie Rowe novels!

Her Rebel Cowboy

NEW YORK TIMES Bestselling Author

Stephanie ROWE

COPYRIGHT

Her Rebel Cowboy (Rodeo Knights, A Western Romance).
Copyright © 2017 by Stephanie Rowe.

Cover design © 2019 by Kelli Ann Morgan, Inspire Creative Services.

ISBN 10: 1-940968-52-6
ISBN 13: 978-1-940968-52-0

To Guinevere Jones. Without you, this book never would have been written, and you know it! I love you, babe!

CHAPTER ONE

AT ANY MOMENT, Wyatt Parker was going to find out what happened three hours ago. He wasn't going to lie. He was scared shitless to get that call—

The bull he was riding jumped to the left, jerking Wyatt off balance. He lost his grip and was ripped over the bull's right shoulder. Swearing, he ducked his head a split second before he hit the ground, face planting into the dirt.

The shock of the crash on his not-quite-healed body kept him motionless for a moment while he waited for the impact to stop reverberating through him. As he lay there, spitting dirt, he realized that he'd missed even the taste of dirt during his two-month suspension.

After endlessly waking up in the middle of the night, sweating his ass off from another nightmare that he was never going to get on another bull again...he was suddenly days away from competition again...or from being banned for life, like his old man.

Banned for life. The words made an icy chill grip his spine. *Banned for life* from the only thing that made his heart beat. Sweat broke out on his brow, but it wasn't from the pain of his crash. It was from the raw terror of having bull riding taken away from him.

He wasn't a praying man, but hell, he'd even thrown up a couple requests to that big, blue western Oregon sky to make sure he covered all his bases. The World Rodeo Championships rules committee was reviewing his appeal today. He knew he was innocent, but he also knew that didn't always matter. According to what he'd heard, the decision had been scheduled to come down three hours ago. His fate was already sealed. All that was left was for someone to tell him what had happened.

Unless the majority of that committee believed his innocence, everything that mattered to him was going to be stripped away from him because of one eight-second ride two months ago.

Eight damn seconds.

"Get up, Wyatt! Hell, man, get up!"

Awareness came roaring back to him, and Wyatt vaulted to his feet just as the bull who'd dumped him lowered his head to impale him. Wyatt lunged to the right, and the horn clipped his right hip, knocking him off his feet. The bull's feet pounded down next to his head, and Wyatt rolled to the side as hooves thudded past him. He scrambled up and sprinted for the fence, hauling himself over the rails as the bull thundered by.

Grinning, Wyatt leaned on the rails, sweat beading down his brow. "Hell, I missed this."

"You're not ready." Brody Hart, who'd been his friend since they were kids, slammed the gate behind the bull, glaring at Wyatt as if it was his damn fault that the bull had almost crushed him. Which it was. He'd had no business taking his time getting up, and they both knew it.

Brody didn't ride the bulls, claiming that bull riding was for assholes who wanted fame, money, and chicks. He stuck with the horses, and the proof of his success was the expansive neighboring ranch he owned with his seven brothers and two sisters, none of whom were related by blood or even paperwork, but were the most loyal family he'd ever known in his life.

Wyatt had always thought he'd had a messed-up childhood...until he'd met Brody and the rest of the Harts, when they were all teenagers. Back then, the Hart clan had been nothing more than a desperate, scared bunch of runaways living under a bridge in downtown Portland,

Oregon, hiding from authorities who wanted to drag them back into the assorted hells that they'd escaped from. The group of runaways had taken the same last name in an attempt to make it more difficult for anyone to pry them apart. They'd trusted no one but themselves...and Wyatt, eventually. Wyatt wasn't a Hart, but the time he'd spent living under that bridge with them, fighting for food and survival, had created a bond that would last forever.

And now Brody was giving him that same look he'd given Wyatt the day he'd said he wanted to ride bulls in the first place, the look that said he was such a stupid ass that it wasn't even worth talking to him.

Man, he loved Brody.

Wyatt grinned. "Shut the hell up, bro." Shaking out the aches from hitting the dirt, Wyatt straightened up, and finished climbing the rails. "I'm fine."

"That bull has been retired for three years," Brody said, watching him through narrowed eyes. "Even I could ride that senior citizen with no hands and blindfolded, but he dumped you on your ass. How's that fine, exactly? Because I'm a little unclear on that logic."

"Just lost my grip on the rope." Wyatt pulled off his helmet. "You know I step up in competition. I'm just feeling my seat."

Brody stared at him. "You were paralyzed less than two months ago. There's no way you should be on a bull already."

Wyatt tensed. "I was paralyzed for only a few hours. I'm fine."

"Bullshit. You don't have your rhythm. I can tell your neck still hurts, and you can't breathe half the time from those damn broken ribs that aren't completely healed. And how's that head? Bet you're seeing stars after that hit you just took."

"My head's fine." Yeah, he'd gotten a slight concussion during his last ride a couple months ago, but it wasn't enough to stop him. He would have been back on the circuit the next weekend if he hadn't been suspended. *Suspended.* Damn.

Brody narrowed his eyes, seeing more than Wyatt was telling him, as he always did. Growing up on the streets, you either got fucked over, or you learned to be the smartest, most observant badass that ever lived. Brody was the latter, and although it had protected the others that had come to him for aid, it was also annoying as hell at times.

"You're riding like shit." Brody clearly decided stating the blatantly obvious was worth his time. It wasn't. "If it's not your head, what's going on?"

"Just rusty." Wyatt had started riding a couple days ago when he'd gotten the news that his appeal was going to be heard this week, determined to be ready if he were reinstated. He'd been pumped to get back on, but it had been ugly. He wasn't going to admit it, but Brody was right. He had no feel for the bull at all. It was like he was no longer connected to the animals that had been a part of his life since he was a teenager. He couldn't figure out what he was doing wrong, and he was running out of time to get his shit together. Three days, to be exact...assuming the committee ruled in his favor.

Which they had to. He was innocent, and they'd see it.

Except he knew damn well that they might not. Innocent people didn't always get cleared, especially when they were the son of the most notorious bull rider who had ever tarnished the sport.

Brody studied him intensely. "The docs say you could die if you get hit like that again."

Yeah, he knew that, and it didn't matter. "Every bull rider could die any time they go out there. It's better to die doing what you love, than spend a life hiding in a cave."

Brody whistled softly. "Hang it up, man. You've had the career. It's not worth it."

Shit. It was so much more complicated than that. "Yeah? You think I should retire? And then what? What the hell else would I do if I walked away?"

"Take Bunny up on her offer to buy this ranch. Turn it into what it's supposed to be." Brody grinned. "Ranch life is good, bro. You'd like it. This place has potential, and if her nephew buys the place, he's going to turn it into some glitzy resort for Hollywood celebs who want to get away from LA. All this will be lost."

Wyatt instinctively glanced at the white ranch house at the top of the hill, the one owned by Bunny Hickerson. He'd known Bunny almost his entire life, and he lived in her bunk house in exchange for running the place since her husband had died a few years back. She was the one who'd given him the chance that had gotten him off the streets, and he'd taken care of her ever since.

But things were changing. Now that her husband was gone, Bunny was ready to retire to Cape Cod, a place she'd always loved. She was putting Sleeping Bull Ranch on the market at the end of the month...which both pissed him off and relieved him.

Once she sold the ranch, Wyatt would no longer be tethered to it. He'd be free to go wherever he wanted and ride bulls until it killed him...which was good. But at the same time, the Hickerson ranch called to him. It felt like the home he'd never had. Shuffled around from relative to relative while his dad was on the WRC tour or in jail, Wyatt had never lived more than a few months in one place as a kid, except the year he'd spent with the Harts. Bunny's place was the first place he'd lived for any length of time, and it had been his anchor ever since.

He liked coming back here after a competition. He liked making sure things ran smoothly. He took pride in the bulls they bred, in seeing Hickerson bulls on the circuit and knowing he had a hand in it. Yeah, it was a small operation, but the baseline was solid. But to own it? To get up in the same place, from the same bed, every damn day for the rest of his life? To be *responsible* for the ranch? No chance. He knew it wasn't his thing. Never would be. He simply wasn't cut out for it. "I don't want it."

Brody sighed. "You want Nathan to get it? Turn it into a resort?"

Wyatt grimaced at the mention of Bunny's relentless nephew. "She won't sell it to him."

"He'll find a way to get it, if for no other reason than to make sure you don't get it. He hates that you're the one she likes."

Wyatt shrugged. "I'm not going to buy the ranch just to block him. Bunny will handle him. She's smart. I'm going back on the tour."

Brody shook his head. "Don't be an ass. Take a lesson from your dad and know when to stop."

Wyatt tensed at Brody's comment, at the reminder of the legacy that haunted him, the one he'd been trying to outrun for twenty years. The one that had come back to bite him in the ass two months ago. His dad, who had cheated, refused to accept his lifetime ban, and then drank himself to death in misery. "Screw that. No way. I'm getting back on the tour."

He couldn't walk away now. He'd fought against his dad's reputation his whole life, and he'd nearly gotten people to forget about it...until two months ago. His bull in the finals had been an absolute beast, giving Wyatt the highest score in history, and a wreck that had nearly broken his body for good. That ride had made him a legend...until it had been discovered that his bull had been drugged into a rage that had resulted in that high score.

The blame had instantly landed on Wyatt's shoulders, as a cheat, just like his old man, and the suspension had come down the next day, while he'd been lying in the hospital.

And now, he needed to prove that he wasn't a cheater, and the only way to do that was to win clean. "I'm going back on the tour, Brody. Drop it. Let's bring another bull in." He swung his leg over the fence and dropped down to the parched earth that was so starved for rain. He glanced at the dark clouds rolling in the distance, calculating how much time they had before the bad weather took over. "I want to get a couple more rides in before the storm hits."

"No."

Wyatt glanced at his friend as he reached the gate. "No, what?"

"No." Brody walked over. "No, I'm not going to help you ride. I've been your friend for too long, Wyatt. I've been watching you ride for two days now, and you're out of sync. You're still hurting from your crash, and your game is off. You don't have it right, and you're gonna get hurt. Bad hurt. Just to prove to a bunch of assholes that you're not a cheat? Well, screw them. It's not worth your life. I can't stop you from riding, but I'll be damned if I'll help you write your own death ticket." He looked at Wyatt. "Brothers tell each other when they're being stupid, so I'm telling you now. You're being stupid."

Wyatt's chest tightened at the brother reference, as it always did. He wasn't a Hart, but he loved that clan as his own family. But that didn't mean they didn't piss him off sometimes. "Brody, I can't practice without you—"

"I know. That's why I'm not helping. See ya, bro." Brody turned to walk toward his truck, then paused, looking toward the left, toward the ranch house.

At the same moment, Wyatt heard the crunch of boots, and he glanced in the same direction Brody was looking. A tall, lean cowboy in a black cowboy hat and jeans was striding down toward the ring from the main house. He recognized him immediately as Jesse Knight, one of the Knight brothers. Jesse's grandfather had founded the World Rodeo Championships circuit, and he and a couple of his brothers owned a detective agency that often assisted the circuit.

Wyatt tensed at the sight of Jesse approaching. Why was he there? Was this about his suspension? There was only one reason he could think of for one of the Knight brothers to be coming here, and that was if there was something out of the ordinary with the ruling on his suspension.

Shit. Wyatt had been so certain he'd be cleared. The presence of Jesse Knight meant he was wrong.

Dead wrong.

And he was about to find out why.

CHAPTER TWO

S WEARING, W YATT HEADED toward the fence, meeting Jesse as he walked up. "Jesse."

"Wyatt." The two men shook hands.

Wyatt stepped back restlessly, not in the mood for meaningless platitudes. "What's up?" He didn't bother with preambles. Only one thing mattered, and that was getting back in the ring. "You're here about the suspension? My appeal didn't go through?"

Jesse tipped his hat back. "Someone juiced that bull you rode."

Wyatt nodded. "I know. It wasn't me." He was aware of Brody walking up to stand beside him, covering his back. Always loyal, even when he was irritated with him. Wyatt fucking loved the Harts. They'd taught him about loyalty when he hadn't even had the first clue what it meant. He'd go through hell and back for every single one of them.

Jesse studied him. "The chemical in the bull's system wasn't designed to give you a ride tough enough to give you a high score. It was meant to get you killed."

Wyatt blinked, startled by the announcement. "What? Kill me? What are you talking about?"

"My brother's a vet. He researched the drug. The only possible use of that drug in the quantities found in that bull's body was to make it uncontrollable, and insanely aggressive. To make its mind snap. It wasn't a fluke he went after you when you were down. If it hadn't been for the clowns, you'd be dead." Jesse cocked an eyebrow. "We also found someone had doctored the coffee of both the clowns working your ride. Neither of them had had time to drink it, but if they had, they both would have been half-asleep and too slow to help you when the bull went after you. It was a setup, Wyatt. An assassination."

Sudden tension gripped Wyatt's shoulders. He could tell from Jesse's face that he was dead serious. "What the hell?"

Beside him, Brody shifted, and Wyatt could feel the tension rolling off him. "Someone tried to murder Wyatt? You think Wyatt was the specific target, or did he just happen to be in the wrong place?"

Jesse glanced at him, his face solemn. "The bull was drugged *after* Wyatt was announced as his rider. Wyatt was the target."

Shit. "That makes no sense. Who the hell would want to kill me?" And why? But even as he asked, a name popped into his head. He swore. Shit. No. It was impossible.

He glanced at Brody, who looked as stunned as Wyatt felt. *Murder? What the hell?*

Jesse shrugged. "I don't know who did it, but that's why I'm here. You got any ideas?"

"No—"

"Yes, you do." Brody interrupted. "You're thinking the same thing I'm thinking."

"Who?" Jesse asked.

Wyatt looked at Brody. "She would never try to kill me—"

"Who?" Jesse repeated the question.

Wyatt looked at Brody for a long moment, then Brody turned to Jesse. "Octavia Kincaid. Wyatt's former fiancée."

A hard, cold sensation settled in Wyatt's gut, that same coldness that had gripped him since the day he'd learned of her betrayal a year ago. He couldn't even hear her name without all the feelings of that moment crashing down upon him.

Jesse raised his brows. "I thought it was an amicable breakup."

"No way," Brody muttered. "She—"

"Enough." Wyatt cut off his friend. There was no way he was going there. She wasn't worth it. Instead, he focused on what mattered to him. "What about the suspension? It's cleared, then?"

Brody swore. "Hell, Wyatt. Let go of the riding. That doesn't matter right now."

"It matters." Wyatt kept his gaze on Jesse. "Well?"

Jesse nodded. "Yeah, you're clear."

"Hell." Relief rushed over Wyatt, so intense that he had to clench his fist. His name was *cleared*. "So, I can ride this weekend?"

Brody swore again. "You're not ready."

Jesse was shaking his head. "Someone tried to kill you. If you go back out there now, before we figure it out, they could get it right this time. Stay low. Keep recovering. Give me a few days to figure it out. I'll need more information on the situation with Octavia, and any other names." He assessed Wyatt carefully. "And how in the hell did you get medical clearance to ride, anyway? I saw that crash. You should be sidelined."

"I'm fine." Had Octavia really tried to kill him? That made no sense. "I don't think Octavia would try to kill me, but I don't know of anyone else. I have no clue." And he didn't. He couldn't even wrap his mind around the fact that someone had tried to kill him. "If it was Octavia, she didn't try to kill me. Jeopardize my ride? Yeah, sure. I could buy that, and there are a few other names I could list." He dropped a few names of competitors who hadn't liked Wyatt's fast rise to the top. "But try murder? No way. No one." But even as he said it, he flashed back to that night a year ago, when the woman he'd trusted, who he'd thought he'd loved, had ripped apart everything that had mattered to him, everything that he'd built up. Octavia had taught him never to trust a woman again, and it was a lesson he was never going to forget.

Jesse met his gaze. "Someone tried to murder you, Wyatt. Accept it, and stay off the bulls this weekend, until I figure it out."

"Stay off the bulls?" Wyatt glanced back over his shoulder at the ring. At the dirt. He was supposed to walk away because some piece of shit tried to take him down? No. Never. He turned back "No chance. I need to ride." He saw the resistance on the faces of both men, but it didn't matter. He had to ride. He knew he had no choice. For reasons that no one but him would ever understand.

Some choices weren't really choices. Some choices were simply fate, burned into a man's bones, a destiny from which there was no deviation, no reprieve, and no salvation.

He was going to ride this weekend. If he died, well, he died. He accepted that possibility. Death had never scared him. It was failing to claim the life he was meant to live that haunted him.

CHAPTER THREE

NOELLE WILDER GRIMACED when she saw her best friend reach for the handle of her fridge. "I haven't been grocery shopping for a while," she warned, trying to preempt the lecture that would be coming as soon as Kate saw the contents.

"Holy crap, girl." Kate Jackson stared into the fridge, her upper lip curling in horror. "Expired eggs, curdled milk, and a plastic container full of something so old I can't even tell what it once was? That's it? That's all you have in here? How do you survive on that? And more importantly, how on earth is that going to inspire a culinary mystery worthy of the hundred thousand copies your last one sold?"

"As soon as the chocolate starts to melt on the stove, the scent will inspire me." Ignoring her throbbing headache, Noelle stared at the computer screen, willing her brain to start working again, for those long-absent ideas to begin to flow.

"No, it won't." Kate slammed the fridge shut. "Face it, girlfriend. Chocolate can't help you this time."

"Of course it can. Chocolate can salvage anything— Hey!" Kate snatched the computer from her lap.

Noelle sighed and glared at her friend. "Really, Kate? How's that helpful?"

"Because staring at blinking cursors on a blank screen for hours on end has been documented to rot the brain cells, and you need all the ones you can still salvage." Kate set the computer on the kitchen counter. "Face it, Noelle. You've even killed chocolate."

Noelle raised her eyebrows. "No one can kill chocolate." Although, if she was honest with herself, she had to acknowledge the truth that if anyone could kill chocolate, she had a feeling that it might be her.

"No?" Kate leaned forward. "Then tell me, what's the first thing that comes to your mind when I mention a very sharp dagger hidden in a molten chocolate lava cake?"

The image of her bed and her favorite fuzzy blanket popped into her head...and that was just not a good thing for a culinary mystery writer. "Oh, God. I didn't see any blood," she said, staring at Kate in horror. "No dead bodies. It makes me want to crawl into my bed and take a nap instead of dealing with it."

Kate sighed and sat down next to her. "You didn't have any visions of what kind of deranged villain would put a dagger in a dessert?"

Noelle groaned. "No. My brain feels like it ran into hiding when I tried to picture the dagger." She closed her eyes and let her head drop back against the couch, suddenly feeling too tired to cope. "That's it then, isn't it? That's what you've been trying to tell me. I can't do this anymore."

"That's exactly what I've been trying to tell you," Kate said gently. "You're dying inside Noelle. Can't you feel it?"

Weariness seemed to strip Noelle of the last vestiges of her enthusiasm, but she opened her eyes and made herself sit straighter. "Don't say that. You don't know what it's like to die. The fact I'm tired isn't the same thing at all—"

"Don't start that with me," Kate snapped. "I know that you spent years trying to keep David from dying. I know you lived that, and I know how much it sucked to spend the first three years of your marriage watching your husband die. I get that. I was here, remember? However, I'm not talking about a physical death, and you know it. I'm talking about your soul, your heart, your spirit."

Noelle bit her lip at the sudden burn of tears in her eyes. "I'm okay," she said stubbornly. "I really am—"

"Sweetie, you've spent the year since David's death trying to keep his dream alive, and it's killing you. Just because he died doesn't mean you have to, as well."

Noelle lifted her chin. "I made him a promise to help his brother and keep his restaurant going. I mean, our restaurant. We opened it together, and it was his dream, I mean, our dream. Don't you remember that? Or did you forget that part?"

"Oh, I remember when you guys decided to open it. I remember when you guys fell in love over the stove. But I also remember when you used to lose yourself in your stories and write until your face glowed with joy, while he pulled most of the weight in the kitchen. I don't see any joy anymore. When was the last time you felt joy?"

"I–" Noelle's voice faded as she tried to remember. She couldn't even remember what joy felt like. All she could feel, all she'd felt for ages, was a tightness in her chest, and a numbness that made every moment and every day the same, day after day after day. No joy. No pain. Just an empty numbness propelled by obligation.

Kate sighed. "Sweetie, David loved the restaurant, but he loved you more. The last thing he would've wanted was for you to live like this, so broken and empty. That restaurant was *his* dream. You did it because you loved him, but when he was alive, you were able to spend a lot of time writing. Now you're there all the time, fighting for a dream that isn't yours. You can't keep doing both."

"Of course I can." Noelle shoved herself to her feet and padded across her bare wood floor to the stove, where the chocolate was beginning to melt perfectly.

"Can you?" Kate didn't bother to keep the skepticism out of her voice. "This book you're working on was due how long ago? How many extensions have you gotten?"

Noelle grabbed a wooden spoon and began to stir the chocolate, watching the rich, creamy substance swirl in her pot. She used to love watching it swirl. Now? She felt nothing. God. When was the last time she felt anything? The day David died. She'd felt something then, but ever since? Nothing. Just endless numbness. "My editor understands."

"I'm sure she does, but she's going to stick around for only so long if you don't deliver. You're a year late on your book, Noelle. A *year*."

"I know!" Noelle set the spoon down. "I'm trying!"

"I know you are, babe, but it's not working, is it?"

Noelle leaned against the kitchen counter and looked at her friend. Suddenly, the weight of the last four years seemed to overwhelm her, and she felt exhausted. "So, maybe I shouldn't write anymore. Maybe I should just go full-time at the restaurant."

Kate's eyebrows shot up. "Really? *That's* your plan? Give up on the one thing that makes you happy, so you can work at a restaurant that's draining your energy and savings? Because that sounds like a fulfilling and brilliant way to spend the rest of your life."

Noelle gritted her teeth, her fingers digging into the counter. "What am I supposed to do? Walk away? Then what happens to Joel? He's the only family David has left, and I promised I'd make sure he was okay. If I close the restaurant, what will happen to him? We both know the only reason he's been sober the last two years is because the restaurant gives him purpose."

Kate shrugged. "So give it to him, then. He's a great chef. He'd be thrilled."

"Give it to Joel? Just walk away from it completely?" Guilt tore through her, a deep, anguished guilt because, for a split second, she'd wanted to cry with relief at the idea of doing that. But how could she? She couldn't. "He needs me to run it. He's a chef, not a business person."

"Let him hire a business manager."

"There's not enough money for that—"

"For heaven's sake, Noelle! Do you hear yourself? You're doing the job for free and putting your own money into it, just because you've convinced yourself that Joel, who's a great chef and has been sober for two years, can't manage without you. Does he really need you? Maybe he needs you to get the hell out of his life so he can stop being David's little brother and find his own strength. Did that ever occur to you?"

Noelle felt like her head was going to explode. She was suddenly too exhausted to cope. "David was the only safe space I ever had in my life, Kate. I won't betray that, or him, or his brother, regardless of the cost to me. This is what I was meant to do. It matters to me. David would've done the same for me."

Kate's face softened. "I know he would have, but would you have ever asked him to give up his dreams until he had no spirit left?"

Noelle stared at her friend. "Of course not. Never."

"So, why is it okay for you to sacrifice yourself that way?"

"I..." Noelle didn't have an answer. Suddenly, it was just too difficult to understand. "I don't know. It just is."

Kate sighed. "Okay, let me present this another way. Maybe you want to sacrifice yourself. That's your choice. But if your goal is to always have a place for Joel to work, you're going to fail there as well. The way it's going now, the restaurant will fail without your supplemental income, but if you don't write a great book soon, you won't have the money to fund it. At the very least, admit that."

Noelle tensed, her stomach clenched with sharp pains as Kate voiced the fear that haunted her day and night. "I know," she whispered. It was very possible that she was going to run out of money. She was already living on savings, and without another book in the pipeline, she was going to be in deep trouble, and then she could do nothing for Joel or David. "I can't fix that, Kate. I can't write anymore. I've tried. I really have." The admission burned as she voiced the fear that had been haunting her constantly for so long. "I can't write anymore." God. It was out there. Acknowledged. *I can't write anymore.*

Kate held up her hand. "No. You can write. It's just that your soul is withering, and you can't write without it. You have to find your muse again, and it has to be now. Or there's going to be nothing left of your soul to call upon."

"My soul?" She wanted to protest, to claim Kate was being melodramatic, but there were some times, in the middle of the night, when she couldn't sleep, that it *did* feel like her soul was withering. The aching, empty void inside her seemed to be growing deeper with every passing day, no matter how hard she tried.

"Yes. You've shut down your soul, and that's just not going to work for a woman whose career depends on baring her rawest emotions on the page. Something has to change."

"I know." Noelle couldn't deny it anymore. "You're right. But what? I don't know what to do."

"I know you don't, but lucky for you, I do." Kate smiled, but there was a fire in her eyes, a gleam of excitement that made Noelle stiffen.

She knew Kate too well not to be afraid of that gleam, and she realized suddenly that the entire conversation had been a clever, well-orchestrated manipulation to back her into the exact corner she was in. She set down the spoon and stared at her friend. "Oh, God, Kate. What have you done?"

Kate didn't even try to look innocent. "Do you know what a house swap is?"

Noelle narrowed her eyes. "You mean, when one person trades two weeks in their New York City condo with someone who has a ski chalet in Colorado? So they live in each other's houses for two weeks?"

"Exactly," Kate pulled a thick, manila envelope out of her purse and slapped it onto the counter. "Girl, you're going to cowboy country. One month on the Sleeping Bull Ranch in Eastern Oregon."

"A ranch?" For one fraction of a millisecond, an image of a sexy, seductive cowboy flashed in Noelle's mind, the same image that she'd fantasized about since she'd been sixteen years old, and read her first cowboy Harlequin romance novel on a sleepover with Kate. Excitement rushed through her, but it was chased away instantly by the reality of her situation. She shook her head. "A month? There's no way. I have to run the restaurant, and I have this deadline. And—"

"You don't have a choice. Remember that whole 'house swap' concept? Well, the owner of Sleeping Bull Ranch, Bunny Hickerson, is going to be living in your lovely Boston abode for the next month. She arrives tomorrow at noon. You don't have anywhere else to live."

Noelle's jaw dropped open. "What? You rented my apartment? Are you crazy? You don't have the right to do that—"

"Oh, but I do. Remember how you and I lived here before you got married? Well, guess who did the automatic renewal every year without bothering to update the name on it? Yes, that would be you, my absent-minded creative friend. I'm still on the lease, so yeah, I can. I did. You don't have a home for four weeks starting tomorrow at noon."

Shock numbed Noelle at Kate's announcement. She didn't know how to respond. A part of her wanted to argue and shut down the entire idea immediately. But at the same time, a deeper part of her that wanted to grab the envelope and run, away from her deadline, away from the restaurant, away from the memories that wouldn't let her go. But she didn't move. How could she take off and go to Oregon? She had obligations. Deadlines. People counting on her.

There was no way she could accept the offer, no matter how badly a part of her burned to do just that.

So, instead of grabbing it, she bit her lip and went back to stirring. "Thanks for trying, but I can't leave. The restaurant and my deadline—"

"Wrong." Kate grinned and pushed the envelope closer, sliding it across the counter toward Noelle. "You aren't accomplishing anything here, my friend, and it's not getting better. Take a few weeks off. Find your spirit. Awaken your muse, and find your own space again."

"But—"

"I'll pop in on Joel every few days just to check on everything, so there's nothing at the restaurant for you to worry about. So, go."

Noelle stared at the envelope, sudden longing surging inside her. How amazing did it sound to get away for a month? To just walk away from all the weight that had been getting so heavy? She bit her lip, guilt rushing through her. "I can't—"

"You can." Kate leaned forward. "And you have to. You're wrecking your career, and the restaurant. You have to step back, Noelle. You have to find you again. It's time." Kate picked up the envelope and held it out. "Just take it, girl. Go find yourself again."

Longing coursed through Noelle, but she didn't move. "I can't just walk away from my life, Kate—"

"Do you want to stay here? Or do you want to get the hell out of here and breathe again?"

Noelle looked around the tiny apartment that she'd been trapped in for the last four years. Three years, taking care of David, and then this last year, fighting with the computer, trying desperately to write. Suddenly, it felt so small and oppressive, a prison crushing her. She thought of the restaurant, of walking in there night after night, knowing that it was sliding into failure, and she couldn't stop it. "Yes," she whispered, barely able to acknowledge the truth even to herself. "I can't keep living like this."

"I know, babe." Kate held out the envelope. "Take it. It's time."

Noelle stared at the envelope, then silently, her hand shaking, she held out her palm. Kate set it in her hand. The moment her fingers closed around the smooth envelope, the hugest sense of relief flooded her, and she knew it was exactly what she needed. "Thanks."

"No problem." Kate winked. "And just so you know, Bunny said the foreman on the ranch is super hot. Single, too."

Heat flooded Noelle's cheeks, and she rolled her eyes as she pressed the envelope to her chest, her heart pounding with life for the first time in so long. "Dating? No way. I've had enough of men." She pointed the envelope at her friend. "I'm going, but it's just to find my muse, not to even look at a man. The last thing I need right now is a complication."

"On the contrary, my dear," Kate said as she leaned back in the chair and beamed at her. "I think complications are exactly what you need. *Exactly* what you need."

CHAPTER FOUR

So, YEAH, APPARENTLY there was a reason why people read novels instead of actually trying to experience the life they were reading about.

Because fantasies had no place in real life. Ever.

Especially fantasies that involved romantic, soul-enriching excursions to ranch country out west.

Noelle had been dreaming about cowboys and the Wild West since she was a kid, and not a single one of those fantasies included driving her rental car off the road and into a flooded ditch during a thunderstorm. Granted, she'd been driving slowly when she'd hit the brakes to avoid a coyote, and the slide down the embankment had been gentle and danger-free, but that didn't change the fact that her car wasn't getting back on the road by itself. And the part about not having any cell service? Yeah, that hadn't made it into even a single fantasy, and for good reason apparently.

Because it kind of sucked.

Noelle sighed, resting her wrists on the steering wheel as she watched the rain hammer onto her windshield. The din of pounding rain sounded like a herd of cattle stampeding across her metal roof, which, again, wasn't exactly how she'd envisioned her first cattle experience.

She'd been sitting in her car for two hours and six minutes, and not a single car had driven by. Not one. She was on some dirt road, not that far from her destination, and apparently, none of the other residents of Eastern Oregon had any business along this particular stretch of road.

So, yay for finding a place where she wasn't going to be harassed by having to deal with people, right? Go her.

She glanced at the dashboard on her car. Almost seven o'clock. It would be getting dark soon, and she so didn't want to spend the night here. She looked again at her directions. How much farther could the ranch be? She was almost there. She could sit there in the car until someone found her clean-picked skeleton, or she could use her body that she was lucky enough to have, and hike the rest of the distance.

The idea of hiking made energy hum through her, a surprising burst of energy that she hadn't felt in a long time. It made her feel powerful, no longer a victim. Taking action felt so much better than waiting to become roadside carnage. Grinning, she quickly leaned into the back seat, dug through her bags for her hiking boots and her raincoat. Within five minutes, she'd changed her shoes, zipped the ranch house key, her phone, the directions, and her wallet into the inside pocket of the coat, and chowed a granola bar.

Thunder rumbled just as she was reaching for the door handle. She hesitated for a split second, then looked around at the car. Another prison, just like her apartment. Suddenly, she couldn't take another second of it. She had to be outside. She had to be moving. She had to be breathing in fresh air. *Now.*

So she shoved open the door, stepped into six inches of muddy, raging water, and got out. The wind hit hard, and the rain thundered down, and she realized it was really brutal out. She hesitated, one hand on the door frame, suddenly unsure what to do. What if it was longer than she thought to the ranch? What if she got lost? There was literally no one to come to aid. No cell service. No cars going past. But, there were coyotes, or at least one. They didn't attack people, though, she was pretty sure. *Crap.* Was she a total fool to get out of the car and start hiking? Or would she be a bigger fool to sit in her car until someone came past?

Probably hiking was the worse choice.

But dammit. She didn't want to sit around anymore. She wanted to move. To live. To feel her body work again.

Screw it.

She was hiking.

With a renewed sense of power, she slammed her door shut and headed up the embankment toward the highway. She made it halfway up the incline, then she felt her boots start to slide. She yelped, and fought for purchase, leaning down to brace her hands on the ground, but as she stood there, her feet slid all the way back down, she lost her grip and landed on her knees, and rode the muddy gravel all the way back down, landing with a sploosh in the muddy river that had trapped her car.

Noelle looked up at the ten-foot embankment of mud and gravel, and suddenly, she started to laugh. Oh, God. This was too insane. Her first day of replenishing her soul, and she was trapped by a hill of shale and mud? Energy rushed through her, a fire that made her entire body feel stronger than it had in years.

She backed up several steps, set her gaze on her goal, and then charged the hill. She made it halfway up again, and then her boots started to slide. She lunged forward, digging her hands into the mud as she fought to scramble up the side. She made it another few feet, sliding backwards almost as often as she made it forward.

Her breath was heaving in her chest, and she fought harder, her feet sliding down almost as fast as she was able to take a step forward. Rain poured over her, running down her neck and under her coat, and mud coated her hands to her wrists. Her jeans were soaked, there was cold mud oozing over the top of her boots, and her hair was glued to her cheeks by the mud and the rain. She was filthy, soaked, exhausted, and hadn't felt so alive in years. Grinning even as her fingernails were scraped by the gravel, she fought against gravity. Inch by inch, she scrambled higher, until she was almost at the top...and then her feet started to go again.

"Crap!" She lunged for the top of the embankment, and just missed it...and started to slide back down again—

A strong hand suddenly grabbed her wrist, jerking her to a stop mid-slide.

She looked up quickly to find a drenched, muddy cowboy in a long jacket, a dripping cowboy hat, and icy-blue eyes staring down at her, his fingers locked around her arm.

Noelle froze, shocked by the sight of him, by the way her belly leapt, by the sudden heat rushing through her body. Dear God, he was straight out of her teenage fantasies. A hot cowboy coming to her rescue?

No, not hot. Calling him hot was kind of like calling a wild, fully grown male mountain lion a cute little kitten. It was a supreme injustice to both the lion and the kitten. The man before her was pure, rugged male...the kind of male that made her want to drop everything, sprint over to him, and surrender every aspect of herself to his raw masculinity.

There was something about the way he was standing there with his duster flapping in the heavy wind, his legs braced against the weight of her body, while the rain dripped off his hat that was just so primal. Delicious. Surreal. Hot. Like he was made of testosterone, Old West charm, and danger...with just a hint of cocky arrogance curving his mouth so seductively that a shiver went down her spine that had nothing to do with the fact she was soaking wet and closing in on hypothermia (yes, it was fifty degrees, but hypothermia wasn't choosy, was it?)

She couldn't quite believe how good it felt to stare at a man and notice how wide his shoulders were beneath his black jacket, or the way his quads bulged beneath his jean-clad thighs as he braced himself, as if his body was made for a life of outdoor roughness. She took a deep breath, wishing that he was close enough for her to catch a scent of him, a heady masculine scent that would make her stomach curl and her belly flutter like it had back when she used to feel alive. But all she could smell was the damp earth, the fresh rain, and the murkiness of the swampy river she'd just waded through...which was just as well.

One more assault to her senses would likely send her romantically barren soul into testosterone-induced shock.

He lifted one eyebrow slowly, amusement flickering in his eyes, and suddenly, she realized she was gawking at him. Like, literally *gawking.* Heat flooded her cheeks, but she had nowhere to hide, nowhere else to look, not when it was his grip on her arm that was keeping her from tumbling back down the embankment to the muddy, bubbly water.

"Ready?" His voice rolled through her. Deep. Masculine. Rich. Her stomach literally vibrated in response.

"Ready? For what?" She had no idea what he was talking about. All she could think of was how kind and warm he sounded, a hint of gentleness in his voice that contrasted so sharply with the strapping strength of his frame, and the ease with which he was keeping her from sliding down the hill.

The amusement in his eyes deepened. "For me to haul you up here so you don't slide down again. Or I can let you go, if you prefer."

"Oh, right." She'd totally forgotten she was still standing at a forty-five-degree angle, several feet below him, on an embankment that was becoming increasingly unstable in the heavy rain. "Hauling me up would be fantastic, thanks."

He flashed her a grin so devastatingly charming that she forgot to breathe, and then he stepped back, using his body to counterbalance her as she scrambled up the last few feet and over the edge. She landed in front of him, her boots thudding on the even ground...and she realized that he was even more solid and tall when she was on his level than he'd looked when he was above her.

For a long moment, she didn't move, and neither did he. His hand was still locked around her arm, and she didn't pull away. They just stood there, the rain hammering down on them, sliding over her face, and down her neck.

She was close enough now to see the heavy whiskers on his face, a beard that he didn't quite allow to grow in. His jaw was hard and strong. His face angular. And his eyes...she forgot about everything else but his eyes. They were a deep, turbulent crystal blue that were so intense they literally took her breath away with the potency burning within them. She knew then that he wasn't simply a sinfully hot cowboy. He was more, something infinitely more complex, burdened by a weight so raw that he made her heart speed up. This man was *alive*, fermenting with power and passion that made her heart clench.

God, how long had it been since she'd felt alive like that?

His gaze traveled over her, across her face, over her muddy, soaking body, moving with a languid interest that made heat burn in her belly. His gaze flicked to her car, angled down in the ditch, and then back to her. "City girl?"

The way he said it didn't sound like an insult. It sounded like a seduction that made him promise to show her exactly how wild the cowboy life could be. She nodded. "Boston."

"Boston." He repeated the word, rolling it ever so slightly with a cowboy twang that made her belly tighten. "So, you must be Noelle Wilder." His gaze settled on her face. "I've been expecting you."

CHAPTER FIVE

YEAH, WYATT HAD been expecting a woman named Noelle Wilder from Boston, but he hadn't been expecting *her.* Not in any way.

When Bunny had told him she was doing a house swap for the next month so she could do some house hunting for her Cape Cod dream home, Wyatt had been annoyed. He didn't have time to babysit a city slicker, not when he had to figure out who the hell had doped his ride, and get his bull riding back on track, but he owed Bunny a lot, so he'd agreed.

He'd figured Noelle Wilder would be a pain in his ass. Afraid to get dirty. Needing shit from him he didn't have to give. Uptight. Maybe on the hunt for an affair with a cowboy that she could tell her friends about, showing up in high heels, makeup, and a need to seduce. He knew about those women. Hell, that was the only kind of woman who ever crossed his path.

Until now.

He hadn't expected the woman standing in front of him. Noelle was wearing jeans and hiking boots. She was soaking wet. Muddy from head to toe. Makeup-free. Rain was glistening on her cheeks, highlighting brown eyes so compelling he'd forgotten to breathe the moment he'd looked into them. She wasn't dressed to impress. She was dressed...for herself...and it had hit him straight in the gut the moment he'd walked to the top of the embankment and seen her struggling to climb it, refusing to succumb to gravity.

And she'd been laughing while she was doing it. *Laughing.*

She made him want to laugh, and he hadn't laughed in a long, damned time.

And now, she gazed up at him, her face glistening with rain. "You were expecting me?" she asked, repeating his words back to him. "Who are you?"

At the sound of her voice, something shifted inside Wyatt. There was such kindness in her voice, a warmth, a lack of pretense...a quiet, deep appreciation for the moment. He couldn't seem to tear his gaze off her face. "My name's Wyatt Parker. I'm the foreman on the Sleeping Bull Ranch. Bunny told me to keep an eye out for you."

"The foreman?" Noelle's eyes widened, and her gaze slipped off his face, checking him out with rapid, nervous interest.

His cock actually tightened at the feel of her gaze sweeping over him. His reaction shocked him. He was used to being checked out by women. The minute he had started having success as a bull rider, the women had flocked to him, wanting only a piece of his ass and his winnings. He'd learned fast and ugly not to trust anyone who looked at him that way, a lesson that Octavia had solidified when he'd thought she was an exception. He didn't even notice anymore when women checked him out...until now. Until Noelle's gaze brushed over him, a tentative, innocent exploration that ignited a fire in him that had been dormant for a long time.

Her gaze shot back to his face, and to his surprise, she pulled free of his grip, took several steps back and set her hands on her hips. She lifted her chin, and he literally felt the wall that she raised between them.

He narrowed his eyes, surprised by the way she tried to put distance between them. Women never did that, not with him. He didn't take it personally, because he knew that any bull rider with a halfway decent career got the same appreciation from women. Which made the fact that Noelle had stepped back a hell of a lot more interesting than if she had stepped forward.

He cocked his head, studying her. "Running the ranch for Bunny is just a part-time gig. I'm a bull rider." He never told anyone he was a bull rider, because he hated being judged by it. But he wanted to see what Noelle would do when she knew. Somehow, he needed to find out what she thought of that fact. "Last year's runner up at the finals." Today's tainted sideliner.

To his satisfaction, Noelle didn't inch forward. She didn't get a flash of interest in her eyes. There was no hint of greed in her face. In fact, her forehead wrinkled. "Can't you die from that?"

Her question made him tense, because, you know, he'd almost died two months ago. "Yes."

It was only because he was watching her so closely that he saw her flinch. It wasn't a superficial, dramatic response designed to stroke his ego about how manly he was. There was a genuine flash of fear and anguish in her eyes, and she physically recoiled, folding her arms across her chest. "I don't understand that," she said. "I don't understand how you could do something that could kill you. Don't you realize what a gift it is to be alive?"

Her voice was almost desperate, edged with a grief that struck him right in his gut. He swore under his breath, and knew then that someone she loved had died on her. Someone who mattered to her. Someone whose death had changed her view of life forever. Suddenly, he saw her differently. He saw the shadows in her eyes, the hollowness of her cheeks, the way she hugged herself, as if she had to hold herself up. He understood why she was taking a month off from her life to hang out on some Oregon ranch. "Who died?" he asked softly.

Shock flashed across her face, and for a second, he thought she wouldn't answer. But she did. "My husband. A year ago. He was sick for three years."

Her voice was tight, guarded, and exhausted. He knew it had been a long three years, and a long year since. "I'm sorry." Protectiveness surged through him, a deep, instinctive need to surround her with his strength, to protect her from the grief trying to hold onto her, to make it safe for her to breathe again.

She nodded. "Thanks." She managed a smile. "But we have to keep living, right? Otherwise it's an insult to those who die young."

He thought of his dad and nodded. "Agreed." Suddenly, he didn't resent Bunny's request to make sure Noelle was safe. He accepted it. He embraced it. In fact, to his surprise, a small part of him actually regretted that he would be leaving the ranch in a few days to compete.

The moment he had that thought, he swore under his breath. He'd already given up everything for a woman once, and he had learned his lesson. God, how he had learned his lesson. He'd known Noelle about sixty seconds, and he was already regretting leaving her? What the hell? He was going to ride this weekend, and nothing was going to keep him home. Not even this woman from Boston, who looked like the weight of life was going to crush her.

He cleared his throat, resisting the urge to close the distance between them and draw her into a hug, to somehow support her. He would make sure she was safe, yeah, but that was it. He wasn't going to step over that line that he'd sworn never to be dragged across again. "Tell you what," he said. "I'll ride back to the ranch, get a tractor, and come back and pull your car out." He liked that plan. It helped and protected her, but put some distance between them, and that power-ful-as-hell tug between them.

She glanced past his shoulder, and he saw her eyes widen when she saw his horse. "You rode out here?"

"Yeah. I was checking fences." He saw her shiver, and he swore, suddenly aware of the pounding rain hammering them both. Her face was streaked with rain, her jeans sodden against her legs, her raincoat no longer beading with rain because it had maxed out its capacity to keep her dry. He frowned. "You should get back in your car and get dry. I'll be back in about an hour." If he rode hard, he could make it home in forty-five minutes. It was pushing it, but he wasn't leaving her out here any longer than he had to.

She blinked, drawing his attention to the raindrops clumping at the ends of her eyelashes. "You want to leave me here?" The question was careful, as if she wasn't sure how that made her feel.

"I don't want to leave you, specifically. I want to help you, but I need to get a tractor to get your car out." He cleared his throat, resisting the urge to throw her on the back of his horse and haul her up against him. "I'll be back as soon as I can."

She looked over her shoulder at the car, and then back at his horse. He saw the flash of fear in her eyes, and he swore. He knew then that she didn't want to wait there. "You'll be safe in the car. Dry. You can turn on the heat." He didn't want her out in the rain on his horse...but at the same time, some part of him didn't want to leave her behind.

Yeah, she would be safe there. Nothing was going to happen. They were already on the ranch property, and no one would be coming by. But hell...it didn't feel right to leave her.

She looked at the horse again, and then back at him. "I'd rather ride with you."

His gut clenched, and he had a sudden image of her riding in front of him on Lightning, leaning back against him while he held her securely in front of him. At the thought of her nestled between his thighs, his gut tightened with the surge of lust he hadn't felt in too damn long. *Shit.* He didn't have time for this, for a woman, for reacting this way. For hell's sake, he had a possible murderer hunting him, and a bull riding career to resurrect in three days. He did not have time to notice her like this. But he couldn't help it. He just couldn't stop staring into her eyes, from wanting to chase away the shadows haunting her, from needing to protect her...

No. He had to keep his distance. He had too much going on. She had to stay in her car, not park herself on his lap for a longer ride in the rain. No way. He opened his mouth to tell her that, but the words that came out weren't what he'd intended. "You want to ride with me?"

The moment he asked the question, he regretted it...and knew it was the only thing he wanted to ask. It might not make sense for a shitload of reasons, but there was nothing more he wanted in that moment than to have his thighs on either side of hers, his arm around her waist, anchoring her back against his chest, his coat tucked around her to keep her protected from the storm. He wanted her where he could make sure she was safe, and the only place that fit that bill right now, was on the back of his horse in his arms.

Relief flashed over her face. "I don't want to be in the car." Her voice was quiet, almost a whisper, but he still heard the desperation. "I would love to ride with you."

His gut shifted at her word choice. *I would love to ride with you.* Shit.

He liked that. He liked that she had no doubt, that she trusted him completely, even though he was a stranger. She was right to trust him. There was no way in hell he'd hurt her. If he took her with him, her safety would be completely dependent on him. *Completely.* Damn. He liked that. No, he didn't like it. He *loved* it. He stood taller, and whistled low under his breath. His mount, Lightning, trotted over, and stopped beside him. Wyatt gathered the reins, and then held out his hand to her.

For a long moment, she didn't move, and he tensed. Was she going to retreat to her car? Decide she was safer in a ditch in her car than on a horse with him? Logic said she was, but something primal deep inside him resisted. "I'll keep you safe," he said quietly.

Her gaze flicked to his, and he didn't miss the flash of yearning in her eyes, coupled with a vulnerability that made his chest tighten. He knew then that no one ever kept her safe. No one ever took care of her. She took care of herself, and the people around her.

He wanted to give her that gift. He wanted it to be him who gave her even a few minutes of feeling like she didn't have to fight her battles herself...or at least this battle, for the next hour. He flicked his fingers, beckoning her toward him. "Come on, Noelle. Ride with me."

She took a deep breath, and she lifted her chin.

He knew then, before she spoke, before she moved, that she was going to say yes. Anticipation roared through him, a fierce, roaring sensation of rightness as she slowly lifted her hand.

His entire body hummed in anticipation as he waited for her to set her hand in his, but the moment he felt her fingers in his, peace settled deep inside him, all the way to his core, and he knew that this woman had come into his life for a reason, and he was going to find out what it was.

CHAPTER SIX

THE MOMENT NOELLE set her hand in Wyatt's, she felt like her world had come to a crashing stop, hovering in suspended abeyance, every one of her senses completely focused on him. His hand was warm, a stark contrast to her frozen fingers. He didn't seem to notice or care how muddy her hands were after her climb up the embankment. Instead of pulling away, his fingers closed around hers, cradling her hand in his.

Her heart seemed to stutter, and heat poured through her, starting in her chest and radiating through her belly and down her arms. Dear God. She wanted him. Not just an attraction, but something deep inside her soul was calling out for him, to him, needing his touch, his kindness...him.

Suddenly terrified, she jerked her hand back and folded her arms over her chest, trying to fight off the longing coursing through her. Her heart ached, and she was suddenly filled with the most haunting sense of loss and emotion, tearing through the shields she had erected so carefully over the last four years, making herself numb enough to handle everything. Suddenly, emotions swelled over her, a flood of every emotion she'd held at bay for so long, all of them triggered by the simple touch of Wyatt's hand.

Tears flooded her eyes, and her breath became labored as she fought to hold herself together. She saw the surprise on his face, and she instinctively turned away, hugging herself as she stumbled back toward the embankment. "I think I'll wait in the car," she managed to croak out. Dear God. What was wrong with her? She couldn't even breathe. Couldn't think. Couldn't talk. There were so many images flashing through her mind. The moment when she found out David was dying. The moment when she'd realized that she would have to live life without him. That sense of loss and loneliness. The need to be loved and supported that she'd crushed so ruthlessly when she'd realized she had to be the strong one. Anger. Loss. Loneliness. Betrayal. And need. God, the *need* was almost overwhelming. A need to be held, to be loved, to be supported, to be understood, to be nurtured, to be accepted exactly as she was.

Somehow, some way, for some reason, Wyatt had unlocked everything inside her that made her human, that made her feel, that made her unable to hide the depth of her need for connection...all of them luxuries she couldn't afford, emotions that made her vulnerable, feelings that terrified her.

She didn't want to feel them. She didn't want to acknowledge how badly she wanted to be more than what she was. She couldn't face how badly she needed her life to be more than she had allowed it to be. She had to become numb again. *She had to.*

She reached the embankment and stumbled over the edge, her feet sliding as she lost her balance. She was vaguely aware of Wyatt calling her name, but she didn't stop. She couldn't stop. The tears were too heavy, and gravity was too strong, dragging her down the embankment in a rush of mud and sliding shale...

Her feet suddenly slipped out from under her, and she yelped as she fell backward–

Right into Wyatt.

His arms snapped around her waist, catching her against him as they slid down the embankment together, the rocks and shale tumbling down into the rising water. They landed with a splash in the water, with her trapped against his chest as they fell backward, with her landing in his lap.

The heat from his body tore through her, and the strength of his frame surrounding her, like a solid shield protecting her, nurturing her, keeping her safe. She knew she had to get up. She knew it was ridiculous to be sitting on the lap of some man she didn't know, but she couldn't make herself move. She just froze, her eyes closed, her fingers wrapped around his forearms. She was trapped by the feel of his body encircling hers, by his warmth penetrating the cold that seemed to go so deeply inside her, by the steady thud of his heart against her back.

The water lapped over their feet, a rhythmic cold undulation over her boots, and rain hammered them, but still, she couldn't move. She felt like she was cocooned in a surreal moment, an oasis in a hurricane where the wind and rain and cold couldn't touch her.

Wyatt shifted, and she felt him lean forward until his face was next to hers, his chin almost resting on her shoulder. "What happened up there?" he asked.

She closed her eyes, gripping his forearms even harder. With him behind her, she couldn't see him. It was as if his strength, the feel of his body against hers was a fantasy she could lose herself in, not a real man that she had to deal with.

"Noelle?" His voice was warm and deep, wrapping around her like a blanket enveloping her heart. "What did I do to spook you like that?"

"I'm sorry," she whispered. "I just...I'll just wait in the car."

He laughed softly, a laugh that felt like a warm caress. "Sweetheart, as heartless as I may be, there's no chance I'm going to leave you behind when you're in tears, drenched, and trapped by a river that's rising faster than I like. When I said you could stay behind earlier, I didn't realize how fast the water was rising. I'm happy to sit here until you're ready to go, but leaving you behind stopped being a possibility when I saw your face after I touched your hand. The fact that the water's rising fast seals the deal."

Noelle scrunched her eyes shut even more tightly, as if closing her eyes could somehow protect her from the kindness he was wrapping around her, that he was making her crave so badly. "I know how to swim. I'll be fine."

He laughed again, drawing a tiny smile from her, because he'd noticed and caught her attempt at humor. "Because swimming upriver in a storm-surge stream is definitely a good plan." His arms tightened around her waist. "I don't mind waiting until you're ready. I've always wanted to sit on this particular embankment during a storm, but I'm always so damn busy I never take the time, so this is all good." He stretched his legs out on either side of hers, as if he were on a tropical beach enjoying the sun. "Nothing like taking time to enjoy life, right?"

This time, she was the one who laughed, a tiny, heart-wrenching laugh that forced the tiniest crack in the emotions threatening to over-whelm her. "The rain is lovely," she agreed. "I especially like how it mixes with the mud as it runs down my neck and under my coat."

"I know. That icy chill is the stuff of fantasies. And getting my ass frozen by cold mud is a damn gift. I can't think of a better place to hang out." As he spoke, the mud gave way, and they both slid a few more feet down into the water.

Wyatt dug his heels in, stopping their descent. Noelle could feel the muscles in his thighs flexing as he braced them, and her heart did a little flip. He was pure strength, rugged, outdoorsy strength, not a man who had already given up on life. So different than what she had lived with for so long.

Noelle opened her eyes and looked at her rental car, askew in the rising water. The water was halfway up the tires, and she could see that it was still rising. "How high is the water going to get?"

"I don't know. It's a hell of a storm coming in." Wyatt's arms were tight around her waist, and he sounded relaxed, as if he could truly spend the next couple hours sitting behind her, holding her, keeping her from sliding the rest of the way into the water.

Noelle sighed. "You're really going to sit here with me until I'm ready to go, aren't you?"

"Yes, ma'am."

"Why?"

He was silent for a moment, and she felt his arm tighten around her waist again. Finally, he spoke. "You want the answer I'd give most people, or the truth?"

From the way he asked the question, she knew the truth was going to be raw and uncensored, a gritty truth that she wasn't prepared to handle. She wanted to be hard and numb again, not open the door to anything that would keep her from pulling herself together. He was a stranger. She didn't want raw and gritty from him, and she didn't know why he'd even offered it.

But as she sat there, tears still mixing with the rain on her cheeks, her heart still aching, her body cold and numb, suddenly she didn't want numb and emotionless anymore. She wanted to feel something. To be forced to feel. To be given the freedom to shiver, cry, yearn, and ache. "Truth," she whispered.

He leaned forward, his breath warm against the side of her neck. "I would sit here for hours until you're ready to get up for one reason."

She looked down at her hands still wrapped around his forearms. "What's that reason?"

"Because you make me want to."

Tears filled her eyes again, but this time, they weren't tears of grief. They were tears of... God. She didn't even know. "Why?"

He sighed. "Because life broke something inside you, and I have never needed anything in my life as much as I need to fix it."

Broken. His words settled inside her. Broken? Was she broken? She closed her eyes. "I didn't feel broken until you took my hand. I thought I was fine."

"We're all like that, until we hit that landmine that blows apart all our pretenses and shields."

Noelle stared at the muddy water bubbling past her. His words made sense. They made her feel normal, as if it was okay for her soul to be broken into so many pieces that it felt like they would never fit together again. She took a deep breath. "Thank you for saying that."

"You're welcome." He fell silent, and the only sound was the storm. The rain hammering on her car. The rush of the water. The roar of the wind. The sound of rain pelting her coat...

And the sound of his breath, steady and even, waiting.

Noelle took a deep breath, and she felt her emotions begin to settle. Her muscles began to loosen, and the tightness in her chest eased. She became aware of his body still framing hers, protective but not overpowering. She glanced at her hands, still tightly gripping his forearms. Why did she want to hold onto him so much? And why did he want to sit here with her? He answered the question, but only partially.

"When I was growing up, Bunny used to tell me that if you tell your sorrows to the rain, it will wash them out of your heart."

"Really? Did it work?"

"I can't remember. I don't think I ever did it. I considered myself too much of a badass to have sorrows, let alone talk about them." There was humor in his voice, a self-deprecating awareness that made Noelle smile.

She lifted her face to the rain, and let it wash over her cheeks. It was cold, but it was also fresh and cleansing. She closed her eyes, feeling each droplet hit her eyelashes. Sorrow and sadness seemed to well up inside her, a grief that wanted to reach out to the rain coming down. She had so much to say to the rain, that she had no words. So she just sat there, letting it wash over her face, until the shivers from the cold penetrated so deeply that she couldn't stop shaking.

Wyatt sighed. "Time to go, Noelle. It's too cold out here. I can feel you trembling."

She didn't want to get up. She didn't want to go with him. She didn't want to stop shivering, because the cold took all her attention, making it impossible to think about David, or about how good it felt to be in Wyatt's arms. But his words made her aware of how badly she was trembling, of how cold she felt deep inside, as if she had finally found the darkest place inside her and unlocked it.

She didn't know why this moment, why this man, why this rain had unlocked the shields she held around her heart, but it had. It hurt. God, it hurt. But at the same time, it felt like the weight of a thousand lifetimes was suddenly lifting from her chest, allowing her to breathe.

She suddenly realized that she wanted to breathe again, truly breathe, no matter how much it hurt to do so.

Wyatt shifted behind her, and she felt him stand up. Deprived of the warmth of his body, cold air rushed across her back, and she suddenly felt a thousand times colder. But just as quickly, he moved in front of her, standing calf deep in the river. His icy blue eyes settled on her face, and her heart seemed to stutter in her chest.

God, she'd forgotten how intense her reaction to him was.

He held out his hands to her. "Let's go."

He didn't give her a choice...and that felt good. She was too tired to make any decisions, to decide when she'd had enough, to be ready to ride with him. She'd been the one making every single decision, even the heart-wrenchingly difficult ones, for the last four years, and it felt good to have someone make one for her, just this time, just this moment. "Okay."

He cocked an eyebrow. "Do I dare take your hand again?"

She laughed, a laugh that felt rusty and good at the same time. "We can try." She set her hands in his. The moment her palms touched his, heat rushed through her, but this time, it didn't feel scary. Maybe it was because he'd sat in the mud with her. Maybe it was because she was too cold to be scared. Maybe it was because the rain had indeed washed away some of her pain. It didn't matter. She just knew that she felt better, and it was because of him.

His eyebrows went up, and then he grinned. "You're still facing me. That's a fantastic start." He gripped her hand tightly. "Let's go, sweetheart. Shelter is calling us." He started up the embankment, his grip strong and firm, his body angled to give her leverage as he used his body as her anchor to follow him up.

Noelle hesitated for only a brief moment, glancing back at her car. Somehow, she knew that once she went up that embankment with him, there was no going back. He was too real, and her reaction to him was too intense. She'd told Kate no complications, and Wyatt was all about complications...but she wanted them. She wanted them with every fiber of her rain-drenched soul.

He paused and looked back at her, his grip still tight on her hand. "Coming?"

She studied him for a long moment. His intense blue eyes. The shadows in his eyes. The warmth in his expression. He was strong and solid, but at the same time, she saw the sorrow in his eyes, and realized suddenly that he needed someone to lean on, just like she did. He'd needed to sit there on that embankment as much as she did. Wyatt was strength, but there was also something broken inside him, something that he needed her to fix.

She relaxed. That was something she knew how to handle: being strong for someone else. She could to do this. Yes, her reaction to him was strong, but she could handle it. She'd been meant to find him, and she knew then that they were meant to help each other. Team healing. Not love. Not lust. Not romance.

She'd come out here to find herself, not fall in love with a cowboy. So what if he was tempting? So what if her heart felt melty? She'd fallen in love once, and it had nearly destroyed her.

Not again.

Not even with him.

He raised his brows. "Noelle?"

She took a deep breath. Go with him, but keep a distance? Yes. She could do that. She had to do it. *She could do this.* "Yes, I'm coming. Let's go."

CHAPTER SEVEN

THEY REACHED THE top of the embankment, and Wyatt didn't let go of her hand even after they were both on solid ground. He turned to face her as she summited, watching her as she reached him. He straightened up, and she realized he was taller than she'd noticed before. She came up to the middle of his chest, and his shoulders were so wide she felt tiny in comparison.

Rightness surged through her, that same rightness as when she'd felt the strength of his quads on either side of her hips. She was startled by how good it felt not to have to be the strong one, the one trying to hold everything together. He gave off the aura of strength and power, and it felt incredible...but even as she thought it, guilt flashed through her. Guilt that she was appreciating his strength, as if it was an insult to David.

She didn't want to compare them. She didn't want David to be less in her memories, just because Wyatt was strong. She wanted to simply appreciate this moment, and not let it get tangled up in all the noise in her head.

"What's wrong?" Wyatt didn't move away, his gaze focused on hers.

"I just–" She stopped. What was she going to say? That she was in love with the fact he was strong and rugged? Because that would sound sane and reasonable, right? Not.

He cocked an eyebrow, studying her as if she was a great enigma he was getting increasingly interested in figuring out.

Heat rushed through her, and instinctively, unable to stop herself, she put her hand on his chest over his heart. He didn't move away, and after a moment, she could feel the steady thump of his heart, strong and solid. Her fingers dug into his chest, as if she could grab onto his life force and hold it in her hand. "You're just so alive," she whispered. "I forgot what that was like." She splayed her fingers, feeling the strength of his muscles where she was used to feeling paper-thin flesh barely stretched over bony ribs. "It's like nothing could ever stop you. It's... amazing." She couldn't keep the wonder out of her voice, and she couldn't make herself break contact.

It just felt so good to be touching a man who was so alive. It made her feel like there was electricity leaping off him into her body, igniting her with strength instead of draining it.

For a long moment, Wyatt didn't react, and they both stood there in the pouring rain, the heat from his body searing her cold palm. She could feel the ripple of his muscles beneath her hand, the movement of his chest as he breathed. How many times had she sat with her hand on David's chest, checking to see if he was only sleeping, or if he was finally gone?

With Wyatt, it was so different. He exuded raw strength and power, a man who seemed like he would never be bested by frailty or disease. Her hand started to tremble, maybe with cold, maybe with the sheer exhaustion of trying to hold onto everything for so long, and knowing that there was suddenly this great strength in front of her, a man who could do things like catch her when she stumbled, even down a slick, muddy embankment.

She looked up at him, and she was startled to see him watching her intently. His head was ducked slightly, as if he were using the brim of his hat to shield her from the rain and even the world. His eyes were inscrutable, and his mouth was in a tight line, but she didn't feel like he was angry. Just intense. Just...God. He was just raw, untamed male, wasn't he? Desire raced through her, a longing to feel his arms around her, to lose herself in the strength of his body, to let him take her away from the memories she couldn't escape.

His gaze dropped to her mouth, and she swallowed, her heart hammering in her chest as she felt the heat from his stare. Dear God, he wasn't going to kiss her, was he? That would be so absurd. She didn't even know him, and...she suddenly became aware of how hot her palm was. Her gaze went to his chest, to her pale hand spread across his chest, and gradual, horrifying awareness flooded her. She was *fondling* a complete stranger in the middle of nowhere...but at the same time, he didn't feel like a stranger. She felt safe with him. Secure. Protected. Like he'd touched a piece of her heart simply by being himself...which made no sense, right?

What was *wrong* with her? Embarrassment flooded her cheeks and she jerked her hand back. "I'm so sorry. I didn't mean to touch you like that. I mean, I don't even know you or—"

He touched his index finger to her lips, silencing her. He shook his head once. "It's okay." Just two simple words were all he said before he moved past her to retrieve his horse. Two simple words muttered in a deep baritone was all he'd offered her, but they rolled through her like a seductive caress that made all the tension and embarrassment disappear.

She took a deep breath, trying to gather herself even as she was unable to tear her gaze from him as he turned toward his horse, murmuring softly to the animal. She caught the name Lightning as Wyatt ran his hand gently over the velvet nose of his horse. Lightning ducked his head, pressing his face against Wyatt's chest, and he bowed his head, murmuring softly to the animal.

Her heart turned over at the moment of intimacy between man and horse, at the trust that so clearly bonded them together. The simple, beautiful connection touched her, and she had to turn her head away to fight off the tears.

God, she wanted a moment like that. A moment with Wyatt bending his head toward hers, holding her quietly, silently promising that he would always look out for her, offering her the strength he carried with him so effortlessly. Not because she was weak, because she wasn't, and she knew that. Not because she needed a man, because she knew she didn't. But because there was nothing as beautiful as that feeling of safety in the arms of someone else who would never, ever walk away if you needed them.

"Noelle?"

Wyatt's deep voice pulled her attention back to him. He was running his palm over Lightning's nose as he watched her. "Have you ridden before?" he asked, mercifully changing the subject to a neutral one, prying her attention away from her thoughts before she could do something absurd like beg him to pat her nose like he was patting his horse's.

Relieved, she nodded. "I rode English as a kid," she said. "I know how to stay on." She glanced at the horse, who had turned his shaggy head to look at her. "Never Western, though."

"Same concept," he said. "Want a leg up?"

Heat flooded her at his suggestion of giving her a boost onto the horse. She wasn't sure she trusted herself to touch him. She glanced desperately at the stirrup, but it was too high. There was no way she would be able to get her foot up there, despite bi-weekly excursions to the yoga studio for a month, two years ago. Who knew that kind of investment wouldn't pay off years later? "Yes, okay."

He grunted his acquiescence and moved beside her. "On three."

"On three." She grasped the saddle and bent her left leg at the knee. His hands closed around her lower leg, just beneath her knee. God, oh, *God*, it felt good to feel his hands on her. It was even more intense than when she'd touched him, because it had been so long since she'd *been* touched by someone else, by a man, one she was attracted to, who made her feel like a woman, soft, vulnerable, and desirable. She closed her eyes, fighting the sudden surge of emotions through her.

"Ready?" he asked.

Ready? To squeeze onto that saddle with him, when the mere touch of his hands on her leg was so overwhelming? No, she wasn't ready. She would never be ready. "Ready." Her voice was shaky, and she hoped that he attributed it to the fact that she was shivering violently from the cold.

"On three." He tightened his grip on her leg. "One. Two. Three."

On three, he boosted her up at the same time that she pushed off. He lifted her easily onto Lightning's back, and she sank down into the deep saddle. The drenched leather sent an icy chill through her jeans almost immediately, but Wyatt swung up behind her before she had time to get cold. His pelvis was up against her butt, and his chaps were cold and wet against the backs of her thighs. As he reached around her to take the reins, she felt like she was being cocooned by his strength, and dammit, it felt too good...the kind of good that she wanted to hold onto forever.

She hadn't had a moment she'd wanted to last forever in a very long time, and it felt amazing.

"Lean back against me," he said, his voice gruff.

She stiffened against her urge to do exactly that. "Um, no, I'm all set—"

"You're not all set. You're shivering. You need protection from the rain."

"Oh..." She suddenly became aware of the rain hammering at her even more fiercely than before. Her teeth were actually chattering now. Silently, refusing to be stupid, she leaned back against him.

His arm went around her belly and he pulled her back against him, cutting off all space between them. "Good?" he asked.

"Yes, great, thanks." It felt so surreal to be held in his arms, to have him taking care of her. It felt so good, too good, so overwhelming that she wanted to cry. But she didn't want to be anywhere else.

CHAPTER EIGHT

WYATT NUDGED HIS horse into a trot, grimacing when the gentle movement of his mount made Noelle rock against him, in a rhythm that was all too tempting. He shifted, trying to pull his hips back, but there was nowhere to go.

He swore, trying not to think about the fact that his arm was just beneath her breasts. Yeah, his forearm might be only millimeters from contact with them, but it was a chasm he wasn't going to cross. What the hell was he doing even thinking about them? He'd seen her tears. He'd seen the loss in her eyes when she'd marveled over the fact he was alive. So what if his entire body had gone into overdrive when she'd touched him? That was no excuse.

She needed someone to rescue her, to help her, not to grope her.

And hell, he had sworn off women the day he'd found out the truth about his ex-fiancée.

And yet, despite both facts, he couldn't stop thinking about how Noelle felt against his chest. He couldn't help but notice the faint scent of flowers that seemed to cling to her. He couldn't help but wrap his jacket more snugly around her, and pull her more tightly against him, so that he could use his body and his jacket to ease the shivers wracking her body.

He had to hold her close, but damn, he didn't have to notice it. He cleared his throat. "So, um, Noelle, what do you do for work?" The moment he asked the question, he grimaced. Work? He'd asked about work? A woman so appealing that she'd taken his breath away with one look of her eyes was in his arms, and he'd asked her about *work*?

But even as he thought it, he felt her relax slightly, as if she, too, was in need of something to take her mind off the intimacy of their position. "I'm a writer. A mystery novelist."

His eyebrows shot up. "Seriously? That's cool as shit."

She laughed softly, relaxing even more against him. "Yes, except I can't think of an idea for my next book. It's been almost a year since it was due, but my brain stopped working."

He didn't need to ask why she'd had writer's block. He could figure it out. "Kind of like how I lost the ability to ride bulls. It's something you've done your whole life, and suddenly, your ability to do it just vanishes."

She looked over her shoulder at him, surprise on her face. "You forgot how to ride bulls?"

Shit. He didn't want to be thinking about the shitstorm of his professional life right now. Grimacing, he shrugged. "Reentry issues. No biggie."

She kept looking at him, and he knew suddenly that she saw so much more than he wanted her to see. So much more than he wanted to see himself. "What happened?" she asked.

He swore again, "Nothing—" But he cut himself off as he spoke, stopped by the expression on her face. She wanted to know. She was struggling, and she needed to connect, to know she wasn't the only one. Swearing, he ground his jaw. "I took a bad crash a couple months ago. The bull was..." He thought of Jesse's visit earlier in the day and swore. "You'd like this, mystery girl. Turns out my bull was drugged, apparently to try to kill me. They suspended me because they thought I'd juiced my ride. Earlier today, they decided that since it was attempted murder, I'm not such a bad guy, and they lifted my suspension. So, I get to ride this weekend, if I can get my damn seat back—"

He stopped as she twisted all the way around, almost sideways on his horse so she could look at him. "Someone tried to *murder* you?"

"Apparently."

Interest gleamed in her eyes, a spark of light that made something tighten in his gut. "That's so cool. Who do you think it was?"

"Cool?" He stared at her. "You think it's cool?"

Heat flushed her cheeks. "Well, I mean, I don't think it's cool on a personal level, but I write mysteries. I've never met anyone in real life who has been almost murdered. What was it like? Were you scared? Is it creepy? Are you always looking over your shoulder now? What if they try again this weekend?"

There was so much excitement in her voice that Wyatt couldn't help but laugh. Suddenly, his stress about the bull riding and Jesse's visit dissipated, chased away by her excitement. "This is *my* potential murder that you find so entertaining. You realize that, don't you?" Somehow, saying it to her took away some of the weight that had been crushing him.

She nodded. "Totally. Do you know who it is? Any ideas?"

He raised his brows. "My friend Brody thinks it's my ex-fiancée, but I don't see her turning to murder."

"Oh...I bet that's weird to have to think about who might want to murder you." She eyed him. "Do you want help? I am an expert on murder, in that 'totally imaginary, far-removed-from-reality' kind of way."

A part of him was tempted to say yes, but he quickly dismissed that thought when he considered the fact that it was actual murder they were talking about. "Thanks, but I don't think getting involved with the potential murderer is exactly what Bunny had in mind when she did the house swap with you. Jesse Knight is an investigator who works for the tour, and he's working on it. If anyone can figure out who it is, it's him."

Even as he spoke, he saw the excitement in Noelle's eyes fade, and he felt her energy sag. Before he could even think about it, he added, "but I'm happy to fill you in, in case you think of something that we don't."

When her face lit up again, he knew why he'd said it. The look on her face was the only reward he needed. He had no idea why he felt so compelled to reach out and try to help this woman, but he did. He had learned long ago not to question his instincts. With Octavia, he had ignored his reservations, and he'd paid the price. With Noelle, there were no reservations. Every instinct was honed in on his need to protect her, to help her, and to wipe away the shadows still clinging to her, so that's what he was doing. At this point, he was too damn bitter and cynical to do anything except follow his gut, and his gut was telling him to take care of Noelle, end of story.

If letting her brainstorm who might've drugged that bull ignited that spirit that she had come here to find, then he was okay with that. He was going to make damn sure she stayed out of danger, but what harm could a little brainstorming cause?

She grinned at him, and he could almost feel her mind cranking into gear, as if years of dust and rust were being shed. "Tell me why you think your ex-fiancée might have tried to kill you. I mean, there are bad breakups and all, but murder seems a little extreme."

Wyatt glanced past her, checking how far they still had to ride. They were nearing the ranch, but they still had a few minutes. He was going to take them straight to the barn, because taking care of his horse was his number one priority, as it would be with any half-decent cowboy. He took a deep breath, gritting his teeth as he thought back to that moment a year ago, when his life had changed, when he had finally stopped believing in anything good.

He shifted his position in the saddle, and Noelle nestled more securely against him. Her body was relaxed, and moving in sync with him, and he liked it. It felt right. He sighed, focusing on the feel of her body against his as he began to speak. "I met Octavia a few years ago. She was working for the tour in the public relations department, so she was at all the events. She seemed cool, not obsessed with the bull riders, like a lot of the women are."

He heard Noelle chuckle. "You guys are considered hotties out there, huh?"

He laughed softly. "Yeah, I guess." There'd been a time when that had felt good, to be treated like he mattered. "My dad was a piece of shit, and he got kicked off the tour for cheating. It took a while to get anyone to see me as anyone but the son of a cheater. Octavia was on my side, and she did a piece on me that changed everything for me. She made me look good, and stood by me, saying I wasn't my old man."

He remembered the day that article had come out. It had blown his mind to see those kinds of words written about him, after all the shit he'd lived with his whole life. "My dad thought I was shit, and I spent my life trying to become good enough to impress him. Bull riding was all he knew, so that was how I planned to do it. I was young and stupid then, thinking that my dad's approval actually mattered, so when Octavia published that article, it paved the way for people on the tour to give me a chance. It felt damn good, really damn good...too good. It made me feel indebted to her, in a way that I should have been too smart to succumb to."

Noelle relaxed against Wyatt as she listened to him. She could hear the edge to his voice, showing her the complexity of his relationship with his father. She felt a slight tinge of jealousy as he spoke about Octavia being the first to believe in him, a surprising emotion, given that she'd just met him.

"No one had ever seen me the way Octavia presented me in her article. Because of her, I became the rising star of the tour, a rookie who had the potential to be the best. I became pretty arrogant, convinced that I ruled the world." He ground his jaw, thinking back to that period of his life, when he was so caught up in the glam and the glory. "I became a complete ass, I got sucked up into all the glamour and glitz, just the way my dad had, so long ago. At the start of my second season, I proposed to Octavia, and she said yes. I thought I had it all. I thought that I'd figured out what mattered."

Noelle glanced over her shoulder, surprised by his comment that he'd become like his dad. "Did you cheat like he did?" Even as she asked the question, she knew the answer. There was no way the man with his arms around her had a dishonest bone in his body. Her soul knew it, without question.

"No, but it was close." His body tensed, and Noelle knew that he was about to get to the nitty-gritty, to the ugly part. "I made the finals of the tour that year. I was the front-runner to win the championship. On the night before the last day of the finals, I was tied for first with two rounds to ride the next night. I was feeling good, and I knew I had a chance to win. Octavia..." He paused, and she felt his arms tighten around her waist. "Octavia came to my hotel room that night. She said she had a chance for us to earn a shit ton of money. She said the odds were in my favor to win, but if I got bucked off the bull, we could both earn two hundred grand."

Noelle stiffened, startled. "She wanted you to throw the finals? After all you had worked to accomplish?"

Wyatt felt the hardness settle in his gut, just like it had that moment when he stared at Octavia, realization dawning. "Yeah, she did. Turns out, she was also shacking up with the bull rider who was tied for first. He wanted to win, and he agreed to split his winnings if I pulled my ride. He got a couple bookies to chip in, and it was set up to be a big payout. Apparently..." The bile churned in his throat, that same sick feeling of betrayal. "Apparently, she made the same offer to the rider in second, who she was also sleeping with. Both of us get bucked off, and her number one wins. She was planning to take out half a million between all the deals. Half a damned million."

Noelle felt sick to her stomach at his words. How could anyone betray someone like that, someone they loved, someone who loved them? "I'm so sorry, Wyatt. What did you do?"

"I turned her in. She lost her job. The other two bull riders denied knowing anything about her plan, so they were cleared. People accused me of making up shit to try to get them kicked off. It got ugly, and we all got bucked off in the final round, and someone else won. Octavia got another job on the tour, but she hates me now, as do the other two bull riders involved, both of whom said I initiated it. Nothing was proven, so we were all cleared, but it got us labeled."

Noelle bit her lip, feeling the tension in Wyatt's body as he spoke. "She betrayed you," she said softly. "She said she loved you, and then betrayed you. That's the worst kind of betrayal."

"Yeah." Wyatt took a deep breath, feeling the way Noelle settled more deeply against him. She didn't pull away, she didn't judge him for being so stupid. She just wrapped her hand around his wrist, an unspoken gesture of support. Something inside him tightened, something deeper than he'd felt in a long time. "Octavia turned on me, not the others. She told everyone it was my idea, and that I'd turned her in after I chickened out. She had no proof, but the seed was planted, especially given my dad. So, yeah, since then, there's an invisible asterisk next to every single ride I take."

And now, thanks to that cursed ride two months ago, there would never be any doubt in anyone's mind that he was a cheater. "Even though I was cleared of that bull ride a couple months ago, the damage is done. Everything I do will be dirty." And he hated that, hated that more than anything. "That's why I'm riding this weekend. I'm not going to walk away and let those bastards take riding away from me." He heard the anger in his voice, and he hated it. He hated that he was pissed, that he let them get to him, but he couldn't stop it.

Noelle was silent for a moment, and the only sound was the hammering of the rain, and the sound of his horse's feet sloshing through the muddy puddles. Then she spoke. "Did your dad really cheat?"

"Yeah. I asked him just before he died. He did." He'd finally posed that question a year ago, when he'd been set up by Octavia. He'd finally realized that maybe his dad's claims of innocence all those years had been true. He'd realized that maybe he'd judged his dad too harshly. He'd had hope for a split second that his dad was worth all the effort he'd put into winning his approval. "He cheated for years before they caught him." He waited for the question again, for her to ask again whether he'd cheated.

But she didn't. She was quiet, and his tension began to rise, wondering what she was thinking. He'd learned long ago not to be held back by what anyone thought of him, to tell people to fuck off if they judged him, but as he sat there with Noelle in his arms, he became increasingly tense, waiting for her response. He realized that he needed her to believe his innocence. No one except Bunny and Brody fully believed his innocence, and suddenly, he needed Noelle to. He didn't know why, but he did.

With every bit of his broken, trampled soul.

CHAPTER NINE

FINALLY, SHE SPOKE. "Getting you kicked off the tour for cheating sounds like something that Octavia, or those other two cowboys would do. Why are you so sure it wasn't them?"

Her question shocked him, making him realize that she hadn't even bothered to wonder about his innocence. She'd accepted it automatically, and had already moved on to figuring out who might have done it. *She believed his innocence.* Sudden emotion rushed through him, a surging turmoil of feelings, and a tightness in his chest. "Because Jesse was convinced it was attempted murder. Murder is different than cheating. Octavia and the others want money, not blood on their hands. They wouldn't do it."

Noelle heard the conviction in his voice, and her heart ached for him. He wanted to believe in Octavia, in the men who were his peers. Despite all the betrayal, both by Octavia and the tour, Wyatt needed to prove to himself he hadn't been completely wrong in believing in them at one time.

She wanted him to be right, but at the same time, she'd written too many mysteries not to know that the most devastating betrayal possible was by those you loved, those you believed in the most. Yeah, in fiction that was the best kind of bad guy to write, but in real life, it happened as well, much too often.

"You believe me, don't you?" His question was quiet, almost a whisper, a question he didn't really want to ask, that he was half hoping she didn't hear.

She heard. Not only did she hear the question he posed, but she also heard the yearning in his soul, the one that needed someone to believe in him. So, she twisted around in the saddle and looked at him, at his icy blue eyes, at the shadows on his face. She saw the man who lived with honor, who had fought for everything against the shadows that weren't his. Her heart turned over, and she set her hands on either side of his face. "I have absolutely no doubt that you are a man of integrity and honor. I don't believe for even a second that you cheated. We'll figure out what happened, and we will clear your name. For good."

He searched her face. "It's impossible to clear my name for good," he said. "It's too tainted. But I'm not walking away. People think I shouldn't ride this weekend, that I shouldn't be back. Screw that. I'm back." But his voice was tense, too tense, and she knew what he was thinking.

"But you can't get your groove, right? Like I can't find my muse?"

He sighed. "Yeah. I need to win the next three events to have a shot at winning the title."

"Which will shut them all up, right?"

He laughed. "Yeah, well, something like that."

"You can't find your rhythm, and I can't find my muse, and we both desperately need to." She settled back against him, sounding thoughtful. "Maybe we were meant to find each other and help each other pull our talents out of the swamp they've sunk into."

Wyatt rested his chin on her shoulder, thinking about that as they neared the ranch. "So, solving my attempted murder might help us both. You can turn my life into a best-selling novel, and I can be freed from the burden and focus on riding, not the bullshit."

"Maybe." She ran her hands over his wrists, feeling lighter than she had in a long time. "I'm not going to lie. In a weird, kind of macabre sort of way, I think the idea of solving your almost murder sounds like fun. But I'm an author, so I'm totally weird and insane like that."

He laughed. "Yeah, well, I'm a bull rider, so I'm off the charts mentally anyway. You have to be to ride." He held out his hand to her. "Let's make a deal. Let's channel our insanity, find the scumbag who tried to get me killed, and then go kick some ass in our professional careers. Deal?"

She set her hand in his, feeling happier than she had in a long time. "I can't believe you aren't horrified by how much fun I think this sounds."

"I can't believe you aren't horrified by the fact you're riding a horse with a guy who has a murderer hunting him, who plans to go against all common sense and ride bulls for the next month just so he can get a shot at a title no one wants him to have."

She smiled as they touched hands. "I was kind of horrified that you were willing to risk death when I first met you—"

"You mean, about an hour ago?"

She laughed. "Yes, about then. I was kind of horrified because I spent three years watching my husband die a horrible death, but I see now that it's your fire and your willingness not to care about death that makes you live." She ran her hand over his wrist, noting how freaking strong it was. He was strong because he wasn't afraid to die, to fail, to crash and burn. "To really live, you have to let the fire inside you burn, don't you?"

She felt his nod against her shoulder, as he flipped her hand over and enfolded it in his. "Yeah, you do. If you kill the fire that makes you who you are, you're dead already. Even if the rest of the entire damn world thinks you should shut it down, you still gotta go forward."

Her heart tightened at his words, and she suddenly realized that that was exactly what she had done for so long. She'd been afraid to live, afraid to be happy, afraid to dance in her life, afraid that to do so would insult David, what he'd gone through, what he'd suffered. How could she be happy when he was gone? When he had suffered? When his brother was teetering on the edge?

God, she wanted to live with fierce passion. She wanted to not worry or obsess about how things might turn out. She wanted to unleash the fire that she'd killed off so long ago. She wanted to not be afraid to be who she was anymore. Ever.

"Barn's up ahead." He pointed past her, and she looked ahead to see two large barns in front of her. Both looked like they'd been well-used, with their faded wood and peeling paint, but they looked sturdy and solid. Functional, not flashy, and she liked them. It felt more her than spending her nights in a fancy restaurant, worrying about whether the linens had been properly pressed, or whether the food was plated with enough aplomb to make even the most discerning diner sigh with appreciation.

She didn't want fancy plates. She didn't care. She wanted fire and life and passion.

"The barn on the left, the big one, is for the bulls. Bunny has a small breeding operation, but she has two great bulls that are turning out some great stock. The barn on the right is for the horses. Can't have a ranch without horses, right?" As he spoke, he turned his head toward the destination in question. "See the house on the hill? That's Bunny's place. That's where you'll be."

Noelle looked up the hill at the white ranch house perched above the barns. It was also old and somewhat faded, but there were brightly colored flowers decorating it. It was a small ranch house, with a huge deck on the right side, looking over the property, including both barns and the two corrals up ahead. She imagined herself sitting out there with her computer, and something softened inside her. Something that felt good. Something that felt strong. Something that felt like *her.* "It's perfect," she whispered.

"Perfect?" Wyatt peered past her, frowning. He'd never considered the house as anything other than a functional building. He narrowed his eyes, trying to see what had put that reverence in Noelle's voice. "The flowers?"

"Everything." Her fingers tightened around his wrists. "I love it. I love this whole place. It's amazing."

Now, that, he understood. He looked across the property as he directed his horse to the barn. He'd spent many, many hours on that property, helping out Bunny, making sure things ran correctly. The place was a nugget, a sliver of gold that just needed the right hand to make it happen. For a split second, he thought of Brody's comment that he should take over when Bunny sold it, but he quickly dismissed it.

He was a bull rider, and he needed to be free to do what he did best, not bound to a ranch that would trap him. So, he simply shrugged. "Yeah, it's a good place."

"Good? It's great." Her voice faded as they neared the barn. "Where do you stay?"

Wyatt nodded to the northwest. "Bunk house behind the bull barn."

She looked over at it, and he followed her glance to the small, two room building. It was small, simple, spartan. Took care of his needs just fine. But as he looked at it, he had a sudden vision of Noelle walking in there, of the way that she would light up that place, making the old building start to breathe in a way it hadn't breathed in a very long time.

Shit. He wanted her, didn't he? He didn't just want her. He needed her. He needed her light. Her energy. Her lack of judgment. He needed the way she made him feel, like he was the breath that made her heart beat.

Bunny would kick his ass if he messed with her guest. Swearing, he directed Lightning into the barn, tightening his arm around Noelle's waist as they rode straight in. He needed to get off that horse, get Noelle up to the house, and disentangle himself from the spell she was casting on him.

He reined his mount to a halt, then swung his leg back to dismount, wanting nothing more than to get away from the temptation that Noelle posed...because a deeper part of him didn't want to move away from her for even a second.

His boots thudded on the wood floor, and he instinctively reached up to help her down. He caught her around the waist as she slid off, steadying her as she lost her balance. Her hips were warm and curvy beneath his palms, and temptation coursed through him.

Swearing, he dropped his hands and stepped back just as she turned to face him. Her cheeks were glistening with rain, her hair plastered to her head, her face pale from the cold. But it was her eyes, always her eyes, that caught his attention. He swore, and moved a step toward her, just enough to trace his fingers along her jaw. "Your eyes are incredible. So much sadness, so much strength, so much courage. So much...realness."

She looked up at him, not moving away from him. "I've felt numb for so long," she whispered, "but in such a short time, you've made my heart start to beat again. I feel like I'm coming to life again, or maybe for the first time ever." She put her hand on his, holding his fingers to her face. "Thank you for that, Wyatt."

He laughed softly. "Sweetheart, you're restoring my faith in humanity. I'm the one who owes you." His smile faded as his gaze settled on her face. The air between them seemed to thicken, and suddenly he knew that despite his best intentions, he was going to kiss her.

Right then.

Right there.

Regardless of whether it was the proper thing to do.

He was going to kiss her, because he was pretty damn certain that if he didn't, his heart would never beat right again.

CHAPTER TEN

WYATT WAS GOING to kiss her.

Noelle's heart started to hammer when she saw the expression on Wyatt's face, and her stomach trembled. She hadn't had a first kiss in years, and she hadn't wanted one.

Until now. Until Wyatt. Until he'd touched her cheek with his fingers, and made her feel alive again.

He waited, and she knew he was giving her a chance to stop him.

She didn't.

After a moment, understanding dawned in his eyes, a realization that she wasn't going to make him stop. A small smile of satisfaction curved the corners of his insanely sexy mouth, and his fingers tightened on her jaw. "My breath of sunshine," he whispered, as he bent his head and leaned toward her.

Noelle's heart leapt the moment she felt his lips touch hers. His kiss was a tender, sweet, decadent caress that flooded her with emotions. Need. Longing. Desire. And a sense of being treasured, as if she were the most precious soul he could ever hold in his arms. He was strong and rugged, a powerhouse that didn't need anything from her...and yet he still wanted her. His fingers stroked along her jaw as he kissed her, his lips evoking swirls of pleasure as she surrendered to him.

With a low groan, he slid his free arm around her waist, drawing her against him. Her belly pressed against his belt buckle, the heat from his body pouring into her. His hold on her was solid and strong, a wall of support that made her feel safe, not threatened, despite his strength.

He angled his head, deepening the kiss, asking for more. With a low sigh of pleasure, she couldn't contain, she kissed him back, allowing herself to melt into his embrace.

It felt so amazing to be kissed by him. To be kissing him back. To feel her body against his solid, muscular frame. To have the raw fire of his being igniting her through his kiss, his touch, and his body.

"God, you taste incredible," he whispered against her lips, just before taking her mouth again, in a kiss that was more about raw need than sweet tenderness.

Heat roared through her, and she slid her arms behind his neck, drawing him closer, needing more from him, from his kiss, from the unapologetic vitality coursing through him. His hands settled on her hips, and then slid down, over her butt. Need hummed through her, a need so strong that her entire body vibrated with it. She wanted him. Needed him. Not just a kiss. She needed everything.

"Noelle." The way he said her name was pure seduction, and, not breaking the kiss, he backed her up with his body, until her back hit the wall of the barn. He pressed his body against her, deepening the kiss until she couldn't think, until she was consumed by the essence of him. Were they going to make love in the barn? Right there? Still in muddy, wet clothes?

Her fingers went to his belt, and she knew the answer was yes. *Yes. YES.*

The lights suddenly went on, a blinding light that made her flinch. Wyatt swore, lifting his head to look behind him...and then he went rigid, his hands tightening on her hips. "Son of a bitch," he muttered.

He whipped around with lightning speed, shoving Noelle behind him, shielding her with his body.

Noelle froze, her heart hammering in sudden fear. Her hands clenched in his shirt, and she leaned to her right to peer around his shoulder.

Standing in the doorway to the barn, wearing jeans, a white cowboy hat, and a leather jacket, was a woman who had a body meant for sinning, and a wardrobe meant for luxury. She was looking right at Wyatt, and from the look of pure venom on her face, Noelle knew exactly who she was. She didn't need to hear Wyatt say it.

But he did anyway. One word that made chills shudder through her. "Octavia."

~

THE MOMENT WYATT saw the expression on Octavia's face, he knew he'd made a major mistake. He'd underestimated her a thousand-fold. She was beyond pissed at him. Pissed enough to try to murder him? Shit. She looked like it...which scared the living hell out of him for one reason, and one reason only: the woman standing behind him.

His entire body went into high alert, and his left hand tightened on Noelle's hip, keeping her behind him. His right hand hung loosely beside his body, ready to fight, ready to defend, ready to protect her. Before this moment, before Noelle, he'd wanted to know one thing: who the hell had tripped his ride, and why. He would have grilled Octavia relentlessly until he had answers.

But with Noelle behind him, he could think of only one thing: defusing the situation and getting Octavia the hell away from Noelle. "What's up, Tav?" He kept his voice as neutral as possible, trying to keep the hostility out of his voice, wanting to give her nothing to play off of.

"You told Jesse Knight I tried to kill you?" Octavia's gaze kept flicking behind him, clearly trying to get a good look at Noelle. "You get me fired from my job, wreck my career, and now try to get a murder rap pinned on me?" Her voice was hard. Ice cold. Ruthless.

Wyatt swore under his breath. "Jesse asked me who hated me. I said you did. Was I wrong?" He couldn't believe he'd fallen for Tav. His entire body recoiled at the sight of her now. Even her body, which pretty much every male who'd ever met her coveted, made his gut turn over. Noelle was so much more beautiful, with her deeply emotional eyes, the beauty of her heart, the way her body filled out her jeans, and her complete honesty about who she was.

Noelle. She was the one he wanted. And she was in danger because of him.

Fuck.

Emotion flashed in Octavia's eyes. "No. You weren't wrong. I do hate you. I trusted you, and you turned me in."

He blinked. "*You* trusted *me?* You tried to get me to give up the championship so your boyfriend could win, and you could take home cash." Just saying the words made that same, deep sense of betrayal settle in his gut. It was more than that she'd been sleeping around on him. It was that he thought she believed he was a good guy, and in truth, she'd seen him as nothing more than the son of a famous cheater, just like every other bastard who'd refused to believe in him.

Noelle put her hand on his lower back, jerking his attention from the moment and back to her. Heat poured through him, a crazy, intense kind of warmth that enveloped him, somehow penetrating the icy coldness that gripped him so tightly. Suddenly, Tav's betrayal didn't hold so much strength, because he knew Noelle believed in him.

This woman he barely knew somehow was willing to see the truth in him that no one else could see. From one simple touch, Noelle had pulled him back from the edge, from the places he'd gone his whole life when someone had seen him as the cheater he'd never been, the cheater whose blood ran in his veins.

The tension inside him settled, and he looked at Octavia, suddenly feeling pity for her, instead of contempt and anger. "You chose your own path, Tav. I had nothing to do with it."

Anger flickered in her eyes. "You walked away from me, instead of helping. We could have been so much."

"No. There was nothing we could have been together." Wyatt didn't want to hear it. He didn't want to go there. Not anymore. "Walk away, Tav. Let it go."

"Let it go?" Anger flashed in her eyes. "You're the one who sent Jesse Knight to my office, asking questions that don't look so good to my bosses. They put me on leave, Wyatt. Suspended, pending investigation. For *murder.* What the hell? You really think I'm capable of murder?"

There was something in her voice, a desperation, a pain that broke through his walls. He suddenly saw the same shadows she lived under, being judged for who she was and what she had done. He knew in that second that she hadn't tried to kill him. "You didn't do it, did you?"

All the fury went out of her. "No," she whispered. "I didn't. I would never have tried to kill you, Wyatt, I swear."

He knew she was telling the truth, but there was something else in her eyes, something that made him tense. "Who did?"

Her gaze flicked away from him for a split second, but it was long enough to reveal the truth. He tensed again. "You know, don't you?" he pressed. "You know who did it?"

"I..." She glanced toward the door, and suddenly Wyatt knew they weren't alone. And from the look on Octavia's face, he knew that he was in trouble. Big trouble. Big *fucking* trouble.

But he wasn't prepared for who walked in.

CHAPTER ELEVEN

NOELLE FROZE WHEN she saw a man emerge from the shadows into the aisle of the barn. He was lean and wiry. A small man with glasses, and the kind of shifty eyes that made fear creep down her spine. There was no way he had the physique to ride a bull, but there was an ominous presence that clung to him, a raw, insidious power that hung over him like a poisoned aura. He nodded at Wyatt as he walked in. "Wyatt."

Wyatt tensed, his hand digging into Noelle's hip. "You?"

The man raised his brows. "Good evening, Wyatt."

"What the hell? You tried to murder me for this ranch? Is that what this is about?" Wyatt sounded incredulous, but from the hard expression on the man's face, Noelle had a feeling Wyatt was right that this was the one who had tried to kill him, but why? Who was this guy?

The man said nothing, and she felt Wyatt tense. He took a deep breath, and when he spoke, he sounded calm and steady, clearly trying to deescalate the situation. "I'm not planning on buying this ranch, Nathan." Wyatt's hand tightened on Noelle's hip. "You can have it."

"It doesn't matter. Bunny won't sell it to me. My own aunt won't sell me the land that should be mine by inheritance."

Awareness dawned on Noelle. This was Bunny's nephew, and he

wanted the ranch. Why on earth would anyone want a ranch so much that they would murder for it? That made no sense.

Nathan's face was dark, almost twisted with hate as he glared at Wyatt. "I spent twenty years being nice to the old bat so that I'd get what I was owed, but she won't sell it to me. She doesn't want a resort property, even though it would make us all rich. She wants to remain true to the spirit of the place. Horses. A ranch. All that bullshit."

"I am not planning on buying the ranch," Wyatt said again, his voice calm and steady. Only the tightness of his grip on Noelle's hip indicated how tense he was.

Nathan circled closer, like a predator stalking his prey, which she found so creepy that she would definitely put it in her next book, assuming she didn't die. Oh, God. Was she going to die? Who would kill over a ranch? That was absurd, right?

Nathan sneered at Wyatt. "I saw Bunny's will two months ago. If she dies, you get it. You get the whole damn place. So, I can't kill her as long as you're around."

The casual way he referenced killing his aunt made fear congeal in Noelle's stomach. Oh, God. Seriously? With all the psychos she'd written about, she had truly failed to do justice to how damn scary it was to be trapped by one.

"She never believed all the rumors about you being a cheat," Nathan continued. "I worked hard as hell, and so did Octavia, to spread those rumors. I got the whole tour labeling you as a cheat, and Bunny still worships you." Bitterness raked across his face. "You're a damned cheat, and you still get the ranch." Then, he reached behind him, grabbed something from his waistband, and raised a gun. "Unless you die before she does. Then I'm all the family she has left, and it's mine."

Wyatt went utterly still, and Noelle froze. She couldn't breathe. Her breath seemed to freeze in her lungs. There was an actual *gun* pointed at them. A *gun*. Dear God. How was this possible?

She'd spent three years with David, trying to help him deal with the fact he was dying. She'd been so certain she understood what it was like to face death, to know what it was like to understand one's mortality, but nothing in her life, or her experience with David, had prepared her for the shock to her body as she stared at that gun.

A thousand thoughts and memories flooded her...and every one was about the life she'd let slip away. About giving up on living, on loving, both herself and others, because she'd been so caught up in duty, or obligation, or all of the noise that life had hammered her with for so long.

Dear God. She was going to die, just like David. Except David had lived fully while he'd been alive. He'd opened his restaurant. He'd saved his brother. He'd married the woman he loved. What had she done? Rotted away for the last year under the weight of guilt and obligation, trying to live David's life for him...not her life. His. Which he had already done, to the best of his ability.

And now...there was a man pointing a gun at her. A man who had done his best to sabotage Wyatt's career, and tried to kill him a few months ago, and now... God, now he looked like he was ready to finish it.

Nathan wasn't bluffing. She could see the fury, the ice-cold anger in his eyes, the absolute sense of entitlement. The ranch belonged to him, and Wyatt was the one standing in his way.

Wyatt.

Suddenly, she forgot about herself. She forgot about her own mortality. Everything was obliterated by the thought of the man still shielding her with his body, the one who had just found out that the rumors that had robbed him of a career he was due had been carefully orchestrated to ruin him.

Wyatt still hadn't moved, but his fingers were digging into her hip almost painfully, the only indication that he'd heard anything Nathan had said. "Noelle," he said softly. "I think you should leave. Nathan and I have some things to talk about."

Her heart tightened. He was trying to get her to safety. He wasn't reacting to anything Nathan had said. He'd somehow managed to stay completely calm, and she knew it was for her sake. How sweet was that? He was every bit as heroic as she'd thought he was.

Nathan didn't lower the gun, but his gaze flicked to Noelle. "Who are you?"

"She's a guest at the ranch," Wyatt answered. "Bunny did a house swap with her, and she just arrived today. She has nothing to do with it. Let her walk away."

Nathan's gaze flicked to her, and she saw the hesitation in his eyes. He didn't want to kill her, a random stranger. Thank God. A murderer with morals, a line he wouldn't cross. Yay for her, right? "Is that true?" he asked her.

Before Noelle could emphatically confirm that yes, indeed, she didn't need to be killed today, Octavia interrupted. "Wyatt was kissing her. I saw them. He had her pinned against the wall and they were getting it on."

Noelle felt the blood drain from her face as Nathan's face darkened. "You fucking liar, Wyatt. Anyone who matters to you becomes fair game." He aimed the gun at Noelle. "You shacked up with the wrong guy, sweetheart. Too bad for you."

Noelle's throat suddenly felt so dry she couldn't talk. "Please let me go. Wyatt's telling the truth. I mean, yeah, he kissed me, but I don't know him." If she could just get out of there, she could call 9-1-1, and–

Wyatt's fingers tightened on her hip. "Nathan, don't make it worse for yourself. Let her go."

"No." Nathan's face darkened. "Fuck you, Wyatt. Just fuck you." He nodded at Octavia. "Get the rope from the tack room." He pointed the gun at Wyatt. "You two, into that stall. Now."

Noelle's heart pounded. Rope? Stall? Wyatt took her elbow and began to move her toward the stall. He was moving slowly, and his body was tense. She knew he was looking for an opening, but there wasn't one, not yet. The guy had a freaking gun. What kind of opening could they get against a *gun?*

As they moved across the aisle toward the stall, she saw a stack of metal cans outside the main door. Gasoline? Dear God, he was going to burn down the barn with them in it. Destroy the ranch and kill the heir at the same time. Why did murder seem so much more fun when she was writing about it in her cute, little condo, than it did when she was faced with it in real life? Honestly. This was not at all the same thing! "Wyatt–"

"I see the gasoline," he whispered.

Noelle felt like she was going to throw up as they moved toward the stall. Behind Nathan, Wyatt's horse had wandered off, nosing through the hay bales at the far end of the aisle in search of a snack. He was near the door, close enough to get out if the barn started burning. Would he leave, or would they all go down? Because it was bad enough for Wyatt and her to die, but a horse, too? That was just wrong on a whole other level.

Anger on behalf of Lightning pulsed through her, chasing away the fear. Burning to death? Really? What kind of asinine plot was that? It was melodramatic, and, quite frankly, much too brutal for her cozy mysteries, which meant it was much too brutal for *real life*. For God's sake, this needed to end now. "Nathan," she said, impressed with how she managed to keep her voice from trembling. "You haven't done anything bad yet. If you walk away, you're still free. It's not worth it over a ranch, and you'll get caught. They always do." Well, not always, but he would be a pretty obvious suspect once the fire marshal figured out it was arson.

Nathan's face was impassive as he watched them. "Shut up, bitch. I don't give a shit what you have to say. You lost the right to have me care when you kissed this cheat."

Okay, that was *it*. She was officially pissed now. "He's not a cheat!" She snapped the words before she could stop herself. "You can spread all the rumors you want, but the reason your aunt believes in Wyatt is because she can see the truth. He's a good man, and killing him will never change that!"

Wyatt swore under his breath when he heard Noelle defend him. Fear ripped through him, a raw terror for her safety. He caught her arm and pulled her behind him. "Don't defend me," he muttered under his breath. "I don't need it."

She glared at him. "Yes, you do. You haven't defended yourself your whole life, have you? You just ride silently, hoping that if you win, people will forget about the rumors. Why don't you just tell them?"

"Because they won't believe me, and I'm not wasting my breath." They were near the doorway to the stall now, and Wyatt could see Octavia coming back down the aisle toward them, several ropes in her hand. Hell. If Nathan got them in the stall, there would be no way out.

He had no doubt that Nathan meant to kill them both. Wyatt had an idea, a sliver of an opportunity that might give Noelle time to get away. He knew it wouldn't be enough to save them both, but it would get Noelle out of there.

Noelle. His gut tightened. She'd mouthed off to a psychopath with a gun to defend him. What was she thinking? She shouldn't have done it, but at the same time, it felt so damn good, good in a way he could barely register, to have her defending him openly, and without fear of reprisal. Just because she believed in him and wouldn't sit back silently when she could right a wrong.

What the hell? He didn't even understand that. There was a gun pointing at her and a problem that wasn't hers, yet she'd made it hers by standing up for him.

And for that, he would do whatever it took to make her safe.

He caught her arms. "Resist me," he whispered under his breath. "Resist going in the stall."

She looked at him sharply, then stopped in place. "I'm not going in there," she announced. "There's no way that I'm going to roll over so that some jerk can kill me easily."

He almost chuckled at the stubbornness on her face. He could feel her trembling, but no one would guess it from looking at her. "Don't make it difficult," he said, loud enough for Nathan to hear. "We can still talk him out of it." He wrapped his arm around her waist, as if he were trying to force her into the stall. The action brought her up against him, close enough for him to whisper under his breath into her ear. "When I say go, run for the doors and don't look back," he muttered, as he continued to make a show of trying to push her into the stall. With her resisting back, it wasn't hard to make a scene.

Her body was warm and soft against his, vulnerable and real, making fear congeal in his gut. He'd never been scared of death in his life, but he was absolutely scared shitless right now at the thought she could get hurt. "My truck is parked in back," he said softly, "and the keys are in the ignition. Drive like hell south and you'll reach a general store. Call the cops from there, and don't come back. Got it?"

"Let me go," she snapped, pushing at him. He wasn't sure if the resistance was for Nathan's benefit, or if she didn't like his plan.

Too bad if she didn't like it. He was getting her the hell out of there. "Got it?" he asked quietly, locking his arms around her waist, a move that brought her tightly against him.

She looked at him. "You come with me," she whispered.

"Won't work that way," he said. "Got it?"

She searched his face.

"We will both die," he snapped, barely able to keep his voice quiet, the fear for her safety was so great. He knew Nathan would believe the false struggle for only so long. "Get the hell out. Got it?"

She looked at him for a long moment, and finally nodded. Relief rushed through him, and for a moment, he paused, sliding his fingers along her jaw. Her skin was so soft, so beautiful, so flawless. "You're the sunshine that I've never seen in my life, until now," he whispered. "Never stop pouring your light into the world. Promise?"

Tears filled her eyes, but she nodded. "Don't die," she whispered. "He doesn't deserve it."

"I know, babe. I know. But sometimes that's the way life is." Unable to stop himself, he bent his head and kissed her. A slow, short kiss that said all the words he didn't know how to say. A thank you for showing him the things he'd never been able to see before this moment. He pulled back, searching her face. He saw confusion and warmth, a kindness that made his heart turn over. He was vaguely aware of Octavia's snort of disgust, and Nathan's command to hurry up, but he didn't care.

All that mattered was Noelle.

He pulled back, and for one endless, agonizingly short moment, he simply stared at her. He saw in her eyes the future that he'd never hoped for, the hope he'd never dared have. On her face, he saw something similar, a warmth directed right at him that seemed to sink deep into his heart...and suddenly, he didn't want to die either.

He wanted a chance with this woman. A chance to see what could happen.

But it wasn't a risk he would take if it meant endangering her.

There would be time only to save her. Not both of them. He had to make the choice. "I wish I had more time with you," he said softly.

Tears filled her eyes. "Not again," she whispered. "God, not again."

He knew she was referring to the man she'd loved and lost, and his heart turned over. Somehow, in the short time they'd been together, she'd put Wyatt in the same place in her heart. Son of a bitch. If he died, it would hurt her.

Screw that.

She didn't get hurt twice.

For her sake, he'd have to live. Resolution flooded him, and he turned toward Nathan and Octavia, his mind rapidly assessing his options. Octavia was furious, but his gut told him she wouldn't kill him. He had to bank on that. Was it worth the risk of being wrong, if it gave him a chance to save his own life?

He felt the way Noelle's fingers were digging into his back, and he knew the answer was yes. For Noelle, he'd do whatever it took to try to stay alive.

CHAPTER TWELVE

IF WYATT WAS GOING to stay alive, he was going to have to come up with another plan. Swearing, he looked past Nathan and Octavia to his horse, who was munching on the hay by the door.

"A few more feet," he said to Noelle, moving her further toward the stall door, changing the angle slightly. Could he really pull off saving both of them? He wasn't sure, but he had to try.

She let him move her, and he whistled softly under his breath. Lightning's head snapped up and he turned to look at Wyatt, his ears perked. His tail stopped swishing, and his attention focused fully on Wyatt, waiting for the next command.

One chance. They would have one chance. Wyatt moved a few more inches to the left, trying to get in the best spot. Octavia's eyes narrowed, and she looked over her shoulder. He swore, aware that Octavia knew how he trained his horses.

It was now...or never. He whistled sharply, two quick blasts, and Lightning exploded into motion, launching into a full gallop, straight at Wyatt. Nathan whirled around, and Wyatt shoved Noelle toward the door. "Go!"

She took off in a sprint, and Wyatt launched himself at Nathan. Lightning plowed into Nathan, knocking him off balance just as Wyatt reached him. Wyatt tackled the other man, reaching for his gun as Lightning thundered past.

There was a deafening blast, and Wyatt gasped as pain shot through his hip. Jesus. He'd been shot?

"Wyatt?" Noelle's horrified gasp ripped through him.

She was still there. Shit. He had to give her time to get away.

Adrenaline rushed through his body, and Wyatt rolled to his side as Nathan started to scramble to his feet. Wyatt tackled him and shoved him to the side, slamming him into the side of the stall. Nathan's head hit first, and he went limp, collapsing on the ground. Wyatt sank beside him, his hand on his hip, gasping for breath.

"Get off him."

He turned his head and saw Octavia pointing the gun at him. Her hands were shaking, and her face was ashen. *Hell.* "Put the gun down, Tav," Wyatt said, keeping his voice steady. "You haven't done anything yet. Let him take the heat."

She shook her head. "Get in the stall, Wyatt."

Wyatt felt Nathan move slightly, and realized the other man was starting to regain consciousness. Swearing, he grabbed Nathan under the arms and staggered to his feet. "I'm putting him in the stall, Tav. You'll have to shoot me to stop me." He intentionally used her nickname, trying to create a bond.

She raised the gun, aiming it at his chest. "I won't let the man I love go to prison. Put him down, Wyatt. Put him down."

Nathan groaned, and Wyatt knew they were almost out of time. Shit—

Movement behind Octavia suddenly caught his eye. He had a split second to see Noelle reach for a small fire extinguisher hanging by the door, before he jerked his gaze off her. Shit. What was she doing?

He couldn't let Octavia turn around and see Noelle. Swearing under his breath, he began dragging Nathan toward the stall again. "You're better than this, Tav. You're brilliantly talented at journalism, and you don't need to be stuck in this life, trying to steal to get money. You can do more. Don't let him drag you down."

"I mean it, Wyatt! Put him down!" She pulled the trigger, and Wyatt jumped as the wood behind his left shoulder splintered.

Hell. She *was* willing to shoot him. Clearly, he wasn't as charming as he'd thought he was. He was going to have to work on that next time he was at the wrong end of a gun.

He saw movement behind her, but he didn't dare draw her attention to Noelle, so he kept his gaze on Octavia. Why the hell wasn't Noelle leaving?

Nathan twisted out of his grip suddenly, and Wyatt swore, knowing that it was over—

Fire extinguisher foam suddenly blasted Octavia in the back. She shrieked and turned around, and got it full in the face. Wyatt slammed his fist into Nathan's face, and hurled him into the stall. He slammed the latch shut, then leapt at Octavia as she stumbled, covering her face with her hands.

He snatched the gun from her hand and turned it on her. "Get down, Octavia."

She immediately dropped to her knees, coughing and gagging. Noelle was behind her in a split second, binding her wrists with the same rope that Octavia had been planning to use on them. Noelle grinned up at him, then looked behind him. Her face went stark in warning. "Nathan's coming—"

Wyatt grabbed the abandoned fire extinguisher and spun around just as Nathan opened the stall door. He hurled the extinguisher at him, catching him square in the chest, knocking him down. This time, Wyatt didn't give him a second chance to get up. He sprinted over with the rest of the rope, and tied him down.

It took only seconds to immobilize him, then Wyatt stepped back, leaving him trussed up like a calf in a roping event. He looked over at Noelle, and then grinned when he saw her standing over Octavia, looking incredibly pleased with herself. "You did great, Noelle."

She beamed at him. "Thanks. I really couldn't bring myself to brain her with the fire extinguisher, but my last book had a particularly soft-hearted villain, so I just did what she did and sprayed instead. It worked just like my research said it would. It was fun." Her smile faded as her gaze settled on his hip. "You're shot?"

The moment she said it, the pain came rushing back. Dizziness slammed into him, and Wyatt sank to his knees, pressing his hand to his hip. Noelle gasped and ran over, catching him as he started to slide to the ground. "I don't have cell service. Where's a phone?"

He bent over, bracing his hands on the floor as he fought for breath. His hip felt warm, and he could feel the blood seeping over his jeans. He'd had many significant injuries over the years, but never had he experienced anything like this. He gritted his jaw, fighting to shut off the pain. Son of a bitch. He'd ignored pain before, but he couldn't believe he'd been able to ignore the gunshot for so long.

Except he could believe it. Noelle's life had depended on him, and a lifetime of ignoring pain had enabled him to save her, to save them. But now that the danger was over...*shit*.

"Wyatt! Where's the phone?"

He gritted his teeth, pressing his hand to the wound. "By the barn doors. I didn't bring mine. Too wet outside." He bowed his head, sinking to the floor as he heard Noelle talking to the operator. His vision began to blur and he swore. Too much blood loss. He had to stop it. Had to find a way. He tried to crawl over to the tack box by the stall, but his legs weren't working–

Noelle was suddenly by his side again, her hands on his shoulders. "Wyatt–"

"Get wraps from the tack box." He gave up trying to crawl and went down on his side. "White cotton. Need to stop the bleeding."

Noelle felt like her heart was going to stop when Wyatt collapsed on the ground. The blood stain was spreading across his stomach with a speed that was terrifying. How had he kept going when he was shot? The strength of his will was astonishing. Incredible. And not surprising.

She'd known he was strong from the moment she'd met him, but now she knew how strong he truly was, both physically and emotionally. He was the rock her soul had been searching for...and now she might lose him.

Fighting off tears, she raced over to a nearby trunk and opened it. Inside were an assortment of what looked like cloth diapers, which she knew were wraps for the horse's legs. She grabbed several and ran back to Wyatt, going down on her knees beside him.

Grimacing, she pressed one of the wraps against his hip, flinching when he let loose a string of profanities. "I thought cowboys were tough," she managed, her hands shaking violently. "And thoughtful. I mean, I just got through almost being murdered, and I need to collapse in emotional anguish now that it's over, and you're not giving me a chance to do that."

He closed his eyes, his face ashen. "I'm a cheating ass," he muttered. "Never said I was a good guy."

His words made her heart ache. "You're not a cheater," she whispered. "Stop labeling yourself. It's over, Wyatt. Don't you realize it's over?"

His eyes flickered open, and she saw that his ice blue eyes were darker now, richer, more complex. "It's not over, babe. It'll never be over."

Her heart sank, and she bent over him, bringing her face close to his. "It's over only if you let it be over. You have to let the past go." As she said it, she thought of David, of Joel, of the restaurant, and she knew she was speaking the truth. Just as Wyatt had to let go of the legacy his father had left him, so did she need to let go of the burden she'd taken on after David's death. "I want to live, Wyatt. I want to truly live. Don't you? Not be trapped by a past full of shadows."

Wyatt searched her face, her beautiful face full of pain and loss and courage...and hope. He saw hope in her eyes, a flash of light that made his own heart start to beat again, a heart that had stopped beating so long ago, long before he'd been shot. He reached up, brushing his finger over her cheeks. "All this time, I thought that winning the championship would make me able to breathe again. I was wrong. It was you."

She smiled. "And a gunshot wound."

He shook his head. "No, it was worrying that you were going to get hurt. It was seeing you defend me against Nathan, despite the gun. You're brave, you don't give a shit what people think, and you made me care if I lived for the first time in my life, because I wanted to stay alive for you." Shit. He couldn't believe he'd just said that aloud.

But when her face softened, he was glad he had. "I'm so glad you did, Wyatt."

His eyelids started to feel too heavy to stay open, and his head fell back on the hard floor. "Noelle?"

"Stay with me, Wyatt. The medics will be here soon."

He knew he was going to lose consciousness any second. He didn't know if he was going to come back. He knew he hadn't known her long enough to feel what he was feeling, to say what he wanted to say, but he was going to say it anyway, because he knew in his gut he was right. He'd lived long enough to see truth when he saw it, and he wasn't going to hide from it. "You saved me, Noelle. Not just my life, but my heart. For that, I will always love you." The words felt right as he said them. She'd broken through the walls in his heart the moment he'd seen her trying to claw her way up that muddy embankment, laughing in amusement. When she'd believed in him when no one else had, she'd won his loyalty forever. And when she'd let him see the real her, her tears, her courage, and her grief, he'd fallen in love with her, completely and irrevocably.

He felt the touch of her lips against his, a feather-light sensuality that went straight into his heart. "You saved me right back, Wyatt, and for that, I will always love you."

He smiled, her words wrapping around his heart. "Just so you know," he muttered, fighting against the lethargy trying to take him, "I'm going to pursue you like a coyote after a rabbit as soon as I can stand up again, so if that doesn't sound good to you, then you better hightail it back east before I get out of the hospital."

He'd give her one last chance, one last opportunity to claim a life without him. One last chance to walk away from the man everyone else thought was a cheater.

But she laughed softly and pressed a kiss to his cheek. "I bet you'd look good running across the Oregon plains in hot pursuit. I think I'll stay around and see if I'm right."

He smiled, his body relaxing at her words. She'd be there when he woke up, and then...yeah...then it was going to get good.

CHAPTER THIRTEEN

Number one.

Number one.

Noelle hung up the phone, unable to stop the tears from streaming down her face. *Number one.* God, how her life had changed–

Footsteps sounded on the front porch, but before she could wipe away the tears, the front door opened. In walked Wyatt, with a new saddle slung over his shoulder. His limp from being shot fourteen months ago was finally gone, and he was as lean and fit as he'd ever been. Behind him was Brody Hart, who was carrying what looked like a large, white cake box.

The minute Wyatt saw her face, he dropped the saddle and strode right over to her. "What's wrong, sweetheart? What happened?" His voice was so tender, so sweet, so concerned that she wanted to cry even harder.

She put her hands on his cheeks, his whiskers prickling her fingers. "How is it that I got so lucky to have you?"

He grinned. "It's a team win, babe." Then he wiped his thumb across her cheeks. "What's wrong? Why isn't my bride smiling the day before her wedding?"

Brody cleared his throat. "I'll just take the cake into the kitchen then, and you can check it out when you're ready." He ducked past them, giving them privacy.

Wyatt didn't even spare his best friend a glance. His entire being was focused on Noelle, making her feel as treasured as he had every day for the last fourteen months. She smiled through her tears. "My agent just called. My new mystery...it hit the New York Times list at number one." *Number one.*

His face lit up, and he let out a loud whoop. "Hot damn, girl! I knew you could do it." He grabbed her around the waist and swung her in a circle, making her burst into laughter as she hung on to keep from flying across the room.

Noelle locked her arms around his neck, beaming up at him. His face was happy and light, a perfect reflection of the joy dancing in her own heart. She loved this man so much, and he poured his love into every moment of life.

Wyatt angled his hat back, then bent his head and kissed her, a beautiful, amazing kiss that made her heart melt every bit as much as it had the very first time he'd kissed her in the barn on that rainy night so long ago.

Noelle clung to him, pouring her love into the kiss, needing to connect with him, to open her heart to this wonderful man who had changed her life. Wyatt's arms locked around her waist, and she melted into his strong body, loving the feel of his muscled strength encasing her in a shield of his love and protectiveness.

After a long moment, and a kiss that consumed her entire being, he pulled back a tiny bit, just enough for her to see his face. "I'm so proud of you, Noelle," he said. "I knew that book was genius when I read it, and I knew the world would see its brilliance."

She sighed and rested her wrists on his shoulders, her hands still clasped behind his neck. "And I knew that you would win that championship. It was so amazing to see you win after all you'd been through."

It had been a difficult off-season, with his recovery from being shot, but Noelle had used that time to make sure the entire bull riding tour understood what Nathan had done to his reputation. By the time Wyatt stepped back into the chute on the first competition of the season, he'd had fans screaming his name, and cowboys vying for a chance to have his back.

And now, he held the title he had coveted for so long, despite all that had happened.

He grinned, a shit-eating grin that never seemed to leave his face. She knew that her cowboy would always have a little bit of rebel in him, a little bit of needing to bask in his awesomeness, and she was just fine with that. A tender-hearted cowboy with a heart of gold and just enough arrogance to accomplish anything he wanted sounded perfect for her.

"Yeah, I got my win," he agreed, "but now it's time to turn this ranch into the brilliant operation that Bunny never had time to turn it into. Speaking of Bunny, has she arrived yet? I know she's dying to meet the woman who finally tamed me."

"Tamed you?" Noelle grinned. "You will never be tamed, Wyatt, and I'd never change that. I love the rebel in you, and the rancher, and the lover, and the man who makes me feel like the most treasured woman in the entire world."

His smile faded and he slid his hand through her hair. "You are, you know. I would trade my life for yours any second of any day."

"I know." She wrinkled her nose. "You almost did once. Let's not do it again, okay?"

His face softened with love. "Deal." He pulled her against him and kissed her again, this time a decadent, sensual kiss that made her think of tousled sheets, moonlight, and secrets shared between lovers. Kate would be arriving in a couple hours with Joel, who had turned the restaurant into a five-star destination in Boston. Bunny would be there momentarily. Brody was waiting in the kitchen, and his entire family was going to be attending as well.

She'd found her home, her man, and her heart...and he had done the same. She smiled up at him. "I love you, Wyatt Parker, and I will love you forever."

He smiled back at her, brushing a lock of hair off her face. "And I love you right back, sweetheart, and I am counting the seconds until you become my wife." He lifted her hand and pressed a kiss to each knuckle. "Forever and always, my love. Forever and always."

~

Did you enjoy Wyatt and Noelle's story? If so, please consider leaving a short review on the eTailer and/or Goodreads. Reviews make a huge difference for authors!

~

Do you want to know when Stephanie has a new book out, is running a sale, or giving away prizes? **Sign up for her private newsletter here!**

~

Keep reading for sneak peeks of other Stephanie Rowe novels!

SNEAK PEEK: A REAL COWBOY NEVER WALKS AWAY

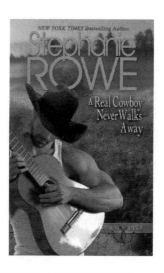

"Beautiful story full of emotion and depth,and
wonderfully written." ~Amber S. (Amazon Review)

When a single mom enlists the help of a handsome stranger during a busy lunch

at her Wyoming café, she has no idea she's just conscripted a world-famous country music star to be her busboy.

~

SHE TRIED.

She *really* tried not to be so aware of him.

But there was no way for Lissa McIntyre to ignore the man sitting at her counter.

When he'd first walked into the café, she'd been a little unnerved by the sheer size of him. He was tall, broad-shouldered, and wore his leather duster as if he were an outlaw from the Old West, owning every joint he walked into. His dark brown hat was low over his eyes, casting his face into shadows, and he moved as if every muscle in his body was primed and ready to pounce...on her.

She never dated. She was careful not to even look at a man in a way that might make him think an overture would be welcome, especially not when she was working and had a café full of cowboys. Men were trouble, dangerous, and a threat to everything that mattered to her, which was a very short list.

And yet, the moment he'd raised his head and looked at her, she'd felt herself falling into the depths of his steely blue eyes. He was pure male, loaded with testosterone. His clothes were old and worn. He was soaking wet. And...God...she couldn't lie. He was insanely, irresistibly sexy. Sensual. Tempting. Every word she would never dare apply to a man had been rushing through her mind for the last hour.

He hadn't said much, except to ask for a refill on his coffee and to thank her each time she refilled his water, but the way he spoke made chills rush down her spine. His voice was deep, almost melodic, filling her with a longing so intense that she wanted to sit down on the stool next to him, prop her chin up on her hands, and ask him to just talk for a while so she could lose herself in the magic of his voice.

Before he'd arrived, she'd been feeling sorry for herself, dreading festival week, and all the chaos and long hours it brought with it. If she didn't need the money, she would shut down for the week and take Bridgette to all the events. Instead, she'd had to pawn her daughter off on her amazing neighbor, Martha Keller, who had become the grand-mother that Bridgette would never have. Martha was the one taking Bridgette to all the events of festival week, while Lissa worked. Of course, it would be worth it when her bank account had enough money in it to make it through another slow winter, but on the first night, she always felt cranky, wondering how she'd ended up with this as her life.

But when her counter cowboy had shown up, he'd been a welcome distraction, drawing her out of her negative thinking and into the present. He made her think of a time when she'd thought life was full of opportunity and sunshine, before everything had crashed down around her. Plus, a little eye candy always made a girl's day brighter, right?

The door jangled again, and she grimaced when she saw another group of competitors from the rodeo walk in. She was already at max capacity, and the crowd was getting boisterous and impatient with the slow service. Even if Katie was here, it would have been tough to keep up, but alone? It was impossible, and she knew it. It wouldn't take much for word to get out about the *Wildflower Café* to the rest of the tourists and competitors. If tonight was a bust, no one would be coming back this week. Fear rippled through her at the thought of losing all that income. She desperately needed a profitable week. *Desperately.*

"Hey." Her counter cowboy waved at her.

She hurried over to him, grabbing her water pitcher as she went. Sweat was trickling down her spine, but she knew she had to find a way to go even faster. "What's up?"

"You got anyone in the kitchen watching those burgers while you're out here?"

She spun around. "Why? Are they burning?" She couldn't afford to burn them. Her customers had already been waiting too long. "I'll go check--"

He stopped her with a hand on her forearm.

She froze, her belly flipping over. His hand wrapped all the way around her arm easily, but his touch was gentle, so gentle that she knew he wasn't trying to trap her. She could pull away if she want-ed...but she didn't want to. "What?"

He gestured at the café. "There's no way you can handle this alone. Want help?"

"Help?" She blinked at him. "Who? You?"

"Yeah. I can cook." He still had his hand on her arm. "I'm too anti-social and bitter to socialize with the public, so I'm not waiting on tables, but I'll flip some burgers."

God, she needed help. There was no way she could manage both the customers and the cooking by herself tonight. A part of her wanted to throw herself over the counter, hug him fiercely, and then put him to work....but there was no way. "I really appreciate the offer, but I don't even know you. I can't have a stranger in my kitchen, but thanks." She started to turn away, but he tightened his grip on her arm.

Her breath caught, and she looked at him. "Yes?"

He hesitated, emotions warring on his face. For a long moment, he said nothing, and she frowned, turning back to face him. "What is it?"

He flexed his jaw, his blue eyes fixed on her face. "You're new to town, right?" he finally said. "You didn't grow up here, did you?"

She blinked at the random question. "I've been here eight years. Why?"

Again, a long moment of silence, as if he were waging some massive internal debate about whether to speak. She leaned forward, her curiosity piqued while she waited.

Finally, he met her gaze. "You know Chase Stockton?" His voice was low, as if he didn't want anyone else to hear.

"Chase?" He was all worked up about Chase? "Of course. He comes in here once a week. He supplies my pies when I don't have time to bake them. Why?" But even as she asked it, his penetrating blue eyes took on new meaning. She'd seen eyes like his before. Exactly like them...on Chase. "You're related to him, aren't you? One of his broth-ers? Aren't there like nine of you or something?"

His face became shuttered, but he didn't pull away. "Yeah." He said nothing else, waiting, watching her face.

"Oh, wow." Relief rushed through her. Chase was one of the nicest guys she'd ever met. Yes, he was intimidating, but there was a kindness beneath the surface that was true and honorable. He'd helped her out on more than one occasion, and she adored his wife, Mira. She'd met his brothers, Steen and Zane, a couple times, and the loyalty between the brothers was amazing. Everyone in the family was incredibly kind, despite the fact that the men were tall, broad-shouldered, and more than a little intimidating when they walked into a room. "Which brother are you?"

He raised his eyebrows, still watching her warily. "Travis."

"Travis Stockton." She frowned, trying to remember if she'd heard anything about him, but she didn't think she had. No matter. The fact he was Chase's brother was enough, given the level of her desperation right now. "Well, if you're as good a guy as Chase, then I trust you in my kitchen."

Surprise flashed across his face. "Really?"

She hesitated. "Why? Is there something about you I shouldn't trust?"

He paused, looking hard at her. "I'm completely fucked up in a lot of ways," he said, his voice hard, almost warning her. "People in this town don't like me."

She raised her brows at his defensiveness. His face was dark and almost angry, and his fingers had tightened around her arm. Her heart turned over, and she wanted to hug him, because she knew what it felt like to suffer under a town's disdain. It was a brutal, horrible way for a child to grow up, and the scars never went away, no matter how hard one tried. "Well, townspeople suck sometimes."

He blinked. "What?"

She shrugged. "Does the fact that they don't like you mean I can't trust you in my kitchen?"

He stared at her for a long moment, then shook his head once. "No. It doesn't."

Of course it didn't. "Then please, please, please help me out tonight. I'm desperate."

A grin flashed across his face then, a smile that was so genuine that her chest tightened. "I'm on it." He slid off the stool. "Give me the ninety second tour, and then I'll be good."

As he stood up, she realized how tall he really was. He towered over her, taller, wider, and so much stronger than she was. He was gritty and tough, a man who wouldn't stand down from anything. She hesitated for a split second, suddenly nervous. Her kitchen was her sanctuary, her world, the only thing that had saved her eight years ago. Having Travis in there felt dangerous, like she was turning over her foundation to someone she barely knew--

He shoved open the kitchen door and disappeared inside, not waiting for a second invitation.

Like it? Get it now!

SNEAK PEEK: UNEXPECTEDLY MINE

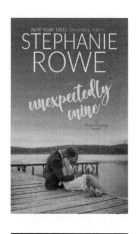

"This book wove...deep
inside my heart and
soul." ~Amy W (Amazon
Review)

CLARE WAS LIFTING the box of cupcakes off the front counter when she became aware of the utter silence of the general store. Even at the funerals of her parents, she hadn't heard this kind of silence in Birch Crossing.

Awareness prickled down her arms, and she looked at Norm, who was in his usual spot behind the front register. She could have sworn that there was amusement crinkling his gray eyes when he nodded toward something behind her.

Clare spun around, and there he was.

Griffin Friesé.

Her mystical knight in shining armor from last night.

Her heart began to race as she met his gaze. His stare was intense, penetrating all the way to her core. She was yanked back to that moment of his hands on her hips, of his strength as he'd lifted her. The power in his body as he'd emerged from his truck during the thundering rain and raging wind. Her body began to thrum, and his expression grew hooded, his eyes never leaving hers, as if he were trying to memorize every feature on her face.

He was wearing a heavy leather jacket that flanked strong thighs and broad shoulders. His eyes were dark, as dark as they'd been last night in the storm. Whiskers shadowed his jaw, giving him a rough and untamed look. His boots were still caked with mud, but his jeans were pressed and clean. His light blue dress shirt was open at the collar, revealing a hint of skin and the flash of a thin gold chain at his throat. His hair was short and perfectly gelled, not messy and untamed like it had been last night. A heavy gold watch sat captive on the strong wrist that had supported her so easily.

Today, he wasn't the dark and rugged hero of last night.

Well, okay, he still was. His power transcended mud, storms, nice watches, and dress shirts.

But he was also, quite clearly and quite ominously, an outsider, a man who did not fit into the rural Maine town of Birch Crossing.

Then he smiled, a beautiful, tremendous smile with a dimple in his right cheek. "How's your daughter?"

A dimple? He had a dimple? Clare hadn't noticed the dimple last night. It made him look softer, more human, more approachable, almost endearing. Suddenly all her trepidation vanished, replaced by a feeling of giddiness and delight to see him. She smiled back. "She's still asleep, but she's okay. Thanks for your help last night rescuing her."

"My pleasure." His smile faded, and a speculative gleam came into his dark eyes. "And how are you?"

No longer feeling like a total wreck, that was for sure. Not with Griffin Friesé studying her as if she were the only thing he ever wanted to look at again. Dear God, the way he was looking at her made her want to drop the cupcakes and her clothes, and saunter with decadent sensuality across the floor toward him, his stare igniting every cell in her body. "I'm fine." She swallowed, horrified by how throaty her voice sounded. "Thank you," she said. "I owe you."

"No, you owe me nothing." He smiled again, a softness to his face that made her heart turn over. "Seeing you hug Katie was plenty."

"Oh, dear Lord," Eppie muttered behind her. "Now he's going to kill Katie, too."

Clare stiffened and jerked her gaze from Griffin. The entire store was watching them in rapt silence, listening to every word. Oh, God. How had she forgotten where they were? Wright & Sons was the epicenter of gossip in Birch Crossing, and everyone had just witnessed her gaping at this handsome stranger.

Assuming her decades-old role as Clare's self-appointed protector, Eppie had folded her arms and was trying to crush Griffin with her glare, for daring to tempt Clare.

Astrid and Emma were leaning against the doorjamb, huge grins on their faces, clearly supportive of any opportunity to pry Clare out of her dateless life of isolation. But Norm's eyes were narrowed, and Ophelia was letting some scrambled eggs burn while she gawked at them. Everyone was waiting to see how Clare was going to respond to him.

Oh, man. What was she doing nearly throwing herself at him? In front of everyone? She quickly took a step back and cleared her throat.

Griffin's eyebrows shot up at her retreat, then his eyes narrowed. "Kill off Katie, *too?* " He looked right at Eppie. "Who else am I going to kill?"

Eppie lifted her chin and turned her head, giving him a view of the back of her hot pink hat.

"The rumors claim that you're in town to murder your ex-wife and daughter," Astrid volunteered cheerfully. "But don't worry. Not all of us believe them."

"My daughter?" Pain flashed across Griffin's face, a stark anguish so real that Clare felt her out heart tighten. Just as quickly, the vulnerability disappeared from his face, replaced by a hard, cool expression.

But she'd seen it. She'd seen his pain, pain he clearly kept hidden, just as she suppressed her own. Suddenly, she felt terrible about the rumors. How could she have listened to rumors about him when he was clearly struggling with pain, some kind of trauma with regard to his daughter?

She realized he was watching her, as if he were waiting for something. For what? To see if she believed the rumors?

She glanced around and saw the entire store was waiting for her response. Eppie gave her a solemn nod, encouraging her to stand up and condemn this handsome stranger who'd saved Clare's daughter. Sudden anger surged inside her. "Oh, come on," she blurted out. "You can't really believe he's a murderer?"

Astrid grinned, Eppie shook her head in dismay, and the rest of the room was silent.

No one else jumped in to help her defend Griffin, and suddenly Clare felt very exposed, as if everyone in the room could see exactly how deeply she'd been affected by him last night. How she'd lain awake all night, thinking of his hands on her hips, of the way his deep voice had wrapped around her, of how he'd made her yearn for the touch of a man for the first time in a very long time.

Heat burned her cheeks, and she glanced uncomfortably at Griffin, wondering if he was aware of her reaction to him. To her surprise, his face had cooled, devoid of that warmth that they'd initially shared, clearly interpreting her silence as a capitulation to the rumors.

He narrowed his eyes, then turned away, ending their conversation.

Regret rushed through Clare as she glanced at Astrid, torn between wanting to call him back, and gratefully grasping the freedom his rejection had given her, freedom from feelings and desires that she didn't have time to deal with.

"I need a place to stay," Griffin said. "A place without rats, preferably."

Griffin's low request echoed through the room, and Clare spun around in shock. Then she saw he was directing his question to Norm, not to her. Relief rushed through her, along with a stab of disappointment.

No, it was good he wasn't asking to stay at her place. Yes, she owed him, on a level beyond words, but she couldn't afford to get involved with him, for too many reasons. Staying at her house would be putting temptation where she couldn't afford it. There was *no way* she was going to offer up her place, even though her renter had just vacated, leaving her with an unpleasant gap in her income stream.

"Griffin stayed at the Dark Pines Motel last night," Judith whispered, just loudly enough for the whole store to hear.

"Really?" Guilt washed through Clare. The Dark Pines Motel was

SNEAK PEEK: UNEXPECTEDLY MINE

quite possibly the most unkempt and disgusting motel in the entire state of Maine. How had he ended up there?

"Well, now, Griffin," Norm said, as he tipped his chair back and let it tap against the unfinished wall. "Most places won't open for another month when the summer folk start to arrive. And the Black Loon Inn is booked for the Smith-Pineal wedding for the next week. It's Dark Pines or nothing."

Griffin frowned. "There has to be something. A bed and breakfast?"

Norm shook his head. "Not this time of year, but I probably have some rat traps in the back I could loan you for your stay.'

"Rat traps?" Griffin echoed. "That's my best option?"

Astrid grinned at Clare, a sparkle in her eyes that made Clare's stomach leap with alarm. She grabbed Astrid's arm. "Don't you dare—"

"Clare's renter just moved out," Astrid announced, her voice ringing out in the store. "Griffin can stay in her spare room. No rats, and it comes with free Wi-Fi. Best deal in town."

Oh, dear *God.* Clare's whole body flamed hot, and she whipped around. *Please tell me he didn't hear that.*

But Griffin was staring right at her.

Of course he'd heard. And so had everyone else.

Like it? Get it now!

A QUICK FAVOR

Did you enjoy this collection of Stockton awesomeness?

People are often hesitant to try new books or new authors. A few reviews can encourage them to make that leap and give it a try. If you enjoyed these Wyoming Rebels books and think others will as well, please consider taking a moment and writing one or two sentences on the etailer to help this story find the readers who would enjoy it. Even the short reviews really make an impact!

Thank you a million times for reading my books! I love writing for you and sharing the journeys of these beautiful characters with you. I hope you find inspiration from their stories in your own life!

Love,
Stephanie

BOOKS BY STEPHANIE ROWE

Do you know why I love to write?

Because I love to reach deep inside the soul, both mine and yours, and awaken the spirit that gives us life. I want to write books that make you feel, that touch your heart, and inspire you to whatever dreams you hold in your heart.

"This book has the capacity to touch 90% of the women's lives. I went through all the fears and anguish of the characters with them and came out the other side feeling the hope and love. I would even say I experienced some healing of my own." -cyinca (Amazon Review)

All my stories take the reader on that same emotional journey, whether it's in a small Maine town, rugged cowboy country, or the magical world of immortal warriors. Some of my books are funnier, some are darker, but they all give the deep sense of emotional fulfillment.

"I adore this family! ...[Wyoming Rebels] is definitely one of my favorite series and since paranormal is my usual interest, that's saying something." -Laura B (Amazon Review)

Take a look below. See what might strike your fancy. Give one of them a try. You might fall in love with a genre you don't expect!

~

CONTEMPORARY ROMANCE

WYOMING REBELS SERIES
(CONTEMPORARY WESTERN ROMANCE)
A Real Cowboy Never Says No
A Real Cowboy Knows How to Kiss
A Real Cowboy Rides a Motorcycle
A Real Cowboy Never Walks Away
A Real Cowboy Loves Forever
A Real Cowboy for Christmas
A Real Cowboy Always Trusts His Heart (Sept 2019!)

A ROGUE COWBOY SERIES
(CONTEMPORARY WESTERN ROMANCE)
A Rogue Cowboy for Her, featuring Brody Hart
(Coming Soon!)

LINKED TO A ROGUE COWBOY SERIES
(CONTEMPORARY WESTERN ROMANCE)
Her Rebel Cowboy

BIRCH CROSSING SERIES
(SMALL-TOWN CONTEMPORARY ROMANCE)
Unexpectedly Mine
Accidentally Mine
Unintentionally Mine
Irresistibly Mine
Mistakenly Mine (Coming Soon!)

MYSTIC ISLAND SERIES
(SMALL-TOWN CONTEMPORARY ROMANCE)

Wrapped Up in You (A Christmas novella)

CANINE CUPIDS SERIES
(ROMANTIC COMEDY)
Paws for a Kiss
Pawfectly in Love
Paws Up for Love

PARANORMAL

ORDER OF THE BLADE SERIES
(DARK PARANORMAL ROMANCE)
Darkness Awakened
Darkness Seduced
Darkness Surrendered
Forever in Darkness
Darkness Reborn
Darkness Arisen
Darkness Unleashed
Inferno of Darkness
Darkness Possessed
Shadows of Darkness
Hunt the Darkness
Awaken the Darkness (Oct 2019)

ORDER OF THE NIGHT
(AN ORDER OF THE BLADE SPINOFF SERIES)
(DARK PARANORMAL ROMANCE)
Edge of Midnight, featuring Thano Savakis
(Coming Soon!)

HEART OF THE SHIFTER SERIES
(DARK PARANORMAL ROMANCE)
Dark Wolf Rising
Dark Wolf Unbound
Dark Wolf Untamed (Coming Soon!)

SHADOW GUARDIANS SERIES
(DARK PARANORMAL ROMANCE)
Leopard's Kiss

NIGHTHUNTER SERIES
(DARK PARANORMAL ROMANCE)
Not Quite Dead

Writing as S.A. Bayne

NOBLE AS HELL SERIES
(FUNNY URBAN FANTASY)
Rock Your Evil

IMMORTALLY CURSED SERIES
(FUNNY PARANORMAL ROMANCE)
Immortally Cursed
Curse of the Dragon
Devil's Curse (Dec 2019)

THE MAGICAL ELITE SERIES
(FUNNY PARANORMAL ROMANCE)
The Demon You Trust

DEVILISHLY SEXY SERIES
(FUNNY PARANORMAL ROMANCE)
Not Quite a Devil
The Devil You Know (Coming Soon!)

ROMANTIC SUSPENSE

ALASKA HEAT SERIES
(ROMANTIC SUSPENSE)
Ice
Chill
Ghost

YOUNG ADULT

MAPLEVILLE HIGH SERIES
(FUNNY CONTEMPORARY ROMANCE)
The Truth About Thongs
How to Date a Bad Boy
Pedicures Don't Like Dirt
Geeks Can Be Hot
The Fake Boyfriend Experiment
Ice Cream, Jealousy & Other Dating Tips

BOXED SETS

Order of the Blade (Books 1-3)
Protectors of the Heart (A Six-Book First-in-Series Collection)
Real Cowboys Get Their Girls (A Wyoming Rebels Boxed Set, with bonus novella!)

For a complete list of Stephanie's books, click here.

STAY IN THE KNOW!

I write my books from the soul, and live that way as well. I've received so much help over the years from amazing people to help me live my best life, and I am always looking to pay it forward, including to my readers.

One of the ways I love to do this is through my mailing list, where I often send out life tips I've picked up, post readers surveys, give away Advance Review Copies, and provide insider scoop on my books, my writing, and life in general. And, of course, I always make sure my readers on my list know when the next book is coming out!

If this sounds interesting to you, I would love to have you join us! You can always unsubscribe at any time! I'll never spam you or share your data. I just want to provide value!

Sign up at www.stephanierowe.com/join-newsletter/ to keep in touch!

Much love,

Stephanie

ABOUT THE AUTHOR

New York Times and *USA Today* bestselling author Stephanie Rowe is the author of more than fifty novels. She's a 2018 winner and a five-time nominee for the RITA® award, the highest award in romance fiction. Stephanie also writes high-octane, irreverent paranormals as S.A. Bayne.

For the latest info on Stephanie and her books, connect with her on the web at:
www.stephanierowe.com
www.sabayne.com

ACKNOWLEDGMENTS

Special thanks to my beta readers and the Rockstars. You guys are the best! There are so many to thank by name, more than I could count, but here are those who I want to called out specially for all they did to help this book come to life: Malinda Davis Diehl, Leslie Barnes, Kayla Bartley, Alencia Bates Salters, Alyssa Bird, Donna Bossert, Jean Bowden, Shell Bryce, Ashley Cuesta, Denise Fluhr, Valerie Glass, Heidi Hoffman, Jeanne Stone, Dottie Jones, Janet Juengling-Snell, Deb Julienne, Bridget Koan, Helen Loyal, Felicia Low Mikoll, Phyllis Marshall, Suzanne Mayer, Jodi Moore, Ashlee Murphy, Elizabeth Neal, Judi Pflughoeft, Carol Pretorius, Kasey Richardson, Caryn Santee, Amber Ellison Shriver, Summer Steelman, Regina Thomas, and Linda Watson. Special thanks to my family, who I love with every fiber of my heart and soul. And to AER, who is my world. Love you so much, baby girl! And to Joe, who teaches me every day what romance and true really is. I love you, babe!

For AER, my shining light.

Made in the USA
Monee, IL
29 December 2020